The Curse of

The India Fan

Mistress of Mellyn
Kirkland Revels
The Bride of Pendorric
The Legend of the Seventh Virgin
Menfreya
The King of the Castle
My Enemy the Queen
The Shivering Sands
The Secret Woman
The Shadow of the Lynx
On the Night of the Seventh Moon
The House of a Thousand Lanterns
The Demon Lover
The Devil on Horseback
The Spring of the Tiger
The Judás Kiss
Lord of the Far Island
The Mask of the Enchantress
The Pride of the Peacock
The Landower Legacy
The Queen's Confession
The Time of the Hunter's Moon
The Road to Paradise Island
Secret for a Nightingale
The Silk Vendetta
Snare of Serpents
The Captive

The Curse of the Kings
The India Fan

Victoria Holt

Diamond Books
An Imprint of HarperCollins*Publishers*,
77–85 Fulham Palace Road
Hammersmith, London W6 8JB

This Diamond Books Omnibus edition first published 1994

The Curse of the Kings © Victoria Holt 1973
The India Fan © Victoria Holt 1988

The Author asserts the moral right to be identified as the author of this work

ISBN 0 261 66278 3

Printed in Great Britain by
BPCC Hazells Ltd

The Curse of the Kings

October 1999

The Curse

When Sir Edward Travers died suddenly and mysteriously, there was consternation and speculation, not only in the neighbourhood of his home, but throughout the country.

Headlines in the newspapers ran: 'Death of Eminent Archaeologist.' 'Was Sir Edward Travers a Victim of the Curse?'

A paragraph in our local paper stated:

> With the death of Sir Edward Travers, who recently left this country to carry out excavations among the tombs of the Pharaohs, it is being asked: Is there any truth in the ancient belief that he who meddles with the resting-place of the dead invites their enmity? Sir Edward's swift and sudden death has brought the expedition to an abrupt end.

Sir Ralph Bodrean, our local Squire and Sir Edward's closest friend, had given financial aid to the expedition and when, a few days after the announcement of Sir Edward's death, Sir Ralph had a stroke, there was further speculation. He had, however, suffered a similar affliction some years before, and although he recovered from this second as he had from the first, he became paralysed in his arm and leg, and his health was considerably impaired. It was, as might be expected, hinted that these misfortunes were the result of the Curse.

Sir Edward's body was brought back and buried in our churchyard and Tybalt, Sir Edward's only son and himself a brilliant man who had already attained some distinction in the same profession as his father, was, of course, chief mourner.

The funeral was one of the grandest our little twelfth-century church had ever seen. There were people present from the academic world as well as friends of the family, and of course the Press.

I was at the time companion to Lady Bodrean, wife of Sir Ralph, a post which did not suit my nature but which my financial needs had forced me to take.

I accompanied Lady Bodrean to the church for the funeral service and there I could not take my eyes from Tybalt.

I had loved him, foolishly because hopelessly, from the time I had first seen him, for what chance had a humble companion with such a distinguished man? He seemed to me to possess all the masculine virtues. He was by no means handsome by conventional standards, but he was distinguished-looking — very tall, lean and neither fair nor dark; he had the brow of a scholar yet there was a touch of sensuality about his mouth; his nose was large and a trifle arrogant, and his grey eyes deep-set and veiled. One would never be quite certain what he was thinking. He was aloof and mysterious. I often said to myself: 'It would take a lifetime to understand him.' And what a stimulating voyage of discovery that would be!

Immediately after the funeral I returned to Keverall Court with Lady Bodrean. She was exhausted, she said, and was indeed more complaining and fretful than usual. Her temper did not improve when she learned

8

that reporters had been to the Court to discover the state of Sir Ralph's health.

'They are like vultures!' she declared. 'They are hoping for the worst because a double death would fit in so well with this foolish story of the Curse.'

A few days after the funeral I took Lady Bodrean's dogs for their daily walk and my footsteps led me out of habit to Giza House, the home of the Traverses. I stood at the wrought-iron gate, where I had stood so many times, looking along the path to the house. Now that the funeral was over and the blinds had been drawn up it no longer looked melancholy. It had regained that air of mystery with which I had always associated it, for it was a house which had always fascinated me, even before the Traverses came to live there.

To my embarrassment Tybalt came out of the house and it was too late for me to turn away because he had seen me.

'Good afternoon, Miss Osmond,' he said.

I quickly invented a reason for being there. 'Lady Bodrean was anxious to know how you were getting on,' I said.

'Oh, well enough,' he answered. 'But you must come in.'

He smiled at me, which made me feel ridiculously happy. It was absurd. Practical, sensible, proud Miss Osmond to feel so intensely about another human being! Miss Osmond in love! How had I ever fallen into such a state and so hopelessly too?

He led me up the path through somewhat overgrown shrubs and pushed open the door with the knocker which Sir Edward had brought from some foreign country. It was cunningly wrought into the shape of a face . . . a rather evil one. I wondered whether Sir Edward had put it there to discourage visitors.

The carpets were thick at Giza House so that footsteps were noiseless. Tybalt took me into the drawing-room where the heavy midnight blue velvet curtains were fringed with gold and the carpet was deep blue with a velvety pile. Sir Edward had found noise distracting, I had heard. There was evidence of his vocation in that room. I knew some of the weird figures were casts of his more spectacular finds. This was the Chinese room; but the grand piano which dominated it brought with it the flavour of Victorian England.

Tybalt signed to me to sit down and did the same.

'We're planning another expedition to the place where my father died,' he said.

'Oh!' I had said I did not believe in this story of the Curse yet the thought of his going back there alarmed me. 'You think that wise?' I asked.

'Surely you don't believe these rumours about my father's death, do you, Miss Osmond?'

'Of course not.'

'He was a healthy man, it was true. And suddenly he was struck down. I believe he was on the verge of a great discovery. It was something he said to me the day before he died. He said: "I believe shortly I am going to prove to everyone that this expedition was very much worth while." He would say no more than that. How I wish he had.'

'There was an autopsy.'

'Yes, here in England. But they were unable to find the cause. It was very mysterious. And now Sir Ralph.'

10

'You don't think there is a connection?'

He shook his head. 'I think my father's old friend was shocked by his sudden death. Sir Ralph has always been somewhat apoplectic and had a mild stroke once before. I know that doctors have been warning him for years to show a little moderation. No, Sir Ralph's illness has nothing to do with what was happening in Egypt. Well, I am going back and I shall attempt to find out what it was my father was on the point of discovering and ... if this had anything to do with his death.'

'Take care,' I said before I could stop myself.

He smiled. 'I believe it is what my father would have wished.'

'When will you leave?'

'It will take us three months to get ready.'

The door opened and Tabitha Grey came in. Like everyone at Giza House, she interested me. She was beautiful in an unobtrusive way. It was only after one had seen her many times that one realized the charm of those features and the fascination of that air of resignation, a kind of acceptance of life. I had never been quite sure of her position at Giza House; she was a sort of specially privileged housekeeper.

'Miss Osmond has called with Lady Bodrean's good wishes.'

'Would you like some tea, Miss Osmond?' asked Tabitha.

I declined with thanks, explaining that I should be going back without delay, or I should be missed. Tabitha smiled sympathetically, implying that she understood Lady Bodrean was no easy taskmistress.

Tybalt said he would walk back with me and this

he did. He talked all the time about the expedition. I was fascinated by it.

'I believe you wish you were going with us,' he said.

'With all my heart.'

'Would you be prepared to face the Curse of the Pharaohs, Miss Osmond?' he asked ironically.

'Yes, I certainly should.'

He smiled at me.

'I wish,' he said earnestly, 'that you *could* join our expedition.'

I went back to Keverall Court bemused. I scarcely heard Lady Bodrean's complaints. I was in a dream. He *wished* that I could join them. Only by a miracle could I do that.

When Sir Ralph died there was more talk of the Curse. The man who had led the expedition and the man who had helped to finance it – and both dead! There must be some significance in this.

And then . . . my miracle happened. It was incredible; it was wonderful; it was like something from a dream. It was as fantastic as a fairy story. Cinderella was to go – not to the ball – but with the expedition to Egypt.

I could only marvel at the wonder of it; and I thought constantly of everything that had led up to this.

It really began on my fourteenth birthday when I found the piece of bronze in Josiah Polgrey's grave.

The Bronze Shield

My fourteenth birthday was one of the most eventful days of my life because on it not only did I find the bronze shield but I learned some truths about myself.

The shield came first. I found it during the hot July afternoon. The house was quiet, for neither Dorcas, Alison, nor the cook and the two maids were anywhere to be seen. I suspected that the maids were exchanging confidences about their sweethearts in their attic bedroom; the cook was drowsing in the kitchen: that Dorcas was in her garden; that Alison was mending, or embroidering; and that the Reverend James Osmond was in his study pretending to prepare next Sunday's sermon and in fact dozing in his chair – now and then being awakened by a sudden jerk of the head or his own genteel snore and murmuring: 'Bless my soul!' and pretending to himself – as there was no one else to pretend to – that he had been working on his sermon all the time.

I was wrong, at least about Dorcas and Alison; they were most certainly in one of their bedrooms discussing how best they could tell the child – myself – for now that she was fourteen years old they believed she should no longer be kept in the dark.

I was in the graveyard watching Pegger, the sexton, dig a grave. I was fascinated by the churchyard. Sometimes I would wake in the night and think of it.

Often I would get out of bed, kneel on the window-seat and look down at it. In the mist it would seem very ghostly indeed and the grey tombstones were like figures risen from the dead; in the bright moonlight they were clearly gravestones but they lost none of their eeriness for that. Sometimes it was pitch dark, and the rain might be teeming down, and the wind howling through the branches of the oaks and buffeting the ancient yews; then I would imagine that the dead had left their graves and were prowling round the churchyard just below my window.

It was years ago that I had begun to feel this morbid interest. It probably started when Dorcas first took me to put flowers on Lavinia's grave. We did that every Sunday. Now we had planted a rosemary bush within the marble kerb.

'That's for remembrance,' said Dorcas. 'It will be green all the year round.'

On this hot July afternoon Pegger paused in his digging to mop his forehead with a red bandana handkerchief and regarded me in the stern way he regarded everybody.

'You'm like me, I reckon. As I stand here, turning over the earth, I think of the one who'll be laid to rest in this deep, dark grave. Like as not I've known 'un all me life – for that's how it be in a parish like St Erno's.'

Pegger spoke in a sepulchral voice. I suppose this was due to his connection with the church. He had been sexton all his life and his father before him. He even looked like one of the prophets from the Old Testament with his mane of white hair and beard, and his righteous indignation against the sinners of

14

the world, into which category all but himself and a very chosen few seemed to fall. Even his conversation had a Biblical flavour.

'This be the last resting-place of Josiah Polgrey. He's lived his threescore year and ten and now he's to face his Maker.' Pegger shook his head gravely as though he did not think highly of Josiah's chance in the next world.

I said: 'God may not be as stern as you, Mr Pegger.'

'You come near to blasphemy, Miss Judith,' he said. 'You should guard well your tongue.'

'Well, what would be the use of that, Mr Pegger? The recording angel would know what was in my mind whether I said it or not — so even to think it might be just as bad, and can you help what you think?'

Mr Pegger raised his eyes to the sky as though he thought I might have invited the wrath of God to descend on me.

'Never mind,' I soothed him. 'Why, you haven't had your lunch yet. It must be two o'clock.'

On the next grave lay another red bandana handkerchief similar to that with which Mr Pegger had mopped his brow, but this one, I knew, was tied about a bottle containing cold tea and a pasty which Mrs Pegger would have made on the previous night so that it would be ready for her husband to bring with him.

He stepped out of the grave and seating himself on the kerb round the next grave untied the knot in the handkerchief and took out his food.

'How many graves have you dug in your whole lifetime?' I asked.

He shook his head. 'More than I can say, Miss Judith,' he replied.

'And Matthew will dig them after you. Just think of that.' Matthew was not his eldest son who should have inherited the doubtful privilege of digging graves of those who had lived and died in the village of St Erno's. Luke, the eldest, had run away to sea, a fact which would never be forgiven him.

'If it be the Lord's will I'll dig a few more yet,' he answered.

'You must dig all sorts of sizes,' I mused. 'Well, you wouldn't need the same size for little Mrs Edney and Sir Ralph Bodrean, would you?'

This was a plot of mine to bring Sir Ralph into the conversation. The sins of his neighbours was, I think, Mr Pegger's favourite subject, and since everything about Sir Ralph was bigger than that belonging to anyone else, so were his sins.

I found our Squire fascinating. I was excited when he passed on the road either in his carriage or on one of his thoroughbreds. I would bob a little curtsey – as taught by Dorcas – and he would nod and raise a hand in a quick imperious kind of gesture and for a moment those heavy-lidded eyes would be on me. Some had said of him – as long ago someone had said of Julius Caesar – 'Hide your daughters when he passes by.' Well, he was the Caesar of our village. He owned most of it; the outlying farmlands were on his estate; to those who worked with him he was said to be a good master, and as long as the men touched their forelocks with due respect and remembered he *was* the master and the girls did not deny him those favours which he desired, he was a good master, which

16

meant that men were assured of work and a roof over their heads and any results which might ensue from his dallying with the maidens were taken care of. There were plenty of 'results' in the village now and they were always granted extra privileges over those who had been sired elsewhere.

But to Mr Pegger the Squire was Sin personified.

Out of respect for my youth he could not talk of our Squire's major qualification for hell fire, so he gave himself the pleasure of touching on his smaller ones – all of which, in Mr Pegger's opinion, would have ensured his entry.

There were house parties at Keverall Court almost every weekend; in various seasons they came to hunt foxes, otters and stags, or to shoot pheasants which were bred on the Keverall estate for this purpose, or merely to make merry in the baronial hall. They were rich, elegant – often noisy – people from Plymouth and sometimes as far as London. I always enjoyed seeing them. They brightened the countryside, but in Mr Pegger's estimation they desecrated it.

I considered myself very lucky to visit Keverall Court every day except Saturday and Sunday. This had been a special concession because the Squire's daughter and nephew had a governess and were also taught by Oliver Shrimpton, our curate. The rather impecunious rector could not afford a governess for me and Sir Ralph had graciously given his consent – or perhaps had raised no objection to the proposal – that I should join his daughter and nephew in their schoolroom and profit from the instruction given there. This meant that every day – except Saturdays and Sundays – I passed under the old portcullis into the courtyard, gave an ecstatic sniff at the stables, touched the mounting-block for luck, entered the great hall with its minstrels' gallery, mounted the wide staircase as though I were one of the lady visitors from London, with a flowing train and diamonds glittering on my fingers, passed along the gallery where all the dead – and some of the living – Bodreans looked down on me with varying expressions of scorn, amusement or indifference, and into the schoolroom where Theodosia and Hadrian would be already seated and Miss Graham the governess would be busy at her books.

Life had certainly become more interesting since it had been decided that I share lessons with the Bodreans.

On this July afternoon I was interested to learn that the Squire's current sin was as Mr Pegger said, 'putting in his nose where God hadn't intended it should go.'

'And where is that, Mr Pegger?'

'In Carter's Meadow, that's where. He wants to set up digging there. Disturbing God's Earth. It's all along of these people who've been coming here. Filling the place with heathen ideas.'

'What are they going to dig for, Mr Pegger?' I asked.

'For worms, I'd reckon.' That was meant to be a joke, for Mr Pegger's face creased into what did service for a smile.

'So they're all coming down to dig, are they?' I pictured them – ladies in silks and velvets, gentlemen in white cravats and velvet smoking-jackets, all with their little spades in Carter's Meadow.

Mr Pegger brushed the pasty crumbs from his coat

and tied the bottle back into the red handkerchief.

'It's digging up the past, they'm saying. They reckon they'm going to find bits and pieces left behind by them as lived here years and years ago.'

'What, *here*, Mr Pegger?'

'Here in St Erno's. A lot of heathens they were, so why any godfearing gentleman should bother himself with them is past my understanding.'

'Perhaps *they're* not godfearing, Mr Pegger; but it's all very respectable. It's called archaeology.'

'What it's called makes no difference. If God had intended 'em to find these things. He wouldn't have covered 'em up with his good earth.'

'Perhaps it wasn't God who covered them up.'

'Then who?'

'Time,' I said portentously.

He shook his head and started to dig again, throwing the soil up on to the bank he had made.

'Squire were always one for taking up with these fancies. I don't like this one. Let the dead bury their dead, I say.'

'I believe someone else said that some time ago, Mr Pegger. Well, *I* think it would be interesting if we found something very important here in St Erno's. Roman remains perhaps. We'd be famous.'

'We weren't meant to be famous, Miss Judith. We were meant to be . . .'

'Godfearing,' I supplied for him. 'So the Squire and his friends are looking for Roman remains close by. And it's not a sudden fancy of his. He's always been interested. Famous archaeologists often come to stay at Keverall Court. Perhaps that's why his nephew is named Hadrian.'

19

'Hadrian!' thundered Mr Pegger. 'It's a heathen name. And the young lady too.'

'Hadrian and Theodosia.'

'They'm not good Christian names.'

'Not like your Matthew, Mark, Luke, John, Isaac, Reuben . . . and the rest. Judith is in the Bible. So I'm all right.'

I fell to thinking of names. 'Dorcas! Alison!' I said. 'Did you know, Mr Pegger, that Theodosia means divinely given? So you see it is a Christian name. As for Hadrian, he's named after a wall and a Roman Emperor.'

'They're not good Christian names,' he repeated.

'Lavinia,' I said. 'I wonder what that means.'

'Ah, Miss Lavinia,' said Mr Pegger.

'It was very sad, wasn't it, to die so young?'

'With all her sins upon her.'

'I don't think she had many. Alison and Dorcas speak of her as though they loved her dearly.'

There was a picture of Lavinia hanging in the rectory on the landing just at the top of the first flight of stairs. I used to be afraid to pass it after dark because I imagined that at night Lavinia stepped out of it and walked about the house. I used to think that one day I would pass it and find the frame empty because she had failed to get back into it in time.

I was such a fanciful child, said Dorcas, who was very practical herself and could not understand my strange imaginings.

'Every mortal man has sins,' declared Mr Pegger. 'As for women, they can have ten times as many.'

'Not Lavinia,' I said.

He leaned on his spade and scratched his white

20

mane of hair. 'Lavinia! She were the prettiest of the rectory girls.'

Well, I thought, that might not have meant a great deal if I was not so familiar with Lavinia's picture, for neither Alison nor Dorcas were exactly beauties. They always wore such sensible clothes – sombre-coloured skirts and jackets, and thick strong boots – so sensible for the country. Yet in the picture Lavinia had a velvet jacket and a hat with a curling feather.

'It was a pity she was ever on that train.'

'In one moment she had no idea what was about to happen and the next . . . she was facing her Maker.'

'Do you think it's as quick as that, Mr Pegger? After all, she would have to get there. . . .'

'Taken in sin, you might say, with no time for repentance.'

'No one would be hard on Lavinia.'

Pegger was not so sure. He shook his head. 'She could have her flighty ways.'

'Dorcas and Alison loved her; and so did the Reverend. I can tell by the way they look when they say her name.'

Mr Pegger had put down his spade to mop his brow once more. 'This is one of the hottest days the Lord have sent us this year.' He stepped out of the hole and sat down on the kerb of the next grave so that he and I were facing each other over the yawning hole. I stood up and peered down into it. Poor Josiah Polgrey who beat his wife and had his children out working on the farm at five years old. On impulse I jumped down into the hole.

'What be doing, Miss Judith?' demanded Mr Pegger.

21

'I just want to see what it feels like to be down here,' I said.

I reached up for his spade and started to dig.

'It smells damp,' I said.

'A fine muss you'll be getting yourself in.'

'I'm already in it,' I cried, as my shoes slipped down into the loose earth. It was a horrible feeling of being shut in with the walls of the trench so close to me. 'It must be terrible, Mr Pegger, to be buried alive.'

'Now you come out of there.'

'I'll dig just a bit while I'm here,' I said, 'to see what it feels like to be a grave-digger.'

I dug the spade into the earth and threw out what it had picked up as I had seen Mr Pegger do. I repeated the operation several times before my spade struck something hard.

'There's something here,' I called.

'You come out of there, Miss Judith.'

I ignored him and went on probing. Then I had it. 'I've found something, Mr Pegger,' I cried. I stooped and picked up the object. 'What is it, do you know?'

Mr Pegger stood up and took it from me. 'Piece of old metal,' he said. I gave him my hand and he pulled me out of Josiah Polgrey's grave.

'I don't know,' I said. 'There's something about it.'

'Dirty old thing,' said Mr Pegger.

'But look at it, Mr Pegger. Just what is it? There's a sort of engraving on it.'

'I'd throw that away . . . sharp about it,' said Mr Pegger.

But *I* would do no such thing, I decided. I would take it back with me and clean it. I rather liked it.

Mr Pegger took up his spade and continued to dig while I tried to wipe the earth from my shoes and noticed with dismay that the hem of my skirt was decidedly grubby.

I talked for a while with Mr Pegger, then I went back to the rectory carrying the piece of what appeared to be bronze with me. It was oval-shaped and about six inches in diameter. I wondered what it would be like when it was cleaned and what I would use it for. I didn't give much thought to it, because talking about Lavinia had made me think about her and what a sad house it must have been when the news was brought to it that Lavinia, beloved daughter of the Reverend James Osmond and sister of Alison and Dorcas, had been killed in the train which was travelling from Plymouth to London.

'She was killed outright,' Dorcas had told me as we stood at her grave while she pruned the roses growing there. 'It was a mercy in a way, for she would have been an invalid for the rest of her life had she lived. She was twenty-one years old. It was a great tragedy.'

'Why was she going to live in London, Dorcas?' I had asked.

'She was going to take up a post.'

'What sort of post?'

'Oh . . . governess, I think.'

'You think! Weren't you sure?'

'She had been staying with a distant cousin.'

'What cousin was that?'

'Oh dear, what a probing child you are! She was a very *distant* cousin. We never hear of her now. Lavinia had been staying with her so she took the train from Plymouth and then . . . there was this terrible accident. Many people were killed. It was one of the worst accidents in living memory. We were heartbroken.'

'That was when you decided to take me in and bring me up to take Lavinia's place.'

'Nobody could take Lavinia's place, dear. You have a place of your own.'

'But it's not Lavinia's. I'm not a bit like her, am I?'

'Not in the least.'

'She was quiet, I suppose, and gentle; and she didn't talk too much, probe or be impulsive, or try to order people about . . . all the things that I do.'

'No, she was not like you, Judith. But she could be very firm on occasions, although she was so gentle.'

'So then because she was dead and I was an orphan you decided to take me in. I was related to you.'

'A sort of cousin.'

'A distant one, I suppose. All your cousins seem to be distant.'

'Well, we knew that you were an orphan and we were so distressed. We thought it would help us all . . . and you too, of course.'

'So I came here and it was all because of Lavinia.'

So considering all this, I felt that Lavinia had had a marked effect on my life; and fell to wondering what would have happened to me if Lavinia had not decided to take that particular train to London.

It was cool in the stone hall of the old rectory, cool and dark. On the hall table stood a great bowl of buddleia, lavender and roses. Some of the rose petals had already fallen on to the stone flags of the hall floor. The rectory was an old house, almost

24

as old as Keverall Court. Built in the early days of Elizabeth's reign it had been the residence of rectors over the last three hundred years. Their names were inscribed on a tablet in the church. The rooms were large and some beautifully panelled, but dark because of the small windows with their leaded panes. There was an air of great quietness brooding over the house and it was particularly noticeable on this hot day.

I went up the staircase to my room; and the first thing I did was wash the soil from the ornament. I had poured water from the ewer into the basin and was dabbing it with cotton wool when there was a knock on the door.

'Come in,' I called. Dorcas and Alison were standing there. They looked so solemn that I completely forgot the ornament and cried out: 'Is anything wrong?'

'We heard you come in,' said Alison.

'Oh dear, did I make a lot of noise?'

They looked at each other and exchanged smiles.

'We were listening for you,' said Dorcas.

There was silence. This was unusual. 'Something *is* wrong,' I insisted.

'No, dear, nothing has changed. We have been making up our minds to speak to you for some time; and as it is your birthday and fourteen is a sort of milestone . . . we thought the time had come.'

'It is all rather mysterious,' I said.

Alison drew a deep breath and said: 'Well, Judith . . .' Dorcas nodded to her to proceed. 'Well, Judith, you have always been under the impression that you were the daughter of a cousin of ours.'

'Yes, a distant one,' I said.

'This is not the case.'

I looked from one to the other. 'Then who am I?'

'You're our adopted daughter.'

'Yes, I know that, but if my parents are not the distant cousins, who are they?'

Neither of them spoke, and I cried out impatiently: 'You said you came to tell me.'

Alison cleared her throat. 'You were on the train . . . the same train as Lavinia.'

'In the accident?'

'Yes, you were in the accident . . . a child of one year or so.'

'My parents were killed then?'

'It seems so.'

'Who were they?'

Alison and Dorcas exchanged glances. Dorcas nodded slightly to Alison which meant: Tell her all.

'*You* were unharmed.'

'And my parents killed?'

Alison nodded.

'But *who* were they?'

'They . . . they must have been killed outright. No one came forward to say who you were.'

'Then I might be anybody!' I cried.

'So,' went on Dorcas, 'as we had lost a sister we adopted you.'

'What would have happened to me if you hadn't?'

'Someone else would have done so perhaps.'

I looked from one to the other and thought of all the kindness I had had from them and how I had plagued them – talking too much and too loudly, bringing mud into the house, breaking their prize crockery; and I ran to them and put my arms about them so that the three of us were in a huddle.

26

'Judith! Judith!' said Dorcas smiling, and the tears – which always came rather readily to her – glistened in her eyes.

Alison said: 'You were a comfort to us. We needed comfort when Lavinia was gone.'

'Well,' I said, 'it's nothing to cry about is it? Perhaps I'm the long-lost heiress to a great estate. My parents have been searching high and low for me . . .'

Alison and Dorcas were smiling again. I had further food for my flights of fancy. 'It's better than being a distant cousin anyway,' I said. 'But I do wonder *who* I was.'

'It is clear that your parents were killed outright. It was such a . . . violent disaster that we heard many people were unrecognizable. Papa went and identified poor Lavinia. He came back so upset.'

'Why did you tell me that I came from distant cousins?'

'We thought it better, Judith. We thought you'd be happier believing yourself related to us.'

'You're thinking I was unclaimed . . . unwanted, and that might have upset me and thrown a shadow over my childhood.'

'There could have been so many explanations. Perhaps you only had your parents and no other relatives. We thought that very likely.

'An orphan born to two orphans.'

'That seems possible.'

'Or perhaps your parents had just come to England.'

'A foreigner. Perhaps I'm French . . . or Spanish. I am rather dark. My hair looks quite black by candlelight. My eyes are much lighter though . . . just ordinary brown. I do look rather like a Spaniard. But then, lots of Cornish people do. That's because the Spaniards were wrecked along our coasts when we destroyed the Armada.'

'Well, all ended well. You came to be as our very own and I can never tell you what a joy that has been for us.'

'I don't know why you're looking so glum. It's rather exciting I think ... not to know who you are. Just think what you might discover! I might have a sister or brother somewhere. Or grandparents. Perhaps they'll come and claim me and take me back to Spain. Señorita Judith. It sounds rather good. Mademoiselle Judith de ... de Something. Just imagine going to see my long-lost family in their wonderful old château.'

'Oh Judith, you romance about everything,' said Dorcas.

'I'm glad she's taking it like this,' added Alison.

'What other way should I take it? I never did like those distant cousins anyway.'

'So you don't feel that you were ... deserted ... unwanted ... unclaimed?'

'Of course not. They didn't know that my parents had been killed. Nobody told them and as they were in a foreign country they weren't missed. They just thought they had slipped out of their lives. As for the little baby ... *me* ... well, they often dream of me. "I wonder what the child is like," they say. "She will be fourteen today. Dear little Judith." But I suppose *you* named me that.'

'You were christened by Papa soon after we brought you to the rectory.'

'Well,' I said, 'it's all very exciting. A nice birthday

surprise. Look at this. I found it. I think when it's cleaned up it will be rather unusual.'

'What is it?'

'I've no idea. What would you say, Dorcas? There are scratchings on it. Look.'

'Where did you find it?'

'In Josiah Polgrey's grave. Mr Pegger was digging it and I had a go ... and lo and behold my spade struck this. I shall clean it up and see what I shall use it for. It's a sort of birthday present from Josiah Polgrey.'

'What an idea! I've seen something like this before,' continued Alison. 'I think it may have some significance.'

'What do you mean, Alison. *Significance?*'

'Sir Ralph would know.'

Dorcas and Alison exchanged looks. Alison said, speaking rather slowly: 'I think, Judith, that you should take it along to Keverall Court and ask if you may show it to Sir Ralph.'

'Whatever for?'

'Because he's interested in this sort of thing.'

'Things that are dug up you mean?'

'Certain things. Of course this may be just nothing ... but there *is* something about it. I think it may be very old indeed and you have stumbled on something important.'

I was excited. It was true there was talk of digging up Carter's Meadow. How interesting if I had been the first to find something!

'I'll take it right away,' I said.

'I should wash first, change your dress and comb your hair.'

I smiled at them. I loved them very much; they were so normal. It was my birthday; they had just told me that I had been unclaimed, my parents had been killed and I might be just anybody; I may have stumbled on something important from centuries ago and they were worried about my changing my dress and making myself presentable to see Sir Ralph!

Under the portcullis, into the courtyard, sniffing the stables and touching the mounting-block for luck; and then into the great baronial hall. The heavy iron-studded door creaked as I pushed it open. How silent it seemed! I stood there for a second or so looking at the two suits of armour on either side of the wide staircase and the weapons on the walls; on the refectory table were pewter utensils, and there was a great bowl of flowers too.

I wondered what Hadrian and Theodosia were doing and what fun I would have tomorrow when I told them what I had found. I had already magnified it into something priceless. The greatest archaeologists in the world were shaking me by the hand. 'We are so grateful to you, Judith. We have been digging for years and never have we found anything quite so wonderful as this.'

I heard the scraping of a chair behind me. I had not noticed Derwent, the footman, dozing in a chair.

'Oh, it's you,' he said.

'I want to see Sir Ralph immediately. It is a matter of the utmost importance.'

He looked at me superciliously. 'Now, miss. This is another of your tricks, I know.'

'It's no trick. I have found something which is

of great value. My aunts (I called Dorcas and Alison aunts; it simplified the relationship) said I was to bring it to Sir Ralph without delay and woe betide anyone who tries to keep this from him.'

I hugged the piece of metal against me and faced him squarely.

'He's taking tea with her ladyship.'

'Go and tell him I am here,' I said imperiously.

Because there had been some talk about Carter's Meadow and Sir Ralph's interest in what could be dug out of the earth was well known, I eventually prevailed on Derwent to go and tell Sir Ralph that I had found something which my aunts thought might be of interest; and consequently within five minutes I was in the library . . . that fascinating room full of Sir Ralph's collection of exotic pieces.

I laid the metal on the table; and from that moment I knew that I had made an impression.

'Good God,' said Sir Ralph; he used oaths of which, I reflected, Dorcas, Alison and the Reverend James would not have approved, 'where did you find this?'

I told him that it was in Josiah Polgrey's grave.

His bushy eyebrows were lifted. 'What were you doing there?'

'Helping to dig it.'

He had two kinds of laughter – one a wild sort of roar and the other inward when his chin shook and I think that was when he was most amused. He was amused in that way now, and pleased. He spoke jerkily always, as though he were in too much of a hurry to complete his sentences.

'H'm,' he said. 'Graveyard, eh?'

'Yes. It's important, isn't it?'

31

'Bronze,' he said. 'Looks prehistoric to me.'

'That's very interesting, I believe.'

'Good girl!' he said. 'If you find anything more, bring it me.'

He nodded in a way which I realized meant dismissal, but I had no intention of being dismissed like that.

I said: 'You want me to leave you my ... er ... bronze?'

He narrowed his eyes and his jaw wagged slightly. 'Yours!' he bellowed. 'It's not yours.'

'I found it.'

'Findings – keepings, eh? No, not with this sort of thing, my girl. This belongs to the nation.'

'That's very strange.'

'Number of things you'll find strange before you're much older.'

'Is it of interest to archaeologists?'

'What do you know of archaeologists?'

'I know they dig and find things. They find all sorts of wonderful things. Roman baths and lovely tiles and things like that.'

'You don't fancy yourself as an archaeologist because you found this, do you?'

'It's doing the same as they do.'

'And that's what you'd like to do, is it?'

'Yes, I would. I know I'd be good at it. I'd find wonderful things that people didn't know were there in the earth.'

He laughed then – the wild roar. 'You fancy archaeologists are constantly finding jewels and Roman villas. You've got a lot to learn. Greater part of the time is spent digging, looking for things of little value –

things like this – the sort of things that have been found times out of number. That's what the majority of them do.'

'I wouldn't,' I said confidently. 'I'd find beautiful things . . . significant things.'

He laid a hand on my shoulder and led me to the door.

'You'd like to know what this is you've found, wouldn't you?'

'Yes. After all *I* found it.'

'I'll let you know when I get the verdict on it. And meanwhile . . . if you find anything else, you'll know what to do with it, won't you?'

'Bring it to you, Sir Ralph.'

He nodded and shut the door on me. I went slowly down through the hall and out into the courtyard. I had lost my piece of bronze but it was pleasant to remind myself that I had contributed to the knowledge of the world.

Although my find was identified as part of a shield, possibly of the Bronze Age, and it appeared that many of its kind had been found before, it brought about several changes which were important.

In the first place it sent up my prestige in the schoolroom. When I arrived for lessons both Hadrian and Theodosia were far more respectful than they had been before. I had always thought Theodosia rather a silly little thing – although she was about a year older than I – Hadrian was slightly older still. They were both fair – Theodosia rather fragile-looking with innocent blue eyes and a chin that receded a little. I was taller than she was and in fact almost as tall as

Hadrian. I never felt the difference in our ages, in fact in spite of the fact that they lived in this mansion and I came from the rectory I was a kind of leader and was constantly telling them what they ought to do.

They had been informed by their father that I had found something of some importance and had had the good sense to bring it along to him. He would like to see them show as much interest as I had.

I spent the morning on and off explaining how I had dug Josiah Polgrey's grave and how I had found the object and drove poor Miss Graham to despair. I drew the object for them. It had become enormous in my mind; it shone like gold. It had belonged to some King, who had buried it in the earth so that I should find it.

I whispered to them that we should all get spades and dig in Carter's Meadow because that was where they thought there was a lot of treasure. That afternoon we found spades in the gardeners' sheds and set to work. We were discovered and reprimanded; but the result was that Sir Ralph decided that we might learn something about archaeology and ordered the long-suffering Miss Graham to give us lessons. Poor Miss Graham was obliged to read up the subject and she did her best in a difficult situation. I was fascinated – far more than the others. Sir Ralph discovered this and his interest in me, which began when I discovered the bronze shield, seemed to grow.

Then Sir Edward Travers and his family came to the old Dower House. The Traverses were already friends of the Bodreans; they had visited Keverall Court many times and Sir Edward was behind the plans for Carter's Meadow. My find had increased that interest and was probably the reason why, since he was looking for a country house, Sir Edward decided on the Dower House.

Sir Edward was connected with Oxford University in some way but was constantly engaged on expeditions. His name was often in the papers and he was very well known in academic circles, but Sir Edward needed a country residence where he could be quiet to compile his finds and set it all out in book form after he returned from one of his trips, usually in far-off places.

There was a great deal of excitement when we heard they were coming. Hadrian told me that his uncle was delighted and that now nothing could stop them digging up Carter's Meadow – parson or no parson.

I was sure he was right for the poor Reverend James was not the man to go into battle. His objections were entirely due to the prodding of his more forceful parishioners. All he wanted was to be able to lead a quiet life and the chief duty of Dorcas and Alison was to keep from him anything that might disturb him. I believe he was delighted by the coming of Sir Edward, for even the more militant of his flock would not dare raise issue with such an important gentleman.

So the Traverses arrived and the Dower House became Giza House.

'Named after the Pyramids, I believe,' said Dorcas, and we confirmed this by looking it up in the encyclopaedia.

The dark old Dower House with the overgrown garden which had stood empty for so long was now inhabited. I could no longer so easily scare Theodosia with stories that it was haunted and dare her and Hadrian to run up the path and look through the windows. It lost none of the strangeness though. 'Once a house is haunted,' I told the nervous Theodosia, 'it's haunted for ever.'

And sure enough it was not long before we began to hear strange rumours of the house which was full of treasures from all over the world. Some of them were very old indeed, so that the servants didn't feel at home with them; and because of these strange things the place was 'creepy'. If it had not been for the fact that Sir Edward was such an important man whose name was often in the papers, they would not have stayed there.

So there was digging in Carter's Meadow and important tenants at Giza House. We learned that although Sir Edward was a widower he had two children – a son, Tybalt, who was grown up and at the University – and a daughter, Sabina, who was about the same age as Theodosia and myself and was therefore to share our lessons.

It was some time before I saw Tybalt but I decided to dislike him before I set eyes on him, largely because Sabina spoke of him with awe and reverence. She did not so much love as adore him. He was omniscient and omnipotent, according to her. He was handsome, in fact godlike.

'I don't believe anyone is as good as that,' I said scornfully, glaring at Hadrian, forcing him to agree with me. Theodosia could think what she liked; her opinion was unimportant.

Hadrian looked from me to Sabina and came down on my side. 'No,' he declared, 'nobody is.'

'Nobody but Tybalt,' insisted Sabina.

Sabina talked constantly and never minded whether anyone was listening or not. I told Hadrian this was because she lived in that strange house with her absent-minded father and those servants, two of whom were very strange indeed, for they were Egyptians named Mustapha and Absalam and wore long white robes and sandals. I had heard from our rectory cook that they gave the other servants 'the creeps' and with all the peculiar things that were in that house and those two gliding about so that you never knew whether they were spying on you and you not seeing them – it was a queer household.

Sabina was pretty; she had fair curls, and big grey eyes with long golden lashes and a little heart-shaped face. Theodosia, who was quite a plain child, very soon adored her. I quickly saw that their friendship strengthened the alliance between Hadrian and myself. Sometimes I used to think it had been better before the Traverses came because then the three of us made a pleasant little trio. I admit that I bullied them a little. Dorcas was always telling me that I must stop trying to organize everyone and believing that what I wanted for them was the best from every point of view. It was a fact that although Hadrian and Theodosia were the children of the big house and I came from the impecunious rectory and had been allowed to have lessons in their schoolroom as a favour, I did behave rather as though I were the daughter of Keverall Court and the others were the outsiders. I had explained to Dorcas that it was just because Hadrian could never make up his mind and Theodosia was too young and silly to have any ideas about anything.

Then there was Sabina, good-natured, her lovely hair always falling into place in a manner most becoming, while my thick straight dark locks were always escaping in disorder from anything with which I tried to bind them; her grey eyes would sparkle with gaiety when she spoke of frivolous things or shine with fervour when she talked of Tybalt. She was a charming girl, whose presence had changed the entire atmosphere of our schoolroom.

Through her we learned of life in Giza House. How her father was shut in his room for days and silent-footed Mustapha and Absalam took his meals to him on trays. Sabina had luncheon in a small dining-room just off the schoolroom at Keverall as I did each day except Saturdays and Sundays, but in Giza House when her father was working she often had meals alone or with her companion-housekeeper, Tabitha Grey, who gave her lessons at the piano. She always referred to her as Tabby and I christened her the Grey Tabby which amused them all; I pictured her as a middle-aged woman, with greying dusty-looking hair, grey skirts and dull muddy-coloured blouses. I was very surprised eventually to meet a striking-looking youngish woman.

I told Sabina that she was no good at describing anything. She had made Grey Tabby sound like a dowdy old woman and I was sure that that wonder hero Tybalt would turn out to be a pale-faced youth with eyes ruined by looking at too much crabbed writing on ancient manuscripts – which he must have done, mustn't he, since he was so clever – round-shouldered and knowing absolutely nothing about anything but long-dead people and what weapons they had used in battle.

'One day you may be able to see for yourself,' said Sabina, laughing.

We could hardly wait. She had so played on our imaginations — particularly mine, which Alison had once said worked overtime — that this miraculous brother of hers was never far from my thoughts. I was longing to see him. I had so built up this picture of the stooping bespectacled scholar that I believed it to be true and had forced Hadrian to do the same. Theodosia took Sabina's version. 'After all,' she said, 'Sabina's seen him. You haven't.'

'People get bemused,' I said. 'She sees him through rose-coloured spectacles.'

We could hardly wait when the time came for him to come down from Oxford. Sabina was exalted. 'Now you will see for yourselves.' One morning she came in in tears because Tybalt was not coming, after all. He was going up to Northumberland on a dig and he would no doubt spend the entire vacation up there. Sir Edward was going to join him.

Instead of Tybalt we had Evan Callum, who was a friend of Tybalt's. Wishing to earn a little money, he was going to spend the period before he went back to the University grounding us in the rudiments of archaeology, a subject in which he was quite proficient.

I forgot my disappointment about Tybalt and threw myself with fervour into my new studies. I was much more interested in the subject than the others. Sometimes in the afternoons I would go down to Carter's Meadow with Evan Callum and he would show me something of the practical work which had to be done.

Once I saw Sir Ralph there. He came over to speak to me.

'Interested eh?' he said.

I replied that I was.

'Found any more bronze shields?'

'No. I haven't found anything.'

He gave me a little push. 'Finds don't come often. You started off with yours.' His jaw wagged in the amused way, and I had a notion that he was rather pleased to see me there.

One of the workers who had come down with the party showed me how to piece a broken pot together. 'First aid,' he called it, until it could be treated properly and perhaps find its way into a museum. He showed me how to pack a piece of pottery which had been put together in this 'first-aid' manner and which was to be sent away to the experts who would restore it and place it in its period where it might or might not betray some little detail of how life was lived five hundred million years before.

I had dreamed of finding something in Carter's Meadow; golden ornaments, things that I had heard had been found in tombs. This was very different. I was disappointed for a while and then I began to develop a burning enthusiasm for the task itself. I could think of little else than the wonder of uncovering the record of the rocks.

Our lessons with Evan Callum were taken in the afternoons, because the mornings were spent with Miss Graham or Oliver Shrimpton learning what were called the three R's: Reading, Writing and Arithmetic. In addition, Theodosia, Sabina and I had to do needlework with Miss Graham and three mornings a week we worked for an hour on our samplers. The alphabet had to be worked, a proverb, our names and the date.

Naturally we chose the shortest proverb we could find but even so the task was laborious. Horrible little cross stitches on a piece of cotton and if one stitch was too large or too small it had to be unpicked and put right. I was in revolt against such time-wasting and I was so frustrated that my sampler suffered through it. There was music and we strummed on the piano under Miss Graham's supervision, but now we had Grey Tabby it was decided that she should give the music lessons. So with our periodic lessons in archaeology our education was running on quite unconventional lines. We had our teachers from three sources – Miss Graham from Keverall Court, Grey Tabby and Evan Callum through Giza House, and from the rectory Oliver Shrimpton. Dorcas was delighted. It was an excellent way, she said, of three families pooling their educational resources and providing an excellent education for the young people involved. She doubted that anywhere in the country a girl was getting such a well-grounded training. She hoped, she added, that I was making full use of it.

What did intrigue me were the sessions with Evan Callum. I told him that when I was grown up I should go with expeditions to the far places of the world. He replied that he thought that as a female I might find this difficult unless I married an archaeologist; but all the same he encouraged me. It was gratifying to have such an apt pupil. We were all interested but my natural enthusiasm was perhaps more intense and more obvious.

I became particularly fascinated by the Egyptian scene. There was so much to be discovered there. I loved hearing about that old civilization; the gods that

41

were worshipped, the dynasties, the temples that had been discovered; I caught my enthusiasm from Evan. 'There's a treasure store in the hills of the desert, Judith,' he used to say.

Of course I pictured myself there, making fantastic discoveries, receiving the congratulations of people like Sir Edward Travers.

I had imagined myself having long conversations with him but he, I must say, was a disappointment. He never seemed to see any of us. He had a strange far-away look in his eyes as though he were looking far back into the past.

'I expect that awful old Tybalt is just like him,' I said to Hadrian.

Tybalt had become a new word which I had introduced into our vocabulary. It meant 'mean, despicable'. Hadrian and I used to tease Sabina with it.

'I don't care,' she said, 'nothing *you* say can change Tybalt.'

I was fascinated by Giza House though, and although I was a hopeless musician I used to look forward to going there. As soon as I entered the house I would become excited. There was something peculiar about it. 'Sinister,' I told Hadrian, who agreed as he usually did with me.

In the first place it was dark. The bushes which surrounded the house might have been responsible for that, but in the house there were so many rich velvet curtains – not only at windows but over doors and alcoves in which were often strange images. It was so thickly carpeted that you rarely heard people come and go and I always had the sensation in that house that I was overlooked.

42

There was a strange old woman who lived at the top of this house in what appeared to be an apartment of her own. Sabina referred to her as old Nanny Tester.

'Who is she?' I demanded.

'She was my mother's nanny and Tybalt's and mine.'

'What's she doing up there?'

'She just lives up there.'

'But you don't want a nanny now surely?'

'We don't turn old servants out when they have served us many years,' said Sabina haughtily.

'*I* believe she's a witch.'

'Believe what you like, Judith Osmond. She's old Nanny Tester.'

'She spies on us. She's always peering out of the window and dodging back when we look up.'

'Oh don't take any notice of Judith,' said Sabina.

Every time I went to the place I looked up to the top window for Nanny Tester. I had convinced myself that it was a strange house in which anything could happen.

The drawing-room was the most normal room, but even that had an oriental look. There were several Chinese vases and images which Sir Edward had picked up in China. There were some beautiful pictures on the walls – delicate and in pastel shades; there were dragons and fat buddhas with sly sleepy looks and thin ones sitting with apparent comfort in a position which I had tried unsuccessfully to copy; there were ladies with inscrutable faces and mandarins with cruel ones. But the grand piano gave the place an air of normality and it was on this that we strummed out our lessons under the tuition of Grey Tabby, who was as enigmatical as one of the Chinese ladies in the cabinet.

Whenever I had an opportunity I would peep into other rooms forcing Hadrian to look with me. He was reluctant, but he was afraid not to do as I wished because he knew that I would call him a coward if he refused.

We had been studying with Evan Callum some of the lore of old Egypt and I was greatly fascinated. He gave us an account of some recent discoveries there in which Sir Edward Travers had been involved; and then he went on to give us a little insight into the history of that country.

When I listened to Evan Callum I would be transported out of the schoolroom into the temples of the gods. I listened avidly to the story of the self-begotten god Ra – often known as Amen-Ra; and his son Osiris who with Isis begot the great god Horus. He showed us pictures of the masks which priests wore during religious ceremonies and told us that each god was represented by one of the masks.

'The idea being,' he explained, 'that the great gods of the Egyptians possessed all the strengths and virtues of men, but in addition they had one attribute of an animal; and this animal was their particular sign. Horus was the hawk because his eyes saw all and quickly.' I pored over the pictures he showed us. I was an apt pupil.

But I think what interested me most were the accounts of burials when the bodies of the important dead were embalmed and put in their tombs and there left to rest for thousands of years. With them would often be buried their servants who might have been killed merely that they might accompany them and remain their servants in the new life as in the old.

Treasure was stored in their tombs that they might not suffer poverty in the future.

'This custom, of course,' Evan explained to us, 'has led to many of the tombs being robbed. Throughout the centuries daring men had plundered them ... daring indeed, for it is said that the Curse of the Pharaohs descends on those who disturb their eternal rest.'

I was very interested to hear how it was possible to keep a person's body for centuries. 'The embalming process,' Evan explained, 'is one which was perfected three thousand years before the birth of Christ. It was a secret and no one has ever really discovered how the ancient Egyptians did it so expertly.'

It was absorbing. There were books with pictures. I was never tired of talking of this fascinating subject; I wanted to ignore other lessons for the sake of going on with Evan.

Sabina said she had seen a mummy. They had had one at Giza once.

Evan talked to her about it and I was a little envious that Sabina who had not taken particular note of it should have had the opportunity which I should have made such use of.

'It was in a sort of coffin,' said Sabina.

'A sarcophagus,' supplied Evan.

'We've still got it, I believe,' said Sabina. 'But the mummy has gone.' She shuddered. 'I'm glad. I didn't like it. It was horrible.'

'It was interesting,' I cried. 'Just imagine. It was somebody who had actually lived thousands of years ago!'

I couldn't get the thought of it out of my mind

and a few days later when we went for our music lesson I decided that I was going to see it. Theodosia was at the piano. She was better than the rest of us and Tabby gave her extra tuition.

I said: 'Now is the time.' And Sabina led us to that strange room. This was the one, of course, which I had heard about, the room which gave the servants 'the creeps' and which they wouldn't enter alone.

I saw the sarcophagus at once. It stood in a corner of the room; it was like a stone trough. Along the top of it were rows of hieroglyphs.

I knelt down and examined them.

'My father is trying to decipher them,' explained Sabina. 'That's why it's here. Later it will go to some museum.'

I touched it wonderingly. 'Just imagine . . . thousands of years ago people made these signs and someone was embalmed and laid inside there. Don't you think that's wonderful? Oh, how I wish they'd left the mummy!'

'You can see them in the British Museum. It's just like someone done up with a lot of bandages.'

I stood up and looked about the room. The walls of one side were lined with books. I looked at their bindings. Many were in languages I could not understand.

I said: 'There's a strange feeling in this room. Are you aware of it?'

'No,' said Sabina. 'You're trying to frighten us.'

'It's because it's dark,' said Hadrian. 'It's the tree outside the window.'

'Listen,' I said.

'It's the wind,' said Sabina scornfully. 'And come on. We mustn't be found in here.'

She was relieved when she shut the door behind us. But I couldn't forget that room.

For the next few days I looked up everything I could find about ancient burials. The others were impatient with me because when I had an idea I was obsessed by it and would talk of nothing else. Sabina was very impatient and Theodosia had begun to agree with everything Sabina said.

She declared she was tired of all this talk about mummies. They were nothing but dead people anyway. She had heard that if they were exposed to the air and the wrappings removed they all crumbled to dust. Why get excited about a lot of dust?

'But they were real people once. Let's go and look at the sarcophagus again.'

'No,' wailed Sabina. 'And this is *my* house, so if you go without me you're trespassing.'

'I believe you're afraid of that room,' I declared.

She indignantly denied this.

I became more and more obsessed and wanted to know exactly what it felt like to be embalmed and laid to rest in a sarcophagus. I forced Hadrian to join me and together we found some old sheets and one of these we cut into strips, and when we all went to Giza House for our music lesson Hadrian and I contrived to have ours first and then we went into the garden where we had hidden our sheets and bandages in an old summer-house. We retrieved them and together we went into the room in which was the sarcophagus. I put the sheet over my head – having cut holes in it for my eyes – and made Hadrian bind me up with the bandages. I scrambled into the sarcophagus and lay there.

My only excuse is that I was young and thoughtless. It just seemed a tremendous joke – and an exciting one too. I thought I was very brave and bold to lie in that sarcophagus alone in the room, for I had twinges of doubt and felt that my boldness might arouse at any moment the wrath of the gods.

It seemed a long time before the door opened. Sabina said: 'Oh, why do you want to keep looking at it . . .' And I knew Hadrian had brought them in as we had arranged.

Then they saw me. There was a bloodcurdling scream. I tried to scramble out of the trough-like receptacle which smelt peculiar and was so cold. It was the worst thing that I could have done for Theodosia, seeing this thing rising from the dead, as she believed, began to scream.

I heard Hadrian shout: 'It's only Judith.'

I saw Sabina was as white as the sheet which was wrapped round me; and then Theodosia slid to the floor in a faint.

'It's all right, Theodosia,' I cried. 'It's Judith. It's not a real mummy.'

'I believe she's dead,' said Sabina. 'You've killed her.'

'Theodosia!' I wailed. 'You're not dead. People can't die like that.'

Then I saw the stranger standing in the doorway. He was tall, and so different from anyone I had ever seen before that for the moment I thought he was one of the gods come for vengeance. He looked angry enough.

He stared at me. What a sight I must have looked – my bandages hanging about me, the sheet still over my head.

From me he looked to Theodosia. 'Good God,' he said and picked her up.

'Judith dressed up as a mummy,' squealed Sabina. 'It's frightened Theodosia.'

'How utterly stupid!' he said, giving me such a look of contempt that I was glad of the sheet to cover my shame.

'Is she dead, Tybalt?' went on Sabina.

He did not answer; he walked out of the room with Theodosia in his arms.

I scrambled out of the bandages and sheet and rolled them into a bundle.

Sabina came running back into the room.

'They're all fussing around Theodosia,' she informed us, and added rather gleefully: 'They're all angry with you two.'

'It was my idea,' I said, 'wasn't it, Hadrian?'

Hadrian agreed that it was.

'It's nothing to be proud of,' said Sabina severely. 'You might have killed her.'

'She's all right?' I said anxiously.

'She's sitting up now, but she looks pale and she's gasping.'

'She was only a bit frightened,' I said.

'People can die of fright.'

'Well, she isn't going to.'

Tybalt came into the room. He still looked angry.

'What on earth did you think you two were doing?'

I looked at Hadrian who waited as usual for me to speak. 'I was only being a mummy,' I said.

'Aren't you a little old for such tricks?'

I felt small and bitterly humiliated.

'You didn't think, I suppose, of the effect this might have on those who were not in the joke?'

'No,' I said, 'I didn't think.'

'It's quite a good habit. I should try it some time.'

If anyone else had said that to me I should have been ready with a pert answer. But he was different ... right from the beginning I knew it.

He had turned to Hadrian. 'And what have you to say?'

'Only the same as Judith. We didn't mean to hurt her.'

'You've behaved very stupidly,' he said; and turned and left us.

'So that's the great Tybalt!' said Hadrian, waiting until he was out of earshot.

'Yes,' I said, 'the great Tybalt!'

'You said he stooped and wore glasses.'

'Well, I was wrong. He doesn't. We'd better go now.' I heard Tybalt's voice as we went down the stairs.

'Who is that insolent girl?'

He was referring to me of course.

Sabina joined us in the hall. 'Theodosia is to go back in the carriage,' she said. 'You two are to walk back. There's going to be trouble.'

She seemed rather pleased about it.

There *was* trouble. Miss Graham was waiting for us in the schoolroom.

She looked worried – but then she often did. She was constantly afraid, I realized later, that she would be blamed and dismissed.

'Young Mr Travers came over in the carriage, with

50

Theodosia,' she said. 'He has told Sir Ralph all about your wickedness. You are both going to be severely punished. Theodosia has gone to bed. Her ladyship is most anxious and has sent for the doctor. Theodosia is not very strong.'

I couldn't help feeling that Theodosia was making the most of the occasion. After all, what was she worried about? She knew now that I had been the mummy.

We went into the library, that room where three of the walls were lined with books and the other was almost all window – large, mullioned, window-seated and with heavy dark green curtains. It was a somewhat oppressive room because so many objects seemed to be huddled together under the enormous glass chandelier. There were carved wooden tables from India and figures with similar carving. Chinese vases and an ornate Louis Quinze table supported by gilded cherubs. Sir Ralph had had this assortment of treasures brought to him from all parts of the world and had gathered them together here irrespective of their suitability. All this I noticed later. At this time I was aware only of the two men in the room. Sir Ralph and Tybalt.

'What is all this, eh?' demanded Sir Ralph.

Hadrian always seemed to be struck dumb in the presence of his uncle so it was up to me to speak. I tried to explain.

'No right to be in that room! No right to play such silly tricks. You're going to be punished for this. And you won't like it.'

I did not want Tybalt to see that I was afraid. I was thinking of the worst punishment that could befall me. No more lessons with Evan Callum.

'Have you nothing to say for yourself?' Sir Ralph was glaring at Hadrian.

'We only . . . pretended.'

'Speak up.'

'It was my idea,' I said.

'Let the boy speak for himself . . . if he can.'

'We . . . we thought it would be a good idea for Judith to dress up. . . .'

Sir Ralph made an impatient noise. Then he turned to me. 'So you were the ring-leader, eh?'

I nodded and I was suddenly relieved because I was sure I saw his chin move.

'All right,' he said. 'You'll see what happens to people who play such tricks. You go back to the rectory now and you'll see what's in store for you.' Then to Hadrian, 'And you, sir. You go to your room. You're going to have the whipping of your life because I'm going to administer it myself. Get out.'

Poor Hadrian! It was so humiliating – and in front of Tybalt too!

Hadrian was severely beaten, which at sixteen was hard to endure.

When I arrived back at the rectory it was to find Dorcas and Alison very disturbed, as they had been already informed of my sinful folly.

'Why, Judith, what if Sir Ralph had refused to have you at Keverall Court again?'

'Has he?' I asked anxiously.

'No, but orders are that you are to be punished and we daren't go against that.'

The Reverend James had retired to his study muttering something about pressure of work. This was trouble and he was going to be out of it.

'Well,' I demanded, 'what are you going to do to me?'

'You are to go to your room and read a book which Mr Callum has sent for you. You are to write an essay on its contents and to have nothing but bread and water until the task is completed. You are to do this if you stay in your room for a week.'

It was no real punishment for me. Dear Evan! The book he chose for me was *The Dynasties of Ancient Egypt* which fascinated me; and our cook at the Rectory in the safety of her kitchen declared that she was not taking orders from Keverall Court; nor was she having me on bread and water. The next thing, she prophesied, would be Dr Gunwen's brougham at the door and nobody was going to make her starve little children. I was amused that I who had often been called a limb of Satan should have suddenly become a little child. However, during that period some of my favourite foods were smuggled in to me. There was a hot steamy pasty, I remember, and one of her special miniature squab pies.

I had quite a pleasant two days, for my task was finished in record time; and I learned later from Evan that Sir Ralph, far from expressing his disapproval of my exploit, was rather pleased about it.

We were growing up and changes came, but so gradually that one scarcely noticed them.

Tybalt was frequently at Giza House. One of my favourite dreams at that time was that I made a great discovery. This varied. Sometimes I dug up an object of inestimable value; at others I found some tremendous significance in the hieroglyphs about the sarcophagus at Giza House, and this discovery of mine so shook the archaeological world that Tybalt was overcome with admiration. He asked me to marry him and we went off to Egypt together where for the rest of our lives we lived happily ever after, piling up discovery after discovery, so that we became famous. 'I owe it all to you,' said Tybalt, at the end of the dream.

The truth was that he scarcely noticed me, and I believed that if ever he thought of me it was as the silly girl who had dressed up as a mummy and frightened Theodosia.

It was different with Theodosia. Instead of despising her for fainting, he seemed to like her for it. She had opportunities for knowing him which were denied me. After lessons were over I went back to the rectory while she, now that she was growing up, joined the family at dinner and the guests were often Tybalt and his father.

Hadrian went off to the University to study archaeology, which was his uncle's choice rather than his. Hadrian had confided to me that he was dependent on his uncle, for his parents were in meagre circumstances. His father – Sir Ralph's brother – had married without the family's consent. Hadrian was the eldest of four brothers and Sir Ralph, having no son of his own had offered to take him and educate him – so Sir Ralph had to be placated.

'You're lucky,' I said. 'Wouldn't I like to go and study archaeology.'

'You were always mad about it.'

'It's something to be mad about.'

54

I missed having Hadrian to order about. He was so meek; he had always done what I wanted.

Then Evan Callum ceased to come to teach because he had graduated and had taken a post in one of the universities. Miss Graham and Oliver Shrimpton continued to teach us and we still had music lessons with Tabitha Grey; but the changes were setting in.

Dorcas tried to teach me a few of what she called 'home crafts', which meant trying to impart a light touch with pastry and showing me how to make bread and preserves. I was not really very good at that.

'You'll need it one day,' she said, 'when you have a home of your own. Do you realize you're nearly eighteen, Judith? Why, some girls are married at that age.'

When she said that there was a little frown on her brow. I believe that she and Alison worried a little about my future. I knew that they hoped I would marry – and I knew whom.

We all liked Oliver Shrimpton. He was pleasant, not exactly ambitious but he had an enthusiasm for his work. He was an asset in the parish and for the last two or three years since the Reverend James seemed to get more and more easily tired he had – as Dorcas and Alison admitted – practically carried the parish on his own shoulders. He got on well with the old ladies and the not so old ones liked him very much. There were several spinsters who couldn't do enough in church activities and I guessed their enthusiasm had something to do with Oliver.

He and I had always been good friends. I had not shone at the subjects he had taught but living under the same roof with him for so long I regarded him as a kind of brother. I sometimes wondered, though, if I had never seen Tybalt I might have been reconciled to the idea of marrying him and going on in the rectory which had been my home all my life – for it was a foregone conclusion that when the Reverend James retired or died, Oliver would come into the living.

I could not talk to anyone of my feelings for Tybalt. They were absurd anyway, for surely it was ridiculous to feel this intense passion for someone who was hardly aware of one's existence.

But our relationship did undergo a change and he began to be a little aware of me. Tabitha Grey was very kindly and she noticed how despondent I was when Evan Callum ceased to teach us. As I grew older she seemed to grow younger. I suppose at fourteen anyone of twenty-four seems very old; but when one is nearly eighteen, twenty-eight seemed younger than twenty-four did at fourteen. Tabitha was Mrs Grey so she had been married. Ever to have called her Grey Tabby was incongruous. She was tall with rippling dark hair and large light brown eyes; when she played the piano her expression changed, something ethereal touched it, and she was then undoubtedly beautiful. She was gentle-natured, by no means communicative; sometimes I thought there was a haunting sadness in her face.

I had tried to find out from Sabina what exactly her position was in the household.

'Oh, she just manages everything,' said Sabina. 'She's there for me when my father and Tybalt are away; and she looks after the servants – and Nanny Tester too, though Nanny won't admit it. She knows quite a lot about Father's work. He talks to her about it – so does Tybalt.'

I was more interested than ever and that gave us something in common. I had one or two talks with her after our music lesson. She became quite animated discussing Sir Edward's work. She told me that on one occasion she had been a member of his party when they had gone down to Kent working on some Roman excavation.

'When Sabina is married I shall go again,' she said. 'It's a pity that you're a girl. If you had been a boy you might have taken archaeology up as a profession.'

'I don't think we have the money for that at the rectory. I was lucky, they tell me, to get the sort of education I have. I shall have to earn some money. What I shall do, I don't know . . . except that I shall probably have to be a governess.'

'You never know what's waiting for you,' she said. Then she lent me some books. 'There's no reason why you shouldn't go on reading and learning all you can.'

It was when I went to Giza House one late afternoon to return some books that I heard music. I guessed Tabitha was playing and, glancing through the window into the drawing-room, I saw her seated at the piano and Tybalt was with her; they were playing a duet. As I watched the duet ended; they turned to each other and smiled. I thought then: How I wish he would smile at me like that.

As people do, they seemed to guess that they were being watched and both of them looked simultaneously towards the window and saw me.

I felt ashamed for being caught looking in but Tabitha waved that aside.

'Come in, Judith,' she said. 'Oh, you've brought the books back. I've been lending these to Judith, Tybalt. She's very interested.'

Tybalt looked at the books and his eyes lit up quite warmly.

'What did you think of them?'

'I was fascinated.'

'We must find some more for her, Tabitha.'

'That was what I was going to do.'

We went into the drawing-room and we talked ... how we talked! I had not felt so *alive* since Evan Callum had left.

Tybalt walked back to the rectory with me, carrying the books; and he went on talking too, telling me of the adventures he had had; and how excited he had been when he had found certain things.

I listened avidly.

At the door of the rectory he said: 'You really are very interested, aren't you?'

'Yes,' I answered earnestly.

'Of course I always knew that you were interested in mummies.'

We laughed. He said goodbye and that we must have another chat. 'In the meantime,' he said, 'go on reading. I'm going to tell Tabitha what books to give you.'

'Oh thank you!' I said earnestly.

Dorcas must have seen us from one of the windows.

'Wasn't that Tybalt Travers?' she said as I started to ascend the stairs.

I said it was; and because she waited for some explanation I went on: 'I took some books back to Giza and he walked back with me.'

'Oh!' was all she said.

The very next day she mentioned him again. 'I've heard that they're expecting a match between Tybalt Travers and Theodosia.'

I felt sick. I hope I didn't show it.

'Well,' went on Dorcas cautiously, 'it's to be expected. The Traverses and the Bodreans have been friends for years. I'm sure Sir Ralph would like to see the families united.'

No, I thought. Never. Silly little Theodosia! It wasn't possible.

But of course I knew that it was highly probable.

Oliver Shrimpton had an opportunity of a living in Dorset. Dorcas and Alison were very upset.

'What we shall do without you, Oliver, I can't imagine,' said Alison.

'You've been wonderful,' Dorcas told him.

He went to see the Bishop, and I have never seen Dorcas and Alison quite so happy as they were when he came back.

I was in my room reading when they came in. 'He's refused it,' they said.

I said, 'Who?'

'Oliver.'

'But what has he refused?'

'I don't believe you're listening.'

'It takes a little time to tear oneself away from ancient Egypt to the rectory of St Erno's.'

'You get too deep into those books. I don't think it's good for you. But Oliver has been to see the Bishop and refused the living. He has explained that he wishes to stay here, and the understanding is that when Father retires he will become rector here.'

'That's wonderful news,' I said. 'Now we shan't have to worry about losing him.'

'He must be very fond of us,' said Dorcas, 'to do so much for us.'

'Fond of some of us,' said Alison significantly.

Evan Callum came down to stay at Giza House with the Traverses. I believe he was invited quite often to Keverall Court.

He called at the rectory to see me and we had a very interesting talk. He told me I had been his most promising pupil and it was a great shame that I had not been able to take up the subject in earnest.

Miss Graham found another post and left; and then lessons were over. It was quite clear that I was never going to be a musician; but I didn't need that excuse now to go to Giza House. I could go into the library there and select books and if they were not some of Sir Edward's precious ones, I could take them home.

I saw very little of Theodosia now. There were many parties at Keverall Court to which naturally I was not invited; and there was entertaining at Giza too which was quite different – although Tybalt and his father often went to Keverall and Sir Ralph and Lady Bodrean visited Giza – but I gathered from Tabitha that there were dinner-parties when the conversation sparkled and of course it centred round the work of those guests – this fascinating absorption with the past.

Life was quite changed for me. I did some of the parish visiting with Dorcas and Alison. I took flowers from the garden to the sick; I read to those whose eyesight was failing; I took food to the bedridden and went off to the town to shop for them in the little trap we called the jingle – a two-wheeled vehicle drawn by our own Jorrocks, who was something between a horse and a pony.

I was settling down to becoming a typical rectory daughter. That Christmas Oliver and I brought in the Yule log and I made the Christmas Bush with Alison and Dorcas. This consisted of two wooden hoops fastened one into the other at right angles and we decorated this framework with evergreens – an old Cornish custom which we continued to follow rather than have the Christmas Tree which, said some of the old folk, was a foreign invention. I went carol singing and when we called at Keverall Court we were invited in for hot pasties and saffron cake and a sip from the great Wassailing Bowl. I saw Theodosia and Hadrian in the great hall and I felt a nostalgia for the old days.

Soon after that Christmas we had a frosty snap – rare with us. The branches of trees were white with hoarfrost and the children could even skate on the ponds. The Reverend James caught a cold and this was followed by a heart attack; and although he recovered slightly, within a week he was dead.

Dorcas and Alison were heartbroken. To me he had been remote for a long time. He had spent so much time in his bedroom; and even when he was in a room with us he scarcely spoke so it was like not having him there at all.

Cook said it was a Happy Release, because the poor Reverend Gentleman would never have been himself again.

And so the rectory blinds were drawn down and

the day came when bells tolled and we lowered the Reverend James Osmond into the grave which Mr Pegger had dug for him and then we went back to the rectory to eat cold ham and mourn.

Fear of the future mingled with the grief of Alison and Dorcas; but they were expectant, looking to me and to Oliver to bring about the obvious solution.

I shut myself in my room and thought about it. They wanted me to marry Oliver, who would become the rector in the Reverend James Osmond's place and we could all go on living under this roof as before.

How could I marry Oliver? I couldn't marry anyone but Tybalt. How could I tell Dorcas and Alison that! Moreover it was only in my wild and improbable dreams that that happy state of affairs could come about. I wanted to explain to them: I like Oliver. I know he is a good man. But you don't understand. I only have to say Tybalt's name and my heart beats faster. I know that they will think marriage with Theodosia a good match – but I can't help it.

Oliver had changed since he had become rector. He was as kind as ever to us; but of course, as Dorcas said to Alison, unless something was *arranged*, they and I would have to move out.

Quite suddenly something was arranged. Poor Alison! Poor Dorcas!

It was Alison who broached the subject. I think Oliver had been trying to but was too kind to do so for fear it would appear that he was asking them to leave.

Alison said: 'Now that we have a new rector it is time for us to go.'

62

As for me, I was dependent on them. They were happy to share everything they had with me but it would be far from an affluent existence.

'But it was always intended that I should be equipped to work if need be,' I said.

'Well,' admitted Dorcas, 'that was one of the reasons why we were so pleased to be able to give you such a good education.'

'We might hear of something congenial,' suggested Alison. It was no use sitting down waiting to hear. I promised myself and them that as soon as they were settled in their new home I would go and find a post.

I was uneasy – not at the prospect of working but of leaving St Erno's. I pictured myself in some household far away from Giza House when I should quickly be forgotten by its inhabitants. And what should I do? Become a governess like Miss Graham? It was the kind of post for which I was most suited. Perhaps as I had had a classical education more advanced than most rectory girls, I might teach in a girls' school. It would be less stultifying than working in some household where I was not considered worthy to mix with the family and yet was that little bit above the servants, which made it impossible for them to accept me. What was there for a young well-educated woman to do in this day and age?

I could not bear to think of the future. I began to say to myself: If I had never found the bronze shield the Traverses might not have come to Giza House. I should never have met Tybalt and Oliver would never have met Sabina. Oliver and I might in time have recognized what a convenient thing it would have been for us to marry and we might have done so. We might have had a peaceful, mildly happy life together as so many people do; and I should have been spared the anguish of leaving everything that was important to me.

Sir Ralph came to the rescue. There was a cottage on his estate which was vacant and he would allow the Misses Osmond to have it for a peppercorn rent.

They were delighted. It had solved half the problem.

Sir Ralph was determined to be our benefactor. Lady Bodrean needed a companion – someone who would read to her whenever required to do so, assist her in her charities, give the help she needed when she entertained. In fact a secretary-companion. Sir Ralph thought that I might be suitable for the post, and Lady Bodrean was ready to consider me.

Alison and Dorcas were delighted.

'After our disappointment everything is working out so well,' they cried. 'We have our cottage and it would be wonderful to have you not too far away. Just imagine, we should be able to see you frequently. Oh, it would be wonderful . . . if . . . er . . . you could get along with Lady Bodrean.'

'Ah, "there's the rub",' I quoted light-hearted. But I felt far from that.

And not without reason. Lady Bodrean, I had always felt, had never really cared for me to join her daughter and nephew in the Keverall Court schoolroom. On the rare occasions when I had seen her I had been met by frosty stares.

She always reminded me of a ship, for with her voluminous petticoats and skirts which rustled as she walked she seemed to sail along without being aware of anyone in her path. I had never tried to ingratiate myself with her, being conscious of a certain antagonism. Now I was in a different position.

She received me in her private sitting-room, a small apartment – as rooms went in Keverall Court – but it was about twice the size of the cottage rooms. It was overcrowded with furniture. On the mantelpiece were vases and ornaments very close together; there were cabinets filled with china and silver and a what-not in one corner of the room full of little china pieces. The chairs were covered by tapestry worked by Lady Bodrean herself. There were two firescreens also of tapestry, and two stools. The frame with a new piece stood close to her chair and she was working at this when I was shown into her room.

She did not look up for quite a minute implying that she found her work more interesting than the new companion. It might have been disconcerting if I had been the timid sort.

Then: 'Oh, it's Miss Osmond. You've come about the post. You may sit down.'

I sat, my head high, the colour in my cheeks.

'Your duties,' she said, 'will be to make yourself useful to me in any capacity which arises.'

I said: 'Yes, Lady Bodrean.'

'You will look after my engagements, both social and philanthropic. You will read the papers to me each day. You will care for my two pomeranians, Orange and Lemon.' At the mention of their names the two dogs reclining on cushions placed in chairs on either side of her and whom I had not noticed when I entered raised their heads and regarded me with contempt. Orange – or it might have been Lemon – barked; the other one sniffed. 'Darlings,' said Lady

Bodrean with a tender smile, but her expression was immediately frosty when she turned back to me. 'You will of course be available for anything I may require. Now I should like to hear you read a passage to me.'

Opening *The Times*, she handed it to me. I started to read of the resignation of Bismarck and the plan to cede Heligoland to Germany.

I was aware of her scrutinizing me as I read. She had a lorgnette attached to a gold chain about her waist and she quizzed me quite openly. The sort of treatment one must expect when one was about to become an employee, I supposed.

'Yes, that will do,' she said in the middle of a sentence so that I knew that engaging a companion was of greater moment than the fate of Heligoland.

'I should like you to start ... immediately. I hope that is convenient.'

I said I should need a day or so to settle my affairs, though what affairs I was not sure. All I knew was that I wanted to postpone taking up my new post for I found the prospect depressing.

She graciously conceded that I might have the rest of that day and the next in which to prepare myself. The day after that she would expect me to take up my duties.

On the way back to the cottage (which had the delectable name of Rainbow Cottage although the only reason known for this was that the flowers which used to be grown in the garden were all the colours of the rainbow) I tried to think of the advantages of my new position, and told myself that while I was going to hate being employed by Lady Bodrean, I would have opportunities of seeing Tybalt.

The Months of Bondage

My room at Keverall Court was close to that of Lady Bodrean, in case she should want me at any time. It was a pleasant enough room – all the rooms at Keverall were gracious, even the smallest – with its panelled walls and mullioned window. And from the window I could see the roof of Giza House, by which I was foolishly comforted.

I had not been in the house long when I came to the conclusion that Lady Bodrean disliked me. She would ring her bell quite often after I had retired for the night and would tell me peevishly that she could not sleep. I must make tea for her, or read to her until she dozed; and I would often sit shivering because she liked a cold bedroom, and she was comfortable enough under her blankets while I was often in my dressing-gown. She was never satisfied with anything I did. If there was nothing of which to complain she was silent; if there was, then she would refer to it over and over again.

Her personal maid Jane commiserated with me.

'Her ladyship seems to have it in for you,' she admitted. 'It's often like that. I've seen it before. A regular servant's got a sort of dignity. There's always housemaids or parlourmaids or lady's maids wanted. But companions and such like – well, that's up another street.'

I suppose some natures could have borne it better

than mine, but I had never been one to accept injustice; and in the old days when I had come to this house I had come on equal terms with Theodosia. It was very hard to accept the new position and it was only the alternative of banishment from St Erno's which made me stay on.

I took my meals alone in my room. During them I usually read the books I had borrowed from Giza House. I didn't see Tybalt during this time for he and his father had gone away for a while on some expedition into the Midlands, but Tabitha always had books for me.

She would say: 'Tybalt thought this would interest you.'

These books, my visits to Tabitha and the knowledge that Dorcas and Alison were happily settled provided the only brightness in my life at that time.

I saw Theodosia now and then. She would have been quite pleasant to me if her mother would have allowed it. There was nothing malicious or proud about Theodosia. She was negative; she took her colour from people about her; she would never be actively unkind; but at the same time she did little to alleviate my position. Perhaps she remembered the past when I had been inclined to bully her.

When I saw Sir Ralph he would ask me how I was getting on and he gave that amused look which I had seen so often. I could not say to him: 'I dislike your wife and I would leave her tomorrow if I did not know that however unhappy I am here I should be far more so elsewhere.'

I went to Rainbow Cottage to see Dorcas and Alison as often as I could. It was an interesting little place about three hundred years old, I think, and it had been built in the days when any family who could build a cottage in a night could claim the land on which it had been erected as their own. It was the custom in those days to collect bricks and tiles and to start building as soon as it was dark and work through the night. Four walls and a roof constituted a dwelling and that was done by morning. After that, the place could be added to. That was what had happened to Rainbow Cottage. When the Bodreans had acquired the cottage they had used it for their dependants and added to it considerably, but some of the old features remained such as the old talfat – a sort of ledge high up on the wall on which children used to sleep and which was reached by a ladder. Now it boasted a moderately good kitchen with a cloam oven in which Dorcas used to bake the most delicious bread I had ever tasted; then there was a copper in which they used to cook the scalded milk to make clotted cream. They were really very happy in Rainbow Cottage with its pleasant little garden; though of course they missed the spacious rectory.

I used to hate leaving them and going back to Keverall Court and my onerous duties, and consoled myself by doing malicious imitations of Lady Bodrean as I paraded round the cottage sitting-room brandishing an imaginary lorgnette.

'And Sir Ralph,' they asked timidly. 'Do you see much of him?'

'Very little. I'm not exactly one of the family, you know.'

'It's a shame,' said Dorcas hotly; but Alison silenced her.

'When you were having lessons there it was so different,' complained Dorcas.

'Yes, I never thought then that I wasn't one of them. But then I hadn't a post, and it was amazing how little I was aware of Lady Bodrean . . . fortunately.'

'It may change,' hazarded Alison.

I was optimistic by nature, and even at that dreary time I had my dreams. They were the usual cliché type. The dinner-party — one of the guests, a lady, was unable to come. They could not sit down with thirteen. Very well, there is the companion. 'She's quite presentable. After all, she was educated here.' And so I went down to dine in a gown which Theodosia found for me (and she had looked frightful in it but it was just right for me) and there I was 'Next to someone you know,' whispered Theodosia. 'Oh!' cried Tybalt. 'How delightful to see you!' And we talked and everyone was aware of how absorbed he was by his neighbour at the dining table and afterwards he would not leave her side. 'How glad I am,' he said, 'that Lady X . . . Y . . . Z . . .' what did her name matter? . . . 'how glad I am that she could not come tonight.'

Dreams! Dreams! But what else was there for me during that unsatisfactory period of my life?

I had read until I was hoarse.

'Your voice is not good today, Miss Osmond. Oh dear, how tiresome! One of the chief duties I look for is your reading.'

She would sit there and in and out went the needle with its tail of red or blue or violet wool and I was sure she was not listening to what I was reading. If only I could have read from one of the books I brought from

Giza House! Sometimes I had the mischievous thought that I would substitute one and see whether she knew the difference.

Sometimes she would lay aside her tapestry and close her eyes. I would go on reading, unsure whether she was awake or not. Sometimes I stopped to see if she had noticed. Often I caught her sleeping; but then she would catch me for she would awake suddenly and demand to know why I was not reading.

I would say meekly: 'I thought you were sleeping, Lady Bodrean. I was afraid I should disturb you.'

'Nonsense,' she would retort. 'Pray go on and *I* will say when we shall stop.'

She kept me reading on that day until my eyes were tired and my voice weary. I began to think of escaping at any price; but I always came back to the thought of going away and never seeing Tybalt again.

Orange and Lemon turned out to be blessings for they needed daily exercise and this gave me the opportunity to get away from the house and it was easy to slip over to Giza House and have a chat with Tabitha.

One day I called and knew immediately that something exciting had happened. She took me into the drawing-room and told me that Sir Edward was planning an expedition to Egypt. It was going to be one of his most ambitious efforts. She hoped to accompany the party. 'Now that Sabina is married,' she said, 'there is no need for me to stay here.'

'You will have some job to do?'

'Not an official job, of course, but I can make myself useful. I can housekeep if that should be necessary and I have picked up quite a lot. I can be useful in a fetch-and-carry sort of way as amateurs are.'

73

I looked at her ecstatically. 'How I envy you!'

She smiled that gentle, sweet smile of hers. 'Lady Bodrean can be trying, I dare say.'

I sighed.

Then she went on to talk about the expedition.

'Will Tybalt be accompanying his father?' I asked.

'Indeed yes. It's going to be one of the most important missions so far. I gather the archaeological world is talking of nothing else. Of course you know that Sir Edward is perhaps one of the greatest men of his profession in the world.'

I nodded. 'And Tybalt is following in his footsteps.'

She looked at me shrewdly and I wondered whether I had betrayed the state of my feelings.

'He is his father all over again,' she said. 'Men such as they are have one great passion in their lives ... their work. It's something that those about them must always remember.'

I could never resist talking about Tybalt.

'Sir Edward seems so much more remote. He hardly seems to see anyone.'

'He does come down from the clouds now and then ... or should I say up from the soil. One should never expect to know men like them in a few years. They're a lifetime study.'

'Yes,' I said. 'I suppose that's what makes them interesting.'

She smiled gently. 'Sometimes,' she went on, 'I have thought that it would be well for such men to live the lives of hermits or monks. Their work should be their families.'

'Did you know Lady Travers?'

'At the end of her life, yes.'

'And you think Sir Edward is happier as a widower than he was as a husband?'

'Did I give that impression? I came to them as a rather privileged housekeeper. We had known them for some years and when the need arose ... I took this post as you have taken yours.'

'And Lady Travers died after that?'

'Yes.'

I wanted to know what Tybalt's mother was like, and as Dorcas and Alison had often told me, I was far from tactful. So I blundered on: 'It wasn't a very happy marriage, was it?'

She looked startled. 'Well ... They had little in common and, as I said, men like Sir Edward perhaps don't make model husbands.'

I was certain then that she was warning me.

She said brightly: 'You remember Evan Callum.'

'Of course.'

'He's coming to visit us. I hear that Hadrian will be returning also. They'll be here soon, both of them. They'll be interested to hear about Sir Edward's expedition.'

I stayed talking although I knew I shouldn't. I wanted to glean all I could. Tabitha was quite animated.

'It would be wonderful if you could come,' she said. 'I am sure you would prefer it to looking after that not very agreeable lady.'

'Oh, if only I could.'

'Never mind. Perhaps some day . . .'

I went back to Keverall Court in a daze. I was dreaming again. That was my only comfort. Tabitha was taken ill; she couldn't go. Someone must take her

75

place, said Sir Edward. 'I know,' cried Tybalt. 'What about Miss Osmond? She was always interested.'

How ridiculous and how unkind to wish an illness on Tabitha!

'I am surprised, Miss Osmond,' said Lady Bodrean. 'I have been ringing my bell for half an hour.'

'I'm sorry. I forgot the time.'

'Forget the time! You are not here to forget time, Miss Osmond. You are not paid for that, you know.'

Oh, why didn't I tell the disagreeable old woman that I would serve her no longer!

Simply because, said my logical self, if you did you would have to do something. You would have to go away and how would you ever see Tybalt if you did?

I had somehow betrayed my inability to accept my position with resignation and this was something Lady Bodrean seemed to have made up her mind to enforce.

She reminded me far more than was necessary that I was a paid servant. She tried to curtail my liberty whenever possible. She would send me on an errand and time me. She would make me walk round the gardens with her carrying her basket while she cut flowers; she would tell me to arrange them – and my efforts in this artistic endeavour had always amused Dorcas and Alison. They used to say, 'If anyone can disarrange a bowl of flowers, that is Judith.' At the rectory it was a joke; here it was a serious matter. If she could humiliate me, she did; and she was seeking and finding many opportunities.

At least, I said to myself, this has taught me what a happy home Dorcas and Alison gave me and I ought to be for ever grateful for that.

76

I shall never forget the day she told me that there was to be a ball at Keverall Court.

'Of course a young lady in my daughter's position must be brought out formally. I am sure you realize that, Miss Osmond, because although you yourself are not in the same position, you did learn something of gracious living when you were allowed to take lessons here.'

'Graciousness is something I miss nowadays,' I retorted.

She misunderstood. 'You were very fortunate to be allowed to glimpse it for a while. *I* always think it is a mistake to educate people beyond their stations.'

'Sometimes,' I said, 'it enables the sons and daughters of erudite churchmen to be of use to their betters.'

'I am glad to see you take that view, Miss Osmond. I have to confess you do not always show such becoming humility.'

She was an exceedingly stupid woman. I had learned that Sir Ralph had married her for her fortune. Why he should have done so was beyond my understanding when he was a rich man in his own right. But what I could understand was why he had acquired his reputation of seeking consolation elsewhere.

'Now,' she went on, 'there will be a great deal for you to do. Invitations to be drawn up and sent out. You've no idea, Miss Osmond, what giving a ball like this entails.'

'I can hardly be expected to,' I replied, 'coming from such a stratum of society.'

'Dear me no. It will be an education for you to learn. Such experience for one in your position is so useful.'

'I shall do my *humble* best,' I retorted with irony.
But that, of course, was lost on Lady Bodrean.

Jane, Lady Bodrean's personal maid, winked at me.
'A nice cup of tea?' she said. 'I've got it all ready.'
She had a little spirit lamp in her room, which she
had made very comfortable. 'Oh, I know how to look
after myself,' she said.
I sat down and she poured out.
'My word, she's got it in for you.'
'I gather my company doesn't give her much pleas-
ure. I wonder she doesn't allow herself the treat of
being rid of it.'
'I know her. She's enjoying herself. She likes tor-
menting people. She was always like that. I've been
with her since before she married. She's got worse.'
'It couldn't have been very comfortable for you.'
'Oh, I know how to handle her. Sugar, Miss
Osmond?'
'Thank you. Yes,' I said thoughtfully, 'she does
seem to dislike me more than is warranted. Mind
you, I am ready to admit I don't perform my duties
with great efficiency. I can't imagine why she doesn't
do what she is always hinting she will. Dismiss me.'
'She doesn't want that. Who's she going to torment
then?'
'There's a fairly large staff to choose from. Surely
from among you all she could find some highly
tormentable type.'
'Oh you joke about it, Miss Osmond. Sometimes
I think you're going to explode, though.'
'So do I,' I said.
'I remember you coming here for your lessons.

78

We used to say, "My word, that one's got more spirit than all the rest of them put together. Regular little firebrand!" And when there was mischief we always used to say, "You can depend on it. That Judith Osmond's at the bottom of that." '

'And now you see the metamorphosis of Judith Osmond.'

'Eh? I've seen it happen before. The nursery governess before that Miss Graham. Nice spirited sort of girl, she was. But she hadn't been here long when things started to happen. Sir Ralph had his eyes on her and when Lady Bodrean got to work ... My word, she changed. In the old days Sir Ralph ... he were a one. No woman safe from him. He's changed a lot too. He's got quieter. I've seen him have some funny dizzy turns too. Slowed him down a bit. There's been some scandals.' She came closer to me and her lively little brown eyes were alight with pleasure. 'Women,' she said. 'Couldn't leave a pretty girl alone. The fur used to fly. That was in the beginning. Many times I've heard ... being in the next room, you know. Couldn't help but hear even if I tried not to.'

I could picture her, ear to keyhole while a young Don Juan of a Sir Ralph stood accused before his wronged wife.

'After a while she seemed to make up her mind that there was nothing she could do about it. He'd go his way, she'd go hers. He wanted a son, of course. And there wasn't another child after Miss Theodosia. So Master Hadrian came to live here. But she ... her ladyship ... seemed to be more of a tartar every day; and once she gets her knife into someone ... she's going to use it.'

I said: 'I should get out, I suppose.'

Jane moved farther towards me and whispered confidentially, 'You could find a better place. I've thought about this. What about Miss Theodosia?'

'What of her?'

'This ball . . . well, it's a sort of coming out. All the fine rich gentlemen of the neighbourhood will be invited. Then they'll have balls and such like goings on. You know what it's all leading up to.'

'Miss Theodosia is being paraded before them . . . in all her charms — and by no means the least of these is the nice golden dowry glittering round her neck. "Young gentleman, show your credentials and make your bid." '

'You always had your answer, didn't you? I used to say to Miss Graham. "My goodness, that one's got a bit of lip, she has." But what I'm getting at is this. Before long they'll find a husband for Miss Theodosia, and then you're her friend . . . so . . .'

'I, her friend. Please don't let Lady Bodrean hear you call me that. I'm sure she would be most indignant.'

'Now you're getting bitter. It's all along of once being treated like one of them and now finding yourself here in a paid job. You have to be clever. Now you and Theodosia were together as children. You were the one who used to order *her* about. Theodosia's not like her mother. Suppose you remind her of your friendship.'

'Ingratiate myself with the daughter of the house?'

'You could become friends with her again and when she marries . . . you see what I mean? Madame Theodosia wants a companion and who better than her old friend. What do you think of it?'

'Machiavellian!' I said.

'You can laugh. But I wouldn't like to think of spending *my* life looking after an old tartar like that.'

'Suppose Theodosia doesn't marry?'

'Theodosia not marry? Of course she will. Why, they've got the man for her already. I heard Sir Ralph talking to her ladyship about it. Quite a to-do there was. She said: "You've got an obsession with those people. I think you wanted Hadrian for Sabina." '

'Oh?' I said faintly.

'I wouldn't mind taking a bet with you, Miss Osmond, that before the year's out the engagement will be announced. After all there's a title. Money, well I'm not so sure of that, but Miss Theodosia will have enough, won't she? When her father dies she'll inherit everything, I reckon. Why, she'll be one of the richest young ladies in the country. Of course, I wouldn't say they're exactly poor, but money's always useful and they say that *he* has poured a fortune into this work of his. A funny way of squandering your money I must say. When you think of what you can do with it . . . and it all goes in digging up the ground in foreign places. They say some of those places are so hot you can hardly bear it.'

I said, although I knew the answer already: 'So for Theodosia they've chosen . . .?'

'The son, of course. Mr Tybalt Travers. Oh yes, he's the one they've chosen for Theodosia.'

I could scarcely bear to sit there and listen to her chatter.

Sir Edward and Tybalt had returned to Giza House and they came to dine at Keverall Court. I contrived to be in the hall when they arrived, pretending to arrange some flowers.

Tybalt said: 'It's Miss Osmond, isn't it?' as though he had to look twice to make sure. 'How are you?'

'I'm the companion now, you know.'

'Yes, I heard. Are you still reading?'

'Avidly. Mrs Grey is so helpful.'

'Good. Father, this is Miss Osmond.'

Sir Edward gave me his vague look.

'She's the one who dressed up as the mummy. She wanted to know what it felt like to be embalmed and placed in a sarcophagus. She's read several of your books.' Now Sir Edward's attention was on me. His eyes twinkled. I think the mummy adventure amused him. He was more like Tybalt now.

I wished that I could have stayed there talking to them. Lady Bodrean had appeared at the top of the staircase. I wondered whether she had heard my voice.

'My *dear* Sir Edward . . . and Tybalt?' She swept down the stairs. 'I thought I heard you talking to the companion.'

I went to my room then and stayed there all the evening. A respite from my tyrant because she was busy with her guests. I pictured them at the dinner table and Theodosia looking pretty in pink satin -- gentle, amenable, with an immense fortune which would be so useful in financing expeditions to exotic places.

I don't think I ever felt quite so hopeless as at that moment, and with the recent encounter with Tybalt fresh in my mind – which confirmed everything I had ever thought him – I was more certain than ever that he was the only man for me. I asked myself whether I should offer my resignation without delay.

But of course that was not my nature. Until he was married to Theodosia I would continue to dream . . . and hope.

I walked the dogs over to Giza House and as I did so a voice called 'Judith.'

I turned and there was Evan Callum coming out of Giza House.

'Judith,' he cried, his hand outstretched to take mine, 'this is a pleasure.'

'I heard you were coming,' I said. 'It is so good to see you.'

'And how is everything with you?'

'Changed,' I said.

'And for the better?'

'The rector died. You know that Oliver married Sabina, and I am now companion to Lady Bodrean.'

He grimaced.

'Ah,' I said with a smile, 'I see you have an inkling of what that means.'

'I worked in the house once, you remember, as a sort of tutor to you all. Fortunately my work did not come under her jurisdiction. Poor Judith!'

'I tell myself fifty times a day not to be sorry for myself. So if *I'm* not, you must not be.'

'But I am. You were the best of my pupils. You had such an enthusiasm; and that is one of the greatest assets in this profession. Enthusiasm! Where would we get without it?'

'Are you accompanying them on this expedition?'

'Unfortunately, no. I'm not experienced enough

for such an honour. There'll be much coming and going between Keverall and Giza, I believe. Sir Ralph is being persuaded to help finance the project.'

'He was always vitally interested. I hope they'll succeed in getting what they want.'

'Tybalt has no doubt of it.' He looked round him: 'How this brings back the old days. You, Hadrian, Theodosia, Sabina. Oddly enough the one who was least interested was Sabina. Have they changed?'

'Sabina has become the rector's wife. I see very little of her. My duties do not give me much time. I visit Dorcas and Alison when I can manage it and I come over here to see Mrs Grey who has been so kind in lending me books.'

'On our subject, of course.'

'Of course.'

'Good. I could not bear for *you* to tire. I hear Hadrian will be home at the end of the week.'

'I didn't know. I am not told such things.'

'Poor Judith. Life's unfair sometimes.'

'Perhaps I've had my share of luck. Did you know that I was found on a train?'

'An abandoned child!'

'Not exactly. It was in an accident. My parents were killed and no one claimed me. I might have gone to an orphanage ... never have met any of you ... never have found a piece of a bronze-age shield and never read any of the books from Giza House.'

'I always thought you were the rector's distant cousin.'

'Many people did. Dorcas and Alison thought it would be kinder to let it be known that I was some sort of distant relation. But I was unknown ... and my great piece of luck was that they took me in and life was wonderful until now. Perhaps I have to pay now for that marvellous piece of luck I had in the beginning. Do you think life works out like that?'

'No,' he said. 'This is just a phase. They come to all of us. But Theodosia's at Keverall, and she's a friend of yours. She would never be unkind, I'm sure.'

'No, but I see little of her. I am always kept so busy dancing attendance on her mamma.'

He gave me a compassionate look.

'Poor Judith,' he said, 'perhaps it will not always be so. It's like a pattern, do you think? We were all here together and now here we are again.'

'I wish I had appreciated the brightness of that pattern when it was being woven by fate – if I may stick to your metaphor.'

'That's often the tragedy in life, don't you think? We don't appreciate the good things when they're with us?'

'I shall in future.'

'I shall hope things change for you, Judith. We must meet . . . often.'

'Oh, but the social barriers will be set up between us because when you visit Keverall Court you will come as a guest.'

'I should soon leap over any barrier they put between us,' he assured me.

He said he would walk with me and I was greatly comforted by his return to St Erno's.

Hadrian arrived at the end of the week. I was in the garden whither I had been sent to gather roses when he saw me and called to me.

'Judith!' He took my hand and we studied each other.

Hadrian had become good-looking – or perhaps he had always been so and I had not particularly noticed before. His thick brown hair grew too low on his forehead – or did I think it was too low because one of Tybalt's most striking features was his high forehead? There was something inherently pleasant in Hadrian and however bitter he became the twinkle was never far from his blue-grey eyes. He was of medium height and broad-shouldered; and when he greeted me, his eyes always lit up in a manner which I found comforting. I felt that Hadrian was one of the people on whom I could rely.

'You've become a scholar, Hadrian,' I said.

'You've become a flatterer. And a companion! To my aunt. How could you, Judith!'

'It's very easily explained. If one does not inherit money one needs to earn it. I am doing precisely that.'

'But you a companion! Cutting roses ... I bet you always cut the wrong ones!'

'How right you are! These red ones I am sure should have been yellow. But I have the consolation of knowing that had I picked yellow, red would have been the chosen colour.'

'My aunt's a tyrant! I know. I don't think it's right that you should be doing this. Who suggested it?'

'Your uncle. And we have to be truly grateful to him for had he not arranged that I should come here, I should be cutting roses or performing some such duty for some other tyrant possibly miles from here – so I shouldn't be chatting with you, nor have seen Evan and ... er ...'

'It's a shame,' said Hadrian hotly. 'And you of all people. You were always such a bully.'

'I know. It's just retribution. The bully now bullied. Hoist with her own petard. Still, it's pleasant to know that some members of the household don't regard me as a pariah now that I have to perform the humiliating task of earning a living.'

'Well, here we are together again. Evan, you, Theodosia, myself . . . and how's Sabina?'

'Playing the rector's wife to perfection.'

'I can't believe it.'

'Life turns out differently from what we expect.'

Theodosia came into the garden. She was in white muslin with pale blue dots on it and she wore a white straw hat with blue ribbons. She's grown quite pretty, I thought with a pang.

'I was saying to Judith that it's like the old times now we're all together,' said Hadrian. 'Evan and Tybalt . . .' I noticed that she blushed slightly, and I thought of Jane's words. It was true then. No, it couldn't be! Not Tybalt and Theodosia. It was incongruous. But she was almost pretty; she was suitable; and she was an heiress. Surely Tybalt would not marry for money. But of course he would. It was the natural order of things. Sabina had not married for money, for Oliver as rector would have little of that useful commodity. How we had changed, all of us. Frivolous Sabina becoming the rector's wife; plain Theodosia to marry my wonderful Tybalt; and myself, the proud one, the one who had taken charge of the schoolroom, to be the companion whose daily bread was service and humiliation.

'Evan, Tybalt, myself, you, Judith, and Sabina and Oliver in their rectory,' Hadrian was saying.

'Yes,' said Theodosia; she looked at me rather shyly apologetic because she had seen so little of me since I had come to Keverall Court. 'It's . . . it's nice to have Judith here.'

'Is it?' I said.

'But of course. You were always one of us, weren't you?'

'But now I am the companion merely.'

'Oh, you've been listening to Mamma.'

'I have to. It's part of the job.'

'Mamma can be difficult.'

'You don't have to be with her all the time,' comforted Hadrian.

'There seems very little time when I'm not.'

'We'll have to change that, won't we, Theodosia?'

Theodosia nodded and smiled.

These encounters lifted my spirits. It was to some extent a return to the old ways.

There was a great deal of talk about the coming ball.

'This will be the biggest we've had for years,' Jane told me. 'Miss Theodosia's coming out.' She gave me her wink. 'Timed, you see, when all these people are here. Lady B. is hoping there'll be an announcement before they go off to Egypt.'

'Do you think that Mr Travers would take his bride with him?'

'There won't be time for that by all accounts. There'll have to be the sort of wedding that takes months to prepare for, I reckon. Her ladyship wouldn't stand for anything else. No quiet little wedding like Sabina and the new rector had. Lady B. wouldn't let her only daughter go like that.'

'Well,' I said, 'we haven't got them betrothed yet, have we?'

'Any day now, mark my words.'

I began to believe she was right when I talked to Theodosia, who since the return of Hadrian was seeing far more of me than she had before. She seemed as though she wanted to make up to me for previously keeping out of my way.

The only time Lady Bodrean was the least bit affable to me was when she talked of Theodosia's coming out ball; I knew at once that she was hoping to make me envious. Theodosia could have had all the balls she wanted if she had left me Tybalt.

'You might go along to the sewing-room,' Lady Bodrean told me, 'and give Sarah Sloper a hand. There are fifty yards of lace to be sewn on to my daughter's ball gown. And in an hour's time I shall be ready for the reading and don't forget, before you go, to walk Orange and Lemon.'

Sarah Sloper was too good a dressmaker to allow me to put a stitch into her creation. There it was on the table – a froth of soft blue silk chiffon with the fifty yards of pale blue lace.

Theodosia was there for a fitting, so I helped get her into the dress. She was going to look lovely in it, I thought with a pang. I could imagine her floating round the ballroom in the arms of Tybalt.

'Do you like it, Judith?' she asked.

'The colour is most becoming.'

'I love dancing,' she said; she waltzed round and I felt we were back in the schoolroom. I went to her and bowed. 'Miss Bodrean, may I have the pleasure of this dance?'

She made a deep curtsey. I seized her and we danced round the room while Sarah Sloper watched us with a grin.

'How delightful you look tonight, Miss Bodrean.'

'Thank you, sir.'

'How gracious of you to thank me for the gifts nature has bestowed on you.'

'Oh, Judith, you haven't changed a bit. I wish . . .'

Sarah Sloper had jumped to her feet suddenly and was bobbing a curtsey, for Sir Ralph was standing in the doorway watching us dance.

Our dance came to an immediate halt. I wondered what he would say to see the companion dancing so familiarly with his daughter.

He was clearly not annoyed: 'Rather graceful, didn't you think, Sarah?' he said.

'Why yes, sir, indeed sir,' stammered Sarah.

'So that's your ball dress, is it?'

'Yes, Father.'

'And what about Miss Osmond, eh? Has she a ball dress?'

'I have not,' I said.

'And why not?'

'Because a person in my position has not great use for such a garment.'

I saw the familiar wag of the chin.

'Oh yes,' he said, 'you're the companion now. I hear of you from Lady Bodrean.'

'Then I doubt you hear anything to my advantage.'

I don't know why I was speaking to him in that way. It was an irresistible impulse even though I knew that I was being what would be termed insolent from one in my position and was imperilling my job.

'Very little,' he assured me, with a lugubrious shake of the head. 'In fact nothing at all.'

'I feared so.'

'Now do you? That's a change. I always had the impression that you were a somewhat fearless young lady.' His bristling brows came together. 'I don't see anything of you. Where do you get to?'

'I don't move in your circles, sir,' I replied, realizing now that he at least bore me no malice and was rather amused at my pert retorts.

'I begin to think that's rather a pity.'

'Father, do you like my gown?' asked Theodosia.

'Very pretty. Blue, is it?'

'Yes, Father.'

He turned to me. 'If you had one, what colour would it be?'

'It would be green, Father,' said Theodosia. 'It was always Judith's favourite colour.'

'That's said to be unlucky,' he replied. 'Or it was in my day. They used to say "Green on Monday, Black on Friday". But I'll swear Miss Osmond's not superstitious.'

'Not about colours,' I said. 'I might be about some things.'

'Doesn't do to think you're unlucky,' he said. 'Otherwise you will be.'

Then he went out, his chin wagging.

Theodosia looked at me with raised eyebrows. 'Now why did Father come in here?'

'You should know more about his habits than I do.'

'I believe he's quite excited about my ball. Judith, Mrs Grey was saying that you were reading books, some of which had been written by Sir Edward

Travers. You must know quite a lot now about archaeology.'

'Enough to know that I'm very ignorant about it. We both have a smattering, haven't we? We got that from Evan Callum.'

'Yes,' she said. 'I wish I knew more.'

She was animated. 'I'm going to start reading. You must tell me what books you've had.'

I understood, of course. She was desperately anxious to be able to talk knowledgeably to Tybalt.

The invitations had been sent out; I had listed the guests and ticked them off when the acceptances came in. I had helped arrange what flowers would be brought from the greenhouses to decorate the ballroom, for it was October and the gardens could scarcely supply what was needed; I had compiled the dance programmes and chosen the pink-and-blue pencils and the silken cords which would be attached to them. For the first time Lady Bodrean seemed pleased and I knew it was only because she wanted me to know what care went into the launching into society of a well-bred girl. She may have noticed that I was downcast at times and this put her into a good humour so that I wanted to shout at her: 'I care nothing for these grand occasions; Theodosia is welcome to them. My melancholy has nothing to do with that.'

I went to Rainbow Cottage when I had an hour or so to spare. Dorcas and Alison always made a great fuss of me; they tried to keep my spirits up with griddle cakes which I used to be rather greedy about as a child.

They wanted to hear all about the ball.

'It's a shame they don't ask you, Judith,' said Dorcas.

'Why should they? Employees are not asked to family balls surely.'

'It's different in your case. Weren't you in the schoolroom with them?'

'That, as Lady Bodrean would inform you, is something for which to feel gratitude and not an excuse for looking for further favours.'

'Oh Judith, is it really unbearable?'

'Well, the truth is that she is so obnoxious that I get a certain delight in doing battle. Also, she is really rather stupid so that I am able to get in quite a lot of barbs of which she is unaware.'

'If it is too bad, you must leave.'

'I may be asked to. I must warn you that I expect dismissal daily.'

'Well, dear, don't worry. We can manage here. And you'd find something else very quickly, I'm sure.'

Sometimes they talked about village affairs. They worked a good deal for the church. Having done so all their lives they were well equipped for the task. Sabina was not really very practical, they whispered, and although she could chatter away to people, a little more than that was expected of a rector's wife. As for Oliver, he was quite competent.

I reminded them that they used to say he had carried the parish on his shoulders when their father was alive.

That was true, they agreed grudgingly. I knew they found it hard to forgive poor Oliver for not marrying me and even more difficult to forgive Sabina for being the chosen one.

It was comforting to remember that they were there in the background of my life.

93

There was a great deal of coming and going between Giza House and Keverall Court. As Sir Ralph was not feeling very well, Tybalt and his father visited him frequently. They were going into the details of the expedition. I quite shamelessly tried to be where I might catch a glimpse of them. Even Sir Edward knew me now and would give me his absent-minded smile, no doubt remembering I was the girl who had dressed up as the mummy.

Tybalt exchanged a word or two with me – usually asking what I was reading. I longed to hear from him about the expedition but naturally I couldn't ask him about that.

Two days before the ball a most extraordinary thing happened.

When I emerged from Lady Bodrean's apartment and was about to go for my daily walk I found Theodosia in the corridor. I fancied she had been looking for me.

She looked excited.

'Hello, Judith,' she said, and there was a little lilt in her voice.

'Were you waiting for me?' I asked.

'Yes, I've something to tell you.'

My heartbeats quickened; my spirits sank. This is it, Tybalt has asked her to marry him. The engagement will be announced at the ball.

She slipped her arm through mine. 'Let's go to your room,' she said. 'You will never guess what it is,' she went on.

I thought: I can't bear it. I've imagined it so many times, but I know I can't bear it. I'll have to go away . . . at once. I'll go and tell Dorcas and

Alison and then I'll get a post far away and never see any of them again.

I stammered: 'I know. You . . . you're engaged.'

She stopped short and flushed hotly, so I knew that although this might not be the surprise she had for me now, it was coming soon.

'You always thought you knew everything, didn't you? Well, clever Judith is wrong this time.'

Clever Judith was never more delighted to be wrong.

She threw open the door of my room and walked in; I followed, shutting the door behind me. She went to my cupboard and opened the door. Hanging there was a green chiffon evening dress.

'What is it?' I cried in astonishment.

'It's your ball dress, Judith.'

'Mine! How could it be?' I went to it, felt the lovely soft material, took the dress down and held it against me.

'It's absolutely right,' declared Theodosia. 'Put it on. I long to see you in it.'

'First, how did it get there?'

'I put it there.'

'But where did it come from?'

'Oh, do try it on first and I'll explain.'

'No, I must know.'

'Oh, you're maddening! I long to see that it fits. Father said you were to have it.'

'But . . . why?'

'He said: "Cinderella must go to the ball." '

'Meaning the companion?'

'You remember he saw us dancing. That day he said to me, "That girl Judith Osmond, she's to go

95

to the ball." I said, "Mamma would never hear of it," and he said, "Then don't tell her." '

I began to laugh. I saw myself at the ball dancing with Tybalt. 'But it's impossible. She will never allow it.'

'This is my father's house you know.'

'But I am employed by your mother.'

'She won't dare go against him.'

'What an unwelcome guest I should be.'

'Only by one. The rest of us all want you to go. Myself, Evan, Hadrian, Tybalt . . .'

'Tybalt!'

'Well, of course he doesn't know yet, but I am sure he would if he did. Hadrian knows, though. He's very amused, and we're all going to have a lot of fun hiding you from Mamma, if that's possible.'

'I don't suppose it is for a moment. I shall be ordered out of the ballroom within an hour.'

'Not if you come as my father's guest, which you will do.'

I began to laugh.

'I knew you'd enjoy it.'

'Tell me what happened.'

'Well, Father said you'd always been a lively girl, and he wished I'd show more of your spirit. He was afraid you didn't have much of a life with Mamma and he wanted you to go to the ball. That's why he wanted to know what colour of dress. It was a secret with Sarah Sloper. I chose the material and Sarah used me as a model. You're a bit taller than I and just a little thinner. We worked on that. And I'm absolutely sure it's a perfect fit. Do put it on now.'

I did so. The transformation was miraculous. It

was indeed my colour. I let down my thick dark hair, and with my eyes shining and colour in my cheeks I would have been beautiful, I thought, but for my nose which was too large. Hadrian always used to laugh at my nose. 'It's a forceful one,' he said. 'It betrays your character. No one who was meek could ever have such a nose. Your powers, dear Judith, are not in your stars but in your nose.' I giggled. In such a beautiful gown I could forget that offending feature.

'You look quite Spanish now,' said Theodosia. 'Your hair ought to be piled high on your head and you should have a Spanish comb. You'd look marvellous then. I wish it were a masked ball. Then it would be so much easier to hide you from Mamma. But she will know it is Father's wish and will say nothing . . . at the ball at least. She wouldn't want a scene there.'

'The storm will come later.'

I didn't care. I would face that. I was going to the ball. I should have a little dance programme with a pink cord and pencil and I would keep it for ever, because I was certain that Tybalt's initials would be on it.

I seized Theodosia in my arms and we danced round the bedroom.

The night of the ball had come. Thank Heaven Lady Bodrean would be too busy to want to be bothered with me. 'My goodness,' Jane had said, 'we're going to have a session. There's her hair to do and I've got to get her into her gown. When it comes to what jewels she's to wear it'll be this and that – and that's no good and what about this. It's a good thing I know how to handle her.'

97

So I was free to dress myself in the close-fitting green satin sheath over which were yards and yards of flowing silk chiffon. Nothing could have been chosen to suit me better. And when I had come up to dress I found that Theodosia had laid the Spanish comb on my dressing-table. Hadrian was there to support me too. I felt that the position had changed since he had come back. I really had friends in the house now.

And on this night of the ball I prepared to enjoy myself.

Sir Ralph and Lady Bodrean stood at the head of the great staircase to receive their guests. Naturally I did not present myself. But what fun it was to mingle with the guests who were so numerous that I was sure I could escape Lady Bodrean's eye. In any case she would hardly recognize me in my finery.

I danced with Hadrian, who said it was rather like some of the tricks we used to get up to in our youth.

'We were always the allies,' he said, 'you and I, Judith.'

It was true.

'I'm sorry,' said Hadrian, 'that it's my aunt you have to work for.'

'Not more sorry than I. Yet it gives me a chance to be at Keverall.'

'You love the old house, don't you?'

'It seems like part of my life. Don't forget I was here almost every day.'

'I feel the same. Theodosia's lucky. It'll be hers one day.'

'You sound envious.'

'I sound as I feel, then. You see I'm a bit of a charity boy myself.'

'Oh, no, Hadrian. You're Sir Ralph's nephew ... almost a son.'

'Not quite.'

'Then, I tell you what you should do,' I said lightly. 'Marry Theodosia.'

'My cousin!'

'Why not? Cousins marry often. It's a very useful way of keeping the property well within the family.'

'You don't think she'd have me, do you? I fancy now her gaze is fixed in another direction.'

'Is that so?'

'Have you noticed her being eagerly intent every time anyone mentions the subject?'

'What subject?'

'Archaeology. She's so excited about this expedition. You'd think she was going on it.'

'Trying to impress someone. Perhaps it's you! After all, it is your subject.'

'Oh no. Nothing of the sort. I'm not the chosen one.'

I couldn't bear to talk of Theodosia and Tybalt so I said quickly: 'Don't you wish you were going out to Egypt with the party?'

'I'd enjoy it in a way. I hear that Sir Edward is very much a lone wolf. He keeps his team in the dark. It's the way some people work. I was talking to Evan about it. We should have been flattered if we'd been asked to join the party, of course. But at our stage it would only be in a minor capacity.'

'And Tybalt?'

'Well, he's the great man's son. I dare say he won't be kept entirely in the dark.'

'I suppose one day he'll be as great as his father.'

'He has the same passionate absorption.'

'I saw him dancing with Theodosia but I didn't see Sir Edward.'

'He'll probably look in later.'

The band had stopped; the dance was over; Hadrian led me to a seat sheltered by pots of palms.

'I feel like a fox in his lair,' I said.

'You mean a vixen,' corrected Hadrian.

'I admit to a kindred spirit with that creature on certain occasions but at the moment I'm far too mellow.'

Evan came up with Theodosia and sat down with us. Theodosia looked at me in my green dress with great pleasure.

'You are enjoying the ball, Judith?' she asked anxiously.

I assured her I was. 'If Sabina were here it would be like schooldays,' I said.

Then Tybalt appeared. I thought he had come to claim Theodosia but instead he sat down. He did not seem the least bit surprised to see me.

Evan then said that he believed Theodosia had promised him this dance. They went off and Hadrian said he had a partner to find; that left Tybalt and myself alone.

'Are you enjoying the dance?' I asked.

'It's not much in my line, you know.'

'I saw you dancing a little while ago.'

'Most ungracefully.'

'Adequately,' I assured him. 'You will be gone very soon,' I went on. 'How you must be longing to set out.'

'It's a most exciting project of course.'

'Tell me about it.'

'You really *are* interested, aren't you?'

'Enormously.'

'We'll go by ship to Port Said and overland to Cairo. We shall stay for a while and then make our way towards the ancient site of Thebes.'

I clasped my hands ecstatically.

'Do tell me more about it. You're going to the tombs, aren't you?'

He nodded. 'My father has been preparing for this project for some time. He was out there several years ago and he's always had the impression that he was on the verge of some great discovery. It's been in his mind for years. Now he's going to satisfy himself.'

'It'll be wonderful,' I cried.

'I think it's the most exciting project that I've ever undertaken.'

'You have been there before?'

'Yes, with my father. I was very inexperienced then and it was a great concession for me to be there at all. My father's party discovered one of the tombs which must have been prepared for a great nobleman. It had been robbed, thousands of years ago. It was very disappointing as you can imagine. All the hard work, the excavating, the probing, the hopes . . . and then to find that the tomb has been so completely cleared that there is nothing left which would help to reconstruct the customs of this fascinating country. I'm getting carried away with my enthusiasm, but it's your fault, Miss Osmond. You seem so interested.'

'I am, tremendously so.'

'So few people outside our little world understand a thing.'

'I don't feel myself to be exactly outside it. I was

101

very fortunate. I took lessons at Keverall Court and as you know Sir Ralph has always been interested in archaeology.'

'Fortunately, yes. He is helping us a great deal.'

'It was he who engaged Evan Callum to give us lessons. Then of course there was what was going on in Carter's Meadow. I sometimes gave a hand there . . . in a very unprofessional way, as you can guess.'

'But you caught the fascination, didn't you? I can hear it in your voice and see it in your face. And I remember how excited you were when you came to the house for books. And I do believe, Miss Osmond, that you are not one of those ridiculously romantic people who believe that this is all digging and finding wonderful jewels and the remains of old palaces.'

'I know such finds are few.'

'It's true. But I am sure you would like to dance. So if you don't mind a little discomfort?'

I laughed and said: 'I'll bear it.'

And there I was, dancing with Tybalt. It was like a dream come true.

I loved him all the more because he kept putting his feet in the wrong places. He apologized and I wanted to cry: Your treading on my toes is bliss.

I was so happy. Alison and Dorcas had said that I had the gift of shutting out everything but the moment and enjoying it to the full. I was glad of it on that night. I would not go beyond this glorious moment when Tybalt's arms were about me and I was closer to him than I had ever been.

I longed for the music to go on and on but it stopped of course and we returned to our alcove where Theodosia was seated with Evan.

I danced with Evan, who said how glad he was to see me there. I told him about how I had found the dress in my cupboard and Sir Ralph had wished me to come to the ball.

We laughed and talked about the old days and later we went to supper and were joined there by Theodosia, Hadrian and Tybalt.

How gay I could be on such an occasion. It was like the old days. I sparkled and made sure that the conversation circled about me. Theodosia was very gentle and did not mind, any more than she had in the schoolroom, the fact that I drew attention from her.

Tybalt was naturally a little aloof from our frivolous chatter. He was more mature than the rest of us and I could not help noticing how insignificant Hadrian and Evan were in comparison. When Tybalt was talking of archaeology he glowed with an intense and single-minded passion which I was sure only a man who could feel deeply would experience. I believed then that if ever Tybalt loved a woman it would be with the same unswerving devotion which he gave to his profession. Because I wanted to see Tybalt animated, glowing with that enthusiasm which thrilled and excited me, I introduced the subject of archaeology and almost immediately he was the centre of a fascinated audience.

When we paused Theodosia said: 'Oh, you are all so clever ... even Judith! But don't you think this salmon is delicious?'

Hadrian then told us a story of a fishing expedition he had enjoyed on the Spey, in the Scottish Highlands, where, he said, the best salmon in the world was caught. He was explaining how he had plunged into the river and pulled in the struggling fish, showing us the size of it at which we all laughingly expressed disbelief, when Lady Bodrean walked past our table in the company of several of the guests.

I was saying: 'Of course, you know that all fishermen double the size of their catch and it wouldn't surprise me if Hadrian trebled his.'

And there she was, her eyebrows raised in astonishment as slowly her outraged feelings were visible in the expression on her face.

There was a silence which seemed to go on for a long time; then she took a step towards our table. The men rose, but she stared incredulously at me. I attempted to put on a calm smile.

One of her guests said: 'Oh, it's Mr Travers, I believe.'

Tybalt said yes it was; and then Lady Bodrean recovered herself. She made introductions, leaving me until last and then: 'Miss Osmond,' she said, almost making my name sound obscene.

Nobody noticed and there were a few moments of polite conversation, and then Lady Bodrean and her party passed on.

'Oh dear!' said Theodosia, very distressed.

'I somehow felt it would happen,' I added, trying to pretend that I was not really perturbed.

'Well,' said Hadrian, 'Sir Ralph has to answer for his guests.'

'What's happened?' asked Tybalt.

I turned to him. 'I really shouldn't be here.'

'Surely not,' he said. 'Your company has made it such an interesting evening.'

That made everything worth while.

'I may well be sent packing tomorrow morning.'

Tybalt looked concerned and I felt absurdly happy.

Theodosia started to explain. 'You see, my father thought Judith should come to the ball and he and I put our heads together. I chose her dress and Sarah Sloper made it . . . but Mamma did not know.'

Tybalt laughed and said: 'There is always some drama surrounding Miss Osmond. If she is not dressing up as an embalmed body and getting into a sarcophagus she is dressing up in a beautiful gown and coming to a ball. And in neither place it seems is she expected to be.'

Hadrian put his hand over mine. 'Don't worry, Judith. You'll weather tomorrow's storm.'

'Mamma can be very fierce,' said Theodosia.

'But,' put in Evan, 'Judith came as the guest of Sir Ralph. I don't see how Lady Bodrean can object to that.'

'You don't know Mamma,' said Theodosia.

'I assure you I do and the outlook seems stormy, but since Judith came at Sir Ralph's invitation I can't see that she has done anything wrong.'

'In any case,' I said, 'this storm is for tomorrow. At the moment it's a beautiful night. There's salmon which we hope was caught in the Scottish Highlands and champagne from the appropriate district. The company is invigorating, so what more could we ask?'

Tybalt leaned towards me and said: 'You live in the moment.'

'It's the only way to live. Tonight I'm a kind of Cinderella. Tomorrow I return to my ashes.'

'I'll be Prince Charming,' said Hadrian. 'The music's starting. Let's dance.'

I did not want to leave Tybalt, but there was nothing else I could do.

'Congratulations,' said Hadrian as we danced. 'You were the calmest of the lot. You put up a good show. I suppose you're really quaking in your glass slippers.'

'I'm resigned,' I said. 'I have a feeling that very soon I shall be back in Rainbow Cottage writing humble letters to prospective employers.'

'Poor Judith. It's hateful being poor.'

'What do you know about that?'

'Plenty. I have my troubles. I have to crave my uncle's benevolence. My creditors are yapping at my heels. I must speak to him tomorrow. So you see, like you, tonight I want to eat, drink and be merry.'

'Oh, Hadrian. Are you really in debt?'

'Up to the eyes. What wouldn't I do to be in Theodosia's shoes.'

'I don't suppose she gets as big an allowance as you.'

'But think of the credit! Did you know that my uncle is fabulously rich? Well, dear Theodosia will inherit all that one day.'

'I hate all this talk about money.'

'It is depressing. It's one of the reasons why I'd like to be rich. Then you can forget there's such a thing in the world as money.

We laughed, danced and joked; but both of us were, I suppose, thinking of what the next day would bring. My ability to live in the moment was only with me when Tybalt was there.

I hoped to see him again, but I didn't; and before all the guests had departed I thought it advisable to return to my room.

I was wrong in thinking that the storm would break in the morning. Lady Bodrean had no intention of allowing it to wait as long as that.

I was still in my ball dress when the bell rang vigorously.

I knew what that meant and I was rather glad because the dress gave me confidence.

I went along to Lady Bodrean's room. She was in her ball gown, too — violet-coloured velvet with a magnificent train edged with fur that looked like miniver. She was quite regal.

'Well, Miss Osmond, what have you to say for yourself?'

'What do you expect me to say, Lady Bodrean?'

'What I do not expect is insolence. You were at the ball tonight. How dared you intrude and mingle with my guests?'

'It is not really very daring to accept an invitation,' I replied.

'Invitation? Have you the effrontery to tell me that you sent yourself an invitation?'

'I did not. Sir Ralph gave instructions that I was to go to the ball.'

'I do not believe it.'

'Perhaps your ladyship would wish me to call him.' Before she could reply I had seized the bell rope and pulled it. Jane came running in. 'Lady Bodrean wishes you to ask Sir Ralph if he will come here . . . if he has not already retired.'

Lady Bodrean was spluttering with rage, but Jane, who, I believe, knew what had been happening, had hurried off to call Sir Ralph.

'How dare you presume to give orders here?' demanded Lady Bodrean.

'I thought I was obeying orders,' I said. 'I was under the impression that your ladyship wished Sir Ralph to come here to corroborate my story, for clearly you did not believe me.'

'I have never in all my life been subjected to such ... such ... such ...'

'Insubordination?' I supplied.

'Insolence,' she said.

I was intoxicated with happiness still. I had danced with Tybalt; he had talked to me; I had conveyed to him my interest in his work. He had said, 'Your company has made it such an interesting evening.' And he had meant that, for I was sure he was not the man to say what he did not mean. So how could I care for this foolish old virago who in a few moments was going to be confronted by her husband who, I knew, would confirm what I had said.

He stood in the doorway. 'What the . . .' he began. Then he saw me and there was that now familiar movement of the jaw.

'What's Miss Osmond doing here?' he asked.

'I sent for her. She had the temerity to mingle with our guests tonight.'

'She was one of them,' he said shortly.

'I think you have forgotten that she is my companion.'

'She was one of your guests tonight. She came to the ball on my invitation. That is enough.'

'You mean you invited this young woman without consulting me!'

'You know very well I did.'

108

'This young woman is under the impression that because she was allowed to have a little education and some of it under this roof that entitles her to special treatment. I tell you I will not allow this. She came here as a companion and shall be treated as such.'

'Which means,' said Sir Ralph, 'that you will make her life unbearable. You will be as unpleasant to her as you know how – and my God, that, madam, is a great deal.'

'You have foisted this person on me,' she said. 'I will not endure it.'

'She will continue as before.'

'I tell you ... that I will not have you force me to have people ... like this in my household.'

'Madam,' said Sir Ralph, 'you will do as I say ...'

He gripped the chair; I saw the blood suffuse his face; he reeled slightly.

I rushed forward and caught his arm. He looked about him and I helped him to a chair. He sat there breathing heavily.

I said: 'I think we should call his valet. He is unwell.'

I took it upon myself to instruct Jane to do so.

Jane hurried away and shortly came back with Blake, Sir Ralph's personal servant.

Blake knew what to do. He loosened Sir Ralph's collar and taking a small tablet from a box put in into his employer's mouth. Sir Ralph lay back in the chair, his face, which had been a suffused purple, becoming gradually paler but the veins at his temples standing out like tubes.

'That's better, sir,' said Blake. Then he looked at Lady Bodrean. 'I'll get him to bed now, my lady.'

Sir Ralph rose shakily to his feet and leaned heavily on Blake.

He nodded at me and a shadow of amusement came into his face.

He muttered: 'Don't forget what I say. I mean it.'

Then Blake led him away.

When the door shut Lady Bodrean turned to me.

'Now!' she said, 'you can see what you have done.'

'Not I,' I replied significantly.

'Go back to your room,' she said. 'I will talk to you later.'

I went back. What a night! She would not get rid of me. She dared not. Nor was I sure that she wanted to. If I went she would be deprived of the joy of making my life miserable. I was sure she did not want that.

But I could cope with her and I did not wish to think of her on such a night. I had so many more memories to brood on.

At the end of that month Sir Edward with his expedition, which included Tybalt, left for Egypt.

Evan went back to the University where he had a temporary post as lecturer in archaeology; Hadrian went to Kent to do some work on a Viking burial ship which had been discovered somewhere along the east coast, and I returned to the monotony of serving Lady Bodrean which was only enlivened by her attempts to humiliate me. But the thought that I had friends in Sir Ralph and Theodosia was comforting. There were no more walks to Giza House because Tabitha had accompanied the party but I walked past it several times. It seemed to have reverted to the old days

110

when we had called it the haunted house. The blinds were drawn down, the furniture under dustcovers, and there were only three or four servants there. The two Egyptians, Mustapha and Absalam, had gone with Sir Edward.

I longed for the return of the expedition. And Tybalt.

I called more often at Rainbow Cottage since I couldn't go to Giza; there was always a welcome there. Dorcas and Alison were delighted when I gave them an account of the ball and the beautiful green ball dress which I had found in the cupboard.

I had long been surprised at their attitude right from the beginning when they had been so delighted that I was to go to Keverall Court. I was young — and although my nose prevented me from being beautiful I could look quite attractive at times. I had assessed myself often in the last months, comparing myself with Theodosia. I had a vitality which she lacked; and my animation was attractive, I was sure. Although my temper was inclined to flare up, any storm was soon over; I had an ability to laugh at life and that meant laughing at myself. I had my very thick dark hair — not easy to handle because it was almost straight; I had large brown eyes with lashes as thick and black as my hair; and fortunately I had a good healthy set of teeth. I was taller than Theodosia and Sabina and inclined to be thin. I lacked Theodosia's pretty plumpness and Sabina's hour-glass figure. Moreover I had youth which was supposed to be a never-failing attraction for ageing roués. Sir Ralph's reputation was far from good. I had heard the blacksmiths talking to some of the farmers about the old days when Sir Ralph was in his prime as a seducer of young maidens. They were immediately silent when I, at that time in the company of Hadrian and Theodosia, had appeared. And yet Dorcas and Alison had been delighted that I was to have a post at Keverall Court.

I reasoned that they believed that Sir Ralph had given up his wild life. He was far too old to pursue it; and, remembering him on that night when he had come to Lady Bodrean's room, I could well believe it. All the same, I did think it rather strange that Dorcas and Alison had so willingly allowed me to go into the lecher's lair.

Now they wanted a detailed account of the ball.

'A dress!' they had cried. 'What a charming idea.'

A further surprise because I had believed that one of the tenets of society was that young ladies did not accept dresses from a gentleman.

This was different. Theodosia had made it so. I had come to the conclusion that Sir Ralph liked me. I amused him in some way, which Theodosia had failed to do.

I was content to have been to the ball and to have enjoyed it. Had I not been presented with the dress I could never have gone.

It was so much easier to accept the cosy outlook I found at Rainbow Cottage rather than to probe the motives of Sir Ralph. For all his faults, he was a kindly man. The servants certainly liked him better than they did his wife. As for myself, I felt fully competent to deal with any situation which might arise. I was fortunate in having Rainbow Cottage so close that I could run straight out of Keverall Court to it, if need be.

So I told them all about the ball. Dorcas was very

interested in the food, Alison in the flower arrangements; and both of them much more interested in what had happened to me.

I danced the waltz round the tiny sitting-room in Rainbow Cottage, knocking over the what-not which resulted in two casualties – the handle of one of Dorcas's little Goss china cups and a finger chipped on her eighteenth-century flower girl.

They were rueful but happy to see me happier; so they made light of the breakages. The cup handle would stick and the finger wouldn't be noticed. And with whom had I danced?

'Tybalt Travers! He's a strange man. Emily's sister who works there says both he and his father give her the creeps.'

'Creeps!' I said. 'The servants there are creep mad!'

'It's a queer sort of house and a strange profession, I think,' said Dorcas. 'Fiddling about with things that people handled years and years ago.'

'Oh, Dorcas, you're talking like some country bumpkin.'

'I know you're very interested in it. And I must say some of the pictures in those books you used to bring here would have given me nightmares. I used to wonder whether we ought to take them away.'

'What pictures!'

'Skulls and bones . . . and I think those mummies are horrible things. And Sir Edward . . .'

'Well, what of Sir Edward?'

'I know he's very well known and very highly thought of but they say he's a bit peculiar.'

'Just because he's different from themselves . . . just because he doesn't go around seducing all the village maidens like Sir Ralph did . . . they think that's odd!'

'Really, Judith, where do you learn such things?'

'From life, Alison dear. Life all around me.'

'You get so vehement every time these Traverses are mentioned.'

'Well, they're doing this wonderful job . . .'

'I do believe you'd like to be out there with them, fiddling about with all those dead mummies!'

'I could imagine nothing I should like more. It would be a little different from dancing attendance on the most disagreeable woman in the world.'

'Poor Judith, perhaps it won't last for ever. Do you know, I think we might manage here. There's quite a big garden. We might grow vegetables and sell them.'

I grimaced at my hands. 'I don't think I have the necessary green fingers.'

'Well, who knows, something may turn up. That young man who used to teach you. He was at the ball, wasn't he?'

'You mean Evan Callum.'

'I always liked him. There was something gentle about him. You used to talk about him a great deal. You were better at his lessons than any of the others.'

I smiled at them benignly. They had made up their minds that marriage would solve my problems. I had failed to bring it off with Oliver Shrimpton so they had chosen Evan Callum as the next candidate.

'I dare say he will be coming down here again. All this interest about the expedition . . .'

'Why doesn't *he* give people the creeps?' I

demanded. 'His profession is the same as Sir Edward's and Tybalt's.'

'He's more . . . . normal.'

'You're not suggesting that the Traverses are not normal!'

'They're different,' said Dorcas. 'Oh yes, Mr Callum will be here again. Sir Ralph, they say, is involved in this Egyptian matter. I heard that he's helping to finance it because his daughter is going to marry Tybalt Travers.'

'Where did you hear that?' I asked.

'Through Emily.'

'Servants' gossip.'

'My dear Judith, who knows more about a family's affairs than the servants?'

They were right, of course. The servants would hear scraps of conversation. I pictured Jane with her ear to the keyhole. Some of them pieced together torn-up letters which had been thrown into waste-paper baskets. They had their ears and eyes open for household scandals.

There was no doubt that the general expectation was that Tybalt was destined for Theodosia.

I went back to Keverall Court thoughtfully.

He doesn't love her, I told myself. I should know if he did. He enjoyed dancing with me at the ball far more than with Theodosia. How could a man like Tybalt be in love with Theodosia!

But Theodosia was rich – a great heiress. With a fortune in his hands such as Theodosia could bring him – Tybalt would be able to finance his own expeditions.

To Sir Edward very little mattered but his work

and Tybalt was following very close in his foot-steps.

This was why the servants in the house had 'the creeps'.

On the day Tybalt married Theodosia I would go away. I would find a post as far as possible from St Erno's and I would try to build a new life out of the ruins of my old one. He might be obsessed by his work; I was by him; and I knew as surely as I knew anything that when I lost him all the savour would go from my life.

Dorcas had said: 'When Judith is enthusiastic about something her whole heart's in it. She never does any-thing by halves.'

She was right; and now I was enthusiastic as I had never been in my life before — enthusiastic for one man, one way of life.

Theodosia, as though to make up for her neglect, sought me out a good deal. She liked to talk about the books she was reading and I could see she was making a great effort to perfect herself in the subject of archaeology.

She would invite me to her room and it often seemed as though she were on the verge of confidences. She was a little absent-minded; sometimes she would seem very happy, at others apprehensive. Once when I was in her room she pulled open a drawer and I saw a bundle of letters tied up with blue ribbon. How like Theodosia to tie up her love letters with blue ribbon! I wondered what was in them. Somehow I could not imagine Tybalt writing love-letters — and to Theodosia!

Dearest Theodosia,

I long for the day when we shall be married.
I am planning several expeditions and these need
financial backing. How useful your fortune will
be . . .

I laughed at myself. I was trying to convince
myself that the only thing he would want from
Theodosia was her fortune. And even if he did,
as if he would write such a letter!

'How is Mamma behaving these days?' she asked
me idly one afternoon when she had invited me to
her room.

'Very much as usual.'

'I expect she had been even worse since the ball.'

'Your expectations are correct.'

'Poor Judith!'

'Oh, we all have our problems.'

'Yes,' she sighed.

'Surely not you, Theodosia.'

She hesitated. Then she said, 'Judith, have you
ever been in love?'

I felt myself starting to flush uncomfortably but
fortunately it was not meant to be a question so
much as a preliminary to confidences.

'It's wonderful,' she went on, 'and yet . . . I'm
a little scared.'

'Why should you be scared?'

'Well, I'm not very clever, as you know.'

'If he's in love with you . . .'

'If! Of course he is. He tells me so every time
I see him . . . every time he writes . . .'

117

I half wanted to make an excuse to escape, half wanted to stay and be tortured.

'I really find archaeology rather boring, Judith. That's the truth, and of course it's his life. I've tried. I've read the books. I love it when they find something wonderful, but it's mostly about tools for digging and kinds of soil and so on and all those boring pots and things.'

'If you're not interested, perhaps you shouldn't pretend to be.'

'I don't think he expects me to be. I shall just look after him. That's all he wants. Oh it will be wonderful, Judith. But I'm worried about my father.'

'Why should you be worried about him?'

'He won't like it.'

'Won't like it! But I thought he was anxious for you to marry Tybalt.'

'Tybalt! I'm not talking of Tybalt.'

This was singing in my ears. It was like listening to some heavenly chorus. I cried: 'What! Not Tybalt. You're joking!'

'Tybalt!' she cried. And she repeated his name with a sort of horror. 'Tybalt! Why I'd be scared to death of him. I'm sure he thinks I am quite foolish.'

'He's serious, of course, which is much more interesting than being stupidly frivolous.'

'Evan is not frivolous.'

'Evan! So it's Evan!'

'But of course it's Evan. Who else?'

I began to laugh. 'And those letters tied up with blue ribbon . . . and all this sighing and blushing. Evan!' I hugged her. 'Oh Theodosia, I'm so happy . . .' I had the presence of mind to add: 'for you.'

118

'Whatever's come over you, Judith?'

'Well, I didn't think it was Evan.'

'You thought it was Tybalt. That's what people think because that's what Father wants. He'd love to see a match between our families. He's always been a great admirer of Sir Edward and interested in everything he does. And he would have loved me to be like you and able to learn about all this stuff. But I'm not like that, and how could anybody want Tybalt when there's Evan!'

'Some might,' I said calmly.

'Then they must be *mad*.'

'So mad that they might think you're mad to prefer Evan.'

'It's good to talk to you, Judith. We don't like to tell Father, you see. You know what families are. You see, Evan's people were very poor and he's working his way up. There was some relative who helped him and Evan wants to pay him back every penny he's spent on him. And we're going to do that. *I* think it's to his credit that he's come so far. It's nothing to be ashamed of. Why, Tybalt inherited all sorts of advantages, whereas Evan worked for his.'

'It's very laudable,' I said.

'Judith, you like Evan, don't you?'

'Of course I do; and I think you and he are ideally suited.'

'That's wonderful. But what do you think Father will say?'

'There's one way of finding out. Ask him.'

'Do you think one could do that?'

'Why ever not?'

'But if he refuses?'

119

'We'll stage an elopement. A ladder against the wall, the bride-to-be escaping down it and then off to Gretna Green, or as that's rather a long way from Cornwall, perhaps a special licence would be better.'

'Oh, Judith, you're always such *fun*. You make everything seem a sort of joke. I'm so glad I've told you.'

'So am I,' I said with heartfelt conviction.

'What would *you* do?'

'I should go to your father and say, "I love Evan Callum. Moreover I am determined to marry him."'

'And suppose he says no?'

'Then we plan the elopement.'

'I wish we could do that now.'

'But you must ask your father first. He may be delighted.'

'He won't be. He's got this fascination for the Traverses. He'd like me to be like you ... crazy about all this digging. I believe he would have gone to Egypt if he'd been well enough.'

'You'll probably go some time with Evan.'

'I'd go anywhere with Evan.'

'What does Evan say?'

'He says that we're going to be married whatever happens.'

'You may be cut out of your father's will.'

'Do you think I care for that? I'd rather have Evan and starve.'

'It won't come to that. Why should it? He has a good job at the University, hasn't he? You have nothing to fear. Even if you don't inherit a vast fortune you will be a professor's wife.'

'Of course. I don't care about Father's money.'

'Then you're in a strong position. You must fight to marry where you please. And you can't begin too soon.'

She hugged me again.

I was so happy. How pleasant it is to work for someone's happiness when doing so contributes to your own!

Theodosia was right when she had said that her father would not be pleased about the wedding.

When she broke the news there was a storm.

Theodosia came to my room in tears.

'He won't have it,' she said. 'He's furious. He says he'll stop it.'

'Well, you have to stand firm if you really want to marry.'

'You would, wouldn't you, Judith?'

'Do you doubt it?'

'Not for a moment. How I wish I were like you.'

'You can be.'

'How, Judith, *how*?'

'Stand firm. No one can make you marry if you won't say the appropriate words.'

'You'll help me, won't you, Judith?'

'With all my heart,' I said.

'I have told Father that he can cut me out, that I don't care. That I love Evan and that I'm going to marry him.'

'That's the first step, then.'

She was greatly comforted and she stayed in my room while we made plans. I told her that the first thing she must do was write to Evan and tell him the state of affairs. We would see what he would say.

'I shall tell him that you know, Judith, and that we can count on you.'

I was surprised to receive a summons from Sir Ralph. When I went to his apartments he was in an armchair in a dressing-gown and Blake was hovering. He dismissed Blake and said, 'Sit down, Miss Osmond.'

I obeyed.

'I have the impression that you are interfering in my daughter's affairs.'

'I know that she wishes to marry,' I said. 'I cannot see that I have interfered.'

'Indeed! Didn't you tell her to come and deliver her ultimatum to me?'

'I did tell her that if she wished to marry she should tell you so.'

'And perhaps ask my permission?'

'Yes.'

'And if I did not give it, to defy me?'

'What she will do is entirely a matter for her to decide.'

'But you in her position would not think of obeying your father?'

'If I decided to marry then I should do so.'

'In spite of the fact that you went against your father's wishes?'

'Yes.'

'I guessed it,' he said. 'Propping her up. That's what you've been doing. By God, Miss Osmond, you have a mighty big idea of your importance.'

'I don't know what you mean, Sir Ralph?'

'At least you admit to some ignorance. I'm glad to see you have a little humility.'

I sat silent.

122

He went on: 'You know that my daughter Theodosia wishes to marry this penniless fellow.'

'I know that she wishes to marry Professor Evan Callum.'

'My daughter will be a very rich woman one day ... providing she obeys my wishes. Do you still think she should marry this man?'

'If she is in love with him.'

'Love! I didn't know you were sentimental, Miss Osmond.'

Again I was silent. I could not understand why he had sent for me.

'You are advising my daughter to marry this man.'

'I? She had already chosen him before I was aware of her intention.'

'I had a match arranged for her ... a much more suitable one.'

'Surely she is the one who should decide its suitability.'

'You have modern ideas, Miss Osmond. In my day daughters obeyed their parents. *You* don't think they should.'

'In most matters. But in my opinion marriage is something which should be decided on by the partners concerned.'

'And my daughter's marriage does not concern me?'

'Not as closely as it does her and her future husband.'

'You should have been an advocate. Instead of which I believe you have a fancy for the profession of the man my daughter would marry ... if I permit it.'

'It's true.'

I saw the movement in his jaw and my spirits rose because again I was amusing him.

'I believe you know that I wanted another marriage for my daughter.'

'There has been a certain amount of speculation.'

'No smoke without fire, eh? I'll be frank. I wanted her to marry but to a different bridegroom. You have your ear to the ground, Miss Osmond, I'm sure.'

'I heard suggestions.'

'And you don't think it's a bad idea that my daughter chose this one? That's it. In fact, Miss Osmond, are you just a little pleased about it?'

'I don't know what you mean.'

'Don't you? This is the second time you've admitted ignorance. That's not like you ... and especially to feign it. You will help my daughter to disobey her father, won't you? You will be pleased to see her become the wife of this young fellow. You're a wily one, Miss Osmond. You have your reasons.'

He lay back in his chair, his face suffused with colour.

I could see that he was laughing. I was overcome by confusion at the insinuation of his words.

He knew that I was delighted that Theodosia was in love with Evan Callum, because I wanted Tybalt for myself.

He waved a hand. I was glad to escape.

A few days later Sir Ralph declared that he would permit an engagement between his daughter and Evan Callum.

Theodosia was in a state of bliss.

'Who could have believed, Judith, that there would have been such a complete turnabout.'

'I think your father is really rather a sentimental man and you're so obviously in love.'

'It's strange, Judith, how little one knows of people who have been close to one all one's life.'

'I don't think you're the first to have discovered that.'

The marriage was to be at Christmas time and Theodosia was plunged into a whirl of preparations.

Lady Bodrean did not approve. I heard her arguing with Sir Ralph about it. I hurried off to my own room but Jane reported afterwards, and I quite unashamedly listened to her account which I suppose was as bad as eavesdropping myself.

'My word,' said Jane, 'did the fur fly! They seem to think he's not good enough for our heiress. "Have you taken leave of your senses?" asks Lady B. "Madam," he says, "I will decide on my daughter's future." "She happens to be my daughter too." "And it is fortunate for her that she has not turned out like you or I'd be sorry for this young man she's going to marry." "So you're sorry for yourself," she says. "No, madam, I know how to look after myself," he says. "You knew how to scatter your bastards all over the countryside." "A man must amuse himself somehow," he said. Oh he's the master all right. If she'd got hold of a meek man, she'd have ruled him. But not our Squire. Then she said, "You told me that she was to marry Tybalt Travers." "Well, I have changed my mind." "That's a sudden turnabout." "She's in love with this fellow." "Love," she snorted. "Something you don't believe in, madam, I know, but I say she shall marry this fellow she's chosen." "You've changed your mind. How long is it since you said: 'I want my daughter to marry the son of my old friend Edward Travers'?" "I've changed my mind, that's all that's to be said . . ." And on and on they went throwing insults at each other. My word, we do see life.'

I thought a great deal about Sir Ralph. I was really quite fond of him.

When Alison and Dorcas heard the news they were astounded.

'Theodosia to marry Evan Callum! How very strange! *You* were so much better at all that work that he's so keen on than she was.'

I could see that they were nonplussed. Another attempt to marry me off had failed.

Evan and Theodosia were married on Christmas Day with Oliver Shrimpton performing the ceremony. I sat at the back of the church between Dorcas and Alison; Sabina was with us.

When the bride came down the aisle on her husband's arm, Sabina whispered to me: 'It'll be your turn next.'

I noticed that her eyes went to Hadrian in the front pew.

Good Heavens! I thought. Is that the way some people are thinking?

As for myself I had always looked upon Hadrian as a brother. I laughed to myself to think of what Lady Bodrean would have to say if she knew that. She would think it highly presumptuous of the companion to think of Sir Ralph's nephew as a brother.

The bridal pair were spending the Christmas and

Boxing nights at Keverall Court. After that they were going to a house in Devon which one of the dons at the University had lent them for their honeymoon. I was allowed to spend the day at Rainbow Cottage, returning early next morning. I wondered at this concession; then it occurred to me that Lady Bodrean probably thought that Sir Ralph, who now quite clearly had become a kind of protector to me, might invite me to the evening's entertainment which was being given to celebrate both Christmas and the wedding.

I spent a quiet day, and in the evening Alison and Dorcas invited one or two of their friends and we had a pleasant evening playing guessing games.

Two days later the radiant bride left with her husband. I missed her. Everything seemed flat now that the excitement of the wedding was over. Lady Bodrean became peevishly irritable and complained continually.

I had an opportunity to talk with Hadrian who was as usual worried about money.

'There's only one thing I can do,' he said, 'and that is find an heiress to marry me as Evan has.'

'I am sure that did not enter his head,' I said hotly.

Hadrian grinned at me. 'With the best intentions in the world, he must have a feeling of relief. Money's money, and a fortune never did any harm to anyone.'

'You're obsessed by money!'

'Put it down to my lack of it.'

And at the end of January he left and it was about that time that Lady Bodrean was indisposed for a few days and I had a little freedom.

Sir Ralph sent for me and said that since Lady

Bodrean did not require my services I might read the papers to him.

So each morning I sat with him for an hour or so and read *The Times*; but he would never let me get very far. I realized that he wanted to talk.

He told me a little about the expedition.

'I should have gone with them, but my doctor said no.' He tapped his heart. 'Couldn't have it giving out, you know. I'd have been a nuisance. Heat would have been too much for me.'

I was able to reply intelligently because of the little knowledge I had acquired.

'It's a pity we couldn't send you up to the University. You'd have done well, I think. Always had a feeling for it, didn't you? That's what's needed — a *feeling*. I always had it myself, but was never anything but an amateur.'

I said that there was a great deal of pleasure to be found in being merely an amateur.

'With Sir Edward it's a passion. I reckon he's one of the top men in his profession ... I'd go so far as to say *the top*.'

'Yes, I believe he is considered so.'

'And Master Tybalt's the same.'

He shot a quick glance at me and I felt the tell-tale colour in my cheeks. I remembered his insinuations about us in the past.

'He'll be another like his father. Very difficult man to live with, was Sir Edward. His wasn't a very happy marriage. There are some men who marry a profession rather than a wife. Always up and off somewhere. When at home, buried in his books or his work. She didn't see him for days at a stretch

128

when he was at home. And he was nearly always away.'

'I suppose she wasn't interested in his work.'

'His work came first. With those sort of men it always does.'

'Your daughter has married an archaeologist.'

'That fellow! I've got his measure. He'll be talking in a class-room all his life . . . theorizing about this and that . . . and when his day's work is over he'll go home to his wife and family and forget all about it. There are men like that – but they're rarely the ones who rise to the top of their profession. Would you like to see some reports of what is happening in Egypt?'

'Oh, I should enjoy that.'

He regarded me with that familiar shake of the jaw.

I read some of the reports to him and we discussed them. How that hour used to fly!

I had slipped into a new relationship with Sir Ralph which used to surprise me sometimes but it had all come about so gradually. That interest which he had always shown in me had become the basis of a friendship which I should not have thought possible.

It was in early March that the news came of Sir Edward's mysterious death and the speculation arose about the Curse of the Pharaohs.

Tybalt's Wife

Sir Ralph was deeply shocked and this shock resulted in another stroke, which impaired his speech. It was then that rumours circulated about the significance of the illness. It was the Curse of the Kings, said the rumours, for it was known that he had backed the expedition financially. He was unable to attend the funeral but a week or so after he sent for me and when I went to his room I was surprised to see Tybalt there.

It was pitiful to see the once robust Sir Ralph the wreck he now was. His efforts to speak were painful and yet he insisted on attempting to do so because there was something he wanted to say.

He indicated that he wished us to sit on either side of him.

'Ju . . . Ju . . .' he began and I realized he was trying to say my name.

'I'm here, Sir Ralph,' I said, and when I laid my hand on his he took it and would not release it.

His eyes turned towards Tybalt, and his right hand moved, for it was with his left that he held mine.

Tybalt understood that he wanted his hand so he laid it in that of Sir Ralph. Sir Ralph smiled and drew his hands together. Tybalt then took my hand and Sir Ralph smiled faintly. It was what he had wanted.

I looked into Tybalt's eyes and I felt the slow flush creeping over my face.

Sir Ralph's implication was obvious.

I withdrew my hand but Tybalt continued to look at me.

Sir Ralph had closed his eyes. Blake tiptoed in.

'I think it would be better, sir,' he said, 'if you and Miss Osmond left now.'

When the door shut on us Tybalt said to me: 'Will you walk to Giza House with me?'

'I must go to Lady Bodrean,' I replied. I was shaken. I could not understand why Sir Ralph should have placed us in this embarrassing position.

'I want to talk to you,' said Tybalt. 'It's important.'

We went out of the house together and when we had walked a little distance from it, Tybalt said: 'He's right, you know. We should.'

'I . . . I don't understand.'

'Why, Judith, what has happened to you? You are usually so forthright.'

'I . . . I didn't know you knew so much about me.'

'I know a great deal about you. It's a good many years since I first met you disguised as a mummy.'

'You will never forget that.'

'One doesn't forget one's first meeting with one's wife.'

'But . . .'

'It's what he meant. He was telling us we should marry.'

'He was wandering in his mind.'

'I don't think he was. I think it has been his wish for some time.'

'It is becoming clear to me. He thought I was Theodosia. He had hoped that you and Theodosia would marry. You did know that, didn't you?'

131

'I think it was talked over with my father.'

'So ... you see what happened. He had forgotten that Theodosia was married. He thought that I was his daughter. Poor Sir Ralph. I'm afraid he is very ill.'

'He is going to die, I fear,' replied Tybalt. 'You have always been interested in my work, haven't you ... vitally interested?'

'Why yes.'

'You see, we should get on very well. My mother was bored by my father's work. It was a very dismal marriage. It will be different with us.'

'I don't understand this. Do you mean that you will marry me because Sir Ralph has implied that he wants you to?'

'That's not the only reason, of course.'

'Tell me some others,' I said.

'For one, when I leave for Egypt, you could come with me. You would be pleased by that, I'm sure.'

'Yet, even that does not seem to me an adequate reason for marrying.'

He stopped and faced me. 'There are others,' he said, and drew me close to him.

I said: 'I would not wish to marry because I would be a useful member of an expedition.'

'Nevertheless,' he replied, 'you would be.'

Then he kissed me.

'If love came into it ...' I began.

Then he laughed and held me tightly against him.

'Do you doubt that it does?'

'I am undecided and I should like some sort of declaration.'

'First let me have one from you because I'm sure

you will do so better than I. You're never at a loss for words. I'm afraid I am . . . often.'

'Then perhaps I shall be even more useful to you. Writing your letters, for instance. I shall be a good secretary.'

'Is that *your* declaration?'

'I suppose you know that I have been in love with you for years. Sir Ralph knew it, I believe.'

'I had no idea I was so fortunate! I wish I had known before.'

'What would you have done?'

'Asked myself whether if you knew me better you might have changed your mind, and wondered whether I dared allow that to happen.'

'Are you really so modest?'

'No. I shall be the most arrogant man in your life.'

'There are no others of any importance . . . and never have been. I shall spend my life if necessary convincing you of that.'

'So you agree to share it with me?'

'I would die rather than do anything else.'

'My dearest Judith! Did I not say that you had a way with words!'

'I have told you quite frankly that I love you. I should like to hear you say that you love me.'

'Have I not made it clear to you that I do?'

'I should love to hear you say it.'

'I love you,' he said.

'Say it again. Keep saying it. I have so long dreamed of your saying those words. I can't believe this is really true. I am awake now, am I? I'm not going to wake up in a minute to hear Lady Bodrean ringing the bell?'

He took my hand and kissed it fervently. 'My

dear, *dear* Judith,' he said. 'You put me to shame. I don't deserve you. Don't think too highly of me. I shall disappoint you. You know my obsession with work, I shall bore you with my enthusiasms.'

'Never.'

'I shall be an inadequate husband. I have not your gaiety, your spontaneity . . . everything that makes you so attractive. I can be dull, far too serious . . .'

'One can never be too serious about the important things of life.'

'I shall be moody, preoccupied, I shall neglect you for my work.'

'Which I intend to share with you, including the moods and the preoccupation, so that objection is overruled.'

'I am not able to express my feelings easily. I shall forget to tell you how much I love you. You alarm me. You are carried away by your enthusiasm always. You think too highly of me. You hope for perfection.'

I laughed as I laid my head against him. 'I can't help my feelings,' I said. 'I have loved you so long. I only want to be with you, to share your life, to make you happy, to make your life smooth and easy and just as you wish it to be.'

'Judith,' he said, 'I will do my best to make you happy.'

'If you love me, if you allow me to share your life, I shall be that.'

He slipped his arm through mine and gripped my hand tightly.

We walked on and he talked of the future. He saw no reason why our marriage should be delayed; in fact he would like it to take place as soon as possible. We were going to be very busy with our plans. Would I mind if after the ceremony we stayed at Giza House and plunged straight into our arrangements?

Would I mind? I cared for nothing as long as I could be with him. The greatest joy which could come to me was to share his life for evermore.

There was astonishment at Rainbow Cottage when I told Dorcas and Alison my news. They were glad that I was to be married but they were a little dubious about my bridegroom. Oliver Shrimpton was so much more eligible in their opinion; and the rumours in St Erno's were that the Traverses were rather odd people. And now that Sir Edward had died so mysteriously they felt that they would have preferred me not to be connected with such a mysterious affair.

'You'll be Lady Travers,' said Alison.

'I hadn't thought of that.'

Dorcas shook her head. 'You're happy. I can see that.'

'Oh, Dorcas, Alison, I never thought it possible to be so happy.'

'Now, now,' said Dorcas, as she used to when I was a child. 'You could never do things by halves.'

'Surely one should not contemplate marriage "by halves" as you say.'

I laughed at her. 'In this marriage,' I said, 'everything is going to be perfect.'

I said nothing at Keverall Court about my engagement. It hardly seemed appropriate with Sir Ralph so ill; and the next day he died.

Keverall Court was in mourning, but I don't think

135

anyone missed Sir Ralph as much as I did. The great joy of my engagement was overshadowed. But at least, I thought, he would have been pleased. He had been my friend, and during the weeks before his death, our friendship had meant a good deal to me, as I believed it had to him. How I wished that I could have sat in his room and told him of my engagement and all that I hoped to do in the future. I thought of him a great deal and remembered incidents from the past – when I had brought the bronze shield to him and he had first become interested in me, how he had given me a ball dress and had defended me afterwards.

Lady Bodrean put on a sorrowing countenance but it was clear that it hid a relief.

She talked to me and to Jane about the virtues of Sir Ralph; but I sensed that the lull in her hostility to me was momentary and she was promising herself that now that I had lost my champion I should be at her mercy. Little did she know the blow I was about to deliver. I was to be married to the man whom she had wanted for her daughter. It was going to be a great shock to her to learn that her poor companion would soon be Lady Travers.

Hadrian came home. I told him the news.

'It's not officially announced yet,' I warned him. 'I shall wait until after the funeral.'

'Tybalt's lucky,' he said glumly. 'I reckon he's fore-stalled me.'

'Ah, but you wanted a woman with money.'

'If you'd had a fortune, Judith, I'd have laid my heart at your feet.'

'Biologically impossible,' I told him.

'Well, I wish you luck. And I'm glad you're getting

away from my aunt. Your life must have been hellish with her.'

'It wasn't so bad. You know that I always enjoyed a fight.'

That night I had a strange intimation from Sir Ralph's lawyers. They wanted me to be present at the reading of his will.

When I called at Rainbow Cottage and told Alison and Dorcas of this they behaved rather oddly.

They went out and left me in the sitting-room and were gone some time. This was strange because my visit was necessarily a brief one and just as I was about to call them and tell them that I must be going, they came back.

Their faces were flushed and they looked at each other in a most embarrassed fashion, and knowing them so well I realized that each was urging the other to open a subject which they found distasteful or distressing in some way.

'Is anything wrong?' I asked.

'There is something we think you ought to know,' said Dorcas.

'Yes, indeed you must be prepared.'

'Prepared for what?'

Dorcas bit her lip and looked at Alison; Alison nodded.

'It's about your birth, Judith. You are our niece. Lavinia was your mother.'

'Lavinia! Why didn't you tell me?'

'Because we thought it best. It was rather an awkward situation.'

'It was a terrible shock to us,' went on Dorcas. 'Lavinia was the eldest. Father doted on her. She was

137

so pretty. She was just like our mother . . . whereas we were like Father.'

'Dear Dorcas!' I said. 'Do get on and tell me what this is all about.'

'It was a terrible shock to us when we heard she was going to have a child.'

'Which turned out to be me?'

'Yes. We smuggled Lavinia away to a cousin . . . before it was noticeable, you see. We told people in the village that she had taken a situation . . . a post of governess. And you were born. The cousin was in London and she had several children of her own. Lavinia could look after them and keep her own baby there. It was a good arrangement. She brought you to see us, but of course she couldn't come here. We all met in Plymouth. We had such a pleasant time and then saw her off on that train.'

'There was an accident,' I said. 'She was killed and I survived.'

'And what was going to happen to you was a problem. So we said you were a cousin's child and brought you here . . . to adopt you, as it were.'

'Well, you are in fact my aunts! Aunt Alison, Aunt Dorcas! But why did you tell me that story about being unclaimed?'

'You were always asking questions about the distant cousins who, you thought, were your close family, so we thought it better for you to have no family at all.'

'You always did what you thought best for me, I know. Who was my father? Do you know that?'

They looked at each other for a moment and I burst out: 'Can it really be? It explains everything. Sir Ralph!'

Their faces told me that I had guessed correctly.

'He was my father. I'm glad. I was fond of him. He was always good to me.' I went to them and hugged them. 'At least I know who my parents are now.'

'We thought you might be ashamed to have been born . . . out of wedlock.'

'Do you know,' I said, 'I believe he really loved her. She must have been the one love of his life. At least she gave him the great solace he needed married to Lady Bodrean.'

'Oh Judith!' they cried indulgently.

'But he has been kind to me.' I thought of the way he looked at me; the amused twinkle in his eyes, the shake of his chin. He was saying to himself: This is Lavinia's daughter. How I wished that he was alive so that I could tell him how fond I had grown of him.

'Now, Judith,' said Dorcas, 'you must be prepared. The reason you are expected to be at the reading of the will is because he has left you something. It may well come out that you are his daughter and we wouldn't want it to come as a shock to you.'

'I will be prepared,' I promised.

They were right. I was mentioned in Sir Ralph's will. He had left a quarter of a million pounds to archaeological research to be used, depending on certain conditions, in whatever way Sir Edward or Tybalt Travers thought fit; he had left an income for life to his wife; to Hadrian an income of one thousand a year; to Theodosia, his heiress, the house on the death of her mother and one half of the residue of his income; the other half was to go to his natural daughter, Judith Osmond; and in the event of the death of one of his

139

daughters her share of his fortune would revert to the other.

It was astounding.

I, penniless, unclaimed at birth, had acquired parents and from one had come a fortune so great that it bewildered me to contemplate it.

Dramatic events had taken place during the recent weeks. I was to be married to the man I loved; and I should not go to him, as I had thought, a penniless woman. I should bring with me a great fortune.

I thought of Sir Ralph taking my hand and Tybalt's and placing them in each other. I wondered if he had told Tybalt of our relationship and of what he intended to do.

I then felt my first twinge of uneasiness.

The truth of my birth was now known through the village. That I was Sir Ralph's daughter surprised few; there was a certain amount of gossip among Oliver's parishioners who recounted how I had been educated with his legitimate daughter and nephew and afterwards taken into Keverall Court, albeit in a humble position. They had guessed, they said, being wise after the event. Alison and Dorcas were alternatively pleased and ashamed. Alison said that she was glad her father had not had to face this scandal; their sister, the rector's daughter, the mistress of Sir Ralph who had borne him a child! It *was* rather scandalous. At the same time I, who meant far more to them than their dead sister's reputation, was now a woman of means whose future was secure. I had also so charmed my father that he had shown the world that I was almost as important to him as his legitimate daughter.

The scandal would die down; the benefits remain.

They had been so anxious for me to marry but now I was about to do so they were, I sensed, not so pleased. As a young woman of means I no longer needed the financial support a husband could give me, and it was for this support that they had selected first Oliver and then Evan for me; and now, before I had known of my inheritance I had become engaged to that rather strange man whose father had recently died mysteriously. It was not what they had planned for me.

When I went to them after the reading of the will they looked at me strangely as though I had become a different person.

I laughed at them. 'You foolish old aunts,' I cried, 'for aunts you have turned out to be, the fact that I'm going to be rich doesn't change me at all! And let me tell you, there is going to be no cheeseparing in this house again. You are going to have an income which will enable you to live in the manner to which you have been accustomed.'

It was a very emotional moment. Alison's face twitched and Dorcas's was actually wet. I embraced them.

'Just think of it,' I said. 'You can leave Rainbow Cottage . . . Sell it if you wish (for Sir Ralph had left it to them) and go and live in a lovely house . . . with a maid or two . . .'

Alison laughed. 'Judith, you always did run on. We're quite happy here and it's our very own now. We shall stay here.'

'Well, you shall never worry about making ends meet again.'

141

'You mustn't go spending all the money before you've got it.'

That made me laugh. 'I believe there's quite a lot of it, and if you think my first thought wouldn't be to look after you, you don't know Judith Osmond.'

Dorcas dabbed her eyes and Alison said seriously: 'Judith, what about *him*?'

'Him?'

'This er . . . this man you plan to marry.'

'Tybalt.'

They were both looking at me anxiously.

'Now that er . . .' began Alison. 'Now that you have this . . . fortune . . .'

'Good Heavens,' I cried, 'you don't think —'

'We . . . we wondered whether he knew . . .'

'Knew what?' I demanded.

'That you . . . er . . . were coming into this money.'

'Aunts!' I cried sternly. 'You are being very wrong. Tybalt and I were meant for each other. I'm passionately interested in his work.'

Alison said with a touch of asperity quite alien to her: 'I hope he's not passionately interested in your money.'

I was angry with them. 'This is monstrous. How could he be . . . Besides . . .'

'Now, Judith, we are only concerned for your good,' said Dorcas.

My anger melted. It was true. All their anxiety was for my welfare. I kissed them again. 'Listen,' I said, 'I love Tybalt . . . love, love, *love!* Do you understand that? I always have. I always will. And we are going to work together. It's the most ideal match that was

142

ever made. Don't dare say anything else. Don't dare *think* anything else . . .'

'Oh, Judith, you always swept everything along with you. I only hope . . .'

'Hope. Who has to hope when one *knows*?'

'So you really love him?'

'Do you doubt it?'

'No. We were wondering about him.'

'Of course,' I said, 'he doesn't show his feelings as I do. Who does?'

They agreed that few did.

'He may seem aloof, remote, cool – but he's not so.'

'It would break our hearts if you weren't happy, Judith.'

'There's nothing to be afraid of. Your hearts are going to remain intact.'

'You really are happy, Judith?' said Alison.

'I'm in love with Tybalt,' I said. 'And he wants to marry me. And that being so how could I possibly be anything but happy?'

It was different at the rectory. Sabina welcomed me warmly.

'Oh, this is *fun*, Judith,' she cried in her inconsequential way. 'Here we are, the old gang all happily tied up together. It is interesting, isn't it? The only one left out is poor Hadrian. Of course we were uneven, weren't we? Three women, and four men. What a lovely proportion – and a rare one. Tybalt wasn't really one of us, though. In the schoolroom, I mean. And dear old Evan and *darling* Oliver . . . well, they were the teachers. I'm so pleased. After all, you did bully us, didn't you, Judith, so Tybalt is just right for

143

you. I always say to Oliver you need someone to bully you. And now you've got Tybalt. Not that he'll bully in the way you did but he'll keep a firm hand. You can't imagine anyone bullying Tybalt, can you? Oh, Judith, aren't you lucky! And I can't think of anyone I'd rather have for my darling perfect brother.'

This was more comforting than the views at Rainbow Cottage.

And she went on: 'It was all so exciting. Sir Ralph and all that . . . and the *money!* You'll be able to go everywhere with Tybalt. My father was always having to get people interested . . . to back his trips, you know. Not that he didn't spend a lot on it himself . . . We'd have been *fabulously* rich, my mother used to say, if it hadn't been for my father's *obsession.*'

So it seemed that whenever my coming marriage was discussed, my recently acquired fortune always seemed to come under consideration.

I couldn't help enjoying my interview with Lady Bodrean.

After the will had been read I presented myself to her. She regarded me as though I were quite distasteful, which I suppose I was.

'So,' she said, 'you have come to hand in your notice.'

'Certainly I have, Lady Bodrean.'

'I expected it would not be long before you did. So I am to be inconvenienced.'

I replied: 'Well, if I was so useful to you, a fact which you very carefully concealed, I would be willing to stay for a week or so until you have replaced me.'

144

Of course he would have preferred his *true* daughter to have made the match – instead of which she must go off with this penniless teacher . . .'

'As I may now presume to correct you, something which was beyond my range before my true identity was discovered, I must remind you that Professor Callum is far from penniless. He holds a good post in one of the country's foremost universities and the term school teacher is hardly the correct one to apply to a lecturer in archaeology.'

'He was not the man Sir Ralph wished his daughter to marry. She was foolish and flouted us – and it seems to me that Sir Ralph then decided that since Theodosia had been so foolish he would offer her chance to you.'

'My future husband is not a prize packet on a dish to be offered round.'

'One might say that there was quite a prize to be offered to him. I am surprised at the manner in which my husband has left his fortune. I would say it is a victory for immorality and extravagance.'

I would not let her see that she had scored. This suggestion that I was being married for *my* money was not a new one.

However, I said goodbye to Lady Bodrean and left her with the understanding that our association as employer and employed was terminated.

I went back to Rainbow Cottage which would be my home until my marriage.

We were to be married very soon. Tybalt insisted. Dorcas and Alison thought it was somewhat unseemly to have a wedding so soon after a funeral; and I had to

146

'You know by now that you were *forced* on me. I had not employed a companion before you came.'

'Then you will have no objection to my leaving immediately.'

She had obviously come to the conclusion that the new turn in my fortunes meant that I would no longer be a good object for oppression and she decided I should go at once, but she pretended to consider this.

That I was Sir Ralph's daughter was, I am sure, no surprise to her. In fact I think his behaviour towards me had convinced her of our relationship and it was for this reason that she had been particularly unpleasant to me. But that Tybalt should have asked me to marry him was something which puzzled her. She had wanted Tybalt for her own daughter and the fact that Theodosia had married Evan Callum and I had won the prize was galling to her.

'I hear you are shortly to be married,' she said, her lip curling.

'You have heard correctly,' I told her.

'I must say I was surprised until . . . er . . .'

'Until?'

'I know that Sir Ralph confided a great deal in Sir Edward. They were close friends. I've no doubt he told him the position and it was for this reason that . . . er . . .'

'You have always been very frank in the past, Lady Bodrean,' I said. 'There is no need to be less direct now that we meet on an equal footing. You are suggesting that Sir Tybalt Travers has asked me to marry him because I am Sir Ralph's daughter?'

'Sir Ralph was eager for a union with that family.

you. I always say to Oliver you need someone to bully you. And now you've got Tybalt. Not that he'll bully in the way you did but he'll keep a firm hand. You can't imagine anyone bullying Tybalt, can you? Oh, Judith, aren't you lucky! And I can't think of anyone I'd rather have for my darling perfect brother.'

This was more comforting than the views at Rainbow Cottage.

And she went on: 'It was all so exciting. Sir Ralph and all that . . . and the *money!* You'll be able to go everywhere with Tybalt. My father was always having to get people interested . . . to back his trips, you know. Not that he didn't spend a lot on it himself . . . We'd have been *fabulously* rich, my mother used to say, if it hadn't been for my father's *obsession.*'

So it seemed that whenever my coming marriage was discussed, my recently acquired fortune always seemed to come under consideration.

I couldn't help enjoying my interview with Lady Bodrean.

After the will had been read I presented myself to her. She regarded me as though I were quite distasteful, which I suppose I was.

'So,' she said, 'you have come to hand in your notice.'

'Certainly I have, Lady Bodrean.'

'I expected it would not be long before you did. So I am to be inconvenienced.'

I replied: 'Well, if I was so useful to you, a fact which you very carefully concealed, I would be willing to stay for a week or so until you have replaced me.'

ever made. Don't dare say anything else. Don't dare *think* anything else . . .'

'Oh, Judith, you always swept everything along with you. I only hope . . .'

'Hope. Who has to hope when one *knows?*'

'So you really love him?'

'Do you doubt it?'

'No. We were wondering about him.'

'Of course,' I said, 'he doesn't show his feelings as I do. Who does?'

They agreed that few did.

'He may seem aloof, remote, cool – but he's not so.'

'It would break our hearts if you weren't happy, Judith.'

'There's nothing to be afraid of. Your hearts are going to remain intact.'

'You really are happy, Judith?' said Alison.

'I'm in love with Tybalt,' I said. 'And he wants to marry me. And that being so how could I possibly be anything but happy?'

It was different at the rectory. Sabina welcomed me warmly.

'Oh, this is *fun*, Judith,' she cried in her inconsequential way. 'Here we are, the old gang all happily tied up together. It is interesting, isn't it? The only one left out is poor Hadrian. Of course we were uneven, weren't we? Three women, and four men. What a lovely proportion – and a rare one. Tybalt wasn't really one of us, though. In the schoolroom, I mean. And dear old Evan and *darling* Oliver . . . well, they were the teachers. I'm so pleased. After all, you did bully us, didn't you, Judith, so Tybalt is just right for remember that that funeral had turned out to be my father's.

When I put this point to Tybalt he said: 'That's nonsense! You didn't know it was your father until afterwards.'

I agreed with him. I was ready to agree with him on anything. When I was with him, I forgot all my misgivings. He was so eager for our wedding, and although he was by no means demonstrative he would look at me in a way which sent me into a state of bliss, for I knew that he was contemplating our future with the utmost pleasure. He took me into his confidence completely about his plans. This bequest of Sir Ralph's was a boon. Such a large sum of money suitably invested would bring in an income which could be entirely devoted to those explorations in which Sir Ralph had always delighted.

He talked a great deal about that other expedition which had ended abruptly and fatally for Sir Edward. He made me see the arid countryside, feel the heat of that blazing sun. I could visualize the excitement when they had found the door in the mountainside and the flight of steps leading down to corridors.

When he talked of ancient Egypt a passion glowed in him. I had never seen him so enthralled by anything as he was by his work, but I used to tell myself that our marriage was going to be the most important thing that ever happened to either of us, even more so than his work. I would see to that.

I was often at Giza House. It seemed different now that it was to be my home. Tabitha welcomed me warmly. She told me at the first opportunity how pleased she was that Tybalt and I were to marry.

'At one time,' she whispered, 'I greatly feared that it might be Theodosia.'

'That seemed to be the general idea.'

'There was a great deal of talk about it. I suppose because of the friendship between Sir Ralph and Sir Edward. And they died within a short time of each other.' She looked very sad. 'I am sure you are the one for Tybalt.' She pressed my hand. 'I shall never forget how you used to come and borrow the books. Those were not very happy days for you, I fear.' I told her that nothing that had gone before was of any more importance. In the last weeks life had given me all that I had ever hoped for.

'And you dreamed your dreams, Judith!' she said.

'I was a great dreamer. Now I am going to live.'

'You must understand Tybalt.'

'I think I do.'

'At times you will feel that he neglects you for the work.'

'I shan't because it's going to be my work too. I'm going to join him in everything he does. I'm as excited as he is about all this.'

'That's as it should be,' she said. 'I hope when you become mistress of Giza House you will not wish me to leave.'

'How could I? We're friends.'

'I have always been a close friend of Tybalt and his father. If I may continue here in my role as housekeeper I should be very happy. On the other hand if you should prefer . . .'

'What nonsense!' I cried. 'I want you to be here. You're my friend too.'

'Thank you, Judith.'

Tybalt said he would show me the house but when he did we didn't get farther than that room in which the sarcophagus had once stood because he would show me books his father had written and plans of sites they had excavated. I didn't mind. I was just so happy to be with him, to listen and to be able to make intelligent comments.

It was Tabitha who showed me the house and introduced me to the staff. Emily, Ellen, Jane and Sarah were the maids, normal girls all four of them, and so like others of their kind that it took me some time to know which was which. But there were three strange people in that house.

I had seen the two Egyptian servants, Mustapha and Absalam, strange, alien, and, I had heard, even sinister; I had listened avidly to the stories I had heard of them in the village.

Tabitha explained to me that Sir Edward liked them to look after him. They would cook him exotic dishes such as she knew nothing of. He had employed them on digs in Egypt and for some reason had taken a fancy to them; he had kept them with him and brought them to England.

She said they had been desolate but fatalistic about his death. They were certain it had come about because he had incurred the Curse of the Pharaohs.

'They are very concerned because Tybalt plans to carry on where his father left off. I think if it were possible for them to dissuade him they would do so.'

When I was presented to them as the future Lady Travers they eyed me with suspicion. They would have seen me some years before racing up the path or round the garden. They probably knew about the mummy incident.

I was prepared for them. Janet Tester was another matter. She was the old woman who had been nurse to Tybalt and Sabina, after fulfilling the same role for their mother; but she remained with them after Lady Travers's death. I remembered Sabina's saying that old Nanny Tester went off into 'funny fits', and her chatter about the old woman had been so interspersed with other matters – in Sabina's habitual manner – that I had not really taken a great deal of notice, because there was so much at Giza House to concern me. I had seen Nanny Tester on one or two occasions and had thought her a peculiar old woman, but as there was so much that was strange in Giza House, she did not seem so unusual as she would have elsewhere.

I had heard stories that the house gave the maids 'the creeps'; and this I had thought had something to do with the strange objects it contained – the sarcophagus, for instance, and that never-to-be-forgotten mummy. Mustapha and Absalam clearly had something to do with it too – and, I began to realize, so had Nanny Tester.

'I must explain Janet Tester to you,' said Tabitha, before she took me up to introduce me to her. 'She's a strange woman. She is really quite old now. She came as nurse to Sir Edward's wife, to whom of course she was devoted. She stayed on to look after Tybalt and Sabina; but when Lady Travers died she was almost demented. You know how it is with some of these nurses. Their charges are as their children. We have to be a bit careful with her . . . and treat her gently.

Her mind wanders a bit. Sir Edward would have pensioned her off but she didn't want to go. She said she'd always been with the family and wanted to stay. There was the ideal apartment at the top of this house, completely shut off from the house. Janet was struck with it and asked to have it. She keeps to herself, although of course we keep an eye on her.'

'What an unusual arrangement.'

'You'll find you're marrying into an unusual family. Tybalt is like his father, far from conventional. Sir Edward never wanted to be bothered with everyday things. He brushed them aside and took the easy way out. Tybalt is very like him in that and lots of ways. It was either a matter of having Janet Tester here or sending her to some sort of home. That would have made her really unhappy. Tybalt goes up to see her ... when he remembers her existence. Sabina comes in quite often. That keeps her happy. Sabina is her pet. It used to be Tybalt but since he's following in his father's footsteps she's turned to Sabina.'

'It sounds as though she didn't like Sir Edward.'

'You know how these old nannies are. She was jealous of him. She had her Miss Ruth – Lady Travers – as a baby; she was always her baby. She resented the intrusion of a husband. Poor Janet. She's getting very old now. She must be eighty. But come and meet her.'

We mounted the stairs. What a silent house it was; our feet sank into those thick carpets which covered every space of floor.

I commented on them and Tabitha said: 'Sir Edward could not endure noise while he was working.'

151

The house was a tall one, and Janet Tester's apartment consisted of several attic-type rooms above the fourth storey.

I was unprepared for the white-haired, gentle-looking woman who opened the door when we knocked; she wore a crisply laundered sprigged muslin blouse and a black bombazine skirt.

Tabitha said: 'Janet, I've brought Miss Osmond to see you.'

She looked at me and her eyes were misty with emotion. 'Come in, come in,' she said.

It was a charming room with its sloping roof, and it was prettily furnished with hand-made rugs on the floor and lots of embroidered cushion covers. There was a fire burning and the kettle on a hob was beginning to sing.

'You'll take some tea with me,' she said, and I replied that I should love to.

'You've heard of me then?' I said.

'Why, bless you, yes. Tybalt told me and I said to him, "Now you tell me what she's like, Tybalt," and all he could say was, "She's enthusiastic about the work." How like him! But I knew. I've seen you often tearing about down in the gardens there. What a one for mischief you were! I'll make the tea.'

'Shall I do that,' asked Tabitha, 'while you and Miss Osmond have a chat?'

The expression in the gentle old face changed startlingly. The eyes were almost venomous, the lips tightened. 'I'll do it, thank you,' she said. 'I'll make my own tea in my own room.'

When she was making it Tabitha gave me a glance.

I imagined she was preparing me for the strangeness she had mentioned in Janet Tester.

The tea was made. 'I always stir it,' she told me, 'and let it stand five minutes. It's the only way to get the right brew. Warm the pot, I used to say to Miss Ruth . . .'

'That's Lady Travers,' explained Tabitha and this remark brought forth another venomous glance.

'And the tea must go into a *dry* pot,' went on Janet Tester. 'That's very important.'

She purred as she poured out the tea.

'Well, I hope you'll be happy, my dear,' she said. 'Tybalt used to be such a good boy.'

'*Used* to be?' I asked.

'When he was a little one he was always with me. He was his mother's boy then. But when he went away to school and started to grow up he turned to his father.'

She shook her head sadly.

'Tybalt had a natural bent for archaeology right from the start,' explained Tabitha. 'This delighted Sir Edward, and naturally Tybalt had so many advantages because of his father.'

Janet Tester was stirring the spoon round and round in her cup. I could sense an uneasy atmosphere.

'And now you're going to marry him,' she said. 'How time flies. It seems only yesterday I was playing peekaboo with him.'

The thought of Tybalt's playing peekaboo was so funny that I couldn't help laughing. 'He's come a long way since then,' I said.

'I hope it's not on the road to ruin,' said Janet Tester, stirring fiercely.

153

I looked at Tabitha who had lifted her shoulders. I decided then that Tybalt's and his father's profession was not a happy subject so I asked about his childhood.

That pleased her. 'He was a good boy. He didn't get into all that much mischief. Miss Ruth doted on him. He was her boy all right. I've got some pictures.'

I revelled in them. Tybalt sitting on a furry rug all but in the nude; Tybalt a wondering two-year-old; Tybalt and Sabina.

'Isn't she a little pet?' doted Nanny Tester.

I agreed. 'Such a little chatterbox. Never stopped.'

I remarked that it was a trait which had remained with her.

'Little minx!' said Nanny Tester fondly.

There was a picture of Tybalt, standing beside a rather pretty woman with lot of fluffy hair who was holding a baby on her lap. 'There they are with their mother. Oh, and here's Tybalt at school.' He was holding a cricket bat. 'He wasn't good at sports,' said Nanny Tester in a disappointed voice. 'It started to be all study. Not like Sabina. They all said she couldn't concentrate. But of course *he* walked off with all the prizes. And then Sir Edward, who'd scarcely noticed the children before, started to prick up his ears.'

She conveyed her feelings by so many gestures – the tone of her voice, a contemptuous flick of the hand, a turning down of the lips, a half closing of the eyes. I had been with her a very short time but I had learned that she disliked Tabitha, and Sir Edward; she had adored Miss Ruth, and while Tybalt, the child, had qualified for her devotion I was not so sure how she regarded the man.

I was interested – greatly so – and I did get

154

the impression that had Tabitha not been with me, I should have understood so much more about Janet Tester.

I sensed Tabitha's relief when we could politely leave; Tabitha went on ahead of me and Janet suddenly caught my hand in hers when we were in the little hall. Her fingers were dry and strong.

'Come again, Miss Osmond,' she said, and whispered: 'Alone.'

As we descended the stairs I said: 'What a strange little woman!'

'So you sensed that.'

'I thought she was not exactly what she seemed. At times she was so gentle – at others quite the reverse.'

'She has a bit of an obsession.'

'I gathered that. Miss Ruth, I suppose.'

'You know what these old nurses are like. They are as mothers to their charges. Far closer to them than their own mothers. She disliked Sir Edward. I suppose she was jealous and because her Miss Ruth had no interest in his work she blamed him for doing it. Very illogical, as you can see. Tybalt's mother wanted him to go into the Church. Of course he was quite unsuited to that profession and from an early age had made up his mind to follow his father. Sir Edward's delight more than made up for Lady Travers's – and Janet's – disappointment. But they bore a grudge against Sir Edward for it. I'm afraid Lady Travers was a rather hysterical woman and I've no doubt she confided a great deal in Janet, who could see no wrong in her. It was a disastrous marriage in many ways – although Lady Travers brought a big fortune with her when she married.'

155

'Money again,' I said. 'It's odd how that subject seems to crop up continually.'

'Well, it's a very useful commodity, you must admit.'

'It seems to have a big part to play in certain marriages.'

'That's the way of the world,' said Tabitha lightly. 'It's good to be out of Janet's rooms. They stifle me.'

Later I thought a good deal about that encounter. I understood Janet's dislike of Sir Edward, but I did wonder why she felt so strongly – and her attitude had betrayed to me that she did – about Tabitha.

The weeks before my wedding were flying past. Dorcas and Alison wanted quite a celebration. They seemed so relieved that they no longer had to preserve the secret of my birth that they were almost like children let out of school. Moreover anxieties for the future had been swept away. The cottage was theirs; I was going to give them an allowance; my future was settled although – in spite of their efforts to hide this – they had misgivings about my bridegroom. Tybalt had little to say to them and their meetings were always uneasy. When I was present I would keep the conversation going but when I went out of the room and returned I would be aware of the awkward pauses when none of them had anything to say. Yet they could chatter away to Oliver naturally about parish affairs and with Evan would talk of the old days and the pranks we used to get up to.

Tybalt was always so relieved when he and I were alone. I was so besottedly in love, always making the affectionate gesture, that his lack of demonstrativeness was not so noticeable as it might have been. Sometimes we would sit close together looking at plans, his arms about me while I nestled close and asked myself whether this was really happening to me; but the conversation was almost always of the work he and his father had been doing.

Once he said: 'It's wonderful to have you with me, Judith.' And then he added: 'You're so absolutely keen. I never knew anyone who was so exuberantly enthusiastic as you.'

'You are,' I said. 'Your father must have been.'

'But in a quieter way.'

'But very intense,' I said.

He kissed me then lightly on the forehead. 'But you express yourself so forcefully,' he said. 'I like it, Judith. In fact I find it wonderful.'

I threw my arms about him and gathered him to me as I used to Dorcas and Alison. I hugged him and cried: 'I'm so happy.'

Then I would tell him about how I had decided to hate him when Sabina had spoken of him in such glowing terms. 'I imagined you stooped and wore spectacles and were pale with lank greasy hair. And then you burst upon us . . . in the mummy room . . . looking fierce and vengeful like some Egyptian god come to wreak vengeance on one who had desecrated the old sarcophagus.'

'Did I really look like that?'

'Exactly — and I adored you from that moment.'

'Well, I must remember to look fierce and vengeful sometimes.'

'And that you should have chosen me . . . is a miracle.'

157

'Oh, Judith, surely you are too modest.'

'Far from it! As you know, I used to dream about you . . . how you suddenly discovered my worth.'

'Which I did in due course.'

'When did you discover it?'

'When I knew that you had come to borrow the books and were so interested. Or perhaps it began when I saw you emerging from those bandages. You looked as though you had suffered a fatal accident rather than embalmment. But it was a good effort.'

I took his hand and kissed it.

'Tybalt,' I said, 'I am going to look after you all the days of your life.'

'That's a comforting thought,' he said.

'I'm going to make myself so important to you that you will hate every moment you spend away from me.'

'I've reached that stage already.'

'Is it true? Is it really true?'

He took my hands in his. 'Understand, Judith, I lack your powers of expression. Words flow from you expressing your innermost thoughts.'

'I know I speak without thinking. I'm sure you never do.'

'Be patient with me.'

'Tell me one thing. Are you happy?'

'Do you think I'm not?'

'Not completely.'

He said slowly: 'I have lost someone who was closer to me, until you came, than anyone else in the world. We worked together; we would be thinking along the same lines together, often without speaking. He is dead, and he died suddenly. He was there one day and the next he was stricken down . . . mysteriously. I mourn him, Judith. I shall go on mourning him for a long time. That is why you must be patient with me. I can't match your exuberance, your pleasure in life. My dear, dear Judith, I believe that when we are married I shall begin to grow away from this tragedy.'

Then I put my head against him and kept my arms tightly about him.

'To make you happy, to give you something to replace what you have lost . . . that shall be my mission in life.'

He kissed my head.

'Thank God for you, Judith,' he said.

There was a little friction between Tybalt and the aunts over the wedding. This, said Alison firmly, could not take place until a 'reasonable' time had elapsed since the deaths of Sir Edward and Sir Ralph.

'Fathers of both bride and groom so recently dead!' said Dorcas. 'You should wait at least a year.'

I had never seen Tybalt express his feelings so forcibly.

'Impossible!' he cried. 'We shall be leaving for Egypt in a matter of months. Judith must come as my wife.'

'I can't imagine what people will say,' Dorcas put in timidly.

'That,' said Tybalt, 'does not concern me in the least.'

Dorcas and Alison were deflated, but afterwards I heard them saying to each other: 'It may not concern him, but it concerns us and we have lived here all our lives and shall do so until the end.'

'Tybalt is unconventional,' I soothed. 'And worrying what people think is really rather unnecessary.'

They did not answer, but they shook their heads over me and my affairs. I was besotted; and they were sure that to let a man see before marriage how much you adored him was wrong. Afterwards, yes. Then it was a wife's duty to think as her husband did, to submit to him in all ways – unless of course he turned out to be a *criminal* – but before the marriage one did not 'make oneself cheap'; it was the custom for a man to go down on his knees before marriage.

I laughed at them indulgently. 'My marriage, as you should know, is going to be like no marriage that ever was. You can't expect me to do what is expected of me.'

When they were with me they grew excited sometimes, for after all a wedding in the family was an event. They produced all manner of objects for my bottom drawer; and they talked about the reception and worried because Rainbow Cottage was too small for it and the bride's house was the necesssary place for it.

I could laugh at them mockingly but I sensed their uneasiness. They did not wish me to wait a year so much for convention but because they thought it would give me time to see clearly as they called it. The fact was that they had chosen Oliver for my husband; Evan was second choice; but Tybalt did not appeal to them at all.

Dorcas caught a cold – something she invariably did when she was anxious; and her colds had to be nursed because they turned to bronchitis.

*

160

Tybalt came hurrying over to Rainbow Cottage. His eyes were glowing with excitement as he took my hands in his. For a moment I thought it was pleasure in seeing me. Then I discovered another reason.

'A most exciting thing has happened, Judith. It's not very far from here. Dorset, in fact. A workman digging a trench has unearthed some Roman tiles. It's quite a find. It seems very likely that this is going to lead to a great discovery. I've had an invitation to go along and give an opinion. I am leaving tomorrow. I want you to come with me.'

'That's wonderful,' I cried. 'Tell me all about it.'

'I know very little yet. But these discoveries are so exciting. One can never be sure what we're going to turn up.'

We walked about the Rainbow garden talking about it. He did not stay long though for he had to go back to Giza House to make some preparations, and I went into Rainbow Cottage to tell the aunts that I was leaving next day.

I was astonished at the opposition.

'My dear Judith!' cried Alison. 'What are you thinking of? How can you – an unmarried woman – go off with a man?'

'The man I am going to marry.'

'But you are not married yet,' croaked Dorcas in a way which implied that she hoped I never would be to Tybalt.

'It wouldn't be right,' said Alison firmly.

'Dear aunts,' I said, 'in Tybalt's words these little conventions don't count.'

'We are older than you, Judith. Why, many a girl has anticipated her marriage to her own bitter

161

cost. She trusts her fiancé, goes away with him and discovers that there are no wedding bells.'

I flared up. 'At one moment you are suggesting Tybalt is marrying me for my money and at the next that he plans to seduce me and then discard me. Really, you are being so absurd.'

'Why, we suggested no such thing,' said Alison firmly. 'And if those sort of things are in your mind, well, Judith, you really ought to stop and consider. No bride should feel her bridegroom capable of such a thing.'

How could I argue with them? I went to my room and started to pack for the next day's trip.

That evening when I was in my room Alison tapped at the door. Her face was strained. 'I'm worried about Dorcas. I do think we should have Dr Gunwen at once.'

I said I would go and fetch him, which I did.

When he came he said that Dorcas had bronchitis and Alison and I were up all night with the bronchitis kettle in Dorcas's room.

I knew the next day that I could not go to Dorset and leave Alison to nurse Dorcas alone, so I told Alison that I was going over to Giza House to explain matters to Tybalt.

Before I could speak, he began to tell me that the finds were even better than had at first been thought. I interrupted him: 'I'm not coming, Tybalt.'

His expression changed. He stared at me incredulously.

'Not coming!'

'My Aunt Dorcas is ill. I can't leave Alison to nurse her. I must stay. She has these turns and it is rather frightening when she does. She is really very ill.'

'We could arrange something. One of the servants could go over to take your place.'

'Aunt Alison wouldn't have that. It wouldn't be the same. I must be there in case . . .'

He was silent.

'Please understand, Tybalt. I want to come . . . to be with you more than anything, but I just can't leave Rainbow Cottage now.'

'Of course,' he agreed, but he was very disappointed. I trusted not in me.

Tabitha came out into the front garden where we were standing.

'I've come to explain that I can't go,' I said. 'My aunt is ill. I must stay here to help.'

'But of course you must,' said Tabitha.

'Would you come in Judith's place?' asked Tybalt. 'I'm sure you'd find it of paramount interest.'

Paramount interest. Was that a reproach? Did he feel that I should have found it of *paramount* interest.

Tabitha was saying: 'Well, since Judith must stay, I will go in her place. You cannot leave your aunts now, Judith.'

Tybalt pressed my arm. 'I was so looking forward to showing you this marvellous discovery. But there'll be plenty of time . . . later.'

'The whole of our lives,' I said.

In a few days, much to our relief, Dorcas began to recover.

She was touched that I had stayed behind to help nurse her and comfort Alison.

I heard her say to Alison when she thought I couldn't hear: 'However impulsive Judith is, her *heart's* in the right place.'

I knew they talked a good deal about me and my coming marriage. I did so want to reassure them; but they had taken it into their heads that Tybalt had asked me to marry him because he had pre-knowledge of my inheritance.

I was greatly looking forward to the day when I would leave Rainbow Cottage naturally because I longed to be Tybalt's wife and in addition I wanted to escape this atmosphere of distrust and to prove to them that Tybalt was the most wonderful husband in the world.

Tybalt and Tabitha were away for two weeks and when they returned they were so full of what they had seen that they talked of little else. I was filled with chagrin because I could not join in their conversation as I would have wished. Tybalt was amused. 'Never mind,' he said, 'when we're married you'll go everywhere with me.'

The wedding day was almost at hand. Sabina had said that we might have a discreet reception at the rectory. After all, Dorcas had been ill and Rainbow Cottage was small and the rectory had been my home and she was Tybalt's sister. 'I insist on it,' she cried. 'I can tell you, Judith, you are the most fortunate woman in the world . . . with one exception because even Tybalt could not be as wonderful as Oliver. Tybalt is *too* perfect . . . I mean he knows everything . . . all about those ancient things, whereas darling Oliver knows about Greek and Latin. Not that Tybalt doesn't too . . . but you couldn't imagine Tybalt's preaching a

164

sermon or listening to the farmers telling him about the droughts and the mothers about their babies . . .'

'What *are* you talking about, Sabina? We're supposed to be discussing my wedding.'

'Of course. It's to be here. I insist. Darling Oliver insists. You'll be married in *his* church and we'll have just a few friends as my father . . . and yours . . . what a surprise and fancy your being Sir Ralph's daughter all that time and our not knowing. I'm not really surprised, though . . . Do you remember the ball? What was I saying? Oh, you're to have your reception in the old rectory.'

It did seem a good idea; and even Dorcas and Alison accepted it, though they insisted that in view of the recent deaths it must just be a quiet family affair.

When I discussed the matter with Tybalt he was rather vague. I could see that it was immaterial to him where we had a reception or whether there was none.

He wanted us to be married, he said. Where and how was unimportant.

He had a surprise for me.

'We'll have a honeymoon. You won't want to go straight back to Giza House.'

'That,' I said, 'is immaterial to *me*. All I ask is that I am with you.'

He turned to face me and with an unusually tender gesture took my face in his hands. 'Judith,' he said, 'don't expect too much of me.'

I laughed aloud — I was so happy. 'Why I expect *everything* of you.'

'That's what makes me uneasy. You see, I am rather selfish, not admirable in the least. And I am a man with an obsession.'

165

'I share in that obsession,' I told him with a laugh. 'And I have another. You.'

He held me against him. 'You make me afraid,' he said.

'You afraid? You are not afraid of anything . . . or anyone.'

'I'm certainly afraid of this high opinion you have of me. Where could you possibly have got it?'

'You gave it to me.'

'You are too imaginative, Judith. You get an idea and it's usually something you want it to be and then you make everything fit into that.'

'It's the way to live. I shall teach you to live that way.'

'It's better to see the truth.'

'I will make this my truth.'

'I can see it is useless to warn you not to think too highly of me.'

'It is quite useless.'

'Time will have to teach you.'

'I said we will grow closer together as the years pass. We shall share everything. I never thought it was possible to be so happy as I am at this moment.'

'At least you will have had this moment.'

'What a way to talk! This is nothing of what it is going to be like.'

'My darling Judith, there is no one like you.'

'Of course there isn't! I am myself. Reckless, impulsive, the aunts would tell you. Bossy, Sabina and Theodosia will agree and Hadrian will confirm that. They are the ones who have known me the longest. So *you* must not have too high an opinion of *me*.'

'I'm glad there are these little faults. I shall love

you for them as I hope you will love me for mine.'

I said: 'We are going to be so happy.'

'I came to tell you about our honeymoon. I'm going to take you to Dorset. They are so excited about this discovery. I long to show it to you.'

I said that was wonderful; but it did occur to me that there would no doubt be a great many people there and a honeymoon on our own might have been more appropriate.

But Tybalt would be there – and that was all I asked.

There was so much to do in preparation even for a 'discreet' wedding, including sessions in Sarah Sloper's cottage which seemed to go on for hours. There was I in my white satin wedding gown with Sarah kneeling at my feet, her mouth full of pins, and as soon as she had it free she would talk all the time.

'Well, fancy it coming to this. You, Miss Judith . . . and *him*. He was for Miss Theodosia, you know, and she gets the little professor and you get *him*.'

'You make it sound as though it's some sort of lottery, Sarah.'

'They do say marriage be a lottery, Miss Judith. And you being Sir Ralph's girl and all. I always guessed that. Why, he had a real fancy for you. And Miss Lavinia. Pretty as a picture she were but I'd say you took more after Sir Ralph.'

'Thank you, Sarah.'

'Oh, I weren't meaning it *that* way, Miss Judith. You'll look pretty enough in your bride's dress. Brides always do. That's why there's nothing I like making better. And is it to be orange blossom? I reckon there's nothing like orange blossom for brides. I had it myself

167

when I married Sloper. That's going back a bit. And I've still got it. Put away in a drawer it be. I look at it now and then and think of the old days. You'll be able to do that, Miss Judith. It's a pleasant thing to do when things don't turn out just as you'd fancied. And don't we all have fancies, eh, on our wedding days?'

'I look on it as a beginning of happiness, not a climax.'

'Oh, you and your talk. Always was one for it. But as I say it's nice to have a wedding day to look back on – as long as it don't make you fretful.' She sighed and went on fervently: 'I hope you'll be happy, Miss Judith. Well, we can but hope. So let's pray the sun'll shine on your wedding day. They do say "Happy the bride the sun shines on." '

I laughed; but this assumption that marriage for me would be a perilous adventure was beginning to irritate me.

On a rather misty October day I was married to Tybalt in the church I knew so well. Oddly enough as I came down the aisle on the arm of Dr Gunwen who had offered to 'give me away', there being no one else to perform this necessary duty, I was thinking of how my knees used to get sore from kneeling on the mats which hung inside the pews for that purpose. An extraordinary thought to have when I was on my way to marriage with Tybalt!

A fellow archaeologist and friend of Tybalt's was his best man. He was named Terence Gelding and was accompanying us to Egypt. On the night before the wedding I had not seen Tybalt. He had gone to the station to meet his friend and bring him back to Giza House where he was spending a few days. Tabitha told me on my wedding morning that they had all stayed up too late talking. I felt that vague tinge of jealousy which I had begun to notice came to me when others shared an intimacy with Tybalt and I was not present. It was foolish of me but I supposed I had dreamed so long of this happening that I could not entirely believe that it was true; there had been covert remarks about my marriage from several directions and it seemed that these insinuations had penetrated even my natural optimism. I could not help feeling a twinge of uneasiness and distrust of this sudden granting by fate of my most cherished desire.

But as I made my vows before Oliver, and Tybalt put the ring on my finger, a wonderful happiness surged over me and I was more completely happy than I had ever been.

It was disappointing that as we came into the porch the rain should begin to pelt down.

'You can't walk out in that,' said Dorcas at my elbow.

'It's nothing,' I said. 'Just a shower and we only have to go over to the rectory.'

'We'll have to wait.'

She was right, of course. So we stood there, I still holding Tybalt's hand, saying nothing, staring out at the rain and thinking: I'm really married . . . to Tybalt!

I heard the whispers behind me.

'What a pity!'

'What bad luck!'

'Not wedding weather by any means.'

A gnome-like creature came walking up from the graveyard. As it approached I saw that it was Mr

Pegger, bent double, with a sack split down one side over his head to keep him dry. He carried a spade to which the brown earth still clung. So he had been digging somebody's grave, and was, I supposed, coming to the porch for shelter until the downpour was over.

When he saw us he pulled up short; he pushed the sack farther back and his fanatical eyes took in Tybalt and me in our wedding clothes.

He looked straight at me. 'No good'ull come of such indecent haste,' he said. 'It's ungodly.'

Then he nodded and walked past the porch with the self-righteous air of one determined to do his duty however unpleasant.

'Who on earth is that old fool?' said Tybalt.

'It's Mr Pegger, the grave-digger.'

'He's impertinent.'

'Well, you see he knew me as a child and no doubt thinks I'm still one.'

'He objects to our marriage.'

I heard Theodosia whisper: 'Oh, Evan, how unpleasant. It's like an . . . *omen*.'

I did not answer. I felt suddenly angry with all these people who for some ridiculous reason had decided that there was something strange about my marriage to Tybalt.

I looked up at the lowering sky and I seemed to hear Sarah Sloper's reedy voice: 'Happy be the bride the sun shines on.'

After a few minutes the rain stopped and we were able to pick our way across the grass to the vicarage.

There was the familiar drawing-room decked out

with chrysanthemums of all shades and starry Michael-
mas daisies. A table had been set up at one end of the
room and on this was a wedding cake and champagne.

I cut the cake with Tybalt's help; everyone applauded and the unpleasant incident in the porch
was temporarily forgotten.

Hadrian made a witty speech and Tybalt responded
very briefly. I kept saying to myself: 'This is the
supreme moment of my life.' Perhaps I said it a little
too vehemently. I could not forget Mr Pegger's eyes
peering at us in that fanatical way from under that
absurd sack. The rain had started again in a heavy
downpour which made itself heard.

Theodosia was beside me. 'Oh, Judith,' she said,
'I'm so glad we're sisters. Isn't life odd? Here you
are marrying Tybalt and this is what they wanted for
me. So Father got his wish that his daughter marry
Tybalt. Hasn't it turned out wonderfully?' She was
gazing across the room at Evan who was talking to
Tabitha. 'I'm so grateful to you . . .'

'Grateful . . .?'

She floundered a little. Theodosia had never been
able to express her thoughts gracefully and often
landed in a conversational morass from which she
found it difficult to extricate herself.

'Well, for marrying Tybalt and making it all come
right so that I need not have any conscience about not
pleasing Father . . . and all that.'

She made it sound as though by marrying Tybalt
I had conferred some blessing on all those who had
been saved from him!

'I'm sure you'll be *very* happy,' she said comfort-
ingly. 'You always knew so much about archaeology.

171

It's a struggle for me to keep up with Evan, but he says don't worry. He's perfectly satisfied with me as I am.'

'You're very happy, Theodosia?'

'Oh . . . blissfully. That's why I'm so . . .' She stopped.

'Grateful to me for marrying Tybalt and making it all work out smoothly. I can assure you I didn't marry him for that reason.'

Sabina joined us.

'Isn't this *fun*? The three of us together. And now we're all married. Judith, do you like the flowers? Miss Crewe arranged them. Most of them came from her garden. Green fingers, you know. And she always makes such a success of the decorations in the church. And here we all are together. Do you remember how we used to talk in the schoolroom? Of course dramatic things *would* happen to Judith. They always did, didn't they? Or perhaps you made it sound dramatic and then you did turn out to be Sir Ralph's daughter . . . Wrong side of the blanket of course . . . but that makes it more exciting. And now you've got Tybalt. Doesn't he look wonderful? Like a Roman god or something . . . He was always different from everybody else . . . and so are you, Judith . . . in a way. But we're sisters now, Judith. And you're Theodosia's sister . . . As I say, it is wonderful!' She gazed at Tybalt with that adoration I had seen so many times before.

'Fancy Tybalt's being a bridegroom! We always thought he would never marry! "He's married to all that *nonsense*," Nanny Tester says. "Like your father ought to have been." I used to point out to her that if Papa had married all that nonsense I wouldn't have been here, nor would Tybalt because archaeology, wonderful as Papa and Tybalt seem to find it, does not produce *people* . . . living ones anyway. Only mummies perhaps. Oh, do you remember the day when you dressed up as a mummy? What a day that was! We thought you'd killed Theodosia.'

They were all laughing. I knew that Sabina would restore my spirits.

'And you said Tybalt stooped and wore spectacles and when you saw him you were struck dumb. You *adored* him from that moment. Oh yes you did, you can't deny it.'

'I'm making no attempt to,' I said.

'And now you're married to him. Your dreams have come true. Isn't that a wonderful *fairytale* ending?'

'It's not an ending,' said Theodosia soberly. 'It's really a beginning. Evan is so pleased because he's been invited to join the expedition.'

'Has he really?' cried Sabina. 'That's a great honour. When he's away you must come and stay.'

'I'm going with him,' declared Theodosia fiercely. 'You don't think I'd let Evan go without me.'

'Has Tybalt said you may? Papa never liked wives around. He said they cluttered and distracted . . . unless they were workers themselves and quite a lot are . . . but you're not, Theodosia. So Tybalt has said you may! I dare say that as he's now a married man himself he has sympathy for others. You'll be company for Judith. Tabitha's going. Of course she's very knowledgeable. There she is talking to Tybalt now. I'll bet you anything you like they're talking about Egypt. Tabitha's beautiful, don't you think? She always seems to wear the right things. Elegance, I suppose. Different from me. That silver grey now ... It's just *right!* Sometimes I think she's the most beautiful woman I've ever seen. You'll have to be careful, Judith,' she added playfully. 'I was surprised that you allowed Tybalt to go off with her to Dorset ... Oh, I know you had to stay behind ... but she's young really. About a year ... possibly two years older than Tybalt, that's all. Of course she is always so quiet ... so restrained ... but it's the quiet ones you have to be wary of, so they say. Oh, Judith, what a way to talk to a bride on her wedding day. You're quite disturbed, I believe. As if I meant it. I was only joking. Tybalt will be the most *faithful* husband in the world! He's too busy anyway to be anything else. The wonder is that he married at all. I'm sure you're going to be wonderfully happy. I think it's a perfect marriage. Your being interested in his world and all that and quite rich so there won't be money problems and Sir Ralph leaving all that money to archaeological research. Wasn't that wonderful! Which sounds horrible in a way as though we're glad he's dead. I'm not. I always rather liked him. What I mean is that it's all worked out so wonderfully well and I *know* you're going to be gloriously happy. You've married the most wonderful man in the world, with one exception of course. But even darling Oliver isn't grand and distinguished like Tybalt ... although he's more *comfortable* and I adore him and wouldn't change him for anyone in the world ...'

'Oh, doesn't she run on,' I said to Theodosia. 'No one else gets a chance.'

'It's revenge for your domineering attitude in the schoolroom and you're only so silent because it's your wedding day and you're not used to the wonder of it.

If you weren't thinking of Tybalt and everything, you would never have allowed me to have the floor for so long.'

'Trust you to make the most of your opportunities. Look, here's Hadrian.'

'Hello,' said Hadrian. 'A family gathering. I must join it.'

'We were talking about the expedition,' said Sabina. 'Among other things.'

'Who isn't?'

'Did you know Evan and Theodosia are coming?' I asked.

'I had heard there was a possibility. It will be like the old days. We shall all be together . . . all except you, Sabina, and your Oliver.'

'Oliver has the church and parish . . . besides, he's a parson, not an archaeologist.'

'So you're going too, Hadrian.'

'It's a great concession. Give me a chance to escape my creditors.'

'You are always talking about money.'

'I've told you before I'm not rich enough to ignore it.'

'Nonsense,' I said.

'And now, Judith, *you've* joined the band of pluto-crats. Well, it will be good experience for us, Tybalt tells me. We'll have to keep together in case this irate god rises from his lair to strike us.'

'Do gods have lairs?' asked Sabina. 'I thought that was foxes. There's a big red one raiding Brent's Farm. Farmer Brent lies in wait with a shotgun.'

'Stop her, someone,' said Hadrian, 'before she flies off at a tangent.'

'Yes,' I said, 'we don't want to hear about foxes.

175

The expedition is of much greater interest. I'm so looking forward to it. It'll soon be time to leave for Egypt.'

'Which is the reason for the hasty wedding,' said Hadrian. 'What did you think of the weird character in the porch?'

'It was only old Pegger.'

'Talk about a prophet of doom. He couldn't have appeared at a less appropriate moment . . . or from his point of view, I suppose, a more appropriate one. He seemed so delighted to be the harbinger of misfortune.'

'I wish everyone would stop hinting at misfortune,' I complained. 'It's most unsuitable.'

'Of course it is,' agreed Hadrian, 'and here comes your reverend husband, Sabina. He'll probably say a blessing and exorcize the evil spirits conjured up by that old ghoul in the porch.'

'He'll do no such thing,' said Sabina, slipping her arm through Oliver's as he came up.

'Just in time,' said Hadrian, 'to prevent this inconsequential wife of yours from giving a dissertation on the duties of a parish priest and where that might lead to Heaven – and Sabina – only knows. I'm going to take the bride away for a cosy tête-à-tête.'

We stood alone in a corner and he looked at me shaking his head. 'Well, well, Judith, this is so sudden.'

'Not you too,' I protested.

'Oh, I don't mean it as old Pegger did. I mean coming into a fortune and marrying at the batting of an eyelid or the twinkling of an eye – to keep the metaphors facial.'

176

I laughed at him. Hadrian always restored my spirits.

'Had I known that you had inherited a fortune I would have married you myself.'

'What a lost opportunity!' I mocked.

'My life is full of them. Seriously, who would have thought that the old man would have left you half his fortune. My pittance was a bit of a blow.'

'Why, Hadrian, it's a pleasant income, and is in addition to what you will earn in your profession.'

'Affluence!' he murmured. 'Seriously, Judith, Tybalt's a lucky devil. *You* and all that money. And there's what my uncle left to the Cause.'

'How I wish I could stop people talking about money for a few moments.'

'It's money that makes the world go round . . . or is that love? And lucky Judith to have both!'

'I can see my aunts making frantic signs.'

'I suppose it's time for you to depart.'

'Why, yes, the carriage will be taking us to the station in less than an hour. And I have to change.'

Dorcas came hurrying up. 'Judith, do you realize what the time is?'

'I was just mentioning it to Hadrian.'

'I think it is time you changed.'

I slipped away with Dorcas and Alison and we went to the room which Sabina had set aside for me. There hung my silver grey grosgrain coat and the skirt of the same material and the white blouse with many frills and the little grey velvet bow at the neck.

Silver grey. So elegant. Yes, when worn by a woman like Tabitha.

'You look lovely,' cooed Dorcas.

177

'That's because you see me through the eyes of love,' I said.

'There'll be someone else who will be looking at you in the same way,' said Alison quickly. There was an almost imperceptible pause before she added: 'We hope.'

I went out to the porch. The carriage was there and Tybalt was waiting for me.

Everyone crowded round; the horse was whipped up. Tybalt and I had started on our honeymoon.

What shall I say of my honeymoon? That it fell short of my expectations? At first it was wonderful and the wonder lasted for two nights and a day. Then Tybalt was all mine. We were very close during that time. We had broken our journey to Dorset and spent the night, and the following day and the next night at a little inn in the heart of the Moor.

'Before we join the dig,' he told me, 'I thought we should have this little respite.'

'It's a wonderful idea,' I told him.

'I thought you were so eager to see this mosaic pavement they've discovered?'

'I'm more eager to be alone with you.'

My frank admission of my devotion amused him and at the same time I fancied made him rather uneasy. Again he stressed that he lacked my powers of expression.

'You must not think, Judith,' he said, 'that because I do not constantly profess my love for you that it isn't there. I find it difficult to speak easily of what I feel most deeply.'

That satisfied me.

I shall never forget the inn in the little moorland village. The sign creaking just outside our window – a gabled one, for the inn was three hundred years old; the sound of the waterfall less than half a mile away sending its sparkling water over the craggy boulders and the big feather bed in which we lay together.

There was a fire burning in the grate and as I watched the flickering shadows on the wall-paper – great red roses – and Tybalt's arms were about me, I was completely happy.

Breakfast was served to us in the old inn parlour with the brass and pewter on the shelves and hams hanging from the rafters. Hot coffee, bread fresh from the oven, ham and eggs from the nearby farm, scones and home-made strawberry jam with a basin of Devonshire cream the colour of buttercups. And Tybalt sitting opposite me, watching me with that look almost of wonder in his eyes. If ever I was beautiful in my life I was beautiful on that morning.

After breakfast we went out on to the moors and walked for miles over the short springy turf. The innkeeper's wife had packed a little hamper for us and we picnicked by a tiny trickling stream. We saw the wild moorland ponies, too scared to come near us; and the only human beings we encountered on that day were a man driving a cartload of apples and pears who raised his whip to us and called a greeting, and another on horseback who did the same. A happy idyllic day and then back to the delicious duckling and green peas and afterwards the cosy bedroom and the flickering fire.

The next day we caught the train to Dorset.

Of course I was fascinated by the Roman site,

but I wanted only one thing in my life at that time and that was to love and be loved by Tybalt. The hotel at which we stayed was full of people who were with the working party, which made it rather different from our Dartmoor haven. I was proud of the respect with which Tybalt was greeted and, although it was brought home to me that I was an amateur among professionals and I was constantly bewildered by technicalities, I was as eager as ever to learn – a fact which delighted my husband.

The day after we reached our hotel, Terence Gelding, Tybalt's best man, arrived. He was tall and rather lean with the same serious and dedicated expression I had noticed among so many of Tybalt's associates. Rather aloof, he seemed a little nervous of me, and I imagined he was not altogether pleased about Tybalt's marriage. When I mentioned this to Tybalt he laughed at me.

'You have such odd fancies, Judith,' he said; and I remembered how often Alison and Dorcas had said the same of me. 'Terence Gelding is a first-class worker, trustworthy too, reliable. Just the kind of man I like to work with me.'

He and Terence Gelding would talk animatedly for long periods, and try as I might to follow their conversation it was not always easy.

When there was a possibility that an amphitheatre might have existed close to the site the excitement was great and a party went out to examine certain finds which might have proved an indication that this was correct. I was not invited to go.

Tybalt was apologetic.

'You see, Judith,' he explained, 'this is a professional affair. If I took you, others would expect to
take people.'

I understood and I determined that in a very short
time I should have learned so much that I would be
considered worthy to join in on such occasions.

Tybalt kissed me tenderly before leaving. 'I'll be
back in a few hours. What will you do while I'm
away?'

'Read a book I've seen here dealing with Roman
remains. Very soon I'm going to be as knowledgeable
as you are.'

That made him laugh.

I spent the day alone. I would have to be prepared for
this sort of occasion, I reminded myself. But, interested
as I was in this absorbing subject, I was a bride on her
honeymoon, and an early Roman floor, even if it was
a geometric mosaic, could not really compare with the
springs and boulders of Dartmoor.

After that he was often at the site with the workers.
Sometimes I went with him. I talked to the more humble members of the party; I studied maps; I even did a
little digging as I had in Carter's Meadow. I watched
first-aid methods in restoration of a plaque on which
was engraved the head of a Caesar. I was fascinated
– but I longed to be alone with Tybalt.

We were two weeks on the Roman site. I believe
Tybalt was reluctant to leave. On our last evening he
spent several hours closeted with the Director of the
expedition. I was in bed when he came in. It was just
after midnight.

He sat on the bed, his eyes shining.

'It's almost certain that there's an amphitheatre,'

he said. 'What a discovery! I think this is going to be one of the most exciting sites in England. Professor Brownlea can't stop talking of his luck. Do you know they've found a plaque with a head engraved? If they can discover whose, it will be a great find.'

'I know,' I said. 'I've seen it being pieced together.'

'Unfortunately there is quite a bit missing. But of course the floor mosaics are most exciting. I would place the date of the black and white at round about 74 AD.'

'I'm sure you'd be right, Tybalt.'

'Oh, but one can't be sure ... not unless there is absolute proof. Why are you smiling?'

'Was I?' I held out my arms to him. 'Perhaps because I was thinking that there are exciting things in life other than Roman remains.'

He came to me at once and for a few moments we embraced. I was laughing softly. 'I know what you're thinking. Yes, there are more exciting things. But I imagine the tombs of the Pharaohs win by a head.'

'Oh, Judith,' he said, 'this is wonderful to be together. I want to have you there with me when we leave.'

'Of course. It was for that reason you married me.'

'That and others,' he said.

'Well, we have discussed that ... now let us consider the others.'

I amused him. My frank enjoyment of our love was something which I am sure would have completely shocked Dorcas and Alison. But then so many people would have considered me bold and brazen.

I wondered if Tybalt did. I asked him. 'You see,'

I explained, 'it has always been almost impossible for me to pretend.'

He said: 'I don't deserve you, Judith.'

I laughed, completely happy. 'You can always try to be worthy,' I suggested.

And I was happy. So was he. As happy as he was on his mosaic pavement or with his broken plaque or ruins of his amphitheatre? Was he? I wondered.

It was foolish of me to have these niggling doubts. I wished that I could forget the Cassandra-like faces of Dorcas and Alison, the hints and innuendoes, the fanatical eyes of old Pegger in the porch. I wished that Sir Ralph had not left me a fortune; then I could indeed have been sure that I had been married for myself.

But these matters could be forgotten ... temporarily. And I promised myself that in time I would banish them altogether.

Then we returned to Giza House.

It was the first week of November when we arrived in the late afternoon, and a dark and gloomy one. The October gales had stripped the trees of most of their leaves; but as the carriage brought us from the station, the countryside seemed unusually silent for the wind had then dropped. It was typical Cornish November weather — warm and damp. As we pulled up at the wrought-iron gates of Giza and descended from the carriage, Tabitha came out to greet us.

'Not a very pleasant day,' she said. 'You must be chilled. Come in quickly and we'll have tea at once.'

She was looking at us searchingly, as though she suspected the honeymoon had not been a success. Why did I get the impression that everyone seemed to have come to the conclusion that Tybalt and I were unsuited?

Imagination! I told myself. I looked up at the house. Haunted! I thought; and remembered teasing Theodosia and frightening her by making her run up the path. I thought of Nanny Tester probably peering out from a top window.

'Giza House always intrigued me,' I said as I stepped into the hall.

'It's your home now,' Tabitha reminded me.

'When we get back from Egypt Judith may want to make some changes in the house,' said Tybalt, slipping his arm through mine. He smiled at me. 'For the time being we must concentrate on our plans.'

Tabitha showed us our room. It was on the first floor next to that room in which I had seen the sarcophagus. Tabitha had had it redecorated while we were away.

'You're very good,' said Tybalt.

In the shadows I saw Mustapha and Absalam. I noticed their dark eyes fixed intently on me. They would be remembering me of course as the rowdy child and afterwards the 'companion' from Keverall Court who came to borrow books. Now I was the new mistress. Or did Tabitha retain that title?

How I wished people had not sown these misgivings in my mind with their sly allusions.

I was left in our room to freshen up while Tabitha returned to the drawing-room with Tybalt. One of the maids brought hot water and when I had washed I went to the window and looked out. The garden had always been chock-a-block with shrubs and the trees made it dark. I could see the spiders' webs on the

184

bushes, glistening where the light caught the globules of moisture as so often I had seen them before at this time of year. The curtains were deep blue edged with gold braid in a Greek key pattern. The bed was large, a four-poster canopied and curtained. The carpet was thick. I remembered Tabitha's saying that Sir Edward disliked noise so intensely when he was working that it was necessary to preserve a hushed atmosphere throughout the house. Bookshelves lined one side of the room. I looked at these. Some of them I had borrowed and read. They all referred to one subject. It occurred to me that this had been Sir Edward's bedroom before he had left for the fatal journey, and it seemed then that the past was enveloping me. I wished that a different room had been chosen for us. Then I remembered that I was the mistress of the house and if I did not like a room I could say so.

I changed my travelling clothes and went down to the drawing-room. Tybalt and Tabitha were sitting side by side on the sofa examining some plans.

As soon as I entered Tabitha jumped up. 'Tea will arrive immediately,' she said. 'I dare say you are ready for it. Travelling is so tiring.'

Ellen wheeled the tea-wagon in and stood by while Tabitha poured.

Tabitha wanted to know how we had enjoyed the honeymoon and then Tybalt began a long explanation of the Roman site.

'You must have had a very interesting time, Tybalt,' said Tabitha, smiling. 'I trust Judith found it equally so.'

She looked at me slightly apprehensively and I

assured her that I had enjoyed our stay in Dorset very much.

'And now,' said Tybalt 'we must begin to work out our plans in earnest. It's astonishing how the time flies when there is so much to do. I want to leave in February.'

So we talked of the trip and it was pleasant sitting there in the firelight while the dark afternoon faded into twilight. I could not help thinking of those occasions when I had dreamed of sharing Tybalt's life.

I'm happy, I assured myself. I've achieved my dream.

My first night in Giza House! One of the maids had lighted a fire in the bedroom and the flickering flames threw their shadows over the walls. How different from those of the Dartmoor cottage; these seemed like sinister shapes which would assume life at any moment. How silent the house was! There was a door behind a blue velvet curtain. I opened this and saw that it led into the room where the sarcophagus had been.

I had gone up in advance of Tybalt; and the room in firelight with only two candles burning in their tall candlesticks on the dressing-table seemed alive with shadows.

I started to wonder about Sir Edward, and his wife who had never lived in this house, for she had died before they came here. And in the attic apartments of this house was Nanny Tester, who would be aware that Tybalt and I had returned from our honeymoon. I wondered what she was doing now and why Tybalt was so long. Was he talking to Tabitha, telling her things which he did not want me to know? What an idea! I must not be jealous of the time he spent with Tabitha. She was a very dear friend; she was almost a mother to him. A mother! She could not have been much more than two years older than he.

It's the house, I said to myself. There's something about this house. Something ... evil. I felt it right from the first before they came here when I used to frighten Theodosia.

Tybalt came into the room, and the sinister shadows receded; the firelight was comforting; the candlelight, I remembered, was becoming.

'What,' he asked, 'are you doing in that room?'

'I found this door. It's the room where the sarcophagus was.'

He laughed. 'You weren't thinking of dressing up as a mummy, were you ... to frighten me?'

'You ... frightened of a mummy! I know you love them dearly.'

'Not,' he replied, 'as dearly as I love you.'

On the rare occasions when Tybalt said things like that, my happiness was complete.

'Do you like the room I had prepared for you?' asked Tabitha next morning. Tybalt had gone to his study; he had a great deal of correspondence to deal with concerning the expedition.

'It's a bit ghostly,' I said.

Tabitha laughed. 'My dear Judith, what do you mean?'

'I always thought there was something rather haunted about Giza House.'

'It's all those trees and shrubs in the garden, I dare

say. That room is the best in the house. That's why I had it made ready for you. It used to be Sir Edward's.'

'I guessed it. And the room which leads from it is where the sarcophagus used to be.'

'He always used that room for whatever he was working on. He often worked late at night when the fancy took him. Would you like to change the room?'

'No, I don't think so.'

'Judith, anything you want you must do, you know. You're mistress of the house now.'

'I can't get used to being the mistress of anything.'

'You will in time. You're happy, aren't you?'

'I have what I've always wanted.'

'Not many of us can say that,' she replied with a sigh. 'And you, Tabitha?'

I wished that she would confide in me. I was sure there were secrets in her life. She was youngish — a widow, I supposed. Life was by no means over for her and yet there was about her a resignation, a subtle secrecy which was perhaps one of the reasons why she was so attractive.

She said: 'I have had my moments. Perhaps one should not ask for more than that.'

Yes, there was something decidedly mysterious about Tabitha.

Christmas was not far off. Sabina said we must celebrate Christmas Day at the rectory, and she would insist on my aunts joining us.

I fancied Dorcas and Alison were a little reproachful. They were so conventional. I think they believed I should have gone to them at Rainbow Cottage or they came to me at Giza House.

I swept all that away by pointing out the convenience of Sabina's suggestion and what fun it would be to be back in the old drawing-room where so many of our Christmases had been celebrated.

The days were passing swiftly. There was Christmas to think of and always of course the expedition. Tabitha and I decorated the house with holly and mistletoe.

'It was something we never did before,' said Tabitha.

The maids were delighted. Ellen told me that it was more like a house since I'd come home. That was a compliment indeed.

They liked me, those maids; they seemed to take a pleasure in addressing me as 'my lady'; it invariably startled me, and sometimes I had to assure myself: Yes, it's true. You're not dreaming this time. This is the greatest dream of all come true.

It was at the beginning of December when the first uneasy situation occurred.

I had never quite understood Mustapha and Absalam. In fact they made me uneasy. I would be in a room and suddenly find them standing close behind me – for they seemed to move about together – having been completely unaware of their approach. I often looked up suddenly to find their dark eyes fixed upon me. Sometimes I would think they were about to speak to me; but then they seemed to change their minds. I was never quite sure which one was which and I believe I often addressed them wrongly. Tabitha could easily tell the difference but then she had known them for a very long time.

I began to think that it was very likely the presence of these two – and Nanny Tester at the top of the house – which had made me feel the house was so sinister.

It was afternoon – that hour when dusk was beginning to fall. I had gone up to our bedroom and on my way saw that the door which led from the corridor into that room which I called the sarcophagus room was ajar. I thought perhaps Tybalt was there, so I looked in. Mustapha, or was it Absalam, was standing silhouetted against the window.

I went in and as I did so, the other Egyptian was standing behind me . . . between me and the door.

I felt the goose-pimples rise on my skin. I was unsure why.

I said: 'Mustapha . . . Absalam, is anything wrong?'

There was a brief silence. The one by the window nodded to the other and said: 'Absalam, you say.'

I turned and faced Absalam.

'My lady,' he said, 'we are your most humble slaves.'

'You mustn't say that, Absalam. We don't have slaves here.'

They bowed their heads.

Mustapha spoke then. 'We serve you well, my lady.'

'But of course,' I replied lightly.

I saw that the door was shut. I looked at that which led into our bedroom. It was half closed. But I knew Tybalt would not be there at this hour of the day.

'We have tried to tell you many times.'

'Please tell me now then,' I said.

'It must not be,' said Mustapha shaking his head gravely.

Absalam began to shake his.

'What?' I asked.

190

'Stay here, my lady. You tell Sir Tybalt. You tell. He must not go.'

I began to grasp their meaning. They were afraid to go back to Egypt, the scene of the tragedy which had overtaken their master.

'I'm afraid that's impossible,' I said. 'Plans are going ahead. They couldn't be altered now.'

'Must be,' said Mustapha.

'I am sure Sir Tybalt would not agree with you.'

'It is death, there. There is a curse . . .'

Of course, I thought, they would be very superstitious.

I said: 'Have you spoken to Sir Tybalt?'

They shook their heads in unison. 'No use. No use to speak to his great father. No use. No use. So he die. The Curse comes to him and it will come to others.'

'It's a legend,' I said, 'nothing more.'

'A legend?' queried Mustapha.

'It is something people fancy. All will be well. Sir Tybalt will make sure of that.'

'His father could not make sure. His father die.'

'It was not because of his work.'

'Not? It was the Curse, my lady. And the Curse will come again.'

Absalam came to me and stood before me. The palms of his hands were together, his eyes raised. 'My lady must speak, my lady must persuade. My lady is the new wife. A husband listens to his beloved.'

'It would be impossible,' I said.

'It is death . . . death.'

'It is good of you to be so concerned,' I said, 'but there is nothing I can do.'

191

They looked at me with great sorrowing eyes and shook their heads mournfully.

I slipped through to the bedroom. Naturally, I told myself, they would be superstitious.

That night as we lay in bed I said to Tybalt: 'The Egyptians spoke to me today. They are very frightened.'

'Frightened of what?'

'What they call the Curse. They believe that if we go to Egypt there will be disaster.'

'If they feel that they must stay behind.'

'They asked me to speak to you. They said a husband loves his beloved and would listen.'

He laughed.

'I told them it was futile.'

'They are very superstitious.'

'Sometimes I'm a little frightened.'

'You, Judith?'

I clung to him.

'Only because of you,' I assured him. 'What if what happened to your father should happen to you?'

'Why should it?'

'What if there is something in this curse?'

'My dear Judith, you don't believe *that*.'

'If anyone else was leading this expedition I would laugh the idea to scorn. But this is you.'

He laughed in the darkness.

'My *dear* Judith,' he said.

And that was all.

I was longing for the days to pass. What dark ones they were before Christmas. There was a great deal

192

of rain and the fir trees glistened and dripped; the soft scented south-west wind blew through the trees and moaned outside the windows. Whenever I saw the Egyptians their eyes seemed to be fixed on me, half sorrowfully, half hopefully. I saw Nanny Tester but only in the presence of Tabitha for she kept mainly to her own apartments and only rarely emerged.

Theodosia and Evan came to stay at Keverall Court for Christmas, and Tybalt and I and Sabina and Oliver were invited for Christmas Eve. Hadrian was there too; he was going to stay until we left for Egypt.

It had long been a custom to sing carols in the Keverall Court ballroom on Christmas Eve and many of the people from the neighbourhood joined the company. Oliver officiated as the Reverend James Osmond used to and it was a very impressive occasion for there was a torchlight procession from the church to Keverall.

After the singing Lady Bodrean's chosen guests went to the hall were we had a supper consisting of the various pies which had been popular for centuries – squab, mutton, beef; and of course hot Cornish pasties. these were all eaten with mead and a beverage known as Keverall Punch which was made in an enormous pewter bowl – the recipe, known only to the steward of Keverall, had been handed down through the last four hundred years. It was rather potent.

I was amused by Lady Bodrean's attitude towards me. When she did not think herself observed she regarded me with a sort of suspicious wonder, but she was all charm when we stood face to face.

After we had partaken of the pies and punch

193

we went to the church for the midnight service and strolled home in the early hours of Christmas Day. It was all as we had done it many times before; and I felt it was good that all the friends of my childhood were gathered together at such a time.

Christmas Day at the rectory was pleasant too. It was amusing to see Sabina presiding at the table where once Alison had sat. There was the turkey with the chestnut stuffing and brandy butter which I remembered used to cause Dorcas and Alison such concern. Sabina showed no such anxiety. She chattered away making us all laugh as we teased her. The plum pudding was ceremoniously carried in with its flaming brandy jacket and followed by mince pies shining with their coating of castor sugar.

Theodosia and Evan with Hadrian were not with us, of course, they being at Keverall Court; so the conversation for once was not of the coming expedition; for this I was grateful because I was sure that Dorcas and Alison would not have enjoyed it.

Afterwards we played charades, miming scenes and childish guessing games at which I excelled and Tybalt did not. Dorcas and Alison looked on and applauded my success, which exasperated while it touched me.

In the early hours of the morning as Tabitha, Tybalt and I walked the short distance from the rectory to Giza House, I found myself wondering whether there would always be the three of us together. I was fond of Tabitha, but there were times when the old saying seemed very apt — two's company; three's a crowd. Was it because when Tabitha was with us Tybalt's attitude towards me seemed to change? Sometimes he seemed almost formal as though he were afraid to

194

betray to her that affection which more and more he was beginning to show when we were alone.

Through the gate, up the path on both sides of which rose the dark shrubs and trees. Into the house – the silent house where up above the strange Nanny Tester lived and in their rooms the Egyptians slept – or did they sleep? Did they lie awake talking of the Curse?

The sprig of mistletoe which hung suspended from the chandelier in the hall looked incongruous in that house of shadows.

January was with us. There was a cold snap, and the hoar-frost glistening on the shrubbery trees gave them a look of fairyland.

Tybalt at the breakfast table going through the mail, frowned and made an exclamation of disgust.

'These lawyers!' he complained.

'What's happened?'

'Sir Ralph's will is taking a long while to settle. It's a clear example of procrastination. It seems as though it's going to be months before everything is clear.'

'Does it matter so much?' I asked.

'You know he has left this trust. We were relying on it. It will make a great deal of difference to the expedition. We shall be less restricted for funds with this additional income. You'll discover, Judith, how money is swallowed up in expeditions like this. We have to employ possibly a hundred workmen. Then of course there are all the other workers. That's why one cannot begin such an undertaking until all these tiresome financial matters are taken care of. We're almost always frustrated by a question of expense.'

'And you can't touch this money or the interest, or whatever it is, until the will is proved?'

'Oh, it will be all right. With such a sum made over to us we shall be able to anticipate. But there will be formalities. I dare say I shall have to go to London. I should have to in any case, but later.'

'So it is only a minor irritation.'

He smiled at me. 'That's true, but minor irritations can mean delays.'

He then began to talk to me in the way I loved and he told me that he believed his father had discovered the way into an unbroken tomb.

'He was so excited. I remember his coming to the house. He had rented a house from one of the most influential men in Egypt who was interested in our operation and allowed us to have his palace, which was a great concession. It's a very grand and beautiful residence with magnificent gardens and a band of servants to look after us. It's called the Chephro Palace. We pay a nominal rent – a concession to independence; but the Pasha is really very interested in what we are doing and eager to help. We shall use this palace again.'

'You were telling me of your father?'

'He came in from the hills. It was night. There was a moon and it was almost as light as day. It's impossible of course to work in the heat of the afternoon and those moonlit nights were made full use of. He was riding a mule and I guessed something had happened. He was a man who rarely showed his feelings, but he showed something then. He seemed exuberant. I thought I would wait until he had washed and changed and had had a light meal which Mustapha and Absalam always prepared for him. Then I would go down and wait for him to tell me. I knew I would be the one he would tell first. I said nothing to anyone for it might have been something he wished kept secret. I knew that a few days before we had been in despair. It was several months earlier that we had discovered the door in the rock; we had penetrated through a corridor only to be led to a tomb which had been rifled probably two thousand years earlier. It had seemed then as though we had come to the end of our quest and all the work and expense would lead to nothing. But my father had had this strange feeling. He would not give up. He was certain we had not discovered all. I was of the opinion that only some tremendous discovery could have made him excited on that day.'

Tabitha had joined us.

'I am telling Judith about my father's death,' he said.

Tabitha nodded gravely; she sat down at the table and propping her elbows on the table leaned her chin on her hands. Her eyes were misty as Tybalt went on:

'I went down when I thought he would be refreshed and then I found him ill. I did not believe it was serious. He was a man of immense physical as well as mental vitality. He complained of pains and I saw that his limbs trembled. I suggested to Absalam and Mustapha, who were very upset, that we get him to bed. This we did. I thought: In the morning he will tell me. That night he died. Before he did I was sent for. As I knelt by his bed I could see that he was trying to tell me something. His lips moved. I was certain he was saying "Go on." That is why I am determined.'

'But why did he die at precisely that moment?'

197

'There was talk of the Curse, which was absurd. Why should he be cursed for doing what many had done before him? He had merely been to the site on which we were working. It was not as though he had violated one of the tombs. It was ridiculous.'

'But he died.'

'The climate is hot; he may have eaten tainted food. That, I can assure you, has happened more than once.'

'But to die so suddenly.'

'It was the greatest tragedy of my life. But I intend to carry out my father's wishes.'

I put out my hand and pressed his. I had forgotten Tabitha. Then I saw that there were tears in her beautiful eyes; and I thought, peevishly I must admit, why are there always the three of us!

During the cold spell Nanny Tester caught a chill which turned to bronchitis, as in the case of Dorcas. I was quite useful nursing her, having had experience with Dorcas. The old woman would lie in bed watching me with her bright, beady eyes; I think she liked to have me there, which was fortunate, for she had what seemed to me an unreasoning dislike for Tabitha. It was really most unfair because Tabitha was considerate in the extreme, but sometimes she would become really restless when Tabitha was in her room.

In February Tybalt went to London to make further arrangements about supplies and to see the lawyers; I had hoped to go with him but he had said that he would have so much to do that he would be able to spend little time with me.

I waved him off at Plymouth station and I couldn't

help thinking of Lavinia's going on that same journey with her baby in her arms and Dorcas and Alison seeing her off. And then an hour later she was dead.

To love intensely was a mixed blessing, I decided. There are moments of ecstasy but it seems that these have to be paid for with anxiety. One was completely happy only when one had the loved one safe beside one. When he was absent one's imagination seemed to take a malicious delight in presenting all kinds of horrors which could befall him. Now I must visualize the piled-up carriages, the cries of the injured, the silence of the dead.

Foolish! I admonished myself. How many people travel on the railways? Thousands! How many accidents are there? Very few!

I went back and threw myself into the nursing of Nanny Tester.

That evening as I sat with Tabitha I told her of my fears.

She smiled at me gently. 'Sometimes it is painful to love too well.'

She spoke as though she knew and I wondered afresh what her life had been. I wondered why she never spoke of it. Perhaps she will one day, I thought, when she gets to know me better.

Nanny Tester was recovering.

'But,' said Tabitha, 'these attacks always leave their mark. After she's been ill she always seems to emerge a little more feeble. Her mind wanders quite a bit.'

I had noticed that. I noticed too that my presence seemed to soothe her, so I used to take up her food and sometimes I sat with her. I would take a book

199

and read or do odd bits of needlework. Sabina used to call often. I would hear her chattering away to Nanny Tester and her visits were always a success.

One day I was sitting by her bed when she said: 'Watch her. Be careful.'

I guessed she was wandering in her mind and said: 'There's no one here, Nanny.' She had asked me to call her this. 'People in the family do,' she explained.

'I could tell you some things,' she murmured. 'I was always one to keep my eyes open.'

'Try to rest,' I said.

'Rest! When I see what's going on in this house. It's him and it's her. She eggs him on. Housekeeper? Friend of the family! What is she? Tell me that.'

I knew then that she was talking about Tabitha, and I had to hear what it was she wanted to tell me.

'Him and her . . .?' I prompted.

'You don't see. You're blind. That's how it often is. Those it concerns most don't see what's under their very eyes. It's the one who looks on . . . that's the one who sees.'

'What do you see, Nanny?'

'I see the way things are between them. She's sly. Oh, so friendly, she is! Friend of the family! House-keeper! We can do without her. There's nothing she does I couldn't do.'

That was hardly true but I let it pass.

'I never knew housekeepers like that one. Sitting down to dinner every night with the family; running the house. You'd think she was the mistress, you would. Then he goes away and what happens? She's called away. Oh, it's some family affair. Family! What

200

family? She'll be called away now he's away . . . I can see it coming.'

She was wandering obviously. 'You watch out, my lady,' she murmured. 'You watch out for her. You're nursing a viper in your bosom, that's what you are.'

The term made me smile; and when I thought of all Tabitha did in the house and how charming and helpful she was I was sure that the old woman had got an obsession, probably because she was jealous.

The house seemed different without Tybalt; the bedroom was full of shadows. A fire was lighted every night and I lay in bed watching the shadows. I often fancied I heard noises in the next room and one night got out of bed to see if anyone was there. How ghostly it looked with the light of the crescent moon faintly illuminating it; the books, the table at which Sir Edward had often worked, the spot where the sarcophagus had stood. I half expected Mustapha and Absalam to materialize. I went back to bed and dreamed that I went into the room and the sarcophagus was there and from it rose a mummy from which the wrapping suddenly disintegrated to show Mustapha and Absalam. They kept their dark eyes on me as they advanced pointing to me; I heard their voices distinctly as they echoed through emptiness. 'Stop him. A man listens to his beloved. The Curse of the kings will come upon you.'

I awoke shouting something. I sat up in bed. There was no light but that from the crescent moon, for the fire was nothing but a few embers. I got out of bed; I opened the door expecting to see the sarcophagus there, so vivid had the dream been. The room was empty. I shut the door quickly and got back to bed.

I thought: When we come back I will change this house. I will have the dark shrubs taken away; I will plant beautiful flowering shrubs like the hydrangeas which grow so luxuriantly here – lovely blue and pink and white blooms and red fuchsias dripping their bells from the hedges. We will replace the darkness by the brightest of colours.

In that mood I slept.

Yes, it was certainly different without Tybalt. Or perhaps I allowed those uneasy thoughts which were in my mind to come uppermost because he was not there to dispel them.

The gloomy house, the hints about Tabitha, the silent-footed Egyptians who followed me with their eyes and although speechless conveyed the message to me every time I saw them: Stop this expedition or face the curse of dead men.

Oh, Tybalt, I thought, come back and all will be well.

Every morning I went hopefully to the breakfast table looking for a note from Tybalt to say that he would be back. None came.

Tabitha had a letter in her hand when I went down.

'Oh, Judith. I'll have to go away for a few days.'

'Oh?'

'Yes, a . . . a relative of mine is ill. I must go.'

'Of course,' I said. 'I haven't heard you speak before of relatives.'

'This one is in Suffolk. It's a long journey. I think I ought to leave at once.'

'Today?'

'Yes, I'll get the ten-thirty for London. I shall have to go to London first of course and from there to Suffolk. You'll manage without me?'

'Yes,' I said. 'Of course I shall.'

She left the table hurriedly. She seemed very embarrassed, I thought. Jenner, the coachman, drove her in the jingle to the station.

I watched her go and I kept thinking of Nanny Tester. What had she said? 'He goes away . . . and she's called away.' But how could she foresee this? But that was what she had done.

I went upstairs to Nanny's apartments. She was standing by the window, her old-fashioned flannelette dressing-gown wrapped about her.

'So she's gone,' she said, 'eh, my lady, she's gone. Didn't I tell you?'

'How did you know?'

'There's things I know, my lady. I've got a pair of eyes in my head that see far and they see for them I care for.'

'So . . . you care for me.'

'Did you doubt it? I cared for you the first minute I clapped eyes on you. I said: "I'll watch over this one all the days of my life." '

'Thank you,' I said.

'It hurts me, though, to see the way you're treated, darling. It hurts right in here.' She struck her hand on where she supposed her heart to be. 'He goes away . . . and she goes to join him. This tale about someone she goes to see . . . Why does it happen when he's away? He's sent for her. They'll be together tonight . . .'

'Stop it! That's nonsense. It's absolutely untrue.'

'You always say that, darling.'

203

'Always! This is the first time you have made such a horrible suggestion to me.'

'Oh,' she said, 'I've seen it. I knew it was coming. Now you should see it too . . . if you look. She's the one he wanted . . . He took you for your money . . . money, money, money . . . that's it. And what for? So that they can go and dig up the dead. It's not right. It's not natural.'

'Nanny,' I said, 'you're not yourself.'

I looked at her wild eyes, her flushed cheeks. It was not without a certain relief that I saw that she was rambling.

'Let me help you to bed.'

'To bed . . . why to bed? It's for me to put you to bed, my precious.'

'Do you know who I am, Nanny?'

'Know you. Didn't I have you from three weeks after you were born?'

I said, 'You're mistaking me for somebody else. I'm Judith, Lady Travers . . . Tybalt's wife.'

'Oh yes, my lady. You're my lady all right. And a lot of good that's done you. I'd have liked to see you wife to some simple gentleman who didn't think more of digging up the dead than his own young wife.'

I said: 'Now I'm going to bring you a hot drink and you're going to sleep.'

'You're good to me,' she said.

I went down to the kitchen and told Ellen to prepare some hot milk. I would take it up to Nanny who was not very well.

'You'd think she'd be better now Mrs Grey's gone,' said Ellen. 'Goodness, my lady, she does seem to hate Mrs Grey.'

I did not comment. When I took the milk up to Nanny she was half asleep.

Tabitha came back with Tybalt. On her way back she had had to go to London and as Tybalt was ready to return they had come back together.

I was uneasy. There were so many questions I wanted to ask; but it was so wonderful to have Tybalt back and he seemed delighted to be with me.

He was in a very happy and contented state. The financial problems had been straightened out. We should be leaving in March instead of February as he had hoped — but it would only mean delaying our start by two weeks.

'Now,' he said, 'we shall be very busy. We must prepare to leave in earnest.'

He was right. Then there was nothing to think of but the expedition.

And in March we left for Egypt.

The Chephro Palace

The Chephro Palace stood majestic, golden-coloured, aloof from the village. I was astounded that the great Hakim Pasha should have put so much magnificence at our disposal.

I was, by the time we arrived, completely under the spell of the strange, arid and exotic land of the Pharaohs. The reality was no less wonderful than the pictures created by my imagination when I had nothing but dreams and a few pictures in the books I had read to guide me.

Several members of the working party had gone on ahead of us; they would be lodged about the site; and they had taken with them a good deal of the equipment which would be needed.

Hadrian, Evan and Theodosia with Terence Gelding and Tabitha were sailing from Southampton with Tybalt and me, but as Tybalt had some business to settle in Cairo, he and I would spend a few days there before joining the party in the Chephro Palace.

The day before we left I went over to Rainbow Cottage. Dorcas and Alison said goodbye to me as though it was our last farewell. Sabina and Oliver had been invited to supper and I could not help knowing how much they wished that I had married Oliver and settled quietly into the life at the rectory which they had chosen for me.

I was rather glad when the evening was over,

and the next day when we joined the SS *Stalwart* at Southampton my great adventure had begun.

It was a fascinating experience to be aboard ship and I couldn't help wishing that Tybalt and I were alone together. Evan and Theodosia I dare say felt the same for themselves; that left Hadrian, Terence and Tabitha. Poor Theodosia was confined to her cabin for the first few days although the sea was not unduly rough considering the time of the year. Conversation was mainly about the expedition and as Theodosia was not present I couldn't help feeling the tyro because it was astonishing how much Tabitha knew.

The Bay, contrary to expectations, was fairly smooth and by the time we reached Gibraltar, Theodosia was ready to emerge. Evan was such a kind and thoughtful husband; he spent a great deal of time with Theodosia and I found myself wondering whether Tybalt would have made me his chief concern if I had suffered from the sea as my half-sister did.

We had a pleasant day at the Rock and went for a trip up to the heights in little horse-drawn traps; we laughed at the antics of the apes and admired the magnificent scenery and the day was a happy one. Shortly after we arrived at Naples. As we were there for two days we took a trip as might have been expected to Pompeii. Excavations were still going on and more and more of that buried town was being revealed. As I walked arm in arm with Tybalt over those stones which until seventy-nine years after the birth of Christ had been streets I was caught up in the fascination of it all; and I said to Tybalt: 'How lucky you are to have this profession which brings these treasures to the world.'

He was delighted that I shared his enthusiasm and he pointed out to me the remains of houses and reconstructed in his mind the manner in which these people had lived under the shadow of Vesuvius before that fatal day when the great mountain had erupted and buried the town for centuries so that it had only emerged just over a hundred years ago when archaeologists discovered it.

When we were back on the ship the discussion continued far into the night on the discoveries of that tragic city.

At Port Said we left the ship and travelled to Cairo – just the two of us – where Tybalt had business to attend to.

I had read a great deal about Egypt and as I had lain in my bed in Rainbow Cottage and at Keverall Court my imagination had transported me to this mysterious land. I should, therefore, have been prepared, yet none of my fancies could compare with the reality and the impact upon me was exhilarating, exciting beyond my dreams.

It was a golden land, dominated by the sun which could be merciless; one was immediately conscious of thousands of years of antiquity. When I saw a goatherd in his long white robes I could believe I was far back in the days of the Old Testament. The country held me spellbound; I knew that here anything could happen – the most wonderful things, the most fearful. It was both beautiful and ugly; it was stimulating, thrilling and sinister.

We stayed at a small hotel which looked out on to the Nile; from my window I could see the river bank and the gold-coloured Mokattam Hills; how different from the green of Cornwall, the misty dampness, the luxuriant vegetation. Here one was aware of the ever present sun – relentlessly burning the land. If green was the colour of England, yellow was that of Egypt. It was the ambience of antiquity which caught my imagination. The people in their white robes and sandalled feet; the smells of cooking food; the sight of disdainful camels picking their dainty ways. I listened in wonder when I first heard the muezzin from the top of his minaret calling the people to prayer; and I was amazed to see them stop wherever they were and pay homage to Allah. Tybalt took me into the *souks* which I found fascinating with him beside me but I think I should have felt them a little sinister had I been alone. Dark-eyed people watching us intently without staring, and one was constantly aware of their scrutiny. Through the narrow streets we wandered, and we looked into the darkened cave-like shops where bakers were making bread coated with seeds and where silversmiths worked over their braziers. There the water-seller demanded attention with the clatter of his brass cups and at the back of the dark openings men sat cross-legged weaving and stitching. In the air the heavy scent of perfumed oils mingled with that of the camel dung which was used as fuel.

I shall never forget that day – the jostling crowds of the noisy streets; the smells of mingling dung and perfume; the side glances from veiled dark eyes; the call to prayer and the response of the people.

'Allah is great, and Mohammed his prophet.' How often I was to hear those words and they never failed to thrill me.

We paused by one of the shops which were like huts open to the street. At the back a man worked cutting and engraving stones and on a stall inside the hut was an array of rings and brooches.

'You must have a scarab ring,' said Tybalt. 'It'll bring you luck in Egypt.'

There were several of them on a tray and Tybalt selected one.

'This is tourmaline,' he said. 'Look at the carved beetle. He was sacred to the ancient Egyptians.'

The man had risen from the back from his work and came eagerly forward.

He bowed to me and to Tybalt. His eyes shone at the prospect of a sale and I listened to him and Tybalt as they bargained ove. the price, while several small children came round to watch. They could not take their eyes from Tybalt and me. I suppose we appeared very strange to them.

Tybalt took the ring and showed me the beetle. About it were hieroglyphs very delicately carved. Tybalt translated, 'Allah be with you.'

'There could not be greater good luck than that,' he said. 'It is what every man should give to the one he loves best when she first comes to this land.'

I slipped the ring on my finger. There were delighted cries of approval from the children. The ring was paid for and we went on our way with the blessings of the stone-cutter ringing in our ears.

'We had to bargain,' said Tybalt. 'He would have been most disappointed in us if we had not.' Then he looked at my ecstatic face and said: 'You are happy today, Judith.'

'I'm so happy,' I said, 'that I'm afraid.'

He pressed my hand with the ring on it. 'If you could have a wish, what would it be?' he asked.

'That I could be as happy as this every day of my life.'

'That's asking a lot of life.'

'Why should it be . . . we are together . . . we have this great interest. I see no reason why we should not always be in this state of happiness. Aren't our lives what we make them?'

'There are certain outside factors, I believe.'

'They shan't hurt us.'

'Dear Judith, I do believe you are capable of arranging even that.'

Back to our hotel and the warm scented night with the smells of Egypt and the great moon which made the night almost as light as day.

These were the happiest days of my life to that time because we were alone together in this exciting land. I wished that we could have stayed there together and not have had to join the others. An absurd wish because it was to join the party that we had come to Egypt.

The next day we went out to the Pyramids – that last remaining wonder of the ancient world; and to find myself face to face with the Sphinx was an experience which enthralled me completely. Mounted somewhat precariously on my camel, I felt exhilarated and I could see how much Tybalt enjoyed my excitement. One hundred thousand men had toiled for twenty years to achieve this wonder, Tybalt had told me; the stone had been quarried from the nearby Mokattam Hills and dragged across the desert. I felt, as everyone

211

else must on witnessing this fantastic sight, speechless with wonder.

When we dismounted, I entered the Pyramid of Cheops and, bending double, followed Tybalt up the steep passage to the burial chamber where the Pharaoh's red granite sarcophagus was displayed.

Then over the sand perched high on our reluctant beasts of burden. I was in an exalted mood when we returned to our hotel.

I think I was as near beautiful as I had ever been that night. We dined at a small table secluded from the rest of the diners by palms. I had piled my dark hair high on my head and wore a green velvet gown which I had had made by Sarah Sloper before I left home. I kept touching the pink tourmaline ring on my finger remembering that Tybalt had said that it was the gift of a lover that good fortune might preserve in a strange land the one he loved best.

Sitting opposite Tybalt, I marvelled afresh at the wonderful thing that had happened to me; and there flashed into my mind then the thought that even if my fortune had been a deciding factor in Tybalt's wishing to marry me, I didn't care. I would make him love me for myself alone. I remembered it being said of our late Prime Minister, Lord Beaconsfield, that he had married his Mary Anne for her money but at the end of their lives he would have married her for love. That was how it should be with us. But I was romantic and foolish enough to hope that it was not for my fortune that Tybalt had married me.

Tybalt leaned forward and took my hand with the scarab ring on it; he studied it intently. 'What are you thinking, Judith?' he asked.

'Just of the wonder of everything.'

'I can see that the Pyramids impressed you.'

'I never thought to see them. So many things are happening that are fresh and exciting. You look suddenly sad, Tybalt. Are you?'

'Only because I was thinking that you won't go on being excited about everything. You'll become blasé. I shouldn't like that.'

'I don't believe I ever would.'

'Familiarity, you know, breeds contempt . . . or at least indifference. I feel since we have been together in Cairo that things which I have seen before seem fresh, more interesting, more wonderful. That's because I'm seeing them through your eyes.'

It was indeed an enchanted night.

The *kebab* served by the silent-footed men in their long white robes tasted delicious. I couldn't believe it was simply lamb on skewers which had been grilled over charcoal. I told Tybalt that the Tahenia sauce into which the meat was dipped and which I discovered later was made of sesame seeds, oil, white sauce and a hint of garlic, tasted like nectar.

He replied prosaically that it was because I was hungry. 'Hunger savours all dishes,' he added.

But I thought it was because I was so happy.

Afterwards we ate *esh es seraya*, which was a delicious mixture of honey, breadcrumbs and cream. We drank rosewater and grenadine with fruit and nuts in it, called *khosaf*.

Yes, that was an evening never to be forgotten. After dinner we sat on the terrace and looked out on the Nile, while we drank Turkish coffee and nibbled Turkish Delight.

The stars seemed to hang low in that indigo sky and before us flowed the Nile down which Cleopatra had once sailed in her royal barge. I wished that I could hold those moments and go on living them again and again.

Tybalt said: 'You have a great capacity for happiness, Judith.'

'Perhaps,' I answered. 'If so, I am fortunate. It means I can enjoy the happiness that comes my way to the full.'

And I wondered then if just as I felt this intensity of pleasure I could feel sorrow with an equal fervour.

Perhaps that was a thought which Tybalt shared with me.

I would not brood on it though – not on this night of nights on the romantic banks of the Nile.

When we arrived at the Chephro Palace the rest of the party had already settled in and Tabitha had slipped into the role of housekeeper.

Hakim Pasha was one of the richest men in Egypt, Tybalt told me, and it was our great good fortune that he felt benign towards our cause.

'He could have hindered us in many ways,' he said, 'instead of which he has decided to be of immense help to us. Hence this palace which he has put at our disposal for just enough rent to preserve our dignity – a very important facet, I do assure you. You will meet him, I dare say, because when my father was here he was a constant visitor.'

I stood in the entrance hall of the Palace and gazed with wonder at the beautiful staircase in white marble; the floor was covered in mosaic tiles of the most beautiful blended colours; and the stained glass in the windows depicted the sea journey of the dead through hideous dangers until they came under the protection of the God Amen-Ra.

Tybalt was beside me: 'I'll tell you the story later. Look, here's Tabitha to welcome you.'

'So you've come!' cried Tabitha. She was looking at Tybalt with shining eyes. 'I thought you never would.'

'It's a long journey from Cairo,' said Tybalt.

'I visualized all sorts of disasters.'

'Which is just what she should not do, don't you agree, Judith? But of course you do.'

'Well, now you're here. I'll take you to your room. Then you can explore the rest of the Palace and I dare say Tybalt will wish to look at the site.'

'You're right,' said Tybalt.

'We'll have a meal then. Mustapha and Absalam are working in the kitchens so I am sure they will mingle a little English cooking with the Egyptian, which might be more agreeable to our palates. But first to your room.'

Tabitha led the way up that grand and imposing staircase and we went along a gallery, the walls of which were decorated with mosaic patterns similar to those in the floor of the hall. These were figures, always in profile, usually of some Pharaohs giving gifts to a god. I had to pause to examine those figures and the beautiful muted colours of the tiles. On the ceiling was engraved the Sun God Amen-Ra; his symbol was the hawk and the ram; and I remembered that Tybalt had told me that the gods of Egypt were said not only to possess all the human virtues, but in addition one from an animal. Amen-Ra had two however, the

Hawk and the Ram. Below him was his son Osiris, God of the Underworld, who judged the dead when they had made their journey along the river; Isis was there – the great goddess beloved of Osiris, and their son Horus . . .

'The figures are so beautifully done,' I said.

'It would be an insult to the gods if they had not been,' added Tybalt.

He slipped his arm through mine and we went into the room which had been prepared for us. I stared at the enormous bed standing on a platform. Mosquito-nets festooned over it from the ceiling like flimsy cobwebs.

'This is the bedroom used by the Pasha himself when he is in residence,' Tabitha explained.

'Should we use it?' asked Tybalt.

'You must. The Palace is in full use and it is only proper that our leader should have the state bedroom. Your father used it, you remember, when he was here.'

She showed us an ante-chamber in which we could wash and generally make our toilet. There was a sunken marble bath, in the centre of which was a statue and three marble steps leading down to the bath; on the walls of this chamber were mosaics depicting nude figures. One side of the room was composed of mirrors, and there was a dressing-table behind gold-coloured brocade curtains; a many-sided mirror reflected my image, and the frame of the mirror was studded with chalcedony, rose quartz, amethyst and lapis lazuli. These stones were, I noticed, in the decorations throughout the bedchamber.

I laughed. 'It is very grand. We shall feel like royalty.'

'The Pasha has given instructions to his servants

that any of our complaints will be met with dire punishment. They are trembling in their shoes.'

'Is he very autocratic?'

'He is the ruler of his lands and he regards his servants as slaves. He expects absolute obedience from them. We are his guests and if we are not treated with respect, that is tantamount to insulting him. He will not accept insults.'

'What happens to offenders?'

'Their bodies are probably found in the Nile. Or they may be deprived of a hand or an ear.'

I shivered.

'It's magnificent. It's beautiful,' I cried. 'But a little frightening. A little sinister.'

'That's Egypt,' said Tabitha, laying her hand on my arm. 'Now perform the necessary ablutions and come down to eat. Then I expect you'll want some sort of conference, eh Tybalt?'

'Well,' said Tybalt when we were alone, 'what do you really think of it?'

'I'm not sure,' I replied. 'I wish it was not quite so grand and this Pasha does sound rather diabolical.'

'He's quite charming. He and my father became good friends. He's a power in these parts. You will meet him soon.'

'Where does he live then since he has given us his palace?'

'My dear Judith, this is but *one* of his palaces. It may well be the most grand, but he would consider it quite ill-mannered not to give it up to us. You have to understand the etiquette. That's very important. Don't look doleful. You will in time. Now let's get cleaned up. I can't wait to hear what's been going on.'

217

It had changed. That other love, his profession, was in the ascendancy.

The dining-room with its heavy curtains was lighted by a chandelier containing about a hundred candles. It was dark now, for there was no twilight hour as at home. But there were others to greet us and add normality to this strange palace, for which I was glad. I laughed to myself, thinking that the verdict of the servants at Giza House would be that it gave them 'the creeps'.

We sat at the big table under the chandelier – Hadrian, Evan, Theodosia, Terence Gelding and others whom I had not previously met but who were all practised archaeologists deeply interested in the task ahead. Tybalt sat at one end of the table, I at the extreme end; and on my right was Hadrian and Evan was on my left.

'Well, here you are at last, Judith,' said Hadrian. 'What do you think of this *kuftas*? Personally I prefer the roast beef of old England but don't let anyone know I said that. Old Osiris might not grant me admittance to heaven when my time comes.'

'You are very irreverent, Hadrian; and I advise you to keep such thoughts to yourself. Who knows who might overhear?'

'There speaks our Judith,' said Hadrian, appealing to Evan. 'She has just arrived and immediately is telling us what we should and should not do.'

Evan smiled. 'On this occasion she's right. You never know what's heard and misunderstood. These servants are no doubt listening and reporting to the Pasha and your jocularity would most definitely be misconstrued as irreverence.'

'What have you been doing while you were waiting for Tybalt?' I asked.

'Going over the site, getting the workmen together, arranging for this and that. There's a great deal to do on an occasion like this. You wait until you go down there and see the hive of industry we've created. She'll be surprised, won't she, Evan?'

'It is a little different from Carter's Meadow.'

'And we do face difficulties,' said Hadrian. 'You see, many of the diggers remember Sir Edward's death and believe that he died because he went where the gods did not wish him to.'

'There is a certain amount of reluctance?'

'It's there, don't you think, Evan?'

Evan nodded gravely.

I looked along the table where Tybalt was deep in conversation with the men around him. Tabitha was sitting near him. I noticed with a pang of jealousy that occasionally she threw in a remark which was listened to with respect.

I felt I had lost Tybalt already.

After the meal Tybalt went out to look at the site and I was permitted to accompany the party. There was a fair amount of work going on in spite of the hour. The full moon and the clear air made it quite bright; it was easier to work at this hour than under the heat of the blazing sun.

The stark hills rising to the moonlit sky were menacing but rather beautiful; the parallel lines of pegs marking the search area, the little hut which had been set up, the wheelbarrows, the forks of the excavators, and the workmen were far from romantic.

Tybalt left me with Hadrian, who smiled at me

cynically. 'Not quite what you expected?' he said.

'Exactly,' I said.

'Of course, you're a veteran of Carter's Meadow.'

'I suppose it is rather similar, although there they were merely looking for bronze-age relics; and here it's the tombs of the dead.'

'We could be on the verge of one of the really exciting discoveries in archaeology.'

'How thrilling that will be when we find it.'

'But we haven't done that yet, and you have to learn to be cautious in this game. As a matter of fact there are lots of things you have to learn.'

'Such as?'

'Being a good little archaeological wife.'

'And what does that mean?'

'Never complaining when your lord and master absents himself for hours at a stretch.'

'I intend to share in his work.'

Hadrian laughed. 'Evan and I are in the profession but I can assure you we're not allowed to share in anything but the more menial tasks. And you think that you will be?'

'I'm Tybalt's wife.'

'In our world, my dear Judith, there are archaeologists . . . wives and husbands are just by the way.'

'Of course I know I'm nothing but an amateur . . . yet.'

'But that is something you won't endure for long, eh? You'll soon be putting us all to shame – even the great Tybalt?'

'I shall certainly learn all I can and I hope I shall be able to take an intelligent interest . . .'

He laughed at me. 'You'll do that. But in addition to

an intelligent interest, take equally intelligent heed. That's my sound advice.'

'I don't really need your advice, Hadrian.'

'Oh yes you do. Now! You're looking for Tybalt, I can see. He'll be hours yet. He might have waited until morning and devoted the first night in the Chephro Palace to his bride. Now had I been in his place . . .'

'You are *not* in his place, Hadrian.'

'Alas! I was too slow. But mark my words, Tybalt's the man he is and so he'll remain. It's no use your trying to make him any different.'

'Who said I wanted to make him any different?'

'You wait. And now let me take you back to the Palace. You must be ready to sink into your bath of chalcedony.'

'Is that what it is?'

'I expect so. Grand, don't you think? I wonder what Lady Bodrean would have thought of it. She wouldn't have approved of it for ex-companions even though it's turned out that you and she are connected – in a manner of speaking.'

'I should love her to see me in my state apartments . . . especially if she had lesser ones.'

'That shows a vengeful spirit, Cousin Judith. You *are* my cousin, you know.'

'The thought had struck me. How are your affairs?'

'Affairs? Financial or romantic?'

'Well both, since you raise the question.'

'In dire straits, Judith. The former because that's their natural state and the latter because I didn't know in time that you are an heiress and missed the opportunity of a lifetime.'

'Aren't you presuming too much? You don't think

221

I would have allowed myself to be married for my money, do you?'

'Women who are married for their money don't know it at the time. You don't imagine the ambitious suitor comes along and, going on his knees, begs for the honour of sharing a girl's fortune, do you?'

'Certainly it would have to be done with more subtlety than that.'

'Of course.'

'Yet you imagine that you only had to beckon my fortune to have it in your pocket?'

'I'm only letting you into the secret now that it's too late. Come on, I'll get you back to the Palace.'

We did the journey back to the river bank on mules where a boat was waiting to take us down the river the short distance to where we alighted on the opposite bank, almost at the gates of the Palace.

When we arrived at the Palace Theodosia came into the hall.

Evan was down at the site, she told us, and Hadrian remarked that he would have to go back. 'You can depend upon it, it will be the early hours of the morning before we return. Tybalt's a hard taskmaster; he works like the devil himself and expects the same of his minions.'

Hadrian went back and when I was alone with Theodosia she said: 'Judith, come to my room with me and talk.'

I followed her along the gallery. The room she and Evan shared was less grand than mine and Tybalt's, but it was large and dark, and the floor was covered by a Bokhara carpet. She shut the door and faced me.

'Oh, Judith,' she said. 'I don't like it here. I hated

it from the moment we came. I want to go home.'

'Why, what's wrong?' I asked.

'You can *feel* it. It's eerie. I don't like it. I can't tell Evan. It's his work, isn't it? Perhaps he wouldn't understand. But I feel uneasy . . . You don't, of course. You never did, did you? I wish they'd go home. Why can't they let the Pharaohs stay in their tombs? That was what was intended! They couldn't have thought, could they, when they went to all that trouble to bury them that people were coming along and going where they shouldn't.'

'But my dear Theodosia, the purpose of archaeology is to uncover the secrets of the past.'

'It's different finding weapons and Roman floors and baths. It's this tampering with the dead that I don't like. I never did like it. I dreamed last night that we found a tomb and there was a sarcophagus just like the one that time in Giza House. And someone rose out of it with bandages unravelling . . .'

'I can't live that down, can I?'

'I cried out in my dream: "Stop it, Judith!" And then I looked and it wasn't you coming out of the thing.'

'Who was it?'

'Myself. I thought it was a sort of warning.'

'You're getting fanciful, Theodosia. I was the one who was supposed to be that.'

'But anyone could get fancies here. There's a sort of shadow of the past everywhere. This Palace is centuries old. All the temples and tombs are hundreds and thousands of years old. Oh, I'm glad you've come, Judith. It'll be better now you're here. These people are so dedicated, aren't they? I suppose *you* are a bit. But I feel I know you and can talk to you.'

I said: 'Are you worried about Evan?'

She nodded. 'I often think what if what happened to Sir Edward should happen to him.'

I had no glib comfort to offer for that. Hadn't I wondered whether it could happen to Tybalt?

I said, 'Of course we get anxious. It's because we love our husbands and one gets foolish when one loves. If we could only take a calm, rational view — look in from outside as it were — we should see how foolish all this talk would be.'

'Yes, Judith, I suppose so.'

'Why don't you go to bed?' I said. 'You're not going to sit up and wait for Evan, are you?'

'I suppose not. Goodness knows what time they'll come in. Oh, it feels so much better since you arrived, Judith.'

'So it should. Don't forget we're sisters — though only half ones.'

'I'm glad of that,' said Theodosia.

I smiled at her, said good night and left her.

I went along the gallery. How silent it was! The heavy velvet gold-fringed curtains shut me in and my feet sank deep into the thickly piled carpet. I stood still, suddenly tense because I had an instinctive feeling that I was not alone in the gallery. I looked round. There was no one there and yet I was conscious of eyes watching me.

I felt a tingling in my spine. I understood why Theodosia was afraid. She was more timid than I — though perhaps less imaginative.

There was the softest footfall behind me. Someone was undoubtedly there. I turned sharply.

'Absalam!' I cried. 'Mustapha!'

They bowed. 'My lady,' they said simultaneously.

Their dark eyes were fixed on my face and I asked quietly. 'Is there anything wrong?'

'Wrong?' They looked at each other. 'Yes, my lady. But it is still not too late.'

'Too late?' I said falteringly.

'You go back. You go home. That is best. You ask it. You are new bride. He cannot refuse his beloved.'

I shook my head.

'You don't understand. This is Sir Tybalt's work . . . his life . . .'

'His life . . .' They looked at each other and shook their heads. 'It was Sir Edward's life . . . and then his death.'

'You must not be concerned,' I said. 'All will be well. When they have found what they seek they will go home.'

'Then . . . too late, my lady,' said Absalam, or was it Mustapha?

The other looked at me with deeply sorrowing eyes. 'Not yet too late,' he suggested hopefully.

'Good night,' I said. 'I shall retire to my room now.'

They did not speak but continued to regard me in their mournful way.

I lay awake. The flickering light of candles showed the ceilings on which had been painted pictures in softly muted colours. I could make out the now familiar outline of Amen-Ra, the great Sun God, and he was receiving gifts from an elaborately gowned figure, presumably a Pharaoh. There was a border of hieroglyphs – strange signs full of meaning. I wondered whether while I was here I might try and learn something of the language; I had a notion that there would be many nights when I lay alone in this bed, many days when I did not see Tybalt.

I must be prepared for this. It was what I had expected in any case; but I did want Tybalt to understand that my greatest wish was to *share* his life.

It was two o'clock in the morning when he came in. I cried out in pleasure at the sight of him and sat up in bed.

He came to me and took my hands in his.

'Why, Judith, still awake?'

'Yes, I was too excited to sleep. I was wondering what you were doing out there on the site.'

He laughed. 'Nothing that would make you wildly excited at the moment. They've just been marking out the proposed areas and making general preparations.'

'You are going on where Sir Edward left off?'

'I'll tell you about it some time. Now you should be asleep.' He kissed me lightly and went into our dressing-room.

But I was not ready for sleep. Nor was Tybalt. We lay awake talking for an hour.

'Yes,' he said during the course of the conversation, 'we are exploring the same ground which my father did. You know what happened. He was convinced that there was an undisturbed tomb in the area. You know, of course, that the majority were rifled centuries ago.'

'I should have thought they would have tried to keep the burial places secret.'

'Up to a point they did, but there were so many workmen involved. Imagine hewing out the rock, making secret underground passages, then the chambers themselves. And think of all the transport that

226

would be needed to bring the treasures into the tombs.'

'The secret would leak out,' I said, 'and then the robbers came. It's odd that they were not deterred by the Curse.'

'No doubt they were, but the fabulous riches found in the tombs might have seemed a worthwhile reward for damnation after death; and since they had been clever enough to find the hidden treasure no doubt they thought they could be equally shrewd in escaping the ill luck.'

'Yet Sir Edward, who was merely working for posterity and to place his finds in some musuem, is struck down whereas robbers who seek personal gain escape.'

'In the first place my father's death had nothing to do with a curse. It was due to natural causes.'

'Which no one seems certain about.'

'Oh come, Judith, surely you're not becoming superstitious.'

'I don't think I am unduly. But everyone must be a little, I suppose, when their loved ones are in danger.'

'Danger. What nonsense is this? It's just a tale.'

'Yet . . . he died.'

He kissed my forehead. 'Foolish Judith!' he said. 'I'm surprised at you.'

'It will teach you not to have too high an opinion of my sagacity where you are concerned. Wise men are fools in love — and you can be sure that applies to women.'

We were silent for a while and then I said: 'I have seen Mustapha and Absalam. They have said I should persuade you to go back home.'

227

That made him laugh.

'It's such nonsense,' he said. 'It was a tale put about to frighten off robbers. But it didn't, you see. Almost every tomb that has been discovered has been tampered with. That's why it's the dream of every archaeologist to find a tomb which is just as it was when closed four thousand years ago or thereabouts. I want to be the first one to set foot in such a burial place. Imagine the joy of seeing a footprint in the dust which was made by the last person to leave the tomb, or a flower offering lying there, thrown down by a sorrowing mourner, before the door was closed, the mountainside filled in and the dead person left in peace for the centuries to come. Oh, Judith, you've no idea of the excitement this could give.'

'We must try to see that your dream is realized.'

'My darling, you speak as though I am a small boy who must have his treat.'

'Well, there are many sides to people and even the greatest archaeologist in the world at times seems as a little boy to his doting wife.'

'I'm so happy to have you here with me, Judith. You're going to be with me all the way. You're going to be the perfect wife.'

'It's strange that you should say that. Did you know that Disraeli dedicated one of his books to Mary Anne, his wife. The dedication said "To the Perfect Wife".'

'No,' he said, 'I'm an ignoramus — apart from one subject.'

'You're a specialist,' I said, 'and knowing so much about one thing you couldn't be expected to know others. He married her for her money but when they were old he would have married her for love.'

'Then,' said Tybalt lightly, 'it must indeed have become a perfect union.'

I thought: If that happened to me I should be content.

Then he started to talk, telling me of customs, fascinating me with the exotic pictures he was able to create. He told me of what had been discovered in tombs which had been partially rifled centuries ago; and I asked why the ancient Egyptians had made such a fine art of the burial of the dead.

'It was because they believed that the life of the spirit went on after death. Osiris, the God of the Underworld and Judge of the Dead, was said to be the first ever to be embalmed and this embalming was performed by the god Anubis. Osiris had been murdered by his brother Set, who was the God of Darkness, but he rose from the dead and begot the god Horus. When a man died he became identified with Osiris but to escape destruction he had successfully to traverse the mythical river Tuat which was said to end where the sun rose in the kingdom of the Sun God Amen-Ra. This river was beset by dangers and no man could navigate it without the help of Osiris. The river was supposed to grow darker as the flimsy craft, in which the soul of the deceased travelled, progressed. He soon reached a chamber which was called Amentat, the place of Twilight, and after he passed through that the horrors of the river increased. Great sea monsters rose to threaten him; the waters boiled and were so turbulent that the boat was in danger of sinking in those horrible waters. Only those who had led good lives on Earth and were valiant and strong could hope to survive —

and only they with the help of Osiris. And if they were lucky enough to survive they at length came to the final chamber where the god Osiris judged them; those whom the god decided were worthy of making a journey to Amen-Ra went on; those who were not, even though they had so far survived, were destroyed. For those who lived on, the tomb was their home. Their Ka, which is the spirit which cannot be destroyed, would pass back and forth into the world and back to the mummy lying in the tomb, and that is why it was considered necessary to make these burial chambers worthy of their illustrious inhabitants that they might not miss the jewels and treasures they had enjoyed during their sojourn on earth.'

I said: 'I can understand why they would not be very pleased with intruders.'

'They?' he said. 'You mean the long-dead members of a past civilization?'

'There must be many people living today who believe in these gods.'

' "Allah is great and Mohammed His Prophet." You will hear that often enough.'

'But there will be many who identify the old gods with Allah. Allah is all-powerful as are Horus, Osiris and the rest. I think people like Mustapha and Absalam believe that Osiris will rise up and strike anyone who intrudes into his underworld.'

'Superstition. My dear Judith, we are employing about a hundred men. Think what that means to these people. Some of them are very poor, as you'll see. These excavations are a godsend to them.'

'You take a practical view, Tybalt.'

'You must too.'

230

'I would, of course, if you weren't involved.'

I heard him laugh in the darkness. He said a strange thing then. 'You love me too much, Judith. It's not wise.'

Then I clung to him and we made love.

And at length I slept.

It was the time of Shem el Nessim which I believe means the Smell of the Breeze and is to celebrate the first day of spring. At home it would be Easter time, I thought, and I pictured Dorcas and Alison with Miss Crewe decorating the church with daffodils and spring flowers – yellow most of them, the colour, we used to say, of sunshine.

Sabina would be chattering away on church affairs and Oliver would be smiling tolerantly and my aunts would be thinking how much more satisfactory things would have worked out if I had been the rector's wife instead of married to a man who had carried me off to share in an expedition in a foreign land.

The days since my arrival had disappointed me a little because I had seen so little of Tybalt. He spent every possible moment at the site. I had longed to accompany him but he explained that, although when there was work which I could do I should be allowed to participate, that time was not yet.

We took our meals in the great banqueting hall of the palace and many of us sat down at the long table. Tybalt was always at the head of it and with him would be the more senior members of the band. Hadrian and Evan were not very experienced, but Terence Gelding, who was several years older than Tybalt, was his right hand. He had been concerned in some of the successful excavations in England and Tybalt once told me that he had become well known in archaeological circles when he had discovered one of the finest Roman pavements in the country, and had also identified the period of some early stone- and bronze-age relics. Tabitha had taken over the housekeeping with efficiency and it was clear she had been here before. This meant that Theodosia and I were together a good deal and we often took drives in the little horse-drawn traps called *arabiyas*. It was known that we were the wives of members of the archaeological party and for this reason we could more or less wander about at our will.

Sometimes we were driven away from the town and we saw the fellaheen working in the fields with oxen and buffalo. They looked dignified in spite of their none too clean long cotton robes and small skullcaps. Often we saw them eating their meal which invariably consisted of unleavened bread and a kind of bean which I discovered was known as Fool.

We would go together in the *souk* and sometimes buy wares which were displayed there. Our presence always seemed to generate excitement because of a hoped-for sale, I supposed; but no one ever tried to force their wares on us.

There was one shop which interested us particularly because seated there was a young girl, wearing a yashmak, bent over a piece of leather on which she was embossing a design.

We paused and she stopped work to regard us over her yashmak intently out of enormous eyes made to look even larger than they were by the heavy application of kohl.

232

She said in tolerable English: 'You ladies like?'

I said that we liked her work very much and she invited us to watch her for a moment or two. I was astonished by the clever way she created a pattern.

'You would like?' she asked, indicating a row of slippers, bags and wallets into which the soft embossed leather had been made.

We tried on the slippers and studied the bags, and the outcome was that I bought a pair of oyster-coloured slippers with a blue pattern and Theodosia a kind of dolly-bag with a cord by which it was drawn up and shut. Her bag was in the same oyster-colour with a pale red pattern.

The girl was delighted with her sale, and as the transaction was completed she said: 'You with English? They dig in the valley?'

I said yes, our husbands were archaeologists and we had the good fortune to accompany them.

She nodded.

'I know, I know,' she said excitedly.

After that we often stopped at her shop and now and then we bought something. We learned that her name was Yasmin, that her father and his before him worked in leather. Her two little brothers were learning to work on it too. She had a friend who dug for us. That was why she was so interested.

Whenever I passed the shop I always looked for her slight figure bent over her work or dealing with a customer. For me she was part of the now familiar life of the *souk*.

Neither of us ever went there alone, however. Although we felt perfectly at ease together, if, as we had done once or twice, we suddenly found ourselves alone, because one of us had paused to look at something or perhaps gone on ahead, an uneasiness would come over us and we would feel suddenly surrounded by an alien people. I knew that Theodosia felt this more intensely than I did. I had seen her when she thought she was lost and there was something near panic in her eyes. But that happened rarely and we usually managed to keep together even though the sights had become familiar to us. I imagined that the people had grown accustomed to seeing us. Although the children would stand and gaze up at us, the adults always passed us, aware of us, we knew, but keeping their eyes averted.

The blind beggars betrayed a certain eagerness as we approached. I couldn't tell why since they were blind. So we never failed to drop a coin into their begging bowls and always would come the grateful murmur: 'Allah will reward you!'

Theodosia's attitude even changed and the feeling which the *souk* could arouse in her became like a delicious terror which children experience. She would cling to my arm, but at the same time she was enjoying the colour and bustle of the markets as we passed men with brown faces and high cheekbones and the kind of noble profile which reminded me of the drawings I had seen on the walls of temples. The women were mostly veiled and all that was visible of their faces were the dark eyes made enormous by the kohl they used. They were often clad in black from head to foot. When we went into the country we would see the women helping the men in the fields. In the early mornings or late afternoons we would take a trip in one of the boats up the Nile and see the women washing their clothes and chattering together as they did so. We often marvelled at the way these women could carry a great jar of water on their heads without spilling a drop and walk so gracefully and in such a dignified manner as they did so.

It seemed that in a very short time the scene had become familiar to me. I was frustrated, though, to be shut out from the main work.

Tybalt smiled at my continual demands to know if there was not *something* I could do.

'This is a very different operation from Carter's Meadow, you know, Judith.'

'I do know that. But I long to have a part in it . . . even if it is only a small part.'

'Later on,' he promised. 'In the meantime would you like to write some of my letters and keep some accounts? It will put you in the picture. You have to know so much, as well as working on the site.'

I would be pleased to do this, I told him; but I did want to share in the active work as well.

'Dear Judith, you were always so impatient.'

So I had to be content with that, but I was determined that it should be only temporarily.

Shem el Nessim was a public holiday and Tybalt was annoyed.

'Just because it's the first day of spring we have to stop work,' he grumbled.

'How impatient you are!' I chided.

'My dear Judith, it's maddening. The cost of this is enormous and this is a sheer waste of a day. As my father always said, they never work as well after a holiday. They take a day or so to recover, so it is more than one day lost.'

235

However, he was determined not to lose time and he and the party were at the site as usual. That was why on this Monday which followed our Easter Sunday Theodosia and I strolled down to the *souk*.

The shops were closed and the streets were different without the sounds and smells and activities of the vendors. There was a small mosque in one of the streets; the door was always open and we had glanced in from the corners of our eyes as we passed. It appeared to be a huge room and we had often seen white-robed figures kneeling on their prayer mats. But we had always averted our eyes because we knew how easy it was to offend people by what would seem prying or irreverence for their religion.

On this day many people were making their way to the mosque. They were dressed differently in their best clothes and although the women kept to their black some of the men wore bright colours.

We paused to watch the snake-charmer who squatted on the cobbles, his pipes in his mouth. We never failed to marvel at the sight of the snake rising from the basket as the music drew it out, fascinated it, soothed it and sent it back into its basket. On this day of Shem el Nessim we noticed the soothsayer for the first time squatting on his mat near the snake-charmer.

As we passed he cried: 'Allah be with you. Allah is great and Mohammed His Prophet.'

I said to Theodosia: 'He is asking to tell our fortunes.'

'I love having my fortune told,' said Theodosia.

'Well then, you shall. Come on. Let's see what the future holds for us.'

Two mats were set out on either side of the

soothsayer. He beckoned first to Theodosia and then to me. Rather self-consciously we sat down on the mats. I was aware of a pair of piercing hypnotic eyes fixed on my face.

'English ladies,' said the soothsayer. 'Come from over the sea.'

There was nothing very remarkable in his knowing that, I thought; but Theodosia was pink with excitement.

'You come with many people. You come here to stay . . . a week . . . a month . . . a month . . . two months . . .'

I glanced at Theodosia. That was almost certain too.

'You will know, of course,' I said, 'that we are with the party who are excavating in the valley.'

He darted a look at Theodosia and said, 'You married lady,' he said, 'you have a fine husband.' Then to me: 'You too, you married lady.'

'We both have husbands. It is hardly likely that we should be here if we had not.'

'From over seas you have come . . . back over seas you must go.' He lowered his eyes. 'I see much that is evil. You must go back . . . back across the seas . . .'

'Which one of us?' I asked.

'You both must go. I see men and women weeping . . . I see a man lying still . . . his eyes are closed . . . There is a shadow over him. I see it is the angel of death.'

Theodosia had turned pale. She started to rise.

'Sit,' commanded the soothsayer.

I said: 'Who is this man you see? Describe him.'

'A man . . . perhaps he is a woman . . . There are men and women. They are underground . . .

237

they feel their way . . . they disturb the earth and the resting-places of the dead . . . and over them is a shadow. It shifts, but it never goes, it is always there. It is the angel of death. I see it clearly now. You are there . . . and you, lady. And now it is near you . . . and now it is over you . . . and it is waiting . . . waiting the command to take whomsoever it will be ordained to take.'

Theodosia was trembling.

'Now it is clear,' went on the soothsayer. 'The sun is bright overhead. It is a white light up there but the angel of death is gone. You are on a big ship . . . you sail away . . . The angel has gone. He cannot live under the bright sun. There. I have seen two pictures. What may be is both of them. Allah is good. The choice is free.'

'Thank you,' I said, and I put coins into his bowl.

'Lady, you come again. I tell you more.'

'Perhaps,' I said. 'Come, Theodosia.'

He stretched out to take the bowl in which I had dropped the money. As his bare arm emerged from his robes I saw the sign on it. It was the head of a jackal. That was the sign of one of the gods I knew, but I could not remember which.

'The blessing of Allah fall on you,' he muttered and sat back on his mat, his eyes closed.

'It would seem,' I said to Theodosia, as we strolled back to the Palace, 'that there are many people who don't approve of our activities.'

'He knew,' she said. 'He knew who we were.'

'Of course he knew. It didn't need superhuman powers to tell that we were English. Nor to guess that we were with the party. We might even have been pointed out to him. Many people in the *souk* know us.'

'But all that talk about the angel of death . . .'

'Fortune-tellers' talk,' I said, 'to be taken with . . . no, not a grain of salt but a sip of *khosaf*.'

'It worried me, Judith.'

'I should never have allowed you to have your fortune told. You thought you were going to hear a gipsy talk about a dark man and a journey across the water, a legacy and three children who will comfort your old age.'

'I thought we might hear something interesting as he is an Egyptian. And instead . . .'

'Come in and I'll make some mint tea. Now that's a drink I do appreciate.'

The fact was that I was a little uneasy. I didn't like this talk of the angel of death any more than Theodosia did.

As Tybalt was at the site with several of the party in spite of the fact that the workmen were not at their posts, and I did not know at what time he would return, I went to bed early and was asleep almost at once. It must have been an hour or so later when I awoke. I started up in terror because I saw a shadowy shape looming up beside my bed.

'It's all right, Judith.'

'Tabitha!'

A candle which she must have brought in with her shone a faint light from the table on which she had laid it.

'Something's wrong,' I cried and my thoughts still lost in vague dreams went to the soothsayer in the

239

souk and the angel of death he had conjured up.

'It's Theodosia. She's had some ghastly nightmare. I was going up to my room when I heard her shouting. I wish you'd come in and comfort her. She seems quite distraught.'

I leaped out of bed and put on the pair of embossed leather slippers I had bought from Yasmin and wrapped a dressing-gown about me.

We went along to the room Theodosia shared with Evan. She was lying on her back staring up at the ceiling.

I went over and sat down beside the bed. Tabitha sat on the other side.

'What on earth happened, Theodosia?'

'I had an awful dream. The soothsayer was there and there was something in black robes like a great bird with a man's face. It was the angel of death and it had come for some of us.'

'It was that old fortune-teller,' I said to Tabitha. 'We shouldn't have listened to him. He was just trying to frighten us.'

'What did he say?' asked Tabitha.

'He talked a lot of nonsense about the angel of death hovering over us.'

'Hovering over whom?'

'The whole party, I imagine, waiting to pounce on which ever one he fancied. Theodosia took it all too seriously.'

'You shouldn't, Theodosia,' said Tabitha. 'They do it all the time. And I don't mind betting that he said Allah was giving you a choice.'

'That's exactly what he did say.'

'He's probably envious of someone who is working

240

for us. This often happens. When we were here last there was a man who was uttering evil prophecies all the time. We discovered that his greatest enemy was earning more working on the site than he was himself. It was pure envy.'

This seemed to comfort Theodosia. 'I shall be glad,' she said, 'when they've found what they want and we can go home.'

'These surroundings grow on you,' prophesied Tabitha. 'People often feel like that at first. I mean those who are not actually involved in the work.'

She began to talk as she used to when I visited her at Giza House and so interesting was she that Theodosia was considerably calmed. She told me how last time she had been here she had seen the celebration of Maulid-el-Nabi which was the birthday of Mohammed.

'The stalls looked so lovely in the *souks*,' she explained. 'Most of them were decorated with dolls made of white sugar and wrapped in paper which looked like dresses. There were processions through the streets and people carried banners on which were inscribed verses from the Koran. The minarets were lit up at night and it was a wonderful sight. They looked like rings of light up in the sky. There were singers in the streets singing praises to Allah and tale-tellers who were surrounded by people of all ages to whom they related stories which had been handed down through the ages.'

She went on to describe these occasions and as she talked I noticed Theodosia's eyelids dropping. Poor Theodosia, she was exhausted by her nightmare!

241

'She's asleep,' I whispered to Tabitha.

'Then let's go,' she replied.

Outside the door she paused and looked at me. 'Are you sleepy?' she asked.

'No,' I told her.

'Come to my room for a chat.'

I followed her. Her room was beautiful. There were shutters at the window, and she opened these wider to let in the warm night air. 'I look down on the courtyard,' she said. 'It's quite beautiful. Cacti grow down there and there are bitter apple trees. They are one of the most useful plants in Egypt. The seeds are used to add flavour to all sorts of dishes and if the fruit is boiled the liquid which is produced makes goatskin watertight.'

'You are very knowledgeable, Tabitha.'

'Don't forget I've been here before, and if you're vitally interested, you do pick up a great deal.'

She turned from the window and lighted a few candles.

'They will probably attract insects,' she said, 'but we need a little light. Now tell me, Judith, does all this come up to expectations?'

'In many ways, yes.'

'But not all?'

'Well, I thought I should probably have more work to do . . . helping . . .'

'It's a very skilled occupation. At the moment it is mainly workmen who are needed.'

'And if they really did find a hitherto undiscovered tomb I suppose I should not be allowed near it.'

'It would be such a find. Only the experts would be allowed to touch anything. But Tybalt was telling

242

me how well you look after his papers and that you are a great help in many ways.'

I felt suddenly resentful that Tybalt should discuss me with her, and then I was ashamed.

She seemed to sense my feelings for she said quickly: 'Tybalt does confide in me now and then. It's because I'm such a friend of the family. You are of the family now and because of this I was saying to Tybalt that you should know the truth.'

'The truth!' I cried.

'About me,' she said.

'What should I know about you?' I asked.

'What only Tybalt and his father knew in their household. When I came to live with them and took the post of companion to Sir Edward's wife, we thought it best that I should be known as a widow. But that is not the case. I have a husband, Judith.'

'But . . . where is he?'

'He is in a mental home.'

'Oh . . . I see. I'm sorry.'

'You will remember that I had a sudden call before we left.'

'When you and Tybalt came back together.'

'Yes, as I had to come back to London we met there and travelled down to Cornwall together. I had had a call because my husband had taken a sudden turn for the worse.'

'He died?' I asked.

A hopeless expression came into her eyes which were large, brooding and very beautiful in the candle-light.

'He recovered,' she said.

'It must be a great anxiety for you.'

243

'A perpetual anxiety.'

'You do not visit him often?'

'He does not know me. It is futile. It brings no pleasure to him and only great unhappiness to me. He is well cared for . . . in the best possible hands. It is all I can do.'

'I'm sorry,' I said.

She brightened. 'Well, they say we all have our crosses to bear. Mine has been a heavy one. But there are compensations. Since I came into the Travers household I have been happier than I ever dreamed of being.'

'I hope you will continue to be.'

She smiled rather sadly. 'I thought you ought to know the truth, Judith, now that you are a Travers.'

'Thank you for telling me. Was it always so . . . from the time you married him? You cannot have been married so many years. You are very young.'

'I am thirty,' she said. 'I was married at eighteen. It was a marriage arranged for me. I was without fortune. My people thought it was a great chance for me because my husband was wealthy compared with my family. Even at the time of our marriage he was a dipsomaniac . . . incurable, they said. It grew steadily worse and when he became violent he was put away. I had met Sir Edward when he lectured on archaeology to amateurs and we became friendly. Then he offered me this post in his household as companion to his wife. It was a great help to me.'

'How very tragic.'

Her eyes were fixed on me. 'But no life is all tragedy, is it? I've had days of happiness, weeks of it . . . even since. But it is one of life's rules that nothing remains on the same level or at the same depth. Change is inevitable.'

'I'm glad you told me.'

'And I knew you would be sympathetic.'

'You will stay with us?'

'As long as I am allowed to.'

'Then that will be as long as you wish.'

She came to me then and kissed me on the forehead. I was moved by the gesture; and as I drew away from her I saw the brooch at her throat. It was a scarab in lapis lazuli.

'I see you have a scarab brooch.'

'Yes, it's supposed to be a protection against evil spirits. It was given to me by . . . a friend . . . when I first came to Eygpt.'

'Which was the last expedition, wasn't it . . . the fatal one?'

She nodded.

'It wasn't very lucky on that occasion,' I said.

She did not answer but I saw her fingers were trembling as she touched the brooch.

'I suppose I should go to bed now,' I said. 'I wonder when they will come back from the site?'

'That's something of which you can't be sure. I'm glad I told you. I didn't think it was right that I should deceive you.'

I went back to my room. Tybalt was not back.

I could not sleep. I lay in bed thinking of Tabitha. Memories from the past intruded into my mind. I remembered walking over to Giza House when I was a companion to Lady Bodrean and seeing Tabitha and Tybalt at the piano together. I thought of their arriving home together after she had been called away; and

245

echoes from Nanny Tester's revelations kept coming back to me.

I wondered who had given her the scarab brooch. Was it Tybalt?

Then a horrible thought crept into my mind. Suppose Tabitha had been free, would Tybalt have married me?

A few days later Theodosia and I visited the Temple, taking a donkey-drawn carriage and rattling on our way over the sandy soil. Here had been the ancient city of Thebes, the centre of a civilization which had crumbled away leaving only the great burial chambers of long-dead Pharaohs to give an indication of the splendour of those days.

Although the Temple was open to the sky it was cooler within the shadows of those tall pillars than without. We examined with wonder the lavishly carved pillars each capped with buds and calyxes. It fascinated us both to study the carvings on the pillars and to recognize some of the Pharaohs depicted there with the gods to whom they were making sacrifices.

Wandering among the pillars we came face to face with a man. He was clearly European and I thought he was a tourist who had, like ourselves, come to inspect this renowned temple.

It was natural on such an occasion that he should speak to us and he said 'Good morning.' His eyes were a tawny colour like so much of the stone we saw in Egypt and his skin was tanned to a pale brown. He wore a panama hat pulled down over his eyes as a shield against the sun.

We were pleased because he was English.

'What a fascinating spot,' he said. 'Do you live here?'

'No. We're with a party of archaeologists working on a site in the Valley. Are you visiting?'

'In a way. I'm a merchant and my business brings me here now and then. But I am very interested to hear that you are with the archaeology party.'

'My husband is leading the expedition,' I said proudly.

'Then you must be Lady Travers.'

'I am. Do you know my husband?'

'I've heard of him, of course. He's very well known in his field.'

'And you are interested in that field?'

'Very. My business is buying and selling *objets d'art*. I'm staying at the hotel not far from the Chephro Palace.'

'It's comfortable, I hope.'

'Very adequate,' he replied. He lifted his hat. 'We may meet again.'

Then he left us and we continued our examination of the pillars.

In due course we returned to our *arabiya*. As we started away we saw the man who had spoken to us getting into his.

'He seemed very pleasant,' said Theodosia.

Next morning Theodosia did not feel well enough to get up; but by midday she was better. We sat on the terrace overlooking the Nile and talked desultorily.

After a while she said to me: 'Judith, I think I may be going to have a baby.'

I turned to her excitedly. 'Why! that's wonderful news.'

A frown puckered her brow. 'That's what people always say. But they don't have to have the babies, do they?'

'Oh, it's uncomfortable for a while but think of the reward.'

'Fancy having a baby . . . here.'

'Well, you wouldn't would you? You'd go home. Besides, if you're not sure, it must be months away.'

'Sometimes I feel we shall be here for ever.'

'Oh Theodosia, what an idea! It'll be a few months at the most.'

'But suppose they don't find this . . . whatever it is they're looking for.'

'Well, they'll have to go home. This is a very costly business. I'm sure that if they don't succeed in due course, they'll know they aren't going to and then we shall all leave.'

'But suppose . . .'

'What a worrier you are. Of course it'll be all right. And it's wonderful news. You ought to be dancing for joy.'

'Oh, you're so capable, Judith.' She began to laugh. 'It's funny, really. *I'm* Mamma's daughter and you know how she manages everyone. You'd think I'd be like her.'

'She may manage everyone, but such people don't always know how to manage their own affairs.'

'Mamma thought she did. And your mother was Lavinia, who was probably very meek. I ought to have been like you and you like me.'

'Well, never mind about that now. You'll be all right.'

'I'm frightened, Judith. It's since we've been here.

I wish we could go home. I just long to see the rain. There's no green here and I want to be among normal men and women.'

I laughed at her. 'Yasmin would think the people in the *souk* were more normal than us, I do assure you. It's a simple matter of geography. You're just a bit homesick, Theodosia.'

'How I wish Evan would lecture in the University and not do this sort of thing.'

'No doubt he will when this is over. Now, Theodosia, you've got to stop worrying. This is the most marvellous news.'

But she did continue to fret; and when it was confirmed that she was indeed pregnant, I could see that this caused her some concern.

Ramadan

It was the time of Ramadan – the months of fasting and prayer. I learned that this was the most important event in the Mohammedan world and that the date varied because of the lunar reckoning of the calendar so that it was eleven days earlier each year. Tybalt, who was always restive at such times because they interfered with the progress of the work, told me that in thirty-three years Ramadan passed through all the seasons of the year successively; but originally it must have taken place during a hot season as the word *ramada* in Arabic means 'hot'.

It began with the rising of the new moon; and until the waning of that moon no food must be eaten between dawn and sunset. Few people were exempt from the rule but babies and invalids were allowed to be fed. In the palace we tried to fall in with the rules and ate a good meal before dawn and another after sunset fortifying ourselves with *herish*, a loaf made with honey, nuts and shredded coconut which was delicious – although one quickly grew tired of it – and we drank quantities of refreshing and sustaining mint tea.

The aspect of the place changed with Ramadan. A quietness settled on the narrow streets. There were three days' holiday although the fast went on for twenty-eight and those three days were dedicated to prayer. Five times a day twenty shots were fired. This was the call to prayer; I was always filled with awe to see men and women stop whatever they were doing, bow their heads, clasp their hands and pay homage to Allah.

Ramadan meant that I saw more of Tybalt.

'One must never offend them on a religious issue,' he told me. 'But it's galling. I need these workers desperately at the moment.' He went through some papers with me and then he put an arm about me and said: 'You've been so patient, Judith, and I know it isn't quite what you expected, is it?'

'I had such absurdly romantic ideas. I imagined myself discovering the entry to a tomb, unearthing wonderful gems, discovering sarcophagi.'

'Poor Judith. I'm afraid it doesn't work out like that. Is it any compensation if I tell you that you have been of enormous help to me?'

'It's the greatest consolation.'

'Listen. Judith, I'm going to take you to the site ... tonight. I'm going to show you something rather special.'

'Then you have made a discovery! It is what you came for!'

'It's not as easy as that. What I do think is that we may be on the trail of something important. Maybe not. We could work for months following what appears to be a clue and find it leads to nothing. But that's the luck of the game. Few know of this, but I'm going to take you into the secret. We'll go down after sunset. Ramadan Moon is nearly full, so there'll be enough light; and the place will be deserted.'

'Tybalt, it's so exciting!'

He kissed me lightly. 'I love your enthusiasm. I wish

251

that your father had had you thoroughly trained so that I could have had you with me at critical moments.'

'Perhaps I can learn.'

'You're going to get a grounding tonight. You'll see.'

'I can't wait.'

'Not a word to anyone. They would think I was being indiscreet or such an uxorious husband that I was carried away by my wish to please my wife.'

I felt dizzy with happiness. When I was with him I wondered how I could ever have doubted his sincerity.

He pressed me to him and said: 'We'll slip away this evening.'

The moon was high in the sky when we left the Palace. What a beautiful night it was! The stars looked solid in the indigo velvet and no slight breeze stirred the air; it was not exactly hot but delightfully warm – a relief after the torrid heat of the days; and up in the sky instead of blazing white light which was the sun was the glory of Ramadan Moon.

I felt like a conspirator, and that my companion in stealth should be Tybalt was a great joy to me.

We took one of the boats down the river and then an *arabiya* took us to the site.

Tybalt led me past the mounds of earth over the brown hard soil to an opening in the side of the hill. He slipped his arm through mine and said, 'Tread warily . . .'

I said excitedly, 'You discovered this then, Tybalt?'

'No,' he answered, 'this tunnel was discovered by the previous expedition. My father opened this up,' He took a lantern which was hanging on the wall and lighted it. Then I could see the tunnel which was some

252

eight feet in height. I followed him and at the end of the tunnel were a few steps.

'Imagine! These steps were cut centuries ago!' I said.

'Two thousand years before the birth of Christ, to be exact. Imagine how my father felt when he discovered this tunnel and the steps. But come on and you will see.'

'How thrilled he must have been! This must have been a miraculous discovery.'

'It led, as so many miraculous discoveries have led before, to a tomb which was rifled probably three thousand years ago.'

'So your father was the first to come here after three thousand years.'

'That may well be. But he found little that was new. Give me your hand, Judith. He came through here into this chamber. Look at the walls,' said Tybalt, holding the lantern high. 'See those symbols? That is the sacred beetle — the scarab — and the man with the ram's head is Amen-Ra, the great Sun God.'

'I recognized him and I am wearing my beetle at the moment. The one you gave me. It will preserve me, won't it, in my hour of danger?'

He stopped still and looked at me. In the light from the lantern he seemed almost a stranger.

'I doubt it, Judith,' he said. Then his expression lightened and he went on: 'Perhaps *I* can do that. I dare say I would manage as well as a beetle.'

I shivered.

'Are you cold?' he asked.

'Not exactly . . . but it is cool in here.' I think I felt then as they say at home as though someone was walking over my grave.

Tybalt sensed this for he said: 'It's so awe-inspiring. We all feel that. The man who was buried here belonged to a world whose civilization had reached its zenith when in Britain men lived in caves and hunted for their food in the primeval forests.'

'I feel as though I'm entering the underworld. Who was the man who was buried here ... or was it a woman?'

'We couldn't discover. There was so little left. The mummy itself had been rifled. The robbers must have known that often valuable jewels were concealed beneath the wrappings. All that my father found here when he reached the burial chamber was the sarcophagus, the mummy, which hadn't been disturbed, and the soul house, which the thieves thought was of no value.'

'I haven't seen a soul house,' I said.

'I hope I will be able to show you one one day. It's a small model of a house usually with colonnades in white stone. It is meant to be the dwelling-house of the soul after death and it is left in the tomb, so that when the *Ka* returns to its home after its journeyings it has a comfortable place in which to live.'

'It's fascinating,' I said. 'I seem to gather fresh information every day.'

We had come to another flight of steps.

'We must be deep inside the mountainside,' I said.

'Look at this,' said Tybalt. 'It is the most elaborate chamber as yet and it is a sort of ante-room to the one in which the sarcophagus was found.'

'How grand it all is!'

'Yet the person buried here was no Pharaoh. A man of some wealth possibly, but the entrance to

254

the tomb shows us that he was not of the highest rank.'

'And this is the tomb which was excavated by your father.'

'Months of hard work, expectation and excitement ... and this is what he found. That someone had been here before. We had opened up the mountainside, found the exact spot which led to the underground tunnel, and when we found it ... Well, you can imagine our excitement, Judith. And then ... just another empty tomb!'

'Then your father died.'

'But he discovered something, Judith. I'm certain of it. That was why I came back. He wanted me to come back. I knew it. That was what he was trying to tell me. It could only mean one thing. He must have discovered that there was another tomb – the entrance to which is here somewhere.'

'If it were, wouldn't you see it?'

'It could be cunningly concealed. We could find nothing here that led beyond this. But somewhere in this tomb, I felt sure, there was a vital clue. I may have found it. Look! You see this slight unevenness in the ground. There could be something behind this wall. We are going to work on it ... keeping it as secret as we can. We may be wasting our time, but I don't think so.'

'Do you think that because your father discovered this he was murdered?'

Tybalt shook his head. 'That was a coincidence. It may have been the excitement which killed him. In any case, he died and because he had decided not to tell anyone ... not even me ... death caught up with him and there was no time.'

'It seems strange that he should die at such a moment.'

'Life is strange, Judith.' He held the lantern and looked down at me. 'How many of us know when our last moment has come?'

I felt a sudden shiver of fear run down my spine.

I said: 'What an eerie place this is.'

'What do you expect of a tomb, Judith?'

'Even you look different here.'

He put his free hand to my throat and touched it caressingly. 'Different, Judith, how different?'

'Like someone I don't know everything about.'

'But who does know everything about another person?'

'Let's go,' I said.

'You are cold.' He was standing very close to me and I could feel his warm breath on my face. 'What are you afraid of, Judith? Of the Curse of the Pharaohs, of the wrath of the gods, of *me* . . .?'

'I'm not afraid,' I lied. 'I just want to be out in the air. It's oppressive in here.'

'Judith . . .'

He stepped towards me. I couldn't understand myself. I sensed evil in this place. All my instincts were crying out for me to escape . . . Escape from what! This mystic aura of doom? From Tybalt!

I was about to speak but his hand was over my mouth.

'Listen,' he whispered.

Then I heard it distinctly in the silence of this place . . . a light footfall.

'Someone is in the tomb,' whispered Tybalt.

Tybalt released me. He stood very still, listening.

'Who is there?' he called. His voice sounded strange and hollow, eerie, unnatural.

There was no answer.

'Keep close to me,' said Tybalt. We mounted the staircase to the chamber, Tybalt holding the lantern high above his head, cautiously going step by step, resisting the impulse to hurry, which might have been dangerous, I supposed.

I followed at his heels. We went into the tunnel.

There was no one there.

As we passed through the door and stepped over the heaps of brown earth, the warm night air enveloped me with relief and a pleasure that was almost bliss.

My legs felt numb; my skin was damp and I was trembling visibly.

There was no one in sight.

Tybalt turned to me.

'Poor Judith, you look as if you've had a fright.'

'It was rather alarming.'

'Someone was in there.'

'Perhaps it was one of your fellow workers.'

'Why didn't he answer when I called?'

'He might have thought you would have been displeased with him for prowling about there at night.'

'Come on,' he said, 'we'll get the *arabiya*, and go back to the Palace.'

Everything was normal now – the river with its strange beauty and its odours, the Palace and Tybalt.

I could not understand what had come over me in the depth of that tomb. Perhaps it was the strangeness of the atmosphere, the knowledge that four thousand years or so before a dead man had been laid there;

257

perhaps there was something in the powers of these gods which could even make me afraid of Tybalt.

Afraid of Tybalt! The husband who had chosen me as his wife! But had he not chosen me rather suddenly — in fact, so unexpectedly that the aunts, who loved me dearly, had been apprehensive for me? I was a rich woman. I had to remember that. And Tabitha . . . what of Tabitha? I had seen her and Tybalt together now and then. They always seemed to be in earnest conversation. He discussed his work with her more than he did with me. I still lacked her knowledge and experience in spite of all my efforts. Tabitha had a husband . . .

There was evil in that tomb and it had planted these thoughts in my mind. Where was my usual common sense? Where was that trait in my character which had always looked for the challenge in life and been so ready to grasp it?

Idiot! I told myself. You're as foolish as Theodosia.

On the river side of the Palace was a terrace and I liked to sit there watching the life of the river go by. I would find a spot in the shade — it was getting almost unbearably hot now — and idly watch. Very often one of the servants would bring me a glass of mint tea. I would sit there, sometimes alone, sometimes joined by some member of our party. I would watch the black clad women chattering together as they washed their clothes in the water; the river seemed to be the centre of social life rather like the sales of work and the socials over which Dorcas and Alison used to preside in my youth. I would hear their excited voices and high-pitched laughter and wondered what they talked

258

of. It was exciting when the *dahabiyehs* with their sails shaped like curved oriental swords sailed by.

Ramadan Moon had waned and now it was the time of the Little Bairam. Houses had been spring-cleaned and I had seen rugs put on the flat roofs of the houses to dry in the sun; I had seen the slaughter of animals on those roof tops and I knew that this was part of the ritual; and that there would be feasting and salting of animals which were to be eaten throughout the year.

I was becoming immersed in the customs of the place and yet I could never grow used to its strangeness.

One late afternoon just as the place was awaking after the siesta Hadrian came out and sat beside me.

'It seems ages since we've had one of our little chats,' he said.

'Where have you been all the time?'

'Your husband is a hard taskmaster, Judith.'

'It's necessary with slothful disciples like you.'

'Who said I was slothful?'

'You must be or you wouldn't complain. You'd be all agog to get on as Tybalt is.'

'He's the leader, my dear Judith. His will be the kudos when the great day comes.'

'Nonsense. It will belong to you all. And when is the great day coming?'

'Ah, there's the rub. Who knows? This new venture may lead to nothing.'

'The new venture?'

'Tybalt mentioned that he had told you or I should not have spoken of it.'

'Oh yes, he showed me.'

'Well, you know that we think we have a lead.'

259

'Yes.'

'Well, who shall say? And if we do find something tremendous, that is going to bring glory to the world of archaeology but little profit to us.'

'Not still worried about money, Hadrian?'

'You can depend on my always being in that state.'

'Then you are highly extravagant.'

'I have certain vices.'

'Couldn't you curb them?'

'I will try to, Judith.'

'I'm glad of that. Hadrian, why did you become an archaeologist?'

'Because my uncle – your papa – ordained it.'

'I don't believe you have any deep feeling for it.'

'Oh, I'm interested. We can't all be fanatics ... like some people I could name.'

'Without the fanatics you wouldn't get very far.'

'Did you know by the way that we are to have a visit from the Pasha?'

'No.'

'He has sent word. A sort of edict. He will honour his Palace with his presence.'

'That will be interesting. I suppose I shall have to receive him ... or perhaps Tabitha.'

'You flatter yourselves. In this world women are of small importance. You will sit with hands folded and eyes lowered, and speak when you are spoken to – a rather difficult feat for our Judith.'

'I am not an Arab woman and I shall certainly not behave like one.'

'I didn't think you would somehow, but when you're in Rome you do as the Romans do ... and I believe that is a rule for any place you might mention.'

'When is the great man coming?'

'Very soon. I've no doubt you will be informed.'

We talked for some time about the old days at Keverall Court – he with a touch of nostalgia.

'There we were,' he said, 'a party of innocent children and now look at us.'

'You sound as though we should be ashamed of our progress!'

'You're not!' he said. 'You married the great Tybalt. From rags to riches, wasn't it, for our Judith?'

'I don't know what my aunts would say if they heard that. I can assure you I was never ragged though often well darned and now and then patched but always with such neatness as to be scarcely discernible.'

'A closely knit community,' he said. 'Sabina and the parson. Theodosia and Evan, you and Tybalt. I am the odd man out.'

'Why, you are one of the party and always will be.'

'I'm one of the unlucky ones.'

'Luck! That's not in our stars but in ourselves, so I've heard.'

'I've heard it too and I'm sure both you and Shakespeare can't be wrong. Didn't I tell you I was one who never seized my opportunities?'

'You could begin now.'

He turned to me and his eyes were very serious.

'In certain circumstances I could.' He leaned forward and patted my hand suddenly. 'Good old Judith,' he went on. 'What a bully you were! Do you bully Tybalt? I'm sure you don't. Now I'm the sort of man who needs a bully in my life.'

I was uneasy. Was this Hadrian's flippant way of

telling me that in the past he had thought that he and I would be the ones to share our lives?

'You used to complain of me enough.'

'It was a bitter-sweet sort of complaint. Promise you won't stop bullying me, Judith.'

'I'll be frank with you . . . as I always have been.'

'That's what I want,' he said.

From the minaret came the voice of the muezzin.

The women by the river stood up, heads bowed; an old squatting beggar on the roadside tottered to his feet and stood in prayer.

We silently watched.

A subtle change had crept over the Palace because the Pasha was coming. There was a growing tension in the kitchens where one heard excited voices; floors were washed with greater vigour than before; and brass was polished to look like gleaming gold. The servants lent to us by Hakim Pasha knew that the tolerant reign of the visitors was temporarily at an end.

Tybalt told me what we must expect.

'He is the governor of these parts, one might say. He owns most of the land. It is because he has lent us his Palace that we are treated so well. He has made it easy for us to get our workmen, and they will know that to work well for us is to work well for the Pasha. So they dare do no other. He was of great assistance to my father. You will see that he comes like a great potentate.'

'Shall we be able to entertain him in the manner to which he is accustomed?'

'We'll manage. After all, we are entertaining him in his own Palace and his servants will know what is expected. I remember when he came before it worked quite smoothly. That was about three weeks before my father's death.'

'How fortunate that he is interested in archaeology.'

'Oh, there is no doubt of his interest. I remember my father's taking him on a tour of the site. He was completely fascinated by everything he saw. I expect I shall do the same.'

'And what will my role be?'

'Just to behave naturally. He is a much travelled man and does not expect our customs to be the same as his. I think you will be amused by his visit. Tabitha will tell you about it. She will remember how he came here when my father was alive.'

I asked Tabitha and she told me that they had been apprehensive but they need not have been for the Pasha had been goodness itself and as eager to please them as they to please him.

Tabitha and I had been to the *souk* and as we were walking back to the Palace, passing the hotel, we saw Hadrian and Terence Gelding sitting on the terrace there drinking with the man whom Theodosia and I had met in the Temple.

Hadrian hailed us and we joined them.

'This is Mr Leopold Harding,' said Hadrian. 'Terence and I stopped here for some refreshment and as Mr Harding knew who we were, he introduced himself.'

'We have met already,' I said.

'Indeed we have,' replied Leopold Harding. 'It was in the Temple when we were sightseeing.'

'You two must be in need of refreshment,' said Terence.

263

'I could do with the inevitable glass of mint tea,'
I replied.

Tabitha agreed that after our walk it would be
welcome. We chatted while it was brought.

Mr Harding told us that he occasionally visited
Egypt on business and he was very interested in the
excavations because antiques naturally interested him
since his business was involved with them. He bought
and sold. 'It's an interesting business,' he assured us.

'It must be,' replied Hadrian, 'and you must be
very knowledgeable.'

'One has to be. It's so easy to get caught. The
other day I was offered a small head — a flat carving
in profile. At first it appeared to be of turquoise and
lapis lazuli. It was so cleverly done that only an expert
would have detected that it was not what it seemed.'

'Are you interested in archaeology?' I asked.

'Only as an amateur, Lady Travers.'

'That's all we are,' I replied. 'Don't you agree,
Tabitha? I discovered that when I came out here.'

'Mrs Grey is more than that,' said Terence.

'As for Judith,' added Hadrian lightly, 'she tries
. . . she tries very hard.'

Terence said gravely: 'Both of these ladies do
a great deal to help the party.'

'You could say that we are amateurs with professional leanings,' I added.

'Perhaps I'm in the same class,' said Leopold Harding. 'Handling objects — some of which are, mostly
wrongly, said to have come from the tombs of the
Pharaohs — arouses an enormous interest. I wonder
whether there is a chance of my being allowed to
look round the excavations.'

'There's nothing to stop you taking a drive along the valley,' Hadrian told him.

'All you would see,' added Terence, 'would be a few shacks containing tools, and men digging. A few heaps of rubble . . .'

'And Sir Tybalt has high hopes of discovering a hitherto undisturbed tomb, I believe.'

'It's what all archaeologists who come here hope,' replied Hadrian.

'Of course.'

'It's going to be a long, hard exercise,' went on Hadrian. 'I feel it in my bones that we are doomed to failure.'

'Nonsense,' retorted Terence sharply, and I added severely: 'This is not a matter of bones but of hard work.'

'They're a very reliable set of bones,' insisted Hadrian. 'And sheer hard work will not put a buried Pharaoh where there was none.'

'I don't believe Tybalt could be mistaken,' I said hotly.

'You are his doting wife,' replied Hadrian.

I wanted to stop Hadrian's talking in this manner before a stranger, so I said to change the subject: 'Have you really dealt with articles which were discovered from tombs, Mr Harding?'

'One can never really be sure,' he answered. 'You can imagine how legends attach to these things. The fact that an object may have been buried for the use of a Pharaoh three thousand years before Christ, gives it inestimable value. As a business man I don't discourage rumours.'

'So that's why you came to Egypt.'

'I travel to many places, but Egypt is a particular treasure store. You must come along to my warehouse one day. It's very small . . . little more than a shed. I rent it when I'm here so that I can store my purchases until I can get them shipped to England.'

'And how long shall you stay here?' I asked.

'I am never sure of my movements. I can be here today and gone tomorrow. If I hear of an interesting object in Cairo or Alexandria I should be off to see it. It makes life interesting, and like you I'm elated when a find comes my way. I had a disappointment a few weeks ago. It was a beautiful plaque which could have come straight from the wall of a tomb — a painted scene showing a funeral procession. The coffin was being carried on the shoulders of four bearers, preceded and followed by servants carrying items of furniture — a bed, a stool, boxes and vessels, the whole inlaid with silver and lapis. A beautiful piece but a copy of course. When I first saw it I was wild with excitement. Alas, it had been made about thirty years ago. It was beautiful but a fake.'

'How disappointing for you!' I cried and Hadrian told them the story of my finding the bronze shield.

'And that,' he finished, 'is why she is where she is today.'

'It is clearly where she enjoys being,' said Leopold Harding. 'You must do me the honour of visiting my little store-room. I haven't a great deal there but some of the pieces are interesting.'

We said we should enjoy that and with an 'au revoir' we left him sitting on the terrace of the hotel.

The Pasha had sent a message that he would dine

with us on his way to one of his palaces and he hoped, while with us, to hear something of the progress which was being made in this wonderful task to which he had given his full support.

With Tabitha and Theodosia I watched his arrival from an upper room of the Palace. It was a magnificent sight. He travelled in a carriage drawn by four beautiful white horses in which he made slow progress, preceded by a train of camels, each of which had bells about its neck so that they tinkled as they walked. Some of the camels were laden with his luggage, polished boxes set with stones and placed on cloths edged with deep gold fringe.

He dismounted at the gates of the Palace. Tybalt, with some of the senior members of the party, was there to greet him. He was then taken into the inner courtyard where he was seated on a special chair which had been brought for him. The back rest of this chair was inlaid with semi-precious stones and while it might have been a trifle uncomfortable was decidedly grand.

Several of the servants were waiting with sweet-meats, large cakes made of wheat and flour and honey fried together, and glasses of tea. Three glasses must be drunk by each – the first very sweet, the second even more so and the third with mint. All the glasses were filled to the brim and it was a breach of etiquette to spill any of the tea. I don't know what would have happened to any of the servants who did so. Fortunately on that occasion none did.

Tabitha told me what was taking place as of course we, as women, were not admitted to this ceremony.

267

But, out of respect for our European customs, we were allowed to sit at table and I was even accorded a place beside the great Pasha.

His fat hands were a-glitter with gems; and it was fortunate that the gem-studded chair was brought in for him, for it was wide and he was very plump. He was clearly delighted with his reception and rather pleased to see the women. He studied us intently, his eyes lingering on us as though he were assessing our worthiness in that field which for him would be the only one suitable for women. I think we all passed – Tabitha for her beauty, no doubt, which was undeniable by any standards, Theodosia for her femininity, and myself? I certainly hadn't Tabitha's looks or Theodosia's fragile charm, but I did possess a vitality which neither of them had, and perhaps this appealed to the Pasha, for of the three he seemed most taken with me. I suppose I was more unlike an Eastern woman than any of them and the difference amused or interested him.

He spoke tolerable English, for as a high official he had often come into contact with our countrymen.

Dinner went on for several hours. The servants knew what should be offered and they were also aware of the enormity of our Pasha's appetite. Unfortunately we were expected to eat with him. *Kebab* was followed by *kuftas*; and I believe they had never during our stay been served with such carefully prepared aromatic sauces. I noticed the expression of fear on the faces of the silent-footed servants as they proffered the food to their master. He was served first, as the guest, and I, next to him, was appalled by the large quantities which he ate. Being a woman, I was not expected to take such large portions. I was sorry for the men.

The Pasha led the conversation. He spoke glowingly of our country, our Queen, and the boon that the Suez Canal had brought to Egyptian trade.

'Think of this great achievement,' he said. 'A canal one hundred miles in length flowing through Lake Timsah and the great Bitter Lakes – from Port Said to Suez. What an undertaking. Moreover it has brought the British in force to Egypt.' His little eyes glinted slyly. 'And what could be a greater pleasure to all concerned? And what has happened since we had the Canal? People come here as never before. You British . . . what a flair for trade, eh! Your Thomas Cook with his steamers up the Nile. Chartering them from our Khedive for the purpose. What a clever man, eh! And what good for Egypt! Now he has a steamer to go between Aswan and the Second Cataract. Such good business for Egypt and we owe it to your country.'

I said that Egypt had so much to offer the discerning visitors in the remains of an ancient civilization which was one of the wonders of the world.

'And who knows what else may be discovered!' he said, his little eyes alight with joy. 'Let us hope Allah smiles on your endeavours.'

Tybalt said that he and the members of the party could never adequately express their gratitude for all the help he had given them.

'Oh, it is well that I help. It is right that I should place my house at your disposal.' He turned to me. 'My ancestors have amassed great wealth and there is a story in the family of how we began to build up our fortunes. Would you like to hear how we began?'

'I should very much like to know,' I told him.

'It will shock you. It is said that long, long ago we were tomb-robbers!'

I laughed.

'That is the story that has been handed down for hundreds of years. A thousand years ago my ancestors robbed the tombs here and so became rich men. Now we must expiate the sins of our fathers by giving all the help possible to those who would open tombs for posterity.'

'I hope one day the whole world will be as grateful to you as we of this party are,' said Tybalt.

'So I continue to placate the gods,' said the Pasha. 'And for my family sign I take the head of Anubis who embalmed the body of Osiris when his wicked brother Set murdered him. Osiris rose again and I honour his sacred embalmer, and he gives my house its sign.'

Conversation then turned to the matter which I was sure was uppermost in the Pasha's mind – the expedition.

'The good Sir Edward suffered a great tragedy,' he said. 'This gives me much unhappiness. But you, Sir Tybalt, will, I know, find what you seek.'

'It is good of you to show such sympathy. I cannot express my gratitude.'

The Pasha patted Tybalt's hand.

'You believe that you will find what you come to seek, eh?'

'It is what I am working for,' replied Tybalt.

'And you will do it, eh, with the help of your genie.' He laughed. It was an expression I had heard often since arriving in Egypt.

'I shall hope my genie will give me his assistance.'

270

'And then you will leave us, eh, and take away with you these beautiful ladies.'

He smiled at me and it was my turn to be patted by the plump ringed fingers. He bent towards me. 'Why, I could wish that you do not succeed.'

'We should have to depart in any case,' said Tybalt with a laugh.

'Then I should be tempted to find some means of keeping you here.' The Pasha was waggish. 'You think I could do it, eh?' he asked me.

'Why, yes,' I replied, 'with the help of your genie.'

There was a brief silence at the table. I guessed I had erred. However the Pasha decided to be amused and he laughed, which was the sign for everyone including the servants to join in.

Then he talked to me about my impressions of the country and asked what I thought of the Palace and if all the servants had pleased me.

We had quite an animated conversation and it was clear that although a few of my answers to the Pasha's questions might have been somewhat unconventional I had made a success.

There was some talk about the excavations in which I did not join. The Pasha having eaten a tremendous meal was nibbling a sweet rather like that which at home we called Turkish Delight. Here it was stuffed with savoury nuts and was quite delicious, or would have been if one had not eaten such a large meal.

The Pasha was to continue his journey to another of his palaces by moonlight as it was too hot to travel by day and before he left he would be taken to the site by Tybalt on a rather ceremonious inspection.

While they were preparing to leave there was a

heart-rending scream from without and hurrying into the court I saw one of the Pasha's servants writhing in agony.

I asked what had happened and heard that he had been bitten by a scorpion. We had been warned to be careful when near piles of stones, for this was where scorpions lurked and their stings were poisonous. I had seen many a chameleon and lizard basking on the hot stones and the geckos came inside the Palace, but I had not yet seen a scorpion.

The servant was surrounded by his fellows who were attending to him, but I shall never forget the terror in his face — whether for fear of the scorpion's sting or for calling attention to himself during the Pasha's visit I was not sure.

Pasha or not, I was going to see that the man had special attention, and before I had left, Alison had supplied me with many home-made remedies which were good, she insisted, for all the dangers I might encounter in a hot dry land.

There was one which was an antidote to wasps, horse-flies and the occasional adder which we found in our Cornish countryside and although I doubted that our mild remedies would work very well on the poison of a scorpion I was determined to try.

So I brought my pot of ointment and as I applied it I noticed on the sufferer's arm that he had been branded with a sign I had noticed before. He immediately grew calmer, and I was sure that he thought there was some special healing power in that jar which I believed had at one time contained Dorcas's special mint jelly.

In any case the man was so sure that he would be cured by this foreign medicine that he seemed to be:

and the dark eyes of his fellow servants regarded me with awe and wonder so that I felt like some accidental witch doctor.

The Pasha, who had come to see me deal with his servant, nodded and smiled approvingly. He thanked me personally for what I had done for his servant.

Half an hour later they left and I watched their departure with Theodosia and Tabitha as I had their arrival. The Pasha walked to the boat which was waiting to take him up-river. The boatmen had decorated it with flags and flowers which they must have gathered, such as stork-bill — a bright purple flower so called because when the petals fell and the centre of the flower was exposed it had the appearance of a stork's bill — and the flame-coloured flowers of the flamboyant tree. Many people had assembled to watch his progress and to call out their homage to him. It was clear that not only the servants of the Palace but the fellaheen of the neighbourhood lived in terror of the powerful Pasha.

Tabitha said: 'It is exactly the same pattern as when he came here before. I think he was quite pleased with his reception and he has taken a fancy to you, Judith.'

'He certainly smiled all the time,' I replied, 'but I noticed that the servants seemed just as terrified when he was smiling as when he was not. It may well be the custom to appear especially benign when you are about to be most venomous. What do we do now? May we retire or are we expected to be here to pay homage when they return from the site?'

'He'll not come back here,' said Tabitha. 'His entourage will set forth and meet him up-river. From there I believe he will go the short distance to his night's destination.'

'Then I shall go to bed,' I said. 'Placating Pashas can be an exhausting experience.'

It was not until early morning that Tybalt came in. I awoke at once.

He sat on a chair, and stretched his legs out before him.

'You must be tired,' I said.

'I suppose so, but quite wakeful.'

'That enormous meal you consumed and all that *khoshaf* I should have thought would have had a soporific effect.'

'I willed myself to remain alert. I had to make sure that all went as it should and no offence be given.'

'I hope I was adequate.'

'So much so that I thought he was going to make me an offer for you. I believe he thought you would be an admirable addition to his harem.'

'And I suppose had the offer been high enough and you could have commanded a tidy sum to be dedicated to your pursuits in the archaeological field you would have readily agreed to exchange me?'

'But of course,' he said.

I giggled.

'Actually,' I said. 'I didn't quite trust all that benignancy.'

'He was very interested in what we were doing and made a thorough examination of the site.'

'Did you show him the new discovery?'

'It was necessary to do so. There had to be some

274

explanation as to why we were working from inside those subterranean passages. It's impossible to keep these matters entirely secret. He was most interested, of course, and asked to be informed as soon as anything is revealed.'

'Do you think that will be soon, Tybalt?'

'I don't know. We have found an indication that there is something beyond the walls of one of the chambers. Because of the inevitability of robbers attempting to break into the tombs it has been known for one burial chamber to be hidden behind another – the theory being that the robbers having found one tomb would believe that was all to be discovered and fail to find the more important site behind it. And if this should prove the case, the one which was being thus protected would doubtless be a very important person indeed. I am convinced that this was what my father was aware of.' Tybalt frowned. 'There was one rather disturbing incident during the tour. You remember when I took you there we heard a footstep?'

'Yes, I do.' It came back to me clearly: the rising of goose-pimples on my flesh, the terror which had overtaken me.

'It happened again,' said Tybalt. 'I was certain that some unauthorized person or persons were somewhere there.'

'Wouldn't you have seen them?'

'They could have avoided us.'

'They might have been hiding in the deep pit over which that rather fragile wooden bridge has been put. Did the Pasha hear it?'

'He said nothing, but I fancy he was alert.'

'He might have thought it was a member of the party.'

'It was a small group of us who went into the tomb. Myself, the Pasha, Terence, Evan with the two servants without whom the Pasha never seems to stir.'

'A sort of bodyguard?' I suggested.

'I suppose so.'

'He might have felt he needed some protection from the gods since the family fortunes were built on tomb-robbing.'

'That's no doubt a legend.'

'What happened to the young man who was stung by the scorpion?'

'He seems to have made a miraculous recovery . . . thanks to you. You'll have a reputation as a sorceress if you're not careful.'

'What a success I am! The Pasha contemplates offering me a place in his harem, and I am possessed of strange powers which I keep enclosed in Dorcas's mint jelly jar. I can see I'm a wild success. I hope I find the same favour in the sight of my true wedded lord.'

'I can give you complete assurance on that point.'

'So much so that I may one day be allowed to share in your work?'

'You do, Judith.'

'Letters! Accounts! I mean the *real* work.'

'I was afraid of this,' he said. 'I knew you always imagined yourself being in the thick of everything. It can't be, Judith. Not yet.'

'I'm too much of an amateur?'

'This is delicate work. We have to go cautiously. It won't always be so. You're learning so much.'

'What of Tabitha?'

'What of her?'

'You seem often to talk of your work to *her*.'

There was an almost imperceptible silence. Then he said: 'She worked a great deal with my father.'

'So she is something more than an amateur?'

'She has had some experience.'

'Which I lack?'

'But which you will have in time.'

'Can I get it if I am not allowed to participate?'

'You will be in time. You must try to understand.'

'I'm trying, Tybalt.'

'Be patient, my dearest.'

When he used that term of endearment, which was rarely, my happiness overcame my frustration. If I was indeed his dearest I was content to wait. It was logical. Of course I could not come into this vast and intricate field and expect to take my place beside him.

'In time I can promise myself, then?'

He kissed me and echoed: 'In time.'

'How long will we be here?' I asked briskly.

'Are you tired of it already?'

'Indeed not. It grows more fascinating every day. I was thinking of Theodosia. She longs to go home.'

'She should never have come.'

'You mean Evan should have left her at home?'

'She is too timid for an expedition of this sort. In any case, if she likes to go home she can at any time.'

'And Evan?'

'Evan has his job to do here.'

'I suppose he's an indispensable member of the community.'

'He is indeed. He's a good archaeologist, really – though inclined to theorize rather than practise.'

'And you do both?'

'Of course.'

'I knew it. I admire you, Tybalt, every bit as much as Pasha Hakim admired me.'

I slept, but I doubt whether Tybalt did. I suspect he lay awake enjoying day-dreams of the glory he was going to find when he broke through into the tomb which would have been left undisturbed – until he came – for four thousand years.

In the early morning Theodosia and I went into the *souk*. The heat was becoming intense. Theodosia suffered from it very much and her desire to go home was becoming an obsession, as were her fears of bearing a child.

I did all I could to comfort her. I pointed out that people here probably went out into the fields and had their babies and then continued working straight away. I had heard such tales.

This consoled her, but I knew she would never be reconciled until we were making plans to go home.

She was torn between her desire to go home or to stay with Evan.

'Where would you go?' I asked. 'To Keverall Court and your mother?'

She grimaced. 'Well, at least there wouldn't be this frightful heat; and Sabina would be there.'

Sabina was going to have a baby too. That would be a comfort for her, of course. Sabina's reactions were quite different from Theodosia's, according to her letters, in which she rambled in the same manner

278

as she talked. It seemed that she was delighted and so was Oliver; and Dorcas and Alison were being wonders. 'They seem to know *everything* about babies — although why they should is a bit of a puzzle, except of course that they had you when you were little and it seems to me, my little Judith, that you were a unique baby. There was never one so bright, intelligent, beautiful, good, naughty (although your naughtiness was something to cluck over), all this according to your aunts of course and I don't believe a word of it!'

How this brought back Sabina and I must confess that I too felt a twinge of nostalgia for those flower-decorated banks with the ragged robin and star of Bethlehem and bluebells giving patriotic colour to the green background and here and there the mauve of wild orchids. So different of course from this hot and arid land; I missed Dorcas and Alison and I should have loved to call in at the old rectory and listen to Sabina's inconsequential chatter.

I looked up at the sky brilliantly blue through the narrow slits between two rows of houses; and the smells and sights of the market caught me and held me in that fascination which never failed.

We went past the shop where Yasmin usually sat, her head bent low over her work, but on that morning she was not there. In her place was a boy; he was bending over the leather, working laboriously.

We paused.

'Where is Yasmin today?' I asked.

He looked up and his eyes were immediately furtive. He shook his head.

'She's not ill?' I cried.

But he could not understand me.

'I dare say,' I said to Theodosia, 'she is taking a day off.'

We passed on.

I was sorry that the soothsayer was seated on the pavement.

He looked up as we passed.

'Allah be with you,' he murmured.

He looked so hopeful that I couldn't pass, particularly when I saw that the bowl in which payment was placed was empty.

I paused and threw something into the bowl and immediately realized my mistake. He was no beggar. He was a proud man who was plying his profession. I had paid, so I must have my fortune told.

So once again we sat on the mats beside him.

He shook his head and said: 'The shadow grows big, my ladies.'

'Oh yes,' I replied lightly, 'you told us about that before.'

'It flies overhead like a bat . . . a big black bat.'

'Sounds rather unpleasant,' I said. He did not understand me but this was to comfort Theodosia.

'And my lady has been blessed. My lady is fertile. Go back to the green land, lady. There you will be safe.'

Oh dear, I thought. This is the worst thing we could have done.

Theodosia rose from the mat and the soothsayer leaned towards me. His fingers like brown claws gripped my wrist.

'You great lady. You say Go and they will listen. You great fine lady. The big bat is near.'

I was looking down at his arm and there on it I

280

saw the brand again – the head of the Jackal. It was similar to that of the man who had been bitten by the scorpion.

I said to him: 'You tell me nothing but this big bat who is hovering around. Is there nothing else?'

'Allah would be good to you. He offers much. Great joy, many sons and daughters, a big fine mansion. . . . but in your green land. Not here. It is for you to say. The bat is very close now. It can be too late . . . for you . . . and for this lady.'

I put more money in the bowl and thanked him.

Theodosia was trembling. I slipped my arm through hers.

'It's a pity we listened to that nonsense,' I said. 'He says the same to everybody.'

'To everybody?'

'Yes, Tabitha has been given the bat treatment.'

'Well, she is one of us, you see. It's threatening us all.'

'Oh come, Theodosia, you're not going to tell me you believe all this. It's the sort of thing that's handed out to everybody.'

'Why should he want to frighten us away?'

'Because we're strangers here.'

'But we're strangers who have our fortunes told and buy certain things in the *souk*. They all seem very happy to see us here.'

'Oh yes, but he thinks we want to be frightened. It makes it all the more exciting.'

'Well, *I* don't want to be frightened.'

'There's no need for you to be, Theodosia. Remember that.'

281

The Feast of the Nile

Tybalt was getting excited. He was certain now that he was on the right track. Those working inside the old tomb had found indisputable evidence that there was another chamber behind the wall which they were now excavating.

We had now been several months in Egypt and it was time, he said, that we had something to show for our labours. This, he was sure, was what we had come for.

'It will be a bitter disappointment,' he said, 'if someone has already been there.'

'But if it has been hidden behind this other tomb can they have been?'

'Not unless there is another entrance, which may well be the case. There'll be another hold-up unfortunately for the Feast of the Nile which must be imminent. The trouble with all these feasts is not only that they exist but that there is no definite date for them. This of course will depend on the state of the river.'

'Why?'

'Well, because it's a sort of placating ceremony. It dates back thousands of years to when the Egyptians worshipped the river. They believed it had to be soothed and pacified so that when the river rose it didn't overflow to such an extent that whole villages were carried away. This has happened frequently and still does. Hence the ceremony.'

'Do they really think that if they perform this ceremony the river will stay within its bounds?'

'It's become a custom now, a reason for a holiday. But it was serious enough in the past. There really was a human sacrifice then. Now they throw a doll into the river – often an enormous life-size beautifully dressed doll. This represents the virgin who used to be thrown into the river in the old days.'

'Poor virgins! They did have a bad time. They were always being thrown to dragons or chained to rocks or something. It couldn't have been a lot of fun being a virgin in the old days.'

'I've no doubt you'll enjoy the ceremony but it is going to hold up work, which is the last thing I want at the moment.'

'I can't wait, Tybalt, for you to take your step into that undisturbed tomb. It will be you, won't it? How happy I shall be for you! It'll be as you wanted it. You will see the footsteps in the dust of the last person to leave the tomb before it was sealed! What a thrill for you and you deserve it! Dear Tybalt.'

He laughed at me in that tender indulgent way I knew so well.

I desperately wanted him to succeed.

We had a day's warning as to when the Feast of the Nile should take place. The waters were rising fast, which meant that the rains in the centre of Africa had been heavy that year; and it was possible to calculate the day when they would reach our neighbourhood.

From early morning the banks of the river became densely populated. There were *arabiyas* everywhere; and some people had travelled in on camels, the bells on the necks of which tinkled gaily as had those on the necks of the Pasha's beasts. Disdainfully they walked down to the river as though they knew they were the most useful animals in Egypt. Their padded feet made it possible for them to walk with equal ease over the pavements and the sand; their wool made rugs and the hooded burnous favoured by so many Arabs, leather was made from their skin and the peculiar odour which seemed to permeate the place came from their dung which was used for fuel.

The great excitement on this day was: How would the river behave? If the floods were great the banks would be under water; if the rain had been moderate, then there would be just the beautiful sight of the river's rising without the dangerous overflow.

But it was a holiday and they all loved a holiday. In the *souks* most of the shops were closed but there would be the smell of cooking food; there would be nutted Turkish Delight for sale; little flat cakes made of fried flour and honey, *herish* loaves and mutton or beef sizzling in a pan over a fire of camel dung and proffered on sticks, when the customer might dip them in the cauldron of steaming savoury sauce; there were the lemonade sellers in their red striped gowns carrying their urn and glasses; there were stalls at which it was possible to buy glasses of mint tea. The beggars had come in from far and wide – blind beggars, legless and armless beggars, the most pitiful sight to take the joy out of a day of gaiety. There they sat; they often raised their sightless eyes to heaven, their begging bowls before them, calling out for *baksheesh* and to Allah to bless those who did not pass the beggars by.

It was a colourful, bustling scene; our party viewed the scene from the highest terrace of the Palace; there we could see it without being part of it.

I sat beside Tybalt with Terence Gelding on the other side of him and Tabitha next to him; Evan was on my left with Theodosia.

Tybalt was saying that it looked as though the river was going to behave. It was to be hoped it would. If there was flooding it might mean that some of his workers would be commandeered to deal with disaster areas and that might mean delays.

Hadrian joined us. I thought he looked a little strained and wondered if he was finding the heat oppressive. Perhaps, I thought, there is a certain amount of tension. It has been so long and there is nothing decided yet. I knew how restive Tybalt was and that every day when he arose he was telling himself that this could be the day of great discovery, but every evening he came back to the Palace disappointed.

The waters of the river looked red as they came swirling by, because they had swallowed some of the rich land as they passed through it. The people shuddered as they pointed out the redness of the water. The blood colour! Was the river in a vengeful mood?

From the minaret rang out the voice of the muezzin. 'Allah is great and Mohammed His Prophet.'

There was an immediate silence as men and women stood where they were, heads bent in prayer.

We were silent on the terrace; and I wondered how many of those people were praying to Allah not to let the waters rise and flood the land. I believed then that although they prayed to Allah and

285

His Prophet Mohammed, many of them believed that the wrath of the gods must be placated and that when the symbol of a virgin was thrown into those seething waters the angry god who made the waters rise would be gratified and bid the river be calm and not wreak its vengeance on the poor people of the land.

We watched the procession wend its way to the river's edge. Banners were held aloft; there were inscriptions on them, whether from the Koran I did not know; perhaps not, I thought, as this was a ceremony which had been handed down from the years before the birth of the Prophet.

In the midst of the procession was a carriage and in this sat the life-size doll which was to represent the virgin. At the river's edge, the doll would be taken from its place and thrown into the river.

I stared at the doll. It was exactly like a young girl – a yashmak hiding the lower part of the face; about the doll's wrists were silver bracelets and she was dressed in a magnificent white robe.

As the procession passed close to us for a few seconds I saw the doll clearly. I could not believe that it was not a real girl; and there was something familiar about her too.

She was lying back in her carriage seat, her eyes closed.

The procession passed on.

'What a life-like doll,' said Hadrian.

'Why did they make the doll with eyes shut?' asked Evan.

'I suppose,' I put in, 'because she knows of her coming ordeal. It's possible that if one was going to be thrown into the river one wouldn't want to

see the crowd . . . all come to witness the spectacle.'

'But it's a *doll*,' protested Hadrian.

'It has to be as realistic as possible, I suppose,'
I said. 'It reminds me of someone. I know. Little
Yasmin, the girl who made my slippers.'

'Of course,' said Theodosia. 'That's who I was
trying to think of!'

'An acquaintance of yours?' asked Hadrian.

'A girl we buy things from in the *souk*. She's
a sweet creature and speaks a little English.'

'Of course,' said Hadrian, 'lots of people here
look alike to us. As we must to them.'

'You and Tybalt, for instance, don't look a bit
alike and Evan is quite different from either of you
and so is Terence and other people too.'

'Don't be argumentative at the crucial moment.
Look.'

We watched. The doll was lifted high and thrown
into the seething waters of the Nile.

We watched its being tossed about and finally
sinking. There was a long-drawn-out sigh. The angry
god had accepted the virgin. Now we could expect
the river to keep within its banks. There would be
no flooding of the land.

Strangely enough, there was not.

Gifts arrived at the Palace – a tribute from the
Pasha and an indication of his good will. For me
there was an ornament — I suppose it could be
made into a brooch. It was in the shape of a lotus
flower in pearls and lapis lazuli and very beautiful
to look at. Both Theodosia and Tabitha had received

similar ornaments but mine was the most elaborate.

Tybalt laughed when he saw them. 'You are obviously the favoured one,' he said. 'That's the sacred flower of Egypt and symbolizes the awakening of the soul.'

'I must write a fulsome letter of appreciation,' I replied.

Theodosia showed me hers, it was feldspar and chalcedony. 'I wish he hadn't sent it,' she said. 'I fancy there is something evil about it.'

Poor Theodosia, she was having a miserable time; she felt ill every morning, but it was the ever growing homesickness that was most alarming. Evan must have been most unhappy. He did tell me that when this expedition was over he thought he would try to remain at home. He thought the quiet University life would suit Theodosia. It seemed that she was indeed getting into a state of melancholy when an unusual gift appeared evil to her.

As we took our walk to the *souk* she explained to me that Mustapha had been horrified when he saw the ornament.

'Mustapha!' I said. 'Oh dear, they are not going to start that "Go home lady" talk again, I hope.'

'He was afraid to touch it. He said it means something about your soul waking up as it can only do when you're dead.'

'What nonsense! The fact is that those two want to go back to Giza House. So they're trying to frighten us into persuading Tybalt to go home. Really they must be half-witted to imagine we can do that.'

'Tybalt would rather see us all dead as long as he could go on looking for his tomb.'

'That's an unfair, absurd and ridiculous thing to say.'

'Is it? He drives everyone hard. He hates all the festivals and holidays. He just wants to go on and on . . . he's like a man who's sold his soul to the devil.'

'What nonsense you are talking!'

'Everybody is saying that there is nothing here. It's wasting money to stay. But Tybalt won't accept that. He's got to go on. Sir Edward died, didn't he? And before he died he knew that he had failed to find what he was looking for. Tybalt has failed too. But he won't admit it.'

'I don't know where you get your information.'

'If you weren't so besotted about him you would see it too.'

'Listen! They're following a clue inside the tomb. There's a possibility that they are going to make the greatest discovery of all time.'

'Oh, I want to go home.' She turned her pale face towards me and so touched with pity for her was I, that I ceased to be angry because of her attack on Tybalt.

'It won't be long now,' I said soothingly. 'Then you and Evan can go back to the University. You will have a dear little baby and live in peace for ever after. Try not to complain too much, Theodosia. It worries Evan. And you know you could go back to Keverall Court. Your mother would be pleased to have you.'

She shivered. 'It's the last thing I want. Imagine what it would be like! She would order everything. No, I escaped from Mamma when I married. I don't want to go back to that.'

'Well, bear up. Stop brooding and seeing evil in

everything. Enjoy the strangeness here; you must admit it's very exciting.'

'I hated that river ceremony. I couldn't get it out of my mind that it was Yasmin they were throwing into the river.'

'How could it have been? It was a doll.'

'A life-size doll!'

'Of course. Why not? They wanted it to look as human as possible. We'll go and see her now and you can tell her how the doll reminded you of her.'

We had reached the narrow streets, and wended our way through the crowds and there was the shop with the leather goods laid out on show. A man was seated in the chair usually occupied by Yasmin. We paused and he rose from his chair, seeing us as prospective customers.

I guessed that he was Yasmin's father.

'Allah be with you,' he said.

'And with you,' I replied. 'We were looking for Yasmin.'

I can only describe the look which passed across his face as terror.

'Please?' he said.

'Yasmin. She is your daughter?'

'No understand.'

'We used to talk to her almost every day. We have not seen her lately.'

He shook his head. He was trying to look puzzled but I felt sure that he understood every word we said.

'Where is she? Why is she not here any more?'

But he would only shake his head.

I took Theodosia's arm and we walked away. I was unaware of crowds, the chattering voices, the tray of unleavened bread, the sizzling meat, the colourful lemonade seller. I could only think of the doll which had been flung into the seething waters of the Nile and which had reminded us of Yasmin. And she had now disappeared.

When we returned to the Palace it was to find that letters had come for us. This was always a great occasion. I took mine to the bedchamber so that I could be quite alone to read them.

First from Dorcas and Alison. How I loved their letters! They usually took weeks to write them and there was a little added each day so that it read like a diary. I could imagine the 'letter to Judith' lying on the desk in the sitting-room and whenever anything worth recording happened either Dorcas or Alison would take up her pen.

Such weather. There's going to be a good harvest this year. We're all hoping the rain keeps off. Jack Polgrey is hiring men from as far afield as Devon for he anticipates a bumper crop.

The apples are going well and so are the pears. it's to be hoped the wasps don't get at the plums. You know full well what they are!

Sabina looks very well. She's in and out a good deal and Dorcas is helping her make the layette — though it's months off yet. My word, I never saw such a cobble. And her knitting. Dorcas unravels what she does every day and then sets it right and I say why not let Dorcas do the whole thing except that Sabina likes to feel she's preparing for the baby.

Dorcas wrote:

It seems so long since we saw you. Do you know this is the first time in our lives that we've been separated like this. We're wondering when you're coming home. We do miss you.

Old Pegger died last week. A happy release for Mrs Pegger, I think. He has been a hard husband and father although we mustn't speak ill of the dead. They had a fine funeral and Matthew's the new sexton. He dug his own father's grave and some think that's not right. They should have got someone else to do it.

Oliver is thinking of getting a curate. There's so much work, and of course in Father's day he had Oliver. He never seems to stop and it's a pleasure to see him holding the parish together.

And so on; the harvest had come in and was up to expectation. Jack Polgrey, who was an extravagant man compared with his cheeseparing father, had given a harvest dance afterwards and there had been fiddlers in the big barn. They had made corn dollies to hang in the kitchen and keep till next year to ensure as good a harvest.

It brought it all back clearly to me and I felt the desire to be there sweeping over me. After all, it was home, and I felt so far away.

There was a letter from Sabina – one of her inconsequential scrawls, mostly about the help the aunts were giving her and how she was looking forward to the baby and wasn't it odd that Theodosia should be in the same condition . . . not odd really but natural, and what about me? Surely I wasn't going to be left out. I was to tell her as soon as I was sure because the aunts were very wistful and wished I would come home and be pregnant and give them a chance of having a new baby in the family for although they were angels and treated her as though she was their niece there would never be anyone who could take the place of their Judith.

I was reading this when there was a knock on the door. Tabitha came in. She was holding a letter in her hand.

She looked at me as though she were scarcely aware of me.

'Tybalt . . .' she began.

'He's at the dig, of course.'

'I thought perhaps . . .'

'Is anything wrong, Tabitha?'

She did not answer.

I jumped up and went to her. I noticed that her hands were trembling.

'Is it bad news?'

'Bad . . . I don't know whether one would call it that. Good perhaps.'

'Do you want to talk?'

'I was hoping Tybalt . . .'

'You could go down to the site if it's all that important.'

She looked at me. 'Judith,' she said, 'it has happened . . . at last.'

'What has happened?'

'He's dead.'

'Who? . . . Oh, is it your husband? Come and sit down. You've had a shock.'

I led her to a chair.

She said: 'This is a letter from the home where they

kept him. He was very ill before we came here. You remember I went to see him. Now . . . he's dead.'

'I suppose,' I said, 'it's what they call "a happy release".'

'He could never have recovered. Oh, Judith, you don't know what this means. At last . . . I'm free.'

I said gently: 'I can understand it. Let me get you something. Perhaps a little brandy?'

'No, thank you.'

'Then I'll send for some mint tea.'

She did not answer and I rang the bell.

Mustapha appeared. I asked him to bring the tea, and in a very short time it came. We sat there sipping the refreshing beverage and she told me of the long and weary years when she had been a wife and no wife. 'It is more than ten years ago that he had to be put away, Judith,' she said. 'And now . . .' Her beautiful eyes were luminous. 'Now,' she added, 'I'm free.'

She was longing to talk to Tybalt. He was the one whom she wanted to tell. There was no opportunity for that when they came in, for Tybalt and the others had stayed late at the site and dinner was ready when they arrived, and immediately the meal was over Tybalt wanted to go back to the site. I watched Tabitha. She wanted to break the news to him when they were alone.

She was waiting for him when he came home that night. It was past midnight. I watched him come in but he did not come up to our room at once. I guessed Tabitha had waylaid him.

I waited. An hour passed and still he did not come.

I asked myself why it should take so long for her to tell him what had happened. Insidious little thoughts like niggling worms – and as obnoxious – crept in and out of my mind. I kept thinking of Nanny Tester's ominous words. She had been rambling in her mind but they *had* come back together on that occasion. I remembered seeing them at the piano. They had looked like lovers then, I had thought. No, that was my imagination. If Tybalt had been in love with Tabitha, why had he married me? Because Tabitha was not free?

And now she *was* free.

The letter from the aunts had brought them back so vividly to my mind. I seemed to see Alison standing there: 'You speak without thinking, Judith. That way a lot of harm can be done. When you're going to burst out with something, it's a good idea to stop and count ten.'

I could count ten now but that would not help. I had to watch my tongue. I must not say anything I would regret. I wondered how Tybalt would react to a jealous wife.

Why should he be with her so long? Were they celebrating her freedom?

A wild rage rose within me. He had married me because he had known that I was Sir Ralph's daughter. Had he? How could he have known? He had married me because he knew that I would inherit money. Had he known? He had married me because Tabitha was not free. *That* he knew.

I had proved nothing, yet why were these thoughts in my mind? Because his proposal had been so sudden? Because I had always known that there was some special relationship between him and Tabitha? Because he

295

was dedicated to his profession and this expedition in particular, and he had needed money to finance it?

I loved Tybalt absolutely. My life had no meaning without him; and I was unsure of him; I suspected he loved another woman who until now had been tied by a cruel marriage. And now she was free.

There was a step outside the . door. Tybalt was coming in. I closed my eyes because I could not trust myself to speak. I was afraid that I might give voice to all these suspicions which crowded into my mind. I was afraid that if I confronted him with my doubts and fears I might find them confirmed.

I lay still, feigning sleep.

He sat down in a chair and remained deep in thought. I knew he was thinking: Tabitha is free.

It must have been an hour that he sat there. And I still pretended to be asleep.

Why does everything seem different with the rising of the sun? Here it was a white blazing light in the sky which one could not look at and at home it was benign and if it could not be relied on to show itself every day it was all the more appreciated when it did. But it only had to appear and fears which had seemed overpowering by night began to evaporate.

How foolish I was! Tybalt loved me. He had made that clear. But at the same time it was possible for him to have affection for others and this he undoubtedly had for Tabitha. She had been a member of his household before I had, a friend of the family, so naturally her affairs would be of deep concern to him. Nanny Tester was feeble-minded. That was obvious. She had taken an unreasoning dislike to Tabitha, and I had built up these suspicions on that.

I could see it all clearly in daylight.

I laughed at myself. I was as bad as Theodosia.

I began to realize that I had felt uneasy ever since the Feast of the Nile. If I could see Yasmin and talk to her as we used to I would feel differently. I did not like mystery.

Theodosia was not feeling well and Tabitha offered to walk with me into the *souk*.

Naturally we talked about her news.

'It seems wrong to feel this relief, but I can't help it,' she said. 'It was no life for him in any case, Judith. He was unaware of who he was for the greater part of the time.'

'I don't think you should blame yourself for being relieved,' I assured her.

'One does, nevertheless. One wonders if there was anything one could have done.'

'What could you have done?'

'I don't know. But I was only happy when I could forget his existence . . . and that seems wrong.'

I glanced at her. But she did look different — younger and there was a shine about her beauty which made it more obvious.

We passed the shop where Yasmin used to sit. The old man was in her place. He looked up and saw me. I knew that he was about to murmur the usual 'Allah be with you!' but he changed his mind. He appeared to be intent on his work.

We went on. As we passed the soothsayer he spoke to us.

Tabitha sat down on the mat beside him.

297

'A great burden has been lifted,' he said. 'You are happy as not for a long time.'

He looked up at me and touched the mat on the other side of him.

'You are loved,' he said to Tabitha. 'You should go away, far away to the land of the rain. You should go . . . and live in great joy . . . for you are loved and the burden has dropped from your shoulders.'

Tabitha's colour had deepened.

I thought: He means Tybalt. Tybalt loves her and she loves Tybalt and she is free . . . though he is no longer so. Why didn't they wait a while? He should not have hurried into marriage for the sake of . . .

The soothsayer's eyes were on me. 'Go back, lady,' he said, 'the bat hovers over you. He hovers like the great hawk, lady. He is there waiting.'

'Thank you,' I said. 'My future is always the same. One of these days I hope I shall have a batless one.'

He did not understand; and we put our money in the bowl and walked away.

'Of course,' said Tabitha, 'he is just the same as the gipsies at home. They give the fortune they think will make the most impression.'

'Well, I am no longer impressed by these premonitions of gloom. And they quite upset Theodosia.'

'These people have a different outlook from us, you know. They rather like the fatalistic approach. They like to visualize danger which is avoided by wisdom. That is what he is giving you.'

'It's most inhospitable. He's always telling me to go home. I do wonder why when I have been quite a good customer. He'd miss that, wouldn't he, if I took this death talk seriously.'

298

'I admit that's a bit odd.'

'At least he was right about the burden dropping from your shoulders. I believe that information about us is passed on to him and he uses it in his prognostications.'

'That would not surprise me,' said Tabitha.

Evan came to me while I was sitting on the terrace late that afternoon. I always enjoyed sitting there and watching the sun set. It fascinated me how it would be there one moment and then gone and the darkness would descend almost immediately. It would make me remember nostalgically the long twilight of home when it grew darker gradually and the evening came almost reluctantly.

Evan said: 'I'm glad I found you alone, Judith. I wanted to talk to you about Theodosia.'

'How is she today?' I asked.

'She's very depressed.'

'Do you think she ought to go home?'

'I'd hate her to and yet I begin to think it might be for the best.'

'She wouldn't want to leave you. Couldn't you go with her?'

'I doubt whether Tybalt would be prepared to release me.'

'Oh . . . I see.'

'I suppose if it were imperative he would, but . . . it's hardly that. The climate doesn't agree with Theodosia and now that she is going to have a child . . .'

'I know, but we shall have left here before that happens.'

'Undoubtedly, but she doesn't seem to get any

better . . . worse, in fact. There is something about the place that has a strange effect on her.'

'Would she perhaps then go home and wait for you to come back?'

'I don't think she would want to go back to our University quarters. She could go to her mother, but you know how things are there. Lady Bodrean never really approved of our marriage. I think Theodosia wouldn't be very happy at Keverall.'

'Perhaps she could go and stay at Rainbow Cottage. The aunts would love to coddle her. Or to Sabina at the rectory.'

'That's an idea; but I know she doesn't want to leave me . . . nor do I want her to.'

'You could ask her anyway.'

'I will,' he said and he seemed a little more cheerful.

The next day I was in the courtyard when a voice whispered: 'Lady.'

I looked round and at first could see no one and then a figure slowly emerged from a bush in the corner of the courtyard. It was a young Arab whom I could not remember having seen before.

'Lady,' he said, 'you have magic in jar.'

He held out his hand, which was bleeding slightly.

'Why, certainly I'll dress it,' I said. 'But the first thing is to clean it. Come inside.'

I took him into a little room which Tabitha used a good deal and which opened on to the courtyard. Here she arranged flowers when we could get them. She had put a spirit lamp there so that it was possible to boil water. I took some from a jar which was kept on a bench and boiled it in a pan. I told the young man to sit down and went up to my room to get Dorcas's ointment.

He watched me as I bathed the wound, which was very slight; and while I was drying it he whispered: 'Lady, I come because I want to talk with you.'

I looked intently into his bright dark eyes; I could see that he was frightened.

'What do you want to say?'

'I want to speak of Yasmin. You very kind to Yasmin.'

'Where is she?'

'She is gone. I pray to Allah to bless her soul.'

'You mean she is dead?'

He nodded and a look of infinite sorrow passed over his face.

'How did she die? Why?'

'She was taken away.'

'By whom?'

He was struggling to understand me and to convey his meaning. It was difficult for him.

'I loved Yasmin,' he said.

'You work on the site?' I said. 'You work for Sir Tybalt Travers?'

He nodded.

'Very good master with very good lady. Very secret.'

I said: 'You can trust me to keep your secret. What is your name?'

'Hussein.'

'Well, Hussein, tell me what you know of Yasmin's disappearance and you can rely on me to say nothing if it is advisable not to.'

'Lady, we love. But her father says No. She is for the old man who keep many goats and sells much leather.'

301

'I see.'

'But love is too strong, Lady, and we meet. Oh, this I dare not say. We have offended the Pharaohs.'

'Oh come, Hussein, the dead Pharaohs wouldn't be offended by two lovers. I dare say they had a few love-affairs in their time.'

'Where can we meet? There is no place. But I work. I am trusted workman. I work inside the old tomb. I am one of Sir Travers's best workmen. I know when there will be workings and when there will not; and when there are not we meet there . . . in the tomb.'

'You are bold, Hussein. Few people would wish to meet in such a place.'

'It is the only place and love is strong, Lady. Nowhere else could we be safe and if her father know he would marry her at once to the man of many goats.'

'I understand, but where is Yasmin?'

'It is the night the great Pasha comes. We are to meet. Together we go to the tomb. But Sir Travers says to me, "Hussein, you are to take a message to Ali Moussa." He is a man who makes tools they use. "And you are to bring back what I ask. I will give you paper." So I must obey and then I cannot go to the tomb. Yasmin went alone . . . and it was the night of the Pasha's coming. I never saw her again.'

'But you talk of her as though she is dead.'

'She is dead. She was thrown into the river on the day of the feast.'

I drew a deep breath. 'I feared it,' I said. 'But Hussein . . . why?'

He lifted his eyes to my face. 'Please tell me,

Lady. You are wise. Why is Yasmin thrown to the crocodiles?'

'Crocodiles!' I cried.

He bowed his head. 'Sacred crocodiles. I have seen sacred crocodiles with jewels in their ears and bracelets of precious stones on their paws.' He looked over his shoulder as though he feared he would be struck dead.

'Who could have done this?' I cried. 'Who could have thrown Yasmin into the river.'

'Big men, Lady. Big strong men of power. She has offended in some way. It is because she is in the tomb, the sacred tomb. It is the Curse of the Pharaohs.'

'But Hussein, the Pharaohs couldn't have done this. Someone else has done it and there must be a reason.'

'I see not Yasmin since the day I am sent to Ali Moussa; but I think she goes to the tomb . . . alone.'

'She is a brave girl.'

'For love one is brave, Lady.'

'You think she was discovered there by someone?'

'I don't know.'

'And when she was thrown into the river she gave no sign of life. She was like a life-size doll.'

'Perhaps she is dead already, Lady. Perhaps she is drugged. I do not know. All I know is that she is dead.'

'But why do this? If anyone wanted to kill her why go to this elaborate method of disposing of her?'

'Lady, you see pictures on these walls. You have

seen the prisoners the Pharaohs bring in from their wars. Have you seen, Lady?'

'I have wondered who the people were. I have seen men tied upside down to the prows of ships on these pictures; and others without a hand or an arm or leg.'

'You have seen, Lady, what happen to those who offend the Pharaoh. They are given to the crocodile. Sometimes they take an arm, a leg . . . and the captive lives on. It shows him and others what happens to him who offends. Sometimes they are thrown to crocodiles. You understand?'

'I can't understand how Yasmin could have offended.'

'She went into the tomb, the forbidden place, Lady.'

'And what about the rest of us?'

He shivered.

'Hussein,' I said, 'are you sure the figure that was thrown into the river was Yasmin?'

'Does the lover not know his beloved?'

I said: 'I knew her but slightly but I thought I recognized her.'

'It was Yasmin, Lady. And I was in the tomb . . . though not on the night she disappeared.'

'You are afraid that they will take you, too?'

He nodded.

'I don't think so, Hussein. They would surely have done so by now. I think somebody was there on the night she went there alone and whoever that was killed her. You should say nothing to anyone of your relationship with her.'

'No, I do not. It was our secret. It is for this reason we choose such a place for our love.'

'You must be clever, Hussein. Do not speak of Yasmin! Do not show your sorrow.'

He nodded, his dark eyes on my face. I was touched and a little afraid by the obvious faith he had in me.

'This,' he pointed to his hand, 'nothing. I come to see wise lady.'

I wanted to protest at such a description but I could see that the only way I could comfort him was by allowing him to believe it fitted.

'I am glad you came to me,' I said. 'Come again if you learn anything.'

He nodded.

'I knew you wise lady,' he said. 'You have magic in jar.'

I could scarcely wait to see Tybalt alone. I wanted to tell him what the boy had told me and ask what could be done about it.

But how difficult it was to see my husband alone! I chafed against the delay. It was late afternoon when I saw him come into the Palace. He looked dejected. He went straight up to our room and I hurried after him. He was sitting in a chair, staring at the tips of his boots.

'Tybalt,' I cried. 'I have something to tell you.'

He looked up rather vaguely I thought, as though he scarcely heard what I said.

I burst out: 'Yasmin is dead.'

'Yasmin?' he repeated.

'Oh, of course you won't know her. She's a girl who made leather slippers in the *souk*. She was thrown into the river at the Feast of the Nile.'

'Oh?' he said.

'This is murder,' I said.

He looked at me in a puzzled way and I realized that he was not giving me his attention.

I cried out angrily: 'A girl has died . . . has been killed and you don't seem to care. This Yasmin was in the tomb that night when the Pasha came and . . .'

'What?' he said. I thought in exasperation: One only has to mention the tomb and he is all attention! That she had trespassed there was of more importance to him than that she had met her death.

I said: 'One of your workmen has been to see me. He is terrified, so please don't be hard on him. They had a meeting-place in the tomb and the girl has died.'

'A meeting-place in the tomb! They wouldn't dare.'

'I am sure he was not lying, but the point is the girl is dead. She was thrown into the river on the day of the Feast.'

Tybalt said: 'They throw a doll into the river nowadays.'

'This time they threw Yasmin. I thought I recognized her. So did Theodosia. And now we know. Tybalt, what are you going to do about it?'

'My dear Judith, you are getting excited about something which is no concern of yours.'

'You mean to say we look on calmly while someone is murdered?'

'This is just a tale someone has told you. Who was it?'

'He was one of the workmen. I don't want you to be hard on him. He has suffered enough. He loved Yasmin and now he has lost her.'

306

'I think you have been the victim of a hoax, Judith. Some of these people love a drama. The story-teller in the *souk* always tells stories which are supposed to be true of lovers who die for love and they make up the stories themselves.'

'I'm sure he wasn't making this up. What can we do about it?'

'Precisely nothing ... even if it's true.'

'You mean we stand by and countenance murder?'

He looked at me warily. 'We are not these people's judges. The first thing one has to learn is not to interfere. Some of their customs seem strange to us ... even barbaric ... but we come here as archaeologists and consider ourselves lucky that we are allowed to do so. One of the cardinal laws is No Interference.'

'In the ordinary way yes ... but this ...'

'It sounds absurd to me. Even in the old days when a girl was thrown into the river as part of the ceremony it had to be a virgin. It seems to me that your Yasmin was not likely to be that since she had been meeting her lover in such an extraordinary place.'

'It was someone who wanted to get rid of her.'

'There are many ways of disposing of bodies other than such an elaborately public one.'

'I think it was a warning.'

He passed his hand wearily over his forehead.

'Tybalt, I don't think you are really paying attention.'

He looked at me steadily and said: 'We have completed the excavation on which our hopes rested. And it has led us to a chamber which is a blind alley. It goes no further. It must have been put there to trick robbers. Well, *we* have been thoroughly tricked.'

'Tybalt!'

'Yes, all our work of the last months has led to this. You may say that our efforts and all the money we have put into this have been wasted.'

I wanted to comfort him; I wanted to put my arms about him and rock him as though he were a disappointed child. It was then that I realized that we were not really as close as the passion we shared had led me to believe.

He was aloof; there was nothing I could say which would not seem banal. I realized in that moment that this work was more important to him than anything else on Earth.

'So,' I said coolly, practically, for my emotions were held completely in check, 'this is the end.'

'This is the ultimate failure,' he said.

To say I was sorry seemed foolish. So I just sat silent.

He shrugged his shoulders and that terrible silence continued.

I knew that he had completely forgotten Yasmin, indeed that he had scarcely given her a thought. I knew that he was scarcely aware of me.

There was nothing in his mind but Failure.

Tragedy on the Bridge

All the next day everyone was talking about going home. It had been one of the most expensive expeditions ever made and it had led to nothing – a blind alley in an already depleted tomb!

Tybalt had made a great mistake. He had been deluded by his father's words before his death. It all came back to that. Because his father had died mysteriously – and it was mysteriously, whatever anyone said about it – Tybalt had believed he was on the verge of a great discovery. So had others. And now they had learned through bitter disillusion, the destruction of hope and the squandering of a great deal of money that they had been deluded.

Theodosia was unfeignedly delighted. The thought of going home was a tonic to her.

'Of course I'm sorry for Tybalt,' she said. 'It's a great disappointment to him. But after all it'll be wonderful to be home.'

Hadrian said: 'Well, so it's all off. We shall soon be home and our great adventure at an end. Has it cured you, Judith? You were so crazy to come out here, weren't you? And it wasn't quite what it seemed. Oh, I know our Judith. You saw yourself leading us all on to victory. Playing the mother superior to the party and finally breaking your way through and discovering the undisturbed tomb of a mighty Pharaoh. And this is the reality.'

'I have found it fascinating.'

'And you haven't minded being an archaeological widow? Some ladies object. I can assure you. And you weren't piqued to be excluded? Do you think I haven't seen you gnashing your teeth! Who wants to take second place to a lot of dead bones – mummified, of course.'

'I soon became reconciled to my position and although it has ended like this, a fact which we must all deplore, I can truthfully say it has been a wonderful experience.'

'Thus spake the good and loyal wife, bravely accepting neglect for the good of the cause.'

'I knew this was what to expect,' I said, 'and I always understood that Tybalt would have to be working most of the time.'

He came closer to me and said: 'I shouldn't have neglected you like that, Judith. And all for nothing!'

I turned on him angrily. 'A loyal supporter of your leader, I see,' I said.

He grinned at me. 'You and I were always good friends, weren't we?'

'Until this moment,' I snapped.

That turned the grin into a laugh. Then he was serious suddenly. 'Don't you believe that. We always were and always will be. If ever you needed me . . .'

'*Needed* you!'

'Yes, my dear cousin. Even the most self-sufficient of us need others at times.'

'Are you hinting something?'

He shrugged his shoulders and gave me that crooked smile of his which I had always found rather endearing. It was there in his serious moments when he was pretending to be light-hearted over something which affected him deeply.

I thought then: He *knows* something. He is warning me. What about? Tybalt!

I said sharply: 'You had better explain yourself.'

He seemed then to decide that he had gone too far. 'There's nothing to explain.'

'But you implied . . .'

'I'm just being my nonsensical self once again.'

But he had succeeded in planting seeds of uneasiness in my mind.

A few days later there was great excitement throughout the Palace. Tybalt was jubilant. He had been following a false clue for months but he had picked up another trail.

He talked to me excitedly about it.

'I have this notion that we have been working in the wrong place. There's something behind the wall which we have yet to probe.'

'What if it's another blind alley?'

'I don't think there could be two.'

'Why not?'

'Oh, for heaven's sake, Judith, why should there be?'

'I don't know, but there was this one.'

'I've got to try it,' he said. 'I won't give up until I've tried it.'

'And that means that we shall stay here for how long?'

'Who can say? But we're going to try.'

The effect on everyone was startling.

People like Terence Gelding and the senior members of the party were delighted. So was Tabitha.

311

Poor Theodosia! She was so disappointed. So was Evan, I believed, but solely on Theodosia's account. He was so kind and tender to her – a husband first, I thought, archaeologist second.

And I knew that in my secret thoughts I was making comparisons.

Theodosia was melancholy. Her hopes of getting home were dashed.

Tabitha said: 'She's upsetting Evan. Tybalt is quite concerned. He says Evan is not concentrating on his work because he is continually worrying about his wife.'

I felt resentful. Why should Tybalt talk to Tabitha about Theodosia? I suspected he talked to her about a great deal. I had come upon them more than once in earnest conversation. I remembered that scene with Hadrian and wondered whether others had noticed these things as I did.

Tabitha was always energetic in smoothing the way for Tybalt. It was she who had the idea that since Theodosia was fretting about a prolonged stay she ought to take more interest in what was going on. She thought it would be a good idea to make up a little party and go for a tour of inspection. Theodosia should be a member of it. Leopold Harding, who called now and then at the Palace and never lost an opportunity of talking to any of us when we met by chance, had asked if he might have an opportunity some time of being taken on a tour of the dig.

'Let Theodosia see for herself how interesting it is,' said Tabitha. 'I'm sure that would help her overcome her nervous fears.'

312

Tabitha spoke to Tybalt who gave his permission and then she arranged the party. To my surprise, Theodosia agreed to join it. She genuinely wished not to worry Evan and was determined to put on a bold face in spite of her fears.

Leopold Harding was very interested in what was happening at the site. Hadrian told me that he had met him once or twice and he always asked how things were going. He had been very sympathetic when we had believed the expedition had failed and had told Hadrian how pleased he was that hopes had been revived.

'He is longing to have a real look round,' said Hadrian, 'and has asked me if there is any hope of his joining this tour. He was delighted when Tybalt gave his permission. He invited me to go along to that store-house of his. Would you like to come?'

I said I would so Hadrian and I went together.

It was a small shop on the edge of the *souk*, heavily padlocked, and I gathered that some of the pieces he had there were very valuable.

The small space inside was full of the most fascinating things. Leopold Harding glowed with enthusiasm as he pointed out various objects.

'Look at this folding stool. It's carved with interlaced foliage. You see the lions' heads on the upper terminals and the claws on the lower ends. I found it here but it might well be Scandinavian. But one never knows what one is going to pick up where. This could be twelfth-century.'

Hadrian had picked up a plaque. 'Why, look at this. I could swear this was genuine.' I saw the

313

profiled figures – a Pharaoh presenting gifts to Horus.

'A lovely piece,' said Leopold Harding, 'and it would fool most people. Wouldn't you think it had been plucked from the walls of a tomb? Not so. It is old – though not old enough. Three hundred years, I'd say. You can imagine how excited I was when that came into my hands.'

Hadrian allowed Leopold Harding to take it from him very reluctantly, I thought.

'Look at this,' went on Mr Harding, picking up a box. 'It's for jewels. See the ivory inlay and the small chequered panels on the lid. This is one of my most valuable pieces.'

We admired the box and went from one object to another. He told us about the difficulties of getting the goods shipped to England and how glad he was when he was able to acquire jewellery or small pieces which he could carry himself.

He showed us some collar-necklets and earrings of lapis and turquoise cut and set in the Egyptian manner. I was fascinated by them. There was one statue which intrigued me. It was of the god Horus with his hawk-like face, and at the feet of the god was a small and beautifully carved figure of a Pharaoh. Over this small figure the hawk-god towered protectively. It seemed to take on life as I looked; it was some five feet in height but as I looked, as though hypnotized, it appeared to grow to enormous proportions. I could not take my eyes from it. There was about it a quality which made me want to escape from it and yet held me there.

When I felt a touch on my shoulder I started. It was Leopold Harding and he was smiling at me.

'Fine, is it not?' he said. 'A wonderful copy.'

'What was the original?' I asked.

'That I never saw, but it was clearly meant to decorate some long-dead Pharaoh's tomb. The sort of image which was put there to ward off tomb-robbers.' He turned to Hadrian. 'But you would know more of that than I.'

'I doubt it,' said Hadrian. 'I have never seen the inside of an undisturbed tomb.'

'That image is certainly a little chilling, don't you agree? Now I want your opinion on this alabaster ornament. The Sphinx, no less. It's rather good. Quite valuable too. It's very cleverly carved.'

We agreed and went on to examine the other interesting articles he had assembled, but I kept thinking of the stone Horus and whenever I turned to look at it, I imagined those hawk's eyes were on me menacingly.

It was certainly an interesting experience and when we left we told Leopold Harding so and thanked him warmly.

'One good turn deserves another,' he said lightly. 'Don't forget you are taking me on a tour of the site.'

The party consisted of Terence Gelding, who was in charge of it, with Hadrian and Evan to assist him, Leopold Harding, the interested guest, Tabitha, Theodosia and myself.

We went to the site in the evening when the workmen were not there.

I could never enter those subterranean passages without a thrill of excitement so I guessed how

315

Theodosia would be feeling. She was now noticeably pregnant and leaned on Evan's arm; but I was surprised how reconciled she was and she seemed almost prepared to enjoy the adventure.

This was an excellent plan and it didn't seem too much to hope that this might induce Theodosia to cast aside her terrors and begin to be what Tabitha called 'a good archaeological wife'.

Terence had one lantern and Hadrian the other – Terence leading and Hadrian taking up the rear.

Theodosia clung to her husband's arm and gingerly picked her steps.

It was cold of course after the heat outside but we had been warned by Terence to bring light coats or wraps.

Terence lifted his lantern high and pointed out wall pictures of the gods and the Pharaohs. I recognized the ram-headed Amen-Ra. Horus the Hawk, or was that Amen-Ra too, for he was both Hawk and Ram? There was Anubis the Jackal, which reminded me of the mark on the arm of the man whose wound I had dressed and also I had seen it on the soothsayer's skin.

Terence was saying: 'This was not the tomb of a very important man. These wall paintings have not been executed with the care that we have seen in some of the palaces – our own palace for one. It was evidently the last resting-place of some minor potentate, a man of wealth, though, because even a secondary tomb must have cost a great deal. It could even be that several people were buried here.'

'And made a sort of syndicate to pay for it?' asked Leopold Harding.

'Wouldn't they have been dead?' asked Theodosia and we were all delighted to hear her express interest.

'No,' said Terence. 'Long before their deaths work was started on the tomb. In the case of a Pharaoh his went on for years and only stopped at the time of his death.'

'When they were ready to use it,' added Hadrian. 'So the longer they lived the better the tomb, which seems hardly fair on the young. To be deprived of life and a fine tomb all at one stroke.'

We proceeded carefully along the narrow passageway, Terence leading. Then the passage opened into a chamber. 'This is not the burial chamber,' said Terence. 'That would be farther on. This pit you see here might have contained something which was removed when the tomb was robbed. It's hard to say. This wooden structure of a bridge was put up by us to be used when we needed to cross the pit to get into the passage just beyond. But first look at the engraving on this wall.'

He held the lantern high and Theodosia, I believe in an endeavour to show Evan that she was unafraid, started to cross that wooden structure which did service as a bridge.

We were all horrified by what happened next. The bridge crumpled; Theodosia was thrown up into the air before she fell, taking part of the bridge with her down into the pit.

There was a terrifying silence which seemed to go on and on but which could only have lasted half a second.

Then I heard Hadrian cry: 'Good God.' I saw Evan. He was scrambling down into the pit; it was not easy

317

to get down for it was a drop of some twelve feet.

Terence took charge. 'Harding, go and get a stretcher somewhere. Get a doctor, someone. Take this lantern.' He thrust it into my hands. 'I'll get down there.' And then he was scrambling down and kneeling with Evan beside the prostrate form of Theodosia.

It was like a nightmare; the gloom of the tomb; the silence all about us; the limp, unconscious Theodosia; the stricken Evan.

Everything seemed to take such a long time. Of course there were difficulties. We did improvise a stretcher but bringing Theodosia out of the pit on it was no easy matter; nor was conveying the stretcher along those passages. Terence proved himself a leader on that night and Tabitha was beside him, cool and authoritative. I did all I could to comfort Evan. He kept saying: 'It's my fault. I should never have let her come here.'

When we finally got Theodosia back to the Palace we put her to bed. Her child was born that night – dead – a five months' girl. But it was Theodosia who gave us such cause for anxiety.

She remained unconscious and Tabitha, who had some experience of nursing, stayed with her while I sat with Evan in an adjoining room trying in vain to comfort him.

I kept saying: 'It'll be all right. You've lost the child but you'll have another.'

'If she comes through this,' said Evan, 'I shall never bring her away from home again. She was terrified. You know how frightened she was. She *sensed* danger. It's my fault.'

318

I said: 'Nonsense. It's not your fault. Of course she came with you. You're her husband.'

'She wanted to go back ... and I kept her here. She was trying hard to adjust herself. Of God, why didn't I go home?'

'You couldn't,' I assured him. 'Your work was here.'

'I did speak to Tybalt. But it was impossible to release me without a lot of trouble. He would have had to find a replacement.'

Tabitha had come to the door. Evan was on his feet. She beckoned us to come in.

I looked at Theodosia's pallid face on the pillows; it was clammy with sweat and I would scarcely have recognized her.

A terrible desolation came to me. She was my sister and I knew she was going to die.

Evan knelt by the bed, the tears running down his face.

Theodosia opened her eyes.

'Evan,' she said.

'My love,' he answered, 'my dear, dear love.'

'It's all right. Evan. I ... I'm not afraid ...'

She was aware of me.

'Judith.'

'I'm here, Theodosia.'

'My ... sister.'

'Yes,' I said.

'It's right over me now, Judith ... the big black bat ...'

'Oh Theodosia ...'

'I'm not afraid, though. Evan, I'm not ...'

I heard Evan whisper: 'Oh God.'

And Tabitha's hand was on my shoulder.

319

'It's all over, Judith,' she whispered.

I stood up.

I could not believe it. Yesterday she has been so well. Only two days ago we had been in the *souk* together.

And now Theodosia was dead.

The effect of Theodosia's death was dynamic.

Had not Sir Edward died? And now another death. This was the Curse of the Pharaohs!

Mustapha and Absalam watched me with great pleading eyes. 'Go home, Lady,' said those eyes. 'Go home before the Curse strikes again.'

Tybalt was distressed. 'This has upset Tabitha,' he said. 'She can't forget that she suggested the expedition. I tell her that she did it to help Theodosia, but that doesn't comfort her.'

I had rarely seen him so affected. For Tabitha! I thought.

What was happening to me? I was growing resentful and suspicious. Now, I was telling myself, he is more concerned with the effect this is going to have on Tabitha than on Evan, whose wife Theodosia was, and on myself who was her sister.

'I have set up an inquiry immediately,' he told me. 'We have to find out how such an accident could have happened. The bridge was used frequently and had been strong enough to hold men and a certain amount of heavy equipment. Why should it have broken when a young woman attempted to cross it? There has to be a logical explanation. If we don't find one, those ridiculous rumours will start up again.'

There was, however, nothing he could do to prevent

that — particularly when it was proved impossible to discover how the bridge had broken.

The Curse had made the bridge fall apart, was the verdict of many. It was the work of the angry gods.

But why should the victim be Theodosia, who had done nothing to offend? It was her first visit to the tomb; she had wanted to go home. If the gods were angry why should they have chosen to wreak their vengeance on her?

Some of the workmen would not go into the tomb, a fact which held up operations considerably.

I was chiefly concerned with Evan, who was beside himself with grief.

He could not concentrate when one spoke to him. His eyes would fill with tears; sometimes he would talk of Theodosia and his happiness with her and the hopes they had shared for the future of their child. It was painful; it was more than that. It was unendurable, and I spoke to Tybalt about it.

I said: 'Evan will have to go home. He can't stay here.'

'We need him here,' said Tybalt.

'Not in his present state surely.'

'He's pretty useless, of course.'

I said sharply: 'He has just lost a wife and child.'

'I know that. I thought perhaps it would be good for him to immerse himself in work.'

I laughed shortly. 'I'm going to make a suggestion,' I said, 'which will horrify you. Everything here reminds him of what he has lost. He must go home at once.'

'What will he do there? He will only mourn for

his wife. Work will help him to overcome his grief.'

'Do you realize, Tybalt, how much Evan loved his wife?'

'He was devoted to her, I know.'

'I dare say you would find it difficult to understand Evan's feelings for Theodosia.'

He looked at me oddly.

'Yes,' I continued sharply, 'I know you would. But *I* understand them. At the moment he is dazed by his grief. We have to help him, Tybalt. He has lost what is most dear to him, more dear than anything you can understand. Work cannot save him. Nothing can save him. I think he must go away from here. Here there are too many memories.'

'Are there not at home?'

'Different memories. Here he keeps thinking of her as she was here . . . all her fears . . . She always wanted to go home. He is reproaching himself. He's on the verge of a breakdown. If you could have seen his face when they brought her out of the pit . . . and then at her bedside when she was dying . . .'

My voice broke; and he patted my shoulder. I looked at him and thought angrily: He is calculating who can be put in Evan's place if Evan is too distraught to continue.

I went on: 'This is not a matter of archaeology. This is a matter of human decency . . . human kindness. I have to look after Evan . . . if others won't.'

'Well, naturally we want to do what is best . . .'

'Yes, I know, the work must go on. No matter what happens, that is important. I know that. But Evan is of no use to you in his present state. I am going to write to my aunts and tell them what has happened. I shall ask them if Evan can go to Rainbow Cottage and there they will nurse him and make him want to live again.'

Tybalt did not answer and I turned from him and said: 'I shall now go and write to my aunts. No matter what you say I shall ask them to take in Evan.'

Tybalt looked at me in astonishment but he said nothing.

I sat down and wrote:

> Dear Aunts, I want you to take Evan and look after him. You will have heard about this fearful accident. Poor Evan is distracted. You know how much he loved Theodosia. I can't believe it. We grew close, particularly out here. She was my sister and we were as sisters. And Evan loved her ...

I had not been able to cry until that moment. Now the tears started to fall down my cheeks on to the paper, smudging the ink. My aunts would weep when they saw it. It was something to weep about.

Poor sad little Theodosia who was frightened of life! All the time she had feared death; and yet when she faced it her last words had been: 'I am not afraid.'

If only she had never set foot on that bridge! But then it would have been someone else. Tybalt! My heart missed a beat. What if it had been Tybalt? Since we had come to Egypt my idyllic dreams had become tinged with doubts, fears, even suspicions. I was remembering too frequently how people had reacted to the announcement of our intended marriage. Some -- including Dorcas and Alison – had suspected Tybalt's motives. It was true that I had become an heiress.

I had always felt that Tybalt withheld some part of himself. I had revealed myself entirely to him, I was sure. He knew of my sudden impulses, my enthusiasms, my faults, my virtues; I had never been able to conceal my feelings for him; my obsession had begun from the moment he had opened the door and seen me rising from the sarcophagus; but although we were now husband and wife in some respects he was a stranger to me. Did he lack human warmth, and that need for others which makes us all so vulnerable and perhaps lovable? How much did he depend on me? How much did he need me?

Why was I tormented by these doubts – I, who had always believed wholeheartedly in my ability to mould the pattern of my life? Why was I failing now when I had everything I had always longed for? The answer was: Because I did not altogether know this man to whom I had given myself completely. I suspected his feelings towards me and the motives which had led him to marry me. I believed that his work came before anything in his estimation . . . before me . . . Before Tabitha?

I had said it. I was jealous. I was unsure of his relationship with Tabitha and his reasons for marrying me. I had built up a nightmare and it was shaping into reality.

I picked up my pen and went on writing resolutely:

I think he needs special care and you could give him that. Will you take him in and care for him and teach him to live again? Sabina and Oliver will help you. Somehow I think that the calm peacefulness of Rainbow Cottage and you two with your philosophy of life can help him. Dearest Alison and dearest Dorcas, will you try?

I knew them too well not to expect an immediate response.

It came.

Evan did not protest; he expressed no surprise. He seemed like a man in a dream ... or a nightmare.

And so he left us and went to Rainbow Cottage.

Ever since the death of Theodosia, Leopold Harding seemed to have attached himself to our party. He was often seen at the site; he used to talk to workers and Hadrian invited him to dine with us. He would ask all sorts of questions and expressed his enormous fascination in the work.

He asked Tybalt if he might look round now and then, and Tybalt gave him permission. He asked intelligent questions. He had evidently read up the subject or cross-examined Hadrian. He and Hadrian were constantly together and we all saw him quite often.

Tybalt's depression had vanished. He felt now that he was on a new trail, success was imminent. He was sure that beyond the wall of the old tomb was the way into another. It had been cunningly concealed but he would find it.

The aunts wrote to me often.

We did hope you would be home before this. It seems that you have been away a very long time. Evan talks a little about it now. He is certainly better than he was on his arrival.

Sabina is very happy. Her baby will be born in a very short time. We are all very excited about it. We never mention it to Evan though. It might make him brood and be sad.

Lady Bodrean is having a memorial set up to Theodosia in the church. There was a Service for her. People are talking as they did when Sir Edward died. Oh dear, I do wish you would come home.

Lady Bodrean asked us up to Keverall Court for tea.

She mentioned you. She said it was odd how you, her companion, had now become a woman of considerable wealth. She was referring to the fact that you had all now that Theodosia was dead.

My heart began to beat fast. It was amazing but I had not thought of that clause in Sir Ralph's will until now. I had twice as much money as I had before and Keverall Court would be mine on the death of Lady Bodrean.

Money had no concern for me except that now and then I wished I had not inherited a fortune and then could have been assured that I had been married for myself.

My aunts were right. Now I was a very rich woman.

She seemed more concerned about your having that money than her daughter's death. I marvel that you were able to stay with her so long. She is not a very agreeable woman. It was very brave of you, dear. Oh, how I wish you would write and say you were coming home.

How their letters brought back the peace of the countryside, the cottage in the quiet cul-de-sac a stone's throw from the old rectory.

Tybalt had said that we must behave as though the tragedy had not taken place. It was the best way to quell the rumours. When we went out, though, people looked at us furtively. They thought we were mad to brave the Curse of the Pharaohs. How much warning did we want? How many more deaths must there be?

Tabitha said to me: 'You don't go into the *souk* much now.'

'I don't want to, Theodosia and I went so often together.'

'They will probably notice that you don't go.'

'Does it matter?'

'I think you should behave as normally as possible.'

'I don't care to go alone.'

'I'll come with you some time.'

The next day she suggested we go.

As we walked we spoke, as we always seemed to, of Theodosia.

'Don't brood, Judith,' said Tabitha. 'I have to stop myself doing that. Remember, I was the one who suggested the tour. If I hadn't . . . she would be here today.'

'Someone else would have died. The bridge was ready to collapse. And how were you to know?'

She shook her head dismally. 'All the same, I can't forget it was my idea.'

'Why should the bridge have broken!' I cried. 'You don't think someone . . .'

'Oh no, Judith!'

'Who could possibly have done such a thing?'

'It was an accident. How could it have been anything else?'

A silence fell between us. I thought: Suppose it were not an accident. Suppose someone wanted to kill Theodosia. Who would gain from her death? I was the one who had become twice as rich.

I said: 'She was my half-sister. I loved her. I bullied her, I know, but I loved her just the same. And now . . .'

Tabitha pressed my arm. 'Don't, Judith. There's nothing to be done. It's over. We must do our best to put it behind us.'

We were in the open market square. There was noise and colour everywhere. The flame-swallower was about to perform and a crowd of excited children hopped round him; the snake-charmer was sitting half asleep, his snakes in their baskets. A juggler was trying to attract a crowd. We went across the square and into that now familiar maze of streets, past the leather shop where Yasmin sat no more, past the meat on sticks and the cauldron of hot sauce . . . and there was the soothsayer.

He eyed us slyly.

'Allah be with you.'

I wanted to move on but Tabitha hesitated. He knew, of course, of Theodosia's death.

'The little lady,' he said, 'she heed not my warning.'

Tears pricked my lids. I could imagine Theodosia so clearly sitting on the mat beside him, her eyes wide with terror.

'I see it,' he said. 'It hovered. It hovers still.' His eyes were fixed on me.

'I do not wish to hear,' I said almost petulantly.

He turned from me to Tabitha.

'A burden has dropped from you,' he said. 'There is happiness now. The obstacle will go and there is the reward if you are wise enough to take it.'

I was about to put money into his bowl but he shook his head.

'No. Not this day. I do not want *baksheesh*. I take only payment for service. I say, Lady, take care.'

We walked away. I was shivering.

'He was right . . . about Theodosia.'

'He is bound to be right sometimes.'

'He is warning me now.'

'But he always warned you.'

'You are the lucky one. You, it seems, are going to get your reward when you have removed the obstacle. Or is it already removed?'

'They talk,' said Tabitha. 'It's a kind of patter. But we must not let them see that we are disturbed. That would be the very way to increase the rumours.'

But I was disturbed . . . deeply disturbed.

How I missed Theodosia! I suffered a certain remorse because when she had been alive I had never let her know how much it meant to me to have been her sister. I used to sit and brood on the terrace where we had often sat together and remember our conversations. Tabitha was no substitute for her; I was unsure of Tabitha.

I was constantly aware of that friendship between her and Tybalt. Once when Tybalt had come back from the site, I was on the terrace and he joined me there. He began to talk earnestly about the work and I listened avidly. But Tabitha joined in. She remembered so much from the previous expedition and she and Tybalt discussed this at length, so that I was shut out. I became apprehensive and resentful. I remembered the aunts' concern about my marriage, Mr Pegger's prophecy, Nanny Tester's suspicions.

I was being unfair. Previously I would have believed nothing but good of Tybalt. He meant everything to me, but I was unsure of him. I had grown jealous and suspicious. I had begun to see Tybalt as a man who could be utterly ruthless in the interests of his work. And would that ruthlessness be only for his work?

Tybalt was becoming a stranger to me.

As I sat on the terrace one day Leopold Harding joined me. He had almost become a member of the party. His enormous interest appealed to Tybalt who was always ready to help amateurs. He now even dined occasionally at the Palace and he used to come to the site and watch the men at work.

He sat down beside me and heaved a sigh.

'What a sight,' he said. 'There's always so much to see on the river. Imagine what it must have been like three thousand years ago!'

'The royal barges,' I said. 'All those wonderful

decorations of people doing strange things ... like carrying stones to build the Pyramids or offering libations to the gods.'

'Why are the figures always in profile?'

'Because they had such handsome ones, I suppose.'

'Is your husband happy with his progress?'

'Each morning he is full of hope. "This will be the day," he feels sure. But so far it has not been, of course.'

'It was so sad about Mrs Callum.'

I nodded.

'So young, just beginning life, you might say, and then that terrible accident. The people at the hotel talk of it constantly.'

'I know they do. They talk of it everywhere.'

'They believe it is the Curse of the Kings.'

'That's absurd.' I was talking as Tybalt would have talked. He was so anxious that these rumours should not be encouraged. 'If it were a curse ... which is absurd anyway ... why let it descend on Theodosia, who was the most inoffensive member of the party?'

'She was a member of the party though.'

'Hardly that. She was the wife of one of them, that's all.'

'But there is a lot of talk. The general opinion seems to be that this expedition, like the previous one, is unlucky ... and it's unlucky because the gods or the old Pharaohs are angry.'

'Well, of course, there will be this talk.'

'I had a letter from England. Theodosia's death was given some prominence in the newspapers. "Another death", it said, and the Curse was mentioned.'

'Another! I see they are referring to Sir Edward's

331

death. People love this sort of mystery. They believe it because they want to.'

'I dare say you are right,' he said. 'I have to go soon. I have sent most of my purchases to England now and very little remains to be done. But it has all been so fascinating. Do you think your husband objects to my prowling round the site?'

'He would say so if he did. He is pleased when people show interest. As long as they don't get in the way.'

'I shall be very careful to avoid doing that. I realize how very knowledgeable you are.'

'When one is with professionals one realizes how little one really does know. Before I married I read a great deal and Evan Callum was at one time our tutor . . . that was for Hadrian, Theodosia and me. You know the relationship, of course.'

'Well, I did hear. You and Mrs Callum were half-sisters, I believe.'

'Yes, and Hadrian a cousin.'

'All childhood friends. You must feel Mrs Callum's loss sorely.'

'I do. And I know Hadrian does.'

'I gather he is very fond of you both . . . in particular you.'

'Oh, Hadrian and I were always good friends.'

'So you studied archaeology in your youth.'

'It was all very amateurish, but I was always particularly interested in the tombs.'

'A fascinating subject.'

'The idea of embalming the bodies is so macabre and clever. No people do it as they did. They perfected the art. I remember reading about it in my rectory bedroom – I was brought up in the rectory – and sitting up in bed shivering.'

'Imagining yourself incarcerated in a tomb?'

'Of course. They didn't do much after the year 500 AD. I wonder why? A gruesome process . . . removing the organs and filling the shell of the body with cassia, myrrh and other sweet-smelling herbs. Then they used to soak it in some sort of soda for about three months before wrapping it in fine linen and smearing it with a sticky substance.'

'It was certainly thrilling to see the inside of a tomb on that fatal night . . . until the accident. What do you think happened about the bridge?'

'It must have been faulty.'

'Do you think someone tampered with it?'

'Who should . . . and for what purpose?'

'To kill someone?'

'Theodosia! Why? What had she done?'

'Perhaps to kill a member of the party?'

'It certainly might have been any one of us.'

'Exactly. So it seems as though it didn't matter which one . . . as long as it was someone.'

'You meant that someone just wanted one of us to die as a sort of warning?'

'It could, of course, have been an accident merely – if it had been anyone else. Mrs Callum's condition helped to make it a fatal one perhaps. You would be far more aware of these things than I. I consider it a great privilege to be allowed these little peeps at what is going on. I shall never forget this visit to Egypt.'

'I don't think anyone who is here will ever forget this expedition. It was the same with the previous one when Sir Edward died. That finished it because he was the leader and they could scarcely have gone on without him.'

'What did he discover?'

'Precisely nothing. But Tybalt believes that he would have, had he gone on. Tybalt was going on where he left off.'

'Well, it's been a great privilege. I have to get back to the hotel so I must leave you. I've enjoyed our talk.'

I watched him walk away. I went into the Palace for the sun was beginning to get hot. I remembered then that I had left Dorcas's pot of ointment in the little room which led off from the courtyard. As I came into it, I heard voices and paused.

Tabitha was speaking. 'Oh yes, it's a great relief to be free. If only it happened before ... and now, Tybalt, it's too late ... too late. ...'

I stood absolutely still. There was a singing in my ears; the courtyard seemed to recede and I felt faint.

Too late! I knew too well what that meant.

I had suspected for some time ... perhaps I had always suspected; but now I knew.

I turned and ran to my room.

I lay on the bed. Tybalt had gone back to the site. I was glad. I did not want to see him ... not yet ... not until I had decided what I must do.

I remembered so many incidents. The manner in which he had looked at her when she sat at the piano; the warning words of Nanny Tester; the time when she had gone up to see her husband and Tybalt had discovered that he must be away at the same time. And she

334

was beautiful and poised and experienced. Compared with her I was plain and clumsy; and I was not patient as she was. I was angry and passionate because he cared more for his work than for me.

She understood perfectly. She was the one he loved; the one whom he would have married had he been free.

But even so, why should he marry me? Why should he not wait for her?

His proposal had been sudden. I had been completely taken by surprise. He had asked me because he knew that I had inherited money from Sir Ralph. It was all becoming very clear . . . too clear for comfort.

And here she was close to him. I wondered how often when I believed him to be working on the site he was with Tabitha. I pictured them together; I seemed to delight in torturing myself. I couldn't bear these imaginings and yet I could not stop myself from creating them.

I felt young and inexperienced. I did not know what I could do.

Of whom could I ask advice? I could not confide in Theodosia now. As if I ever could have! What would she have known of my problem – she with her innocence and her inexperience of life and her doting Evan who had loved her faithfully and would have done so to the end of her days. Dorcas and Alison knew nothing of relationships like this; and they would nod their heads and say, 'I told you so. We never liked him. We felt something was *wrong*.' That would not do. Sabina? I could hear her voice coming to me over space. 'Of course Tybalt is wonderful. There is no one

like him. You ought to be glad he married you . . .
because he did do that. But of course you don't know
enough and Tabitha does and she is beautiful . . . and
she was always in the house . . . really like his wife
. . . only she had that husband and he couldn't marry
her because of him. At least you are Tybalt's wife and
Lady Travers, aren't you? So I suppose that ought to
be enough . . . After all he's not like other people, is
he . . .?'

How foolish to let my mind run on with these
imaginary conversations. But I could not stop myself.
In whom could I confide?

I wanted to talk to someone. I wanted to say:
What can I do?

I thought of Hadrian. We were fond of each other
in a cousinly way although he had hinted at stronger
feelings on his part. Did he really mean that? I believed
he did. He bantered about it, but it was Hadrian's way
to banter. We had always been allies; we had protected
each other when we were children – I protecting him
more than he did me, because I seemed to be able to
do it better than he could, and he, being a boy, was
more often blamed. Dear, uncomplicated Hadrian!

Yet I could not tell even him of my fears, because
I could not bear to discuss Tybalt. It was bad enough
that I, in my private thoughts, could build up such
a monstrous fabrication. He had asked me to marry
him suddenly; I was an heiress and now Theodosia's
death had made me a very rich woman. Theodosia's
death! Oh no, I would not accept such absurdly wicked
thoughts. Anyone might have stepped on to the bridge.
Yet it *had* been Theodosia and her death had made
Tybalt's wife a very rich woman. Tybalt needed money

336

for his work. Was this why he had married a rich wife? If Tabitha had been free . . . But her release had come too late. 'Too late . . .' I could hear her voice with that note of sadness in it . . . that deep and bitter regret.

I stood between them. If I were not here Tybalt and Tabitha could marry, and who would inherit a rich wife's fortune but her widower!

My imaginings were becoming fantastic.

Premonition

I don't know whether I imagined it but from that time I began to feel that I was often followed. I was nervous. I was afraid to be by myself in a lonely part of the Palace; footsteps began to sound stealthy, and in the silence I would find myself looking over my shoulder furtively. This was unlike me. I had been the one to laugh at the stories of the big black bat. I had teased Theodosia but now it seemed that I had inherited her fears as well as her money.

Yet I had an irresistible urge to come face to face with my fears. I wanted to know because at the back of my mind was the thought: It is Tybalt. He wants to be rid of me. And on the heels of that thought was another: That's a lie. He cares more for his profession than for you, which is natural since he loves another woman. But he would never harm you. You know that.

But I was not sure which side of the question was the true one and because it was imperative to my peace of mind, to my future happiness, to find out, I could not resist the temptation to frighten myself.

It was in this mood that alone I took an *arabiya* to the Temple. I left my driver and told him to wait for me.

As I entered the Temple I was aware of the stillness all about me. I was the only person, it seemed, who

338

had come here today. I stood among the tall pillars and remembered the day when Theodosia and I had come here together.

I tried to give my entire attention to the carvings which depicted the history of Egypt; I was not really concentrating though; I kept listening for the sound of footsteps; for the sudden swish of robes; I don't know what it was but I had a strange sensation that I was not here alone and that something evil was close to me.

I studied the elaborate carving on the pillar. There was King Seti with his son who was to become Rameses the Great. And on another carving was Queen Hatshepsut.

I was sure someone was close to me . . . watching me. I fancied I heard the sound of deep breathing. He had only to stretch out a hand and catch me.

I felt my heart thundering. I must get out of this maze of pillars; I would get right out into the open. With all speed I must make my way to my *arabiya* and tell my driver to take me back to the Palace.

Thank God the *arabiya* and the driver would be waiting. If I did not return they would know that I was missing. But would they?

The pillars of the ancient ruined temple were close together like trees in a forest. Someone could be standing behind one of them, close to me, yet I would not see him if he were using one as a shield. At any moment murderous hands could seize me. I could be buried here in the sand. And the driver of my *arabiya*? A little money exchanging hands. Not a word to be said about the lady he had brought out to the Temple. It would be very simple. If a girl could disappear from a shop in the *souk* and be thrown into the river in place of a doll, surely I could be disposed of. But I was the wife of the leader of the expedition. There would have to be some explanation which could be fabricated ... He had been ready enough to accept the fact that Yasmin had been murdered and regard it as of little importance. But this would be his wife. A wife of whom he wished to rid himself?

That was the thought which had been in my mind; and here in this sinister and ancient Temple I could come face to face with my real fears. Perhaps I could also come face to face with a murderer.

Yes. Someone *was* close. A shadow had fallen across my vision ... a tall shadow. Someone was stalking me. The pillars protected him from my view, but suddenly he would catch me; his hands would be about my throat and I would look up into his face. Tybalt's face? No, no. That was going too far, that was being absurdly wild. It was someone who was trying to stage another accident. Someone who wanted us to go from here ... Someone who had tampered with the bridge ... who had killed Theodosia and now it would be so much more effective to kill the wife of the leader.

I stood very still, trying to calm myself. I was being dramatic, stupid, letting my imagination run away with me. Hadn't Dorcas and Alison said I used to do that and that I would have to stop it?

There was one thing of which I was certain. I was afraid.

I started to run; I touched the pillars as I passed.

I emerged from the shadow of the pillars into the open. The sun hit me like a blow. It sent little chinks of brilliant white light through the weave of my chip straw hat.

I had almost fallen into the arms of Leopold Harding, who was coming towards me.

'Why, Lady Travers, what's wrong?'

'Oh . . . nothing. I didn't see you.'

'I saw you come rushing out of the Temple. I was just about to go in.'

'Oh,' I said, 'I'm glad you came . . .' I was thinking: Perhaps *he*, that anonymous murderer, heard your *arabiya* arrive, perhaps that was why he allowed me to escape. I added quickly: 'It's worth a second visit.'

'A wonderful old place. Are you sure you are all right?'

'I think I was a little overcome by the heat.'

'You shouldn't rush about, you know. Would you like to take a walk round with me?'

'Thank you, but I think I'll go back to the Palace. My *arabiya* is waiting for me.'

'I shall not allow you to go back alone,' he said.

I was glad of his company. It helped to dispel my absurd fears. He talked about practical matters such as how he had succeeded in making his arrangements for the despatching of his goods.

'It has been a very successful trip,' he said. 'It is not always so. Of course one buys a lot of stuff which we call "run-of-the-mill". One makes a small profit and this makes these transactions worth while. But occasionally there are the real finds.'

'Have you any this time?'

'I think so . . . yes, I think so. But one is never sure, and however fine the piece one has to find the buyer for it. That's business. Here is the Palace. Are you all right, Lady Travers?'

'Perfectly, thank you. It was the heat, I think.'

'Very trying and exhausting. I'm glad I was there.'

'Thank you for your kindness.'

'It was a pleasure.'

I went to my room and lay on the bed. The fear still hung over me.

Had I been right? Was it a premonition which had set my skin pricking and the goose-pimples rising? Had I really been in danger? Was, as the soothsayer would have said, the big black bat hovering over me? Or was I imagining this, because I had discovered that my husband loved another woman and wanted to be rid of me?

I must have been there for ten minutes when there was a knock on my door. I sat up hurriedly while the door opened slowly, stealthily. A pair of dark eyes were watching me.

'Lady would like mint tea? Lady very tired.'

Mustapha was regarding me pityingly.

I thanked him. He stood for a few moments and then he bowed and left me.

The intense heat of the day was over. I put on my shady straw hat and went out. People were rising from their beds where they had slept behind shutters which kept out the sun. The market square was getting noisy. I heard the weird music of the snake-charmer's pipes. I saw the snake beginning to rise from its basket for the benefit of the little crowd who had assembled to watch.

I paused by the story-teller – cross-legged on his

mat, his dark hypnotic eyes dreamy. The faces of his listeners were rapt and attentive; but as I approachd they seemed aware of me. In my cotton blouse, my linen skirt and my big straw hat I was alien. The story-teller even paused in his narrative.

He said in English for my benefit: 'And where she had died there grew a fair tree and its flowers were the colour of her blood.'

I dropped some coins into the bowl as an expression of my appreciation.

'Allah be with you,' he murmured; and the people drew back for me to pass.

I went on into the *souk*. The soothsayer saw me and dropped his eyes to stare down at the mat on which he sat.

On through the narrow streets I went, past the open shops with their now familiar smells; and I was aware of eyes that watched me, furtively almost. I belonged to those who had twice felt the wrath of the dead. I was one of the damned.

I went back to the Palace.

During the last few days I had neglected the paper-work I did for Tybalt. I did not want him to know that anything was wrong so I decided that everything must be in order as it had been in the past.

There were papers in his bureau which he had left for me to put away. They were notes of the day's progress – each dated; and I had filed them in a sort of briefcase in perfect order so that he could refer to them and find what he wanted without a moment's delay. He had told me that this particular case, which was a very fine sealskin, had belonged to his father. It was lined with black corded silk.

I had noticed some time before that the stitching of the lining had come apart and I had made up my mind that at some time I should mend it. I decided that I would do it now.

I took out needle and thread, emptied the case of its papers and set to work, but as I thrust my hand inside the lining I realized that there was something there.

At first I thought it was a sort of packing but as it was crumpled I drew it out and to my surprise saw that it was a sheet of paper with writing on it. It was creased and as I smoothed it out, certain words caught my eye. It was part of a letter and it was signed Ralph.

. . . an expensive project even for you. Yes, I'll subscribe. I wish I could come with you. I would but for this heart of mine. You wouldn't want an invalid on your hands, and the climate would just about finish me. Come round tomorrow. I want to talk to you about that plan of ours. It's something I've set my heart on. Your son and my daughter. He's getting so like you that I could sometimes believe it is you sitting there talking about what you're going to do. Now I'm leaving a tidy sum to your cause on condition that your son marries my daughter. Those are the terms. No marriage, no money. I've set my heart on this. I've had the lawyers work on it so that on the day my daughter marries your son the money goes to your cause. Tell the boy what depends on it. A daughter of mine and a son of yours! My dear fellow, your brains and my vitality! What a combination we'll have for the grandchildren. See you tomorrow, Ralph B.

I stared at the letter. The words seemed to dance

a mad dance like the dervishes in the market place.

'A daughter of mine and a son of yours.' He had meant Theodosia at the time. Tybalt knew the terms of the will. And of course when Sir Ralph had become so taken with me and Theodosia had wished to marry Evan, he had offered me as the bride. It was for this reason that he had sent for Tybalt. He would have explained to him. 'Judith is my daughter. The will stands if you take her.' And Sir Ralph who had loved me had known that I wanted Tybalt. He had given Tybalt to me even though Tybalt had had to be bribed to take me.

It was all becoming clear . . . heartbreakingly clear.

Theodosia had married for love. Poor Theodosia, who had enjoyed married bliss so briefly! And I had married Tybalt and the settlement had been made.

And now that the money was safe in the coffers of the 'Profession', Tabitha was free.

Tabitha had always been a strange woman, full of secrets. And Tybalt . . . what did I know of Tybalt?

I had loved him for years. Yes, as a symbol. I had loved him from the moment I saw him in my foolish, impetuous way. I loved him no less now. But I had had to learn that he was ruthless where his profession was concerned. And where his marriage was concerned too?

What had come over me?

I went to the window and opened the shutters. I could look out beyond the terrace to the river. White-robed men; black-robed women; a train of camels coming into the town; a shepherd leading three sheep, carrying a crook, looking like a picture I had seen in Dorcas's Bible. The river dazzling in the bright sunshine; up in the sky a white blazing light on which none dared gaze; the hot air filling the room.

Then from the minaret the muezzin's cry. The sudden cessation of movement and noise as though everyone and everything down there had been turned to stone.

It is this place, I thought. This land of mystery. Here anything could happen. And I longed then for the green fields of home, the golden gorse, the soft caressing south-west wind; the gentle rain. I wanted to throw myself into the arms of Dorcas and Alison and ask for comfort.

I felt alone here, unprotected; and an ominous shadow was creeping closer.

I was passionate in my emotion. Hadn't Dorcas always said I was too impulsive? 'You jump to conclusions,' I could hear Alison's voice. 'You imagine some dramatic situation and then try to make everything fit it. You should stop that.'

Alison was right.

'Look at it squarely . . .' Alison again. 'Look it right in the face. See the worst . . . as it really is, not as you're trying to make it, and then see what is best to do.'

Well, I am jealous, I said. I love Tybalt with a mad possessiveness. I want him all to myself. I do not want to share him even with his profession. I have tried to be proficient in that profession. Ever since I was a child and loved him I have been interested. But I am an amateur and I can't expect to be taken into the confidence of these people who are at the head of their profession. I am jealous because he is at the site more than with me.

346

That was logical and reasonable. But I was forgetting something.

I had heard Tabitha's voice: 'It's too late, Tybalt, too late.'

And I had read Sir Ralph's letter to Sir Edward. A bribe to marry his daughter. A quarter of a million pounds for the cause if he did so.

The money had been passed over. It was safe in the hands of people who would use it to further the cause. And now Tabitha was free. I had served my purpose.

Oh no. I was being ridiculous. Many people married for money; loving one woman, they married another.

But they did not murder.

There. I had faced it. Could I really suspect Tybalt and Tabitha of such a criminal deed? Of course I could not. Tabitha had been so kind to me. I remembered how sorry she had been because I had had to work for the disagreeable Lady Bodrean; she had lent me books; she had helped me improve my knowledge. How could I suspect her? And Tybalt? I thought of our marriage, our love, our passion. He could not have feigned that, could he? True, he had never been so eager, so fervent, so completely in love as I and I had accepted that as a difference in our natures.

But was it so?

What did I know of Tabitha? What did I know of Tybalt?

And here I was, with evil thoughts chasing themselves round and round in my head. I had inherited Theodosia's fear. I knew how she had felt when she had listened to the soothsayer. I understood the terror that had gripped her.

347

We had come to a strange land. A land of mystery, of strange beliefs, where the gods seemed to live on wreaking their vengeance, offering their rewards. That which would have seemed ridiculous at home was plausible here.

Theodosia's premonitions of disaster had proved to have substance. What of mine?

I could not stay in my room. I would go and sit on the balcony.

On the way down I met Tabitha, going up to her room.

'Oh hello, Judith,' she said, 'where have you been? I was looking for you.'

'I took a little walk in the market and then came back. It was so hot.'

'I must just have missed you. I was out there too. What do you think the soothsayer told me this time: "You will have your bridegroom," he said. "It will not be long now." So you see I'm fortunate.'

'No black bat for you then?'

'No, a husband, no less.'

'Should I congratulate you ... both. Who is the bridegroom to be?'

Tabitha laughed; she lowered her eyes; then she said: 'It is a little premature to say. No one has asked me. Perhaps that's to come.'

She was smiling secretly as she passed on upstairs.

I had begun to shiver as I had in the Temple. I went out into the hot air but I felt cold and could not stop the shivering.

I did not tell Tybalt about the letter. I hid it in a little box of embossed leather which I had bought

348

from Yasmin some time before. I had mended the case and filed the letters in order.

Leopold Harding came to say goodbye. He said he had already stayed longer than he had intended to.

'Meeting you all and talking to you made it so fascinating. Even now I find it hard to tear myself away.'

Tybalt told him that he must visit us in England.

'I shall take you up on that,' was the reply.

There was to be a conference which would be held at the hotel. I gathered that the funds which had been set aside for this expedition were getting low and it had to be decided whether work could be continued.

Tybalt was anxious. He was afraid it would be voted to discontinue, something which he could not accept.

'To stop now . . . at this stage would be the utmost folly,' he said. 'It was what happened to my father. There has been a fatal accident but that could have happened anywhere. It's these absurd rumours.'

He went off with Terence, Hadrian and other members of the party to the hotel. The Palace seemed very quiet without them.

It was during the morning that one of the servants came to tell me that a worker from the site had come to see me. He had hurt himself and wanted me to dress his wound with my now famous salve.

When I went down to the courtyard I found the young man whose wound I had dressed before and whom I knew as Yasmin's lover.

'Lady,' he said, and held out his hand. It was

grazed and bleeding a little. I told him to come in and I would boil some water and wash it before anointing it with my salve and bandaging it.

I knew that the hand was not badly hurt; and had perhaps been grazed purposely. He had something important to tell me.

'Yasmin will never come back,' he said. 'Yasmin is dead. Yasmin was thrown into the river.'

'Yes, I know that now.'

'But, Lady, you do not know why.'

'Tell me.'

'Yasmin was found in the tomb. I was not with her that day, or I would be dead. Because she was found where she should not be she was taken away and killed. I know because I have confession from the man who did it. He dared do nothing else. It was the order. And then there came another order. There must be an accident. There must be a warning because it is important to some . . . that you go away.'

'I see,' I said. 'And who gave these orders?'

The boy began to tremble visibly. He looked over his shoulder.

'You may tell me,' I said. 'Your secret would be safe with me.'

'I dare not tell,' he said. 'It would be death.'

'Who should know you told?'

'His servants are everywhere.'

'Everywhere. Not here.'

'Yes, Lady, here . . . in this house. You see their mark . . .'

'The Jackal?'

'It is the sign of Anubis — the first embalmer.'

I said: 'The Pasha?'

350

The boy looked so frightened that I knew I was right.

'So,' I said, 'he gave orders that Yasmin should be killed; and then that one of us should have an accident which could be fatal on the bridge. One of his servants could easily have tampered with the bridge. But why should he?'

'He want you away, Lady. He want you leave it all. He fears . . .'

But he would not go on.

'So Yasmin died,' I said, 'and my sister died.'

'Your sister, Lady. She your sister?'

I nodded.

He was horrified. I think more by the fact that he had betrayed this information to me than by the death of Theodosia, and that she should turn out to be my sister might mean that I would want to take a personal vengeance.

He said suddenly: 'Yasmin, she wait for me in a secret place . . .'

'A secret place?' I said quickly.

'Inside the tomb. There is a small opening not far from the bridge. We have not worked in that small opening so I thought that is our spot. That was where she would have been waiting for me. That was where we lay together.'

I tied the bandage and he said: 'I tell you, Lady, because you good . . . you good to me . . . good to Yasmin. And there are orders that there should be more accidents . . . that all may know the Curse is alive, and the Kings are angry . . . with those who defile their resting-places.'

I said: 'Thank you for telling me.'

'You will tell the Sir. But not tell that I told. But

351

you will tell him and go away ... and then you will be safe.'

I said: 'I will tell him.'

'He will go then for fear it should be you who will die next, for you are his beloved.'

I felt sick with horror. I wanted to be alone to think.

I wished Tybalt were here so that I could tell him what I had discovered. He should have listened to me, I told myself angrily. When Yasmin disappeared he had not appeared to be interested. But her disappearance concerned us all.

The Pasha! He wanted us out of the way. Why? I thought of his sitting at the table, eating, paying compliments, assessing our feminine attributes. He had lent us his Palace. Why, if he did not want to help us? To have us under his eyes; that was why. His servants waited for us and reported everything we did. It was becoming very clear.

And little Yasmin, what had she done to deserve death? She had been found in the tomb waiting for her lover. In the little alcove, which I had not noticed but which Yasmin's lover had described.

I remembered suddenly that the soothsayer had the brand of the Jackal on his arm. So he too was the servant of the Pasha. Was it his task to predict death and disaster ... to drive us away?

I must talk to Tybalt. I must tell him what I had heard. But he was at a conference. I would have to wait for his return.

The Palace was becoming really sinister. How did we know who was watching us, listening to every word we uttered? Silent-footed servants following us, reporting on everything we did!

352

All the servants were the Pasha's servants. They would all have their duties. There were only two we had brought with us: Mustapha and Absalam.

And what of them?

I must find out. I went to my room and rang the bell. Mustapha came and I asked him to bring me mint tea.

I stood beside him as he laid it on the table. I said: 'There is an insect. Oh dear! It's gone up your arm.' Before he could move I drew up his loose sleeve. It would be on the forearm where I had seen the others.

My little ruse had told me what I wanted to know. On Mustapha's forearm was the brand of the Jackal.

I said calmly: 'I don't see it now. The insects here are a pest, and their stings can be so poisonous. people are always coming for my ointment. However, it's gone.'

Mustapha's suspicions had not been aroused, I was sure.

He thanked me and left me with my tea.

I sat there sipping it and thinking that if Mustapha was the Pasha's man so must Absalam be.

Then my thoughts went to Sir Edward. He had died in the Palace. He had eaten food prepared by Mustapha or Absalam or both and he had died.

If he had a doctor to attend him, that doctor could have been the Pasha's man.

Tybalt was in danger as his father had been. We were all in danger.

Sir Edward had discovered something in the tomb and that had necessitated his immediate death. So far it seemed that Tybalt had not found what his father had, as no attempt had been made on his life. But if Tybalt were to make that discovery . . .

I began to shiver. I must see him. I must make him listen, for I was sure that what I had discovered was of the utmost importance.

Within the Tomb

How quiet the Palace seemed. How long would the conference go on? There was no one about. I might have tried to find Tabitha, but I had no desire to confide in her for I no longer trusted her. I no longer knew whom to trust.

I went to my favourite seat on the terrace and as I sat there I saw someone coming up the steps towards me. To my surprise it was Leopold Harding.

'I thought you had gone,' I said.

'No, there was a slight hitch. Business, you know. I have just come from the hotel. I have a message from your husband.'

I stood up. 'He wants me to go there?'

'No. He wants you to meet him at the site.'

'Now?'

'Yes, now. At once. He has gone on.'

'Then the conference is over?'

'I don't know, but he asked me to give you this message as I had a few hours to spare before leaving.'

'Did he say where at the site?'

'He told me exactly. I said I would take you there.'

'But where was it?'

'It's better if I show you.'

I picked up my hat which was on the seat beside me and without which I never went out.

I said: 'I'm ready. I'll come now.'

He was already leading the way out to the river. We took one of the boats and went to the site.

The valley looked grim under the glare of the late afternoon sun. In spite of the windlessness there always seemed to be a fine dust in the air.

The place seemed deserted because the men were not working today. I had understood from Tybalt that they were awaiting the outcome of the conference.

We came to the opening in the hillside which was the way into the tomb, but to my surprise Leopold led me past that.

'But surely . . .' I began.

'No,' he said. 'I am quite sure. I was here yesterday and your husband was showing me something. It is here . . .'

He led me into what looked like a natural cave but which could well have been hollowed out. To my amazement there was a hole in the side of this cave.

He said: 'Let me help you through here.'

'Are you sure?' I began. 'I have never been here before.'

'No. Your husband has just discovered that it is here.'

'But what is this hole?'

'You will see. Give me your hand.'

I stepped through and was surprised to find myself at the top of a flight of steps.

'If you will let me help you we will descend these stairs.'

'Is Tybalt here, then?'

'You will see. There are lanterns here. I will light them and then we can have one each.'

'It seems strange,' I said, 'that you, who are a stranger here . . .'

He smiled. 'Well, Lady Travers, I have explored a little. Your husband has been very kind to me.'

'They knew of this place, then. Is it connected with the tomb?'

'Oh yes, but I don't think it was considered worth exploring until now.' He handed me a lantern and I could see steps which had been cut out of the earth. They turned and there facing us was a door. It was half open.

'There,' said Leopold Harding as we went through. 'This is the spot. I'll go ahead, shall I?'

Tybalt had never mentioned this place to me. It must be a new discovery. But then lately I had been aloof. I was not able to prevent myself being so; for while I could not bring myself to talk of my suspicions, at the same time I could not behave as though they did not exist.

We were in a small chamber not more than eight feet in height. I saw that there was an opening ahead and I went towards this. I looked up and saw three or four steps.

I mounted these and called: 'Tybalt, I'm here.'

I was in another chamber; this one was larger than the other. It was very cold.

The first shadow of alarm touched me. 'Tybalt,' I called. My voice sounded rather shrill.

I said: 'There is nobody here.'

I looked over my shoulder. I was alone.

I said: 'Mr Harding, I think there's been a mistake. Tybalt isn't here.'

There was no answer. I started down the steps. I

went back to the smaller chamber. Leopold Harding was not there either.

I went back to the opening. It was completely dark because the door was shut.

I called: 'Mr Harding. Where are you?'

There was no reply.

I went to the door. I could see no handle, no bolt ... nothing with which to open it. I pushed it. I tried to pull it. But it remained fast shut.

'Where are you? Mr Harding, where are you?'

No answer. Only the hollow sound of my own voice.

I knew then what it meant to have one's flesh creep. It was as though thousands of ants were crawling over me. I knew that my hair had risen on my scalp. The awful realization had come to me. I was alone and only Mr Harding knew I was here.

Why? Who was he? Why should he do this? My imagination was running wild again. It was so senseless. He had stepped outside for a moment. He would come back. Why should a tourist, an acquaintance merely, shut me in a tomb?

I tried to be calm. I lifted the lantern and looked about me ... at the steps cut out of the earth, at the earth walls of the little chamber. Tybalt must be here. He would come out in a moment.

Then I remembered my suspicions of Tybalt. Could it be that he had had me brought here ... to rid himself of me? But why did he send Leopold Harding to bring me here? Who *was* Leopold Harding? Why did Tybalt not bring me himself? Because he did not wish to be seen coming here with me? When I did not return ...

Oh, this was folly. This was madness.

To be shut in a tomb alone could drive one mad.

358

I set down the lantern and banged my fists on the door. it did not give one little bit. How was it shut? How had it opened? All Leopold Harding had appeared to do was to push it and we stepped inside. It was as easy as that. And now it was fast shut and I was on the wrong side of it.

He must be hiding to tease me. What a foolish trick. I remembered myself suddenly rising from the sarcophagus in Giza House. I could almost hear Theodosia's shrieks.

Oh God, let somebody come. Don't let me be alone in this place.

Tybalt must be here somewhere. It was better to look . . . to assure myself before I allowed this creeping terror to take a grip on me.

I picked up the lantern and walked resolutely towards the steps. I descended them and was in the larger chamber. I must explore this. There might be a way out here. Tybalt might be somewhere beyond, waiting for Leopold to bring me to him.

I held my lantern high and examined the walls of the chamber; there was no decoration on them, but I saw that there was an opening. I went through this and was in a corridor.

'Tybalt,' I called. 'Are you there, Tybalt?'

No answer.

I lifted my lantern. I saw that these walls had been decorated. Rows of vultures were depicted there, their wings stretched as though they hovered. Now I had reached yet another chamber. I examined it with care. There seemed to be no outlet from this one. I had come to the end of my exploration; and there was no one here.

I felt my legs trembling and I sank down on to the floor. Now I knew a fear that I had never known before. I had been brought here for some purpose. All the warnings I had received, all the premonitions, they had some meaning. I should have heeded them.

But why should Leopold Harding wish to trick me? Why had he lied to me? I remembered coming out of the Temple and running straight into that man. He had been the one who had stalked me there. He had meant to kill me – Oh, but this was a better idea!

Had Tybalt ordered him to do this, and who was he that he must take his orders from Tybalt?

I was sure something moved overhead. Something was looking down at me. I held up the lantern.

On the ceiling had been carved a great bat with enormous wings. Its eyes were of some sort of obsidian and the light of the lantern catching them had made them seem alive.

I fancied I could hear the soothsayer's voice: 'The bat is hovering . . . waiting to descend.'

I stared up at it – hideous, malevolent; and I said to myself: 'What is to become of me? What does it mean? Why have I been brought here?'

I was cold. Or was it fear that made me shiver so violently that I could not keep still? My teeth chattered . . . an unearthly sound.

I could not bring myself to stand up and go back. I was fascinated by that hideous bat on the ceiling of the chamber.

Now I could make out drawings on the walls. There was a Pharaoh offering a sacrifice to one of the gods. Was it Hathor, the goddess of love? It must be because there she was again and her face was that of a cow, and I knew the cow was her emblem.

I was so cold. I must move. I stood up unsteadily. I examined the walls. There might be a way out of this place. There *must* be a way out. Now I could see the drawings on the walls more clearly. There were pictures of ships and men tied upside down on their prows. Prisoners, I remembered. And with them were men without one or more limbs. And there was the crocodile who had maimed them, sly, ugly, with a necklace about his neck and earrings hanging from his ears.

Where was I? At the entrance to a tomb? Then if I was at the entrance it must lead on. Somewhere ahead perhaps was a burial chamber and in it the stone sarcophagus and inside the sarcophagus the mummy.

One can grow accustomed to anything . . . even fear. Fear! Terror! Horror! These were creeping up on me and yet I felt calmer than I had at the first realization that I was alone in this gruesome place.

I walked a few paces. If there was a way out of this chamber . . . but to what would it lead . . . only to a long-dead mummy. What I needed was a way out into the open . . . the fresh air.

I thought: There is little air in here. I shall use what there is in a short time. I shall die; and I shall lie here for ever until some archaeologist decides to explore this place just in case it leads to a great discovery; and his discovery will be my dead body.

'Nonsense,' I said as I had said so many times to Theodosia, 'there must be something I can do.'

The very thought inspired me with courage. I would

not sit here quietly and wait for death. I would find the way out if it was to be found.

I picked up the lantern. I examined the walls again. I now saw some significance in the wall drawings. This was meant to depict the progress of a soul along the River Tuat. There was the boat on a sea from which rose hideous sea monsters, snakes with double heads, waves which enveloped the vessel; but above was the God Osiris, God of the Underworld and Judge of the Dead. This meant that he was giving his protection to the traveller in the boat and he would conduct him through the turbulent seas of the Tuat to the Kingdom of Amen-Ra.

There was an opening in the wall. My heart leaped with hope. Then I saw that it was merely an alcove, similar in size to that one in which Yasmin and her lover had lain together.

As I examined it my foot touched something. I was startled and immediately thought of some of the horrible creatures I had seen rising from the River Tuat. I stooped and looked down. What I saw was not a hideous serpent but a gleaming object.

A matchbox! A small, gold box. What a strange thing to find in such a place. It was no antique piece. It belonged to this century. I turned it over in my hand and I saw the name engraved on it: 'E. Travers.'

Sir Edward's matchbox! Then he had been here!

I felt dizzy with this discovery. My incarceration was already having its effect. I could not think clearly. Sir Edward had been here at some time. What if it was the night when he had died? Had he died because he had been here? But he had gone back to the Palace. He had told no one what he had seen, but Tybalt knew he had found something . . . something which excited him. Then he had eaten something which had been prepared for him. Who prepared his food? Mustapha and Absalam – those two who were branded with the Jackal, servants of the Pasha.

Sir Edward had been murdered. I was certain of that. And he had been murdered because he had been here. It would have been at the orders of the Pasha . . . who had ordained that he should die just as he had commanded that Yasmin be killed and thrown into the river and that there should be an accident at the bridge which would show that the Curse was in force.

The Pasha wanted to drive us away; he wanted our expedition to end in failure. Why? Because there was something which he did not want us to discover. If the Pasha's interest in archaeology really existed, why should he be ready to kill rather than allow discoveries to be made.

Because *he* wished to make them?

In my present state of fear and panic memories of the past seemed clearer than they normally were. I recalled vividly the Pasha's plump face, his shaking jowls, his lips greasy from the food he was eating; he had looked sly as he murmured: 'There is a legend that my family founded its fortune on robbing tombs.'

Could it possibly be that he continued to build up his fortune in this illegal way?

If that was so he would not be very friendly towards archaeologists who might expose him. Was that why he offered his Palace, why his servants waited on us, why they had orders to frighten us away?

I knew that that was the answer.

But it did not answer the pressing question: Why was it necessary to bring me here?

I thought, Leopold Harding is another of his servants. In the papers they will be reading: Wife of Archaeologist disappears! Lady Travers, wife of Sir Tybalt, left the Palace where the party of archaeologists are lodged and has not been seen for two days ... three days ... a week ... a month ... She can only be presumed dead. How was she spirited away? This is another instance of the Curse of the Kings. It will be remembered that a few months ago the wife of one of the archaeologists suffered a fatal accident.

I could see Dorcas reading that. Alison with her. I could see their blank, miserable faces. They would be truly heartbroken.

It must not be. I must find a way out of it.

I clutched Sir Edward's golden matchbox as though it were a talisman.

Darkness! Was the lantern growing dim? What should I do when the oil ran out? Should I be dead by then?

How long could one survive in an atmosphere such as this?

My feet were numb. With fear or cold I could not know. Above me the eyes of the great bat glittered ... waiting ... waiting to descend.

'Oh God,' I prayed, 'help me. Show me what to do. Let Tybalt come and find me. Let it be that he wants me to live ... not to die.'

Then I thought, when we are in need of help why do we always tell God what to do? If it is His will, I will come out of this place alive — and only then.

I think I was a little delirious. I thought I heard

footsteps. But it was only the beating of my own heart which was like hammer strokes in my ears.

I talked aloud. 'Oh, Tybalt, miss me. Search for me. You will find me if you do. You will find that door. Why should there be such a door? Something will lead you to me . . . if you want to find me . . . desperately . . . you must. But do you want to find me? Was it by your order? No . . . I don't believe that. I won't believe that!'

I could see the old church now with the tower and the gravestones tottering over some of them. 'You can't read what's on them.' That sounded like Alison's voice. 'I think that they should be removed . . . but you can't disturb the dead . . .'

'You can't disturb the dead. You can't disturb the dead.' It was as though a thousand voices were chanting that. And there was the boat all round me and the sea was boiling like the water in the big black saucepan that used to be on the kitchen fire at the rectory when Dorcas or Alison was making Irish stew or boiling the Christmas puddings.

This was delirium. I was aware of it, but I welcomed it. It took me away from this dark and fearsome place. It took me back to the schoolroom where I teased the others; it took me to the graveyard where old Pegger was digging a grave.

'And who's that for, Mr Pegger?'

'It be for you, Miss Judith. You was always a meddler and now look where it 'as brought you . . . to the grave . . . to the tomb . . .'

There were the echoing voices again. 'To the tomb,' and I was back in this cold place of death and terror.

'Oh God, help me. Let Tybalt find me. Let him love me. Let it have been a mistake . . .'

'There's a wedding at the church,' said Dorcas. 'You must come with us, Judith. Here is a handful of rice. Be careful how you throw it.'

And there they were coming down the aisle . . . married by the Reverend James Osmond. Tybalt and Tabitha . . .

'No!' I cried; and I was back again in the tomb.

My limbs were stiff. I tried to get up. I would try to get out.

As I stood, I kicked something. It was the matchbox which I had dropped. I stopped to pick it up; as I did so the wall seemed to move.

I'm imagining something, I told myself. I'm delirious. In a moment I shall be opening the door of my bedroom at the rectory.

The door did open. I fell against it. I was in a dark passage, facing another door.

Some impulse made me bang on this door.

The small hope which had come to me brought back with it panic because I realized full well what was happening to me then in a flash of clarity. I was trapped. I had been led here and the purpose could only be to kill me. I was losing my strength. The lantern would not remain alight for ever. And I could not get out.

I kicked the door. I tried to open it. But it did not move.

I sank down beside it. But at least the door which led to the chamber was open and might that let in more air?

I stumbled along the passage. It was short and

came to an abrupt end. It was nothing that I had discovered; only another blind alley. I went back and kicked at the door in fury. And then I sank down and covered my face with my hands.

There was nothing I could do ... nothing but wait for death.

I lost consciousness. I was sitting in the half-open doorway and in the chamber beyond the great bat was waiting.

How long? I wondered.

The light of the lantern was growing fainter. It would go out at any moment.

When the darkness came, what should I do?

I would be frightened perhaps because then I should not be able to see anything at all ... not even the eyes of the bat in the ceiling.

In sudden panic I rose again. I stumbled to that door. I cried: 'Help me. Help me. God, Allah, Osiris ... anyone ... help me.'

I was half sobbing, half laughing, and I kicked and kicked with all the strength of which I was capable.

And then ... the miracle happened. There was an answer.

Knock, knock ... on the other side of that blessed door.

With all my strength I knocked back.

There was the answering knock. Now I could hear noises beyond that wall. Someone knew I was here. Someone was coming to me.

I sank back. While I could hear that blessed noise I knew they were coming. It increased. The door trembled. I sat back watching it, the tears falling down my cheeks, the babble of words on my lips.

'Tybalt is coming. He has found me. I shall be free . . .'

I was happy. Had I ever known such exultation? Only when one is about to lose it does one realize how sweet life is.

The lantern was flickering. Never mind. They are coming. The door is moving.

Soon now.

Then I was no longer alone. I was caught up.

'Judith . . .'

It was Tybalt, as I had known it would be. He was holding me in his arms and I thought: I did not die of fear, but I shall die of bliss.

'My love,' he said. 'Judith, my love.'

'It's all right, Tybalt,' I said, comforting him. 'It's all right . . . now . . .'

The Great Discovery

During the days that followed I lived in a kind of daze.

There were times when I was not sure where I was and then Tybalt would be beside me . . . always Tybalt, holding me in his arms, reassuring me.

I had suffered a severe shock; and I was constantly told that everything was all right. All I had to do was remember that. And Tybalt was with me. He had come to me and rescued me; and that was all I must think of as yet.

'It is enough,' I said.

I would lie still clinging to his hand; but when I dozed I would often awake shouting that the black bat was in the ceiling and that his eyes were glittering. I would find myself crying 'Help. Help. God . . . Allah . . . Tybalt . . . help me.'

It had been a terrible ordeal. There could be few who had been buried in one of the tombs of the Pharaohs and come out alive.

Who had done this to me? That was what I wanted to know. Where was Leopold Harding? And why had he taken me down into that underground vault and left me there?

Tybalt said: 'We shall know in time. He has disappeared but we shall find him.'

'Why did he do it, Tybalt? Why? He said he was

taking me to you. He said you had asked for me to come.'

'I don't know. It is a mystery to us all. We are trying to find him. But he has disappeared. All you need think about now is that you are safe and I shall never allow you to be lost again.'

'Oh, Tybalt,' I said, 'that makes me very happy.'

Tabitha was by my bed.

'I want to tell you something, Judith,' she said. 'You've been talking a great deal. We were shocked to know what was in your mind . . . how could you have believed such things possible. Tybalt knows I'm talking to you. We think it best so that you should understand right away. You thought that Tybalt and I were lovers. My dear Judith, how could you? I love Tybalt, yes . . . I always have . . . as I would love a son if I had one. I came to the household, as you know, when my husband was put into a home. Sir Edward's wife was alive then, but ill. Oh, I know it was wrong but Sir Edward and I loved each other. Nanny Tester knew it and spied on us. She was devoted to Sir Edward's wife and she hated me. She hated Sir Edward too. When Lady Travers died she blamed me. She all but suggested that I had murdered her. Sir Edward and I were lovers. As you know, I accompanied him on some of his expeditions. We would have married had I been free. But I was not . . . until it was too late . . .'

'I understand now,' I said.

'My dearest Judith. You were always so besotted about Tybalt, weren't you? He realizes how lucky he is. You never did things by halves, as your aunts used to say. So you had to love Tybalt with that fierce possessiveness. Such determination as yours had to have its effect. Even Tybalt was vulnerable. He confided to me long before he asked you that he wanted to marry you . . . that was when you were Lady Bodrean's companion . . . and I must admit you didn't fit into the role very comfortably. There was nothing meek about you, which is a quality one always associates with companions.'

'I can see,' I said, 'that my wild and foolish imagination built up the situation.'

'It was not a real one . . . It did not exist outside your imagination, remember that. I've something else to tell you too. Terence Gelding has asked me to marry him.'

'And you've accepted?'

'Not yet. But I think I shall.'

'You'll be happy, Tabitha. At last.'

'There's something I want to tell you. I never saw Tybalt work so hard or so fervently as when they were pulling down that door which separated him from you . . . not even when he believed himself to be on the verge of the biggest discovery of his career. No, I have never before seen that purpose, that desperate need . . .'

I laughed. 'I do believe I must be of greater importance to him than a Pharaoh's undisturbed tomb after all.'

'I am sure of it,' said Tabitha.

Tybalt was by my bed.

'As soon as the doctor has seen you we are going home. I have asked Dr Gunwen to come out and make sure that you are fit to travel.'

371

'You have sent for Dr Gunwen! And we are going home. Then is the expedition over?'

'Yes, it's over for me.'

'My poor Tybalt.'

'Poor! When you are here . . . alive and well.'

Then he held me against him.

'At least,' I said, 'I found happiness that I never dreamed possible.'

He did not answer but the way in which he held me told me that he shared my joy.

'Where is Hadrian?' I said. 'Why doesn't Hadrian come to see me?'

'Do you want to see Hadrian?' asked Tybalt.

'But of course. He is all right, isn't he?'

'Yes,' he said. 'I'll send him to you.'

I saw the change in Hadrian at once. I had never seen him as sober before.

'Oh Hadrian!'

'Judith.' He took my hands, kissed me on both cheeks. 'That! To happen to you. It must have been frightful.'

'It was.'

'The swine!' he said. 'The utter swine. Better to have put a bullet through your head than that. Judith, you'll forget it in time.'

'I wonder whether one ever forgets such an experience.'

'You will.'

'Why did he do it, Hadrian?'

'God knows. He must be a madman.'

'He seemed sane . . . an ordinary merchant who was excited to come across an expedition like ours, because in a way it was a link with his business. What could have been his motive?'

'That we shall have to find out. Thank God the conference ended when it did . . . about the time you and Harding entered that place. They had agreed that there was to be an extension of a few more weeks and when we came back to the Palace Tybalt wanted to tell you this. One of the servants had overheard Harding telling you that Tybalt wanted him to take you to him on the site and that you had gone off with him. Tybalt was alarmed. I think he has been more uneasy than he has let us know about a lot of things. We went to the site. We searched for you. We thought it was hopeless but Tybalt wouldn't give up. He kept going over and over the same ground. And finally we heard the knocking.'

'What *could* have been his motive? I believe he tried to kill me in the Temple one day.'

'But how could your death possibly profit *him*?'

'It's so mysterious.'

'There was Theodosia. Do you think that was Leopold Harding?'

'No, that was the Pasha and his servants.'

'The Pasha!'

'One of the workmen . . . Yasmin's lover . . . warned me. Yasmin was discovered in the tomb and they killed her. She was there on the day the Pasha came to us. You remember the Feast of the Nile.'

'Good God, Judith. We're in a maze of intrigue.'

'Theodosia's death could have been anyone's death. She was the unfortunate one. The bridge had been tampered with because the Pasha wanted a victim. It didn't matter which.'

373

'But the Pasha has helped us.'

'He wants us out of this place. It may well be that he will attempt to kill another of us.'

Tybalt came in and sitting on my bed regarded me anxiously.

'You've been tiring Judith,' he accused Hadrian.

I revelled in his concern but insisted that I was not tired and that we had been talking of Leopold Harding and the Pasha and once again looking for a reason why the attempt had been made on my life.

Tybalt said: 'In the first place Harding must have known something about the layout of the ground.'

'He had been there on several occasions,' I reminded him.

'He knew too much. He must have acquired the knowledge from somewhere.'

'It is certain,' I said, 'that Leopold Harding was not what he seemed. Tybalt, I wonder if that boy – Yasmin's lover – knows anything. It was he who told me that the Pasha wanted to drive us away.'

'We'll send for him,' said Tybalt.

'On some pretext,' I warned. 'No one must know that he is suspected of helping us. How can we be sure who is watching us?'

The boy stood before us. We had decided that I should be the one who questioned him because I had won his confidence.

'Tell me what you know of Leopold Harding,' I said.

The manner in which he looked over his shoulder assured me that he knew something.

'He comes at times to Egypt, Lady.'

'He has been here often then? What else?'

'He is a friend of the Pasha. Pasha give him beautiful things.'

'What beautiful things?'

'All beautiful things. Jewels . . . stones . . . furniture . . . all kinds. Leopold Harding goes away and comes back to the Pasha.'

'He is a servant of the Pasha then?'

The boy nodded.

'Thank you,' I said. 'You have served me well.'

'You very goody lady,' he said. 'You good to Yasmin. You were shut in the tomb.' His big dark eyes filled with horror.

'But I came out,' I said.

'You very great wise lady. You and the great Sir will go back to the land of the rain. There you will live in peace and joy.'

'Thank you,' I said. 'You have done me good service.'

Dr Gunwen arrived. He sat by my bed and talked to me. I asked how Dorcas and Alison were and he said: 'Making preparations for your return.'

I laughed.

'Yes, I'm going to prescribe an immediate return. I've spoken to your husband. I want you to be back there . . . a nice long rest in the country you know well. Help the rector's wife with the bazaar and jam-making sessions.'

'It sounds wonderful,' I said.

'Yes, get away from these foreign parts for a bit. I think then I shall be able to pronounce an immediate cure. There's nothing wrong with you, you know. Only that sort of incarceration can have a devastating effect.

I think you're strong-minded enough to suffer fewer ill effects than most.'

'Thanks,' I said. 'I'll live up to that.'

'Tybalt,' I said, 'we're going home.'

'Yes,' he answered. 'Doctor's orders.'

'Well, the expedition was over, wasn't it?'

'It's over,' he said.

I lay against him and thought of green fields. It would be autumn now and the trees would be turning golden brown. The apple-tree in Rainbow Cottage would be laden with russets and the pears would be ready for gathering. Dorcas and Alison would be fussing about the size of the plums.

I felt an inexpressible longing for home. I would turn Giza House into the home I wanted it to be. Darkness should be banished. I never wanted darkness again. I would have bright colours everywhere.

I said: 'It will be wonderful to be home with you.'

Now that I was well and we were making our preparations I learned more of what had happened.

Mustapha and Absalam had disappeared. Had they heard my explanations of how I suspected the Pasha? There was more than that. There was great excitement because in that narrow passage, which I had stumbled into and which they had entered when they broke the wall of the alcove in which Yasmin had been discovered, there was evidence that there was something beyond, and that the passage was not a blind alley after all.

It was the greatest discovery of the expedition and

376

it was clear that Sir Edward had been aware of this on the night that he died.

Tabitha told me that Terence was taking over the leadership because Tybalt had decided to come home with me.

I said: 'No. I can't allow it.'

I stormed into our bedroom where he was putting some papers together.

'Tybalt,' I said, 'you're staying.'

'Staying?' He wrinkled his brow.

'Here.'

'I thought we were going home.'

'Did you know that they are probably on the verge of one of the greatest discoveries in archaeology?'

'As a budding archaeologist, you must learn never to count your chickens before they are hatched.'

'Archaeology is all counting chickens before they're hatched. How could you go on with this continual work if you didn't believe it was going to be successful? That passage leads somewhere. You know it. It leads into a tomb. A very important one, because if it wasn't important why would they have gone to all the trouble with the subterfuge of blind alleys all over the place?'

'As usual, Judith, you are exaggerating. There were three blind alleys.'

'What does it matter? Three is a great many. It must be a wonderful tomb. You know it. Confess.'

'I think that maybe they are on the verge of a great discovery.'

'Which was the purpose of this expedition.'

'Why, yes.'

'The expedition which you had been planning ever since your father died.'

377

He nodded.

'And he died because he got too close. He was there in that place where I was.'

'And because you were there we have been led to this.'

'Then it wasn't in vain.'

'My God, I'd rather never have found the way.'

'Oh Tybalt, I believe that. But you're going to stay now.'

'Dr Gunwen wishes you to go back as soon as possible.'

'I won't go.'

'But you must.'

'I won't go alone and you are not coming with me.'

'I'm getting ready to leave now.'

'I will *not* have it,' I said. 'I will *not* let you go now. You are going on. It's *your* expedition. When finally you reach that tomb, when you see the dust there undisturbed for four thousand years ... and perhaps the footprint of the last person to leave ... *you* are going to be the first. Do you think I would allow Terence Gelding to have that honour?'

'No,' he said firmly. 'We are going back.'

But I was determined that it should not be so.

That was a battle of wills. I was exultant. It seemed so incongruous. I was standing out against his giving up that which I thought he would rather sacrifice anything for than miss.

I thought: I am loved ... even as I love.

I simply refused to go. I wanted to stay. I could not possibly be happy if we left at this stage. I made Dr Gunwen agree with me and I finally won the day.

*

378

It is well known what happened. That was *not* the discovery of the century.

Tybalt's expedition found the tomb a few days before the Pasha's men working from a different part of the hillside reached the burial chamber.

What treasures there would have been! It was clearly the burial place of a great King.

The Pasha had been working towards it for some time; he knew that there was a way in through the chambers in which I had spent those terrifying hours; that was why when Sir Edward discovered it he had died. He knew too that the alcove in which Yasmin had been discovered was a way into the corridor and it may have been that he thought she had discovered something. Her death was a warning to any of his workpeople who might have thought of exploring the subterranean passages.

Alas, for Tybalt's great ambition. There was the sarcophagus, the mummy of the Pharaoh, but robbers – perhaps the Pasha's ancestors – had rifled the tomb two thousand years before; and all that was left was a soul house in stone which they had not thought worth taking.

We heard that the Pasha had left for Alexandria. He did not come to bid us farewell. He would know through his servants that we had unravelled the mystery of Sir Edward's death and that of Theodosia.

We came back to England.

There was great rejoicing at Rainbow Cottage. I had asked that the aunts should not be told of my adventures because, as I said to Tybalt, we shall go off to other places together and they would fret all the time and say 'I told you so' which is what I could not endure.

A few days after we had arrived home there was a paragraph in the Press about an Englishman, a successful dealer in antiquities – mainly Egyptian – who had been found drowned in the Nile. His name was Leopold Harding. Whether his death was due to foul play was not certain. Head injuries had been discovered but these could have been caused by his striking his head against the boat when it was overturned. As a dealer in rare objects his clients had been mainly private collectors.

It was clear that he had been one of the Pasha's servants, just as those who had tampered with the bridge, the soothsayer, and Mustapha and Absalam had been. Harding disposed of priceless objects which the Pasha may have taken from tombs in the past, for naturally it would take him years to dispose of articles of this nature. Many would have to be broken up and if there were jewels decorating them these would have to be sold separately, and these transactions would be carried out under the cover of legitimate business.

The Pasha had clearly been hoping to make the discovery of a lifetime. Sir Edward had found the same trail, so he had died through Mustapha and Absalam. Then Tybalt had arrived to take up where his father had left off and Theodosia had died as a warning. As we remained, Leopold Harding had been ordered to kill me. He had failed. The Pasha did not like failures; moreover, he was no doubt afraid that Harding, over whom he would have less control than he had over servants of his own race, might betray the fact that he had been commanded to kill me.

So Leopold Harding had been murdered as Yasmin had.

The adventure was behind me. Leopold Harding had attempted to take my life and had instead taken away my fears. Because of what he had done to me I had greater understanding than I had ever had before.

And Tybalt too. He will never of course be the man to show his feelings; and when perhaps he is most moved he is most reticent.

But for Leopold Harding and the Egyptian expedition, I might have gone on for years doubting Tybalt's love for me for he could never have expressed in words what he did when he came to get me and when he was ready to give up his life's ambition when he believed it – erroneously it turned out – to be within his reach.

'My poor Tybalt,' I said, 'I did want you to make the great discovery.'

'I made a greater one.'

'I know. Before, you thought you wanted more than anything in the world to find the greatest treasure ever known to the world.'

'But I did that,' he said. 'I discovered what you meant to me.'

So how could I but be grateful to all that had gone before? And how could I not rejoice when I looked forward to the richness of the life we would lead together?

The India Fan

Sept. 1989
July 1994
Oct. 1999

ENGLAND
AND FRANCE

The Big House

I had always been fascinated by the big house of Framling.
Perhaps it had begun when I was two years old and Fabian
Framling had kidnapped me and kept me there for two
weeks. It was a house full of shadows and mystery, I
discovered, when I went in search of the peacock feather
fan. In the long corridors, in the gallery, in the silent rooms,
the past seemed to be leering at one from all corners,
insidiously imposing itself on the present and almost –
though never quite – obliterating it.

For as long as I could remember Lady Harriet Framling
had reigned supreme over our village. Farm labourers standing respectfully at the side of the road while the carriage,
emblazoned with the majestic Framling arms, drove past,
touched their forelocks and the women bobbed their defer-
ential curtsies. She was spoken of in hushed whispers as
though those who mentioned her feared they might be
taking her name in vain; in my youthful mind she ranked
with the Queen and was second only to God. It was small
wonder that when her son, Fabian, commanded me to be
his slave, I – being only six years old at that time – made
no protest. It seemed only natural that we humble folk
should serve the Big House in any way which was demanded
of us.

The Big House – known to the community as 'The House'
as though those dwellings which the rest of us occupied
were something different – was Framling. Not Framling
Hall or Framling Manor but simply *Fram*ling, with the
accent on the first syllable which made it sound more
impressive. It had been in the possession of the Framlings
for four hundred years. Lady Harriet had married into the

389

family most condescendingly, for she was the daughter of an Earl, which, my father told me, meant that she was Lady Harriet instead of simply Lady Framling. One must never forget that, for the fact was that she had married beneath her when she became the wife of a mere baronet. He was dead now, poor man. But I had heard that she never allowed him to forget her higher rank; and although she had come to the village only when she was a bride, ever since she had considered it her duty to rule over us.

The marriage had been unproductive for years – a source of great annoyance to Lady Harriet. I guessed she constantly complained bitterly to the Almighty about such an over-sight; but even Heaven could not ignore Lady Harriet for ever, and when she was forty years old, fifteen years after her wedding day, she gave birth to Fabian.

Her joy was boundless. She doted on the boy. It was simple logic that *her* son must be perfect. His slightest whim must be obeyed by all underlings; and the Framling servants admitted that Lady Harriet herself would smile indulgently at his infant misdemeanours.

Four years after the birth of Fabian, Lavinia was born. Although, being a girl, she was slightly inferior to her brother, she was Lady Harriet's daughter and therefore far above the rest of the community.

I was always amused to see them come into church and walk down the aisle – Lady Harriet followed by Fabian, followed by Lavinia. They would be watched with awe while they took their places and knelt on the red and black prayer mats embroidered with the letter F; and those behind were able to witness the amazing spectacle of Lady Harriet's kneeling to a Higher Authority – an experience which made up for everything else the service lacked.

I would stare in wonder as I knelt, forgetting that I was in church, until a nudge from Polly Green reminded me and recalled me to my duty.

Framling – the House – dominated the village. It had been built at the top of a slight incline which made one feel that it was on the alert, watching for any sins we might commit. Although there had been a house there in the days of the Conqueror, it had been rebuilt over the centuries and there was hardly anything left of the pre-Tudor building. One passed under a gatehouse with its battlemented towers into a lower courtyard where plants grew out of the walls, and in iron-banded tubs shrubs hung over in artistic profusion. There were seats in the courtyard on to which leaded windows looked down – dark and mysterious. I always fancied someone was watching behind those windows – reporting everything to Lady Harriet.

One went through a heavily studded door into a banqueting hall where several long-dead Framlings hung on the walls – some fierce, some benign. The ceiling was high and vaulted; the long polished table smelt of beeswax and turpentine; and over the great fireplace the family tree stretched out in all directions; at one end of the hall was a staircase leading to the chapel and at the other end the door to the screens.

During my tender years it seemed to me that all of us in the village rotated like planets round the glorious blazing sun that was Framling.

Our own house, right next to the church, was rambling and draughty. I had often heard it said that it cost a fortune to heat it. Compared with Framling, of course, it was minute, but it was true that although there might be a big fire in the drawing-room, and the kitchen was warm enough, to ascend to the upper regions in winter was like going to the arctic circle, I imagined. My father did not notice. He noticed very little of practical matters. His heart was in ancient Greece and he was more familiar with Alexander the Great and Homer than with his parishioners.

I knew little of my mother because she had died when I was two months old. Polly Green had come as a substitute; but that was not until I was just past two years old and had had my first introduction to the ways of the Framlings. Polly must have been about twenty-eight when she came.

She was a widow who had always wanted a child, so that just as she took the place of a mother to me, I was to her the child she never had. It worked very well. I loved Polly and there was no doubt whatever that Polly loved me. It was to her loving arms that I went in my moments of crisis. When the hot rice pudding dropped into my lap, when I fell and grazed my knees, when I awoke in the night dreaming of goblins and fierce giants, it was to Polly I turned for solace. I could not imagine life without Polly Green.

She came from London – a place in her opinion superior to any other. 'Buried myself in the country, all for you,' she used to say. When I pointed out to her that to be buried one had to be under the earth in the graveyard, she grimaced and said: 'Well, you might as well be.' She had contempt for the country. 'A lot of fields and nothing to do in them. Give me London.' Then she would talk of the streets of the city where something was always 'going on', of the markets, lighted by night with naphtha flares, stalls piled high with fruit and vegetables, old clothes and 'anything you could think of', and all the costers shouting in their inimitable way. 'One of these fine days I'll take you there and you can see for yourself.'

Polly was the only one among us who had little respect for Lady Harriet.

'Who's she when she's out?' she would demand. 'No different from the rest of us. All she's got is a handle to her name.'

She was fearless. No meek curtsey from Polly. She would not cower against the hedge while the carriage drove past. She would grasp my hand firmly and march on resolutely, looking neither to the right nor the left.

Polly had a sister, who lived in London with her husband. 'Poor Eff,' Polly would say. '*He*'s not much cop.' I never heard Polly refer to him as anything but He or Him. It seemed that he was unworthy of name. He was lazy and left everything for Eff to do. 'I said to her the day she got engaged to him: "You'll sup sorrow with a long spoon if you take that one, Eff." But did she take a bit of notice of me?'

I would shake my head solemnly, because I had heard it before and knew the answer.

So in the early days Polly was the centre of my life. Her urban attitudes set her aside from us rural folk. Polly had a way of folding her arms and taking a bellicose stance if anyone showed signs of attacking her. It made her a formidable adversary. She used to say she would 'take nothing from nobody' and when I pointed out, having been initiated into the intricacies of English grammar by my governess, Miss York, that two negatives made an affirmative, she merely said: 'Here, are you getting at me?'

I loved Polly dearly. She was my ally, mine entirely; she and I stood together against Lady Harriet and the world.

We occupied the top rooms of the rectory. My room was next to hers; it had been from the day she had come and we never wanted to change it. It gave me a nice cosy feeling to have her so close. There was one other room on the attic floor. Here Polly would build up a nice cosy fire and in the winter we would make toast and bake chestnuts. I would stare into the flames while Polly told me stories of London life. I could see the market stalls and Eff and Him, and the little place where Polly had lived with her sailor husband. I saw Polly waiting for him to come home on leave with his baggy trousers and little white hat with *HMS Triumphant* on it and his white bundle on his shoulder. Her voice would quaver a little when she told me of how he had gone down with his ship.

'Nothing left,' she said. 'No little 'un to remind me of him.' I pointed out to her that if she had had a little 'un she wouldn't have wanted me, so I was glad.

There would be tears in her eyes, which made her say briskly: 'Here. Look at me. You trying to make me soft in me old age?'

393

But she hugged me just the same.

From our windows we looked down on the churchyard . . . tottery old grave stones, some of them, under which lay those who had long since died. I used to read the inscriptions and wondered what the people who lay there were like. Some of the writing on the stones was almost obliterated, so old were they.

Our rooms were big and wide with windows on either side. Opposite the graveyard, we looked on the village green with its pond and seats where the old men liked to congregate, sometimes talking, sometimes sitting in silence staring at the water before they shuffled off into the inn to drink a pint of ale. 'Death on one side,' I pointed out to Polly, 'and life on the other.'

'You're a funny bit of baggage, you are,' Polly would often reply, for any fanciful remark produced that comment.

Our household consisted of my father, myself, my governess Miss York, Polly, Mrs Janson the cook-housekeeper, and Daisy and Holly, two lively sisters who shared the housework. I learned later that the governess was there because my mother had brought a little money into the family which had been set aside for my education and I was to have the best possible, no matter what hardship had to be endured to attain this.

I loved my father but he was not as important in my life as Polly was. When I saw him walking across the graveyard from the church to the rectory in his white surplice, prayer book in hand, fine white hair made untidy by the wind, I felt a great desire to protect him. He seemed so vulnerable, unable to take care of himself, so it was odd to think of him as the guardian of his spiritual flock – particularly when it contained Lady Harriet. He had to be reminded of meal times, when to put on clean clothes, and his spectacles were constantly being lost and found in unexpected places. He would come into a room for something and forget what it was. He was eloquent in the pulpit, but I was sure the villagers at least did not understand his allusions to the classics and the ancient Greeks.

'He'd forget his head if it wasn't fixed on his shoulders,' was Polly's comment in that half-affectionate, half-contemptuous tone I knew so well. But she was fond of him and would have defended him with all the rhetoric of her colourful language – sometimes quite different from ours – if the need arose.

It was when I was two years old that I had the adventure of which I could remember so little. I had had the story by hearsay, yet it made me feel I had some connection with the Big House. If Polly had been with me at the time, it would never have happened; and I believe it was due to this that my father realized I must have a nurse who could be trusted.

What happened is an indication of the nature of Fabian Framling and his mother's obsession with him.

Fabian would have been about seven at the time. Lavinia was four years younger and I had been born a year after she was. I had heard details of the story because of the friendship between our servants and those of Framling.

Mrs Janson, our cook-housekeeper, who worked so well for us and instilled discipline into the house and kept us all in some order, told me the story.

'It was the strangest thing I ever heard,' she said. 'It was young Master Fabian. His lordship leads them all a fine dance up at the House . . . always has done. Lady Harriet thinks the sun, moon and stars shine out of his eyes. She won't have him crossed. A little Cæsar, that's what he is. He'll have his own way or there'll be ructions. Heaven knows what he'll be like when he's a bit older. Well, his little majesty is tired of playing the old games. He wants something new, so he thinks he'll be a father. If he wants it . . . it's going to be. They tell me up there that he expects everything he wants to be his. And that's no good for anyone, mark my words, Miss Drusilla.'

I looked suitably impressed, for I was eager for her to get on with the story.

'You were put in the rectory garden. You could toddle round and that was what you liked to do. They shouldn't have left you. It was that May Higgs, flighty piece, she was. Mind you, she loved little ones . . . but she was courting that Jim Fellings at the time . . . and he came along. Well, there she is giggling with him . . . and didn't see what was happening. Master Fabian was determined to be a father and a father had to have a child. He saw you and thought you would do. So he picked you up and took you to the House. You were his baby and he was going to be your father.'

Mrs Janson put her hands on her hips and looked at me. I laughed. It seemed very funny to me and I liked it. 'Go on, Mrs Janson. What happened then?'

'My goodness, there was a fine how-do-you-do when they found you'd disappeared. They couldn't think where you'd got to. Then Lady Harriet sent for your father. Poor man, he was in a rare flummox. He took May Higgs with him. She was in tears, blaming herself, which was only right that she should do. Do you know, I think that was the start of the rift between her and Jim Fellings. She blamed him. And you know she married Charlie Clay the next year.'

'Tell me about when my father went to the House to fetch me.'

'Well, talk about a storm! This was one of them tornados. Master Fabian raged and he fumed. He wouldn't give you up. You were his baby. He had found you. He was going to be your father. You could have knocked us all down with feathers when the rector came back without you. I said to him, "Where's the baby?" and he said; "She's staying at the Big House, only for a day or so." I said, shocked-like, "She's only a baby." "Lady Harriet has assured me that she will be well looked after. Miss Lavinia's nurse will take care of her. She will come to no harm.

Fabian flew into such a rage when he thought he was going to lose her that Lady Harriet thought he would do himself some harm." "You mark my words," I said, "that boy — Lady Harriet's son though he may be — will come to a bad end." I didn't care if it got back to Lady Harriet. I had to say it.'

'And so for two weeks I lived in the Big House?'

'You surely did. They said it was real comical to see Master Fabian looking after you. He used to wheel you round the gardens in the push chair which had been Miss Lavinia's. He used to feed you and dress you. They said it was really funny to see him. He's always been such a one for rough games . . . and there he was playing the mother. He would have overfed you if it hadn't been for Nanny Cuffley. She put her foot down, took a firm hand for once and he listened. He must have been really fond of you. Goodness knows how long it would have gone on if Lady Milbanke hadn't come to stay with her young Ralph who was a year older than Master Fabian. He laughed at him and told him it was like playing with dolls. It didn't make any difference that this was a live one. It was a girl's game. Nanny Cuffley said Master Fabian was really upset about it. He didn't want you to go away . . . but I suppose he thought it was a slur on his manhood to look after a baby.'

I loved the story and asked to have it repeated many times.

It was almost immediately after that incident that Polly came.

Whenever I saw Fabian — usually in the distance — I would look at him furtively, and in my mind's eye see him tenderly caring for me. It was so amusing; it always made me laugh.

I fancied, too, that he looked at me in a rather special way, although he always pretended he did not see me.

Because of our standing in the village — the rector was on a level with the doctor and solicitor, though of course chasms separated us from the heights on which the Framlings dwelt – as I began to grow older I was invited to have tea now and then with Miss Lavinia.

Although I did not exactly enjoy these occasions, I was always excited to go into the house. Before those little tea-parties I knew very little of it. I had only seen the hall because it had rained once or twice when the garden fête was in progress and we were allowed to shelter from the rain in the House. I shall always remember the thrill of leaving the hall and mounting the stairs, past the suit of armour, which I imagined would be quite terrifying after dark. I was sure it was alive and that when our backs were turned it was laughing at us.

Lavinia was haughty, overbearing, and very beautiful. She reminded me of a tigress. She had tawny hair and golden lights in her green eyes; her upper lip was short and her beautiful white teeth slightly prominent; her nose was small and very slightly turned up at the tip which gave a piquancy to her face. But her glory was in her wonderful abundant curly hair. Yes, she was very attractive.

The first time I went to have tea with her stands out in my mind. Miss York accompanied me. Miss Etherton, Lavinia's governess, greeted us and there was an immediate rapport between her and Miss York.

We were taken to tea in the schoolroom, which was large with panelled walls and latticed windows. There were big cupboards there which I guessed contained slates and pencils and perhaps books. There was a long table at which generations of Framlings must have learned their lessons.

Lavinia and I regarded each other with a certain amount of hostility. Polly had primed me before I left. 'Don't forget, you're as good as she is. Better, I reckon.' So with Polly's words ringing in my ears, I faced her more as an adversary than a friend.

'We'll have tea in the schoolroom,' said Miss Etherton, 'and then you two can get to know each other.' She smiled at Miss York in an almost conspiratorial manner. It was

398

clear that those two would like a little respite from their charges.

Lavinia took me to a window seat and we sat down.

'You live in that awful old rectory,' she said. 'Ugh.'

'It's very nice,' I told her.

'It's not like this.'

'It doesn't have to be to be nice.'

Lavinia looked shocked that I had contradicted her and I felt that ours was not going to be the easy relationship which that between Miss York and Miss Etherton showed signs of becoming.

'What games do you play?' she asked.

'Oh . . . guessing games, with Polly my nurse and with Miss York. We sometimes imagine we are taking a journey through the world and mention all the places we should pass through.'

'What a dull game!'

'It's not.'

'Oh yes it *is*,' she affirmed as though that were the last word to be said on the matter.

The tea arrived, brought in by a maid in starched cap and apron. Lavinia dashed to the table.

'Don't forget your guest,' said Miss Etherton. 'Drusilla, will you sit here?'

There was bread and butter with strawberry jam and little cakes with coloured icing on them.

Miss York was watching me. Bread and butter first. It was impolite to have cakes before that. But Lavinia did not observe the rules. She took one of the cakes. Miss Etherton looked apologetically at Miss York, who pretended not to notice. When I had eaten my piece of bread and butter I was offered one of the cakes. I took one with blue icing on it.

'It's the last of the blue ones,' announced Lavinia. 'I wanted that.'

'Lavinia!' said Miss Etherton.

Lavinia took no notice. She regarded me, expecting me,

I knew, to give the cake to her. Remembering Polly, I did not. I deliberated, picked it up from my plate and bit into it.

Miss Etherton lifted her shoulders and looked at Miss York.

It was an uncomfortable tea-time.

I believe both Miss York and Miss Etherton were greatly relieved when it was over and we were despatched to play, leaving the two governesses together.

I followed Lavinia, who told me we were going to play hide-and-seek. She took a penny from her pocket and said: 'We'll toss.' I had no idea what she meant. 'Choose heads or tails,' she said.

I chose heads.

She spun the coin and it landed on the palm of her hands. She held it where I could not see it and said, 'I've won. That means I choose. You'll hide and I'll seek. Go on. I'll count ten . . .'

'Where . . .' I began.

'Anywhere . . .'

'But this house is so big . . . I don't know.'

' 'Course it's big. It's not that silly rectory.' She gave me a push. 'You'd better go on. I'm starting to count now.'

Of course she was Miss Lavinia of the Big House. She was a year older than I. She seemed very knowledgeable and sophisticated; and I was a guest. Miss York had told me that guests often had to be uncomfortable and do things they would rather not. It was all part of the duty of being a guest.

I went out of the room leaving Lavinia counting ominously. Three, four, five . . . It sounded like the tolling of the funeral bell.

I hurried on. The house seemed to be laughing at me. How could I possibly hide in a house of whose geography I was ignorant?

For a few moments I went blindly on. I came to a door and opened it. I was in a small room. There were some chairs, the seatbacks of which had been worked in blue and yellow needlepoint. It was the ceiling which attracted my attention; it was painted and there were little fat cupids up there seated on clouds. There was another door in this room. I went through it and I was in a passage.

There was no place to hide there. What should I do? I wondered. Perhaps make my way to the schoolroom, find Miss York and tell her I wanted to go home. I wished Polly had come with me. She would never have left me to the mercy of Miss Lavinia.

I must try to retrace my steps. I turned and went, as I thought, back. I came to a door expecting to see the fat cupids on the ceiling; but this was not so. I was in a long gallery, the walls of which were lined with pictures. There was a dais at one end on which stood a harpsichord and gilded chairs.

I looked fearfully at the portraits. They seemed like real people regarding me severely for having trespassed into their domain.

I felt the house was jeering at me and I wanted Polly. I was getting near to panic. I had the uneasy notion that I was caught and never going to get away. I was going to spend the rest of my life wandering about the house trying to find my way out.

There was a door at one end of the gallery. I went through this and was in another long passage. I was facing a flight of stairs. It was either a matter of going on or going back to the gallery. I mounted the stairs; there was another passage and then . . . a door.

Recklessly I opened this. I was in a small dark room. In spite of mounting fears I was fascinated. There was something foreign about it. The curtains were of heavy brocade and there was a strange smell. I learned afterwards that it was sandalwood. There were brass ornaments on carved wooden tables. It was an exciting room and for a moment I forgot my fears. There was a fireplace and on the mantelshelf a fan. It was very beautiful in a lovely shade of blue with big black spots. I knew what it was, because I had seen pictures of peacocks. It was a fan made of peacock feathers. I felt an urge to touch it. I could just reach it by standing on tiptoe. The feathers were very soft.

Then I looked about me. There was a door. I went to it. Perhaps I could find someone who would show me the way back to the schoolroom and Miss York.

I opened the door and looked cautiously in.

A voice said: 'Who is there?'

I advanced into the room. I said: 'It is Drusilla Delany. I came to tea and I am lost.'

I went forward. I saw a high-backed chair and in it an old lady. There was a rug over her knees which I felt showed she was an invalid. Beside her was a table strewn with papers. They looked like letters.

She peered at me and I looked back boldly. It was not my fault that I was lost. I had not been treated as a guest should be.

'Why do you come to see me, little girl?' she asked in a high-pitched voice. She was very pale and her hands shook. For a moment I thought that she was a ghost.

'I didn't. I'm playing hide-and-seek and I am lost.'

'Come here, child.'

I went.

She said: 'I have not seen you before.'

'I live in the rectory. I came to tea with Lavinia and this is supposed to be a game of hide-and-seek.'

'People don't come to see me.'

'I'm sorry.'

She shook her head. 'I am reading his letters,' she said.

'Why do you look at them if they make you cry?' I asked.

'He was so wonderful. It was ill fortune. I destroyed him. It was my fault. I should have known. I was warned . . .'

I thought she was the strangest person I had ever met. I had always sensed that extraordinary things could happen in this house.

I said I should have to go back to the schoolroom. 'They

402

will wonder where I am. And it is not very polite for guests to wander about houses, is it?'

She put out a hand which reminded me of a claw and gripped my wrist. I was about to call for help when the door opened and a woman came into the room. Her appearance startled me. She was not English. Her hair was very dark; her eyes deep-set and black; she was wearing what I learned later was a sari. It was a deep shade of blue rather like the fan and I thought it beautiful. She moved very gracefully, and said in a pleasant sing-song voice: 'Oh dearie me. Miss Lucille, what is this? And who are you, little girl?'

I explained who I was and how I came to be here.

'Oh, Miss Lavinia . . . but she is a naughty, naughty girl to treat you so. Hide-and-seek.' She lifted her hands. 'And in this house . . . and you find Miss Lucille. People do not come here. Missie Lucille likes to be alone.'

'I'm sorry, I didn't mean to.'

She patted my shoulder. 'Oh no . . . no . . . it is naughty Miss Lavinia. One of these days . . .' She pursed her lips, and putting the palms of her hands together, gazed up at the ceiling for a moment. 'But you must go back. I will show you. Come with me.'

She took my hand and pressed it reassuringly.

I looked at Miss Lucille. The tears were slowly running down her cheeks.

'This part of the house is for Miss Lucille,' I was told. 'I live here with her. We are here . . . and not here . . . You understand?'

I didn't but I nodded.

We went back by way of the gallery and then through parts which I had not seen before and it seemed to me some little time before we reached the schoolroom.

The woman opened the door. Miss York and Miss Etherton were in deep conversation. There was no sign of Lavinia.

They looked startled to see me.

'What happened?' asked Miss Etherton.

'They play hide-and-seek. This little one . . . in a house

403

she does not know. She was lost and came to Miss Lucille.'

'Oh, I *am* sorry,' said Miss Etherton. 'Miss Lavinia should have taken better care of her guest. Thank you, Ayesha.'

I turned to smile at her. I liked her gentle voice and her kind black eyes. She returned my smile and went gracefully away.

'I hope Drusilla didn't . . . er . . .' began Miss York.

'Oh no. Miss Lucille lives apart with her servants. There are others . . . both Indian. She was out there, you know. The family has connections with the East India Company. She is a little . . . strange now.'

Both governesses looked at me and I guessed the matter would be discussed further when they were alone.

I turned to Miss York and said: 'I want to go home.'

She looked uneasy but Miss Etherton gave her an understanding smile.

'Well,' went on Miss York, 'I suppose it is about time.'

'If you must . . .' replied Miss Etherton. 'I wonder where Miss Lavinia is. She should come and say goodbye to her guest.'

Lavinia was found before we left.

I said: 'Thank you,' in a cold voice.

She said: 'It was silly of you to get lost. But then you are not used to houses like this, are you?'

Miss Etherton said: 'I doubt there is another house like this, Lavinia. Well . . . you must come again.'

Miss York and I left. Miss York's lips were pursed together. But she did say to me: 'I should not care to be in Miss Etherton's shoes from what she told me . . . and the boy is worse.' Then she remembered to whom she was talking and said it had been really quite a pleasant visit.

I could hardly call it that, but at least it had held elements of excitement which I should not easily forget.

Although I was not eager to visit the house again, its fascination for me had increased. Whenever I passed it I used to wonder about the strange old lady and her companion. I was consumed with curiosity, for I was by nature inquisitive; it was a trait I shared with Polly.

I used to go down to my father's study on some days when he was not busy. It was always just after tea. I almost felt I was one of those things like his spectacles which he forgot about from time to time; it was when he needed his spectacles that he looked for them and when a sense of duty came over him he remembered me.

There was something lovable about his forgetfulness. He was always gentle with me and I was sure that if he had not been so concerned about the Trojan Wars he would have remembered me more often.

It was quite a little game talking with him, the object being for him to get on to some classical subject and for me to steer him away from it.

He always asked how I was getting on with my lessons and whether I was happy with Miss York. I thought I was doing quite well and told him that Miss York seemed satisfied.

He would nod, smiling.

'She thinks you are a little impulsive,' he said. 'Otherwise she has a good opinion of you.'

'Perhaps she thinks I am impulsive because she is not.'

'That could be so. But you must learn not to be rash. Remember Phæton.'

I was not quite sure who Phæton was but if I asked he would take possession of the conversation, and Phæton could lead to some other character from those old days when people were turned into laurels and all sorts of plants and gods became swans and bulls to go courting mortals. It seemed to me such an odd way of going on and in any case I did not believe it.

'Father,' I said, 'do you know anything about Miss Lucille Framling?'

A vague look came into his eyes. He reached for his spectacles as though they might help him to see the lady.

'I did hear Lady Harriet say something once . . . Someone in India, I think.'

'There was an Indian servant with her. I saw her. I got lost playing hide-and-seek and I found her. The Indian took me back to Miss York. It was rather exciting.'

'I did know that the Framlings were somehow connected with India. The East India Company, I suppose.'

'I wonder why she is shut off like that in a wing of the house.'

'She lost her lover, I think I heard. That can be very sad. Remember Orpheus who went down to the underworld to search for Eurydice.'

I was so preoccupied with the mystery of Miss Lucille Framling that I allowed my father to win that session and the rest of the time was taken up by Orpheus and his trip to the underworld to find the wife who had been snatched from him on their wedding day.

In spite of that unfortunate beginning my acquaintance with Lavinia progressed, and although there was always a certain antipathy between us, I was attracted by her and perhaps most of all by the house, in which anything might happen; and I never entered it without the feeling that I was embarking on an adventure.

I had told Polly about the game of hide-and-seek and how I had met the old lady.

'Tut-tut,' she said. 'There's a nice little madam for you. Don't know how to treat her guests, that's for certain. Calls herself a lady.'

'She said the rectory was small.'

'I'd like to get her carrying coal up them stairs.'

I laughed at the thought.

Polly was good for me. She said: 'You're a sight more of a little lady than she is. That's for sure. So you just stand up to her. Tell her a thing or two and if she don't like it, well, there's no harm done, is there? I reckon you could enjoy yourself somewhere nice with me . . . more than that old house. Time for it to go to the knacker's yard if you was to ask me.'

'Oh, Polly, it's the most marvellous house!'

'Pity it's got them living in it that don't know their manners.'

I used to think of Polly when I went into the House. I was as good as they were, I reminded myself. I was better at my lessons. That had slipped out. I had heard Mrs Janson say that that Miss Lavinia led Miss Etherton a nice dance and refused to learn when she didn't feel like it, so that that young lady was at least a couple of years behind some people. I knew who 'some people' implied and I felt rather proud. It was a useful piece of knowledge to be remembered when I was in the presence of Lavinia. Moreover, I knew how to behave better than she did, but perhaps she knew and refused to act as she had been taught. I had been in Lavinia's company long enough to know that she was a rebel.

Then there was Polly's admonition to give her as good as I got, so I did not feel quite so vulnerable as I had on that first occasion.

My father constantly said that all knowledge was good and one could not have too much of it. Miss York agreed with him. But there was one piece of knowledge that I could have been happier without.

Lady Harriet had smiled on my friendship with Lavinia and therefore it must persist. Lavinia was learning to ride and Lady Harriet had said that I might share her lessons. My father was delighted and so I went riding with Lavinia. We used to go round and round the paddock under the watchful eyes of Joe Cricks, the head groom.

Lavinia enjoyed riding and therefore she did it well. She took a great delight in showing how much more proficient she was than I. She was reckless and did not obey orders as I did. Poor Joe Cricks used to get really scared when she disregarded his instructions and she was very soon ordering him to take her off the leading rein.

'If you want to feel good on your mount,' said Joe Cricks, 'don't be afraid of him. Let him see that you are the master. On the other hand . . . there's dangers.'

Lavinia tossed her tawny hair. She was fond of the gesture. Her hair was really magnificent and this called attention to it.

'I know what I am doing, Cricks,' she said.

'I didn't say as how you didn't, Miss Lavinia. All I says is . . . you have to consider the horse as well as yourself. You may know what you're doing but horses is nervous creatures. They get it into their heads to do something you might not be expecting.'

Lavinia continued to go her own way; and her very boldness and assurance that she knew better than anyone else carried her through.

'She's going to be a good horsewoman,' was Joe Cricks's comment. 'That's if she don't take too many risks. Now, Miss Drusilla, she's a more steady party. She'll come to it in time . . . then she'll be real good.'

I loved the lessons, trotting round the paddock, the excitement of the first canter, the thrill of the first gallop.

It was one afternoon. We had had our lessons and had taken the horses back to the stables. Lavinia dismounted and threw her reins to the groom. I always liked to stay behind for a few minutes to pat the horse and talk to him, which was what Joe had taught us to do. 'Never forget,' he said. 'Treat your horse well and the chances are he'll treat you well. Horses is like people. You have to remember that.'

I came out of the stables and started across the lawn to the house. There I was to join Lavinia in the schoolroom for tea. Miss York was already there enjoying a tête-à-tête with Miss Etherton.

There were visitors in the house. There often were, but they did not concern us. We hardly ever saw Lady Harriet – a fact for which I was extremely grateful.

I had to pass the drawing-room window which was open

and I caught a glimpse of a parlourmaid serving tea to several people. I went hurriedly past, averting my eyes. Then I paused to look up at that part of the house which I thought must be Miss Lucille's quarters.

As I did so I heard a voice from the drawing-room. 'Who is that *plain* child, Harriet?'

'Oh . . . you mean the rector's daughter. She is here quite frequently. She comes to keep Lavinia company.'

'Such a contrast to Lavinia! But then, Lavinia is so beautiful.'

'Oh yes . . . You see there are so few people . . . I gather she is quite a pleasant child. The governess thinks so . . . and it is good for Lavinia to have the occasional companion. There aren't so many people here, you know. We have to make do with what we can get.'

I stared ahead of me. *I* was the plain child. *I* was here because they couldn't get anyone else. I was stunned. I knew that my hair was a nondescript brown, that it was straight and unmanageable . . . so different from Lavinia's tawny locks; my eyes were no colour at all. They were like water and if I wore blue they were bluish, green greenish . . . and brown . . . just no colour at all. I knew I had a big mouth and an ordinary sort of nose. So that was plain.

And of course Lavinia was beautiful.

My first thought was to go into the schoolroom and demand to be taken home at once. I was very upset. There was a hard lump in my throat. I did not cry. Crying for me was for lighter emotions. Something within me was deeply hurt and I believed that the wound would be with me for ever.

'You're late,' Lavinia greeted me.

I did not explain. I knew what her reaction would be.

I looked at her afresh. No wonder she could behave badly. She was so beautiful that people did not mind.

Polly, of course, noticed my preoccupation.

'Here, don't you think you'd better tell me?'

'Tell you what, Polly?'

409

'Why you look about as happy as if you've lost a sovereign and found a farthing.'

I could not hold out against Polly, so I told her. 'I'm plain, Polly. That means ugly. And I go to the House only because there is no one better here.'

'I never heard such a load of nonsense. You're not plain. You're what they call interesting, and that's a lot better in the long run. And if you don't want to go to that house, I'll see you don't. I'll go to the rector and tell him it's got to stop. From what I hear you'd be no worse without them.'

'How plain am I, Polly?'

'About as plain as Dundee cake and Christmas pudding.'

That made me smile.

'You've got what they call one of them faces that make people stop and take a second look. As for that Lavinia, or whatever she calls herself, *I* don't call her all that pretty when she scowls – and my goodness she does a good bit of that. I'll tell you what. She'll have crows' feet round her eyes and railway lines all over her face the way she goes on. And I'll tell you something else. When you smile your face all lights up. Well, then you're a real beauty, you are.'

Polly raised my spirits and after a while I began to forget about being plain, and as the House always fascinated me, I tried not to remember that I was only chosen because there was no one better available.

I had caught glimpses of Fabian, though not often. Whenever I did see him I thought of the time when he had made me his baby. He must remember, surely, because he would have been seven when it happened.

He was away at school most of the time and often he did not come home for holidays but spent them with some schoolfriend. Schoolfriends came to the House sometimes but they took little notice of us.

On this occasion – it was Easter time, I think – Fabian was home for the holidays. Soon after Miss York and I arrived at the House it began to rain. We had tea and Lavinia and I left the governesses together for their usual chat. We were wondering what to do when the door opened and Fabian came in.

He was rather like Lavinia only much taller and very grown up. He was four years older than Lavinia and that seemed a great deal, particularly to me who was a year younger than Lavinia. He must therefore have been twelve and as I was not yet seven, he seemed very mature.

Lavinia went to him and hung on his arm as though to say, This is my brother. You can go back to Miss York. I shan't need you now.

He was looking at me oddly – remembering, I knew. I was the child whom he had thought was his. Surely such an episode must have left an impression even on someone as worldly as Fabian.

'Will you stay with me?' pleaded Lavinia. 'Will you tell me what we can do? Drusilla has such silly ideas. She likes what she thinks are clever games. Miss Etherton says she knows more than I do . . . about history and things like that.'

'She wouldn't have to know much to know more than you do,' said Fabian, a remark which, coming from anyone else, would have thrown Lavinia into a temper; but because Fabian had said it, she giggled happily. It was quite a revelation to me that there was one person of whom Lavinia stood in awe, not counting Lady Harriet of course, of whom everyone was in awe.

He said: 'History . . . I like history, Romans and all that. They had slaves. We'll have a game.'

'Oh, Fabian . . . really?'

'Yes. I am a Roman, Cæsar, I think.'

'Which one?' I asked.

He considered. 'Julius . . . or perhaps Tiberius.'

'He was very cruel to the Christians.'

'You need not be a Christian slave. I shall be Cæsar. You are my slaves and I shall test you.'

411

'I'll be your queen . . . or whatever Cæsars have,' announced Lavinia. 'Drusilla can be our slave.'

'You'll be a slave, too,' said Fabian, to my delight and Lavinia's dismay.

'I shall give you tasks . . . which seem to you impossible. It is to prove you and see whether you are worthy to be my slaves. I shall say, Bring me the golden apples of the Hesperides . . . or something like that.'

'How could we get them?' I asked. 'They are in the Greek legends. My father is always talking about them. They are not real.'

Lavinia was getting impatient as I, the plain outsider, was talking too much.

'I shall give you the tasks to perform and you must carry them out or suffer my anger.'

'Not if it means going down to the underworld and bringing out people who are dead and that sort of thing,' I said.

'I shall not command you to do *that*. The tasks will be difficult . . . but possible.'

He folded his arms across his chest and shut his eyes as though deep in thought. Then he spoke, as though he were the Oracle of whom my father talked now and then. 'Lavinia, you will bring me the silver chalice. It must be a certain chalice. It has acanthus leaves engraved on it.'

'I can't,' said Lavinia. 'It's in the haunted room.'

I had never seen Lavinia so stricken, and what astonished me was that her brother had the power to drive the rebellion out of her.

He turned to me. 'You will bring me a fan of peacock feathers. And when my slaves return to me, the chalice shall be filled with wine and while I drink it my slave shall fan me with the peacock feather fan.'

My task did not seem so difficult. I knew where there was a peacock feather fan. I was better acquainted with the house than I had once been and I could find my way easily to Miss Lucille's apartments. I could slip into the room where I knew the fan to be, take it and bring it to Fabian. I should do it so quickly that he would commend me for my speed, while poor Lavinia was screwing up courage to go to the haunted room.

I sped on my way. A feeling of intense excitement gripped me. The presence of Fabian thrilled me because I kept thinking of the way in which he had kidnapped me, and there I had been, living in the house for two weeks just as though I were a member of the family. I wanted to astonish him with the speed with which I carried out my task.

I reached the room. What if the Indian was there? What would I say to her? 'Please may I have the fan? We are playing a game and I am a slave.'

She would smile, I guessed and say: 'Dearie, dearie me,' in that sing-song voice of hers. I was sure she would be amused and amenable; but I wondered about the old lady. But she would be in the adjoining room sitting in the chair with the rug over her knees crying because of the past which came back to her with the letters.

I had opened the door cautiously. I smelt the pungent sandalwood. All was quiet. And there on the mantelshelf was the fan.

I stood on tiptoe and reached it. I took it down and then ran out of the room back to Fabian.

He stared at me in amazement.

'You've found it already?' He laughed. 'I never thought you would. How did you know where it was?'

'I'd seen it before. It was when I was playing hide-and-seek with Lavinia. I went into that room by accident. I was lost.'

'Did you see my great-aunt Lucille?'

I nodded. He continued to stare at me.

'Well done, slave,' he said. 'Now you may fan me while I await my chalice of wine.'

'Do you want to be fanned? It's rather cold in here.'

He looked towards the window from which came a faint draught. Raindrops trickled down the panes.

'Are you questioning my orders, slave?' he asked.

As it was a game I replied: 'No, my lord.'

'Then do my bidding.'

It was soon after that when Lavinia returned with the chalice. She gave me a venomous look because I had succeeded in my task before she had. I found I was enjoying the game.

Wine had to be found and the chalice filled. Fabian stretched himself out on a sofa. I stood behind him wielding the peacock feather fan. Lavinia was kneeling proffering the chalice.

It was not long before trouble started. We heard raised voices and running footsteps. I recognized that of Ayesha.

Miss Etherton followed by Miss York burst into the room.

There was a dramatic moment. Others whom I had not seen before were there and they were all staring at me. There was a moment's deep silence and then Miss York rushed at me.

'What have you done?' she cried.

Ayesha saw me and gave a little cry. 'You have it,' she said. 'It is you. Dearie, dearie me . . . so it is you.'

I realized then that they were referring to the fan.

'How could you?' said Miss York. I looked bewildered and she went on; 'You took the fan. Why?'

'It . . . it was a game,' I stammered.

'A game!' said Miss Etherton. 'The fan . . .' Her voice was shaking with emotion.

'I'm sorry,' I began.

Then Lady Harriet came in. She looked like an avenging goddess and my knees suddenly felt as though they would not hold me.

Fabian had risen from the sofa. 'What a fuss!' he said. 'She was my slave. *I* commanded her to bring me the fan.'

I saw the relief in Miss Etherton's face and I felt a spurt of laughter bubbling up. It might have been mildly hysterical but it was laughter all the same.

Lady Harriet's face had softened. 'Oh, Fabian!' she murmured.

Ayesha said: 'But the fan . . . Miss Lucille's fan . . .'

'I commanded her,' repeated Fabian. 'She had no alternative but to obey. She is my slave.'

Lady Harriet began to laugh. 'Well, now you understand, Ayesha. Take the fan back to Miss Lucille. No harm has been done to it and that is an end to the matter.' She turned to Fabian. 'Lady Goodman has written asking if you would care to visit Adrian for part of the summer holiday. How do you feel?'

Fabian shrugged his shoulders nonchalantly.

'Shall we talk about it? Come along, dear boy. I think we should give a prompt reply.'

Fabian, casting a rather scornful look at the company which had been so concerned over such a trivial matter as the borrowing of a fan, left with his mother.

The incident was, I thought, over. They had been so concerned and it seemed to me that there was something important about the fan, but Lady Harriet and Fabian between them had reduced it to a matter of no importance.

Ayesha had gone, carrying the fan as though it was very precious, and the two governesses had followed her. Lavinia and I were alone.

'I have to take the chalice back before they find we had that, too. I wonder they didn't notice, but there was such a fuss over the fan. You'll have to come with me.'

I was still feeling shocked because I had been the one to take the fan, which was clearly a very important article since it had caused such a disturbance. I wondered what would have happened if Fabian had not been there to exonerate me from blame. I should probably have been banned from the house for evermore. I should have hated that, although I never felt welcome there. Still, the fascination was strong. All the people in it interested me . . . even Lavinia who was frequently rude and certainly never hospitable.

415

I thought how noble Fabian had looked pouring scorn on them all and taking the responsibility. Of course, it *was* his responsibility, and it was only right that he should take the blame. But he had made it seem that there was no blame, and that they were all rather foolish to make such a fuss.

Meekly I followed Lavinia to another part of the house which I had never seen before.

'Great-Aunt Lucille is in the west wing. This is the east,' she told me. 'We are going to the Nun's room. You had better watch out. The Nun doesn't like strangers. I'm all right. I'm one of the family.'

'Well, why are you frightened to go alone?'

'I'm not frightened. I just thought you'd like to see it. You haven't got any ghosts in that old rectory, have you?'

'Who wants ghosts anyway? What good do they do?'

'A great house always has them. They warn people.'

'Then if the Nun wouldn't want me, I'll leave you to go on your own.'

'No, no. You've got to come, too.'

'Suppose I won't.'

'Then I'll never let you come to this house again.'

'I wouldn't mind. You're not very nice . . . any of you.'

'Oh, how dare you! You are only the rector's daughter and he owes the living to us.'

I was afraid there might be something in that. Perhaps Lady Harriet could turn us out if she were displeased with me. I understood Lavinia. She wanted me with her because she was afraid to go to the Nun's room alone.

We went along a corridor. She turned and took my hand. 'Come on,' she whispered. 'It's just along here.'

She opened a door. We were in a small room which looked like a nun's cell. Its walls were bare and there was a crucifix hanging over a narrow bed. There was just one table and chair. The atmosphere was one of austerity.

She put the chalice on the table and in great haste ran out of the room, followed by me. We sped along the corridors and then she turned to regard me with satisfaction. Her natural arrogance and composure had returned. She led the way back to that room where a short time before Fabian had sprawled on a sofa and I had fanned him with the peacock feather fan.

'You see,' said Lavinia, 'we have a lot of history in our family. We came over with the Conqueror. I reckon your family were serfs.'

'Oh no, we were not.'

'Yes, you were. Well, the Nun was one of our ancestresses. She fell in love with an unsuitable man . . . I believe he was a curate or a rector. Those sort of people do not marry into families like ours.'

'They would have been better educated than your people, I dare say.'

'*We* don't have to worry about education. It is only people like you who have to do that. Miss Etherton says you know more than I do although you're a year younger. I don't care. *I* don't have to be educated.'

'Education is the greatest boon you can have,' I said, quoting my father. 'Tell me about the Nun.'

'He was so far below her that she couldn't marry him. Her father forbade it and she went into a convent. But she couldn't live without him, so she escaped and went to him. Her brother went after them and killed the lover. She was brought home and put in that room which was like a cell. It has never been changed. She drank poison from the chalice and she is supposed to come back to that room and haunt it.'

'Do you believe that?'

'Of course I do.'

'You must have been very frightened when you came in for the chalice.'

'It's what you have to do when you're playing Fabian's games. I thought that since Fabian had sent me the ghost wouldn't hurt me.'

'You seem to think your brother is some sort of god.'

417

'He is,' she replied.

It did seem that he was regarded as such in that household.

When we walked home, Miss York said: 'My goodness, what a to-do about a fan. There would have been real trouble if Mr Fabian hadn't been behind it.'

I was more and more fascinated by the House. I often thought of the nun who had drunk from the chalice and killed herself for love. I talked of this to Miss York, who had discovered from Miss Etherton that Miss Lucille had become quite ill when she discovered that the peacock feather fan had been taken away.

'No wonder,' she said, 'that there was all that fuss about it. Mr Fabian should never have told you to take it. There was no way that you could know. Sheer mischief, I call it.'

'Why should a fan be so important?'

'Oh, there is something about peacock's feathers. I have heard they are unlucky.'

I wondered whether this theory might have something to do with Greek mythology and if it did my father would certainly know about it. I decided to risk a lecture session with him and ask.

'Father,' I said, 'Miss Lucille at the House has a fan made of peacock's feathers. There is something special about it. Is there any reason why there should be anything important about peacock's feathers?'

'Well, Hera put the eyes of Argus in the peacock's tail. Of course you know the story.'

Of course I did not, but I asked to hear it.

It turned out to be another of those about Zeus courting someone. This time it was the daughter of the King of Argos and Zeus's wife, Hera, discovered this.

'She shouldn't have been surprised,' I said. 'He was always courting someone he shouldn't.'

'That's true. He turned the fair maiden into a white cow.'

'That was a change. He usually transformed himself.'

418

'On this occasion it was otherwise. Hera was jealous.'

'I'm not surprised ... with such a husband. But she should have grown used to his ways.'

'She set the monster Argus who had one hundred eyes to watch. Knowing this, Zeus sent Hermes to lull him to sleep with his lyre and when he was asleep to kill him. Hera was angry when she learned what had happened and placed the eyes of the dead monster in the tails of her pet peacocks.'

'Is that why the feathers are unlucky?'

'Are they? When I come to think of it, I fancy I have heard something of that nature.'

So he could not tell me more than that. I thought to myself: It is because of the eyes. They are watching all the time ... as Argus failed to do. Why should Miss Lucille worry so much because the eyes are not there to watch for her?

The mystery deepened. What an amazing house it was, which had a ghost in the form of a long-dead nun and a magic fan with eyes to watch out for its owner. Did it, I wondered, warn of impending disaster?

I felt that anything could happen in that house; there was so much to discover and, in spite of the fact that I was plain and only asked because there was no one else to be a companion to Lavinia, I wanted to go on visiting the house.

It was a week or so after the incident of the fan that I discovered I was being watched. When I rode in the paddock I was aware of an irresistible urge to look up at a certain window high in the wall and it was from this one that I felt I was being overlooked. It was a shadow at the window which was there for a moment and then disappeared. Several times I thought I saw someone there. It was quite uncanny.

I said to Miss Etherton: 'Which part of the house is it that looks over the paddock?'

'That is the west wing. It is not used very much. Miss Lucille is there. They always think of it as her part of the house.'

I had guessed that might be so and now I was sure.

One day when I took my horse to the stable, Lavinia ran on ahead and as I was about to return to the house, I saw Ayesha. She came swiftly towards me and taking my hand looked into my face.

She said: 'Miss Drusilla, I have waited to find you alone. Miss Lucille wants very much to speak to you.'

'What?' I cried. 'Now?'

'Yes,' she answered. 'This moment.'

'Lavinia will be waiting for me.'

'Never mind that one now.'

I followed her into the house and up the staircase, along corridors to the room in the west wing where Miss Lucille was waiting for me.

She was seated in a chair near the window which looked down on the paddock and from which she had watched me.

'Come here, child,' she said.

I went to her. She took my hand and looked searchingly into my face. 'Bring a chair, Ayesha,' she said.

Ayesha brought one and it was placed very near Miss Lucille.

Ayesha then withdrew and I was alone with the old lady.

'Tell me what made you do it,' she said. 'What made you steal the fan?'

I explained that Fabian was a great Roman and that Lavinia and I were his slaves. He was testing us and giving us difficult tasks. Mine was to bring a peacock fan to him, and I knew there was one in that room, so I came and took it.

'So Fabian is involved in this. There are two of you. But you were the one who took it and that means that for a while it was in your possession ... *yours*. That will be remembered.'

'Who will remember?'

'Fate, my dear child. I am sorry you took the fan. Anything else you might have taken for your game and no harm

420

done, but there is something about a peacock's feathers . . .
something mystic . . . and menacing.'

I shivered and looked around me. 'Are they unlucky?' I
asked.

She looked mournful. 'You are a nice little girl and I am
sorry you touched it. You will have to be on your guard
now.'

'Why?' I asked excitedly.

'Because that fan brings tragedy.'

'How can it?'

'I do not know *how*. I only know it does.'

'If you think that why do you keep it?'

'Because I have paid for my possession.'

'How do you pay?'

'I paid with my life's happiness.'

'Shouldn't you throw the fan away?'

She shook her head. 'No. One must never do that. To do
so is to pass on the curse.'

'The curse!' This was getting more and more fantastic. It
seemed even wilder than my father's version of the maiden
being turned into a white cow.

'Why?' I asked.

'Because it is written.'

'Who wrote it?'

She shook her head and I went on: 'How can a feather
fan be unlucky? It is after all only a fan, and who could
harm the one who had it? The peacock whose feathers it
was must be dead a long time ago.'

'You have not been in India, my child. Strange things
happen there. I have seen men in bazaars charm poisonous
snakes and make them docile. I have seen what is called the
Rope Trick when a seer will make a rope stand on end
without support and a little boy climb it. If you were in
India you would believe these things. Here people are
too materialistic; they are not in tune with the mystic. If
I had never had that fan I should be a happy wife and
mother.'

'Why do you watch me? Why do you send for me and tell me all this?'

'Because you have had the fan in your possession. You have been its owner. The ill luck could touch you. I want you to take care.'

'I never thought for an instant that it was mine. I just took it for a while because Fabian commanded me to take it. That was all. It was just a game.'

I thought: She is mad. How can a fan be evil? How could someone turn a woman into a white cow? My father seemed to believe this, though, which was extraordinary. At least he talked as though he believed it. But then the Greeks were more real to him than his own household.

'How can you be sure that the fan is unlucky?' I asked.

'Because of what happened to me.' She turned to me and fixed her tragic eyes on me, but they seemed to be staring past me as though she were seeing something which was not in this room.

'I was so happy,' she said. 'Perhaps it is a mistake to be so happy. It is tempting the fates. Gerald was wonderful. I met him in Delhi. Our families have interests there. They thought it would be good for me to go out for a while. There is a good social life among the English and the members of the Company — that is the East India Company — and we were involved in that. So was Gerald and his family. That was why he was out there. He was so handsome and so charming . . . there could never have been anyone like him. We were in love with each other from the first day we met.'

She turned to smile at me. 'You are too young to understand, my child. It was . . . perfect. His family were pleased . . . so were mine. There was no reason why we should not be married. Everyone was delighted when we announced our engagement. My family gave a ball to celebrate the occasion. It was really glittering. I wish I could describe India to you, my dear. It was a wonderful life we had. Who would have guessed that there was a tragedy waiting to spring up on us? It came suddenly . . . like a thief in the night, as it says in the Bible, I believe. So it came to me.'

'Was it because of the fan?' I asked tremulously.

'Oh, the fan. How young we were! How innocent of life! We went to the bazaar together, for when we were officially engaged that was allowed. It was wonderful. Bazaars are so fascinating, although I was always a little afraid of them though not with Gerald, of course. It was thrilling . . . the snake charmers . . . the streets . . . the strange music . . . that pungent smell which is India. Goods to sell . . . beautiful silks and ivory . . . and strange things to eat. It was exciting. And as we went along we saw the man selling fans. I was instantly struck by them. "How lovely they are!" I cried. Gerald said: "They are very pretty. You must have one." I remember the man who sold them. He was badly crippled. He could not stand up. He sat on a mat. I remember the way he smiled at us. I did not notice it then but afterwards it came back to me. It was . . . evil. Gerald unfurled the fan and I took it. It was doubly precious to me because he had given it to me. Gerald laughed at my delight in it. He held my arm tightly. People looked at us as we passed along. I suppose it was because we looked so happy. Back in my room I opened the fan. I put it on a table so that I could see it all the time. When my Indian servant came in, she stared at it in horror. She said, "Peacock feather fan . . . Oh no, no, Missie Lucille . . . they bring evil . . . You must not keep it here." I answered, "Don't be silly. My fiancé gave it to me and I shall always treasure it for that reason. It is his first gift to me." She shook her head and covered her face with her hands as though to shut out the sight of it. Then she said, "I will take it back to the man who sold it to you . . . though now it has been yours . . . the evil is there . . . but perhaps a small evil." I thought she was crazy and I wouldn't let her touch it.'

She stopped speaking and the tears began to run down her cheeks.

'I loved the fan,' she went on after a while. 'It was the

first thing he gave me after our engagement. When I awoke in the morning it was the first thing I saw. Always, I told myself, I will remember that moment in the bazaar when he bought it for me. He laughed at my obsession with it. I did not know it then, but I do now. It had already cast its spell on me. "It is only a fan," said Gerald. "Why do you care so much for it?" I told him why and he went on, "Then I will make it more worthy of your regard. I shall have something precious put in it, and every time you see it you will be reminded of how much I care for you."

'He said he would take it to a jeweller he knew in Delhi. The man was a craftsman. When I received the fan back it would indeed be something to be proud of. I was delighted and so happy. I ought to have known happiness like that does not last. He took the fan and went into the centre of the town. I have never forgotten that day. Every second of it is engraved on my memory for ever. He went into the jeweller's shop. He was there quite a long time. And when he came out . . . they were waiting for him. There was often trouble. The Company kept it under control but there were always the mad ones. They didn't see what good we were bringing to their country. They wanted us out. Gerald's family was important in the country . . . as my family were. He was well known among them. When he came out of the jeweller's they shot him. He died there in the street.'

'What a sad story. I am so sorry, Miss Lucille,' I said.

'My dear child, I see you are. You are a good child. I am sorry you took the fan.'

'You believe all that was due to the fan?'

'It was because of the fan that he was in that spot. I shall never forget the look in my servant's eyes. Somehow those people have a wisdom we lack. How I wish I had never seen that fan . . . never gone into the bazaar that morning. How blithe and gay I had been . . . and my foolish impulse had taken his life and ruined mine.'

'It could have happened somewhere else.'

'No, it was the fan. You see, he had taken it into the

jeweller's shop. They must have followed him and waited for him outside.'

'I think it could have happened without the fan.'

She shook her head. 'In time it came back to me. I will show you what was done.' She sat there for a few moments with the tears coursing down her cheeks. Ayesha came in.

'There, there,' she said. 'You shouldn't have brought it all back to yourself. Dearie me, dearie me, it is not good, little mistress . . . not good.'

'Ayesha,' she said. 'Bring the fan to me.'

Ayesha said: 'No . . . forget it . . . Do not distress yourself.'

'Bring it please, Ayesha.'

So she brought it.

'See, child, this is what he did for me. One has to know how to move this panel. You see. There is a little catch here. The jeweller was a great craftsman.' She pulled back the panel on the mount of the fan to disclose a brilliant emerald surrounded by smaller diamonds. I caught my breath. It was so beautiful.

'It is worth a small fortune, they tell me, as if to console me. As if anything could. But it was his gift to me. That is why the fan is precious.'

'But if it is going to bring you bad luck . . .'

'It has done that. It can bring me no more. Ayesha, put it back. There. I have told you because, briefly, the fan was yours. You must walk more carefully than most. You are a good child. There. Go and rejoin Lavinia now. I have done my duty. Be on your guard . . . with Fabian. You see, he will take some of the blame. Perhaps because you were in possession of it for such a short time it will pass over you. And he, too, would not be considered free of blame . . .'

Ayesha said: 'It is time to leave now.'

She took me to the door and walked with me along the corridors.

'You must not take too much notice of what she says,' she told me. 'She is very sad and her mind wanders. It was

425

the terrible shock, you understand. Do not worry about what you have heard. Perhaps I should not have brought you to her, but she wanted it. She could not rest until she had talked to you. It is off her mind now. You understand?'

'Yes, I understand.'

And I said to myself: What happened made her mad.

And the thought of the ghostly nun in the east wing and the mad woman in the west made the house seem more and more fascinating to me.

As time passed I ceased to think about the peacock feather fan and to wonder what terrible things might befall me because it had once been in my possession. I still visited the House; the governesses remained friendly; and my relationship with Lavinia had changed a little. I might still be plain and invited because I was the only girl in the neighbourhood of Lavinia's age and my station in life was not too lowly for me to be dismissed entirely, but I was gaining a little superiority over Lavinia because while she was exceptionally pretty I was more clever. Miss York boasted a little to Miss Etherton and on one occasion when Miss Etherton was ill, Miss York went over to the House to take her place until she recovered; and then the gap between myself and Lavinia was exposed. That did a lot for me and was not without its effect on Lavinia.

I was growing up. I was no longer to be put upon. I even threatened not to go to the House if Lavinia did not mend her ways; and it was obvious that that was something she did not want. We had become closer — even allies, when the occasion warranted it. I might be plain but I was clever. She might be beautiful but she could not think and invent as I could; and she relied on me – though she would not admit it – to take the lead.

Occasionally I saw Fabian. He came home for holidays and sometimes brought friends with him. They always ignored us; but I began to notice that Fabian was not so unaware of my presence as he would have us believe.

Sometimes I caught his furtive glance on me. I supposed it was due to that adventure long ago when I was a baby and he had kidnapped me.

It was whispered now that Miss Lucille was mad. Mrs Janson was very friendly with the cook at the House so, as she said, she had it 'straight from the horse's mouth'. Polly was like a jackdaw. She seized on every bit of dazzling gossip and stored it up so that she could, as she said 'piece things together a treat'.

We used to talk about the House often, for Polly seemed as fascinated by it as I was.

'The old lady's mad,' she said. 'Not a doubt of it. Never been right in her head since she lost her lover out in India. People must expect trouble if they go to these outlandish places. It turned Miss Lucille's head all right. Mrs Brent says she's taken to wandering about the House now . . . ordering them around like they was black servants. It all comes of going to India. Why people can't stay at home, I don't know. She thinks she's still in India. It's all that Ayesha can do to look after her. And she's got another black servant there.'

'That's Imam. He comes from India too. I think she brought him with her when she came home . . . with Ayesha, of course.'

'Gives me the creeps. Them outlandish clothes and black eyes and talking a sort of gibberish.'

'It's not gibberish, Polly. It's their own language.'

'Why didn't she have a nice British couple to look after her? Then there's that haunted room and something about a nun. Love trouble there, too. I don't know. I think love's something to keep away from, if you ask me.'

'You didn't feel like that when you had Tom.'

'You can't find men like my Tom two a penny, I can tell you.'

'But everyone hopes you can. That's why they fall in love.'

'You're getting too clever, my girl. Look at our Eff.'

'Is he still as bad?'

Polly just clicked her tongue.

Oddly enough, after that conversation, there was news of Him. Apparently he had been suffering, as Polly said, from 'Chest' for some time. I remember the day when news came that he was dead.

Polly was deeply shocked. She wasn't sure what this was going to mean to Eff.

'I'll have to go up for the funeral,' she said. 'After all, you've got to show a bit of respect.'

'You didn't have much for him when he was alive,' I pointed out.

'It's different when people are dead.'

'Why?'

'Oh, you and your "whys" and "whats". It just is . . . that's all.'

'Polly,' I said. 'Why can't I come to the funeral with you?'

She stared at me in amazement.

'You! Eff wouldn't expect that.'

'Well, let's surprise her.'

Polly was silent. I could see she was turning the idea over in her mind.

'Well,' she said at length, 'it would show respect.'

I learned that respect was a very necessary part of funerals.

'We'd have to ask your father,' she announced at length.

'He wouldn't notice whether I had gone or not.'

'Now that's not the way to speak about your father.'

'Why not, if it's the truth? And I like it that way. I wouldn't want him taking a real interest. I'll tell him.'

He did look a little startled when I mentioned it.

He put his hands up to his spectacles which he expected to have on his head. They weren't there and he looked helpless as though he couldn't possibly deal with the matter until he found them. They were, fortunately, on his desk, and I promptly brought them to him.

'It's Polly's sister and it shows respect,' I told him.

'I hope this does not mean she will want to leave us.'

'Leave us!' The idea had not occurred to me. 'Of course she won't want to leave us.'

'She might want to live with her sister.'

'Oh no,' I cried. 'But I think I ought to go to this funeral.'

'It could be a morbid affair. The working classes make a great deal of them . . . spending money they can ill afford.'

'I want to go, Father. I want to see her sister. She's always talking about her.'

He nodded. 'Well, then you should go.'

'We shall be there for a few days.'

'I dare say that will be all right. You will have Polly with you.'

Polly was delighted that I was going with her. She said Eff would be pleased.

So I shared in the funeral rites and very illuminating I found it.

I was surprised by the size of Eff's house. It faced a common round which the four-storied houses stood like sentinels. 'Eff always liked a bit of green,' Polly told me. 'And she's got it there. A little bit of the country and the horses clopping by to let her know she's not right out in the wilds.'

'It's what you call the best of both worlds,' I said.

'Well, I won't quarrel with that,' agreed Polly.

Eff was about four years older than Polly but looked more. When I mentioned this Polly replied: 'It's the life she's led.' She did not mention Him because he was dead and when people died, I realized, their sins were washed away by the all-important respect; but I knew it was life with Him which had aged Eff beyond her years. I was surprised, for she did not seem to be the sort of woman who could be easily cowed even by Him. She was like Polly in many ways; she had the same shrewd outlook on life and that sort of confidence which declared that none was going to get the better of her before anyone had attempted to do so. During my brief stay I recognized the same outlook in others. It was what is referred to as the cockney spirit; and it certainly seemed to be a product of the streets of London.

That visit was a great revelation to me. I felt I had entered a different world. It excited me. Polly was part of it and I wanted to know more of it.

Eff was a little nervous of me at first. She kept apologizing for things. 'Not what you're used to, I'm sure,' until Polly said: 'Don't you worry about Drusilla, Eff. Me and her get on like a house afire, don't we?' I assured Eff that we did.

Every now and then Polly and Eff would laugh and then remember Him lying in state in the front parlour.

'He makes a lovely corpse,' said Eff. 'Mrs Green came in to lay him out and she's done a good job on him.'

We sat in the kitchen and talked about him. I did not recognize him as the monster of the past; I was about to remind Polly of this, but when I attempted to she gave me a little kick under the table to remind me in time of the respect owed to the dead.

I shared a room with Polly. We lay in bed that first night and talked about funerals and how they hadn't known how ill He had been until He had been 'took sudden'. I was comforted in this strange house to be close to Polly because below us in the parlour lay 'the corpse'.

The great day came. Vaguely I remember now those solemn undertakers in their top hats and black coats, the plumed horses, the coffin 'genuine oak with real brass fittings', as Eff proudly explained.

It was piled with flowers. Eff had given him 'The Gates of Heaven Ajar' which I thought a little optimistic for one of his reputation – before death, that was. Polly and I had hurried to the flower shop and bought a wreath in the shape of a harp, which seemed hardly suitable either. But I was learning that death changed everything.

There was a solemn service, with Eff being supported on one side by Polly and on the other by Mr Branley to whom she let rooms in the house. She drooped and kept touching her eyes with a black-bordered handkerchief. I began to think that Polly had not told me the truth about Him.

There were ham sandwiches and sherry which was taken in the parlour – blinds now drawn up and looking quite different without the coffin – a little prim and un-lived-in but without the funereal gloom.

I learned that there was a great bond between Polly and Eff although they might be a little critical of each other – Polly of Eff for marrying Him and Eff of Polly because she had 'gone into service'. Father, Eff hinted, would never have approved of that. Mind you, Eff conceded, it was a special sort of service and Polly was almost one of the family with that rector who never seemed to know whether he was standing on his head or his heels, and Eff admitted that I was 'a nice little thing'.

I gathered that Eff was in no financial difficulties. Polly told me that it was Eff who had kept things going in the house on the common. *He* hadn't worked for years because of his Chest. Eff had taken lodgers. The Branleys had been with her for two years and they were more like friends than tenants. One day, of course, when the little nipper grew up they would have to consider getting a place of their own with a garden, but just now the Branleys were safe.

I realized that Eff's fondness for the Branleys was largely due to 'the nipper'. The nipper was six months old and he dribbled and bawled without reason. Eff allowed them to keep his perambulator in the hall – a great concession of which Father would never have approved – and Mrs Branley would bring him down so that he could have his airing in the garden. Eff liked that; and I gathered so did Polly. When he lay in his pram Eff would find some excuse to go into the garden and gaze at him. If he was crying – which was often – they would babble nonsense at him. 'Didums want his Mumums then?' or something like that, which sounded so strange on their lips as they were both what Mrs Janson would have called 'sharp-tongued'. They were completely changed by this baby.

431

It occurred to me that the great lack in the lives both of Polly and Eff was a baby of their own. Babies seemed to be very desirable creatures – even Fabian had wanted one.

I remember very well an occasion two days after the funeral. Polly and I were going back to the rectory the next day. Polly had been making the most of our last day and she had taken me 'up West', which meant the West End of London.

We were in the kitchen. I was seated by the fire and I was so sleepy that I dozed off.

Vaguely I heard Polly say: 'Look at Drusilla. She's half asleep already. Well, we did a bit of traipsing about, I can tell you.' Then I really did doze.

I awoke suddenly. Eff and Polly were at the table, a big brown earthenware teapot between them.

Eff was saying: 'I reckon I could take two more people in here.'

'I don't know what Father would have said, you taking in lodgers.'

'They call them paying guests . . . in the sort of place I'll have. Did you know, Poll, the Martins next door are going and I reckon I could take on that place.'

'Whatever for?'

'More paying guests, of course. I reckon I could make a real business out of this, Poll.'

'I reckon you could.'

'Mind you – I'd need help.'

'What'll you do . . . get someone to come in with you?'

'I'd want somebody I know. Somebody I could trust.'

'Nice business.'

'What about you, Poll?'

There was a long silence. I was quite wide awake now.

'The two of us would make a regular go of this,' said Eff. 'It would be a nice little venture. You in service . . . well, you know Father would never have liked that.'

'I wouldn't leave Drusilla. She means a lot to me, that child.'

'Nice little thing. No beauty . . . but she's sharp and I reckon she's got a way with her.'

'Sh!' said Polly.

She looked in my direction and I immediately closed my eyes.

'Well, that won't go on forever, Poll. I reckon sisters ought to stick together.'

'If it wasn't for her I'd be with you like a shot, Eff.'

'You like the sound of it, do you?'

'I'd like to be here. The country's dead dull. I like a bit of life.'

'Don't I know that! Always did, always will. That's you, Poll.'

'While she wants me I'll be there.'

'You think about it, that's all. You don't want to be at the beck and call of others all your life. You was never one for that.'

'Oh, there's not much of the beck and call there, Eff. He's soft . . . and she's like my own.'

'Well, it would be a good life. The two of us working together.'

'It's nice to know you're there, Eff.'

So a new fear had come into my life. There would come a day when I should lose Polly.

'Polly,' I said to her that night when we had retired. 'You won't go away from me, will you?'

'What you talking about?'

'You might go in with Eff.'

'Here! Who's been listening to what she wasn't meant to? Pretending to be asleep. I know. I rumbled you.'

'But you won't, will you, Polly?'

'No. I'll be there as long as I'm wanted.'

I hugged her, holding her tightly for fear she would escape from me.

It would be a long time before I forgot Eff's holding out the bait of freedom to Polly.

The French Affair

The years passed and I was fourteen years old, doing much the same as I had always done. Miss York was still with me and Polly was my guide, comforter and mentor. I still paid my periodic visits to the House, but I was no longer so subservient to Lavinia. I only had to hint that I would refuse to come and she changed her hectoring ways. She had a faint respect for me — although she would never admit it. I had helped her through one or two scrapes and that gave me an advantage.

Polly and I were closer together. We had paid several visits to Eff, who now had the house next door and was doing well with her paying guests. She seemed to have grown in importance and presided over her two houses in a very gracious and genteel manner. Polly had to admit that Father would have had very little to complain of. The Branleys had gone and been replaced by the Paxtons. 'Much better,' commented Eff. 'Mrs Paxton always wraps her rubbish before putting it in the dustbin. Mrs Branley never did. Though I must say I miss the nipper.' So apart from the loss of the baby, the change really was for the better.

'Eff'll do well,' said Polly. 'All this is right up her street.'

And I knew that, but for me, Polly would have been with Eff, keeping all those paying guests in order and secretly laughing with Eff over their little foibles.

But Polly had sworn never to leave me while I wanted her, and I trusted Polly.

Then life started to change. An architect came to the House because there was something wrong with the structure of the east wing and it had to be put right by an expert who would know how to restore it in a suitable manner.

This was Mr Rimmel and he and Miss Etherton became very friendly. Lady Harriet was unaware of this until it had gone too far and Miss Etherton announced her engagement to Mr Rimmel and notice to Lady Harriet that she would be leaving in a month to prepare for her wedding.

Lady Harriet was incensed. Apparently there had been a succession of governesses before Miss Etherton's arrival and she had been the only one who had stayed. 'People are so inconsiderate,' said Lady Harriet. 'Where is their gratitude? All these years she has had a good home here.'

But Miss Etherton, secure in the love of Mr Rimmel, was by no means dismayed. She was beyond Lady Harriet's disapproval now.

In due course she went. Two governesses came but neither of them stayed more than two months.

Lady Harriet then declared that it was rather absurd to employ two governesses when there were two girls virtually of the same age living so close. She had been impressed by Miss York's efficiency and she saw no reason why the young woman should not teach Lavinia and me at the same time.

My father hesitated and said he would have to consult Miss York, which he did. Miss York, like the two governesses whose stay at the House was brief, was not eager to undertake the education of Lavinia; but in due course, attracted by the offer of a larger salary and no doubt overwhelmed by the dominating personality of Lady Harriet, she agreed; and as a result Lavinia sometimes came to the rectory and I went to the House, where we took lessons together. Miss York, buoyed up by the knowledge that she could to some extent make her own terms, refused to take up residence at the House and insisted on regarding the rector as her employer.

So Lavinia and I did our lessons together.

I was not displeased, for the schoolroom was the scene of my triumphs. Miss York was constantly shocked by Lavinia's ignorance, and though Lavinia often copied my work, and I helped her on many occasions, she was very much my inferior in the schoolroom.

I was at heart quite fond of Lavinia, though I could not understand why. Perhaps it was a feeling of familiarity, for we had known each other for so many years. She was arrogant, selfish and domineering; but I took that as a sort of challenge. I was rather flattered to find that she secretly relied on me. I think I knew her better than anyone else did; thus I became aware of a trait in her character which without doubt was the reason why certain things happened to her.

She was governed by a deep sensuality and she had matured early. She was a woman at fifteen whereas I, in spite of my superior knowledge, was physically a child. She had a small waist and was always at great pains to accentuate her figure, which was showing signs of nubility. She had always been excessively proud of her gorgeous hair. She had perfect white teeth and was fond of displaying them; she would bestow her smiles right and left so that people might see and admire them, which gave a false impression of affability.

Because she had failed academically she had decided that learning was for those who lacked physical charms.

It dawned on me that Lavinia had a perpetual love-affair with the opposite sex. She blossomed when men were near. She smiled and sparkled – showing her teeth and tossing her hair and was an entirely different person.

I saw Fabian now and then. He had been away, first at school, then at the university. Sometimes he came home, almost always bringing a friend with him. I would see him riding out or perhaps in the house when I was having a lesson there.

When Lavinia talked of the young men who came to the House with her brother her eyes would sparkle and she would giggle a good deal. Fabian took no notice of me, and I supposed he had forgotten that time when he had looked after me and made such a fuss when they wanted to take me away. Although it was just a child's game, I had liked to think it had made a special bond between us.

A few days after my fifteenth birthday I met Dougal Carruthers. I was taking the short cut across the churchyard to the rectory when I noticed the door of the church was open and as I came nearer I heard the sound of footsteps on the flagstones. I thought perhaps my father was there and that he should be making his way home as Mrs Janson would be displeased if he were not at the table punctually for lunch. One had constantly to remind him of such matters.

I stepped into the church and saw a young man standing there gazing up at the roof.

He turned as I entered and smiled at me.

'Hello,' he said. 'I was just admiring the church. It's very attractive, isn't it?'

'I believe it is one of the oldest in the country.'

'Norman, obviously. And excellently preserved. It is wonderful how these old places stand up to time. Do you know the history of the place?'

'No. But my father does. He is the rector.'

'Oh . . . I see.'

'He would be only too delighted to tell you anything you wanted to know.'

'How kind!'

I was debating with myself. If I took him home to meet my father we should have to invite him for lunch and Mrs Janson did not welcome unexpected guests at mealtimes. On the other hand, if we did not ask him to lunch my father would keep him talking and miss his. In either case we should invoke Mrs Janson's displeasure.

I said: 'Why don't you come and see my father sometime? He will be free this afternoon. Are you staying near here?'

'Yes,' he said waving his arm, 'here.' I thought he was indicating the local inn where I believed they occasionally put up paying guests.

I left him in the church and went home. Over lunch I told my father that I had met a man in the church, and he was interested in the architecture and history of the place.

437

My father brightened, sensing an encounter with someone who shared his enthusiasm.

'He's coming this afternoon. I said you'd see him.'

I waited for the young man to arrive, for I feared if I did
not my father would have forgotten he was to see him and
I felt I was needed to make the introduction.

In due course he arrived and my father received him de-
lightedly. To my surprise, he told us that he was staying at
Framling. I left my father with him and went over to ride.

Lavinia and I were good horsewomen but we were not
allowed to ride without a groom in attendance. Reuben
Curry, the head groom, usually accompanied us. He was a
taciturn man, quite immune to Lavinia's wiles; and he kept
a firm hand on us. He was an interesting man, very religious.
His wife, I had heard from Polly or Mrs Janson, had
'gone astray' when a gipsy encampment rested nearby.
Apparently there was one among the gipsies who was 'a
fascinating fellow. All white teeth and gold earrings and he
could play the fiddle a treat. All the maids were in a twitter
about him and as he was up to no good a certain amount
of harm was done. Goodness knew what went on.' Mrs
Janson wouldn't have put anything past him. And Reuben's
wife . . . well, she got carried away by the fellow and the
truth was he took advantage of her; and when the gipsies
went off at the end of the summer, they left a little something
behind. The 'little something' was Joshua Curry – a bundle
of mischief from the day he was born. Another such as his
father, it was reckoned, and one for the maids to beware
of.

Having heard of Joshua's colourful beginnings, I was
interested in him. He had black curly hair and sparkling
dark eyes which were always smiling and alert for what I
could only guess. He was so dark, brown-skinned, lithe and
unlike anyone else I knew.

On this occasion when Lavinia and I arrived at the
stables, Joshua was there alone. He grinned at us as we
entered. I noticed the change in Lavinia at once, for

although he was only a servant, he was a member of the opposite sex. She dimpled and her eyes shone.

Joshua touched his forelock but not in the way most of them did. He gave the impression that he was doing it as a kind of joke and it did not really mean respect.

'Are our horses saddled?' asked Lavinia haughtily.

Joshua bowed. 'Oh yes, my lady. All waiting for you.'

'And where is Reuben?'

'He's working. I'm here, though. I reckon I could be your escort today.'

'It is usually Reuben or one of the older men,' said Lavinia, but I could see that she was secretly pleased.

'Well, today it's yours truly . . . that's if you young ladies will have me.'

'I suppose we must,' said Lavinia languidly.

We went to the horses. I mounted, using the mounting block. I looked back at Lavinia. Joshua was helping her into the saddle. It seemed to take quite a little time. I saw his face close to hers and noticed how his hand rested on her thigh. I thought she might be angry at the familiarity, but she was by no means so. The colour had heightened in her cheeks and her eyes were sparkling.

'Thank you, Joshua,' she said.

'I answer to the name of Jos,' he told her. 'More friendly, don't you think?'

'I hadn't thought about it,' said Lavinia, 'but I suppose it is.'

I saw his hand on her arm.

'Well then, Jos it is.'

'All right,' she said. 'Jos.'

We rode out of the stables and soon we were cantering along. Lavinia let me go ahead so that she was behind with Jos. I heard her laughing, and I thought how strange that was. She was usually so haughty with the servants.

She was more inattentive than ever at her lessons. She was continually studying her face in a looking-glass, combing her hair, pulling out little tendrils and letting them

439

spring back, smiling to herself as though she were hoarding some secret.

'I despair of teaching that girl anything,' sighed Miss York. 'For two pins I would go to Lady Harriet and tell her it's a hopeless task. Really, she gets worse than ever.' Lavinia did not care. A smugness had settled on her. She was content with life. Something had happened. I was sorry I was the one to discover what.

Dougal Carruthers had formed a firm friendship with my father and during his stay at Framling he came several times to see us and once to lunch.

He told us he was staying for three weeks at the House and that his father had been a great friend of Sir William Framling; they were connected with the East India Company and he would shortly be leaving the country. He confessed to my father that he would rather have studied medieval art and architecture. He shrugged his shoulders, adding that it was a tradition that sons of the family should go into the Company just as Fabian Framling would eventually do.

Mrs Janson was not displeased. She reckoned she could put on as good a lunch as Mrs Bright of the House. All she wanted was notice and this time she had it.

I liked Dougal. He was very charming to me and did not treat me as Fabian and his friends had – not unkindly or rudely, but simply as though I did not exist.

Dougal had a pleasant habit of glancing my way when he was talking, thus giving the impression that he included me in the conversation, and when, occasionally, I offered a comment, he would listen with attention.

I wished that I had paid more attention when my father talked of the antiquity of our Norman church, so that I could have contributed more.

Once Fabian came to the rectory with him. They sat in the garden and took wine with my father. Dougal and my father were soon deep in conversation and that left me to talk to Fabian.

I saw that he was studying me with a certain interest and I said: 'Do you remember when you kidnapped me?'

He smiled. 'Yes, I remember. I thought if I wanted a baby, all I had to do was find one.'

We laughed.

'And you found me,' I said.

'I think you must have been a very tolerant baby,' he went on.

'I don't remember anything of it. I was rather flattered when I heard of it. Flattered to have been chosen, I mean. But I suppose any baby would have done.'

'You seemed to me a suitable subject for adoption.'

'I believe there was a great fuss.'

'People always make fusses if something unconventional happens.'

'Well, you wouldn't have expected my family to let me go without a word, would you?'

'No. But I kept you for two weeks.'

'I have heard the story often. I wish I had been aware at the time.'

'You would probably have protested if you had known what it was all about. As it was, you took it very calmly.'

I was very pleased because it seemed that in talking of the matter, we had broken through some barrier. I imagined that he felt the same and that our relationship would be easier from now on.

We suddenly became involved in the general conversation and after a while Dougal and he left. Dougal was leaving Framling the next day and at the end of the week Fabian would be gone, too.

I could not resist telling Lavinia that they had called.

'Well, they didn't come to see *you*,' was her comment.

'I know that, but they came and I was there to talk to them both.'

'Dougal is *lovely*, but he's only interested in old things.' She grimaced. I imagined she had flaunted her flaming hair before him and had expected him to be overcome by admiration. I was rather pleased that, presumably, he had not been.

I said: 'Fabian talked about that time he abducted me.'

'Oh, that,' she said. 'That's all rather boring.'

But I could see that my meeting with Dougal rankled. She was quite annoyed when we rode out that afternoon.

Jos was with us. I think he contrived to be our guardian whenever he could; and the fact that he accompanied us rather than Reuben usually put Lavinia in a good mood.

She was very wayward that afternoon. She was both haughty and familiar with Jos; he said little and just smirked at her.

We came to a field across which we always galloped, and it was a competition between Lavinia and me to see who reached the other side first.

I set off and was well ahead. When I came to the edge of the field I pulled up and looked round. I was alone.

Amazed, I called out: 'Lavinia, where are you?'

There was no answer. I cantered back to the other side of the field. When I had started off on my gallop they could not have accompanied me.

I rode around looking for them; but after half an hour I went back to the stables. There was no sign of them. I did not want to go back to the House alone, for there might be a fuss. We were not supposed to ride without a groom. It was at least half an hour before they returned.

Lavinia looked flushed and excited. She assumed an annoyed expression.

'Wherever did you get to?' she demanded. 'We've been looking for you everywhere.'

'I thought you were galloping across the field after me.'

'What field?'

'You know – where we always gallop.'

'I can't think what happened,' said Lavinia. She smirked and I was quick enough to see the exchanged glances between her and Jos.

I suppose, had I been wiser and more experienced in the

442

ways of the world, I should have guessed what was going on. It would have been obvious to an older person. But I really believed there had been a misunderstanding and that they had not realized I had broken into a gallop.

Polly was in close conversation with Mrs Janson and Mrs Janson was saying: 'I've warned her time and time again. But does she take any notice? That Holly was always a flighty piece . . . and now I believe she's taken leave of her senses.'

'You know what girls are,' soothed Polly.

'Well, that girl's courting trouble, that's what. And a nice thing that'll be.'

When I was alone with Polly I said: 'What's Holly doing?'

'Oh . . . just being silly.'

'It sounded as if it was rather dangerous.'

'Oh, it's dangerous all right . . . with one like that.'

'Who . . . like Holly?'

'No . . . him.'

'Tell me about it.'

'You've been listening again. Little pitchers have long ears.'

'Polly, I'm quite a sizeable pitcher and my ears are normal size, but they work as well as anyone else's. Stop treating me like a child.'

Polly folded her arms and looked at me intently.

'Growing up fast,' she said, with a hint of sadness.

'I'm not going to be a child forever, Polly. It's time I learned something about the world.'

She regarded me shrewdly. 'There might be some truth in that,' she said. 'Young girls have to watch out. Not that I'm worried about you. You're sensible. Been brought up right, you have. I've seen to that. It's that Jos . . . He's one of that kind . . .'

'What kind?'

'He's got a way with him. He'll always have girls after him, and it seems to me that's about all he thinks of. Perhaps that's why he gets what he wants.'

I was thinking of the way he looked at Lavinia and how

she accepted familiarities from him which I am sure, as Lady Harriet's daughter, she should not have done.

'And Holly?' I asked.

'She's being silly over him.'

'Do you mean he's courting Holly?'

'Courting her! Courting her for one thing . . . and that won't involve a wedding ring. I reckon the silly girl has given what he's after already . . . and that's no clever thing for any girl to do, I can tell you.'

'What are you going to do about it?'

Polly shrugged her shoulders. 'Me! What can I do? I could speak to the rector. Might just as well speak to a brick wall as speak to him. Mrs Janson's done her best. Well, we shall see. Perhaps she'll find him out before it's too late.'

Ignorant as I was, I did not realize the implications of the situation. Holly might dally with Jos as Jos's mother had with the gipsy and there could be a similar result.

But Jos was not a wandering gipsy; he could hardly wander off and shirk his responsibilities.

I wished I had not been the one to find them.

The grounds surrounding the House were large and in some places wild and uncultivated. Beyond the shrubbery was a part which was somewhat isolated. There was an old summerhouse there which I had discovered by accident. When I asked Lavinia about it she had said: 'Nobody goes there nowadays. It's locked. There's a key somewhere. One day I'll find it.' But that was a long time ago and she had never done anything about it.

On this particular day I went over to join Lavinia. It was early afternoon – a rest period for Miss York and I knew that Mrs Janson 'put her feet up for an hour' at that time; I suspect Mrs Bright of the House did the same.

A somnolent atmosphere hung over the house. It was very quiet. Lavinia was nowhere about. She should have met me at the stables but she was not there. Her horse was, so I knew she had not gone without me.

I thought she must be somewhere in the gardens, so I decided to look round before going into the House.

I could not find her and my steps eventually led me to the shrubbery and thus it was that I came on the old summerhouse. The place had always attracted me in a morbid way. I believed it was said to be haunted and that was why people did not go there often.

I paused at the door and thought I heard a sound within. It was a long, low chuckle which made me shiver. It sounded ghostly. I turned the handle of the door and to my surprise it opened. Then I saw who was there. It was no ghost. It was Jos and Lavinia. They were lying on the floor together.

I did not want to notice details. I felt myself get very hot. I shut the door and ran and did not stop running until I reached the rectory. I felt sick. I glanced at my face in a mirror. It was scarlet.

I could not believe what I had seen. Lavinia . . . proud, haughty Lavinia . . . doing *that* with a servant!

I sat down on my bed. What should I do? Lavinia might have seen me. She would have heard the door open. What ought I to do? How could I tell anyone – and yet how could I not?

The door opened and Polly came in.

'Heard you running up . . .' She stopped and stared at me. 'Why, what is it? What's the matter?'

She came and sat on the bed beside me and put an arm round me.

'You're upset,' she said. 'You'd better tell old Polly about it.'

'I don't know, Polly. I can't believe it. I don't know whether she saw me or not. It was awful.'

'Come on. Tell me.'

'I think I ought not to tell anyone . . . ever.'

'You can tell me as it's as good as if you'd kept it to yourself . . . only better because I know what's best to do. Don't I always?'

'Yes, you do. Only swear you won't do anything . . . without telling me.'

'Cross my heart.'

'Swear it, Polly.'

'Here.' She licked her finger and rubbed it dry. 'See me finger's wet, see me finger's dry, Cross my heart and never tell a lie,' she finished with a dramatic gesture.

I had heard Polly swear that before and I knew she would keep her word.

'I couldn't find Lavinia,' I said. 'I went to look for her. You know that old summerhouse . . . the haunted one . . . someone killed herself in it years ago . . .'

Polly nodded.

'She was in there . . . with Jos. They were . . . on the floor together . . . and . . .'

'No!' cried Polly, aghast.

I nodded. 'I saw them clearly.'

Polly rocked gently back and forth. 'This is a nice sort of how-di-do. I can believe anything of them two. A regular pair. I'd like to see her ladyship's face when she hears of this.'

'You mustn't tell her, Polly.'

'What! Let them go on till he leaves his signature on the family tree! That wouldn't be one for the drawing over the fireplace, I can tell you.'

'She'd know that I told. I can't tell tales.'

Polly sat quietly thinking. 'Nor can you let this go on. And I wonder how far it *has* gone. She's a little . . . er . . . madam, that one. As for him, I reckon he's his father all over again and no girl would be safe from him . . . unless she had her head screwed on right, of course. I reckon it's got to be stopped. There could be big trouble . . . and I wouldn't like even Lady Harriet to have that foisted on her.'

'Perhaps I should speak to Lavinia.'

'Not you. You keep out of it. You'd make her worse. I know her kind. We've got to do something, though. You leave it to me.'

'Polly, you won't tell I saw them, will you?'

446

She shook her head. 'I've given you my promise, haven't I?'

'Yes, but . . .'

'Don't you worry, my love. I'll find some way and you can bet your life I'll see that you are not mixed up in this.'

Polly was most inventive. She found the way.

It was a few days later. I went over to the House as usual. Lavinia was not to be found; nor was Jos. I hurried back to the rectory and told Polly, who was waiting to hear.

She told me to go to my room and read because she wanted me out of the way.

I heard what happened later.

Polly let Holly know that her lover was in the Framling haunted summerhouse with another woman. Holly wouldn't believe her at first, but after a while she went to investigate. Polly's assumption had been right. Holly came upon Jos and Lavinia, as Lavinia told me later, in *flagrante delicto*. Poor Holly, she had been deceived by her lover and her impulse on finding him in such a position with another woman – even though she was Miss Lavinia – aroused her unbridled fury.

She shouted at him, cursing him and Miss Lavinia. He could not escape because he was not fully dressed and it was the same with Lavinia.

Holly's shouting was heard and several of the servants came hurrying, thinking a burglar had been caught.

It was disastrous, for it became a matter which could not be hidden from Lady Harriet herself.

Lavinia and Jos had been caught in the act.

There was certain to be a big storm.

I did not see Lavinia for some days. Polly told me what had happened and she had it from the horse's mouth via Mrs Janson, who had had it from Mrs Bright. Lavinia was confined to her room and something big was about to take place.

Jos could hardly be dismissed as he was known as

Reuben's son although he wasn't – so he would have to stay in the stables because Reuben was too useful to be dispensed with and it was not fair that the sins of the children should be visited on their elders, even though it was the other way round in the Bible. If he had been caught with any of the servants it would have been a venial sin – but Miss Lavinia!

'I always knew what she was,' commented Polly. 'Plain as the nose on your face. You can be sure your sins will find you out . . . and Madam Lavinia's have surely done that.'

We waited to see what would happen and we did not have to wait long.

Lady Harriet sent for my father and they were in conference for a long time before he returned home. As soon as he came back he asked me to go to him.

'As you know,' he said, 'you were always intended to go away to school. Your mother and I used to plan for you before you were born. It mattered not whether you turned out to be a boy or a girl, we both believed absolutely in the necessity of education and your mother wanted the best for our child. As you have heard, there is some money – not a great deal but perhaps adequate – and that has been set aside for your schooling. Miss York is a very good governess and Lady Harriet will do all in her power to find her another place, and with such a recommendation it should not be difficult. Polly . . . well, she has always known that she could not be with you permanently and I believe she has a sister whom she can join . . .'

I stared at him. It was not the thought of school which appalled me. I could only think of the loss of Polly.

'Lavinia will accompany you. Lady Harriet approves of the school and the two of you will be together.'

Then I understood. Lady Harriet had decreed that Lavinia must go away. There must be an end to this disastrous affair with Jos. Separation was the only answer – and I was to go with her. Lady Harriet ruled our lives.

I said: 'I don't want to go away to school, Father. I am

448

sure Miss York is a wonderful teacher and I can do just as well with her.'

'It is what your mother wanted for you,' he said sadly. I thought: And it is what Lady Harriet wants!

I went straight to Polly. I flung my arms round her and clung to her.

'Polly, I can't leave you.'

'Better tell me,' she said.

'I'm going to school. Lavinia and I are going.'

'I see. I see. This is because of madam's little prank, eh? I shouldn't think school is going to stop that one. So you are going away to school, eh?'

'I won't go, Polly.'

'It might be good for you.'

'What about you?'

'Well, I've always known this would come to an end one day or another. That was certain sure. I'll go to Eff. She's always on at me to come. There's nothing to fret about, lovey. You and me . . . we'll always be friends. You'll know where I'll be and I'll know where you'll be. Don't be so downhearted. School will suit you, and then when you have your holidays you can come and stay with me and Eff. Eff would be so proud. So . . . look on the bright side, there's a love. Life goes on, you know. It never stands still and you can't be Polly's baby forever.'

It was getting better already.

Miss York took the news philosophically. She had been expecting it, she said. The rector had always told her that one day I should have to go away to school. She would find another post and the rector had said she must stay at the rectory until she did. Lady Harriet had promised to help her find another situation, so she was as good as fixed up.

It was about a week after Lavinia's exposure that I saw her.

She was smoulderingly resentful. She looked more like a tigress than a spoiled kitten. Her eyes were slightly red so I knew she had been crying.

'What a fuss!' she said. 'It was that awful girl Holly.'

'Holly wasn't any different from you. Jos had made fools of you both.'

'Don't you dare call me a fool, Drusilla Delany.'

'I shall call you what I like. And you are a fool to do what you did – with a groom, at that.'

'You don't understand.'

'Well, everybody else does and it is why we are being sent away.'

'You are being sent as well.'

'That is only because you are going. I have to be with you.'

She snorted. 'I don't want you.'

'I dare say my father could send me to another school.'

'My mother would not allow that.'

'We are not your mother's slaves, you know. We have freedom to do what we want to. If you are going to be objectionable I shall ask my father to send me away without you.'

She looked a little alarmed at that.

'They treat me like a child,' she said.

'Jos didn't.'

She began to laugh. 'He is a rogue,' she said.

'That's what they all say.'

'Oh . . . but it was so exciting.'

'You should be careful.'

'I was . . . if that woman hadn't come and found us in the summerhouse . . .'

I turned away. I wondered what she would say if she knew what had led up to her discovery.

'He said I was the most beautiful girl he had ever seen.'

'I think they all say that. They think it will get them what they want more quickly.'

'They don't! And what do you know about it?'

'I've heard . . .'

'Shut up,' said Lavinia, and seemed near to tears.

We made a sort of truce. We were both going into a

strange place and the only familiar things about us would be each other. We were both a little pleased that we should not be alone.

We talked a good deal about school.

We spent two years at Meridian House. I fitted in quite well. I was immediately noticed as a bright child, and as such attracted the attention of the teachers. Lavinia was backward for her age, and showed no inclination to change that state. Moreover, she was arrogant and moody, which did not make her popular, and the fact of her exalted parentage – which she was apt to stress at first – was a deterrent rather than an asset. She had always expected those about her to fit in with her ways and it never occurred to her that she must adapt to others.

There was a boys' school close by and occasionally we saw the boys playing games on the green near the school. This caused a certain amount of excitement among a section of the girls, particularly on Sundays when we went to the village church for the morning service and the boys occupied the pews immediately opposite us. Of course, Lavinia was to the fore among those girls who had a marked interest in the boys. Notes were smuggled across the aisle and Sunday morning church was the high spot of the week for some girls, for a reason which would not have pleased the vicar or our formidable headmistress, Miss Gentian.

It was during our second year at Meridian House that Lavinia experienced her second disaster and it was inevitable that it was of a nature similar to the first.

She ignored me for a good deal of the time, remembering me only when she needed help with her work. She had her own little community and they were known as 'the fast set'. They regarded themselves as adult and worldly; they were very daring and knowledgeable of the facts of life. Lavinia was queen of this little band, for although most of them could only theorize on the topic nearest their hearts, Lavinia had had practical experience.

When she was very angry with me she would sometimes refer to me in a tone of complete contempt as 'You . . . *virgin!*'

I often thought that if Lavinia had been one of that despised sect I might be at home cosily doing my lessons with Miss York and with dear Polly to run to when an emergency arose.

Polly wrote to me in a rather laborious hand. She had learned to write when Tom had gone away to sea so that she could keep in close touch with him. Her words were often misspelt but the warmth of her feeling came through to comfort me.

I often thought of her and Eff during that time and in the summer holidays I did go to see them. I stayed a week and it was wonderful to be with Polly. She and Eff were doing well. Both had an aptitude for business. Polly was soon on friendly terms with the paying guests and Eff supplied the essential dignity which was part of keeping everyone in order.

'We're what Father would have called a good team,' Eff told me. She was particularly pleased at that time, for 'Downstairs No 32' (which was what she called the tenants of the lower floor in the most recently acquired house) had brought a nipper with them. They were very content and had the garden for the pram, which was a very comfortable arrangement, and Eff and Polly could pop in at any time and gurgle over the child. Eff always referred to her tenants as 'Top Floor 30', 'First Floor 32', and so on.

They were wonderful days while Polly listened to my news about school and I learned the backgrounds and idiosyncrasies of Top Floor to Basement Room.

For instance, Top Floor left the tap running and First Floor wouldn't do her part of the stairs properly; even Downstairs No 32 hadn't really come out of the top drawer, but of course they were forgiven a great deal because they had brought the nipper.

'He's a regular little fellow, he is. You should see the

smile I get from him when I go out there.' So I gathered that, as previously in the case of the Branleys, the nipper made up for his parents' shortcomings.

Going 'up West' with Polly, looking at the big shops, walking through the market on a Saturday night when the flares were lighted and the faces of the costers gleamed scarlet in their light, looking at the rosy apples piled on the stalls, listening to the cries of 'Fresh herring, cockles and mussels', past the old quack who swore his remedies would cure falling hair, rheumatic pains and all the ailments that the flesh was heir to . . . it was the greatest excitement and I loved it.

Polly made me feel that I was the most important person in the world to her and it was comforting, even when we parted, that I felt I had not lost her forever.

She loved me to talk about my life. I told her about Miss Gentian, the absolute ruler of us all. 'A real tartar, that one,' commented Polly, chuckling, and when I imitated Mademoiselle the French mistress, she rolled about with glee and murmured: 'Them foreigners. They're real cautions. I reckon you have a real lark with her.' It all seemed incredibly amusing – much more funny than it was in reality.

When I left, Eff said: 'Mind you come again.'

'Think of it as your home, love,' said Polly. 'I'll tell you this: Where I am . . . that will always be your home.'

What a comfort that was! I should remember it always.

During the last term I spent at Meridian House, Lavinia and two other girls were caught coming in late at night. They had bribed one of the maids to let them in and were caught in the act by a mistress who, having a toothache, had come down to the medical stores to get something to soothe it. Her arrival in the hall had coincided with the surreptitious opening of the door and the conspirators were caught red-handed.

There was a terrible scene. Lavinia crept up to the bedroom she shared with me and another girl. We had to be in the secret, of course, for it was not the first time it had happened.

Lavinia was shaken. 'There'll be trouble over this,' she said. 'That sly Miss Spence. She caught us coming in.'

'Did Annie let you in?' I asked. Annie was the maid. Lavinia nodded.

'She'll be dismissed,' I said.

'Yes, I suppose so,' said Lavinia carelessly. 'I reckon we'll be for it tomorrow. You wait until old Gentian hears.'

'You shouldn't have involved Annie.'

'How would we have got in otherwise?'

'You should not have used her.'

'Don't be idiotic,' snapped Lavinia; but she was very worried.

And with good reason. The reverberations were greater than we had feared. Poor Annie was dismissed immediately. Miss Gentian had the girls involved brought to her, and according to Lavinia had gone on and on about how ashamed she was that girls from her school should have behaved in such a cheap and common manner. They were finally sent to their rooms after being told that this was not the end of the matter.

The term was almost over and the day before we returned Lady Harriet received a letter stating that Miss Gentian was of the opinion that Lavinia would be happier at another school and she regretted there would be no place for her at Meridian House next term or in the foreseeable future.

Lady Harriet was furious that a school should have refused to take *her* daughter. She would not allow that to pass. Lady Harriet and Miss Gentian were like two commanders going into battle. Lady Harriet began by writing to Miss Gentian suggesting that perhaps her letter had been a little unconsidered. She, Lady Harriet, was not without influence and she had wished her daughter to remain at Meridian House for at least another year. Miss Gentian replied that she was sure Lavinia would be happier elsewhere in such a manner that she implied that she herself would also be happier in that event.

Lady Harriet suggested that Miss Gentian come and see

454

her that they might talk the matter over in a friendly fashion. Miss Gentian replied that she had many commitments but if Lady Harriet cared to come to see *her* that might be arranged, but she thought she ought to point out that she had given much thought to the problem and in her mind Lavinia was not suited to Meridian House and the matter was settled.

Lady Harriet came to the rectory to see what report Miss Gentian had given me.

'Drusilla has worked well. Her mathematics leave much to be desired but she is improving in this field. She is making good progress generally.' It was clear that I was not included in the edict of excommunication. I had enjoyed the school. I was interested in my studies and the feeling of competition which I had missed at home spurred me on to do better. True, I was not very much interested in sport, but Miss Gentian herself was not either. I fancied I had now and then caught a gleam of approval in her eyes when they rested on me. Moreover, I had not been caught illegally consorting with members of the boys' school. Lady Harriet was more concerned than ever to find that I was making a success of my scholastic career.

She took the unprecedented step of going to see Miss Gentian, but she came back defeated. I think she must have learned about the escapade and this made her feel deflated. Her fears that her daughter might be turning into a nymphomaniac were being confirmed. If it had been possible for me to feel sorry for such an exalted being, I should have done so.

But she did not hesitate long before taking action. She sent for my father. I was not present at the interview but I heard of it later.

She told my father that what girls needed was a finishing school. She had been inquiring among her friends and she knew of a good one in France. The Duchess of Mentover had sent her daughter there, and knowing the Duchess one knew also that she would never send her daughter to a school which was not everything it should be.

Meridian House had been a bad choice. That Miss Gentian was far too domineering. What girls wanted to learn if they were to do well in after-life was social grace.

My father feebly protested that it was a good education that he and his late wife had wanted for me and he believed that I was getting that at Meridian House. I had, according to my reports, been doing very well. Miss Gentian had written to him personally.

'Foolish woman!' said Lady Harriet. 'She is evidently eager to keep one of the girls I sent to her.'

'I thought that if Drusilla stayed on another two years, say . . .'

'Quite wrong, Rector. Girls need a good finishing school. They must go to this one in France recommended by the Duchess.'

'I fear it will be beyond my means, Lady Harriet.'

'Nonsense. I will pay the extra. I would like Drusilla to be with Lavinia. They had been *such* friends over many years. It will be a good thing for them both to go together.'

After a good deal of hesitation, my father gave in. My mother had been concerned solely with education. 'Polish' was not something which had come into her mind. Erudition was one thing; social graces another. Presumably Lavinia would have a season in London when she emerged with a sufficiently high gloss upon her; then she would be presented at Court. No such future was envisaged for me.

I see now that my father wanted me to be prepared to look after myself when he died. There would be a little money – a very little – just enough for me perhaps to live in a very modest fashion. I wondered whether he was aware that I was plain and might never marry. Lady Harriet had evidently assured him that though my circumstances were very different from those of Lavinia, I should be better equipped to face the world with that veneer which could only be obtained at one of the schools to which she was suggesting I should go; and as she was prepared to pay what would be extra to the cost of Meridian House, it was finally decided that I should accompany Lavinia.

The chosen establishment was the Château Lamason, the very name of which excited me, and in spite of the fact that I should be beholden to Lady Harriet, I could not help being thrilled at the prospect of being there.

Jos had been spirited away. He had gone, Lavinia told me with a grimace, to the stables of a friend of Lady Harriet. But Lavinia and I could talk of little but the prospect before us. For the first time we were going abroad.

'It is not like an ordinary school,' she explained. 'It's for people who will be coming out. There won't be stupid lessons and that sort of thing.'

'No, I know. We are going to be polished.'

'Prepared to go into society. That won't be for you, of course. They will all be aristocracy over there.'

'Perhaps I should be better at Meridian House.'

I only had to suggest that I might not accompany her for Lavinia to become placating. I knew how to deal with her now and she was so easy to read that I often had the upper hand.

The last thing I wanted was to miss this tremendous adventure. I was as excited about Château Lamason as Lavinia was.

I went to stay a few days with Polly before I left. We laughed about the polish. Eff thought it was 'ever so nice' and told everyone that I was staying with them before I went off to my finishing school. She particularly enjoyed talking of me to Second Floor No 32 who 'fancied herself' and was always explaining that she had 'known better days'.

The summer holidays were coming to an end and we were leaving in September. A day before our departure I was summoned to Lady Harriet's presence. She received me in her sitting-room; she was seated in a high chair rather like a throne and I felt I ought to curtsey.

I stood uncertainly on the threshold of the room.

'Come in, Drusilla,' she said. 'You may sit down.' Graciously she indicated a chair and I took it.

She said: 'You will shortly be leaving us for the Château Lamason. It is one of the best finishing schools in Europe. I have chosen it very carefully. You are very fortunate. I hope you realize that.'

Now that I was growing up Lady Harriet's divinity had decreased a little. I was seeing her as a woman who created a sense of power which people accepted because she was so determined that they should. My feelings for her would never be the same as they had been before the battle with Miss Gentian. Miss Gentian had clearly shown that Lady Harriet was not the mighty figure she had made herself out to be and Miss Gentian had won the war between them. It was like the case of Napoleon and Wellington and it had taught me that Lady Harriet was not invincible.

'Well, Lady Harriet,' I said, 'I was very happy at Meridian House and Miss Gentian thought I should do well there. I should have liked to stay.'

Lady Harriet looked astonished. 'That is nonsense, my child. It was an ill choice.'

I raised my eyebrows. An admission of failure? It was Lady Harriet who had chosen Meridian.

She was ever so slightly disconcerted, and laughed dismissively. 'My dear *child*, you are going to be so grateful that you had a chance of going to Lamason. That Gentian woman has no sense of the needs of society. Her great ambition was to stuff her pupils' heads with facts which would be no use to them after their schooldays.' She waved a hand as though to dismiss Miss Gentian. 'You and Lavinia will be far from home. You are a sensible girl and . . . er . . .' She did not say plain, but she meant it. 'I want you, my dear, to keep an eye on Lavinia.'

'I am afraid, Lady Harriet, that she will not take any notice of what I say.'

'There you are wrong. She thinks very highly of you.' She paused and added: 'And so do I. Lavinia, you know, is very beautiful. People flock about her because of that . . . and who she is. She is a little . . . impulsive. I shall rely on you, my dear, to –' she gave me a little smile '– to look after her.' She laughed lightly. 'Your father is delighted that you are to have this opportunity and I know you are very grateful. Girls need polish.' I felt myself laughing inwardly. I must remember every word of this interview and store it up so that I could give Polly an accurate account when we met. I pictured myself taking the role of Lady Harriet. I would tell Polly that I expected to feel like the Cromwellian table in the Framling hall after an application of beeswax and turpentine.

I felt a little triumphant to discover so much about Lady Harriet. She was uneasy about her daughter and she found it humiliating to admit to the rector's plain little daughter that her own daughter was less than perfect. Polly had said that both Lavinia and Fabian Framling would have to pay for all the coddling they had had in their childhood, and all that 'Lord God Almighty stuff' would have to be knocked out of them. 'Who are they when they're out?' she demanded. 'No different from the rest of us. That's not the way to bring up children. They want loving, but brought up sharp now and then. They want cuddles too . . . not coddling.' Poor Lady Harriet, so sublimely aware of her superiority and making the most fearful mistakes with her offspring!

'You will find a spell at the Château Lamason will be a great asset to you in after-life. Your father understands and that is why he is so eager to accept my offer for you. I want you to keep an eye on Lavinia. She is too . . . warm-hearted and inclined to make unsuitable friends. You are more thoughtful, more serious. It is only natural that you should be. Just be a good friend to her. There now, you may go.'

I took a ready leave of Lady Harriet and joined Lavinia.

'What did Mama want?' she demanded.

'She was just saying that you were warm-hearted and inclined to make the wrong friends.'

She grimaced. 'Don't tell me she was asking you to be my nursemaid. What nonsense!'

I agreed that it was.

*

459

We left England with four other girls who were going to the Château Lamason in the charge of Miss Ellmore, one of the mistresses.

Miss Ellmore was middle-aged, very genteel, the daughter of a professor; and when she was no longer young she found herself without means and had been forced to earn her own living. She was employed at the château, not because of her academic qualities, I learned later, but because she was a lady.

She was rather a sad person, and somewhat harassed by her task of looking after six girls in their mid-teens.

For us it was an exciting adventure. We all met at Dover, to which port Lavinia and I had been taken by the Framling coachman and head groom, and we were delivered safely into the custody of Miss Ellmore.

At the Paquet Hotel, the grooms departed and we were introduced by Miss Ellmore to our travelling companions. They were Elfrida Lazenby, Julia Simons, Melanie Summers and Janine Fellows.

I was immediately interested in Janine Fellows because she was quite unlike the other three. Elfrida, Julia and Melanie resembled so many of the girls I had already met at Meridian House – nice and ordinary, though with their separate identities of course, but there was a similarity between them. But right from the first I noticed the difference in Janine.

She was of small stature and very slim, with reddish hair and light sandy lashes; her skin was milky white and faintly freckled. I felt I should have to wait, to know whether I was going to like Janine or not.

It was clear from the start that they were all very interested in Lavinia. They could not stop looking at her. I had already noticed that most people turned to have a second glance at her when passing . . . particularly men. Lavinia was aware of this and it always put her into a good mood.

We crossed the Channel. Miss Ellmore told us what we must do and what not.

'We must all keep together, girls. It would be disastrous if one of us were lost.'

The crossing was smooth and my excitement increased when I saw the coastline of France looming up.

It was a long journey across France and by the time we reached the Château Lamason, I felt I knew my travelling companions well . . . except Janine.

Château Lamason was right in the heart of the Dordogne country. We left the station and drove through what seemed like miles of beautiful country to reach it, past forest land, streams and fields.

And there was the château. I could hardly believe we were going to live in such a place. It was so impressive and so romantic. Close by were the forests and steep hills down which little waterfalls tumbled. The great stone château looked ancient and formidable with its pepperpot towers at either end and its thick stone bastions.

I caught my breath in amazement. It was like stepping into another age. Miss Ellmore was clearly pleased by my obvious awe and as we drove under an arch and into a courtyard she said: 'The château was owned by Madame's family for hundreds of years. They lost a great deal during the Revolution but this one was left alone, and she decided to turn it into a school for young ladies.'

We alighted and were taken into a great hall where numbers of girls were assembling for the opening of the term. Many of them apparently knew each other well. There were several middle-aged ladies, rather like Miss Ellmore. They had an air of doing something not quite natural to them because they had come down in the world.

Mademoiselle Dubreau showed us the rooms which had been allotted to us. There were to be four in a room. Lavinia and I were to share with a French girl whose name was Françoise and a German girl, Gerda.

Miss Ellmore had said: 'You two are together as you are friends, but Madame likes to mix nationalities. It is an excellent way of improving your understanding of languages.'

Françoise was about eighteen and pretty. I saw Lavinia examining her with some intenseness which almost immediately turned to complacency. The French girl might be pretty but she could not compare with Lavinia's flamboyant tawny beauty. The German girl, Gerda, was plump and had no pretensions to good looks.

'Two plain, two purl,' I commented inwardly and thought as I often did: I'll tell that to Polly.

We unpacked and chose our beds. Françoise was not a newcomer to the château so she was able to tell us a little about it.

'Madame,' she said, 'is a very fierce lady. The rules . . . oh so many . . . You wait and see. But we have our fun, yes? You understand?'

I understood and translated for Lavinia. 'What sort of fun?' she wanted to know.

Françoise raised her eyes to the ceiling. 'Oh . . . there is fun. In the town. It is near. We take coffee at the café. It is good.'

Lavinia's eyes sparkled and the German asked in stilted French what the food was like.

Françoise grimaced, which I supposed was not very flattering to the chef. Gerda was a little dismayed, so I guessed the reason for her somewhat full figure.

I quickly realized that life at the château would be far from dull. To be in such surroundings in itself was exciting to me. The château dated back to the fourteenth century and many of its old features remained. There were turrets and winding spiral staircases which led to various dark passages; and the hall had obviously once been the centre of life in the château. Although there was a huge fireplace, one could see where the original one had been, right in the centre of the hall with a vent above to let out the smoke. There was even an *oubliette*, from which it was said that at certain times strange noises could be heard from the ghosts of those who had been incarcerated there to be forgotten. But it was the people who attracted me most.

Madame du Clos reigned over the château like some medieval queen. As soon as I saw her, I recognized her as one of those formidable women cast in the same mould as Lady Harriet and Miss Gentian. Known simply as Madame, she was by no means tall but she gave an impression of grandeur. Clad in black — I never saw her in any other colour — her person glittered with jet which hung from her ears and rose and fell over her impressive bosom. She had small hands and feet and sailed rather than walked, her voluminous skirts making a gentle swishing noise as she moved. Her small dark eyes darted everywhere and she missed little, as we were to discover. Her dark hair, piled high on her head, was always immaculate; her nose was long and patrician; she bore a striking resemblance to many of the portraits which were in various parts of the château. They were undoubtedly members of the great family of du Clos, a certain branch of which had managed to survive the Revolution; her grandfather, we were soon to discover, had been an intimate friend of Louis XVI and Marie Antoinette; they had lost their estates — apart from this château — in the débâcle, but some of them had contrived to retain their heads. Madame had decided to turn the château into an exclusive finishing school, thereby bestowing a great privilege on those who were fortunate enough to gain admission to her establishment, and at the same time restoring her own fortunes sufficiently to enable her to live among the remains of her one-time glory.

On the first day we were all assembled in the great hall, where we were addressed by Madame and reminded of our great good fortune in being here. We should be instructed in the art of social grace; we should be ladies taught by ladies and by the time we left Château Lamason we should be prepared to enter any society with ease. All doors would be open to us. Lamason was synonymous with good breeding. The greatest sin was vulgarity, and Madame du Clos would make aristocrats of us all.

The majority of the girls were French; next came the

English, followed by Italian and German. We were to be given certain tuition which would enable us to make light conversation in French, English and Italian. Beside Madame on a dais sat three mistresses: Mademoiselle Le Brun, Signorina Lortoni and our own Miss Ellmore. They would lead the girls in appropriate conversation and as they were all well bred, their speech would be that which was spoken in the highest circles of society. We were also instructed by Signor Paradetti who taught us singing and the pianoforte, and Monsieur Dubois, the dancing master.

We learned a great deal from Françoise. She was eighteen years old, almost a year older than Lavinia. This was to be her last term and she was leaving to marry the man of her parents' choice. He was thirty years older than Françoise and very rich. It was for this reason that the marriage had been arranged, and he was eager for it, for in spite of his money he was not of a noble family. Françoise explained that he would become ennobled, and her impoverished aristocratic family would benefit from his wealth.

Gerda said she thought it was a mercenary arrangement.

Françoise shrugged her shoulders. 'It makes sense,' she said. 'He marries into a noble family; I marry into a wealthy one. I am tired of being poor. It is terrible. Always there is talk of money . . . money for roof . . . damp coming in the bedrooms . . . spoiling the Fragonard and the Boucher in the music room. Alphonse will change all that. I hope never to hear talk of money any more. I only want to *spend* it.'

Françoise was philosophical and realistic. Gerda was different. I supposed there was plenty of money in her family's iron works and it seemed possible that she would be allied with another giant in industry.

It was interesting listening to it all. We used to talk at night. Those nights remain vividly in my memory . . . lying there in the darkness with perhaps only the light of the stars to give our room with its high ceiling and panelled walls an eerie look. I remember the comfort of those four beds in each corner of the room and the knowledge that we were not alone.

I felt very much the odd one out. They were all richer than I, even Françoise. What was the daughter of a country rector doing here? I knew the answer. I was here to look after Lavinia and I owed the experience to her waywardness. I had my duty to do. Yet when I saw her casting interested looks at Monsieur Dubois I wondered how I should be able to protect her from future follies. It was, of course, what I was here to do. I should never have been given the opportunity to be in this exalted place but for the fact that Lady Harriet had selected me for this purpose.

Françoise and Lavinia talked together quite a lot. They discussed men, a subject dear to the hearts of both. I would see them whispering together. I believed that Lavinia had told Françoise about her experiences with Jos. It was the reason why she had been sent away really, although of course she had first gone to Meridian House; but from there she had been expelled for going out with boys.

In the darkness of our dormitory Lavinia would tell of her adventures, stopping short at certain points and saying: 'No, I can't go on ... not in front of Drusilla. She is too young yet.' She did not mention Gerda, whose deep breathing and occasional snore indicated that she was asleep. It was her way of denigrating me.

Françoise told us all that several girls had grown rather romantic about Monsieur Dubois.

'He's really quite good-looking,' commented Françoise. 'Some of the girls are quite mad about him.'

I was quite interested in Monsieur Dubois — not that I felt that fascination which some of the girls seemed to. He was just a rather slight little Frenchman with very smooth dark hair and jaunty mustachio. He wore very ornate waistcoats and a signet ring on his little finger which he always looked at with affection when he beat time with his hands.

'One ... two ... three ... the lady turns ... four ... five ... six ... she faces her partner ... Come, ladies, that will *not* do. Ah, Gerda, you have the feet of lead.'

Poor Gerda! She was not very good at it. Perhaps that

was not very important as the iron master might not be all that concerned with dancing. In Françoise's case it was different. In the noble châteaux of France she would be expected to lead the dance.

Some of us had to take the part of men in the dance. Gerda was usually assigned to that role. She disliked the ritual in any case and lumbered round on reluctant feet.

Lavinia had always danced well and had done it with a sensuous abandon. Monsieur Dubois was quick to notice this and when he was demonstrating he invariably chose Lavinia to partner him.

She would move close to him, sinuously and meaningfully. I wondered whether in my role of guardian I should speak to her about it. She was showing too clearly how she felt about Monsieur Dubois.

He was quite tender to her, always implying that he liked her very much. But he was like that with all the girls. He had a way of letting his hand rest on one's shoulder or even round one's waist. Monsieur Dubois seemed to like all girls so much that it was difficult to know whether he liked any one in particular. But it did seem that he paid Lavinia just a little more attention.

Françoise said: 'He only comes to school to teach. I expect he's got a wife and six children somewhere.'

'I think he is very attractive,' said Lavinia. 'He told me I was the most beautiful girl in the school.'

'He tells others that,' said Françoise.

'I don't believe it,' retorted Lavinia. 'He looked really sincere.'

'Don't fall in love with him,' warned Françoise. 'It is all on the top . . . how you say it?'

'On the surface,' I supplied. 'He doesn't mean anything. He is just being polite to the girls who throw themselves at him.'

Lavinia scowled at me.

But the affair did not progress, much to Lavinia's chagrin and my relief.

Françoise was right when she said that Monsieur Dubois would be too much afraid of losing his job to take any of his little flirtations to a logical conclusion.

Because of the distance from home we were only to return once a year. At first the time went very slowly and then it began to fly past.

I enjoyed the life; so did Lavinia. It was more or less up to ourselves to learn if we wanted to. I was very eager to improve my languages, so I soon became fluent in French and had quite a smattering of Italian. I enjoyed the dancing and singing lessons and I was doing quite well at the piano.

There was a good deal of freedom.

Sometimes in the afternoons we would go into the little town of Perradot. One of the mistresses would take us in the wagon, which would hold about twelve of us, and the wagon would be left in the square while we wandered round. It was a lovely little town with a river running through it, over which was a small but attractive bridge. There were shops, including a café where delicious cakes were sold, and in the hot weather we would sit under the gaily coloured sunshades and watch the people pass by. On Fridays there was a market in the square and so there was always a number who wanted to go on that day. One could buy clothes on the stalls, shoes, sweets, cakes, eggs, vegetables and cheeses. The place always seemed to be permeated by the smell of hot crusty bread which the *boulanger* used to rake out of his cave-like oven to sell to the waiting customers.

What we liked best was to go into the *pâtisserie*, choose our cake and then bring it out and sit at one of the little tables under the coloured sunshade, and drink a cup of coffee and watch the people go by.

We became acquainted with many of the tradespeople and market stall-holders and we were known throughout the town as *Les jeunes filles du château*.

Life formed itself into patterns: language classes, which were more or less optional; dancing and music, essential, as were deportment and conversation. There was a *thé*

467

dansant once a week, at which Madame herself presided.

Time was passing. We had arrived at Lamason in September and it was not until the beginning of the following July that we returned to England for the summer holidays, escorted by Miss Ellmore. We were to return in September for another year and then we should be ready to take our place in the highest society.

I was rather shocked by the sight of my father. He looked rather wan and had aged more than a year warranted.

Mrs Janson told me that he had been ailing during the winter, and there was talk of getting a curate to help him.

'He's had some funny turns,' she said. 'I haven't liked the look of him at times.'

I talked to my father. He assured me that all was well. I said that perhaps I should not go too far away but he would not hear of that. He was pleased about the languages and music, but he thought some medieval French history might have been included in the curriculum.

Lady Harriet was delighted by the change she saw in Lavinia. I was sent for and took tea with her and Lavinia. Fabian was at home but he did not join us. Lady Harriet asked me a number of questions about the school and she sat listening with obvious approval. I was glad, for I should have hated it if she had decided that we were not to return.

I learned through Mrs Janson that Miss Lucille was madder than ever. She was more or less shut up now in her part of the house. Some of the staff had seen her wandering around looking like a ghost. They said she had lost all sense of time and was often heard calling for her lover.

I also resumed my acquaintance with Dougal Carruthers, who was very affable when he saw me. I was now seventeen years of age – adult one might say – and I was learning what a difference that made to one's relationships. Dougal's attitude had changed towards me subtly. I quite enjoyed the change.

He came to see my father and talked a great deal about Norman architecture, Norman customs and so on. My father was delighted to have met a kindred spirit and was more animated than he had been for a long time.

Fabian, too, had changed towards me. He took more notice of me and asked questions about the château.

The four of us went riding together and I could see that Lavinia was annoyed because Dougal talked more to me than to her. It was the first time any young man had shown interest in me and that rankled with Lavinia.

'He's only being polite,' she said. When we rode out she would endeavour to get beside him, which left me with Fabian. I always felt that he was a little embarrassed with me because of that long ago time when he kidnapped me – and he was a little ashamed of it.

I was glad to have a week with Polly. She pretended to be blinded by the sight of me, which was because of the old joke about polish.

'My word, someone's been rubbing you up a bit. I can't see nothing for shine.'

Everything was going well with the two houses. Polly and Eff were, as Polly told me, quite well-to-do in the neighbourhood – ladies of substance. The houses were full of good payers and Eff had her eyes on another house in the same row.

' "Expansion", that's what she calls it. Father always said Eff had a head for business.' Downstairs No 32 had left some months before and it had been a bit of a wrench because of the loss of the nipper. But they had found a good replacement in Mr and Mrs Collett, a good steady couple, too old for nippers, alas, but you had to count your blessings.

There was the usual round of markets and 'up West' and everything we had done before; and it was good to be with Polly, and wonderfully comforting to know that the bond between us was as strong as ever.

I said a sad farewell knowing that it would be a year before I saw her again.

In September we returned to Lamason.

There were changes. Françoise had left and must be

married to her rich elderly husband by now; and in her place in our dormitory was Janine Fellows.

I did not know whether I was pleased or repelled by this, for I was still not sure whether or not I liked Janine. Françoise had been a good companion; she had been entertaining and her knowledge about the château had helped us along in our first days. Her nonchalant acceptance of her fate, her philosophical views of life, her realism and lack of sentiment had intrigued me. I felt I had learned a good deal from Françoise. Gerda, of course, was not the most interesting of room mates. Her preoccupation with food had always bored me a little; she was too phlegmatic and intent on her creature comforts, but she was never malicious and was fundamentally good-hearted. Lavinia of course was my familiar; and now there was Janine.

Her presence had changed the atmosphere of our dormitory. It had been cosy and rather exciting with Françoise; now I felt there was something malevolent there.

In the first place she and Lavinia seemed to take an instant dislike to each other and what made it a little sinister was that Janine rarely showed this. It was only now and then that it came out, in certain flashes of temper with Lavinia and sly sarcasm from Janine.

Janine was plain and that gave her something in common with me. Her reddish hair was fine and straight, hardly ever tidy; her eyes were small, very light blue and her fine eyebrows made her look perpetually surprised.

She seemed to turn to me more for friendship. Gerda was interested mainly in herself and her eyes would become glazed and vague when other subjects were raised; she never made trouble; neither did she contribute anything to companionship.

So naturally Janine talked to me more than any of the others simply because Lavinia, like Gerda, was not interested in anything but her own desires, Gerda's for food and Lavinia's for admiration.

Lavinia had renewed her admiration for Monsieur

Dubois, perhaps because there was no other male available. Janine noticed this and her lips always twitched with amusement every time he was mentioned.

Lavinia was an excellent dancer and Monsieur Dubois still chose her when he wished to demonstrate how a step should be danced. Lavinia revelled in this, twirling round, swaying from side to side, pressing closer than was necessary to Monsieur Dubois, raising her beautiful eyes to his face and then allowing the lids to fall over them showing her long curling lashes, which alone would have made a beauty of her.

'Monsieur Dubois is a born flirt,' said Janine. 'It's part of his trade. Of course he knows what girls he can flirt with. He wouldn't dare with some. You can't see him trying it on with the Princess, can you?'

The Princess belonged to the ruling house of some obscure middle European country and Madame was especially proud of her title.

'I should hardly think he would want to,' said Lavinia.

'My dear, he doesn't want to with any of us. It's just his way of keeping us happy. If he sees a girl wants to flirt, he flirts. It's what he has been paid to do.'

Lavinia was not subtle in conversation and Janine was too clever for her. She nearly always lost in these verbal battles. But she continued with her wooing of the dancing master.

She was the best dancer and the most outstanding beauty of the school – or certainly the most flamboyant one. She was now at the zenith of her youth. Eighteen years old, full-hipped, full-bosomed, with the tiniest of waists. Sometimes she wore her hair hanging down her back caught back by a bow of ribbon; sometimes she piled it high on her head with little tendrils nestling against her white neck. Hardly anyone could stop taking a second glance at Lavinia.

One day Janine came in bursting with excitement. She waited until Lavinia was with us until she spoke of what was amusing her.

471

She had followed Monsieur Dubois to his home. She had waited for him and kept a safe distance. She saw his home, his wife and four children; she overheard the greeting between him and his wife, for Janine spoke fluent French. They embraced, she said, like lovers who had been separated for months. 'How was it today, Henri?' 'Oh, not bad . . . not bad at all, *mon chou.*' 'How many silly girls were chasing you today?' 'Oh . . . the usual. It is always so. Such a bore. You must bear with it, my angel. I must keep the little girls happy. It is a nothing . . . all in the matter of the work, eh.'

'I don't believe it,' said Lavinia hotly.

Janine shrugged her shoulders, as though it were immaterial to her whether Lavinia believed her or not.

Janine sought me out.

'You're different from the others,' she said. 'They are silly frivolous nonentities, most of them. As for your friend Lavinia, I don't know how you endure her.'

'I've known her all my life.'

'Far too long,' commented Janine.

'Her mother pays some of my fees. My father couldn't afford to send me here. You are right in saying I am different from the others. I am. I am not rich and destined for a grand marriage.'

'Thank your lucky stars for that.'

Janine had a way of ferreting out secrets. I was often amazed at myself for being so frank with her. She was an avid listener — rare among self-centred girls. I was soon giving her a picture of Lady Harriet and our village.

'Spoilt brat,' she commented of Lavinia.

'Lady Harriet sees herself and everything connected with her as perfect, and that includes her daughter.'

'She must be mentally blind. Lavinia hasn't much above the neck beyond her curly hair and her pretty face.'

'I suppose that makes up for a good deal.'

'She is too . . . *physical* for her own good. It wouldn't surprise me if she got herself into some mess sooner or later.

472

She's so blatant about men. Look at the way she throws herself at Monsieur Dubois.'

'She didn't like what you said about him and his wife. Was it true?'

She looked at me and laughed. 'In a way,' she said.

'So you made it up!'

'I'm sure it goes something like that. I've seen them in the market together. They are very devoted. He must be bored with silly romantic girls throwing themselves at him; and she must be grateful to have such a desirable husband.'

Janine confided to me about herself. I was not sure whether I believed her. The story, according to her, was quite romantic. She was the illegitimate offspring of two people in very high places. She hinted at royalty.

'They couldn't marry, you see. He – my father – was to make a very grand marriage for political reasons. That is how it is with the royals. My mother was a lady of the Queen's Bedchamber. She, too, was to marry into high circles. However, I happened. I was born in a clinic run by the woman whom I call Aunt Emily. She is not my aunt at all; but I was brought up there and always called her Aunt Emily. I was to have the best education. It was paid for by my parents but I was meant to believe that I owed everything to Aunt Emily. Aunt Emily has close connections with the Court. She is known to be discreet. People come to her . . . if they don't want it known . . .'

I said it was very interesting while only half believing it. I could not imagine why, but I felt sorry for her. I fancied she was always trying to prove something to herself. She was not very popular with the other girls; and as, after all, she was one of the quartet which shared our room, I seemed to be with her more than anyone else.

It was a week or so after our return to Lamason . . . a lovely golden September afternoon. We had gone into the town on the wagon and then dispersed going our various ways. We were at the *pâtisserie*. There was myself, Janine, Lavinia and a girl called Marie Dallon. We had chosen our cakes and had seated ourselves under one of the sunshades. Charles the *garçon* had brought our coffee.

We were laughing together when a man strolled by. He paused to look at us. He half-smiled. Lavinia immediately responded for, if a little mature, he was very good-looking in a dark, rather Italianate way. I noticed how his eyes rested on Lavinia; but there was nothing unusual in that.

'Good afternoon,' he said. 'Forgive me. I was so enchanted. I heard your laughter and I saw you all sitting there . . . looking so happy. It is unforgivable of me . . . but please forgive me.'

'You are forgiven,' said Lavinia, flashing a smile at him.

'Then I am indeed happy.'

I thought he would bow and pass on but he did not. He was still looking at Lavinia.

'Tell me,' he went on, 'are you not the young ladies from the château?'

'You are right,' cried Lavinia.

'I have seen girls from the château in the past. Today I have just arrived here . . . on my way to Paris. And I see that it is just the same. I rejoice. There are still young ladies from the château and . . . they grow more enchanting than ever. I would make a request.'

We looked at him enquiringly.

'It is that I may be allowed to stay here . . . just for a little moment . . . so that I may continue to look at you . . . and perhaps talk a little.'

Janine, Marie and I looked at each other a trifle uneasily. Heaven knew what would be the result if we were discovered in conversation with a strange man. It would be disastrous, quite outside the laws of Lamason; and the mistress who had brought us might appear at any moment.

But Lavinia was saying: 'If you can become invisible when our dragon of a mistress comes into sight, do. You will have to stop talking to us if she comes along. Then we can say you are just someone who sat here after we had been served with our coffee so we could not move away.'

'How delightfully devious!' He sat down. The *garçon* came and he ordered coffee.

'I think we are safe,' said Lavinia, leaning her arms on the table and studying him intently. Her very attitude was inviting.

'I shall be watchful and at the first appearance of the dragon I shall summon my magical powers and become invisible.'

Lavinia laughed, throwing back her head and displaying perfect teeth.

'Now you must tell me about the Château Lamason. Are the rules there very strict?'

'In a way . . . but not as bad as school,' said Lavinia.

'For which you are very grateful?'

'Oh yes,' I said. 'It enables us to come into the town like this.'

'And meet interesting people,' added Lavinia, smiling at him.

We talked. He asked a good many questions about us and the school, and in return he told us that he was the Comte de Borgasson. His château was some fifty miles from here. It was one of those which had escaped the Revolution.

'Like Lamason,' I put in.

'Yes . . . that is so.' He gave me a grave smile, but he could not for long keep his eyes from Lavinia.

During that first encounter he established himself as an aristocrat with a castle some fifty miles away, a large estate which included vineyards. He was young, unmarried; his father had just died and he had inherited the title and large estates.

'My student days are over,' he said. 'I have to be serious now.'

It was quite an adventure. I was sure Lavinia had enjoyed it, particularly as he had shown so clearly that she was the one among us who held his attention.

When we saw Mademoiselle coming towards us we all rose innocently, murmured goodbye to our handsome companion and joined the others at the wagon.

I saw Lavinia look round as I clambered in. I saw the

475

Comte lift his hand. Lavinia was smiling secretly as we drove back to the château.

We saw the Comte the next time we went into town and he took coffee with us in the same way as he had before. There was a great deal of light-hearted chatter. This time he sat next to Lavinia.

Perhaps because I knew her so well, I guessed she had a secret. She often disappeared and we were not sure where she was. She was very absentminded and seemed no longer aware of the charms of Monsieur Dubois. She danced with a kind of abandon but she never sought to make him choose her as she had in the past by moving a little forward and flicking back the hair from her face.

I did not see the Comte again and I forgot about him until one day I met him near the château. He smiled at me in a rather absentminded way as though he were trying to remember who I was. I was not surprised, for during our encounters he had had eyes for no one but Lavinia.

She continued in a kind of euphoric mood; she was less querulous; she would often sit twirling a lock of her hair, staring into space and smiling.

I asked her one day what was happening.

She gave me a rather contemptuous look.

'Oh, *you* wouldn't understand.'

'If it is so very profound I wonder you do.'

'This isn't silly old school work. This is life.'

'Oh . . . that,' I retorted. 'Has Monsieur Dubois discovered that he no longer loves his wife and four children and dreams only of you?'

'Don't be silly. Monsieur Dubois! That little dancing master! Do you think he is a real man? Oh, you might . . . knowing so little about them.'

'Of course *you* know a great deal.'

She smiled secretly.

'So it is something to do with men,' I said.

'Hush,' she replied, quite good-temperedly.

I should have been prepared.

476

One day when we all went to the town she did not come. She said she had a headache. I should not have believed her. She looked quite radiant on that occasion.

When we returned she was not in our room and it was sometime before she came in. She was very flushed. I cannot understand now why I was so blind. After all, I had seen it all before with Jos.

Christmas had come. It was celebrated in the traditional manner at Lamason, and most of the girls remained at the château, because it was too far to go home; so it was a merry time.

Janine told me that she had seen the Comte again. He was quite near the château. He had not seemed to recognize her. Janine said: 'He looked a little purposeful.'

A few days later I was alone with Lavinia and I told her that Janine had seen him.

She smirked a little and said: 'Can you keep a secret?'

'Of course. What is it?'

'I'm going to be married.'

'Married, of course you will be. When Lady Harriet has found a husband for you.'

She shook her head. 'Did you think I couldn't find one for myself?'

'You certainly give the impression that you are on the lookout.'

'I didn't have to wait very long, did I?'

'What do you mean?'

'I am going to marry the Comte.'

'The Comte! Do you mean that man who spoke to us in the town?'

She nodded gleefully.

'But what of your mother?'

'She will be delighted.'

'Have you told her?'

'No, Jean Pierre thinks it better not . . . just yet. Not until we have decided how to break the news.'

'Jean Pierre?'

477

'The Comte, of course, silly. Just think of it! I shall be the Comtesse de Borgasson, and I shall live in a wonderful château. He is very rich. He will go to England and see Mama. He noticed me at once . . . that first afternoon and he knew that I was for him. Isn't it wonderful?'

'Well, it sounds as if . . .'

'As if what? Are you jealous, Drusilla?'

'Of course not.'

'You must be. Everyone will be jealous of me.'

'Well, you hardly know him.'

She looked very wise. 'In these matters it is not how long you know people. It is how deeply you know them. Don't tell anyone yet . . . especially Janine.'

'Why do you have to keep it secret?' I asked.

'It's only for a while. I shouldn't have told *you* but you know how I seem to tell you things.'

She was certainly ecstatically happy. She was more pleasant to me. She did not come on the wagon in the afternoons and I guessed she was keeping some secret rendezvous with the Comte. I wondered where. Perhaps he had his carriage which would wait for her in a secret place and carry her off . . . to where? I did feel a twinge of uneasiness.

Janine said: 'What's happened to Lavinia? She's changed.'

'Has she?' I asked innocently.

'Don't tell me you haven't noticed.'

'Well, you never know what mood she will be in.'

'Something has happened,' said the all-seeing Janine. There were suspicions in her eyes. Her overweening curiosity had been aroused; and when Lavinia's mood changed once more she was the first to notice.

Lavinia looked a little pale; she was absentminded; sometimes when one spoke to her she did not seem to hear.

I thought something must have gone wrong with the romance and was making up my mind to ask her when she told me she wanted to speak to me . . . urgently.

478

'Come into the garden,' she said. 'It's easier there.'

As it was February the weather was cold. We had discovered that although the summers here were hotter than in England, the winters could be far colder. In season the gardens were quite glorious with bougainvillaea and oleander and many-coloured plants. But this was, after all, winter. In the gardens during the month of February, we were less likely to be interrupted than anywhere else.

I met her there. 'Well, what is it?' I asked.

'It's the Comte,' she replied.

'I can see it is not good news. Has he called off the engagement?'

'No. I just haven't seen him.'

'He's probably been called away on important business . . . that large estate and all that.'

'He would have let me know. He was supposed to meet me.'

'Where?'

'At that little hut place. You know it . . . about half a mile away in the forest.'

'That broken-down old shed! That was where your meetings took place, then?'

'Nobody goes there.'

I was becoming uneasy. It was getting to look like the Jos affair.

'So he didn't arrive . . .'

She shook her head. I could see she was trying to hold back the tears.

'How long is it since you've seen him?'

'It's three weeks.'

'That is a long time. I have no doubt someone else will turn up. If not, you will have to give your attention to Monsieur Dubois.'

'You don't understand.' She looked at me steadily and burst out: 'I think I am going to have a baby.'

I stared at her in horror. My first thoughts were of Lady Harriet. Her shock . . . her reproaches. Lavinia had been

479

sent away to escape that sort of thing; and I had been sent with her to protect her.

I said: 'You must marry him . . . at once.'

'I don't know where he is.'

'We must get a *message* to that château of his.'

'It is three weeks since I saw him. Oh, Drusilla, what am I going to do?'

I was immediately sorry for her. All her arrogance had been wiped away. There was only fear; and I was flattered that she had turned to me for help. She looked at me wheedlingly as though I could certainly find the solution. I was pleased that she held me in such esteem.

'We must find him,' I said.

'He loved me so much, Drusilla. More than anyone he has ever known. He said I was the most beautiful woman he had ever seen.'

'I think they all say that to everyone.' I thought of a sharp retort, but I spoke gently for there is something more than ordinarily pathetic about the arrogant when they are brought low. I was looking at a very frightened girl, as well she might be.

'Drusilla,' she begged, 'you will help me?'

I did not see how, but it was gratifying that the normally overbearing Lavinia should turn to me with that innocent belief in my ability to solve her problem.

'We have to think about it,' I said. 'We have to give our minds to it.'

She clung to me desperately. 'I don't know what to do. I've got to do something. You will help, won't you? You're so clever.'

I said: 'I'll do all I can.'

'Oh, thank you, Drusilla, thank you.'

My mind was occupied with her problem. I thought: The first thing to do is to find the Comte.

I went into the town on the wagon with the girls that afternoon. Lavinia stayed behind pleading a headache. Perhaps a real one on this occasion.

480

I chose my cake and when Charles came out with the coffee I seized the opportunity to talk to him.

'Do you know Borgasson?' I asked.

'Oh yes, Mademoiselle. It's some fifty miles from here. Did you think of taking an excursion? It is hardly worth a visit.'

'There is an old château there . . . owned by the Comte de Borgasson . . .'

'Oh no, Mademoiselle, there is no château . . . just a few little farms and some small houses. Just a village . . . No, not worth a visit.'

'Do you mean to say that there is no Château de Borgasson?'

'Certainly there is not. I know the place well. My uncle lives there.'

Then I began to see clearly what had happened. Lavinia had been duped by the bogus Comte; and the significance of her position was borne home to me.

I had to tell her. I said: 'Charles, the *garçon*, says there is no château in Borgasson; there is no Comte. He knows because his uncle lives there. You have been deceived.'

'I don't believe it.'

'He would know. And where is the Comte? You'd better face up to the truth, Lavinia. He was pretending all the time. He merely wanted you to do . . . what you did. And that is why he talked of marriage and all that.'

'He couldn't have . . . not the Comte.'

'Lavinia, the sooner you face facts the better . . . for the easier it will be for us. We have to look at this as it really is and not as you would like it to be.'

'Oh, Drusilla, I am so frightened.'

I thought: I'm not surprised at that. She relied on me. I should have to do something. But what?

People began to notice the change in her. She was looking pale and there were shadows under her eyes.

Miss Ellmore said to me: 'I think Lavinia is unwell. Perhaps I should have a word with Madame. There is a good doctor here ... a friend of Madame ...'

When I told Lavinia this she fell into a panic.

'Don't worry,' I said. 'Pull yourself together. It would be fatal if she sent for the doctor. They would all *know*.'

She tried, but she was still pale and wan.

I told Miss Ellmore that she was considerably better.

'Girls do go through these phases,' said Miss Ellmore; and I felt we had got over that fence.

It was inevitable that Janine should notice.

'What's wrong with our forlorn maiden?' she asked. 'Has the noble Comte deserted her? Are we witnessing the symptoms of a broken heart?'

It suddenly occurred to me that the worldly Janine might be able to help us and I asked Lavinia if I might tell her.

'She hates me,' said Lavinia. 'She would never help me.'

'She would. She hated you because you were more attractive than she was. Now that you are in deep trouble she wouldn't hate you so much. People are like that. They don't hate people half as much when they fail. And she might be able to help.'

'All right, tell her. But make her swear not to tell anyone else.'

'Leave it to me,' I said.

I went to Janine. 'Will you swear not to divulge it to a soul if I tell you something?'

Her eyes glistened at the prospect of sharing a secret. 'I promise,' she said.

'Lavinia is in deep trouble.'

I must say I did not like the light of pleasure that came into Janine's eyes.

'Yes ... yes ...' she urged.

'The Comte has gone.'

'I always knew he was false. All that talk about the title and the estates ... at the first meeting. Go on.'

'She is going to have a baby.'

'What?'

'I'm afraid so.'

'My goodness! What a story! Well, well. It serves her right. She was anybody's for the taking. All that attraction she is supposed to have for the opposite sex. What is it? Just . . . I'm easy. Smile at me and I'm willing.'

'What are we going to do?'

'We?'

'We've got to help her.'

'Why should we? She has never been particularly pleasant to us.'

'It's just her way. She's different now.'

'Of course she is.' Janine was thoughtful. 'What could we do? We can't have the baby for her.'

'There'll be a terrible scandal. You can't imagine what her mother is like. There is already a mad aunt in the house who believes peacock's feathers are unlucky.'

'What's that got to do with it?'

'It just means it will be awful for her if she has to go home and tell them she is with child.'

'Being biblical about it may sound very fine but it doesn't alter anything.'

'I persuaded her to let me tell you because I thought you might help.'

I could see that that had flattered Janine.

She began to laugh. 'I'm just thinking of the fuss there'd be. It just serves Madam Lavinia right. When you think how arrogant she has always been, lording it over us all . . . and now this. "Pride goeth before a fall." I reckon this will put an end to that grand marriage her mama has in mind for her. Wealthy gentlemen do like to think they are getting a virgin.'

'Janine . . . please . . . try to help.'

'What can I do?'

I used the tactics Lavinia employed with me. 'You're clever. You know something about the world. You might think of something.'

'Well,' she said grudgingly. 'I might.'

*

483

Janine did give her mind to the matter. She talked with Lavinia, discovered when the baby was likely to appear, and when Lavinia calculated that it might be in August, Janine said with an air of wisdom: 'Well, it will be in the holidays. That's something to be thankful for.'

We looked at her eagerly.

'You see,' she explained, 'it gives you a chance to have the child and no one know.'

'How?' pleaded the newly humble Lavinia.

'If you could leave here at the beginning of July when the term ends . . . My goodness, it will be seven months. Can we hide it so long?'

'We'll have to,' I said.

'I will. I will,' said Lavinia, like a drowning woman clutching a lifebelt which has just been handed to her.

'There is my Aunt Emily,' went on Janine.

I turned excitedly to Lavinia. 'Janine's aunt runs a clinic where people go to have babies . . . among other things.'

Lavinia clasped her hands as though in prayer.

'Aunt Emily is very discreet,' said Janine.

'Where is it?' asked Lavinia.

'Near the New Forest.' Janine's eyes were sparkling. 'Listen. We'll go there. You must tell your people that you have been invited to stay . . . you might say at the Princess's place.'

'That would please Lady Harriet,' I said.

'And you are to go there from Lamason when the term breaks up.'

Lavinia nodded excitedly.

'I will write to my aunt and see if she will have you. If she will, you must write to your people and tell them that you will be staying at the Princess's mansion in . . . wherever it is. It is very remote, I know. I had never heard of the place. When we leave here we will go together to my aunt's clinic, and there you will have your baby.'

'It is wonderful,' cried Lavinia. 'Thank you, Janine.'

I said: 'And when the baby is born?'

Lavinia's face fell.

'Adoptions are arranged,' said Janine. 'You might have to pay . . .'

'I would manage,' said Lavinia. I knew she was already compiling a letter for her mother. She was going to stay with a noble Princess; she needed new clothes – French clothes and they were rather expensive. Lady Harriet would be delighted at the thought of her daughter's visiting royalty, however remote.

It seemed that we were getting somewhere with the help of Janine. That took us up one step. But perhaps what was more important was what we were going to do with the baby afterwards.

Then I had a brilliant idea. My thoughts went back to that tall house opposite the common. I saw Polly and Eff with the 'nippers'. Polly would do anything to help me; she had always said so. But she would not be so ready to do anything for Lavinia whom she had always disliked; and I fancied that she might not be displeased to see Lavinia in that spot of trouble which she had prophesied for her. But if *I* asked her she would surely help.

I mentioned this. Lavinia was overcome with relief. She said what good friends we were to her and she did not know what she would have done without us.

It was amazing to see her in this humble mood.

And from then on we became the three conspirators.

I must say that Lavinia played her part well, which could not have been easy. There was a certain anxiety about her health but fortunately the true state of affairs had not occurred to anyone in authority.

I was on tenterhooks lest they should guess. We bought a voluminous skirt in the marketplace. It was very concealing. Spring came; we were all three deeply involved in the enterprise and Lavinia was able to sit outside the *pâtisserie* without being overcome by bitter memories.

We were to leave at the end of that term, having completed our allotted span. The three of us could scarcely wait, so eager were we to put our plan into action.

Janine had had a reply from her Aunt Emily, who said that it was not the first time this sort of thing had overtaken an unwary girl like Lavinia, and we could rely on her.

Polly wrote back. She and Eff would, of course, take in the little baby when it was born. Eff was really good with little babies and ought to have had some of her own but there had been Him to look after. It seemed that He, being sometime dead, had lost a good deal of that sanctity which had descended on him when he was recently expired. However, the news was good. Polly and Eff would take the child in. It was only later that the reason emerged that Polly was so quick to offer help because she thought the child was mine.

So the plans were laid. It was pathetic to see the way in which Lavinia relied on us. Both Janine and I enjoyed that.

The weeks were passing. In a short time we should be on our way to put the first part of our venture into practice. Sometimes I wondered whether Madame had been aware. She did not say anything, but I fancied that she would rather whatever was going on took place away from Lamason. She would want no scandal attached to that most impeccable of institutions.

So the day came when we said goodbye to our fellow students, exchanged addresses and promised to write and see each other if we ever found ourselves in close vicinity.

We travelled with Miss Ellmore to England. I did see her glance once or twice at Lavinia and we held our breath in case she had noticed, but like Madame, Miss Ellmore wanted no complications while we were in her care.

She had been told that we were going to stay for a brief visit with Janine; and it was left at that.

When she had put us on the train we were almost hysterical with relief. We laughed and laughed and could scarcely stop ourselves. Lavinia was in good spirits. We had success-

486

fully eluded disaster which had at times seemed imminent; and she owed it to us.

In due course we arrived at Candown close to the New Forest. The Firs was a large white building set among trees. Aunt Emily received us graciously, but her eyes immediately went to Lavinia.

'We will get you to your room,' she said. 'You, Miss Delany, can share with Miss Framling. Janine will show you and then I must have a talk with Miss Framling. But first we will get you settled in nice and comfy.'

She was a large woman with a breezy yet soothing manner which I thought from the first did not quite match the rest of her. She was slightly unctuous. She had light sandy hair and piercing eyes which were between green and blue. As soon as I saw her I thought that was how Janine would look in thirty years' time and I could not believe that there was not some blood relationship between them. In spite of her attempt to create what she would call 'a comfy atmosphere', there was a certain sharpness about her, a certain coldness in her eyes, and an aggressive point to her nose gave a look of alertness to her face; she reminded me of some kind of bird — a crow or, I thought with a certain uneasiness, a vulture.

But we had successfully completed what seemed to us the most hazardous part of the adventure and must rejoice.

Janine took us to our room. It had blue curtains and the furniture was of light wood. It was a pleasant room and there were two beds in it.

'I am glad you are sharing with me,' said the newly humble Lavinia.

Janine said: 'You'll be all right now. You've just got to wait until your time comes.'

'It's another month ... at least I think so,' replied Lavinia.

'You can't be sure,' Janine told her. 'Aunt Emily will soon find out. She'll get Dr Ramsay to have a look at you.'

Lavinia shivered slightly.

487

I said soothingly: 'It will be all right. I know it will.'

Lavinia swallowed and nodded. Now that the difficulties of getting her here had been successfully accomplished she was beginning to brood on the ordeal before her.

A tray of food was sent up to us. Janine brought it and shared the food with us.

When we had eaten, she told Lavinia: 'Aunt Emily wants to see you as soon as we've finished. She just wants to discuss a few things.'

In due course she took Lavinia off to see Aunt Emily. I was left alone in the room. I went to the window and looked out on a garden. There was a seat there among the shrubs and two people sat on it. One was a very old man. Although seated, he leaned forward on a stick and I could see that his hand was shaking; every now and then his head gave a little jerk. Beside him was a girl of about Lavinia's age; she was obviously pregnant. They did not speak together; they just sat staring into space. They looked as though they were bewildered.

A shiver ran through me. I had a sudden feeling that the walls were closing round me. From the moment I had entered I had had a premonition of evil . . . and that had not been soothed by the breezy presence of Aunt Emily.

In a few weeks, I reminded myself, it will be over. The baby will be with Polly and we shall all go home. Lavinia was away for the best part of an hour and when she came back she looked a little frightened.

I said: 'Well?'

'It's going to cost a great deal. I hadn't thought of that.'

'But we haven't got the money.'

'I don't have to pay it all at once. She'll give me time. I've got to give her some money now . . . to start with. It's almost all I've got.'

'I didn't think about the money,' I said. 'Janine didn't say how much it would cost.'

'I'll have to find it somehow.'

'Perhaps you should tell your mother.'

'No!'

'What about your brother?'

'I couldn't tell him I'd got myself into this mess. I shall have to pay for your bed and board, too.'

'I could go home.'

'Oh no, no. Promise you won't go.'

'Well, if it is going to cost money we haven't got . . .'

'I can pay. She'll give me time. I told her what I'd got and she said she would open an account. I shall have to send her something every month. Oh, Drusilla, why did I ever get myself into this?'

'Ask yourself. You knew how it was with Jos.'

'Oh, Jos!' She smiled faintly. 'He was only a stable boy but . . .'

'Not quite so dangerous as a bogus French aristocrat.'

'I don't know how I could have been so taken in.'

'I do,' I said. 'You are bemused by flattery. After this, you'll have to be more sensible.'

'I know. Oh, Drusilla, you are my best friend.'

'You didn't seem to think so before this happened.'

'I always did. But it is things like this which test friendship.'

'Well, you only have to wait now for the baby and then we'll leave. You'll have to pay Polly something too. You can't just have children and send them off for someone else to keep.'

'Polly was always so fond of you.'

'But she wasn't so fond of you. You were always rather arrogant with her.'

'I didn't know.'

'Well, she didn't like you.'

'She's only helping because *you* asked her. Oh, Drusilla, what should I do without you?'

'Or Janine,' I reminded her.

'I know. You have both been . . . wonderful.'

'Don't get emotional. Remember the baby.'

She smiled at me gratefully.

*

489

Those few weeks I spent at Aunt Emily's clinic were the strangest I had ever known.

I was not sure whether I was aware of the sinister atmosphere at that time or whether I built it up afterwards.

There were twelve patients staying there and there was nothing ordinary about any of them. There were four other young women expecting babies. They were always called by their Christian names, which in itself was significant. They were under a cloud and their identity was a secret known only to themselves. But I learned a little about them during our stay at The Firs.

I remember Agatha, a bold beauty, mistress of a wealthy merchant and much to her chagrin she had conceived his child. She had a rather curious cockney voice and a loud laugh. She was the only one who was not particularly reticent about her life. She told me she had had numerous lovers but the father of the child was the best; he was oldish and grateful for her favours and in exchange for them was ready to lavish his wealth upon her. 'Suits me, suits him,' she said, giving me a wink. And in her presence it seemed to me that normality returned; and because I wanted to rid myself of that feeling of unreality I used to meet her in the gardens and we would sit on a seat while she did most of the talking. She knew I was merely accompanying Lavinia, who had been the victim of a little miscalculation, as she said with another of her winks.

'Bound to have happened to her sooner or later,' she said. 'She'll have to watch out and get the wedding ring soon. These little bastards can be most inconvenient.'

She had successfully summed up Lavinia's character.

Another of the pregnant ladies was Emmeline, sweet-faced and gentle, no longer very young – about thirty, I should imagine. I discovered a little about her, too. She was nurse to a querulous invalid lady and she had fallen in love with the lady's husband and he with her. She had been genteelly brought up and I could see that she regarded her present position as a sin. Her lover came to see her. I was rather touched. It was clear to me that there was a genuine affection between them. They used to sit in the garden holding hands; he was very tender towards her.

I fervently hoped that the querulous wife would die and they would be able to marry and live in respectable happiness ever after.

There was one young girl who was expecting a baby. She had been raped and used to cry out at night; she was terrified at the sight of men. Her name was Jenny and she was only twelve years old.

Then there was Miriam. I think in time I grew to know Miriam better than any of the others. There was something intense about her. She was reticent and did not want to know anyone. She was locked in with her own tragedy.

I found the days long and strange. Lavinia rested a good deal. Janine had certain duties which Aunt Emily expected her to perform; but I was there more as an onlooker. I could not help feeling that I was in some way in a world of shades, among people who would one day escape from it and resume their normal personalities. At the moment they were unreal . . . lost souls in a kind of underworld, fearing Hell and hoping for a sight of Heaven.

Miriam used to sit in the garden quite often, alone and brooding. At first she did not encourage me to sit with her, but it might have been that she sensed my sympathy and the temptation to talk to someone was too strong to resist.

Gradually I learned her story. She was passionately in love with her husband. He was a sailor. They had longed for a child and that blessing had been denied them. It was a sadness, but not a great one because they had each other. She loved him deeply; she lived through one separation after another waiting for the reunion. Her cousin had said she must not stay at home and brood during his absences, but go out a little. She had had no great desire to but finally she had been persuaded.

She looked at me with tragic eyes. 'That is what makes it all so stupid . . . so pointless.'

491

Tears coursed down her cheeks. 'To think that I have done this to him.'

I said: 'Don't talk of it if you'd rather not.'

She shook her head. 'Sometimes I feel better for talking. Sometimes I think I'm dreaming and this is a terrible nightmare. What am I doing in this place? If only I hadn't gone . . . if only . . .'

'That is what so many people say.'

'I couldn't bear him to know. It would kill him. It would be the end of everything we had.'

'Wouldn't it be better to tell him? What if he should find out?'

'He never will.' She became fierce suddenly. 'I'd kill myself rather.'

'This baby . . .'

'It came about in the most silly way. I didn't know the man. They had given me too much to drink. I wasn't used to it. I told him about Jack – that's my husband – and he said his name was Jack. I don't know what happened. He took me somewhere. I woke up next morning with him beside me. I nearly died. I dressed . . . I ran out. I wanted to wash everything out of my mind. I didn't want to remember that night. I wanted to pretend it hadn't hap-pened. And when I found I was pregnant because of it I just wanted to die.'

I put my hand over hers. She was trembling. I said: 'Why don't you tell him? He would understand. You love him so much and he loves you. Surely he would forgive you.'

'I could never face him. You see, it was perfect . . . and now . . .'

I said: 'You wanted a child.'

'*His* child.'

'This is your child.'

'I should hate it. It would always be a reproach.'

'You were innocent. They gave you too much to drink. You weren't used to it and that happened. I am sure that if your husband really loved you he would understand.'

'He would not. He could not. We were everything to each other.'

'And what of the baby?'

'I shall get someone to adopt it.'

'Poor little baby!' I said. 'It will never know its mother.'

'You are too young to understand what was between Jack and me. No child could ever mean more to me than he does . . . not even his. I have thought and thought. I have to do it this way.'

'But it is making you very unhappy.'

'I don't expect ever to be happy again.'

'You should try, I am sure. It was one little moment when you were off guard. It wasn't as though you took a lover.'

'It would seem like that.'

'Not if you told him.'

'He would never understand.'

'Why don't you try? That poor little baby . . . to be born unwanted. That is the most terrible tragedy of all.'

'I know. My sin is heavy on me. I have thought of taking my life.'

'Please don't talk like that.'

'If I did it would break Jack's heart, and if he knew of this it could never be the same between us. He would never believe me entirely. He is passionate and jealous. He so much wanted a child . . . and to think that another man gave me what he couldn't . . . I know Jack. You don't. You're too young to understand these things.'

And so she talked to me and again and again she went over her problems. I tried to advise her but, as she said, I was too young to understand.

I thought a great deal about those children who would be born in Aunt Emily's clinic – the unwanted ones – and I thought of my own parents who had planned my education while they were waiting for me; and I thought of Lady Harriet who had long upbraided the Almighty for denying her offspring, and who had rejoiced so wholeheartedly when her prayers had been answered that she spoiled her

493

children to such an extent that Lavinia had come to this pass.

There were other patients besides the women who were expecting babies. There was the poor old man whom I had seen from my bedroom window sitting on the seat, on the first day I had come. I learned that he had been a great scientist in his day, but he had had a seizure which had robbed him of his mind; and he was at this place because he was unwanted by his family and had been put here to await death because it was the most convenient way of disposing of him. There was one woman who lived in a world of her own. Her manner was haughty and she believed she was reigning over a large household of servants. She was known as the Duchess. There was George Thomson who was always laying fires in cupboards. He caused a great deal of anxiety and had to be watched. He had never attempted to light the fires but there was always the fear that he might.

They were like people from a shadow world.

I often wondered about Janine who had been brought up in this place by an aunt whose relationship to her she denied. The house was bright. There were blue curtains and white furniture everywhere and yet somehow it seemed a dark and mysterious place, and I never felt at ease in it. I would wake in the night sometimes and start up in fear. I would gaze at that other bed where Lavinia lay, her beautiful hair spread out on the pillow. Her sleep was often troubled. I wondered how often she thought of her lover, swaggering up to us outside that *pâtisserie* with his tales of grandeur, his sole motive being the seduction of gullible girls. And those weeks of pleasure had led to this. What a lesson! I wondered if Lavinia would ever learn it.

She had been seen by Dr Ramsay – a small man with dark, rather frizzy hair, some of which grew out of his nose and ears. He had examined her, declared her to be in good health and had said that all was going reasonably well and that we could expect the baby during the second week of

August. This was good news. We had thought it would be two weeks later.

I told myself: Soon we shall be out of this strange place. Here I felt shut away from the real world. It would be good to be back in the natural world, for the idea struck me that anything could happen here. Yet Aunt Emily seemed determined to create a homely atmosphere. She was always bright and breezy and wanting to know if we were 'comfy'. If only she had not had those sharp blue-green eyes which seemed to betray something to me which I would rather not know.

The days seemed normal enough; it was during the night when I heard strange noises. The little girl would suddenly cry out in terror; and the scientist would wander about tapping his stick, murmuring to himself that there was something wrong in the laboratory; the Duchess sometimes walked in her sleep and we would hear her giving orders to the bust of George IV in the hall, thinking it was her butler.

It was a house of contrasts; the robust Agatha with her accent of the streets of London; gentle Emmeline awaiting the visits of her lover. Yes, it was a mysterious world, and while I found it of absorbing interest in a morbid sort of way, I longed to escape from it.

I knew that tremendous problems awaited us . . . or at least Lavinia, when we were out of here. I guessed that all the people here were paying Aunt Emily a considerable sum of money for her services; and even though Lavinia was to be allowed to pay over a period of time, it would not be easy for her.

There was something strange about most of the people here. It was the sort of nursing home where people who had something to hide went . . . except those like the Duchess and the old man whose people sent them here to get them out of the way. It was very pathetic and I could not get out of my mind the thought that it was also sinister.

I did not greatly like the doctor. There was something

secretive about him. He looked to me like a man who had something to hide.

Janine was different here. She had to help her aunt and was often sent to look after the patients. There was one young man who was made her special charge. He was the Honourable Clarence Coldry and was quite clearly mentally deficient. He had a beaming smile and was delighted if anyone spoke to him. He himself had difficulty in speaking; his tongue seemed too large for his mouth; there was something dog-like about him.

I had an idea that Janine was not very happy. She did not seem like the same girl who had been to school with us. I sensed a scheming nature behind Aunt Emily's smiles and she was very watchful of Janine.

I was longing to get away. It seemed as though we had been here for months. We took little walks, Janine and I. Lavinia was so cumbersome – her voluminous skirts could not have shielded her now – that she could not accompany us.

'Soon you'll be gone,' Janine said to me once. 'It can't be long now. Lavinia is almost ready to deliver the goods.'

I winced. I was more fond of that yet-to-be-born baby than any of them. I did not like to hear it referred to as 'the goods'. 'And I shall still be here,' she said with a little grimace.

'Well, it is your home,' I reminded her.

She nodded grimly. 'Aunt Emily has plans for me.'

'Not the Honourable Clarence!'

'Afraid so.'

'Oh, Janine . . . you couldn't!'

'Perhaps. After all, he is an Hon.'

'He wouldn't want to marry.'

'I have to make him rely on me.'

'Janine, why do you stay here?'

'It's where I was born. I have lived here all my life . . . except when I was at school.'

'Your aunt must have been fond of you to send you to Lamason.'

'She is not my aunt. It's my real family who pay.'

'They would not want you to marry Clarence.'

'It's Aunt Emily who has the say.'

'She seems very powerful. I hope she will give Lavinia time to pay.'

'She will. Though if there was any delay in the payments she might decide to approach Lady Harriet.'

'She mustn't do that. I don't think Lavinia realized it was going to be so costly.'

'Mistakes always are . . . in one way or another. After all, she was in a real mess. We got her out of it . . . you and I. What would she have done if we hadn't brought her here? There will be the baby's keep too. Mind you, she's been lucky. Can't expect any more than she's got.'

'At least we have come so far,' I said.

And I thought again: It can't be long now.

It was soon after that when Lavinia awoke one night to find her pains had started.

The doctor and Aunt Emily came to her room. I had hastily put on some clothes and was sent to arouse one of the maids who knew something about childbirth and had assisted before.

It was not a difficult birth. Lavinia was young and healthy and the next day her little girl was born. A cradle had been set up in our room.

'We are rather full at the moment,' explained Aunt Emily apologetically to me. I did not mind sharing the room which had become a nursery. I was fascinated by the baby.

Lavinia was greatly relieved to have come through her ordeal. During the first day she sat up in bed smiling and marvelling with the rest of us at the baby.

She had many visitors — Emmeline, Agatha and the Duchess; the latter mistook Lavinia for her daughter and kept calling the baby Paul. Miriam did not come.

There was to be a short respite for Lavinia before we moved on. I was conscious of an immense relief. Lavinia

497

had come through safely. I had heard tell of many things which could go wrong in childbirth and I had had some anxious moments wondering what action we could take if anything of that nature happened to Lavinia. But there was no longer need to worry on that score. She was perfectly well and the baby appeared to be flourishing. Moreover, the end of our stay in the house was certainly at hand.

For the first few days we gave ourselves up to marvelling at the baby. It was like a miracle to me that such an enchanting creature could have come out of that sordid little affair. Even Lavinia succumbed to her charm and looked rather proud and almost happy to have produced her. I loved her red wrinkled face, her screwed-up eyes and the tufts of dark hair, her little hands and feet all equipped with delicate pink-tinted nails.

'She has to have a name,' I said. 'She is like a little flower.'

'We'll call her Flower and as she is half French she shall be Fleur.'

'Fleur,' I repeated. 'It seems to suit her.'

So Fleur she became.

I had written to Polly to tell her that the baby was born and that it was a little girl named Fleur. Polly wrote back that they couldn't wait to get the baby. Eff was so excited; she had everything ready . . . cradle, bottles and nappies. Eff was very knowledgeable about babies' needs; she did think the name was a bit outlandish and would have liked Rose or Lily or perhaps Effie.

'You're on your own, now,' said Janine. 'I've got your address. I'll write.'

Aunt Emily took a cosy farewell and at the same time presented Lavinia with the outstanding account which depressed Lavinia every time she looked at it.

She and I were to take the baby to London. Polly would meet us at the station. Eff would be at home preparing the welcome.

In due course we arrived. I was carrying the baby. I was less awkward with her than Lavinia was. And so Polly saw us. She cried out: 'Drusilla!' Then she was beside me, her eyes brimming over with love and hugging me and the baby at the same time.

'So here you are with that little love. And you . . . Let's have a look at you. You're looking well.'

'And you, too, Polly. It's wonderful to see you.'

'You bet,' said Polly. 'And wait until Eff sees the nipper.'

Her greeting to Lavinia was less warm. I was glad that Lavinia was suitably subdued and did seem to be aware of what she owed to Polly and her sister.

Polly had a cab already waiting for us and we all got in and drove to the house on the common, where Eff was waiting for us.

Eff had changed. She was quite stately now. They had taken the house across the road and now had three houses which they let very profitably. It took me some little time to learn who the tenants were because there were now the various floors One, Two and Three, and so on.

Their joy over the baby eclipsed all else. Eff took charge. I could see that Polly was a little baffled. She kept looking at me intently; and of course the presence of Lavinia was a mystery to them and it put a certain restraint on them. Lady Harriet's invisible presence seemed to brood over us; and I supposed even Polly was not quite immune from that. Eff apologized for everything to Lavinia, for she was far more aware of the grades of society than Polly would admit to being; and however much they disliked Lavinia, she was still Lady Harriet's daughter.

We stayed only a few days and I wrote to my father from London and Lavinia wrote to Lady Harriet. We said we had now returned from Lindenstein and were breaking the journey in London. We should be home within a few days.

Murder in Fiddler's Green

❦

I was further shocked to see the deterioration in my father. He now walked with a stick, but he said he was still capable of carrying on. He had many good workers in the village who were of inestimable help to him.

He wanted to hear about Lindenstein; he believed the *schloss* was very ancient, Gothic in fact.

'It must have been fascinating for you, my dear. A great opportunity. You were wise not to miss it.'

I parried his questions about the place and told myself I must find a book on it if that were possible, and learn something about it. I upbraided myself for my folly in not trying to do this earlier. But, of course, we had had too much to contend with.

Mrs Janson said he had been ailing last winter and she dreaded the one to come. She was glad I was home. 'You ought to be here,' she added significantly. 'I was a bit worried when I heard you wasn't coming straight home but were going gadding about with foreign princesses.'

'There was only one princess, Mrs Janson,' I reminded her.

'One's enough. You ought to have come straight home. I don't mind telling you, I'm glad school's done with. How was Polly?'

'Very well.'

'I reckon she was glad to see you.'

I said she was.

So, I was finished with school now. I was the polished article. What difference it had made to me I was not sure, except that I knew I was no longer the innocent girl who had gone to France.

That night as I lay in my familiar bed I had muddled dreams.

Faces seemed to swim in and out of my mind. The Duchess . . . the scientist . . . the old man with his fires . . . all waiting for Death . . . and so many of the women for a new life to begin. I pictured Agatha's cheerful grin, Emmeline's wistful looks and Miriam's tortured face. I was aware of Aunt Emily's secret smile as she smiled at me as though she were saying: You'll never escape . . . you will be here for ever . . . cosy . . . cosy . . .

I awoke crying out: 'No, no.'

Then I realized I was in my own familiar bed and it was only a dream. I was free.

Lavinia came over the next day.

'Let's ride,' she said and we rode out together, for being finished young ladies we could ride – as long as there were two of us – without a groom in attendance.

She said: 'It's the only way I can really feel safe to talk. There are so many people around. I feel they might be listening. My mother is talking about a London season.'

'She doesn't guess anything?'

'Of course not. Why should she?'

'My father asks awkward questions about Lindenstein.'

'Oh, it's too far away for people to know about. A London season, think of that!'

'Do you want it?'

'Of course I want it. I want to marry a rich man so that I can pay off Aunt Emily. The woman's a shark.'

'You didn't think that when you went to her.'

'I didn't know it was going to cost so much.'

'How long is it going to take you to pay?'

'More than a year . . . unless I can get Mama to top up my allowance.'

'Why don't you ask Fabian?'

'I couldn't tell him what I wanted it for and he'd want to know.'

'Couldn't you tell him it's a secret?'

'You don't understand Fabian. He wants to know everything. That's how he has always been. No. I'll have to pay it out of my own allowance until I find a rich husband.'

I looked at her wonderingly that she could talk so. Did she never think of little Fleur? Did she not want to be with her baby sometimes?

I asked her.

'Oh yes,' she replied, 'but I can't, can I? Those two will look after her. They love her already.'

'I shall go down and see them soon. I want to see Fleur, too.'

'Oh, good! You can let me know how she is.'

I marvelled at how rapidly she was regaining her old assurance. The submissive, fearful Lavinia was fast disappearing. She had overcome her misfortune and was, I could see, ready for adventure again.

She could think of little but the coming season. How she would revel in it. She was already regaining her healthy looks; she was even preening herself, certain that she would become the debutante of the season.

I went once or twice to Framling. I saw Lady Harriet, who was gracious in a detached sort of way. I was no longer of importance in her scheme of things. I had served my purpose as Lavinia's steadying companion over the school years and was now relegated to my proper position – the rather plain rector's daughter.

Lavinia's excitement grew. Such plans there were. Lady Harriet was having her schooled in certain accomplishments. She would soon be leaving with Lavinia for their London residence and there Lavinia would be put through her paces, learning how to curtsey, how to dance the new fashionable dances, and certain matters of deportment; and of course she must visit the court dressmakers. She was to be presented in the spring.

All through the winter I saw little of Lavinia. I had written several letters to Polly and she reported the progress of Fleur. The child was flourishing. There wasn't a baby like

502

her on the common. She and Eff took it in turns to wheel her out; and they had that nice bit of garden at the back where she could be in her pram.

She already knew them, and did she kick up a fuss when she wanted a bit of a cuddle!

I imagined there would be plenty of 'bits of cuddle' for Fleur and I rejoiced as I had throughout my life for the good fortune which had brought me Polly.

Christmas came – always a busy time for us at the rectory. There were the usual services – midnight mass on Christmas Eve, the carol service and before that the decorating of the church, organized by church workers but my father had to be present, of course. We had friends from the neighbourhood to dinner on Christmas Day. They were the doctor, his family and the solicitor and his wife.

There was a good deal of entertaining at Framling. Fabian was home. I saw him once or twice. He would call a greeting and give me that somewhat cryptic smile which I had come to expect from him.

'Hello, Drusilla,' he said. 'Finished school now?'

'Yes,' I told him.

'Now you are really a grown-up young lady.'

What was there to say? He smiled as though it were a great joke that I had grown up.

He did not stay long at Framling. I heard from Mrs Janson, who had it from the Framling cook, that he would be going to India soon; and that he was in London most of the time in the offices there, learning about the East India Company with which the Framling family had been concerned ever since it came into existence.

I wrote to Polly and sent Christmas presents to them, among them a little jacket for Fleur. Polly wrote back but her letters were full of how the baby was getting on, how she smiled at Polly first only Eff wouldn't have it, that that was not a smile. It was only a bit of wind, said Eff, determined to be the first to win recognition from the baby. In February, Lavinia and Lady Harriet went to London.

The weather was extremely cold and my father caught a chill which turned to bronchitis. He was quite ill and most of my time was spent nursing him.

A curate came to help out. He was Colin Brady, a fresh-faced, earnest young man who was quickly popular with the household. Mrs Janson cosseted him and the others followed her lead. He was very much liked in the neighbourhood.

I was pleased that he had come, for willingly he took all the onerous tasks from my father's shoulders; he very quickly became part of the household.

He and I got along well together. We both enjoyed reading and discussing what we had read. There was an air of innocence about him which I found refreshing. He would discuss his sermons with me and he always listened to my ideas. I seemed to take more part in church affairs than I had when my father was in charge.

His health was improving, but as Mrs Janson said, he had to take care. We never allowed him to go out if the wind was cold; it was really quite touching to see how Colin Brady was always there when there was a question of my father's doing something which would be too much for him, and doing it himself in an unostentatious way.

I was very grateful to him and very glad that he was there until I began to notice the surreptitious looks which came to us, not only from Mrs Janson but from the servants and certain of the parishioners. They had decided that the ideal solution was for me to marry Colin and that he should take over completely, thus solving the future of my father, Colin and myself in one swoop.

The result was that they had spoilt my pleasant relationship with the curate. I liked him very much but the thought of what was in people's minds concerning us made me less comfortable in his presence.

With the coming of the spring my father was almost back to normal.

504

'He's a marvel,' said Mrs Janson. 'They say creaking doors go on for a long time.'

Fabian came to Framling and with him was Dougal Carruthers. Lady Harriet and Lavinia were still in London. I was writing regularly to Polly and received news of the baby. I told Polly that I wanted to come and see them but in view of my father's health I had not been able to before. But now that he was better I wanted to arrange a visit. Polly wrote back that the baby was a little love, bright as a button, and did she know how to get her own way! I was not to worry about *her* and when I did come I could be sure of a big welcome.

Dear, dear Polly! What should I have done without her? What would Lavinia have done? I imagined her now being presented to the Queen, going to balls and parties; she would have completely forgotten the bogus Comte, just as she had Jos. But could she have forgotten Fleur? I could not believe even Lavinia would do that.

I decided that I would go to London during the following week.

Dougal called to see my father. He stayed to tea and my father greatly enjoyed his visit. I was pleased to see him so animated, looking as well as he had before the winter.

When Dougal left I conducted him to the hall and thanked him for calling.

'But it was a pleasure,' he said.

'It has done my father so much good. He has been rather ill and that makes him low in spirit.'

'I hope I may come again.'

'Please do. My father will be delighted to see you at any time.'

'You too, I hope.'

I did not expect him to come again so soon, but the next afternoon he presented himself. It was another pleasant tea-time and my father said: 'Do come and dine with us. There is so much we have to talk about.'

'I should greatly enjoy that,' replied Dougal, 'but I am a guest at Framling. I could hardly leave my host.'

'Bring him too,' said my father rashly.

'May I? I am sure he would be delighted to come.'

Mrs Janson was slightly less than delighted. She did not like the idea of entertaining 'them up at the House', and of course Sir Fabian would be our guest.

I said: 'Don't worry. Just forget who he is.'

'The trouble with them Framlings is they never let you forget who they are.'

And so Fabian came to dine.

He took my hands and held them for a few moments in a warm grip.

'Thank you for letting me come,' he said, somewhat insincerely, I thought, for I was sure he was not in the least grateful to be invited to our humble dwelling.

'Mr Carruthers suggested it,' I told him.

He raised his eyebrows as though he were amused. In fact I was beginning to feel that most of the time he regarded me with amusement.

'The rector has an astonishing knowledge of ancient Greece,' said Dougal. 'He has some quite unusual ideas.'

'How fascinating!' said Fabian, continuing to smile at me.

I took them to the drawing-room where my father was seated in his chair. Colin Brady was with him.

'I think you all know each other,' I said.

'I don't think we have met,' said Fabian, eyeing Colin closely.

'Mr Brady came to help my father when he was ill and we are hoping he is going to stay with us.'

'That must be useful,' said Fabian.

'And Mr Brady . . . this is Sir Fabian Framling.'

Colin was a little in awe of Fabian. He knew he came from the influential family which ruled the village.

Soon we were seated at table. Mrs Janson had excelled herself and the maids had been given detailed instructions how they were to behave.

Dougal was in conversation with my father, with Colin Brady now and then throwing in a remark. Fabian turned to me.

'Did you enjoy Lamason?' he asked.

'It was a most interesting experience,' I told him.

'I think my sister found it so, too.'

'I am sure she did.'

'And now you are back . . . what shall you do?'

'I suppose . . . I just go on living here.'

He nodded.

My father was talking about the ancient civilizations which flourished for a while and then passed away.

'It is a pattern,' said Dougal. 'Empires rise and fall. I suppose the most significant fall was that of the Roman Empire. All over Europe you can see the remains of that civilization . . . in spite of the fact that its fall was followed by the Dark Ages.'

Then I heard my father say: 'Drusilla was at Lindenstein only recently.'

'Lindenstein,' said Dougal. 'Now that is a very interesting spot. You remember it, Fabian.' He turned to me. 'Fabian and I did a kind of grand tour. We visited all the conventional places, didn't we, Fabian? But we did stray from the beaten track now and then. Actually we were quite near Lindenstein.'

I felt myself flushing a little. I was always uncomfortable when there was reference to our deceit. I wanted to change the conversation quickly.

'Tell us what you think of Florence, Mr Carruthers,' I said. 'I have always felt it must be the most fascinating city in the world.'

'There are many who would agree with you,' replied Dougal.

My father said: 'How I should love to stroll along the Arno where Dante met Beatrice.'

'What do you think of Lindenstein, Miss Delany?' asked Fabian.

'Oh . . . very interesting.'

'That medieval *schloss* . . .'

'That is where Drusilla stayed, isn't it, Drusilla?' said my father. 'The Princess was at school with Drusilla and Lavinia. She invited them. It was a great experience.'

'Yes,' I said with feeling. 'We had a great experience.'

My father had turned the conversation back to Dante; and Colin and Dougal joined in.

Fabian said quietly to me: 'An amazing little country . . . Lindenstein. Those mountains . . . stark and grim . . . don't you think?'

'Oh yes,' I said.

'And the *schloss*. Extraordinary architecture . . . all those towers . . .'

I nodded.

'It must have been very interesting to stay in such a place.'

I nodded again.

He was regarding me intently. I wondered if Lavinia could have confided in him after all; and I felt suddenly angry that I should have been burdened with her secret.

When I left the men with the port I went to my room. Fabian Framling always disconcerted me. It was the way in which he looked at me as though he were trying to remind me how vulnerable I was.

When they were taking their departure my father said: 'This has been a pleasant evening. I rarely meet people who are interested in my hobbies. Do please come again.'

'You must dine at Framling,' said Fabian.

'Thank you,' I said, 'but my father should not be out in the evening.' I was looking at Dougal. 'It is better for you to come here.'

'That I shall certainly do . . . when I am asked.'

'I hope you will be here for a little while yet,' said my father.

'I think so,' answered Fabian. 'I doubt we shall be leaving the country until the end of next year.'

'Next week — it is next week, is it not, my dear? — Drusilla is going to London.'

'Oh?' said Fabian, his gaze on me.

'It is to stay with her old nurse,' explained my father. 'You know how strong these ties are.'

'Yes,' said Fabian. 'Then perhaps we may come when Miss Drusilla returns.'

'There is no reason why you should not come when I am away,' I said. 'Mrs Janson will take care of things, and my father would enjoy your company.'

'I shall invite you,' said my father.

Then they took their leave.

My father said what a delightful evening it had been and Colin Brady agreed with him. Mrs Janson was not displeased. Her verdict was that the Framlings were just like anybody else and she wasn't afraid of *him*. As for the other one, he was a perfect gent and no one could take objection to him.

I felt I had come through the evening tolerably well although I had had certain qualms when they began to talk about Lindenstein.

I was growing excited about my coming visit to London. The prospect of seeing Polly again always filled me with joy and now there was the baby as well as Eff. I went down to the town, which was about a mile out of the village. I had a pleasant morning shopping and bought a little jacket and bonnet and a pair of bootees for Fleur and a pair of bellows for Polly and Eff because I could see they had had some difficulty in getting the kitchen fire to draw up.

As I was coming out of the shop a carriage drove by. I knew it was from Framling because I had seen Fabian driving it around. It was drawn by two spirited grey horses and he liked to go at great speed.

I saw Fabian in the driver's seat and to my surprise he pulled up.

'Miss Delany.'

'Oh . . . hello,' I said.

'You have been shopping, I see.'

'Oh yes.'

'I'll drive you back.'

'Oh, that is not necessary.'

'Of course I'll take you back.'

He had leaped down from the seat and taken from me the bag which contained my purchases. As he did so the contents fell out and there on the pavement were the bellows, the baby's jacket, bonnet and the bootees.

'Oh dear,' he said, stooping to pick them up. 'I hope no harm is done.'

I flushed hotly. He stood there with the bootees in his hand.

'Very pretty,' he commented, 'and they are all safe.'

'Really,' I stammered, 'there's no need to take me home.'

'But I insist. I like to show off my horses, you know. They really are a superb pair. You can sit beside me. Then you can see the road better. You'll enjoy it.'

He carefully put my purchases in the carriage and helped me up.

'Now,' he said. 'Off we go. I shall not take you directly home.'

'Oh, but . . .'

'Again I insist. You'll be home just as soon as you would if you had walked. And you will have the pleasure of seeing Castor and Pollux in action.'

'The heavenly twins . . .' I murmured.

'They are as like each other as twins only to look at. Pollux has a bit of a temper and Castor is inclined to be lazy. But they know the master's touch.'

The horses broke into a gallop and he laughed as we gathered speed.

'Just cling to me if you're scared,' he said.

'Thanks,' I replied. 'But I'm not.'

'And thank you for the compliment. It is well deserved in fact. I know how to manage my horses. By the way, I haven't seen you riding lately.'

'Not since I returned.'

'Why not?'

'We don't have a stable at the rectory.'

'But you used to ride regularly.'

'That was when Lavinia was at home.'

'My dear Miss Delany, you don't have to ask permission to use a horse from the Framling stables. I thought you understood that.'

'It was different when Lavinia was here. I rode with her.'

'There is no difference at all. Please, whenever you wish, ride the horse you have always had.'

'Thank you. That is very good of you.'

'Oh no. After all, you are a great friend of my sister. Do you envy her, preening in London?'

'I don't think I should greatly care for the process.'

'No, I dare say not. But please ride when you want to.'

'You are very kind.'

He gave me a sideways, rather sardonic smile.

'Tell me about Lamason,' he said.

'Oh, it is supposed to be a very fine school.'

'Where they turn hoydens into young ladies.'

'I think that is the idea.'

'And do you think they have done a satisfactory job on you and Lavinia?'

'I cannot speak for Lavinia. You should ask her.'

'But yourself?'

'That is for others to judge.'

'Do you want to hear my judgement?'

'Not particularly. It could not be a true one because you scarcely know me.'

'I feel I know you very well.'

'I can't think why. I have so rarely seen you.'

'There have been significant moments. Do you remember when you took the peacock fan?'

'On your orders, yes. Tell me, how is your Aunt Lucille?'

'She has grown very feeble. She is lost to this world and exists only in her own.'

'Does she still have the Indian servants?'

'She does. They would never leave her and she would be completely lost without them.'

'I'm sorry,' I said.

There was a brief silence; then he said: 'You will be going to London soon.'

The carriage lurched and I fell against him clutching his coat.

He laughed. 'All's well. I told you you were safe with me.'

'I really think I should be home. I have a great deal to do.'

'You have to prepare for your visit to London.'

'Yes, that and other things.'

'How long shall you stay?'

'Oh . . . about a week.'

'You are very fond of your old nurse.'

'She is not really old. Polly is one of those people who never will be.'

'Your loyalty does you credit.'

'Is it so very creditable to express one's true feelings?'

'No, of course not. There. You see how docile I am. I'll have you at the rectory door in three minutes.'

'Thank you.'

He pulled up sharply at the grey stone house, leaped down and helped me out. He took my hands and smiled at me.

'I hope the gifts are acceptable.'

'What gifts?'

'The bellows and the baby's clothes.'

To my annoyance I flushed again.

I took the bag he handed me, said 'Thank you,' and went into the house.

I was disturbed. He had always disturbed me. It was a pity he had seen my purchases. I felt he had looked at them cryptically. I was wondering what he had thought.

*

512

My father said was it wise of me to travel to London alone?

'My dear Father,' I replied, 'what harm could befall me? I shall get on the train under the eye of Mr Hanson, the station master, and Mr Briggs, the porter. Polly will be waiting for me at the other end. I am grown up now, you know.'

'Still . . .' said my father.

'I shall be all right.'

At last he agreed that I could come to no harm and I set out with my case containing the gifts and the little bit of luggage I was taking with me.

I sat in the carriage by the window and closed my eyes while I contemplated the pleasure of a reunion with Polly and seeing Eff and the baby again.

The door opened. Fabian was getting into the carriage.

He grinned at me. 'I had to go to London unexpectedly. This is fun. We can travel together. Why, you don't look very pleased to see me.'

'I hadn't expected to . . .'

'Surprises are pleasant, don't you think?'

'Sometimes.'

He sat opposite me and folded his arms.

'I am sure your father would be pleased. I believe he is a little anxious about your travelling alone. Young ladies don't usually, do they?'

'I am of the opinion that we are not so fragile as some try to pretend.'

'I wonder why?'

'Oh, it is a masculine idea . . . meant to show the superiority of men.'

'Do you really believe that?'

The train was beginning to move out of the station.

'Believe what?' I asked.

'In masculine superiority.'

'Certainly not.'

'They are inferior, then?'

'I did not say that.'

'That is gracious of you.'

'No . . . just common sense. The sexes are meant to complement one another.'

'Doesn't it say that in the Bible? But I believe there are some occasions when the subservient role of the female is expressed. St Paul . . .'

'Oh, St Paul! Wasn't he one of those who found women a temptation and blamed them for being that?'

'Did he? I think your Biblical knowledge is greater than mine. It all comes of being such a polished young lady.'

'Thank you.'

'How long shall you be staying in London?'

'A week, I think. I do not like leaving my father longer.'

'He was very ill in the winter, I believe. I understand your anxiety. The curate is a very worthy young man, I gather.'

'He is very helpful and popular with the parishioners, which is very important.'

'It is important for us all to be popular.'

'But particularly with someone in his position. For instance, I don't suppose you care very much whether you are popular or not.'

'I do . . . where some people are concerned.' He smiled at me in that quizzical manner with which I was familiar.

He sat back, still smiling. 'This is really a pleasant way of travelling. Usually I regret the time spent on it.'

'You will be doing a good deal of travelling, I dare say.'

'Oh, you mean India where I shall be going at some time.'

'Soon, I suppose.'

'Probably at the end of the year. Carruthers will go too. You see, our families are connected with the East India Company.'

'I had heard.'

'From Carruthers, I suppose. I know he is a frequent visitor at the rectory.'

'He gets on well with my father. They have shared interests.'

'We have been brought up with the idea that we shall

514

eventually go into the Company. My uncle . . . my father's brother . . . has offices in London. I go there now and then . . . gleaning experience, you might say.'

'It must be interesting.'

'The Company . . . oh yes. It is part of history, of course. It goes back years and years. As you know, trading with India started when Vasco da Gama discovered the eastern passage and cast anchor off Calicut. But the Portuguese never started a trading company; they left that to us. Did you know that Queen Elizabeth granted us a charter to trade? It was on the very last day of the sixteenth century. So you see we have our roots in the past and it is obligatory in the family to carry on.'

'You must be very proud of your ancestors.'

'We do have our share of sinners.'

'All families have that.'

'Some more than most. Now I imagine yours is very worthy . . . just the occasional peccadillo perhaps.'

'It might be better not to enquire.'

'I am sure you are right, but with a family like ours it all seems to be recorded. We know that an ancestor was one of those who founded the Company and we know something of the lives of those who followed him. People are unexpected, don't you agree? Those who appear so virtuous often have their secrets and the villains often a grain of goodness.'

I said: 'Tell me about the merchandise. What commodities do you deal in?'

'We send out bullion, woollens, hardware and such things to India and we bring back silks, diamonds, tea, porcelain, pepper, calico, drugs and so on.'

'I see. You are traders.'

'Exactly. But we have become very powerful. You see, we were not content with trading. We wanted to rule, and we have taken part in quarrels between Indian princes, supporting one against another. We have gained power and some would say that the East India Company is the true ruler of India.'

'Do the Indians resent this?'

'Naturally some of them do. Others see the advantages we have brought them. The French had an East India Company, too. That is the reason for the trouble between our two countries.'

'It seems to me that this ambition for power causes a great deal of trouble.'

He nodded. 'You see why, do you not, that it is a family tradition.'

'Yes, I do,' I said, 'with a family like yours.'

'Well, enough of the Company and my family. What of you? What do you propose to do now you are home?'

'Do? What could I do?'

'You tell me.'

'At the moment I am helping to run the rectory and look after my father. There are a great many duties which fall to the rector's family. I suppose that is what I shall continue to do.'

'You have no plan . . . no ambition? To travel, perhaps? You have already been to France . . . and Lindenstein.'

I replied hurriedly: 'I suppose one waits to see what happens.'

'Some of us are impatient and prod fate. Are you one of those?'

'That is something I have to find out. Up to now I have never done any prodding. Have you?'

He leaned towards me. 'I am continually doing it. If I want something I make an effort to get it.'

'It is all that ambition and lust for power. It is because you belong to the Framlings and the East India Company.'

'Not entirely. It is my pushing nature.'

I laughed and he said: 'How different you are when you laugh. Did you know that you look a little severe in repose?'

'I did not know I was particularly so.'

'Perhaps it is only when you see me.'

'I can't think why you should induce solemnity.'

'Perhaps because you disapprove of me?'

'Why should I?'

'I can think of a few reasons.'

'Then I don't know them.'

'Don't look expectant. I am not going to tell you. I should not be so foolish as to increase your disapproval.'

'The disapproval is entirely of your imaginings. How could one disapprove of someone one did not know?'

'Perhaps through ill repute.'

'I know nothing of that.'

'There! Now you are severe again. I feel we are getting to know each other well on this journey.'

'Why should being in a train do that which all the years living as neighbours has failed to do?'

'There is something very intimate about trains.'

'Is there?'

'Don't you feel it?'

'I suppose we have talked together more than we ever did before.'

'There you are, you see. You can't get away from me.'

'Nor you from me.'

'Oh, but I don't want to.'

I laughed. 'I think we must be near our destination.'

'Five more minutes,' he said. 'Alas! What a short journey it has seemed. Most enlivening. How fortunate that we had a carriage to ourselves. I will tell you something. It wasn't luck. I had the foresight to tip the guard.'

'Why?'

'Obvious reasons. I thought it would be interesting to get to know each other. People would have spoilt our little tête-à-tête.'

'I can't understand why you took the trouble.'

'I take a lot of trouble to do what I want. Didn't I tell you that I'm a prodder?'

I was a little startled and faintly alarmed. I did not know what was in his mind. It seemed to me that he might be preparing to indulge in a little light flirtation. No doubt he thought that I was an innocent maiden ready to fall into the arms of the all-powerful lord of the manor. If Lavinia had learned little from her experience, I had learned a great deal.

I said coolly: 'I can't imagine why you should take the trouble.'

'I'll tell you later.'

'In the meantime, here we are.'

He took my case.

'I can manage, you know,' I said.

'I wouldn't think of allowing you to carry it.'

It seemed to me that he was taking a proprietorial attitude already.

I should have to be wary of him. He was the type of person who thought he had only to beckon to a girl and she would come running. He was Sir Fabian, rich and powerful; and his mother had made him feel — as they used to say – the little Cæsar.

I tried to take my case from him, but he resisted, smiling. We walked along the platform and there was Polly waiting for me.

She stared in amazement to see me with a man, and her amazement turned to dismay when she recognized him.

I ran to her and she embraced me. 'Oh Polly,' I cried, 'how wonderful to see you.'

'Well, it's not like a smack in the chops to me neither.'

She was restrained because he was there.

'It's Sir Fabian, Polly. He kindly carried my bag.'

He bowed to Polly. 'Miss Delany and I met on the train.'

'Did you now?' said Polly, very faintly bellicose. She had never approved of the Framlings. *Who were they when they were out?* she was thinking, I knew. *Or on trains and carrying people's bags. Up to no good, shouldn't reckon.* I knew her so well that I was aware of her thoughts.

'Well thank you, Sir Fabian,' I said. 'It was good of you.'

'We'll get a cab and be home in a tick,' said Polly.

'I shall see you home,' he said. 'I shall get the cab.'

'There is no need . . .' I began.

'But I insist.' He spoke as though his word was law. It was faintly irritating. I felt an urge to snatch my case from him and tell him we did not need his help. But if I did that might betray something which I ought to hide.

I was aware of the imperious manner in which he hailed the cab and in a very short time we were on our way to the common.

I tried to chat to Polly as I should have done if he had not been there. I asked about Eff. Eff was flourishing. Doing very well. Might even take on No. 10 Maccleston if the old man living there moved out. Eff had always had her eyes open.

Neither of us mentioned the baby but I knew Polly was longing to talk of her, as I was.

I was glad when that journey was over. He alighted and carried my bag to the door. Eff was waiting to open it. She cried out with pleasure when she saw me and then stepped back at the sight of Fabian.

He raised his hat and bowed.

'This is Sir Fabian Framling, a neighbour of mine,' I explained. 'I saw him on the train and he has been very helpful.'

I could see she was wondering whether he should be asked in for a cup of tea and a piece of the special sultana cake she had baked for the occasion; her only hesitation was because of his title and perhaps his undeniable presence.

I said quickly: 'It was kind of you, Sir Fabian. Thank you so much.' And with that I turned away; and he, with another bow, went back to the waiting cab.

We went inside.

'Well, I never,' said Polly. 'You could have knocked me down with half a feather when I saw who he was.'

She shook her head. She was bothered; I would tell her as soon as I had an opportunity that there was no need for alarm.

Eff said: 'I know who you'll be wanting to see. I'd have her here but she's having her nap, and I don't want to disturb her, else there'll be ructions, eh, Poll?'

519

'You bet,' said Polly.

'Well, what about a nice cup of tea first. I've got some muffins.'

As we sat over tea and muffins I heard of the increasing prosperity of the business and how the baby grew more beautiful every day.

At length she was brought down by Eff and I held her in my arms while she gazed at me wonderingly, her little hands curled round my finger and what could have been a smile of contentment on her pinkish face. She had changed a good deal from the day when Lavinia and I had brought her here. She was getting on for nine months old – quite a personage. I had always been distressed by the unwanted babies, but this one, at least, thanks to Polly and Eff, was overwhelmed with love.

Fleur had vivid blue eyes and the almost black hair she had been born with had lightened considerably. It was dark brown with tawny lights in it – inherited no doubt from Lavinia. She was clearly a contented baby and that was something to be happy about.

Being with Fleur made me wonder about the other babies who had been born round about the same time. What had happened to Emmeline? Her child would have had a happy home, I was sure. And the poor little girl who had been raped? Surely her family would look after her child. And Agatha? She would know what to do. She was warm-hearted and would never desert her child. Mostly I thought of Miriam who would have to give up hers for the sake of not disturbing her marriage. That seemed the saddest case of all.

But I was delighted to see Fleur here. She would not miss her parents because she could not have two more devoted people to care for her than Polly and Eff.

The bellows were seized on with joy. 'That kitchen fire never did draw like it ought,' said Eff.

The bonnet was immediately tried on and Fleur was very interested in the bootees.

'Nice for her afternoon nap,' said Polly. 'She's starting to toddle now. I reckon she thinks she's done enough shooting round on her hands and knees.'

'Don't you think she's a little angel?' said Eff.

I said I did.

'Eff spoils her, really,' said Polly.

'I like that!' retorted Eff. 'Talk about the pot calling the kettle black!'

It was all so comforting, so much what I had expected from them. Polly was still the anchor in my life.

She was uneasy, though. I sensed that. When she came to my room that night, after Eff had retired, she talked very seriously to me.

She said: 'I've been worried about you, Drusilla. I didn't like to think of you in that foreign place. I didn't know what was happening. Fleur . . . she's Lavinia's. I know that now. At first I thought she was yours.'

'Oh Polly!'

'Well, that's why we took her in so prompt. I said to Eff, "This is my girl and she's in trouble. We're going to help her all we know how and if that means having the baby here, well, then we'll have the baby here." '

'I thought of you immediately. I remember how you and Eff always liked babies.'

'We do. But having one of your own is something that has to be thought about.'

'You didn't hesitate.'

'No . . . As I told you, I thought it was yours.'

'You've always been wonderful to me, Polly . . . always.'

'I know now she's that Lavinia's. That saucy baggage. Just like her. Gets into trouble and gets someone else to sort it out for her.'

'Lady Harriet took over a big part of my school bills. I was there to be with Lavinia.'

'I know. That sort think they own the world and everyone in it. Now there's that Fabian . . . or whatever he calls himself.'

521

'Everyone else calls him Fabian. It's his name.'

'*Sir* Fabian, if you please.'

'He inherited the title from his father. He's been a sir ever since his father died.'

'Silly way of going on ... Little children getting airs. No wonder they grow up thinking they are Lord God Almighty.'

'Do you think he does?'

'Clear as daylight.'

'That's not always very clear.'

'Now you're being clever and I want to talk serious, like. It's about Fleur.'

'Oh, Polly, hasn't Lavinia sent you any money?'

'It's not money we're after. What I wanted to say was that Fleur ... well, she is one of them Framlings when all's said and done. She's all right now. Wouldn't know the difference between Buckingham Palace and the rookeries ... as long as we're there to look after her and give her a kiss and a cuddle ... she's all right. But when she grows up a bit, is this place going to be good enough for her?'

'It will be good enough if you and Eff are there. She loves you both. Look how contented she is when you're there.'

'Oh, she's a loving little thing. No bones about that. But there'll come a time when she'll have to be told who she is and something done about her education and all that.'

'Let's leave it at that, Polly. When I get a chance I'll talk to Lavinia.'

'And there's you.'

'What about me?'

'What are you going to do?'

'What do you mean, Polly?'

'You know what I mean. Rector's not well, is he? How long can he go on working? I reckon this Colin Brady will take over. Do you like him?'

'You are not trying to do a little matchmaking, are you, Polly?'

'People have to be serious about these things. I'd like to

see you settled, I would. You'd be happy with some little ones. Oh, I know. I've seen you with Fleur. There's some who are natural mothers and you are one of them.'

'You are going too fast, Polly.'

'Well, you like him don't you, this Colin Brady?'

'Yes.'

'And he's a good man.'

'I dare say he is.'

'You don't want to let some people pick you up when they think they will and like as not drop you when they get a little tired.'

'To whom are you referring?'

'That *Sir* Fabian.'

'Oh, there is no question of his picking me up. He just happened to be on the train.'

'Some people have a way of making things happen when they want them to.'

I thought of what he had said about prodding, and he had certainly contrived the meeting. I felt rather pleased and excited that he had bothered to do so, which ought to have irritated me, but it didn't.

Gradually she wormed the story of Lavinia's betrayal and downfall from me.

'That one had trouble coming to her if ever anyone had. Perhaps this will be a lesson to her. Could be . . . though I doubt it. She's got mischief written all over her, that one. She'll be in trouble again sooner or later. And to think that Sir Fabian is our Fleur's uncle and doesn't know it!'

'Of course he doesn't know there is a Fleur.'

'Bit of a shock to him if he did. I'm not surprised that Lavinia went to all them lengths to keep her little secret. I've always been sorry for girls in trouble but I can't say I'm getting out my sackcloth and ashes for her.'

And so we talked, and it was as comforting to me as it used to be in the old days when we sat in the room at the rectory with the churchyard on one side and the village green on the other.

Polly and I had our trips 'up West'; I bought some clothes, and some gloves for Polly and a scarf for Eff. I had my allowance which came from the money my mother had left. It was not very much but at least I was not penniless. I told Polly I was going to send her half of what I had to help with Fleur, but she was indignant. 'You'll do no such thing! If you attempt to do that I'll send it right back . . . pronto . . . and Eff and me 'ull be most put out.'

She told me how they loved having the baby. It was important . . . particularly to Eff. Eff loved the business but she often said she'd missed something. She had put up with Him for years and she would have forgiven him all his little ways if he had given her a baby. But it seemed he wasn't any good . . . even at that. Polly, too, had been disappointed in that respect.

'But now we've got Fleur,' she said, 'and if that Lavinia ever wanted her back she wouldn't get her. I'd fight to the death for Fleur . . . so would Eff . . . and Eff always wins . . . always has and always would. Father used to say that.'

I often thought of Lavinia and wondered what she was doing and if she ever gave a thought to the child. I doubted it. She had recklessly conceived the child for her own gratification and as casually cast her off without seeming to realize how fortunate she had been to find people to take the burden from her shoulders.

During that week, I would wheel the baby out on the common. I used to sit on a seat and think of everything that had happened over the last two years. Often in my mind I went back to the little town, choosing my pastry and bringing it out on a plate to sit under the sunshade and wait for Charles to bring the coffee. I could recall with vividness the day the so-called Comte had strolled up to us. I could see Lavinia smiling provocatively at the handsome intruder in her secretive manner. I remembered so well that inner satisfaction of hers. I should have guessed that the Comte was false and all he wanted was a brief love-affair.

While I was dreaming thus and Fleur was dozing in her

pram, I was suddenly aware that someone had sat down on the seat beside me. I turned and with a mingling of exhilaration and consternation I saw that it was Fabian.

'Sir Fabian . . .' I stammered.

'Oh, please,' he said, 'not so formal. I'm simply Fabian to my friends.'

'What . . . what are you doing here?'

'Rejoicing in this happy turn of fortune. How are you faring? You look well. Such a rosy colour in your cheeks. Is that due to the London air or reunion with your devoted nurse?'

I did not answer and he went on: 'What a pretty child! Whose is it?'

'She has been adopted by Polly.'

'She is an unusual woman, your Polly. The bonnet suits her.' He looked at me rather roguishly. 'It was a good choice.'

'Yes, it was.'

'And the little socks.'

'She is really too old for those so it wasn't such a good choice. She will soon be toddling and she needs shoes for that.'

'You should have thought of that. How enterprising those two are! They have their own houses and they take it upon themselves to adopt a child. Most unusual! Tell me, have they acquired No 10 Maccleston yet?'

'No, but it will come. Are you on business down here?'

He looked at me with a half-amused smile. 'I see you suspect me of playing truant. I happened to be in the neighbourhood and when I came across the common I remembered you were staying here. Luckily I saw you. I was surprised. First the baby carriage disconcerted me. I thought it must be some young mother . . . and then I realized that no one could look quite as you did . . . and I rejoiced. When are you returning? I believe you said you would stay for a week. Friday would be a week exactly.'

'Yes. I expect it will be then.'

'I hope you are having a rewarding week.'

'Extremely so.'

Fleur had awakened and after regarding us gravely for a few moments decided that she had been ignored long enough and started to whimper. I took her out of her pram and she was immediately smiling. I bounced her up and down a little which she obviously enjoyed. She showed great interest in Fabian and stretching out towards him took hold of one of the buttons on his coat. She looked up at him, staring intently into his face.

'Is that an expression of disapproval?' he asked.

'I am not sure, but it is certainly one of interest.'

Fleur laughed as though she found him amusing.

'She will soon be talking,' I said. 'She wants to say something to you but she just cannot get the words.'

'She's a nice creature.'

'I think so and so do Polly and Eff.'

'Eff?'

'Short for Effie.'

At the mention of Eff Fleur began to mumble, 'Eff, Eff . . . Eff.'

'You see,' I said, 'she is already beginning to speak.'

'It did not sound like speech to me.'

'Oh, you have to listen carefully. She is saying Eff.'

'Effeff . . . eff,' said Fleur.

'What is her name?' he asked.

'Fleur.'

'A little French flower. Is she French?'

'Polly did not say.'

'But they gave her a French name.'

'I think she may have had that before she came to them.'

I tried to persuade her to relinquish the button but she refused to do so, and when at length she did her hand shot out and gripped his ear.

'She clearly likes you,' I said.

'I wish she would find another way of expressing her fondness.'

'Come, Fleur,' I said. 'It is time we went home. Polly will be waiting for you and so will Eff. They will be cross if I keep you out too long.'

'I have an idea,' he said. 'Take the baby back and let me give you luncheon.'

'It is kind of you,' I replied, 'but I have such a short time left. I must be with Polly.'

'Because you will soon be leaving. All right. We'll travel back together.'

I did not answer. I put a mildly protesting Fleur back into the pram and turned to him. He stood there hat in hand, bowing.

'Goodbye,' I said.

'*Au revoir*,' he replied meaningfully.

I did not tell Polly I had met him on the common. I knew it would disturb her.

It was the following morning. Polly and I were breakfasting. Eff took hers very early, which often meant that Polly and I could talk as we loved to do. I think Eff knew this and was glad to make herself scarce and give us the opportunity.

Polly had been glancing through the paper and she cried as soon as I appeared, 'Here, what do you think of this?'

I sat down expectantly.

'There's been a big fire at the place . . . that Firs. Nursing Home it calls it . . . in the New Forest.'

She started to read: ' "Firs Nursing Home. Terrible fire, believed to have been started by one of the patients. The fire was well under way before it was discovered. Mrs Fletcher the proprietress lost her life. It is not yet known how many died, but the fire was very intense and it is feared that several lives were lost. Many of the inmates were suffering some infirmities . . ." '

I sat staring ahead. Had Janine been one of the victims? I wondered how many women awaiting their babies had perished. I thought of the Duchess and the young man whom Aunt Emily had intended for Janine. I imagined that one day George had lighted one of those fires he had laid so many times in cupboards and such places.

I told Polly about George.

'Thank goodness it didn't happen when you were there,' she said.

All that day I could not stop thinking of The Firs and Aunt Emily, Janine and the people I had known.

It might so easily have happened while we were there.

I scoured the papers later that day and all those I could find on the next. I supposed it was not considered of enough interest to be given more than the initial space.

The day for my departure arrived.

An hour before the train was due to leave, Fabian appeared at the door with a cab to take us to the station in time to catch the three o'clock train. It was the only one that afternoon, so he knew I should be taking it.

Eff opened the door when he knocked. Her surprise was obvious; she was greatly impressed. She liked distinguished people to come to the house. As she said, it went down well with the neighbours.

There was nothing to be done but to accept his offer with a good grace. Polly came with us to the station but of course his presence prevented intimate conversation between us.

He was very affable to her and when we arrived he insisted that the cab driver should wait to take her back; and he paid for the journey.

Polly said: 'There's no need for that.'

But he waved aside her protests and even Polly had to fall in with the arrangement, though she resented it and I knew was disturbed to see me sitting with him in the carriage.

He seemed very pleased with his manœuvring.

'It was a pleasant visit,' he said, as we moved out of London. 'I always enjoy being with them.'

'A most unusual pair of ladies and there is the baby, too. I could see how much you liked her. A pleasant child. I fancy she looked a little French.'

'Oh, did you think so?' I forced myself to say.

'Oh yes. And the name Fleur. I don't know whether it is used much in France, but it is certainly charming, don't you think?'

'Yes, I do.'

'It makes one wonder who could abandon such a child. I should like to know the story behind her birth. A liaison, I imagine . . . with both participants realizing that they had made a mistake.'

'Perhaps.'

'Most certainly, I would say. Did you hear how those two worthy ladies undertook the adoption?'

'I don't know how such things are done.'

I looked out of the window.

'You find the view interesting,' he said.

'The Home Counties are very pleasant,' I replied.

'They are indeed. There is an air of peaceful prosperity about them. Nothing rugged . . . all neat and pleasant. It always seems to me that even the trees submit to conventions. How different from Lindenstein!'

I felt sick with apprehension. He had guessed something and he was determined to bait me. He was teasing me as a cat teases a mouse before the final death stroke.

'Oh . . . Lindenstein,' I murmured, trying to sound nonchalant.

'Rather flat, I thought when I saw it. Stark, in fact. Rather surprising when you consider its position. Not quite what one would have expected.'

He was trying to trap me. I remembered snatches of that conversation when he had visited us and there had been mention of the mountainous country.

I was growing very uncomfortable under his scrutiny.

I turned from the window and met his gaze. There was a faint amusement in his eyes. Was he telling me that he knew I had never been to Lindenstein? I could see that he was working things out. Lavinia and I had left school at the end of term; we had said we were visiting the Princess;

we had been away for two months; and there was a mysterious baby — French — who had been taken in by my devoted nurse.

I imagined he was fitting things together and thinking he had the solution. The inference would seem obvious to him. I felt indignant. I wanted to tell him to stop his insolent probing and ask his sister for the explanation.

I said coldly: 'I suppose everywhere is different from what we expect it to be. Perhaps it is not wise to compare.'

'Odious, aren't they ... comparisons? ... Or is it odorous?'

'It depends on which source you are consulting.'

'That is true, of course, but in either case it means they are rather obnoxious.'

He continued to regard me with amusement. Surely he must consider Lavinia's involvement in this. Knowing her — as he must — he could not believe that she would be ready to make any sacrifice for a friend. If I had been the one who was forced to hide, she would never have gone to such lengths to help me.

I wanted to shout at him: 'You Framlings take up such an attitude of superiority when you are the ones who cause all the trouble.'

He must have seen that I was shaken and when he spoke it was rather tenderly. 'I hope there is an improvement in your father's health when you return.'

'I hope so. Of course his duties are considerably lightened by the coming of Colin Brady.'

'Oh, the curate. I hear he is quite a success.'

'That's true and it is very fortunate that he is there. There are some days when my father is unable to work and that distresses him. But Mr Brady takes on all the duties and a great load off my father's shoulders.'

'I suppose he will want a living of his own one day.'

'He certainly will.'

He nodded and again he was giving me that probing look.

'I dare say you have a great deal in common.'

I raised my eyebrows.

'Both in Holy Orders, so to speak. You by accident of birth and he by choice.'

'I suppose you could say that.'

'And you are obviously good friends.'

'One could not be anything else with Mr Brady. He is so friendly with everyone.'

'An admirable young man.'

Again the almost derisive smile. I was annoyed with him. First he had decided that I had had a liaison in France and that Fleur was the result and now he was contemplating marrying me off to Colin Brady. It was really quite impertinent . . . assuming the role of lord of the manor taking care of the underlings.

I wanted to tell him that I had not sought his company and that I did not care for his assumptions; but of course I did nothing of the sort; and in due course he changed the subject.

He talked about India, a subject which clearly fascinated him, the scenery and the people. He had not yet seen it, he told me, but he was learning so much about it that he felt he was beginning to know it.

I was interested to hear about the people, caste system, the power of the Company, the markets and the exotic goods which could be bought there. I was quite beguiled, but I could not forget our previous conversation and the implication that Fleur was the result of an indiscretion on my part; and, of course, I could not tell him that it was his sister and not I who was at the centre of that sordid tragedy.

In due course the train steamed into our station. One of the grooms from Framling had brought the carriage and Fabian drove me to the rectory.

He took my hand and smiled at me as he said goodbye. It had been a most interesting and illuminating visit, he told me, with double-edged meaning.

I felt very uneasy and I could not get out of my mind the

thought of the fire at The Firs and wondering who of the strange people I had known, had been its victims. Had Janine been one of them?

Mrs Janson told me that all had been as well as could be expected at the rectory during my absence. The rector had had one rather bad turn but she hadn't thought it necessary to interrupt my holiday. That Mr Carruthers had been over once or twice and his visits seemed to do the rector a power of good. There they had been, huddled over some old maps and things that Mr Carruthers brought and it was like a tonic for the rector. And, of course, Mr Brady was there to look after everything, so she could say it had all gone off rather well.

During the next week or so my friendship with both Dougal Carruthers and Colin Brady seemed to take a new turn.

Dougal came often and my father was eager for me to join them in their discussions.

'You will find it all so interesting,' he said. 'Of course, Mr Carruthers's forte is the Anglo-Saxons . . . a little late for me, but I am finding it all absorbing. He has a good knowledge of early European history, which is very necessary to the period, of course. You will find his conversation quite fascinating.'

I was rather surprised that this was so. He brought books for me to read and I was glad of the diversion, for I had been more upset than I had realized by those encounters with Fabian. I could not stop thinking about him and his insinuations. When Lavinia returned I would tell her that she must explain to her brother what my part had been in the adventure. It was clear that he had pieced things together and come up with what he thought was the right solution. I did not want him to think that first I could have been involved in such a sordid affair and secondly that I should abandon my child . . . even to a trusted nurse. Lavinia would *have* to explain.

I wished I could stop thinking of Fabian. He intruded constantly into my thoughts. I was not sure of my feelings towards him and sometimes they came close to dislike. I dreaded meeting him, which was always possible as we lived so close to each other; on the other hand, I hoped I should.

He made me feel alive, on the defensive as no other had ever done before. It was rather alarming because of Fleur; but our meetings had been an exhilarating experience.

I wished I could stop thinking of the fire at The Firs. Janine was constantly in my mind. What had become of her? She knew where we were so perhaps she would get in touch. I believed her aunt had amassed a fortune and surely she would have left Janine well provided for. I wished there had been more news in the papers.

My friendship with Dougal was developing and I began to think that he came to the rectory to see me as well as my father.

The interest of probing into the past took hold of me for a time; it was because I needed to keep my mind from dwelling on Fabian and what he might be thinking about me — if he gave me another thought. Perhaps it was presumptuous of me to think that he would, but he had seemed deeply interested at the time, which might be because of his sister's involvement. Moreover, I had muddled dreams in which The Firs featured. I was back in that half-world surrounded by strange people. I saw George laying his fires and in the middle of the night creeping out and lighting one. I dreamed of waking up, suffocating smoke in my lungs. How dreadful for those poor people caught in such a place!

Colin's attitude was changing towards me too. Church matters brought us together. He would always discuss them with me – what hymns should be chosen for special services, who should have which stall at the annual bazaar, and when the Framlings should be asked when we might make use of their grounds.

I imagined I could see plans forming in Colin's mind. It was only natural that they should. He was a young curate in search of promotion. This would seem the perfect parish for him. Parsons needed wives; promotion was easier for them if they had the right one. The rector's daughter would be considered highly acceptable, and the likelihood was that, married to me, the living would be his.

I thought, as most girls do, of marriage; but I had learned in the Framling garden that I was plain and I knew that plain girls did not attract husbands as readily as pretty ones. I had told myself that if no one wanted to marry me I did not care. I would be my own mistress and not have to consider the vagaries of any man.

My chances, if any, would be few, and as Polly would say, no sensible girl would turn them away without consideration; but I had made up my mind that I would prefer not to be married at all than because it was a convenient solution for Colin Brady.

I had to admit at the same time that I had been thinking just a little romantically of Dougal Carruthers. He was moderately good-looking, gentle and courteous to everyone. Mrs Janson was always delighted if he stayed to lunch. She was also very fond of Colin Brady, but I believed she had a special admiration for Dougal Carruthers.

I was becoming very interested in history and he brought books for me to read which we discussed. One day he suggested that we rode to Grosham Castle which was about eight miles away. It would be a day's outing and Mrs Janson could give us a picnic lunch to take with us. She was delighted to do this. Leave it to her, she said. She knew just what was wanted.

So early in the morning we set out from the Framling stables. It was a lovely summer's day, not too hot, with a gentle breeze; and we made our leisurely way to the castle.

Dougal did not want to hurry. He liked to savour the countryside. He was interested in wild life. We walked our horses side by side so that it was easier to talk. He told me that he was not looking forward to going to India. He would rather stay at home. He would have liked to be attached to some university and pursue his studies.

We reached the castle at about noon. The sun was getting warm and as we had made an early start we decided to take a quick look at the ruins and after that refresh ourselves with what Mrs Janson had prepared for us. After that we could explore more thoroughly.

Grosham was a shell although the walls were intact, and riding up to it one would have no idea that the interior had been destroyed.

We picked our way over the jutting stones – part of an inner wall – past broken columns over grass which was growing where once there had been a tiled hall.

Dougal's indignation was great, for it was not natural age and decay which had ruined Grosham but Cromwell's soldiers.

In the shadow of the castle we opened the picnic basket, to find legs of roasted chicken with salad, and crusty bread with a pot of butter. There was fruit to follow and a bottle of Mrs Janson's homemade elderberry wine.

We were hungry and the meal tasted especially delicious.

I did enjoy talking with Dougal, and as I had been reading a great deal more since I had known him I was able to talk with confidence.

I had rarely seen him so indignant. 'To think that castle might be in perfect condition today but for that . . . vandal.'

'You are referring to the self-righteous Oliver, of course.'

'I hate to see beautiful things spoilt.'

'But he thought they were sinful.'

'Then he must have been a fool.'

'I think he is not generally regarded as such.'

'People can be wise in some ways and foolish in others.'

'That's true. Cromwell did raise an army and taught peasants how to fight. He did win a war and governed the country for a time.'

'He destroyed beautiful things and that is unforgivable.'

'He made war and destroyed people, which is worse. But

he believed he was right, that he had God on his side. Can people be blamed for doing what they think right?'

'It is arrogant to think one is right when so many people have differing views.'

'It is difficult to understand whether he was right or not. Some historians agree, others take the completely opposite view. It is not easy to form a judgement on such a man. About people like Nero and Caligula there are no possible doubts. But your opinion on Oliver Cromwell must be your own.'

'He destroyed beautiful things,' insisted Dougal, 'and that is something for which I cannot forgive him. When people kill in the name of God I feel more strongly against them than I would if they were openly cruel. That castle is just one example. When you think of what he did all over the country . . .'

'I know. But the point is that he *thought* he was right and that he was doing the best for the people.'

'I suppose you have a point. I love beauty so passionately. I cannot bear to see it destroyed.'

'I believe that beautiful things mean more to you than they do to most people. Cromwell saw them as sinful because people worshipped them more than they did God.'

He became animated in discussion. There was a faint colour in his pale, rather ascetic face. I thought: I believe I could be very fond of him. He is the sort of person who becomes more interesting as one knows him. I could picture myself taking up his interests and making them mine. It would be a rich and rewarding way of living. Already he had opened up new ideas in my mind. He was a man of intellect, a lover of humanity except those who vandalized beautiful things. I had never seen him show such indignation towards a living person as he did towards Oliver Cromwell.

He seemed to follow my thoughts. He said: 'It has been a great pleasure to me to know you and your father.'

'It has been a great pleasure to us to know you.'

'Miss Delany . . . it seems absurd to address you so

536

formally when there is such friendship between us. Perhaps I shall call you Drusilla.'

'It seems a good idea,' I replied, smiling.

'What an excellent picnic this is.'

'I shall tell Mrs Janson what you say. She will be delighted.'

'Drusilla . . .'

I never knew what he intended saying, for just at that moment we heard the sound of a horse's hoofs approaching and as Dougal paused in surprise, Fabian rode up.

'Hello,' he called. 'I knew you were coming here so I thought I'd join the party. Food! What an excellent idea!' He dismounted and tied up his horse with ours. 'Are you going to invite me to join you?'

I felt a faint annoyance. I had been serenely contented listening to Dougal and now this man had arrived to put me on the alert, to destroy that serenity.

I could not help saying: 'It seems you have invited yourself, Sir Fabian.'

'I guessed you wouldn't mind my joining you. Is that chicken?' He stretched out a hand and took a leg. 'The bread looks delicious,' he added.

'It was made by Mrs Janson.'

'An admirable cook, Mrs Janson, as I learned when I had the pleasure of dining at the rectory. How good it tastes. I am so glad I came along.'

'How did you know where we had gone?' asked Dougal.

'Ha! Devious methods. I shall not tell you. I might want to use the same again. It's a wonderful old ruin, is it not? I am not surprised it aroused your interest. Outside perfect and inside . . . not quite what you would expect. It is like some people who present an innocent face to the world and hide secrets.'

He was looking straight at me.

I said: 'We were discussing Oliver Cromwell.'

'An unpleasant fellow, I always thought.'

'There is one who would agree with you, Dougal,' I said.

537

'Drusilla had a good word to say for him.'

I read his thoughts. Drusilla: Dougal? He had noticed the use of Christian names and was considering the significance of this. He looked faintly displeased.

'And so . . . Drusilla . . . admired the man?'

I replied: 'He believed he was right in doing what he did and that has to be taken in consideration when assessing people.'

'You are very fair-minded. I, of course, have to be grateful to him for leaving us Framling intact.'

'He was a strong-minded man with firm views.'

'It is a necessity for a ruler. Is that wine? I wonder if I might partake.'

I poured a little into a small tumbler which Mrs Janson had thoughtfully provided. 'I am afraid it is one I have used,' I told him. 'Mrs Janson naturally believed there would be only two of us.'

'I am delighted to share your glass,' he said, smiling at me. He sipped the wine. 'Nectar of the gods,' he murmured. 'Your Mrs Janson is a most excellent provider.'

'I will pass on your compliments. I am sure she will be gratified.'

'How delightful this is! We should do more of it. Al fresco picnics! What an excellent idea. Whose was it? Yours . . . Dougal's or Drusilla's, eh?'

'Mrs Janson naturally provided some food since we should not be returning to luncheon.'

'A most thoughtful lady! Yes, certainly we should do more of this. You and Drusilla will be able to tell me of the antiquities we should explore. I confess to being something of an ignoramus in these matters. But I am always ready for instruction.'

Since he had come he dominated the conversation. The pleasant intimacy had gone. After we had packed up the remains of the meal and explored the castle it seemed different. *He* was there, making me uneasy now and then, and now and then casting his amused glance on me. It

538

seemed to be a speculative glance and it both irritated and disturbed me.

The magic had gone out of the afternoon and he had a way of making our comments about the castle sound pretentious.

We curtailed the exploration considerably and thus returned to the Framling stables an hour or so earlier than we had expected to.

Two days later, Dougal came to the rectory. My father expressed his great pleasure and Mrs Janson brought out wine and her special wine-biscuits into the drawing-room where we were.

She purred rather like a cat to show her pleasure. She liked distinguished visitors to come to the rectory and Dougal was certainly one of those.

As soon as she had gone I poured out the wine.

Dougal said: 'I have come to tell you I shall be leaving tomorrow.'

'I hope you will be coming back soon,' replied my father.

'I hope to. This is a matter of trouble in the family. My cousin has had a fall from his horse and is rather badly injured. I must go to see him.'

'Is he far from here?' I asked.

'About seventy miles. It's a place called Tenleigh.'

'I have heard of it,' said my father. 'Some Roman remains were discovered nearby ... on the Earl of Tenleigh's land, I believe.'

'Yes, that is so.'

'Very interesting. Fine mosaic pavings and baths. What a wonderful race the Romans were. They brought benefits to the lands they occupied, which is, of course, what a conqueror should do. It was a great tragedy that they should have become decadent and their empire fade away.'

'It is the fate of many civilizations,' Dougal commented. 'It is almost like a pattern.'

'One day there might be one to break free of the pattern,' I suggested.

'That may well be,' agreed Dougal.

'We shall miss your visits,' my father told him.

Dougal smiled from my father to me. 'I shall miss them, too,' he said.

I was a little sad that he was going away. I went to the door with him to say goodbye. He took my hands and held them firmly.

'I am sorry to have to go just now,' he said. 'I was so enjoying our meetings. I was planning some more excursions like those to the castle. There are so many interesting places all over England. It has been such a pleasure.'

'Well, perhaps when you have seen your cousin . . .'

'I shall be back. You may be assured of that. I shall insist on being invited.'

'I dare say my father would be pleased if you stayed with us. We can't offer you the grandeur of Framling, of course.'

'I should so much enjoy that but wouldn't it be putting you out?'

'Not in the least. There is plenty of room at the rectory and Mrs Janson would enjoy cooking special meals for you.'

'It would not be the food I came for. Food for the mind is another matter.'

'Well think about it.'

He looked at me earnestly and went on: 'Drusilla . . .' He stopped and I looked enquiringly at him. Then he went on: 'Yes, I should so much like to stay here. I'll just get over this matter and then . . . we'll talk.'

'I should like that,' I said.

He leaned towards me and kissed me lightly on the cheek. Then he had gone.

I felt a sudden contentment. The relationship between us had deepened and that gave me a feeling of great serenity.

The future seemed suddenly promising.

*

I thought a good deal about Dougal during the days which followed. I believed that in time he would ask me to marry him. Dougal was a thoughtful person. He was serious-minded; he would not make hasty decisions. That he was attracted by me, I knew; yet our friendship had grown steadily and I felt that was the best way it should grow. Ever since I overheard that comment in the Framling gardens I had recognized the fact that I was plain and that no man was going to fall violently in love with me on account of my beauty, for I had none. But relationships were formed in other ways and I believed that one founded on mutual understanding would be firmer than a blinding passion for a beauty.

Dougal had been away for a week. Fabian was in London, a fact for which I was glad. I could well do without his disturbing presence. I was becoming obsessed by the thought of Janine and my dreams about The Firs kept recurring. I had an idea that if I went to the New Forest and saw the place for myself, I might discover something from the local people. Janine had been so close to us during those anxious months and had done so much to help us, I just could not forget her.

I was in constant communication with Polly, who kept me informed of Fleur's progress, and I wrote to her and told her of my concern about Janine and how I could not forget the fire at The Firs and the terrible tragedy which had overtaken all those people among whom for a short time I had lived.

Polly had an idea. What if I came to London? She and I could take a trip to the place. Eff would be in sole charge of Fleur, which would please her; and so it was arranged.

I left the rectory and this time travelled alone to London. Polly was at the station to meet me and there was the usual affectionate greeting.

Then there was the joy of seeing Fleur and Eff again. Fleur had grown amazingly; she now toddled and could even say something which sounded like Eff . . . Poll . . . yes and no. Quite emphatically this last. She was enchanting and seemed very satisfied with life.

Eff and Polly vied for her affection and she gave it with regal unconcern; and it was quite clear to me that no mother could give a child more love than did those two dear people.

Polly had made plans for our visit. She suggested we go the next day and spend the night at one of the inns nearby. She had discovered through Third Floor Back in one of the houses – who most fortuitously knew the district – that The Feathers was the best one and she had taken the precaution of booking two rooms for the night.

This was progress and Polly and I in due course set out on our voyage of discovery.

We arrived in the late afternoon and decided that on the following morning we should visit the site.

In the meantime we were able to have a little conversation. First of all we talked to the chambermaid. She was a middle-aged woman who had worked at The Feathers when she was a girl and then when her children were off her hands she came in the afternoons. She lived only a few yards from the hotel.

'So,' I said, 'you know the district well.'

'Like the palm of my hands, Madam.'

'You must remember the fire.'

'At The Firs?'

'Yes.'

'Oh, that wasn't so long ago. My goodness, what a blaze that was! It happened in the night.'

'We read about it in the paper,' said Polly. 'It was quite a piece of news, that.'

'It was a strange place. Used to give me the horrors every time I passed by.'

'Why?' I asked.

'I dunno. That Mrs Fletcher ... As a matter of fact, before I came back here ... just when my youngest was old enough not to need me at her heels all the time ... I worked there for a bit.'

'Oh,' I said faintly, fearing suddenly that she might have seen Lavinia and me.

'Best part of five years ago, that was.'

I was relieved.

'Why did it give you the creeps?' asked Polly.

'I can't rightly say. There was something about it. It was all them old people. You get the feeling that they are all there waiting for death to come along and take them. It gives you the shivers in a way. People used to say they were put there because their families did not want them. And a funny lot they was . . . and there'd always be one or two who had come there to have a baby . . . on the quiet, if you know what I mean?'

I certainly knew what she meant.

'And the fire?' I prompted.

'Lit up the whole place. I was in bed and I said to my old man, "Jacob, something's going on." He said, "Go to sleep," and then he realized there was a funny smell and a sort of light in the room. "Snakes alive," he said and he was out of that bed in a flash. He was out there helping them. The whole village seemed to be out there. Oh, it was a night, I can tell you.'

'There were a lot of casualties, were there not?' I asked.

'Oh yes. Well you see, this batty old man had started fires in one of the downstairs cupboards and the whole of the ground floor was well on the way to being destroyed before it spread about. They were all burned to death . . . Mrs Fletcher herself among them.'

'All?' I asked. 'Everyone?'

'Everyone in the place. It was too late to rescue them. Nobody knew the place was on fire until it was well on the way.'

'What a terrible tragedy.'

I did not sleep that night. I kept on thinking of Janine and how easily it might have been the end for Fleur, Lavinia and me.

The next day Polly and I made our way to The Firs. The

gate with The Firs on it in brass letters, was open. Memories rushed back as I went up the drive. The walls were surprisingly still standing in some parts. I looked through the windows on to the scorched pile.

Polly said: 'It makes you think. I'll tell Eff we've got to be specially careful. Make sure all the fires are out before we go to bed. Watch out for candles. Them paraffin lamps could turn over as soon as you could say Jack Robinson . . . and then it would be a case of God help you.'

It was difficult to recognize the place. I tried to work out which room would have been Lavinia's and mine, which Mrs Fletcher's sanctum on the first floor and Janine's room . . . and that of Emmeline and the others.

It was impossible, and Polly thought we should not try to mount the remains of the staircase.

'You'd only have to take a look at that and it would collapse.'

I was thoughtful and sad, remembering so much.

Polly said: 'Here. Let's go. We've had enough of this.'

It was as I stood with Polly among the debris that I heard quick footsteps coming along the drive. A middle-aged woman came into sight. I saw her before she saw us. Her face was pale and her eyes tragic. She stood for a few moments looking up at the grim remains. Then she saw us.

'Good morning,' I said.

'Oh . . . er . . . good morning.'

'Like us, you are looking at the burned-out house.'

She nodded. She looked as though she were fighting to conceal her emotion.

Then she said: 'Did you have . . . someone . . . someone who perished?'

'I don't know,' I replied. 'There was a girl I used to know at school. Mrs Fletcher was her aunt.'

She nodded. 'It was my daughter who was here. We didn't know she was. It wouldn't have mattered. She could have told me. She was so bright . . . a lovely girl . . . to go like that.'

I guessed the story. It was similar to others. The daughter

would be going to have a baby and she had come here in secret and here she had died.

'Such a tragedy,' said the woman. 'It should never have happened.'

'It doesn't really help us to come here,' I replied.

She shook her head. 'I have to. When I found out she was here and died in the fire ... I would have done anything ...'

Polly said: 'Things like that happen sometimes. It's hard to know why. Makes you bitter. I *know*.'

The woman looked enquiringly at her.

'My husband was lost at sea.'

It is amazing how someone else's tragedy can make one's own seem lighter. The woman certainly looked a little comforted.

'Have you been here before?' I asked.

She nodded. 'I can't seem to keep away. I just had to come.'

'Do you know anything about the people who died?'

'Only what I've heard from others.'

'There was a young girl with whom I was at school. I wonder if you knew whether she was saved.'

'I wouldn't know. I only know that my daughter was there and it happened to her ... my girl.'

We left her there, contemplating the ruins as though by doing so she could bring her daughter back.

We walked slowly to The Feathers. There was a stretch of grass in front of a pond and on this sat two old men. They were not talking ... just staring into space.

Polly and I sat down on the seat and they regarded us with interest.

'Staying there?' said one of the men, taking his pipe from his lips and jerking it towards The Feathers.

'Yes,' I replied.

'Nice place, eh?'

'Very nice.'

'Used to do pretty well before the fire.'

545

'That must have been terrifying.'

One of the old men nodded. 'Reckon it was the vengeance of the Lord,' he said. 'The lot they had up there. Sodom and Gomorrah . . . that's what it was. They got their just deserts.'

'I heard there were several old people there.'

The old man fiercely tapped his head. 'Not right up there. Offended against the Lord in some way. It was the punishment of the Lord, that's what I reckon. Her . . . she was a queer one . . . and all them women . . . no better than they should be.'

I was in no mood to enter into a theological discussion. I said: 'Did you hear if there were any survivors?'

The two old men looked at each other. The religious fanatic said with satisfaction: 'All burned to a cinder . . . taste of hell fire that's waiting for 'em.'

Polly said ironically: 'You're destined for the heavenly choir, I reckon.'

'That's so, Missus. Good churchgoer all me life. Regular every Sunday . . . night and morning.'

'My goodness,' said Polly. 'You must have a good record. Wasn't there any time you did a bit of sinning?'

'I was brought up in the shadow of the Lord.'

'Oh, I reckon the recording angel would have looked the other way when you got up to your little bits of mischief.'

I could feel a real antagonism building up between them and I guessed that if I were going to get any information from them this was not the way to do it.

'So everyone there died,' I said.

'Here,' put in the other. 'Wasn't there some niece or something, Abel?'

I said eagerly: 'Her name was Janine Fletcher. Do you know what became of her?'

'Oh, I remember,' said the man to Abel. 'You know that young woman . . . wasn't she out of the place on a visit or something? That's right. She was the only one who didn't die.'

'It was God's will,' said Abel.

I was excited. I turned to his companion. 'So she didn't die?'

'No . . . that's it. She came back. There was some sort of to-do about insurance and that sort of thing.'

'It wasn't insured,' said Abel. 'They was like the foolish virgins, unprepared when the bridegroom came.'

'Doesn't sound much like a wedding to me,' commented Polly.

'Do you know where she went?' I asked.

'Can't tell you that, Miss.'

I could see that that was all the information we could get. I rose as Abel began reminding me about the rewards of evil. I said: 'We must get back.'

Polly agreed.

'I reckon,' she said, as we walked away, 'that that Abel's got a nasty surprise waiting for him when he gets to Heaven.'

I felt our journey had not been wasted. We had not discovered where Janine was but we knew she was still alive.

I had not been back at the rectory for more than two days when, to my surprise, Fabian called.

In all the years he had not called before, except with Dougal, and I was surprised to see him.

I must have shown my surprise.

'I heard that you had been to London,' he said. 'I came to assure myself of your safe return.'

I raised my eyebrows. 'That was extraordinarily kind of you.'

'I was concerned. Had you told me I should have made my visit coincide with yours.'

'The journey is not long and I was met at the other end.'

'By the inestimable Polly, I guess. And how is her sister and that enchanting ward of theirs?'

'Very well.'

'That is good. I have news of a friend of yours.'

547

'Really?'

'Dougal Carruthers.'

'What news?'

'He has become an exalted gentleman overnight.'

'What do you mean?'

'You were aware that his cousin had an accident. Alas, the cousin died from his injuries.'

'Were they close friends?'

'Relations.' He smiled sardonically. 'That is quite a different thing. They say that one chooses one's friends but one's relations are thrust upon one.'

'There is often a stronger bond between relations than friends.'

'The proverbial blood being thicker than the proverbial water.'

'Exactly.'

'Well, I don't think the cousin . . . or to give him his full name, the Earl of Tenleigh . . . had very much in common with our friend Dougal. He was the hunting man – more at home on a horse than on his own two legs. Athletic, all physical activity and a brain that hardly ever got any consideration and had begun to pine away from neglect. Ah, I'm speaking ill of the dead and perhaps shocking your conventional heart just a little.'

I smiled. 'Not in the least,' I said. 'But how has Mr Carruthers become an exalted gentleman?'

'By the death of the cousin. You see, the Earl was the son of Dougal's father's elder brother so he got the title and the family estates. Dougal's father was just a younger son. I gathered from Dougal that he was rather pleased about that. Like his son, he was the studious type. I am not sure what his obsession was. The Byzantine Empire, I fancy. Dougal takes after him with his Anglo-Saxons and Normans. Alas for Dougal! The present has impinged on the past. He will have to tear himself away from Hengist and Horsa and Boadicea most likely and think a little about his obligations to the present.'

'I dare say he will enjoy it. He will probably have the money to continue with his research in the way he wanted it.'

'Great estates are demanding and he may not find it so easy. In any case I thought I ought to warn you that we shall doubtless see little of him from now on. These things change people, you know.'

'I do not believe they will change him.'

'He's too wise, you think?'

'I do think that. He would never be arrogant.'

I looked at him and he smiled. 'As some people are,' he murmured.

'Yes, as some people are.'

'Well, we shall see. But it will mean that he will not be here to enjoy those little picnics in ruined places. I thought I should warn you.'

'Thank you.'

'It is a pity that the picnics cannot continue.'

'There was only one . . . in which you shared.'

'Into which I forced myself. It would be rather pleasant not to have to do that. Why do we not have a picnic of our own . . . you and I?'

'It would be quite impossible.'

'Whenever I hear that word I am always challenged to disprove it.'

'You are not interested in ruins.'

'You could teach me.'

I laughed at him. 'I don't think you would relish the idea of being taught anything.'

'You are mistaken. I am avid for knowledge . . . particularly the kind which you can supply.'

'I don't quite know what that means.'

'Now you are looking like a teacher . . . a little severe . . . rather displeased with the bad boy and wondering whether to give him a hundred lines or make him stand in the corner with the dunce's cap on his head.'

'I am sure I implied nothing of the sort.'

549

'I shall see if I can discover a ruin you have never seen . . . and tempt you.'

'Don't bother. I am sure I should not be able to come with you.'

'I shall never give up hope,' he said, and added: 'Teacher.'

'If you will excuse me I have several things to do.'

'Let me help you.'

'You could not, really. They are parish matters.'

'Which you perform with Mr Brady?'

'Oh no . . . he has his own affairs. You have no idea what has to be done in a rectory . . . and with my father not so well we are very busy.'

'Then I must detain you no longer. I will see you very soon. *Au revoir.*'

When he had gone I could not get him out of my thoughts. It made me forget Dougal's elevation to high rank and fortune. Then I began to consider that and wonder what difference it would make to him and our relationship which was just beginning to flower into something deeper.

Colin Brady said to me: 'We should be thinking about the summer fête.'

'Everyone knows it is to be on the first Saturday in August. It always has been. Most of them have been working for months getting things together for the stalls.'

'The rector was saying that it is the custom to ask permission of the Framlings to hold it in the grounds and if it is wet to use the hall. I suppose it's big enough?'

'Oh yes. It's vast. There have only been a few occasions in my memory when we have had to go inside. The Framlings know about it. It's a tradition and Lady Harriet has always granted permission most graciously.'

'Yes, but your father says it has to be asked for. That is also a part of the tradition.'

'Yes, I suppose so.'

'Well, Lady Harriet is in London with her daughter. We shall have to make the request to Sir Fabian.'

'I should hardly think that was necessary.'

'But he should be asked.'

'It would be different if Lady Harriet were there. She is a stickler for convention.'

'I think it would be wise to ask Sir Fabian . . . just as a gesture. Perhaps you would go and get his formal consent.'

'If you are passing . . . it would only be a matter of looking in.'

'Well, I have to go and see Mrs Brines today. She has been confined to her bed for several weeks and is asking to see me. Also I have a good deal to sort out . . . so if you could see your way . . .'

There was no reason why I should not do it except that I felt uneasy about approaching Fabian. But I could not refuse without explaining, so I thought I would go over, quickly make the request and get it over.

Sir Fabian was at home, I was told. I asked if they would tell him that I had merely come to ask his permission for the fête to be held in the grounds if fine and if wet in the hall. I would not take up much of his time.

I was hoping the maid would come back and say that permission was granted so that I could be on my way. Instead she came back with the news that Sir Fabian was in his study and would be pleased to see me there.

I was ushered across the great hall to the staircase. His study was on the first floor.

He rose as I entered and came towards me smiling. He took both my hands.

'Miss Delany! How nice to see you. You've come about the fête, they tell me.'

The maid went out shutting the door and that feeling of mingled excitement and apprehension was with me.

'Do please sit down.'

'I shan't stop,' I said. 'It's a formality, really. Lady Harriet usually grants permission for the grounds to be used and if it is wet, the hall.'

'Oh my mother always deals with that sort of thing, doesn't she?'

'There is nothing to be dealt with really. Framling has always been used for the fête. I just want to get formal permission, so I will say thank-you and goodbye.'

'But you haven't got my permission yet.'

'It is really taken for granted.'

'Nothing should ever be taken for granted. I should like to discuss this with you.'

'But there is nothing to discuss. It is the same every year. So I may take it as granted . . . ?'

He had risen and I immediately did the same. He came close to me.

'Tell me,' he said, 'why are you afraid of me?'

'Afraid? Of you?'

He nodded. 'You look like a frightened fawn who has heard the approach of a tiger.'

'I do not feel in the least like a frightened fawn. Nor do you strike me as being tigerish.'

'Then a bird of prey, perhaps . . . a rapacious eagle, ready to swoop on a helpless creature. You know, you should not be frightened of me, for I am very fond of you and the more I see you the fonder I grow.'

'That is good of you,' I said coolly. 'But I must go.'

'It is not good of me. It is an involuntary emotion and one for which I cannot personally take credit.'

I laughed with an attempt at lightness.

'Well,' I said, 'I take it we can go ahead with plans for the fête.'

He put his hands on my shoulders and drew me towards him.

'Sir Fabian?' I said in surprise, drawing back.

'You know how I feel about you,' he said. 'Isn't it obvious?'

'I have no idea.'

'Aren't you curious to know?'

'It is not really of great interest to me.'

'You don't give that impression.'

'Then I am sorry if I misled you.'

'You haven't misled me in the least, for I know a good deal about you, my dear Drusilla. After all, we have been acquainted all our lives.'

'In spite of that I would say we hardly know each other.'

'Then we must remedy that.'

He drew me towards him with a strength I could not resist and kissed me on the lips.

I flushed and encouraged the anger which arose in me. I said: 'How dare you!'

He smiled mockingly. 'Because I am a very daring person.'

'Then please keep your daring displays for others.'

'But I want to show them to you. I want us to be good friends. I am sure that could be very pleasant for both of us.'

'It would not be so for me.'

'I promise you it will.'

'I do not believe in your promises. Goodbye.'

'Not yet,' he said, taking my arm and holding it fast. 'I think you like me just a little.'

'Then that assumption must be due to your good opinion of yourself.'

'Perhaps,' he said. 'But you are not indifferent to my undeniable charm.'

'I do not wish to be treated in this flippant manner.'

'I am not in the least flippant. I am in deadly earnest. I am very fond of you, Drusilla. You have always interested me. You are different . . . so serious . . . so dedicated to learning. You make me feel humble and that is such a new experience with me that I find it exciting. It is growing more and more impossible for me to hide my feelings.'

'Goodbye,' I said. 'I shall tell the church committee that permission has been granted in the usual way.'

'Stay a while,' he pleaded.

'I do not wish to. I will not be treated like this.'

'Your maidenly modesty is most effective.' He paused and raised his eyebrows. 'But . . .'

I felt myself flushing. I read the suggestions in his eyes.

I wrenched myself free and walked to the door; but he was there before me, standing with his back to it, mocking me.

'I could detain you,' he said.

'You could do no such thing.'

'Why not? This is my house. You came here willingly. Why should I not keep you here? Who would stop me?'

'You seem to think you are living in the Middle Ages. Is this some idea of *droit de seigneur*?'

'What an excellent notion! Why not?'

'You had better step out of the past, Sir Fabian. You and your family may have the idea that we in this place are your serfs, but that is not the case and if you attempt to detain me as you suggest I shall . . . I shall . . .'

'Bring in the law?' he asked. 'Would that be wise? They probe, you know.'

'What do you mean?'

He looked at me slyly and I knew he had been planning something like this. He had only been waiting for the opportunity and I, foolishly, had given it to him. He thought he had discovered a secret in my past and he was going to use it against me. I wanted to shout at him: 'Fleur is not my child. She is your sister's.' I almost did; but even at such a time I could not bring myself to break my promise to Lavinia:

He was so gratified at my discomfiture that he released his hold. I dashed past him out of the room and hurried down the staircase into the hall and out of the house. I did not stop running until I reached my room at the top of the rectory. I flung myself on the bed. My heart was beating furiously. I was very deeply disturbed.

I was so angry. I hated him. It was a sort of blackmail. *I have discovered your secret. As you are the sort of girl who can have a love-affair before you are out of the schoolroom, why are you so outraged when I make certain suggestions to you?*

It was too humiliating.

I heard the news from Mrs Janson. Lavinia and Lady Harriet had come home.

Lavinia sent a message over. 'You must come at once. I want to talk to you. Meet me in the garden where we can get right away from people.'

I sensed an urgency in her message. She would not be so anxious to see me if she did not want something from me. Perhaps, I told myself, it was merely because she wanted to boast of her successes in London. But had her season been so successful? There was no news of an engagement to a duke or a marquess. I was sure Lady Harriet would aim for the highest stakes.

I was chary of going to Framling after that encounter with Fabian, and I was therefore glad that she suggested a meeting in the garden.

She was waiting for me. There was a change in her, or perhaps I had forgotten how beautiful she was. Her skin was milk-white; her cat-like eyes with the dark lashes were arresting, but it was her magnificent hair which was her crowning glory. She wore it high on her head and little tendrils escaped from the mass on her forehead and in the nape of her neck. She was wearing a green gown which was most becoming to her colouring. She was, in fact, the most beautiful girl I had ever seen.

'Oh, hello, Drusilla,' she said. 'I've got so much to tell you.'

'You have had a successful season?'

She grimaced. 'One or two proposals but no one Mama thought good enough.'

'Lady Harriet would set high standards. None but the highest in the land for her beautiful daughter. Did you see the Queen?'

'When I was presented and once at the opera and once at a ball for charity. She danced with Albert. Drusilla, that fire . . .'

'You mean at The Firs?'

'I was so relieved.'

'Lavinia! A lot of people died!'

'Those people . . . well, life wasn't much for them, was it?'

'They might have thought so, and there were people there who were going to have babies as you were. I met the mother of one of them when I went down.'

'You went there?'

'I wanted to see what had happened. Polly came with me.'

'All those demands for payment . . .'

'Well, it was what you owed. What would you have done without her?'

'I know . . . but it cost a lot and *I* had to find the money.'

'It was your affair.'

'I know, I know. But it's Janine.'

'Janine? I gathered she wasn't there on the night of the fire.'

'I wish she had been.'

'Oh . . . Lavinia!'

'You haven't heard what I'm going to tell you. It's Janine I'm worried about. I have seen her.'

'So she is all right?'

'It's far from all right. There was I thinking I was free of all that and then Janine turns up.'

'Did she come to see you?'

'She certainly did. There were pieces in the paper about the debutantes and I was mentioned. They called me "the beautiful Miss Framling". Every time they mentioned me they called me that. She must have seen it. Oh, Drusilla . . . it was awful.'

'How? What do you mean?'

'She's asked for money.'

'Why?'

'Because she says she is very poor and I've got to help her or else . . .'

'Oh no!'

'But yes. She said if I didn't, she would put a piece in the paper about Fleur.'

'She couldn't.'

'She could. I never liked her.'

'She got you out of your trouble.'

'She just took us to that dreadful place . . . that awful aunt of hers who kept demanding money.'

'You can't do what you did and get away without paying for it.'

'I know. Well, Janine is living in London. She's got some miserable place. It's all she can afford. She said how lucky I was and she wanted me to give her fifty pounds, and then she would say nothing of what she knew about me.'

'It's blackmail.'

'Of course it's blackmail. You are not supposed to submit to that sort of thing, but what could I do? Mama would have been furious.'

'I dare say she would have known how to deal with Janine.'

'I knew how to deal with her. I had to give her fifty pounds to keep her quiet. I did . . . and I haven't heard any more of her.'

'It is terrible to think of Janine's stooping to that.'

'It was awful. I had to pretend I was going to the dressmaker and I went to this place where she lives. It's in a little house in a place called Fiddler's Green. It's in a row of little houses. She's got rooms there. She says it's all she can afford. She said she wouldn't have asked if she hadn't been desperate. You see, the fire burned down the house which belonged to her aunt and all the contents of the place, too. Her aunt hadn't insured the place. She had only just succeeded in buying the house and all she had was tied up in it . . . so there was nothing much for Janine. She said fifty pounds would set her on her feet. I found it hard to get the money together but I did. And that's the end of it.'

'I hope so,' I said.

'Of course it will be.'

'Blackmailers have a habit of coming back and asking for more.'

'I shan't give her any more.'

'You should never have given her anything in the first place. What you should have done was confessed to your mother. It is always unwise to submit to blackmail. I've heard that said many times.'

'By people who are not being blackmailed, I suppose.'

'Perhaps.'

'Well, it was worth it to me to shut her up. She said she was going to marry that Hon . . . whatever his name was . . . and she would have been set up for life, for he was quite rich. But he died in the fire. It was just good luck for Janine that she was away that night.'

I was thoughtful. 'Lavinia,' I said, 'you will have to confess.'

'Confess? Why ever should I?'

'Because it's got to come out. There's Fleur.'

'She's all right. She's happy with those two nice old women.'

'For the moment. But she will have to be educated. Polly and Eff will have to be paid for keeping her. Why don't you tell your mother?'

'Tell my mother! I don't think you know my mother.'

'I assure you that everyone around here knows Lady Harriet very well.'

'I just can't think what she would do.'

'She would be horrified but she would certainly do something, and something has to be done.'

'I could never tell her.'

'Your brother has seen Fleur.'

'What?'

'I went to London and he was on the train. He saw where I was staying. He came there one day when I was taking Fleur out in her pram.'

She had turned pale.

'He was suspicious,' I said. 'I want you to tell him the truth because he suspects the baby is mine.'

She tried to disguise the look of relief which came over her face.

I went on: 'You must tell him. He can't go on with this half-truth.'

'*You* didn't tell him!'

'Of course not. But I do object to his sly references, and I think you ought to tell him the truth right away.'

'I couldn't possibly tell him.'

'Why not? I don't suppose he has led a blameless life.'

'It's all right for men. It is girls who have to be so pure.'

'Obviously there are some who are not. I don't suppose you are the only one who has indulged in pre-marital adventures.'

'Oh, Drusilla, I do rely on you.'

'Far too much. I am not going to be insulted by your brother.'

'He wouldn't *insult* you.'

'He would and he has . . . and I want him to know the truth.'

'I . . . I'll think about it.'

'If you don't tell him, I might be tempted to.'

'Oh, Drusilla . . . first Janine and now you . . .'

'This is quite different. I'm not blackmailing you. I am merely asking you to tell the truth.'

'Give me time. Just give me time. Oh, Drusilla, you have always been my best friend. Promise you won't say anything . . . yet.'

'I wouldn't say anything without telling you first but I won't have your brother hinting . . . at things.'

'However did you let him guess there was a baby!'

'I told you . . . he followed me.'

'But why should he follow *you*? It could only be that he suspected something like this. It's not as though . . .'

'I am the sort of girl men follow?' I finished for her. 'Nobody could be interested in *me*, of course.'

'Well . . .' she began.

'Don't feel you have to wriggle out of that,' I said. 'I know I'm not the beauty you are.'

'Well, there is that Mr Brady. Mama thinks it would be most suitable.'

'Do thank her for her concern,' I said.

'She likes everything to run smoothly in the neighbourhood.'

'I am sure she does. But I don't propose to be someone's neat ending to a problem.'

'Oh . . . look who's coming.'

I looked and saw Dougal approaching us.

'Mama invited him,' went on Lavinia. 'Do you know, he is an earl now. Mama insisted that he come and stay.'

I was pleased to see him. My friendship with him had been so refreshing and promising. His regard for me restored my faith in myself.

'Oh . . . Drusilla . . . Lavinia,' he said. He was smiling at us. Lavinia was standing a little apart. The faint wind ruffled the tendrils and as she put up a hand to her hair the green material of her loose, rather Grecian-style gown flapped round her, clinging to her figure.

Dougal could not take his eyes from her. I saw the light in them and I remembered his adoration of beautiful objects.

He looked rather startled as though he were seeing something for the first time. It was the new Lavinia in her studiedly simple gown with her escaping curls and her tigerish eyes.

I knew in that moment that he had fallen in love with her or that he was on the brink of doing so.

The moment passed. He was smiling his gentle smile at me, asking how my father was, telling me that he would be soon coming to see us if he might.

I said my father would be delighted.

'I have discovered two new books on the Conquest,' he said. 'I must bring them over.'

I was not thinking so much of the Norman Conquest as of Lavinia's.

I did not go into the house with them. I excused myself. 'There is so much to do at the rectory.'

'Even now you have that nice curate,' said Lavinia a little roguishly. 'I hear you and he get on very well together.'

'He is very efficient,' I said.

'I am so glad you came and that he is so nice,' said Lavinia. 'Well, see you soon, Drusilla. Drusilla and I are the greatest friends,' she went on, turning to Dougal. 'We always have been.' Some spirit of mischief seemed to take hold of her. I think she knew of my feelings for Dougal. She was also aware that he had just been blinded by her great beauty. A few moments before she had been terrified that her secret might be revealed; but now she had forgotten the past and was revelling in the present. Admiration always stimulated her. 'Drusilla and I were at school together. It was in France.'

'I know,' Dougal told her.

'That sort of thing draws people together,' went on Lavinia. 'We had some exciting times there, didn't we, Drusilla?'

She was laughing at me, triumphing over the spell she had cast on Dougal. She would have heard rumours of his attachment to the rectory and its inhabitants; she was savouring her triumph to such an extent that she forgot to be anxious about Janine.

I felt angry, humiliated and hurt. I went back sombrely to the rectory.

Mrs Janson said: 'That Lady Harriet is making a dead set at that Mr Carruthers . . . oh, beg his pardon, the Earl of Tenleigh, if you please. Well, it stands to reason. That Miss Lavinia goes up to London. The most beautiful debutante they say . . . the Debutante of the Season. All very well, but where's this duke what Lady Harriet thinks she's going to get? All that season and not one in sight. I reckon that won't please her ladyship. An earl will have to do, and what's she doing going up to London when she's got one right on her own doorstep? I can tell you there are some goings on up at the House. Lady Harriet says he must come. She insists . . . and earl as he is, he can't refuse Lady Harriet. I reckon something will come of this. Lady Harriet will see to it.'

That was what I overheard and when I appeared she was silent. I was sure that long ago they had paired me off with Dougal as a first and Colin Brady as a second.

Mrs Janson liked Dougal and he had been a frequent visitor. They were sure he was as they said 'sweet on me'. But now Lady Harriet was making a rare fuss of Dougal. Mrs Janson had it from the maids there. 'Now that he's got this title and the money it's been a leg up for him. Before, he was just a friend of Sir Fabian's . . . treated just like one of them young boys from the school. Now it's a different matter. We didn't see him so much then . . . Why, there was a time when he seemed to make the rectory his home.'

He did come over to bring the books he had spoken of. My father was delighted to see him and they had long discussions together. I went in and joined them. I did fancy he was a little subdued with me. He made a special effort to include me in the conversation, whereas previously it had been done without effort. I remembered how we had talked just before he left when I had been foolish enough to think that he was on the point of making a declaration.

It was a bitter blow to my pride rather than to my deep emotions. I was not sure what I really felt about Dougal except that he was a very pleasant and interesting friend. I had allowed myself to envisage a future with him and I had believed it could be very rewarding. How foolish I had been! Of course he liked to talk to me about things which interested him; and he would never be able to talk to Lavinia in that way. But that was not love. It was not what people married for. The beauty of Lavinia had suddenly struck him and he could not help but marvel at it.

I did not go over to the stable, for I would not avail myself of Fabian's offer. I wanted to take nothing from him. Moreover, I avoided Framling for fear of meeting him.

I was in the rectory garden one day when he came riding by.

'Drusilla,' he called. 'It is such a long time since I saw you.'

I merely replied: 'Good morning,' and turned to go into the house.

'I trust you are well. And your father?'

'Thank you, yes.'

'You know, of course, that Dougal is here.'

'He has been to see my father.'

'And you too, I dare say. I know what good friends you are.'

I did not answer.

'I hope you are not still put out with me. I think I rather allowed my feelings to get the better of my good manners.'

Still I did not answer.

'I am sorry,' he went on humbly. 'You must forgive me.'

'It is of no importance. Please forget it.'

'You are very generous.'

'I must go in now.'

'There is so much to do at the rectory.' He spoke mockingly, finishing my sentence for me.

'That is true,' I retorted sharply.

'There is quite a flutter of excitement at the House,' he went on.

In spite of myself I waited to hear what had caused this.

'We are expecting them to announce it shortly.'

I felt the blood rushing to my head.

'Lavinia and Dougal,' he added. 'My mother is delighted.'

I looked at him steadily, my eyebrows raised.

He nodded smiling – was it maliciously? 'My mother says there is no need to delay . . . long. Why should they? It is not as though they are strangers. They have known each other for a long time. They have suddenly realized how they feel. People do, you know. My mother is all for an early wedding. I am sure you will be pleased for them, for you know them both so well.'

'It is most . . . suitable.'

563

'That's what my mother thinks.'

I thought angrily: Yes, since Dougal acquired a title and a fortune and the London season did not produce anyone of higher rank.

'I dare say Lavinia will be coming over to tell you the good news. Dougal too, perhaps. They will want you to give them your blessing.'

I felt a great need to get away from his probing eyes. I knew what he was telling me. *You have lost Dougal. My mother will never let him slip out of her hands now. It was different before he came into this glory.*

He raised his hand, inclined his head, and murmuring, '*Au revoir*,' rode off.

A month after the arrival of Dougal at Framling the engagement was announced between the Earl of Tenleigh and the beautiful Miss Lavinia Framling, the debutante of the season.

I did not go to Framling to congratulate Lavinia. She came to me. I could see at once that she was disturbed.

'What's the matter?' I asked. 'You don't look like the happy betrothed.'

'It's that woman . . . Janine. She wants more money.'

'I told you how it is with blackmailers. You should never submit in the first place.'

'Why should this have happened to me?'

'You have to learn that you must pay for your sins.'

'I only did what a lot of people do.' She was aggrieved and I felt a sudden anger sweep over me. She had had so much and now she had taken Dougal. I had analysed my feelings for him and I was desperately hurt. But I was honest enough to admit to myself that it was mainly my pride which had been wounded. It had been hard for me to realize that at first, for I had enjoyed his friendship and I had thought of eventual marriage as a pleasant prospect. It would have been a wonderful experience to be loved by a man whom I could trust.

But could I have trusted him if our close relationship, which might have developed into a serious commitment, could have been shattered by the appearance of a girl just because she happened to be outstandingly beautiful?

I whipped up my anger against Lavinia. These Framlings seemed to think the whole world was made for them. Lavinia believed she could commit the great indiscretion, have a child even and everyone should cover up for her and leave her to sail happily on. As for her brother, he had thought he could insult me and then come along and behave as though nothing untoward had happened.

I was tired of the Framlings.

'And,' Lavinia was saying, 'don't preach to me.'

'I'm sorry, Lavinia. You must get yourself out of your own troubles.'

'Oh, Drusilla.' She had run to me and flung her arms round my neck. 'Help me, *please*. I know you can. I didn't mean to say those silly things. I'm at the end of my tether. I am really. If Mama or Dougal found out ... I'd just kill myself ... I've thought about jumping out of my window.'

'You'd land on the furze bush, which would be very uncomfortable.'

'Oh, help me, *please*, Drusilla.'

'How can I?'

'I thought you might see her.'

'I? What good would that do?'

'She likes you. She thinks you're interesting. She told me you were worth a dozen of me. I know she's right.'

'Thanks. I'll remember that. But talking to her would do no good.'

'It might ... if you did.'

'What could I say?'

'You could tell her how good I've been so far and if she would wait a little time ... until I'm married ... I'll be very rich and I'll do something for her then. I will. I promise.'

'I don't think she would believe in your promises, Lavinia.'

'You promise for me. Tell her you'll be a sort of witness and you'll make sure she gets the money. It is only a matter of waiting.'

'I think you should go to your mother or your brother or Dougal and tell the truth.'

'How could I? Dougal might refuse to marry me.'

'I believe he is a very understanding young man.'

'He wouldn't understand. He'd be furious. He believes in perfection.'

'He has a shock waiting for him when he marries you.'

'I am going to try to be a good wife to him.'

What a fool he is! I thought. He wants to marry Lavinia without knowing her. Even the village idiot would know better than that; and Dougal is supposed to be clever! Well, he would discover, I thought, with a certain satisfaction – and Lavinia was not the sort to change just because she was married to the indulgent husband he would probably be.

Lavinia went on pleadingly: 'We've been such good friends . . . ever since we met.'

'I remember the time well. You were not the most charming of hostesses. It is rather unwise of you to recall that occasion if you are trying to show the loving nature of our relationship.'

'Stop being clever, Drusilla. You are too clever and always showing off. Men don't like it. I never do that.'

'You are showing off, as you call it, all the time.'

'Yes, but only in the right way. Drusilla, stop beating about the bush. Do say you'll help me. I know you will in the long run. You are just making me suffer.'

'But what can I *do*?'

'I told you. Go and see Janine. Explain to her.'

'Why don't you?'

'How could I go to London? You could . . . easily. You can just say you have gone to see Polly.'

I hesitated. I always felt better after a visit to Polly. She would understand how I felt about Dougal's engagement. I had no need to go into explanations with Polly. I could talk to her as I could to myself. I should see Fleur. The child was beginning to get a hold on me. She could pronounce her version of my name. Polly had written: 'You should hear Eff go on at her. "Who's got a nice Aunty Drusilla, eh? Whose Aunty Drusilla is coming to see her soon?" That's how she goes on.' Yes, it would be wonderful to be with Polly, Eff and Fleur. Moreover, I had a raging curiosity to see Janine.

Lavinia could see that I was wavering.

'You love Fleur,' she said. 'She's a little darling.'

'How do you know? You never see her.'

'I'm going to . . . when I get this sorted out. When I know Dougal better I'll tell him. I will really. I know he'll say I can have her with me.'

'That would be the last thing Fleur would want. Don't you understand that children are not pieces to be moved round a board as people want to for their convenience?'

'You're being the governess again.'

'Somebody has to try to teach you a few facts of life.'

'I know. I'm wicked. But I can't help it. I'm trying to be good. Once I'm married to Dougal I shall settle down. Oh, please . . . *please*, Drusilla.'

'Where does she live?'

'I've written it down. I went there to take the fifty pounds. I'll tell you how to get there. It's not so very far from Polly's place.'

I took the address. 'Fiddler's Green, No. 20,' said Lavinia. 'It's easy to find.'

'Did you take a cab?'

'Yes, I did. The driver looked surprised but I made him wait for me to come back. I didn't want anyone to know where I was. It was awful . . . and then . . . her. She sneered at me. She kept calling me the Countess. Then she told me I had to find the money, for if I didn't come with it she was

567

going to let the world know what I had done. She said I had deserted my child and a lot of other unpleasant things. I said I hadn't. I'd found a good home for the child. She said, "Drusilla found that. You would probably have left her on someone's doorstep so that you could go on with your life." I told her she was wrong. I did care about Fleur and when I was married I was going to take her. I know it will be all right once I am married.'

'I shall not come to your wedding, Lavinia. It's such a mockery really. Have you thought how you are deceiving Dougal? You will be standing there in virginal white . . .'

'Oh, shut up. Are you going to help me or not? Can't you see how miserable I am?'

'I can't do anything. *I* haven't any money.'

'I'm not saying give her money. I just know if you talked to her she'd listen to reason.'

'No, she wouldn't.'

'She would. She has always admired you. I know you can persuade her. Please, Drusilla, go to London. You know how you like to see Polly and Fleur. Please, Drusilla.'

And then I knew I had to go.

I considered what I should say. It gave me something to think about. The wedding plans were going ahead as Lady Harriet did not see why there should be any delay. I might not be exactly in love with Dougal but I did not want to hear about them.

I said to my father: 'I think I will go and see Polly.'

'I know.' He smiled. 'You want to go and see that child they have adopted. You are very fond of her, are you not?'

'Well, yes . . . and I am very fond of Polly.'

'A good woman,' he said. 'Somewhat forthright but good at heart.'

I went, and as usual, Polly was delighted to see me. I did not tell her where I intended to go for I felt she would try to dissuade me. She would think I should not involve myself further in Lavinia's affairs. I had done so once and that had brought them Fleur and she could not regret that; but, as she would have said, once is enough.

I took a cab to Fiddler's Green. The driver looked at me in surprise but did not comment. I asked him to wait for me – not outside the house but a little distance away.

He looked at me as though he thought I was on some nefarious mission. I wondered whether Lavinia had had the same experience.

I found my way to No. 20 Fiddler's Green. It was a tall house showing signs of what must have been an attempt at grandeur; but now the stucco was broken away and what should have been white was a dirty grey. Four steps leading to the front door were broken away; two mangy-looking stone lions stood on guard. Lavinia had told me to knock three times, which meant that I wanted Janine who was on the third floor.

I did so and waited. It seemed a long time before Janine appeared.

She stared at me for a few seconds in amazement. Then she cried: 'Drusilla! Whatever made you come here?' She lifted her shoulders. 'You'd better come in,' she added.

I was in a dingy passage with a staircase facing me. The carpet on the stairs was showing signs of wear and was threadbare in places.

We went up three flights and the carpet grew shabbier as we rose. She threw open a door to disclose a fairly large room, sparsely furnished. She turned to me, grimacing. 'Now you see how the poor and needy live.'

'Oh Janine,' I said, 'I'm so sorry.'

'Just my luck. Everything went wrong with me.'

'I've wanted to know what happened since I heard of the fire.'

'Everything lost . . . Aunt Emily dead . . . and all those people with her. That stupid George. It was his fault, you know. I told her how dangerous he was and that we should all be burned in our beds one night.'

'Yes, he was certainly dangerous.'

'Dangerous! He destroyed everything for Aunt Emily . . . and for me, too. I was going to marry Clarence . . . Oh, I know he was simple, but he adored me. He would have given me anything . . . anything I asked. And then he died . . . killed by that stupid George.'

'He didn't know what he was doing. Oh, Janine, what a blessing that you weren't there on that night.'

'Sometimes I've almost wished I had been.'

'Don't say that.'

'I do say it. How would you like to live in a place like this?'

'Do you have to?'

'What do you mean . . . do I have to? Do you think I would if I didn't have to?'

'Surely there is something you can do? People of education usually become governesses.'

'Well, I don't intend to.'

'What will you do then?'

'I'm planning. It made me mad when I saw all that fuss over Lavinia Framling. When you think of her . . . and that child . . . and there she is queening it over everyone. It's not fair.'

'One has to make up one's mind that life never is fair.'

'I intended to get something out of it anyway.'

'She told me you had asked her for money.'

'She would! And why shouldn't she give me something? I helped her. Where would she have been without me? I reckon the noble Earl would not be so keen if he knew he was getting soiled goods.'

'Don't be bitter, Janine.'

'It's not so much bitterness as sound thinking. She has everything. I have nothing. Well then, I think it is about time I took a share.'

'You will regret this, Janine.'

'I am sure I shall not. I want to start a business. I could, I am sure. Making hats. I think I'm quite clever at it. I know someone who has a little shop. If I could find the money I could go in with her. I have to have the money and I don't see why Miss Lavinia Framling should not provide me with some of it.'

'You'll need more than fifty pounds.'

She looked cunning. 'I intend to have it.'

'It's blackmail, you know, and that is a crime.'

'Would she take me to court? That would be nice, wouldn't it? Miss Lavinia Framling bringing a charge against someone who knew she had an illegitimate child whose existence she was keeping secret. I can see her doing that, can't you?'

'Janine, it is not the way.'

'You tell me another.'

'I should think you could work . . . work and save. You'd be happier that way.'

'I certainly should not. In some ways you are a simpleton, Drusilla. The way you've worked to keep that little matter a secret . . . and all for her. She's thoroughly selfish. Do you think she would have helped you in the same way?'

'No.'

'Then why bother? Let her pay up or take what's coming to her.'

She looked fierce and very angry and I knew there was nothing I could say to divert her.

I looked round the room and she noticed my glance.

'Grim, isn't it?' she said. 'You can see why I want to get out of it.'

'I do, of course, and I am very sorry. Where were you that night?'

'You remember the Duchess?'

'Yes, I do.'

'Her family decided they would take her back. They might have been ashamed of themselves dumping her on Aunt Emily like that – but I think perhaps it was something to do with money. They wanted to have her under their noses so that she couldn't make a will leaving it all to someone else. They didn't trust Aunt Emily. They weren't far wrong on that one. I had to take her home. There was no one else. It was too long a journey to make in one day so I was to stay the night at the family's stately home. It was a bit different from this, I can tell you.'

I nodded.

'So, you see, that's what happened. Everything gone in the fire. The house would have been mine. That was worth something. I could have started some business. But I shouldn't have had to because I should have married Clarence. I'd have been set up for life, and now . . . nothing. The place wasn't insured. How could Aunt Emily have been so foolish with madmen like George about!'

'But you were lucky not to be there.'

'If you can call it luck.'

'I've come to ask you to think again.'

She shook her head. 'No, she's got to pay. She has to give me some of what she's got.'

'She doesn't have a large allowance.'

'Then I want a share of what she's got and when she marries her noble lord . . .'

'Do you mean you will go on demanding money? You told her that the fifty pounds she gave you would be all.'

'Well, it's not. I'm desperate, Drusilla. I'm not going to let a chance like this go by.'

'You won't do it, Janine, I know you won't. You'll stop it. Whatever you feel — and I do understand your bitterness — it is wrong.'

'It's right for me. It's time someone taught Lavinia Framling a lesson. She always thought she was superior to the rest of us because of that red hair.'

'Oh Janine! Listen. I shall come to see you again. I could take you back with me to the rectory. You could have a holiday with us. We might be able to find some work for you to do. We know a number of people and if you were recommended by a rector it would be a help. You could stay with us until you found work. Leave this place . . .'

572

She shook her head. 'You are good, Drusilla,' she said rather gently. 'You are worth twenty of Lavinia.'

I smiled. 'My value has gone up. You told Lavinia twelve.'

'I overestimated her. Actually she's not worth anything at all. I'm sorry for this earl. He's going to have a nice dance with her. She's one who can't leave the men alone. I've seen one or two of those in my time.'

'I think she may settle down when she marries.'

'I know you were top of the class, Drusilla, but you are a babe in arms when it comes to the facts of life.'

'Do listen to me.'

'I have.'

'So you are going on with this . . . blackmail.'

'I'm going on getting money until I set myself up.'

'It's a mistake.'

'I'll be judge of that. Did you keep a cab waiting?'

'Yes.'

'You'd better go, then. He might not wait. He wouldn't believe anyone who came here would be able to pay him. He'll think you've made off.'

'He didn't seem to think so and he said he would wait.'

'I appreciate what you have done.'

'If I hear of anything I shall come along and let you know.'

She smiled at me and shook her head.

And that was all I could do at that time with Janine Fletcher, but I did not give up hope.

I avoided telling Polly where I had been. I knew she would have disapproved and told me to keep away. But I was sorry for Janine. I think in a way I always had been. She had had such a strange life; there appeared to have been little affection from Aunt Emily. Janine had been sent to an expensive school because Aunt Emily had had plans for a rich marriage and she must have intended to select one of her clients for her. Poor Clarence had been an ideal young man for the case. Unaware of what was going on, affectionate to anyone who showed him kindness and rich into the bargain. He was like a puppet to be manipulated and Aunt Emily had performed the manipulation with skill. And now . . . instead of making a desirable marriage poor Janine was alone and penniless; so she had taken to that most despicable of crimes: blackmail.

I wrote to Lavinia and told her that I had made little headway with Janine. She was adamant.

I could imagine Lavinia's dismay on reading that letter. She would rage against Janine and perhaps against me for failing to perform the mission satisfactorily. But she had to know the truth.

Polly said: 'Is anything wrong, love?'

'No. Why should there be?'

'You seem . . . thoughtful. You can tell me, you know. That Dougal . . . he seems a bit of a fool to me . . . to be taken in by that Lavinia. I like a real man, I must say, one who can see what's what and is not going to make a fool of himself. I think you were a little bit fond of him.'

'He is a very charming man, Polly, and clever.'

She sniffed. 'Bit of a jackass, if you ask me.'

'Lots of men fall in love with beauty. Lavinia is really lovely. Going to Court has done a great deal for her and she has some exquisite clothes.'

'Men don't marry clothes-horses . . . not if they've got any sense.'

'Polly, I was not in love with Dougal Carruthers and he did not throw me aside to marry Lavinia. He had never asked *me* to marry him.'

'I thought . . .'

'Then you thought wrongly. Lavinia will be a countess. Can you see me as one?'

'Why not? I reckon you could be Queen of England if you wanted to.'

'I don't think Prince Albert would think so. And I shouldn't fancy him either . . . even if Her Majesty was willing to abdicate in my favour.'

'Oh, you!' she said smiling. 'But you know there's nothing you can't tell me.'

I tried to forget Lavinia's affairs. I concentrated on Fleur, who was more enchanting than ever. I used to sit by the kitchen fire in the evenings and neither Polly nor Eff omitted to mention every day how well the fire drew nowadays, throwing a glance at the bellows which had pride of place nearby. I listened to their cosy talk while they heated the poker and put it red hot into the stout; and then I felt a certain peace. Somewhere at the back of my mind was the fact that I should always find a home where I would be loved and cherished. I had Polly, Eff and Fleur. In my most despondent moments I should never forget that.

One day Eff said: 'Second Floor 32 says her relation is the Honourable Mrs Somebody.'

'Honourable my foot,' said Polly. 'That one's always going on about her high class relations.'

'She's got breeding,' said Eff. 'I know about these things.'

On such matters Polly had to bow to Eff's superior knowledge. 'Well, what about her?' she added conceding the point by implication.

'This cousin . . . or somebody's going abroad. Oh, hoity toity, she is . . . connected with the highest in the land. This cousin or whatever she is is looking for a companion to take abroad with her . . . have to be a lady and know how to manage things.'

I had been in a soporific mood watching the leaping flames and seeing pictures in them, when suddenly I was alert. A companion to travel . . . to get right away. Janine, I said to myself.

'It sounds like a good post,' I said aloud.

'Good post!' retorted Eff. 'It's one in a million. Now if I had been young . . . before I met Him . . . it's just the sort of thing I would have jumped at.'

'Why, you always hated foreigners, Eff,' said Polly with a little laugh.

'They're all right in their own country and that's where I'd be seeing them.'

I was still thinking of Janine.

I said excitedly: 'One of my old schoolfellows is rather hard up. She is looking for a post. I was with her the other day.'

'You didn't say,' said Polly. 'Did you run into her somewhere?'

'Yes. I know she needs work. I wonder if . . .'

'I tell you what,' said Eff. 'You find out if she'd like the job and I'll have a word with Second Floor 32. Perhaps we could arrange a meeting.'

'I should like to do that.'

'Do you know where she lives?'

'Yes, I have her address. I might write.'

'It would be a feather in Second Floor 32's cap if she found this educated young woman and she turned out to be just what they was looking for.'

I asked a few questions about Second Floor 32 who was, according to Eff, 'the genuine article, a lady who had come down in the world'.

If I wrote to Janine she would tear the letter up, I guessed. If I talked to her it might just possibly be different. Perhaps I flattered myself but I did imagine I had made some impression on her.

The next day I took a cab and did the same as before. I was deposited in the same spot and made my way to No. 20 Fiddler's Green. I walked quickly, making up my mind what I would say to Janine as I went along.

As I came into the street I noticed a group of people standing near No. 20. They looked at me curiously as I approached. I mounted the broken steps and knocked three times on the door.

It was opened by a man. He said: 'What do you want?'

'I have come to see my friend Miss Janine Fletcher,' I told him.

His expression became alert. 'You'd better come in,' he said.

576

I went in. A woman opened a door and looked at me.

'Better wait here,' said the man.

He went up the stairs. It was very strange. I could not understand what it meant. The woman was looking at me. 'Terrible, ain't it?' she murmured. 'A young woman like that.'

'What happened?'

'She must have been up to something. It's not good for the house.'

I was getting very worried. I knew something awful had happened to Janine.

I heard the sound of a carriage drawing up at the door.

'That's them,' said the woman. 'They've come to take her away.'

'I don't understand,' I said.

There was a knocking on the door. As the woman went to open it the man who had let me in appeared on the stairs.

There were two men at the door carrying a stretcher.

'It's all right,' said the man on the stairs. 'Come up.'

They went up the stairs carrying the stretcher. The woman had retreated into her room but she left the door open. I was still standing in the hall.

There was a movement from upstairs. The men emerged with the stretcher; they were carrying someone on it this time – a body covered with a sheet. As they passed me I caught a glimpse of sandy-coloured hair. It was matted with blood.

I knew that under that sheet lay Janine.

A man followed the stretcher-bearers down the stairs. He came to me and said: 'I am a police officer. I am here to investigate the death of Miss Janine Fletcher. What are you doing here?'

'I came to see her.'

'You are a friend of hers?'

I felt sick. I tried to suppress the thought which persisted in my mind. I was telling myself that Lavinia had done this. She would never get away with it . . . never.

'I was at school with her,' I heard myself say.

'Do you visit her often?'

'No. I came once before.'

'When?'

'Three days ago.'

'And she was all right then? Did she seem frightened? Worried?'

I shook my head.

'Where do you live?'

I gave him the rectory address.

'You have come some way to visit Miss Fletcher.'

'I am staying with my old nurse for a few days.'

A younger man had joined us and the first said to him: 'Take the lady's address. We shall be wanting to ask you a few questions, so we shall be visiting you at some time. Please remain in London.'

'Well, I have to go back . . .'

'We must ask you to stay. You may have something important to tell us. It is necessary.'

I murmured: 'I'll stay.'

My legs were trembling and I felt myself sway a little. I wanted to run away from this macabre scene. There was so much I wanted to know. How had this happened? Who had done it? Whom did they suspect? I kept saying to myself: You would never do this, Lavinia. You always left others to do your dirty work.

The man turned to the other who had joined us: 'Oh, Smithson,' he said, 'take the young lady to the cab she is alleged to have waiting for her.' And to me: 'One of our men will be wanting to ask you a few questions about your relationship with the deceased. It's just a formality.'

I was only too glad to escape. I noticed the young man who was accompanying me was young and he looked a little nervous.

'Bit of a shock,' he said as we walked away.

'I feel . . . shaky.'

'I'm a bit nervous myself,' he admitted. 'It's my first murder.'

578

Murder! It was a word that set me shivering. I could not believe it. Janine! To think that we had all been to school together and now . . . in a short time Lavinia had become a mother and Janine . . . a corpse. I tried to shut out the idea that these two facts were in some way connected.

As we moved away a young man approached us. He took off his hat and bowed.

'May I ask you if you are a friend of the young lady?' he asked.

I thought he was another policeman and I said: 'Yes.'

'Would you tell me your name?'

I told him and he produced a notebook from his pocket.

'Do you live near here?'

'No . . . in the country. I'm just staying here.'

'Interesting. Did you know the young lady well?'

'We were at school together. I have just told your people this.'

'Just a few questions. We have to get this right, you see.' He went on: 'Whereabouts in the country?'

I gave him the address of the rectory.

'So you are the rector's daughter?'

I nodded.

'And you were at school together. Have you any idea why anyone would want to kill your friend?'

'No,' I said emphatically.

My escort nudged me. 'You're talking to the Press,' he whispered.

'You needn't worry about that, Miss,' the other assured me. 'Just a few questions, that's all.'

I stammered: 'I thought you were connected with the police.'

He smiled disarmingly: 'There is a sort of connection,' he said.

'I don't want to say anything more. I know nothing about this.'

He nodded, smiling, and lifting his hat walked away.

I felt I had behaved in a very indiscreet manner.

The young man walked with me to where the cab was waiting. He came with me back to the house.

'You should never talk to the Press,' he said. 'We don't like it. We like to give them the information we want them to have.'

'Why didn't you tell me sooner?'

He blushed. He did not like to admit that the identity of the reporter had not immediately dawned on him.

His parting words struck a note of doom. 'I reckon you'll be hearing from us soon,' he said. 'They'll have to check up and all that.'

Polly and Eff were in the hall wondering what had happened.

'Here,' said Polly, 'what's all this? Who was that young man with you?'

'A policeman,' I said.

Polly turned pale.

Eff said: 'Police here. What's police doing with respectable people? What are the neighbours going to think?'

Polly interrupted her. 'Get a drop of brandy. Can't you see how upset she is?'

I was lying on my bed and Polly was seated beside me. I had told her everything that had happened.

'My goodness,' she murmured. 'This is something. Murder, eh? That Janine, she was a nasty piece of work if you was to ask me, going round blackmailing people.'

'I feel sure her death has something to do with that, Polly.'

'Shouldn't be surprised. Do you reckon that Lavinia had a hand in this?'

I shook my head. 'I can't believe that.'

'I'd believe anything of that piece of goods . . . and this will put paid to her and her great romance if it's true. I reckon not even the mighty Framlings would be able to hush this up.'

'Oh, Polly, it's terrible.'

'I only hope to God you can keep out of it. What a pity you went there. Don't want to be mixed up in this sort of thing.'

'I'm afraid I am involved now, Polly.'

'That Lavinia . . . she spells trouble. I think there's a very good chance she has had a hand in this.'

'I can't believe it, Polly. She would lie if necessary . . . but I am sure she could not commit murder. She could never bring herself to do it. Where would she get a gun?'

'They'd have guns at Framling. That wouldn't be hard for her. I reckon she's capable of doing anything to save her own skin. I'm not telling Eff any of this. She'd go stark raving mad if she thought we'd be having the police here.'

'Perhaps I'd better go back to the rectory.'

'It would be worse still there. No, I'm keeping you here till this blows over.'

I just clung to her. I was bewildered and frightened. I could not get out of my mind the thought of Janine lying under that sheet . . . dead.

The police came. They asked more questions. What did I know of Janine's life? What friends had she? I told them I knew nothing of her friends. I had met her only a few days ago for the first time since we left school.

'She was the daughter of a Miss Fletcher who ran a nursing home.'

'That was her aunt,' I said.

The two policemen exchanged glances.

I thought: They discover everything. They will learn who Fleur is. This is going to be terrible for Lavinia . . . and just when she is about to get married.

I was so relieved when they went, but there was worse to come. Polly saw it first in the morning paper and she knew then that it was no use trying to keep it from Eff.

She read it to me in a shaky voice: '"Who was Janine Fletcher? Why should someone take this young girl's life? I had the opportunity of speaking with an old school friend of hers. This was Miss Drusilla Delany who is at present staying with her one-time nurse." They've given this address.' Polly went on: '"She is the daughter of the rector of Framling and was on a visit to her schoolfriend when she found her lying on a stretcher being conducted out of her lodgings. Janine had been shot through the head. Miss Delany said she knew of no one who would want to kill her friend. Janine was the daughter of Miss Emily Fletcher who ran an exclusive nursing home for the well-to-do in the New Forest. Police at the moment are saying nothing but it is rumoured that they have hopes of an early arrest."'

Polly finished reading and looked at me in dismay.

'Oh Polly,' I said, 'it's terrible.'

'I wonder if they'll find out about Fleur. Police has noses for sniffing out nasty titbits.'

'It would be terrible just as the wedding is about to take place. I do hope Lavinia is not involved in this. I am sure she isn't, but all sorts of things could come out.'

'It might be better for that earl or whatever he is to know something about the girl he's marrying before the ceremony. He'll find out quite enough after, I shouldn't wonder.'

'Oh, Polly . . . I'm frightened.'

'Nothing for you to be frightened of. If anything comes out you've got to stand up and tell the truth. Never mind covering up for Madam Lavinia. It's time she came out in the open.'

It was comforting to be with her, but I felt I should return to the rectory, for I knew how concerned Eff was for the respectability of the house. Polly was, too, but her love for me overcame her desire for respectability.

It was the day after we read that piece in the paper when Fabian appeared at the house. I heard the knock and I had an uneasy feeling that it might be the police. I went to open it and there was Fabian.

'Good afternoon,' he said, stepping into the hall without invitation. 'I want to talk to you.'

'But . . .' I began.

'Where can we go?' he asked.

I took him into the parlour, that prim little room with the straight velvet-backed chairs and the sofa to match, the what-not with the precious ornaments on it — dusted only by Eff — the marble mantelpiece and the aspidistra in the big brown pot on the table standing by the window and the paper flowers in the vase in the fireplace. It was the unlived-in room, the sanctum of respectability used for callers, interviewing would-be tenants and sometimes, on very special occasions, Sunday afternoon tea.

'What has brought you here?' I asked.

'Need you ask? I've seen the paper. This girl . . . Janine . . . what has she to do with you?'

'If you read the paper you would know that we were at school together.'

'The girl's been murdered . . . and you were there at the time.'

'I arrived after she was dead.'

'After she was murdered,' he said. 'Good God! What does it mean?'

'I think that is what the police are deciding.'

'But you have been mentioned in regard to this case.'

'I happened to be there. I was questioned.'

'The police don't question just to be sociable, you know. The fact that they questioned you means they think you know something.'

'I did know her. I was going to call on her.'

'For what purpose?'

'Purpose? She was an old schoolfriend.'

'Just renewing acquaintance? I want to know the truth. Do you hear me? You can't go on lying forever. You'd better tell me. I insist on knowing.'

At that moment the door burst open and Polly stood there. She told me afterwards that she had heard him come in and had been listening at the door.

She stood there, her cheeks aflame, her arms akimbo.

'Now, Sir High and Mighty Whatever your Name is, I'm going to tell you a few things. I'll not have you coming here and upsetting my girl. She's worth the lot of you all tied up in a bundle, and I wouldn't give you tuppence for it either.'

He was taken aback but I saw the amused look in his eyes.

'Polly!' I said reproachfully.

'No. You let me have my say. I've had enough of this if you haven't. I'm going to tell these Framlings a thing or two. Coming here . . . upsetting you. He's going to have the truth.'

'Nothing would please me more,' said Fabian.

'Oh! You won't be so pleased when you hear it, I can tell you, and if them policemen come here trying to trap Drusilla into saying what they want, I'll tell them, too. Drusilla's done a lot for your sister. Whose child do you think it is we've got here? Your sister's, that's whose. Drusilla tried to help her and gets insulted for it. Who was it went away with her to that home? Pretending they were at Princess something or other's place? Who was it brought the baby to me? It was plain to me when they come here that your sister didn't know the difference between a baby and a pound of butter – and cared just about as much. So I am not having you here bullying Drusilla. You go back and bully your sister. She's the cause of the trouble.'

He said: 'Thank you for telling me.' He turned to me: 'This is true, I suppose?'

'Of course it's true,' cried Polly. 'Are you calling me a liar?'

'No, Madam, but I thought a little corroboration might be in order.'

'Now we're in this bother and it's all along of your sister. So don't you start accusing Drusilla of nothing because I won't have that either.'

'You are quite right,' he said, 'and I am indebted to you. It is an unpleasant situation and I want to do all I can to help.'

584

'H'm,' said Polly, slightly mollified. 'It's about time, too.'

'Yes. Once more you are right. Do you think I might have a little talk with Miss Delany?'

'That's for her to say.'

'Yes, certainly,' I said.

I was trembling slightly. Polly's revelations had staggered me, but I was glad that he knew, and that I was not the one who had betrayed Lavinia.

Polly said: 'Well, I'll take myself off.' She looked at me. 'Will you be all right?'

'Yes, Polly, thank you.'

The door shut on us.

'A redoubtable lady,' he said. 'So now I have the truth. I think you should tell me more about this. You see, I am deeply involved through my sister. It happened in France, did it?'

'Yes.'

'A Frenchman?'

I nodded.

'You knew him?'

'I saw him once or twice.'

'I see. And my foolish sister asked for your help.'

'Janine Fletcher was a girl at school. She had an aunt.'

'So you lied about going to Lindenstein. I knew you hadn't been there, of course.'

'Yes. You tried to trap me. And you had some idea of what really happened.'

'When I saw the child . . .'

'And you thought that I . . .'

'It seemed hard to believe.'

'Yet you did.'

He did not answer; then he said: 'This girl . . . Janine . . . what do you think happened?'

'I don't know.'

'You came along just after. Why?'

'I was trying to talk to her.'

'About Lavinia. Was she blackmailing Lavinia?'

585

I was silent. I did not want to betray her, but of course Polly had already done that.

He was serious now. 'My God!' he said. 'But she wasn't here. She was at Framling. It must have been . . . someone else.'

'You mean . . .'

'Did that woman have other girls there in the same position?'

'There were some.'

'What a mess! It was a pity you were seen there. I am glad I know. I shall keep in touch. I shall be in London. I'll give you the address of my place in town. Get a message to me if anything develops.'

He looked really anxious. I imagined he was thinking of the scandal if anything came out about Lavinia's staying at the nursing home and for what reason. That would be headline news. I only rated a mention and a short paragraph. Lavinia's reputation would be in ruins. I could see that her brother was prepared to prevent that at all costs.

I felt a certain relief. I had great confidence in his powers to help. He would be strong and resourceful. Of course he was only concerned in protecting his sister but in doing so he would look after me at the same time.

He said he would go now. He took my hands and smiled at me; it was almost like an apology for his behaviour in the past. I was glad that at last he knew the truth and I had not been the one to tell him.

There was no news of the case — just brief references. The police were pursuing their enquiries. There were no more visits from them.

Fabian called at the house. Eff let him in. She was not at all displeased.

'Eff's a rare one for a title,' Polly explained. 'You'll hear her going on to Second Floor about *Sir* Fabian calling. She thinks it's good for the house. He looks the part too. I hope he's behaving right.'

586

'Oh yes,' I assured her.

'Don't you put up with any old truck from him.'

'No, I won't.'

He wanted to talk to me about the child, he told me. Those two women had looked after her from birth, had they? I told him they had.

I knew by his attitude that he had a respect for Polly. I think he quite enjoyed her manner of dealing with him although what she had to impart had been unpalatable. He had seemed faintly amused to contemplate the rector's daughter having stepped out of line; it was not quite so amusing for his own sister.

'It's a little girl, isn't it?'

'Yes. You should meet your niece. Apart from that one encounter on the green, you have not seen her.'

'I want to meet her. And those two have looked after her, fed her . . . clothed her . . .'

'They have also loved her,' I said.

'Poor child! What would she have done without them . . . and you?'

'Lavinia would have had to make some arrangements but none could have been so good for Fleur as Polly and her sister.'

'I want to make sure that they are compensated for what they have done.'

'You mean . . . money?'

'I did mean that. They cannot be wealthy enough to take care of other people's children. It must be a costly business.'

'They are, as they would say, comfortably off. They let rooms and Eff is a good business woman. Polly, too. They work hard and enjoy the fruits of their labours. They might be offended if they thought you believed they were in need of money.'

'But they have taken the child!'

'They did that for me, because . . .'

'Because they made the same mistake as I did. You see,

I was not such a villain after all if Polly . . . who is so close to you . . . Well, perhaps that sort of thing can happen to anyone.'

'Perhaps.'

'We all have our unguarded moments.' He was smiling at me quizzically. Then he said briskly: 'I shall find a way of recompensing these good women. Will you talk to them for me? I am afraid I should never be allowed to state my case. They might listen to you.'

I said I would speak to them.

They were both rather indignant when I told them.

'Who does he think he is?' demanded Polly. 'We don't want his money. We've had Fleur since she was a baby. She's ours . . . If you took money from a man like that you'd have him dictating . . . telling you what you'd got to do. No, we're not having that.'

Eff conceded: 'It was good of *Sir* Fabian to suggest it.' She always made the most of the 'Sir' when talking to Second Floor 32 and fell into the habit with us.

'Look, Polly,' I said, 'you're all right now . . . but suppose things didn't go so well. You have to think of Fleur and there will be school and all that.'

'I wouldn't want her going to one of them foreign places. A lot of good it did to that Lavinia.'

But Eff was more practical. I think Polly's emotions dulled her perception to some extent. She had marked Fabian out as a smooth seducer and she had made up her mind that he had designs on me. She was very wary of him.

However, when Fabian suggested that he should set up an account for them on which they could draw at any time they needed money for Fleur, they at length agreed.

'Not that we'll touch it,' said Polly.

'But it's nice to know it's there,' added the practical Eff.

During the following week I saw a good deal of him. I had to admit that he was a help and that he comforted me. The

588

fact that he was there and knew the truth took a great weight off my mind.

No one else from the police came to see me. There was little in the papers about the case. It was good to know that if any crisis arose Fabian would be there.

I grew to know a little more of him. He used to visit the house and Eff, with a certain pride, would serve tea in the parlour. I think she was rather proud to show it off. When he was coming fresh antimacassars were put on the velvet chairs and there was an extra polish on the brass; the ornaments on the what-not were carefully dusted. 'We don't want that Sir Fabian to think we don't know what's what.' I was secretly amused at the thought of his examining the little bits of china on the what-not and assessing the brightness of the brass of the candlesticks. But I liked to see Eff's pleasure in entertaining a titled gentleman, and Polly's suspicions of him, which were an indication of her love and concern for me.

He seemed to change a little. He met Fleur who took quite a liking to him, which surprised me, for he found it difficult to communicate with her and appeared to make no attempt to do so.

'Say hello, Sir Fabian,' Eff urged; and Fleur did with a halting charm. She put her hands on his knees and gazed up at him with a sort of wonder. It was very amusing. I thought there was a look of the Framlings about Fleur. She had failed to inherit Lavinia's tawny hair but, I thought, like her mother, she would be a beauty.

'A pleasant-looking child,' was Fabian's comment.

'She seemed to sense that she was related to you,' I told him.

'Surely not?'

'Who knows? You are her uncle.'

Eff brought in tea which I took alone with Fabian. I guessed Polly was hovering. As she would say, she wouldn't trust him and he might get up to some 'hanky-panky'.

We talked of Lavinia's coming marriage which would be

589

very soon now. Lavinia would have heard of Janine's death, as it had been extensively reported in the papers. I wondered what she was thinking. If I knew her she would be mightily relieved on one hand, but on the other she must be wondering what could come out about Janine. I wondered if it occurred to her that if Janine was blackmailing her she might be doing the same to other people. Surely she must be suffering some anxiety.

Fabian would have to return for the wedding.

'I think,' he told me, 'you would be expected to attend.'

'I am not sure whether that is necessary. She will have heard about Janine. I wonder how she is feeling.'

'She doesn't let much worry her but even she must be having some uneasy moments. Thank God she was in Framling when the woman was killed and there can be no question of accusations being brought against her.'

'Do you think she will tell Dougal?'

'No, I do not.'

'Do you think she should?'

'It is a matter for her to decide.'

'Shouldn't he know?'

'I can see you are a stickler for morality.'

'Aren't you?'

'I am for good common sense.'

'And morality does not always fit in with that?'

'I would not say that. Each situation has to be judged on its own. You cannot generalize about such matters.'

'Do you think it is right . . . or even wise . . . for a woman who has a child to marry and not mention that child to her husband?'

'If the woman in question was a virtuous one she would not have had the child in the first place, so you must not expect exemplary conduct from her afterwards. It is a matter for Lavinia to decide.'

'And Dougal . . . isn't he being deceived?'

'Yes. But perhaps he would prefer not to know.'

'Do you really think so? Would you in similar circumstances?'

'I find it exceedingly difficult to put myself in Dougal's place. I am not Dougal. I am myself. Dougal is a good, worthy man. I am sure he has lived an exemplary life. I cannot say the same for myself. Therefore I take a different view from the one he would take. I believe that it is better to get through life as easily as one can . . . and if ignorance is more soothing than knowledge, let's remain in the dark.'

'What a strange philosophy!'

'I am afraid you disapprove of me.'

'I am sure there are very few things you are afraid of and my approval or disapproval is not one of them.'

'I would always welcome your good opinion.'

I laughed. I was feeling much easier with him. I looked forward to his visits and I was continually warning myself not to become too interested in him. I had had one warning with Dougal. He had seemed the perfect gentleman; Fabian was not that but I found him, if anything, more interesting. The subjects raised by Dougal had fascinated me, but it was Fabian himself who attracted me.

I was on dangerous ground. Polly knew it; that was why she was watchful.

It was evening. Fleur was in bed, I was sitting with Polly and Eff by the kitchen fire. Eff had just commented on how well it was drawing these days, when there was a knock on the door.

Eff rose in dismay. She never liked anyone to catch her using the kitchen as a living-room.

'One of the tenants,' she said in dismay. 'First Floor Back, bet you anything.'

She composed herself, putting on the special dignity she reserved for tenants, and went to the door.

Polly followed her with me in the wake.

It was not First Floor Back but one of the others, and she was clutching a newspaper.

591

'I thought you might not have heard the latest,' she was saying excitedly. 'It's the Janine Fletcher case.'

We all went into the parlour. Polly had seized the newspaper and spread it out on the table. We all gathered round. It was on the front page, Stop Press News.

'"Startling Developments in the Janine Fletcher Case. Police think they have solution."'

That was all.

'Well, well,' said Eff. 'It was kind of you, Mrs Tenby.'

'Well, I thought you'd want to know. And Miss Delany . . . you'd be interested, seeing as how you knew the poor thing.'

'Yes,' I agreed.

'Now we have to wait and see what it's all about,' said Polly.

Eff with the utmost dignity was ushering Mrs Tenby into the hall.

'Well, thank you for letting us know.'

When she had gone we sat in the kitchen asking ourselves what it could mean and we were later than usual going to bed.

I went in to see Fleur as I always did every night. She was fast asleep clutching the little doll Eff had bought for her and from which she refused to be parted. I bent and kissed her; she murmured something in her sleep and I felt a great relief because Fabian knew and that meant that her future was assured.

I lay awake for a long time wondering what new development there had been and whether I should see Fabian next day.

We had the papers early and there it was for us to read. It was a further shock for me and I felt more deeply involved that I had before. Dramas . . . tragedies . . . are taking place frequently. One reads of them and sometimes they seem unreal because they happen to vague people whom we can only imagine; but when they concern someone we know, that is different.

What I read saddened me greatly, although it must have brought intense relief to Lavinia.

They had found the murderess — not by any great detective work on the part of the police, but through the confession of the one who had killed Janine.

KILLER OF JANINE FLETCHER CONFESSES

It was written in flowery prose.

In a little house on the outskirts of Wanstead, near Epping Forest, James Everet Masters lay dying of self-inflicted wounds. Beside him was the body of his wife, Miriam Mary Masters. She had been dead some hours.

They were known as the happiest couple in the neighbourhood. James was a seaman. Neighbours tell how his wife used to wait for his return and how each time he came home it was another honeymoon for them. Why should she then have decided to take her life by consuming an overdose of laudanum? It was because she could not face the consequence of a reckless act which took place during one of James's absences at sea.

Double Suicide

was the next headline.

Miriam could no longer tolerate the situation in which she found herself and decided she could not go on living. So, carefully writing two letters — one to James and one to the coroner — she confessed to the killing of Janine Fletcher. In that to her husband she gave her reasons for doing so.

I love you, James.

The letter she wrote to her husband explained what happened. One night when James was at sea she had been persuaded by friends to go to a party. She had not wanted to, and, little realizing that she was setting out on a path which would lead to misery and finally death, unused to alcohol, she took too much and was unaware

593

of what was happening to her. Some person took advantage of the poor girl's state and seduced her, with the result that she became with child. Miriam was desperate. How to tell James? Would he understand? She greatly feared that he would not. Her happiness was in ruins. She tried to plan a way out. She had heard of Mrs Fletcher's Nursing Home in the New Forest. It was expensive but discreet. She decided there was no alternative but to go there and get the child adopted when it arrived. Janine Fletcher, known as the niece of the owner of the nursing home, was there when Miriam had her baby. Janine knew her secret. The child was born and adopted. Miriam came home to put the past behind her. And so she did until Janine Fletcher turned up in her life.

It is not an unfamiliar story. Janine wanted money to keep quiet. Miriam paid . . . once or twice . . . and then she found she could not go on paying. Greatly she feared the consequences. She could not face telling James. She acquired a gun. She went to Janine's rooms and shot her dead. She managed to get away without being seen. But she realized she could not live with such a secret, so she wrote those letters.

Star-Crossed Lovers. They were Romeo and Juliet. He came and found her dead. He read her letter. He was prostrate with grief. He would have understood. He would have forgiven. Perhaps they would have found the child and he would have been a father to it.

Too Late. She had killed Janine Fletcher. She must have realized, while she might have lived on weighed down by the sin of adultery, she could not by that of murder. So the star-crossed lovers died, and the mystery of who killed Janine Fletcher is solved.

Fabian called later in the morning.

'You've heard the news?' he said.

'Yes,' I said. 'I was deeply touched.' I remembered Miriam

so well. I remembered her misery and I thought how cruel life had been to her.

'You seem shaken,' he said.

'I *knew* her. She was there when we were there. She was such a gentle person. I cannot think of her as a murderess.'

'It closes up the case. We can breathe more easily now. Good God! It would have been certain to come out. Lavinia could have been caught up in all this. So could you. I was daily expecting something to be disclosed. And now it's all over.'

I said: 'She loved her husband . . . deeply. And he must have loved her. He could not contemplate living without her. She made a deep impression on me.'

'She must have been an unusual woman . . . to take that gun and shoot her enemy.'

'It all seems so unnecessary. If only she had told her husband! If only Janine had tried to work for her living and not turned to blackmail! If only Lavinia had not been carried away by that man!'

'If only the world was a different place and everyone in it perfect, life would be simpler, wouldn't it?' He smiled at me ruefully. 'You look for perfection,' he went on. 'I believe you will have to do with something less. I am going to cheer you up. I am going to suggest that you have luncheon with me. I think we have something to celebrate. The case is over. I can tell you I have had some uneasy moments!'

'For Lavinia,' I said.

'For you also.'

'I had nothing to fear.'

'It is never good to be connected with what is unsavoury. It leaves something behind. People remember . . . vaguely. They forget details . . . who was who . . . what part they played. It is a great relief that it is over.'

'I can't stop thinking of Miriam.'

'She took what she thought was the best way out of her dilemma.'

'And destroyed her life and that of her husband.'

595

'Alas. It was her choice. It is a sad story. I will call for you at twelve-thirty.'

Polly was pleased by the news.

'My goodness, it gave me the willies . . . thinking what was going to happen next . . . and now you are going to lunch with *him*.' She shook her head. 'You want to be careful with that one. I wouldn't trust him as far as I could throw a goose feather.'

'That might float in the air for quite a long time, Polly.'

'It would come down pretty soon, I reckon. Take care.'

'Oh, Polly, I will.'

In the restaurant where we lunched he was treated with deference. He was in good spirits. Naturally he had never met Miriam and her tragedy meant little to him except an ending to a situation which could become dangerous.

'Isn't it strange?' he said. 'You and I have been acquainted since you were two years old and it is only now that we know each other. It took this little matter to bring us together. I very much regret that I shall soon be leaving England.'

'You are going to India?'

'Yes, by the end of this year or the beginning of next. It is quite a journey.'

'Have you ever done it before?'

'No. But I have heard a great deal about it. There are always people at the House connected with the East India Company and they discuss it constantly.'

'You will go part of the way by ship, of course.'

'One has to decide whether one will take the long haul round the Cape or disembark, say, at Alexandria and take the trek across the desert to Suez where one can board an East Indiaman.'

'Which you will do, I suppose.'

'We take that route, yes. It saves time, but I believe crossing the desert can be a little hazardous.'

'I am sure it will be of the utmost interest.'

596

'I feel certain of that too. But in a way I shall be sorry to leave England.'

He smiled at me significantly and I felt myself flushing faintly. I could not forget that time when he had, as I believed, made a rather veiled suggestion to me.

'I don't know when your friend Dougal, our bridegroom, will be coming out,' he went on. 'He was to have done so but it may be that his new commitments will keep him in England.'

'Whereabouts is the ancestral home?'

'Not very far from Framling. I would say some thirty or forty miles.' He looked at me intently. 'I dare say you will be invited to visit. Perhaps you will enjoy that.'

He had a way of insinuating meaning into his conversation. He implied that he knew of my feelings for Dougal and was translating them into aspirations and hopes. I felt indignant. It was a mood I was often verging on with him.

'Of course the newly married couple may wish to be alone for a while, but doubtless that will pass. Then I am sure you will be an honoured guest.'

'Lavinia will have new interests. I dare say she will have little time for me.'

'But you and Dougal were so interested in antiquities. It is hardly likely that he will lose his enthusiasm for those after the first delights of marriage are over.'

'It remains to be seen.'

'As so much does. You are very philosophical.'

'I did not know that.'

'There is a great deal we do not know about ourselves.'

He began to talk about India and the Company. He thought he might be away for several years. 'When I come back,' he said, 'you will have forgotten who I am.'

'That's hardly likely. Framling and its inhabitants have dominated the village for as long as I can remember.'

'Perhaps you will have married and gone away . . . I wonder.'

'It seems hardly likely.'

'What seems unlikely today can be inevitable tomorrow.' He lifted his glass and said: 'To the future . . . yours and mine.'

He was disturbing. He was implying that he knew I had cared for Dougal and that I was sad because Lavinia and Lady Harriet had taken him from me. I could not explain to him that, though I liked Dougal and we had been good friends and I had perhaps been a little piqued because he had seemed to forget me when he had been overwhelmed by Lavinia's beauty, I was far from heartbroken.

He leaned forward across the table. 'Do you know,' he said, 'I have always had a special interest in you?'

'Really?'

He nodded. 'Ever since I kidnapped you and took you to Framling. Did you ever hear how I cared for you during those two weeks?'

'I did hear of it.'

'Don't you think there is some significance in that?'

'The significance is that you were a spoilt child. You had a whim. I was there and I did as well as any other so you took me to your home, and because you had to be indulged you kept me there . . . away from mine.'

He laughed. 'It shows a purposeful character on my part.'

'Rather that you were surrounded by those who allowed you to indulge your whims.'

'I can remember it. A little baby. You weren't much more. I enjoyed my part as the father figure . . . and what I am saying is that it gave me a special interest in you. That's natural enough.'

'I believe you have a natural interest . . . if a fleeting one . . . in most young women.'

He laughed at me. 'Whatever you say, I think our little adventure makes a special bond between us.'

I shook my head. 'Nothing of the sort.'

'You disappoint me. Don't you feel it?'

'No,' I replied.

'Drusilla, let's be friends . . . good friends.'

'One can't make friendship to order.'

'One can give it a chance. We live close together. We could see a great deal of each other. This . . . incident . . . has brought us closer together, hasn't it?'

'I hope it has taught you a little about me which you did not know when you jumped to certain conclusions.'

'It has taught me a good deal about you and I am eager to learn more.'

I thought I knew what he was leading up to . . . not quite so crudely as he had done once before when he came to conclusions about me . . . but it was there all the same.

In my mind's eye I could see Polly's warning face. She did not trust him. Nor did I.

I started to talk about India and he told me more about that country, until I said it was time I left.

I was surprised at myself. I did not want the luncheon to end. Yet I knew Polly was right. I must beware of this man.

When I returned to the house she studied me a little anxiously. I must have shown signs of the elation his company always seemed to inspire in me.

I could not stay with Polly indefinitely and in due course I had to return home.

The wedding day was close.

Lavinia was caught up in a whirl of excitement. I went over to see her and she greeted me with a show of affection and talked excitedly about the wedding and the honeymoon until she was able to get me alone.

'Oh, Drusilla,' she burst out, 'if you only knew what I went through.'

'Others did, too, Lavinia.'

'Of course. But I was just going to get married.'

'Poor Miriam went through a good deal.'

'Fancy her doing that! I couldn't believe it.'

'Poor girl. She came to the point when she could endure no more.'

'I was terribly worried. What if the police had put my

599

name in the paper! They did have bits about me . . . but in a different way. You know they called me the most beautiful debutante of the year.'

'I had heard it.'

'Dougal was very proud. He adores me, of course.'

'Of course,' I said.

'It's going to be such fun. We are going to India.'

'So both you and your brother will be there.'

She grimaced. 'He's been a bit touchy about all this business. Lectured me about Fleur and all that. I told him I'd arranged for her to be well looked after. What else could I do?'

'You might have brought your daughter home and looked after her.'

'Don't talk nonsense. How could I?'

'Make a confession, turn over a new leaf and become a devoted mother. Fleur is lovely.'

'Is she? Perhaps I'll go and see her one day.'

'Polly wouldn't want you to. She'd say it was unsettling the child.'

'Unsettle her to see her mother!'

'Certainly, when that mother has left her with others to get her out of the way.'

'Oh, shut up. You talk like Fabian. I've had enough of that. It's over. Miriam saw to that.'

'She was certainly your benefactress.'

'That's a funny way of seeing it.'

'It's how you see it. Can you imagine the anguish she suffered?'

'She ought to have told her husband.'

'As you have told Dougal?'

'That's different.'

'Everything that happens to a Framling is different from that which happens to other people.'

'Stop it. I want to talk to you about the wedding. We're going to Italy for our honeymoon. Dougal wants to show me the art treasures.' She grimaced.

Poor Dougal! I thought. Then I felt an anger against him. How could he have been so stupid as to marry someone who was so utterly incompatible as Lavinia was?

How self-centred she was! She had hardly spared a thought for Miriam, except to be gratified because she had removed the one who was a threat to herself.

I had daydreams at that time. I dreamed that Dougal realized his mistake, that he came back to the rectory to resume our pleasant friendship, that the relationship between us strengthened.

It was strange that there were three men who were important in my life. There was Colin Brady, who would be prepared to marry me because it would be so convenient and a step towards acquiring the living with which my father was rapidly becoming too ill to continue; there was Fabian who had hinted clearly that he would like to indulge in some sort of relationship with me . . . an irregular one, of course. Marriage would not come into it. I had no doubt that Lady Harriet, who had so capably acquired a noble title for her daughter, would have even greater ambitions for her son. He might resist, of course; he would not be so malleable as Lavinia. Lady Harriet must have realized by now that her adored son had as strong a will as her own. That was something I should remember. Just suppose he really did care for me, he would only have to decide to marry me. Lady Harriet, outraged and bitterly disappointed as she would be, would have, nevertheless, to bow to his wishes. It was impossible. He might be sufficiently attracted to me to enjoy a light love-affair but there could be no question of a marriage between the heir of Framling and the humble girl from the rectory. And then there was Dougal. Dougal had the manners of a gentleman and the morals, too. I could have been proud to care for Dougal. I could have shared his interests. But he had seen beauty and succumbed. If I were wise I should agree with Polly and say to myself: I have been lucky. Suppose it had happened later when I had become more deeply involved?

Polly had said before I left: 'Men are funny things. There's the good and the bad, the faithful sort and them that can't stop running after women even if they know they're sitting on a keg of gunpowder. It's choosing the right one to start with that's the thing.'

'If there is a choice,' I reminded her.

'There's a choice whether to or not. That's where it comes in. And there's some I wouldn't touch with a barge pole.'

I knew Fabian was one of those; but Dougal hadn't been; and he was soon to be joined in matrimony with Lavinia who might well be, as Polly had mentioned, one of those who was sitting on a keg of gunpowder. It was almost certain that that marriage would not run smoothly.

The wedding day dawned. It was a great day for the village. My father performed the ceremony. The church was decorated with flowers of all descriptions which had been sent down from nearby nurseries who had chosen their best blooms for the purpose. With them had come two ladies to arrange the flowers, much to the disgust of the Misses Glyn and Burrows who had always previously dealt with the decoration of the church.

It was very impressive. Lavinia was a breathtakingly beautiful bride, Dougal a handsome bridegroom. The guests were numerous.

I sat at the back of the church. I saw Lady Harriet, resplendent in her wedding finery and Fabian with her, extremely distinguished. I felt like a wren among peacocks.

And so Lavinia was married to Dougal.

Janine was dead. Fleur's future was taken care of; I felt it was the end of an episode.

INDIA

A Perilous Journey Across the Desert

That happened two years ago. They had been two uneventful years and life had taken on a grey monotone. Each day I rose in the morning knowing exactly what the day would bring. There was no light and shadow. The excitement was whether it would be fine for the summer fête or whether the bazaar would make more profit this year than last.

Fabian had left for India earlier than had been expected and went off soon after Lavinia's wedding day.

It was absurd, but it seemed very dull without him. Why it should when I had seen so little of him and had taken such pains to avoid him, I could not imagine. I should not regret his going. He was, as Polly would have said, a menace.

Although I had often been irritated by Lavinia, I missed her too. Framling seemed different without them. I wondered whether Lady Harriet missed them and I was surprised that she had allowed both her darlings to leave her. She gave herself up to the task of ruling the village with more energy than ever. Colin Brady was quite a favourite with her, which I guessed was because he was more conventional than my father had been. He was a subservient young man. 'Oh yes, of course, Lady Harriet'; 'Thank you for telling me, Lady Harriet'. I wanted to shout at him: You don't have to be quite so blatantly humble. I am sure the living will be yours in time.

There was another reason for depression. My father's health was deteriorating. He became tired very easily and I had to be grateful to Colin for his care of him. Colin was to all intents and purposes playing the part of rector. It must be noticed and his reward must come.

I heard Lady Harriet say once: 'Such a pleasant young man! The dear rector can be a little odd, you know. All that preoccupation with dead people ... and those who have been dead so long. He has his own parish to think of. You'd think that would be enough for him.'

She called at the rectory now and then, feeling it was her duty to do so. She would cast her probing eyes over me.

I knew her thoughts. She liked everything to be rounded off neatly. My father had been ailing for some time and like Charles the Second was an unconscionable time a-dying. I was his unmarried daughter and there was a young man living in the rectory. The solution was obvious in Lady Harriet's view, and in such circumstances those concerned should realize this and accept what was offered them.

My father had a slight stroke. It did not incapacitate him entirely but his speech thickened a little and he lost some use of his arm and leg; he had become a semi-invalid.

I nursed him with the help of Mrs Janson and two of the maids. I could see, though, that I was moving towards some climax.

Dr Berryman, who had always been a good friend to us, told me he feared my father could have another stroke at any time and that it could be fatal.

So I was prepared.

I used to spend a lot of time reading to him. It was what he enjoyed most and this duty certainly increased my knowledge of Greek and Roman history; after that, each day I woke up and wondered what it would bring, for I knew the existing state of affairs could not last.

Lady Harriet invited me to Framling to take tea with her. I sat in the drawing-room while my stately hostess presided behind the lace-covered table on which was the silver tray with silver teapot, thin bread and butter and a fruit cake.

A parlourmaid took the cup containing the tea which Lady Harriet had poured for me. While the maid remained conversation was guarded, but I knew it was not simply to take tea that I had been summoned.

She talked of Lavinia and how much she was enjoying India.

'The social life there must be very exciting,' she went on. 'There are so many people from the Company out there. I believe the natives are so grateful to us. And so they should be. Ingratitude is something I cannot tolerate. The Earl is well and the dear young people are blissfully happy together ... especially after the birth of little Louise. Dear me. Imagine Lavinia . . . a mother!'

I smiled grimly to myself. Lavinia had been a mother far longer than Lady Harriet realized.

She talked of little Louise and how she at least would have to come home sometime. It would be a little while yet but children couldn't live in India all their childhood.

I sat listening and agreeing as docilely as Colin Brady might have done.

When we had finished tea and the tray was removed Lady Harriet said: 'I am a little anxious about the state of affairs at the rectory.'

I raised my eyebrows slightly as though to question why.

She smiled at me benignly. 'I have always kept an eye on you, my dear, ever since your mother died. It was so sad. A child left like that. And your father . . . I am very fond of him but his head is in the clouds . . . just a little. Most men find it difficult to care for a child . . . but he particularly so. So I have watched over you.'

I had not noticed the attention and was rather glad that I had not – but of course I did not really believe in it.

'Your father is very frail, my dear.'

'I am afraid so,' I said.

'There comes a time when facts have to be faced . . . however painful. Your father's health is failing. It is time Mr Brady took over entirely. He is an excellent young man and has my full support. He entertains very warm feelings towards you. If you and he married it would be a relief to me and such a happy solution to the problems which will inevitably face you. As the rector's daughter you know our ways . . .'

I felt indignant at the manner in which my future was being disposed of.

I said with a certain hauteur: 'Lady Harriet, I have no wish to marry.' I wanted to add: And I shall certainly not do so because it is a relief to you.

She smiled indulgently as though at a wayward child.

'You see, my dear, your father is no longer young. You are of an age to marry. I have spoken of the matter to Mr Brady.'

I could imagine it and his response: 'Yes, Lady Harriet, if you think I should marry Drusilla, I shall certainly do so.'

I felt angry and roused up all the stubbornness in my nature.

'Lady Harriet,' I began, but I was saved from giving vent to my anger, which would probably have meant that I should be exiled from Framling for ever, by a commotion outside the room.

I heard someone say: 'No . . . no, Lady Harriet is in there.'

Lady Harriet rose and swept to the door. She flung it open and started back, for standing there was a wild figure whom I recognized at once. Her hair hung down her back in some disarray; she was wearing a loose nightgown and her feet were bare.

'What does this mean?' demanded Lady Harriet.

The woman I had known as Ayesha came hurrying forward, and my memory went back to the first time I had seen Miss Lucille who had talked to me about the peacock feather fan.

'I would speak to her,' she cried wildly. 'She is here. Ah . . .' She was looking at me, stumbling towards me. Ayesha held her back.

'Miss Lucille . . . come to your room. It is better so.' I remembered the sing-song voice which had impressed me all those years ago.

Miss Lucille said: 'I want to talk to her . . . There is something I must say.'

Lady Harriet said briskly: 'Take Miss Lucille back to her bedroom. How could this have happened? I have ordered that she should be kept to her own apartments, which is so necessary for her health.'

I had risen and the poor demented woman stared at me. Then she smiled rather tenderly. 'I want . . . I want . . .' she began.

Ayesha murmured: 'Yes, yes . . . later on . . . We shall see. We shall see . . .'

Ayesha took her gently by the hand and led her away; as she went she turned her head and looked at me helplessly.

Lady Harriet was extremely put out.

She said: 'I cannot think what happened. She is far from well. I do everything I can to care for her and that they should have let her come down . . .'

Clearly the scene had shaken her as well as myself. Her thoughts had strayed from me and my affairs. What was happening at Framling was of far more consequence.

'Well, my dear,' she said, dismissing me, 'you will think about it . . . and you will see what is best.'

I was glad to get away and went thoughtfully home.

It was a real problem facing me, and although I would do anything rather than accept Lady Harriet's solution, I had to admit that the future looked rather bleak.

Two days later Colin Brady asked me to marry him.

I did a good deal of walking. I should have liked to ride but I had no horse of my own and although Fabian had long ago given me access to the Framling stables, in view of my inability to fall in with Lady Harriet's views, I did not feel I could make use of the offer.

I had come home after a walk and was taking a short cut

across the churchyard when I saw Colin coming out of the church.

'Ah, Drusilla,' he said. 'I did want to have a word with you.'

I guessed what was coming.

I looked at him steadily. He was by no means ill-favoured. His face shone with virtue; he was the sort of man who would walk in the paths of righteousness all his life; he would make no enemies, except those who were envious of his virtues; he would bring comfort to the sick and ailing; he would introduce a touch of laboured humour, and many a young woman would be eager to spend a lifetime caring for him. Marriage with him was as much as an impecunious parson's daughter could hope for.

I don't know what I did hope for, but I did feel that I ought to face the world alone rather than with someone who had been more or less ordered to marry me, and whom I had been advised to accept because it was the best thing for me.

'Hello, Colin,' I said. 'Busy as usual, I see.'

'Parish affairs. They can be demanding. The rector was looking less well, I thought, this morning.' He shook his head.

'Yes,' I answered. 'I am afraid he is very weak.'

He cleared his throat. 'It seems to me a good idea if you and I . . . well, in view of everything . . . it seems a good solution . . .'

Again that irritation arose in me. I did not want marriage to be a solution.

'Well,' he went on, 'you know this place. And I . . . I have grown to love it . . . and to love you, too, Drusilla.'

'I think,' I told him, 'you have been talking to Lady Harriet. Perhaps I should say she has been talking to you. One doesn't exactly *talk* to Lady Harriet. One listens.'

He gave a little titter and coughed.

'What I was really going to say was that you and I could . . . get married.'

'And you mean you could take over the rectory.'

'Well, I think it would be a successful answer to all our problems.'

'I feel one should not undertake marriage as an answer to problems, don't you?'

He looked puzzled. He said: 'Lady Harriet has intimated . . .'

'Oh, I know what she intimated, but I wouldn't want to marry just because it is convenient.'

'It is not only that . . .' He took my hand and looked earnestly at me. 'I am very fond of you, you know.'

'I like you too, Colin. I am sure you will make an excellent job of it all when you take over completely. Well, you really have done that already. As for myself, I am not sure that I want to marry . . . yet.'

'My dear girl, you mustn't think like that. Everything will be all right, I do assure you. I do not want to hurry you. If we could be engaged . . .'

'No, Colin. Not yet.'

'I know you have a great deal on your mind. You are worried about your father. Perhaps I have spoken too soon. Lady Harriet . . .'

I wanted to scream at him: Lady Harriet is not going to govern my life if she governs yours.

'Lady Harriet,' I said calmly, 'likes to arrange people's lives. Please try to understand, Colin, that I want to manage my own.'

He laughed. 'She is a very forceful lady . . . but kind at heart, I think, and eager for your welfare. I have spoken too soon. I know you are very anxious about your father. We will speak together later.'

I let it go at that, but I wanted to shout at him: I'll never marry you.

That seemed unkind. He was gentle and good-hearted. I shouldn't let him see how angry I was because he had made himself a tool of Lady Harriet. Perhaps he was wise. He had his way to make in the world and he knew he could not afford to ignore those such as Lady Harriet when they crossed his path, for they could be instrumental in making or breaking his career.

I went to the paddock a good deal. It was in Framling land but rarely used. I found a certain peace there. I could see the west wing, that which housed Miss Lucille. I thought a great deal about that strange encounter of ours all those years ago. She had remembered and when she came down to the drawing-room where I was having tea with Lady Harriet, she had come to see me.

I brooded on the past and tried to look into the future. It was growing of some concern to me. My father was getting more and more frail. He looked forward to that period of the afternoon when I would read to him for a couple of hours, for his greatest affliction was his failing eyesight which robbed him of his contact with the world of books. When he dozed off while I was reading I knew he was very weak indeed, for he so much looked forward to these sessions. I would let the book lie in my lap and look at his face, peaceful in repose. I would imagine his coming here with my mother and the hopes they had had and how they had planned for me. And then she had died leaving him alone and he had given himself to his books. How different it would have been had she lived!

And now here he was at the end of his life and I should be alone in the world. No, I would have Polly. Polly was like a raft to a drowning person, Polly was the guiding star of my life.

I knew that my father could not live long. I knew that Colin Brady would step into his shoes; and there was no place for me here — where I had lived all my life — unless it was as Colin's wife.

Perhaps some would think the wise thing to do would be to take what was offered to me.

No, no, I said to myself. Why should I feel this revulsion? Colin is a good man. I should be content with him. But I had compared him with others and found him wanting —

Dougal who had made me think our friendship was ripening to something stronger; Fabian who promised excitement and who had made it clear what sort of relationship there would have to be between us.

It was foolish to think of these two. They were not to be compared with Colin. Colin would never be overwhelmed by beauty as Dougal had been; it would never occur to him to indulge in a less than respectable relationship.

Sometimes I thought I was foolish to turn from Colin. Lady Harriet was right. Marriage with him might well prove not only the best but the only solution.

While I sat leaning against the hedge of the paddock I often found myself looking up at a certain window and remembering how, years ago, Miss Lucille used to look down on us having our riding lesson.

One day I saw the curtains move. A figure stood at the window looking down at me. Miss Lucille. I lifted a hand and waved. There was no response and after a while I saw her move away as though she were being led.

I saw her often after that. I would be there usually in the afternoons and often at the same time. It was like an arrangement between us.

I was getting more and more uneasy about my father. He talked now and then of my mother and I felt he was finding great satisfaction in living in the past.

'Everything she was going to do was for you,' he told me dreamily when he had nodded off when I was reading and had awakened suddenly to find that I had stopped. 'She so much wanted a child. I was glad she lived long enough to see you. I never saw anything more beautiful than her face when she held you in her arms. She wanted everything for you. She wanted you well settled in life. I'm glad Colin Brady is here. He's a good man. I'd trust him as I feel I can trust few others.'

'Yes,' I agreed, 'he has been good.'

'He'll take over when I'm gone. It's right that he should. He'll be better at the job than I was.'

'You are very much liked here, Father.'

'Too forgetful. Not really cut out to be a parson.'

'And you think Colin is?'

'To the manner born. He's got it in his blood. His father and grandfather were both in the Church. Drusilla, you could do far worse . . . and you couldn't do better. He's a man I'd trust with you.'

'A lot of people seem to think it would be convenient if I married Colin Brady.'

'The rectory would always be your home.'

'Yes. But does one marry for a home? Did you?'

He was smiling, his mind drifting back to the days when my mother was alive.

'You could do far worse,' he murmured.

They were all concerned for my future and the answer seemed obvious to them . . . even to my father.

One day when I was in the paddock Ayesha came to me. I was startled to see her. She smiled at me and said: 'You come here often.'

'It's so quiet and peaceful.'

'Quiet . . . peaceful,' she repeated. 'My mistress sees you. She looks for you.'

'Yes, I have seen her.'

'She wishes to speak to you.'

'To me?'

She nodded. 'She has never forgotten you.'

'Oh . . . you mean . . . that time I took the fan.'

'Poor soul. She lives much in the past. She is ill, I fear . . . very ill. She talks of joining Gerald . . . He was her lover. It is wonderful to see with what joy she contemplates the reunion. Shall we go? You see, she watches us from the window. Very much she wishes to speak with you.'

I followed Ayesha into the house and up the great staircase, hoping that we should not meet Lady Harriet on the way.

Through the long passages we went and came to the door

of that room in which I had found the peacock feather fan. It was still in its place.

Miss Lucille was standing by the window. She was in a dressing-gown, her feet in slippers.

'I have her here for you,' said Ayesha.

'Welcome, my dear,' said Miss Lucille. 'How happy I am to see you here. It is a long time since we met face to face. But I have seen you.' She waved her hand vaguely in the direction of the window. 'Come and talk with me.'

'Sit down here,' said Ayesha, settling Miss Lucille in her chair and drawing up another for me.

'Tell me, my dear,' said Miss Lucille. 'Life has not been good . . .?'

I hesitated. I was not sure. Had it been good? In parts, perhaps.

'Much has happened that is not good?' she persisted.

I nodded slowly. All that trouble with Lavinia . . . the ordeal with the police . . . the sadness of Janine . . . the tragedy of Miriam . . . the disappointment with Dougal . . . the encounters with Fabian.

'You should never have had it in your possession,' she went on. 'There is the toll . . .'

I realized she was talking about the peacock fan.

'Do you ever think of it?' she asked. 'The beauty of those feathers. Do you remember the jewels . . . the good and the evil . . .? So beautiful . . . but beauty can be evil.'

Ayesha was standing by the chair, watching her mistress closely. She was frowning a little and I believed that meant she was anxious.

Miss Lucille half-closed her eyes and began to tell me the story of her lover as she had told me once before and as she spoke the tears began to run down her cheeks.

'It was the fan . . . If only we had not gone into the bazaar that day. If only he had not bought it for me . . . if only he had not taken it to the jeweller . . . how different everything would have been! And you, my child, you should never have let it cast its spell on you.'

615

'I don't think it cast a spell on me. I only borrowed it for a little while.'

'It did. I know. I felt the weight lifted from me.'

She closed her eyes and seemed to fall asleep.

I looked questioningly at Ayesha, who lifted her shoulders. 'That is how she is,' she whispered. 'She wanted so much to see you and when you come she forgets what she wanted to say to you. She is content now. She has seen you. She talks of you now and then. She is concerned for you. She makes me tell her about your life at the rectory. She is concerned because your father is so ill.'

'I wonder she remembers me.'

'It is because she likes you and because of the fan. She is obsessed by the fan.'

'Why does she attach such importance to it?'

'She sees it as the source of trouble.'

'I am surprised she does not get rid of it.'

She shook her head. 'No. She believes she cannot do that. It would not get rid of the curse, she says. That goes on forever.'

'But if she believes . . .'

'It's an old superstition and because of what happened after she had it . . . it was because of it, she believes, that she lost her lover. It has taken possession of her.'

'It is very sad. I think I should go now. Lady Harriet would not be pleased to find me here.'

'Lady Harriet has gone to London. She is very happy. Her son is coming home . . . for a brief visit. There is some business to which he must attend. It is to be a short stay but she is delighted that she will see him . . . if only for a little while.'

I felt my heart leap and I was alive again. A brief visit! I wondered if I should see him.

'There will be much entertaining. There will be some grand people here. Invitations go out. It is not good for Miss Lucille. She is always restive when there are people in the house.'

I was wondering if his stay in India had changed him.

'I think I should go now,' I said.

Ayesha glanced at Miss Lucille. 'Yes,' she said. 'It is a deep sleep now. She sleeps most of the time.'

'I have to read to my father. He will be expecting me.'

'Yes,' she said. 'Come. I will take you out.'

She led me out through the hall and I went quickly home. I had almost forgotten the visit and the strangeness of Miss Lucille . . . because Fabian was coming home.

That night my father took a turn for the worse. Since he had had his stroke he had been slightly paralysed and unable to speak clearly. The doctor told us it could not be many weeks before the end.

I was with him most of the time and I could see death coming closer and closer.

Polly wrote. If anything happened I should come to her immediately. We'd talk. There would be a lot to say. I wasn't to rush into anything. Polly was the only one who seemed to think that marriage with Colin Brady was not the most desirable thing that could happen to me.

Fabian arrived at Framling the day my father died. I heard from Mrs Janson that he was home. I was with my father at the end. He held my hand and I could see that he was at peace.

Colin Brady was very good. He took charge with sympathy and efficiency and if he thought he was a step nearer to his goal he did not show it.

Lady Harriet was displeased that the rector should die just as she was preparing for her son's return. Immersed as she was in parish affairs, the event was to say the least inconvenient. I imagined her mentioning the fact somewhat reproachfully in her prayers. There should have been a little more consideration from On High towards one who had always unflinchingly done her duty.

I heard from Mrs Janson that she had been planning important festivities ever since she had heard that her son

617

was coming home. Lady Geraldine Fitzbrock, with her parents, was coming to stay at Framling and it was an important visit. The Fitzbrocks were of lineage as impeccable as Lady Harriet herself and it was quite clear that she had settled on Geraldine Fitzbrock for Sir Fabian.

I wondered about him now and then, but mostly my thoughts were preoccupied with the past. There was so much in the house to remind me of my father. It seemed oddly quiet and alien almost, now that he was lying in his coffin behind the drawn blinds of the sitting-room. Everywhere there was something to bring back memories ... his study with the book-lined walls; those books with the bookmarks in his favourite places. I kept thinking of him hunting for his spectacles when he wanted to remind himself of a particularly beloved passage ... living in another age, halfheartedly trying to tear himself away from it and come back to the affairs of his parish.

I should have been prepared. I could see his furrowed brow when he contemplated me. He had been deeply concerned about my future – as I supposed I should be. In his unworldly heart he had believed I would marry Dougal. How he would have welcomed him as his son-in-law, visualizing long visits when they would delve into the past together. Dougal had been a young man not greatly endowed with worldly goods at that time – a scholar, a man of great gentleness, lacking ambition, a man made in my father's own mould.

Looking back, I realized how disappointed he must have been when it had not turned out as he wished. Not only had he been deprived of a son-in-law whom he would have welcomed, but there was the problem of his daughter's future which had become an anxiety. Then he had hoped I would marry Colin Brady. That would have been a very sensible conclusion. Colin Brady, true, would have been second best but very acceptable all the same.

People were thinking that I should take what I could get. Opportunity came rarely in life and when it did must not be lightly turned aside. Lady Harriet had implied that I was foolish. I dare say I was. It was not that I disliked Colin Brady. No one could, really. He was so kind and considerate to all. He would be the perfect priest. But somehow at the back of my mind was the feeling that if I did 'the sensible thing' I would regret it, for I would be choosing a way of life which would be so predictable that it would rob me of all the excitement which made up the savour of living.

If I had never known Dougal . . . if I had been a more conventional person . . . perhaps I should have married Colin. But I was myself; and instinctively I rebelled against the suggestion of marriage in such circumstances.

Fabian came over to the rectory to see me. He looked really concerned. 'I am so sorry,' he said.

'Thank you. It was not unexpected.'

'No. But a shock nevertheless.'

'It was good of you to call.'

'But of course I called.'

'I hope your stay in India was successful.'

He lifted his shoulders.

'And shall you be here long?' I went on.

'No. Briefly. Very briefly.'

'I see.'

'And you will be making . . . plans?'

'I shall have to.'

'I am sure you will. If there is anything we can do up at Framling . . .'

'Nothing, thank you. Mr Brady is a great help.'

'I was sure he would be. I hear the funeral is tomorrow. I shall be there.'

'Thank you.'

He smiled at me and soon after left.

I was glad when he went. I did not want him to see how emotional I was. I almost wished that he had not come to see me.

The church was full when my father was buried.

Lady Harriet with Sir Fabian were in the Framling pew.

I could think of nothing but my father, and I kept going over all the little things I remembered of him. A feeling of desolation swept over me. I had never felt so lonely in my life.

Colin Brady was brisk and businesslike. He conducted the mourners back to the rectory and we drank mulled wine and ate sandwiches prepared by Mrs Janson. An air of solemnity enveloped the house.

It was no longer my home. It could be, of course, if I married Colin. I had to think very seriously what I should do.

The will was read. There was little to leave but what there was was mine. The solicitor told me that it would provide me with a minute income — not enough to live on in any degree of comfort, but something to fall back on if need be. He added that he expected I should have already considered the situation which must be no surprise to me.

I said I was considering.

I was aware of the expectancy around me. Mrs Janson looked prophetic. I was sure she thought I was going to marry Colin Brady and the household would go on in the way it always had. They knew my ways; they were fond of me; they did not want a stranger in the house.

It seemed inevitable to them, for it was clear that Mr Brady was willing and where would I find a more suitable husband? It was high time I settled down and there was the right place just waiting for me.

Colin talked to me on the night of the funeral. I was sitting by the window staring out on the graveyard and an infinite sadness had taken possession of me. I had come to the end of a path and I did not know which way to go. And there was the easy road to take and everyone was pushing me towards it.

'What a sad day,' he said. 'I know what your father was to you. I was fond of him. He was a wonderfully good man.'

I nodded.

'After all these years you have been together, except of course when you were at school.'

Ah, there was the point. What had happened then had changed me. If I had stayed all my years in the rectory would I have felt differently? It seemed that I had briefly stepped into a world where people did wild things and paid for them; but it had made me see that there was more to life than being comfortable and living one day after another, quietly, unadventurously, almost like waiting for death.

'It's a great blow to you,' he was saying. 'Drusilla, won't you let me share it with you?'

'You are doing that,' I told him. 'You have taken on everything and done it perfectly.'

'I would be only too happy to care for you from now on.'

I wanted to say that I did not particularly want to be taken care of. I felt capable of looking after myself. I wanted life to be adventurous, exciting . . . I was not looking for comfort, pleasant as it might be.

'There could be an early wedding. Lady Harriet has said that would be best.'

'I do not allow Lady Harriet to run my life, Colin.'

He laughed at me. 'Of course not. But she is important, you know. Her word carries weight.' He looked a little anxious. 'She is worried about you. We are all worried about you.'

'You must not be. You must leave me to plan for myself.'

'But you have had a great shock. I don't think you fully realize that. I want you to know you just have to say the word. I won't hurry you. This is your home. It should always be your home.'

'Oh, rectories are like tied cottages. They go with the job.'

'Yes, that is so.' He looked so earnest. I had learned that he was a man who hated indecision; and I knew I could never marry him and that it was only fair to tell him so.

'Colin,' I said, 'I have to tell you that I shall never marry you.'

He looked taken aback.

'I am sorry,' I went on. 'I am fond of you . . . but differently.'

'Drusilla, have you thought . . .? Just contemplate. Where will you go?'

I said on the spur of the moment: 'I shall go to stay with Polly for a while. I shall discuss my future with her. She knows me well. She will advise me.'

'I am thinking of what is best for you and what will make a happy solution. It is clear, Drusilla, you must marry me.'

'I cannot do it, Colin. You are good and kind and have done a great deal for my father and me. But I cannot marry you.'

'Later perhaps . . .'

'No, Colin. Please forget it.'

He looked abashed and I added: 'I am most sincerely grateful to you for everything and for asking me.'

'You are distraught just now.'

'No,' I said almost angrily, for it seemed he was saying I must be foolish to refuse him. But somehow I managed to convey to him that I meant what I said.

I said: 'I want to retire now. It has been a stressful day.'

He said he would send one of the maids up with hot milk for me to drink. I tried to protest but he waved that aside; and later the milk was brought to my room.

I sat by the window looking out. In the distance I could see the lights of Framling. I felt lonely and lost. There would be revelry there. The Lady Geraldine and Fabian would dance together, ride together, talk . . . not today, of course, out of respect for my father, but later. It was Lady Harriet's wish that he should marry her. I wondered if he would. He would be the first to agree that it was suitable.

I told myself angrily that he was the sort of man who would marry *suitably* and indulge his fancies somewhere else . . . with lesser mortals who would be good enough for a light divertissement but not for marriage.

I said to myself: I will go to Polly.

The next day I saw Fabian ride by with a young woman whom I presumed was Lady Geraldine. She was tall and handsome. She had rather a loud voice and they were chatting animatedly together. I heard Fabian laugh.

I went into the house and put some things together into a bag. I did not know how long I should stay but I must make up my mind what I was going to do before I returned.

With Polly I found the comfort I was so sorely in need of.

Fleur was now five years old. She was a sensible child and full of high spirits. 'Up to a trick or two,' was Eff's fond comment and Polly added that she was as sharp as 'a wagonload of monkeys'.

She welcomed me. Both Polly and Eff always referred to me in near reverent terms when they spoke of me to her and it had its effect. I spent a lot of time with her. I found some books in a second-hand shop . . . books which I had had as a child . . . and I started to teach her; she was an apt pupil.

I began to think I could make a happy life for myself with Polly and Eff. I had my little income which would suffice. I could teach Fleur and we could all be happy together.

Polly was worried about me.

'What will you be doing?' she asked.

'I have time to make up my mind, Polly,' I replied. 'I don't have to rush into anything.'

'No. That's a mercy.'

'I'd like to stay here for a while. I love being with Fleur. It takes my mind off things.'

'Well, for a bit, but it's no life for a young lady as has been educated like you have. Where are you going to meet anyone here?'

'Your mind runs on familiar lines. Are you thinking of getting me married?'

'Well, it's a lottery, they say, but there is a chance of the right number coming up . . . and if it does, well, there's nothing like it.'

'I'm sure you're right, Polly.'

'It's a pity about that Colin.'

'I couldn't marry him just because it provided the good solution.'

'Nobody's asking you to.'

'Oh yes, they are. Lady Harriet for one and Colin Brady for another.'

'Oh, *them* . . .'

'I know you're different, Polly, but good solution though it might be, I couldn't do it.'

'Then let's go on from there. You're not still thinking of that Dougal. A nice one he'd be . . . leading a girl up the garden path and then liking the flowers in the garden next door.'

'Oh, Polly,' I laughed, 'it wasn't quite like that.'

'How else, I'd like to know. There he was coming to see you and the rector and that Lavinia comes along and gives him the glad eye . . . and it's whoops and away.'

I couldn't help laughing, which showed how little I minded that it had happened that way.

'He'll rue the day he ever came into his fortune.'

'Perhaps not, Polly. She's very beautiful and let's face it . . . I'm not.'

'You're as God intended you to be.'

'Aren't we all?'

'And you're as good-looking as any. There's some men as can't resist that Come Hither look and they are the ones to avoid, so thank your lucky stars you fell out of that one. I wouldn't touch that Dougal with a barge pole even if he come crawling back on his hands and knees.'

'A spectacle, I assure you, we are unlikely to see.'

'He'll soon be seeing he's made a mighty mistake. He'll

be wishing he hadn't been so daft. You take my word for it.'

'I think Lavinia may have changed now she has a child.'

'Leopards don't change their spots, so I've always heard.'

'Lavinia is not a leopard.'

'She's as likely to change as one of them. Mark my words, he's regretting that hasty step. But it's you we've got to think of.'

'I'm happier here than I could be anywhere else, Polly.'

'For a while, yes . . . but something has to be done.'

'Let's wait, shall we? Let's wait and see.'

She nodded.

The days passed. Fleur brought a lot of pleasure. We played games together. Then when she was in bed asleep I would sit with Polly and Eff and listen to their racy talk about the tenants.

'We do see life,' said Eff with a chortle.

Polly agreed, but I could see she thought it was not the life I should be leading.

Then the letter came from Lady Harriet. Her family crest was on the envelope and Eff hoped the postman noticed it. She would bring Lady Harriet into the conversation next time she talked to Second Floor No. 32.

I stared at the letter for a few seconds before opening it, wondering what Lady Harriet would have to say to me.

My dear Drusilla [she had written],

I have been quite concerned about you. Poor Mr Brady is most distressed. I only hope you will not regret your hasty decision. The best thing you could have done was to marry him and continue in your rectory home. I am sure in time you will come to regret your stubborn attitude.

However, I have a proposal to make. Lavinia is very happy in India. She has little Louise, as you know, and I am delighted to tell you that she has just given birth to another — a little boy. Lavinia would like you to go

625

out and help her. I must say she has made me see that this could be quite a good thing. I am sending a nanny out to her. I do not care that my grandchildren should be brought up by foreigners. She has an ayah at the moment, but I want her to have a good English nanny. I have found the right person for the post and I am sending her out almost immediately. Lavinia has expressed a wish that you should go out to be a companion to her and I am of the opinion that this is an excellent idea. It would serve Lavinia's needs and your own. Lavinia wishes the children to be taught in an English manner and she believes that as well as being a companion for her you could instruct the children.

Lavinia and her husband, the Earl, expect to return to England in two years' time. I am sure you will decide that this will be an excellent opportunity for you. I shall expect an early decision. The nanny will be leaving at the beginning of next month and it would be most convenient if you travelled out together, so there are three weeks for your plans to be made. I shall appreciate an early reply.

I stopped reading the letter. I felt numb with surprise and a certain tingling excitement. To go to India! To be with Lavinia and the children. I should see Dougal and Fabian.

Polly came and saw me staring into space.

'News?' she enquired.

'Polly . . .' I cried. 'It's amazing.'

'Well?'

'This is from Lady Harriet.'

'Interfering again?'

'You could say that . . . but in a rather exciting way. Polly, she is suggesting I go to India.'

'What?'

'I should be a sort of governess to Lavinia's children and a companion to her.'

Polly stared at me in amazement.

'That Lavinia,' she said.

I read the letter to her. I could hear the thrill of excitement in my voice as I did so. It seemed to me that the Framlings had always been a great influence in my life.

Polly said: 'When do you have to say?'

'Soon. I should leave in less than a month.'

'H'm,' said Polly.

We talked it over for hours but I think I had long before made up my mind that I should go. Polly came round to the idea very soon.

'It knocked me off my feet at first. India. It's such a long way. But perhaps it would be for the best. It's no life for you here . . . much as we like to have you. A girl of your education . . . she shouldn't be stuck here. Fleur . . .? We'd been thinking of getting a governess for young Fleur. We want her to be educated, you know. And we can use the money *he* put by for her. I don't see why we shouldn't. After all, he's her uncle. We wouldn't take anything for ourselves, but Fleur's different. She's got to have the best.'

Eff agreed with Polly. It was no place for me here. Eff reckoned it was a bit risky going off to foreign places but Lavinia had gone and she seemed to have survived.

I was going to write to Lady Harriet but as there was such a little time I thought it simpler to return. I had my room in the rectory still and many of my possessions were there, so it was the best place from which to make my arrangements.

Two days after receiving the letter I was on my way back.

I went straight to the rectory. Mrs Janson had news to impart. Framling was in mourning.

'It's that Miss Lucille. She had a few funny turns and this last one was too much for her. It finished her off. I always say one funeral begets another.' She often became biblical in her role as seer. 'First the dear rector and then Miss Lucille. Well, it seems this was a happy release for her. We

627

were hoping for a wedding, but I suppose that would be rushing things a bit.'

'A wedding?'

'Lady Harriet was all for Fabian marrying Lady Geraldine, but he had to go back to India . . . or somewhere. He had to cut his stay a bit shorter than he thought. I'll tell you what.' She was the seer once more. 'I reckon there's some understanding. She'll be going out there to him and they'll be joined in holy wedlock, you see.'

'Is that so?' I said. 'I want to see Lady Harriet immediately. She wrote to me suggesting that I should go to Miss Lavinia in India.'

'My goodness gracious me! Indeed . . . indeed! I don't know . . . but I reckon if the Framlings are there . . .'

'I think I should go now. I do need to let her know.'

Lady Harriet received me at once.

'My dear Drusilla, I was expecting you.'

'It seemed quicker to come than to write.'

'And your decision?'

'I want to go, Lady Harriet.'

A smile of satisfaction spread across her face.

'Ah. I thought you'd be sensible . . . this time. There will be so many arrangements to be made. Alas, we are now a house of mourning.'

'I am so sorry. I heard about Miss Lucille.'

'Poor dear creature. It was really a happy release. We shall be concerned with the funeral, but in the meantime we will set our plan in motion. I shall write immediately to Lavinia. I know she will be delighted, and I am sure you will be able to teach Louise. It is a relief to me to *know* who will be in charge of her. Alice Philwright will be coming here for a few days and it would be a good idea for you to get to know her as you will be travelling together. I think you will be safe with her. She has travelled before and has been looking after children in France. You will go by ship to Alexandria and there travel across country to another ship . . . at Suez, I think. But there will be more details later. In the meantime you will have certain things to prepare . . . your personal things at the rectory and so on. I don't know quite what arrangements you will make . . . but I will leave that to you.'

She went on talking, obviously pleased that at last I had fallen in with her decisions and seen the wisdom of following the plans she had made for me. There was little she liked better than arranging the lives of others.

I made my way back to the rectory. Colin was very kind. He was quite pleased with life. He had stepped into my father's shoes and was generally accepted throughout the neighbourhood. My father had been loved more for his foibles than his efficiency. Colin exuded goodwill and bon-homie; he mingled jollity with seriousness, which was very becoming to a man of the cloth. He was ideal for the job.

Moreover, he was already displaying interest in the doc-tor's daughter Ellen. She was a few years older than he was but had all the qualifications a parson's wife should have, plus the approval of Lady Harriet. What could be more suitable when Colin's only lack to make him an ideal rector was a wife? He was obviously on the way to acquiring one.

He bore me no rancour for refusing his offer. He told me that there was plenty of room in the attics for me to store anything I wished and after my stay in India I could decide what I wanted to do with it. He would pay me a good price for the furniture in the house which he was now taking over and that would save him the trouble of getting his own furniture and at the same time be a help to me.

This all seemed very reasonable and I was grateful to Colin for being so helpful in a practical way. I had to rid myself of all sentimental feeling about my old home and accept the fact that this was the best way.

My excitement grew and as the days passed I realized this was exactly what I needed. I wanted to get right away. My life had come to a dead end. I should experience new scenes, new people.

There was a great deal in the papers at this time about

war with Russia. It had been coming to a boiling point for some time and now we were definitely at war.

Despatches were being sent home about the terrible conditions in the Crimea and a Miss Florence Nightingale had gone out there with a party of nurses. I had read about it, and when I was with Polly I had seen soldiers marching through London on the way to the wharf for embarkation. People cheered them and sang patriotic songs, but I am afraid I was so immersed in the dramatic change in my own fortunes that I paid less attention than I would otherwise have done.

I went to the church when Miss Lucille was buried. Colin took the service and I hovered in the background. I was aware that Lady Harriet might think it presumptuous of me to assume the status of a friend.

While the coffin was lowered in the grave I caught a glimpse of Ayesha who looked very sad and lost. I went over to speak to her.

She smiled at me and said: 'She would be glad you came. She often talked of you.'

'I felt I had to come,' I said. 'Although I saw very little of her I never forgot her.'

'No. And now she is gone. She was glad to go. She believed she would join her lover. I hope she will. I hope she will find happiness again.'

The mourners were dispersing and I went slowly back to the rectory.

The next day one of the Framling servants came over to the rectory. Lady Harriet wished to see me at once.

I went over immediately.

'This is rather unexpected,' Lady Harriet said. 'Miss Lucille has left something to you.'

'To me!'

'Yes. Ayesha tells me that you interested her when you came to play with Lavinia.'

'I did see her once or twice since then.'

'Well, she has requested that one of her possessions should be passed on to you. I have told them to bring it here.'

Just at that moment one of the servants came in. She was carrying a case which she laid on the table.

'This is the object,' said Lady Harriet. 'There were instructions in her will that it should go to you.'

I took the case.

'Open it,' said Lady Harriet.

I did so. The sight of the peacock feathers was not really a surprise to me. I knew before I opened it that this would be her bequest to me. I touched the beautiful blue feathers and as I did so I felt a faint shudder of revulsion.

I could not resist taking out the fan and unfurling it. I touched the little spring in the mount and disclosed the emerald and diamonds I had seen before.

Lady Harriet was beaming at me.

'Worth, I have heard, a small fortune,' she said. 'Well, you may regard it as your nest-egg.'

'Thank you, Lady Harriet,' I said.

She inclined her head. 'Miss Lucille was a somewhat eccentric lady. A tragedy in her youth affected her deeply. I can comfort myself by the thought that I always had her well looked after to the best of my ability.'

So I came back to the rectory carrying the peacock feather fan.

Ayesha came to see me.

She was very sad. She had spent a great many years looking after Miss Lucille. We walked in the rectory garden, for she did not wish to come into the house.

I asked her what she would do now.

She told me she would decide later. Miss Lucille had left her well provided for, so money was not a problem. She might return to India. She was not sure. Although she had been expecting Miss Lucille's death it was still a shock to her. She had permission to stay at Framling until she had decided what she would do.

She talked about Miss Lucille – her kindness and gentleness and her terrible grief.

'She always said you must have the fan,' she said. 'She thought it the best way of disposing of it as you had already had it in your possession.'

'But she thought it brought ill luck.'

'She had listened to legends. She was told those stories after her lover died . . . and in her grief she accepted them. Perhaps it assuaged her grief to believe that it was to be. You see, she blamed herself. She had wanted the fan and he had bought it for her; she had been so attracted by it that he wanted to embellish it for her, and while he was actually dealing with this he met his death. It was the only way she could stop blaming herself, to blame the fan . . . which in her eyes represented fate.'

'I could never understand why she did not destroy it if she thought it brought evil.'

'It was because she thought it would bring more bad luck if she did so. It carried the curse; she had suffered; it would harm her no more. She believed too that you had suffered through your connection with it. There was gossip at the House. She heard some of it. She was interested and pleased when she thought you might marry Mr Carruthers who became the Earl. When he became engaged to Lavinia she was sure this was due to the curse of the fan. It had robbed her of her lover and now you. She said: "The curse worked on her, poor child. She has paid the price. She is young. She has many years to live. But she has paid the price . . . so she is now free from its evil."'

'It doesn't seem to be very logical reasoning.'

'Poor lady, she was never reasonable. Her tragedy changed her. It touched her mind.'

'It seems a strange legacy . . . to pass on evil.'

'She felt it was best. The fan would harm you no more. You had already paid the price. She felt it was best with you.' Ayesha touched my hand lightly. 'You are no dreamer. You have . . . what is it they say, two feet on the ground.

You will see that this is a nonsense. And in the fan is the jewel. It is there when you need it. We never know in this life what will happen to us. Who knows? One day you might be in need of money . . . desperately in need. Then you sell the jewel . . . and when the jewel is gone what is it but a few peacock's feathers. You will be wise, as my poor mistress never could be. Remember this. We make our own luck. If you believe in ill luck, it will surely come. Mistress Lucille, she was stricken and she made no attempt to cast off her grief. She nursed it; she nourished it. She told herself that it was the curse of the peacock's feathers . . . and what did she do? She preserved the fan; she liked to look at it. At times she asked me to bring it to her and she would unfurl it and gaze at it until the tears rolled down her cheeks. You have much sense. You will know that Miss Lavinia's marriage to the Earl was in no way connected with the fan.'

'Of course I do. But I was not deeply involved. I suffered from hurt pride, not a broken heart.'

'And who knows, it may be in a few years' time you will say: That was good for me, that is when you find great happiness. Believe this will be so, and it will come. You are going to India. It will seem very strange to you. I shall pray for you . . . that all good may come your way.'

After that she talked awhile of India, of the strange sights I should see. She told me of the religion, the conventions, the different castes and the old customs.

'The women, ah,' she said, 'they are the slaves of the men. You will know that the world over the man wants to dominate. It is so here in England . . . but in India doubly so. There was a time when widows burned themselves to death on their husband's funeral pyres. That was the custom of Suttee but it is so no longer. The Governor General Sir William Bentinck made it against the law. But the people do not like their customs changed . . . especially by foreigners.'

'It was good to abolish such a custom.'

'Yes . . . that and Thuggery . . . but there are those who

do not care what is good, only that their old laws are being interfered with.'

'It is bringing civilization to the land. Surely they want that?'

She looked at me and shook her head, her dark eyes mournful.

'They do not always want what is good. They want what is theirs. Ah, you have much to see and you will understand . . . Miss Lavinia will be glad to see you, I know.'

We talked on about my journey and India. I said we must meet again before I left.

I spent a busy time preparing. I was in close touch with Framling and constantly being sent for by Lady Harriet to be grounded in what I must do.

She had already written to Lavinia who would be getting ready to welcome me, and during one of our meetings she let drop the news that Lady Geraldine, she was sure, would soon be travelling out to India 'for a certain purpose', she added slyly; and I felt a little twinge of anger because everything worked out as Lady Harriet wished it to, and even Fabian seemed to consider it imperative to obey her.

We were to stay two nights in London and I should spend those with Polly and Eff. It was what I wanted, as I wished to say a proper farewell to them. Lady Harriet had thought it an excellent idea as we should have to go to London in any case.

About a week before we were due to leave Alice Philwright came to Framling. I was summoned to meet her.

She was a tall woman about thirty years of age, by no means beautiful but her face suggested character. She looked a little formidable and extremely efficient. Lady Harriet had interviewed her personally and was pleased with what she had discovered.

First we had tea with Lady Harriet during which the conversation was predictable, mainly given over to Lady

Harriet's views on the upbringing of children; but later when we were alone together we came to know each other, which was a pleasure for me and I hoped for Alice.

She told me that she was one of those women who did not care for interference in the nursery and if it had been Lady Harriet's children she was to care for she would have declined the post without hesitation. 'I will not be told what to do in my nursery,' she declared. 'And I decided that one would not be able to stir outside her ladyship's ideas, which I fear might be a little antiquated in any case.'

I laughed and assured her that it would be quite different with the Countess.

'You know her well, I suppose.'

'Very well. We were at school together.'

'Oh. So the friendship goes right back.'

'Oh yes . . . earlier than that. They used to send to the rectory for me to come and play with Lavinia.'

'Lavinia is our Countess?'

I nodded. 'She was rather a spoilt child, I'm afraid.'

'Spoilt! Under that martinet!'

'She thought her children were formed in the same divine mould as herself.'

'And this is my new mistress!'

'I am convinced that you will have a free hand in the nursery.'

'I believe there is a brother, too.'

'Oh yes, Sir Fabian. I doubt he will be aware of us.'

'He is going to be married, Lady Harriet tells me.'

'I had heard that. A lady of impeccable lineage will be going out to marry him.'

'That will be interesting.'

'Apparently there was not time to arrange the marriage when he was home, for he was called away on sudden business.'

'Connected with the East India Company, I gathered.'

'Yes, that is so.'

'I suppose we shall get there all right. This war might

make things a little difficult . . . transport and troopships going out to the Crimea and all that.'

'I hadn't thought of that.'

'Well, we shall wait and see.'

'Are you looking forward to going?' I asked.

'I always look forward to new children. I've had two families so far and it is a wrench when you leave them. One has to steel oneself not to become too emotionally involved with them, and remember all the time that they are not your children although you're inclined to think of them as such.'

'I have never lost touch with my nanny,' I told her. 'And I never shall. In fact she is the best friend I have.'

I talked about Polly often, and the house and Eff.

'She was lucky,' said Alice. 'She had somewhere to go. Nannies, governesses . . . they spend their lives with other families and never have one they can call their own.'

'Unless they marry.'

'Then they cease to be nannies and governesses. It's a strange thing. In my profession we understand children . . . we love children . . . we would make the best mothers . . . but we rarely marry. Men are notorious for turning away from the women who would make the best wives and falling in love with some flighty creature because she looks pretty in moonlight . . . and often they regret it later.'

'I see you take a cynical outlook on life.'

'That comes with increasing years. You wait.'

'Oh, you are not so very old.'

'Thirty-three. Considered to be most definitely on the shelf. Mind you, there is still a chance . . . a very slight one . . . that someone might see one and take to one. But very, very remote.'

She laughed as she made these pronouncements; and I felt we were going to get along very well together.

There was one more session with Lady Harriet. We were given letters for Lavinia which I was sure were full of admonitions. I went round the neighbourhood saying good-

636

bye to my friends; I took a last leave of Ayesha and then we left.

Polly and Eff were waiting to give us a good welcome.

Alice Philwright was to spend the two days in their house. They had said it would be an easy matter to put her up. I think Polly was secretly pleased to have the opportunity of assessing my companion. I was delighted that they seemed to like each other from the start. Alice was completely at home in the kitchen and even partook of a glass of poker-heated stout.

She talked of her children in France and Italy and confessed that she was finding it hard to imagine what an Anglo-Indian menage might be like.

Polly said: 'I'm glad you're going with her.' And afterwards to me: 'She's a good sensible woman, that one. I was afraid they were going to send you out with some young flighty piece.'

I reminded Polly that flighty pieces rarely worked as nannies.

'You find all sorts anywhere these days,' was her comment.

I had brought the peacock feather fan with me. I showed it to Polly.

'It was left to me by Miss Lucille.'

'H'm,' said Polly. 'Pretty.'

She opened her eyes and gasped when I showed her the jewels.

'That must be worth a pretty penny.'

'I believe so, Polly. Lady Harriet referred to it as a nest-egg.'

'Well, that's nice to have, I must say.'

'I want you to keep it for me. I didn't know where else to leave it.'

'I'll take care of it. I'll put it in a safe place, never fear.'

I hestitated. I did not tell her that it was supposed to be unlucky. I knew she would have laughed at the idea in any case; and I think secretly I wanted to forget it.

She said: 'I wish I was going with you. Take care of yourself. And look out for that Fabian. I expect you might run into him while you're there.'

'I don't suppose I shall see much of him. He'll be engaged on business matters.'

'He's the sort who'd bring himself forward and I wouldn't touch him with a barge pole.'

'I believe you've said that before.'

'Well, I'll say it again. And remember this. We're always here. If they try any hanky-panky . . . either of them . . . I never did trust anyone by the name of Framling . . . you just let me know . . . and I'll be waiting for you when the ship comes home.'

'That's a comfort, Polly.'

'Remember it. There's always a home for you here.'

'I will remember it,' I said. 'Goodbye, Polly, and thank you for coming to the rectory and being there all those years.'

'Well, we was made for each other, wasn't we? Now take care and come back soon.'

'Two years, Polly. It's not long.'

'I'll count the days.'

And shortly after that we sailed on the *Oriental Queen* for Alexandria.

Alice and I stood side by side on the deck until the last piece of land which was England was out of sight. Then we went down to the cabin we shared.

It was small and cramped, but, as we realized later, we were lucky to have it to ourselves. But I was too excited to think about such details then. We were on our way to . . . adventure.

I had had very little experience of travelling. True, I had crossed the Channel once or twice on my way to and from Lamason. I was immediately reminded of that secretive journey back to England with Janine and a pregnant Lavinia.

That set me thinking of Lavinia and wondering whether marriage had changed her and what surprises I had waiting for me at my destination. But that seemed a long way off. There was so much to be experienced first.

Within less than an hour of our departure the sea became very rough and continued so all through the Channel and into the Bay of Biscay. We had to curb our inclination to explore for a while, for it was difficult enough to stand upright on the ship.

When we did mingle with our fellow passengers we found them pleasant enough; many of them knew each other as they had made the journey several times on the ship; that rather set us apart and it was quite unusual that two women should be travelling alone, for Alice, although of a more mature age than I, was still comparatively young. I was sure Lady Harriet would not have approved if it had not fitted in so well with her plans to send us out.

However, there we were and in a few days we did learn a little about the people on board.

There were two girls – of different families – going out to get married. It was a fairly frequent happening, I understood. There was Fiona Macrae, a Scottish girl who was going to marry a soldier, and Jane Egmont whose husband would be one of the officials of what was referred to as The Company.

I kept thinking of Lady Geraldine who would be coming out on some future voyage to join Fabian. I fell to wondering whether I should see him and what his attitude towards me would be. I wondered whether he would approve of my coming out to be with his sister.

Alice and I were naturally very much together and I learned a little about her. Once she had been engaged to be married. She had not then decided that she would become a nanny. She had lived with her married sister and brother-in-law in Hastings. She had not been very happy; not that her family had not been kind to her; but she had felt an intruder. And then she had met Philip. Philip was an artist.

He had come down to Hastings for his health. He had a weak chest and the sea air was said to be good for him.

She met him when he was seated on the shore painting a rough sea. Some of his equipment had blown away and landed right at her feet; she had rescued it and returned it to him.

'There was this howling wind, I remember,' she said. 'It tore at you. I thought he was crazy to be working in such weather. They were sketches he was making. He was pleased that I'd caught them and we talked and got on well. Then we used to meet every day.' Her eyes grew tender and she was like a different woman, soft, gentle and feminine. 'We were to have been married. He told me that he was not strong. He had consumption. I planned to nurse him. I was sure I could bring him back to health. He died . . . a month before we were to have been married. Ah well, that's life. Then I decided I wanted to look after people . . . little ones . . . and I became a nanny. It didn't seem as if I were going to get any children of my own so I had to make do with other people's.'

We did share confidences very quickly. I told her about Colin's proposal and Lady Harriet's conviction that it was the best solution for me and that I was stubborn and foolish not to take it.

She grimaced. 'You have to be careful of the Lady Harriets of this world. They are all manipulators. I'd never be manipulated. Good for you that you weren't either.'

'I never shall be.'

'You were right to refuse him. Marriage lasts a long time and it's got to be the right one. Perhaps you meet that one . . . once in a lifetime. Perhaps he doesn't even notice you. But if he's the one, no one else will do.'

I did not tell her about Dougal who had failed me before I had time to fall in love, nor did I mention Fabian whom I never seemed to be able to get out of my thoughts.

Our first stop was Gibraltar.

It was wonderful to be on dry land. A certain Mr and Mrs Carling invited us to go ashore with them. I think they were sorry for two women travelling alone.

We had a very pleasant day inspecting the Rock and the monkeys and it was exciting to be in a foreign place; but the British flag flew over it so we still felt we were part of home.

Sailing along the Mediterranean was peaceful. We sat on deck basking in a mild sunshine. It was on one of those occasions that we made the acquaintance of Monsieur Lasseur.

I had noticed him once or twice about the ship. He was of medium height, verging on middle age, with black hair and dark eyes which seemed to dart everywhere as though he were afraid of missing something.

He had always given me a pleasant smile and bow with a cheerful good-morning or whatever time of the day it was. I gathered that he was French.

As we were coming into port at Naples and I was leaning over the rail watching our approach – I was alone; I was not quite sure where Alice was – I was aware of him standing beside me.

'An exciting moment, is it not, Mademoiselle, coming into port?'

'Yes, indeed it is,' I answered. 'I suppose one feels the excitement because it is all so new.'

'I feel it . . . and it is not new to me.'

'Do you travel this way frequently?'

'Now and then . . . yes.'

'You are going to India?'

'No. I go as far as Suez.'

'I believe we have to travel across the land from Alexandria.'

'That is so. A little . . . lacking in comfort. How will you like that?'

'Everything is so new and exciting to me that I don't think I shall notice the discomfort.'

'You are very philosophical, I see. And the . . . older lady . . . your sister, perhaps?'

'Oh no.'

'Not so? Then . . .'

'We are travelling together. We are both taking up posts in India.'

'That is interesting. May I ask . . .? But I am curious. It is just that on board . . . well, the conventions do not apply in the same way. We are here together . . . we are one family . . . So I can be like the uncle . . . the elder brother *peut-être*.'

'That is a pleasant suggestion.'

'You have not made many friends yet.'

'So many people seem to know each other already and married couples drift together. I suppose it is unusual to find two women like us travelling alone.'

'Refreshing, shall we say? Refreshing. Now I am going to ask you: are you going ashore at Naples?'

'Well, I am not sure . . . You see . . .'

'I know. Two ladies alone. Now I am going to be very bold.'

I raised my eyebrows.

'I am going to say this. Why do I not conduct you two ladies ashore? Two ladies to go ashore by themselves . . .' He lifted his hands and gravely shook his head. 'No . . . no . . . that is not good. These people, they say, "Here come two ladies . . . we will charge them more." And perhaps there are other bad things they practise. No, no, ladies should not go ashore without protection. My dear young lady, I offer you that protection.'

'That is good of you. I will speak to my friend.'

'I shall be at your service,' he replied.

At that moment I saw Alice. I called: 'Alice, Monsieur Lasseur is kindly offering to escort us ashore.'

Alice's eyes widened with pleasure. 'What an excellent idea! I was wondering what we were going to do.'

'Mademoiselle, the pleasure is mine.' He looked at his

watch. 'Let us meet say . . . in fifteen minutes. I think we shall be allowed to leave the ship then.'

So that day in Naples was spent in the company of the gallant Frenchman. He talked to us a great deal. He was a widower and childless. He had interests in Egypt and would stay in Suez for some time on business.

He contrived to find out a certain amount about us. He had an intent way of listening which made us feel that what we had to say was of the utmost interest to him.

There was about him an air of authority. He shepherded us through the hordes of chattering people, among whom were countless small boys begging or trying to sell us articles. He waved them all aside.

'No, Miss Delany,' he said, 'I see you are feeling sorry for these piteous waifs, but believe me they are professional beggars. I have heard that they do very well from gullible visitors.'

'There is always a possibility that they may be as poor as they look.'

He shook a finger at me. 'Trust me,' he said. 'If you gave to one you would have them all round you like vultures and you may be sure that while you were concerned with your almsgiving some little fingers would find their way into your pockets.'

He hired a little carriage drawn by two small horses and we were driven through the town. Monsieur Lasseur obviously knew the place well; and as we drove under the shadow of the great mountain Vesuvius, he talked interestingly of its menace. We said we wondered why people continued to live so close to it.

'Ah,' he replied, 'they were born here. Where one's native land is . . . that is where one wants to be . . . except adventurous young ladies who would go to the other ends of the earth.'

'It is because their work takes them there,' pointed out Alice.

'To India . . . land of strange spices and unsolved mysteries.'

643

Then he talked about Vesuvius and the great eruption which had destroyed cities like Pompeii and Herculaneum. He was interesting.

He took us to a restaurant and we sat outside under gaily coloured umbrellas and watched the people passing by. He made us talk and I found myself telling him about the rectory and Lady Harriet and how I had been to my finishing school in France. Alice said little about herself and it suddenly occurred to me that he did not prompt her to do so, although he listened avidly to what I told him.

I thought perhaps I was talking too much and made up my mind to ask Alice when we were alone if this had been so.

Finally it was time to return to the *Oriental Queen*. It had been a most enjoyable day.

I said to Alice when we were alone: 'Do you think I talked too much?'

'He certainly encouraged you to.'

'I noticed you said little about yourself.'

'I thought he did not want to hear. It was you in whom he was interested.'

'I wonder . . . if he really is, or whether he was just being polite.'

'Oh, there is no doubt that he was very interested in what you said, and yet . . .'

'And yet what?'

'Oh . . . just a thought. I am not sure that I trust him.'

'In what way?'

'He seems a little speculative . . .'

'I did not get the idea that he was the least bit . . . flirtatious.'

'No. That is what makes it rather odd.'

'Oh Alice, you are being dramatic. I think he is just a lonely man who wants companionship. He travels a great deal. He probably becomes friendly with people for a few weeks and then forgets all about them.'

'H'm,' said Alice, but she was rather thoughtful.

*

In due course we arrived at Alexandria, where we left the *Oriental Queen*, boarded a steam barge and sailed up the canal to Cairo.

Monsieur Lasseur had explained to us what would happen. We should spend one night in a hotel – preferably Shepheard's – and from Cairo we should make our journey across the desert to Suez in a sort of covered wagon. These wagons were in constant use carrying people to where they could embark on the next stage of the journey by sea.

It was very exciting to be on dry land after so much time at sea and we were impressed by the grandeur of the hotel which was unlike any we had seen. It appeared to be dark and shadowy and silent-footed men in exotic robes glided about watching us intently with their darting dark eyes.

Monsieur Lasseur told us that there was a constant stream of travellers – mostly going to and from India.

From the moment we entered the hotel, I noticed the man. He was in European dress, and was tall and broad which made him immediately noticeable. When we came into the hotel after leaving the carriage which had brought us there in the company of the other passengers who were taking the route to India, he seemed to be aware of us. He rose from the chair in which he had been sitting and came close to the desk where we were being asked our names and were designated our sleeping quarters.

'Miss Philwright and Miss Delany,' said the clerk at the desk. 'Your room is on the first floor. It is small but as you see we are very crowded. Here is your key.'

The tall man was very close to us then. I wondered what he was doing there as he was not one of our party. But Alice was pulling at my arm. 'Come on,' she said. 'It's only for one night. We shall be leaving early in the morning.'

Excited as I was, I slept well and I was awakened very early next morning by Alice telling me it was time we got up.

The trip across the desert was to be made in those covered wagons which were very much as Monsieur Lasseur had described them. They were drawn by four horses and we were told that there were several caravanserais in the desert where we could rest while the horses were changed. Six people rode in each wagon.

Monsieur Lasseur said: 'Let us go together. I feel I must keep an eye on you two young ladies. I know from experience how uncomfortable these journeys can be. The drivers are very handy with their whips and their one aim seems to be to get the wagon to the caravanserai as quickly as possible. I am afraid you will find the journey somewhat exhausting.'

'As I have already told you, Monsieur Lasseur, it is all so new to us that we are ready to face a little discomfort,' I reminded him.

I shall never forget riding through Cairo in the early morning. The buildings looked mysterious in the half-light. We passed elegant mosques, one of the palaces of the Khedive, and latticed houses which would have delighted Dougal who would have seen the Saracen influence in their shadowy walls. Because it was so early the city had not sprung to life, which it would shortly do. I saw just a few donkeys led by small barefooted boys. There was a hush over the place; but the sun was about to rise and in the light of dawn Cairo looked like an enchanted city as though it belonged in the Arabian nights and I could well imagine a loquacious Scheherazade entertaining her Sultan behind the doors of some ancient palace.

There were six of us in the wagon; myself, Alice, Monsieur Lasseur, Mr and Mrs Carling and to my surprise the tall man whom I had noticed in the hotel.

I wondered if he was going to join the steamer which was taking us to India or whether his destination, like that of Monsieur Lasseur, was merely Suez.

Soon the desert closed round us. It was now light enough to see the miles of sand. It was golden in the dawn light. I was fascinated. Then the driver whipped up his horses and we had to concentrate on keeping our seats.

'I told you,' said Monsieur Lasseur, 'it was hardly a comfortable journey.'

We laughed as we were flung against each other. Mrs Carling said it was a mercy it could not last for long, and Mr Carling commented that when one undertook such a journey one must be prepared for discomforts. Monsieur Lasseur commented that there were certain things in life which were wonderful to anticipate and look back on, but less agreeable to experience, and travel often proved to be one of them.

The tall man smiled benignly on us. He seemed to divide his interest between Monsieur Lasseur and me and whenever I looked up I would find his eyes fixed gravely on one of us.

The horses rattled on.

'What happens if the wagon overturns?' I asked.

'Which,' added Mr Carling, 'it might well do if it goes on like this. I don't think our driver realizes what he is putting us through.'

'His idea is to get rid of one load, receive his money and then on to the next,' explained Monsieur Lasseur.

'But if there is an accident surely that would delay him,' I suggested.

'Oh, he is confident that Allah will look after him.'

'I wish I shared his confidence,' said Alice.

We were all relieved when the horses pulled up. Poor things, they must have been very weary . . . I knew we all felt considerably battered and we welcomed the short respite before the ordeal started again.

As we alighted I noticed the tall man stayed close to us.

The heat of the desert was intense, for it was round about noon. We had been going for some six hours and were glad of the shelter, although our resting place was like a hut, but the stables adjoining it were extensive.

Beverages were served and I was glad to see that there

647

was tea. There was food — bread and meat of some indefinable kind, which I declined.

We sat at tables — the six of us who had shared the wagon. I saw no one else from the ship's party and I presumed they would come later as ours had been one of the first wagons to leave Cairo.

'At least we have come safely through the initial stage of the journey,' said Alice.

The tall man replied: 'There is still more of the same to come.'

'I should not think it would be any worse,' went on Alice with a grimace.

The man lifted his shoulders.

'I have heard of frequent breakdowns on the way,' put in Monsieur Lasseur.

'How awful,' I said. 'What would happen then?'

'You wait until the message gets through and they come with another wagon.'

'What if we didn't get to Suez in time to catch the ship?'

'They would find some means of getting you there,' said the tall man.

'We don't know your name,' I told him. 'And it does seem as if we are to be fellow passengers on this hazardous journey.'

He smiled. He had very white teeth. 'It's Tom Keeping,' he said.

'So . . . you are English.'

'Did you not think so?'

'I wasn't sure.'

Monsieur Lasseur said: 'I will find out when we are leaving.'

He went to the table where a man who was obviously taking charge of the place was sitting.

Tom Keeping said: 'I am an interloper. Your party have all come out from England, is that so?'

'Yes, we all sailed together.'

'And Monsieur ... I forget his name ... the French gentleman.'

'Monsieur Lasseur. Yes, he was with us also.'

'And all good friends. People quickly become friends when they are travelling, I believe.'

'They are thrown very much together,' I explained.

'That must be so.'

Monsieur Lasseur came back.

'We are leaving in half an hour.'

'We had better brace ourselves,' said Alice.

The next part of the journey was as hazardous as the first. I noticed that there was a pathway across the desert. Presumably it had been made by the wagons and if the drivers had kept to this it would have been moderately comfortable, but the frisky horses, maddened no doubt by the frequent applications of the whip, kept straying into the sand which sent up clouds of it over the wagon.

Several times during the trip to the second caravanserai I thought we were going to be overturned, but by some magic we survived and after what seemed an interminable journey we reached the second of our resthouses.

As we were making our way into the caravanserai Monsieur Lasseur slipped his arm through mine and drew me slightly away from the others.

He said: 'That was a real shake-up. I feel quite bruised, don't you?'

I told him I did.

'I think,' he went on, 'I could get a better conveyance for us. Don't say a word. I couldn't take the others ... only you and Miss Philwright.'

As he was talking Tom Keeping came up close behind us.

I said: 'How could we leave the Carlings? They should be the ones to travel more comfortably.'

'Let me arrange this,' went on Monsieur Lasseur. 'I'll find a way.'

I felt a little uneasy. I wished that I could have asked

Alice for her opinion. It was not just the fact of the two of us going off with Monsieur Lasseur. We had travelled with him and knew him well. How could we explain to the Carlings who were less able to stand up to the journey than we were?

We sat down and refreshments were brought to us.

Tom Keeping said: 'I have a bottle of wine here which I brought with me. Would you care to join me?'

I declined, so did Alice and Mrs Carling. We preferred tea, although it was not very good. Mr Carling hesitated and finally said he, too, would take the tea.

That left Monsieur Lasseur and Tom Keeping. The latter went to the end of the room and procured a tray and two glasses, pouring the wine into them.

He brought it back to the table and offered one to Monsieur Lasseur.

'To a successful journey,' said Tom Keeping, lifting his glass. 'May we all arrive safe and sound at our destinations.'

We chatted for a while and then Monsieur Lasseur left us. He looked at me and he went rather conspiratorially. Mr and Mrs Carling were so tired that they were dozing off. There was a small room where we could wash and freshen up a little before we began the next phase of our journey. I signed to Alice to accompany me there.

I said to her when the door had closed: 'Monsieur Lasseur has plans. He thinks he can get a better carriage for us but he can't take us all.'

'Then he had better take the Carlings. They are elderly and we can stand up to it better than they can.'

'I mentioned that, but he wants to take us.'

'Why? We have endured the greater part of it?'

'He seems to be going to a lot of trouble.'

'It would be nice to travel in comfort, but it would be impossible to leave the Carlings. Mr Keeping will be all right but I really think Mrs Carling has had enough.'

'Yes, we'll insist that he takes them.'

'I don't think he'll be eager to do that. He wants to show *you* what a resourceful gentleman he is.'

'I think he wants to be more comfortable himself. He said he was going to the stables to arrange it all.'

'Well, let's see what happens.'

We washed and prepared ourselves for the resumption of the journey.

When we went back to the table Mr and Mrs Carling roused themselves and went off to the rest-room. There were two of them naturally, one for men and one for women.

It was some time before Mr Carling emerged with Tom Keeping and as soon as I saw them I knew that something was wrong. Tom Keeping came quickly to the table at which Alice and I were sitting.

'I am afraid something has happened to Monsieur Lasseur,' he said.

We half-rose. 'What is it?'

'Oh, don't get alarmed. He is a little unwell. I think it may be something he has eaten at the last stopping-place. It happens now and then. I am afraid he will be unable to continue with us.'

'But . . .' I began.

'Perhaps there is something which we could do,' said Alice.

'My dear ladies,' said Tom Keeping, 'we have to catch the steamer. I believe Monsieur Lasseur's business was in Suez. If he is a day late in arriving that could be of little moment. For us to arrive after the steamer had sailed would be disastrous.'

'But what can we do . . .?'

'He is in good hands. They are used to this sort of calamity here. They will look after him. He will catch a later wagon.'

'Where is he now?'

'In the men's rest-room. There is a little room there where people can lie down. He has asked me to convey his best wishes to you and tell you not to worry about him.'

'Perhaps we could see him . . .' I began.

'Miss Delany, he would not wish that. Moreover, the wagon is leaving at any moment now. If you miss it there may not be room on the next.'

Mr Carling said: 'This is the most uncomfortable journey I have ever undertaken.'

'Never mind, Father,' said Mrs Carling. 'We've come so far and this part is nearly over. Only one more lap to do.'

Mr Keeping hurried us to the wagon and we were soon galloping across the desert.

In due course we arrived at Suez where we spent a day waiting for the rest of the wagons to arrive. To our amazement, Monsieur Lasseur did not come. Alice and I wondered a great deal about him. It was strange. Who would have thought that such a seasoned traveller would have eaten something which did not agree with him? It would have been understandable if it had happened to one of us.

The P & O steamer was waiting for us. We went on board and settled into our small cabin for two, immensely relieved that we had survived the hazardous journey across the desert.

In due course we sailed and Monsieur Lasseur did not arrive.

We discussed him a great deal during the first days at sea.

'He was very attentive to us,' I said to Alice.

'I always felt he had a motive,' she said.

'Just friendliness. He liked helping two defenceless females who ought not to have been travelling on their own.'

'I could never quite understand him and his disappearance was most mysterious.'

'I wonder how he felt about not being able to get to Suez?'

'He'll only be a few days late and as he hadn't a ship to catch I don't suppose it mattered all that much.'

'It seemed so strange. We were with him most of the time and then . . . he disappeared.'

'Tom Keeping seemed to think it was a very ordinary occurrence. The food doesn't always agree with us. I don't suppose standards of hygiene are what they should be. But I thought he would be the sort who would be fully aware of all that and act accordingly.'

'I think Tom Keeping did not care very much for him.'

'Perhaps the feeling might have been mutual. However, Monsieur Lasseur disappeared and it is doubtful that we shall ever hear of him again.'

We saw Tom Keeping every day. I had a feeling that he was watchful of us and had instituted himself as our protector in place of Monsieur Lasseur.

The seas were calmer and the voyage enjoyable; one day seemed to slip by after another and there was a similarity between them. Many of the passengers who had been on the *Oriental Queen* were still with us and it seemed just a change of scene. But we had picked up a few passengers at Suez and there were friendly exchanges between us as we sailed down the Red Sea to Aden.

The heat grew great and I remember lazy days when we sat on deck and, as Alice said, recovered from the gruelling time we had endured in the desert.

Tom Keeping often joined us. I noticed that Alice was getting very friendly with him. He was most pleasant to us both, but I detected that while he regarded me more as an object in need of protection he had a great admiration for Alice.

He was an experienced traveller. He told us that he had done the journey from India to England and back many times.

'Most of the people who are going out are in the Army or in the Company; and I think the greater number are in the Company.'

'And you,' I asked, 'are in the Company?'

'Yes, Miss Delany. I am a Company man and I shall be making my way to Delhi as soon as we land.'

'We shall be staying in Bombay for a while,' Alice told him. 'But I believe that our employer may travel round a bit so we might well find ourselves in Delhi.'

'It would please me very much if you did,' he said.

He knew, of course, to whom we were going. Fabian, it appeared, was well known to him.

'You must know India well,' said Alice.

'My dear Miss Philwright, I don't know anyone who is not a native of the country who knows India well. I often wonder what goes on in the minds of the natives. I don't think anyone can be sure . . . any European, that is.'

He talked vividly. He made us want to see the lush green country, the big houses with their lawns dominated by the spreading banyan trees, the stately pipal and feathery tamarind, but most of all to see the people . . . the mixed races, the several castes, the customs which were so different from our own.

'I have a feeling that many of them resent our presence,' he told us, 'although the more sensible of them know that we bring trade and a better style of living. But intruders are never popular.'

'How deeply do they resent foreigners?'

'That is something we cannot be sure of. We are dealing with an inscrutable race. Many of them consider themselves to be more civilized than we are and they resent the intrusion of our foreign ways.'

'And yet they endure you.'

Tom Keeping smiled at me wryly. 'I sometimes wonder for how long.'

'You mean they might turn you out?'

'They couldn't do that, but they might try.'

'That would be dreadful.'

'You express it mildly, Miss Delany. But what a topic! India is safe in the hands of the Company.'

I shall never forget our time in Aden. It was brief. We

were only stopping for a few hours, but Tom Keeping said he would take us for a short drive.

How menacing it seemed as we sailed towards it. The black cliffs rising starkly out of the sea seemed to threaten us.

We were on deck, Alice and I, with Tom Keeping beside us.

'It looks as though we are sailing into the gates of hell,' Alice remarked.

'You feel that, do you? Do you know what they say of this place? That Cain – who slew Abel – is buried here and that since such a notorious murderer was laid here, the atmosphere of the place has changed. It has become evil.'

'I could well believe that,' I said. 'But I imagine it was rather gloomy before.'

'No one has left word to tell us so,' replied Tom Keeping. 'And I think the story got about because it has such a forbidding aspect.'

'Oh, I certainly believe legends attach themselves to things and places because they seem to fit,' said Alice.

The few hours we spent in Aden were very pleasant. We were under the protection of Tom Keeping and I was glad. Alice seemed to be changing; she looked younger. I thought: Can it be that she is falling in love with Tom Keeping?

They talked a great deal together and sometimes I felt like an intruder. It was strange. Alice was the last person I should have thought who would have allowed herself to be taken by romantic storm. Perhaps I exaggerated. Just because two people obviously liked each other, that was no reason to conclude that they were contemplating marriage. Alice was far too sensible to take a shipboard friendship seriously, and I was sure Tom Keeping was, too. No. It was just that their personalities were congenial. They struck me as two of the most sensible people I had ever known; quite different from Lavinia and her bogus Count.

655

Tom Keeping told us that he would make his way across land from Bombay to Delhi. Travelling was not easy in India. There was no railroad and therefore journeys were tedious and only taken from necessity. Doubtless he would travel by *dâk-ghari*, a sort of carriage drawn by horses; there would be many stops en route, often in places offering inadequate comfort.

'I believe it was you who warned us that travelling was often uncomfortable,' I said.

'It is something I have learned through experience.'

The sea voyage was coming to an end. There were long warm calm days as we crossed the Arabian Sea, and then we forgot our cramped cabin, the stormy seas and the ride through the desert when we had rather mysteriously lost Monsieur Lasseur.

I noticed that Alice was growing a little sad as we were nearing our destination and I believed it was at the prospect of saying goodbye to Tom Keeping. He did not seem to be touched by the same melancholy, although I did feel he had enjoyed his friendship with us and particularly with Alice.

He had always given me the impression that he had taken on the role of protector and I told Alice that I often thought of him as Tom Keeper rather than Tom Keeping. She laughed and said she felt the same.

And then at last we were nearing the end of our long journey.

I was excited by the prospect of seeing Lavinia again . . . and perhaps at some time Fabian. I wondered how I should feel about Dougal. Whichever way I looked at it, I knew it would be far from dull.

'You will be met, I am sure,' said Tom Keeping. 'So . . . the time has come for us to say our farewells.'

'How long will you stay in Bombay?' I asked.

'Only for a day or so. I have to make arrangements to leave for Delhi immediately.'

Alice was silent.

There came the last evening. In the morning we should disembark.

As we lay in our bunks that night, I asked Alice how she felt about arriving at our destination.

'Well,' she said rather wistfully, '*it's* really what we set out to do, isn't it?'

'Yes. But the journey was an adventure in itself!'

'Well, it is over now. And here we are. Now we have to begin our duties.'

'And remember we are no longer independent.'

'Exactly. But work will be good for us.'

'I wonder if we shall see Tom Keeping again.'

Alice said nothing for a few moments, and then: 'Delhi is a long way from Bombay. You heard what he said about the difficulties of journeys.'

'It is so strange. When you travel with people you get to know them so well . . . and then they are gone.'

'I think,' said Alice soberly, 'that is something you have to accept from the start. Now we should try to sleep. We have a long day ahead of us.'

I knew she was afraid of betraying her feelings. Poor Alice. I thought she had begun to care for Tom Keeping. And he might have done for her if they could have remained together. But now he seemed concerned with his business. I thought of Byron's lines:

'Man's love is of man's life, a thing apart,
'Tis woman's whole existence.'

The next day we reached Bombay.

657

The Approaching Storm

There was bustle the next morning. I was accustomed now to these arrivals in port. People seemed to change their personalities and it was almost as though those who had been close friends for weeks now slipped back into the role of strangers. One realized that what had appeared to be a deep friendship was only a pleasant but passing acquaintance.

Poor Alice! She was aware of this but she was a brave and sensible woman. She would never admit that she had allowed herself to entertain warm feelings towards a man whom she might never see again.

And there we were on that crowded quay.

One of the officials from the dock approached us and asked if we were Miss Delany and Miss Philwright. If so, there was a carriage waiting to take us to our destination. A few paces behind him was a most dignified Indian in a white puggaree and a long blue shirt over baggy white trousers. He ignored the official and bowed low.

'You Missie Delany?' he asked.

'Yes,' I replied eagerly.

'I come for you and Missie Nannie.'

'Oh yes . . . yes . . .'

'Follow please.'

We followed our impressive leader as he shouted orders to two coolies who appeared to be part of his entourage.

'Coolie bring bags . . . Missie follow,' we were told.

And we felt that we were well and truly being treated like honoured arrivals.

A carriage was waiting. It was drawn by two grey horses, standing patiently in the care of another coolie.

Tom Keeping left us there, having more or less handed us over. I noticed that he held Alice's hand firmly and seemed reluctant to let it go. I watched her smile at him unflinchingly. I liked Alice more and more as I began to know her better.

We were helped into the carriage by our gracious protector; our hand luggage was passed to us and we understood that our main baggage would be delivered in due course. Such was the outstanding presence of our man that we were confident everything would be in order.

The memory of that drive stays with me still. I suppose it was because it was my first glimpse of India.

The heat beat down on us. There were people everywhere – noisy, colourful. It was quite unlike anything I had ever seen before. Small boys seemed to be darting all over the streets. I thought we should run some of them down but our driver skilfully avoided them, although on one occasion he shouted something which sounded like a string of curses and the miscreant turned and gave him a look of intense dismay which I was not sure was due to his narrow escape or the awfulness of the curses.

How colourful were those streets – the buildings white and dazzling and very grand; and in the side streets of which we had a fleeting glimpse the contrast of dark little hovels and people squatting on the pavements . . . poor old men who seemed nothing but rags and bones, little children naked save for a loin cloth . . . searching in the gutters . . . for food, I imagined. I was to learn later that however much I was impressed by the grandeur, there would almost always be the accompanying shadow of appalling poverty.

I wanted to stop and give all I had to the mother with the child in her arms and another pulling at her tattered skirts. Our driver drove furiously on, heedless of the effect this had on us. I supposed he had seen it all so many times that he accepted it as normal.

There were stalls filled with produce which I did not always recognize and people in various styles of costume.

I learned afterwards that they belonged to different castes and tribes; the Parsees with their umbrellas; the Brahmins, the Tamils, the Pathans, and others. Darting everywhere were the coolies, presumably seeking to beg or earn a little money for some form of labour. I saw women, white-veiled, wrapped up in plain shapeless robes and here and there those of lower castes with their beautiful long black hair hanging down their backs moving with infinite grace. I thought how much more attractive they were than the *purdah* women whose charms, I supposed, were kept for their masters alone.

We said little as we were both intent on the scene about us and eager to miss nothing. We drove on for some miles and passed several beautiful houses, at length pulling up before one of these.

It was a most impressive residence — dazzlingly white, surrounded by a veranda on which were two white tables and chairs. Over the tables were green and white sunshades.

There were steps leading to the veranda.

As we approached, white-clad servants came running out of the house. They surrounded the carriage, chattering excitedly.

Our magnificent driver descended, threw the reins to one of the white-clad servants and waved his hand to silence the chatter. He then began to issue orders in a tongue we did not understand. He was immediately obeyed, which did not surprise me at all.

We mounted the steps, he marching ahead of us.

Alice whispered to me: 'One feels there should be trumpets . . . not for us but for him.'

I nodded.

We were led from the veranda into the house.

The contrast in temperature was amazing. It was almost cool. The room was large and darkish, the windows being built into recesses. I realized that this was to keep out the heat of the sun. On the wall of the room was a large fan which I learned after was called a *punkah*. This was manipulated by a boy in the regulation long white shirt and baggy trousers. I imagined he had been idling, for at our approach he was on his feet vigorously working the *punkah*.

The lordly one threw a scathing glance in his direction and I guessed there would be a reprimand at a more suitable moment.

'Missie Nannie go to room ... in nursery,' said our gentleman. 'Missee Delany come to Memsahib Lady Countess.'

Alice looked surprised but one of the servants immediately snatched the bag she was carrying and hurried off. Alice followed him. I was left.

'You Missie Delany. You come,' I was told.

I was taken up a flight of stairs. Through one of the windows I caught sight of a courtyard. There was a pool on which lotus blossoms floated, and chairs and a table were out there with the green and white sunshade.

We paused before a door. My guide scratched on it.

'Come in,' said a voice I recognized.

'Missie come,' said the guide, smiling with the satisfaction of a hero who has triumphantly completed an almost insuperable task. 'I bring Missie,' he added.

And there was Lavinia standing before me.

'Drusilla!' she cried.

I ran to her and we embraced. I heard the grunt of self-congratulation as the door closed on us.

'You've been so long.'

'It is a long journey.'

'I'm so glad you've come. Let me look at you. Still the same old Drusilla.'

'What did you expect?'

'Just what I see ... and I'm glad of it. I thought you might have developed into some terrible old bluestocking. You were a little like that.'

'I never expected *you* would so such a thing! Now let me look at you.'

She took a few steps back, shook out her magnificent

hair which had been loosely tied back with a ribbon, turned her eyes upwards in a saintly manner and posed for me.

She was plumper but as beautiful as ever. I had forgotten how striking she was. She was clad in a long loose lavender-coloured teagown and it suited her . . . in fact everything always suited Lavinia.

I felt that she had staged our meeting and was acting it as though it were a scene in a play and she was the heroine.

'You haven't changed a bit,' I said.

'Well, I hope not. I work on it.'

'India suits you.'

She smirked. 'I'm not sure. We're going home in two years' time. Dougal can't wait. He hates it here. He wants to go home and study some dry old thing. Dougal just doesn't know how to enjoy himself.'

'People don't always find enjoyment in the same things.'

She raised her eyes to the ceiling — an old habit of hers, I remembered. 'Trust Drusilla,' she said. 'You've been here five minutes and the conversation has already taken a psychological turn.'

'That's just a plain simple fact.'

'What's simple to clever you is profound to a numbskull like me. The point is, Dougal can't wait to get home.'

'Where is he now?'

'In Delhi. They are always going somewhere. It's the old Company making its demands. I'm sick of the Company. Fabian is there, too.'

'In Delhi? Why aren't you there?'

'Well, we were in Bombay and we're to stay here for a while. I think in time we may be going to Delhi.'

'I see.'

'Now, tell me about home.'

'It's just as it was except that my father died.'

'I heard that from Mama. You were supposed to marry the good Colin Brady and keep up the parsonic tradition. I heard all about that, too. You were not very sensible,

662

which meant that you did not do what she had planned for you.'

'I see you are well informed in Framling parish matters.'

'Mama is a great letter-writer. Both Fabian and I get periodic missives from home. One thing she cannot see from there is whether her orders are carried out or not . . . which is a mercy.'

'She has always arranged everything. It is her mission in life.'

'She arranged my marriage.' She looked a little sulky.

'You went willingly to the altar.'

'It seemed all right then, but I'm a big girl now. *I* decide what I am going to do.'

'I'm sorry it didn't work out well.'

'Are you? You know, he ought to have married you. You'd have got on well. You would have liked all that talk about olden times. It is just up your street. I can see you getting excited because someone dug up a pot which was used by Alexander the Great. I wouldn't care whether Alexander or Julius Cæsar used it. To me it would just be an old pot.'

'You're unromantic.'

That made her laugh. 'I like that. I'm terribly romantic. I'm having quite a good time . . . romantically, as a matter of fact. Oh, I'm so glad you're here, Drusilla. It's like old times. I like to see you look at me disapprovingly. It makes me feel so gloriously wicked.'

'I suppose there are . . . admirers?'

'There always have been admirers.'

'With disastrous results.'

'I have already told you I am a big girl now. I don't get into silly scrapes any more.'

'That at least is a mercy.'

'You're looking prim again. What is it?'

'You haven't asked about Fleur.'

'I was coming to that. What about her?'

'She is well and happy.'

'Well, what is there to be so disapproving about?'

'Just that you happen to be her mother and are somewhat casual about the relationship.'

'I have to remind you, Miss Delany, that I am now your employer.'

'If you feel like that I will return to England at the earliest possible moment.'

She burst out laughing. 'Of course you won't. I'm not letting you go now. You've got to stop here and put up with it all. Besides, you'll always be my old friend Drusilla. We've been through too much together for it to be any other way.'

I said: 'You didn't see Fleur before you left. In fact, have you seen her at all since Polly took her?'

'The good Polly didn't want me unsettling her. Those were your own words.'

'You know that Fabian is aware.'

She nodded. 'I've been lectured on my folly.'

'I hope you didn't think I told.'

'He said it was Polly who told because he had come to conclusions about you. He seemed to be more angry about that than anything else.'

'He has been good,' I said. 'He has deposited a sum of money for Fleur to be used at Polly's discretion . . . for her education and all that. They are going to have a governess for her. She has to be educated.'

'That's fine. What have we got to worry about? And that dreadful Janine was murdered. That worked out very well.'

'For you perhaps — hardly for her.'

'Blackmailers deserve their fate.'

'Have you thought of poor Miriam?'

'I didn't remember her very much. You were the one who was running round getting to know them all while I was in acute discomfort awaiting the birth. It was a horrible place and I'm so glad it's all over.'

'Shall you tell Dougal?'

'Good Heavens, no. Why should I?'

'I thought perhaps you might want to see Fleur and have her with you ... though Polly and Eff would never allow that. Or ease your conscience perhaps.'

'Conscience is something one has to learn to subdue.'

'I am sure that is one lesson at which you have excelled.'

'There goes Drusilla again. Oh, I mustn't remind you of our respective positions or you'll get huffy and I don't want that. Besides, I like those stern asides. They are pure Drusilla. I'm glad you're here. What about this nanny Mama has sent out with you?'

'She is very good. I like her enormously. She is sensible and I am sure absolutely trustworthy.'

'Well, that's what I expected since Mama found her.'

'We got on very well.' I started to tell her about our journey and the hazardous ride across the desert and the disappearance of Monsieur Lasseur, but I saw that her attention strayed. She kept glancing in the mirror and patting her hair. So I stopped.

I said: 'What about the children?'

'The children?'

'Oh, have you forgotten? You have two born in wedlock. We have already discussed and dismissed your illegitimate offspring.'

Lavinia threw back her head and laughed.

'Typical Drusillaisms,' she said. 'I love them. I'm not going to give you the pleasure of being dismissed for impertinence to your mistress, so don't think I am. You have been chosen for me by my determined Mama and my overbearing brother approves of the decision ... so you will have to stay.'

'Your brother?'

'Yes, as a matter of fact it was he who suggested it in the first place. He said to me, "You used to get along well with that girl from the rectory. You went to school with her. I dare say you would be amused to have her here." When he said that, I didn't know why I hadn't thought of it before. I said, "How would she come?" You know Fabian. He

665

replied, "By steam to Alexandria and then on from Suez."
I didn't mean that, of course. I said, "Why? How could
she?" "Well," he said, "she's a very erudite young woman.
She could teach the children. That's what genteel well-
educated young women of flimsy means do – and the
rectory girl is exactly that."'

She laughed and I felt a foolish elation. *He* had suggested
it. It must have been when he had come home and was
courting Lady Geraldine that he had spoken to Lady
Harriet.

I wanted to ask about Lady Geraldine, but I felt this was
not the moment to do so. Lavinia, by no means clever
academically, would be an adept at discovering one's feelings towards the opposite sex.

So I just said: 'Oh . . . was it like that?'

'Coming from Mama it is like the passing of an Act of
Parliament, and the approval of Fabian is like the signature
of the Monarch. So you see it becomes law.'

'You don't always take their advice, I'm sure.'

'That is why sin is so enticing to me. If I hadn't such a
forceful family it wouldn't be half as much fun. My dear
virtuous Drusilla, so different from your erring friend, I
can't tell you what joy it is to have you here. It was delightful
that the command from Framling should coincide exactly
with my wishes. I'm going to have lots of fun.'

'I hope there are not going to be more predicaments
like . . .'

She put her finger to her lips. 'The subject is closed. I'm
out of that one. Seriously, Drusilla, I'll never forget the part
you played in it. Then I snatched Dougal from right under
your nose.'

'He was never mine to snatch.'

'He could easily have been. I reckon if he hadn't suddenly
become important in Mama's eyes he might still be delving
in his books and paying his snail-like courtship to you. He
might not have arrived at proposing yet. Speed is not
Dougal's greatest strength. But the progress would have

666

been steady ... and so right for him really and it might have been a solution for you. Better than that priggish old Colin Brady whom you had the good sense to refuse. But then you would always have good sense. At the same time, Dougal would have been happier without his grand title. Poor Dougal! I could feel almost sorry for him. Swept off his snail's path to marry the woman who was the most unsuitable in the world for him. Still, it was Mama's decree and that is like the laws of the Medes and the Persians which you would know of.'

I was suddenly very happy to be here. I felt life had been dull too long. I was alive again. Everything was strange, a little mysterious — and Fabian had suggested that I should come.

I wondered why. For the convenience of the Framlings, of course. Lavinia needed a companion, perhaps someone to rescue her from the result of possible peccadilloes, of which there would certainly be many here where there were more opportunities than there had been in a French finishing school. And I had proved myself very useful once. Fabian would remember that.

Therefore one of the decrees which had ordered the marriage of Dougal and Lavinia was now extending to me. I was to leave everything and report for duty — so here I was.

I was afraid she would see my elation and connect it with Fabian, so I said: 'I should like to see the children.'

'Drusilla has spoken. I shall indulge her whim just to show how pleased I am to have her here. I will take you to the nursery.'

She led the way from the room up a staircase; we were at the top of the house where the nurseries were ... two huge rooms with smallish shrouded windows set in embrasures. There were heavy drapes which gave a darkness to the room.

I heard voices and I guessed Alice was already there, making the acquaintance of her charges-to-be.

Lavinia took me to a room where there were two small beds, mosquito-netted, and there was the inevitable *punkah* on the wall.

The door to the communicating room was opened and a small dark woman in a sari emerged and with her was Alice.

'This,' I said, 'is Miss Alice Philwright. Alice, this is the Countess.'

'Hello,' said Lavinia in a friendly fashion. 'I am glad you are here. Are you introducing yourself to the children already?'

'It is the first thing I always do,' said Alice.

They went into the room. The slight dark woman stepped aside to let us pass. She looked apprehensive and I believed that she feared our arrival meant her departure. I smiled at her and she returned my smile. She seemed to read my thoughts and to thank me for them.

Louise was enchanting. She reminded me a little of Fleur, which was not surprising as they were half-sisters. She had fair curly hair and delightful blue eyes; her nose was small and pretty but she lacked the tigerish look which I had noticed when I first saw Lavinia, who at that time would have been very little older than Louise. She was a pretty child but she had missed her mother's great beauty. She was a little shy and stayed close to the Indian woman to whom she was clearly attached. The boy was about a year old. He was taking his first steps and a little uncertain of his balance.

Alice picked him up and he studied her intently, and seemed to find her not unpleasing.

'Louise will be your pupil, Drusilla,' said Lavinia.

'Hello, Louise,' I said. 'We are going to learn some wonderful things together.'

She regarded me solemnly and when I smiled she returned my smile. I thought we should get on well together. I had always been attracted by children and although I had had little contact with them I seemed to have a natural empathy with them.

668

Lavinia watched us a little impatiently. I felt sad for her children. Their affection for the ayah was obvious, but Lavinia appeared to be almost a stranger to them. I wondered how Dougal was with them.

Lavinia did not want to linger in the nursery. She insisted on taking me away.

'There is so much to arrange,' she said. She turned a dazzling smile on Alice. 'I can see you are going to manage everything perfectly.'

Alice looked gratified and I guessed she was assuming – correctly – that there would be no – or very little – interference in the nursery.

I went to my room to unpack and I was aware of a feeling of exhilaration such as I had not felt for a long time.

Each day was a new adventure. I had arranged that at first two hours' tuition for Louise would be enough and Lavinia was ready to agree with anything I suggested. I went riding with her in a carriage through the town, past the burial place of the Parsees where their bodies were left in the dry hot air so that the vultures might leave nothing but their bones. I was fascinated by so much that I saw and I wanted to savour it to the full. Everything was so new and exotic.

Occasionally Alice and I ventured out together. We liked to walk through the streets which were a continual fascination to us. We were assailed on all sides by the beggars whose conditions appalled and distressed us. The deformed children worried me more even than the emaciated-looking men and women who exposed their infirmities to win one's sympathy and cash. Alice and I used to take a certain amount of money out with us which we would give to what we considered to be the worst cases, but we had been warned many times that when we were seen to give we should be pestered unmercifully. We accepted this and eased our consciences.

There seemed to be a plague of flies which settled on the

goods for display, on the white garments of the veiled women, the pink and yellow turbans of the dignified gentlemen, and – most disconcertingly – on the faces of the people who apparently were so accustomed to them that they ignored them.

We watched the snake-charmer piping his rather dismal tunes; we strolled through street after narrow street, past coolies, water-carriers with their brass pots on their shoulders, past donkeys laden with goods; sometimes we heard the strains of unfamiliar music mingling with the shouts of the people. Most of the shops were frontless and we could see the wares spread out before us, presided over by their owners who would do their best to lure us to pause and examine. There were foodstuffs, copperware, silks and jewellery. Presiding over these last was a plump man in a glorious pink turban smoking a *hookah*. Cattle often lumbered through the streets, small boys ran among us, often naked except for a grubby loin cloth, like mischievous gnats darting around seeking the right moment to rob the vulnerable.

Alice and I bought some Bokhara silk which we thought amazingly cheap and which was very beautiful. Mine was blue and pale mauve, Alice's biscuit colour. Lavinia had said that my clothes were awful and that there was a very good *durzi* who made up materials with speed and efficiency at a very low price. She would help me to choose a style which would suit me and he would be only too pleased to come to the house. All the Europeans used him; all one had to do was tell him what was wanted. He could be paid the price he asked without the usual native haggle. Praise meant as much to him as the money.

Lavinia took quite an interest in my appearance; she was enthusiastic about my clothes. I felt she had some motive. Lavinia, I believed, would always have a motive.

She moved in an Army and Company set, for these two appeared to work closely together. The Company was more than just a trading company. It was part of the government of the country, it seemed, and the Army was there to support it. It stood for British interests in India.

Lavinia was contented and that meant something. I was certain she had a lover. I had come to realize that Lavinia was the sort of woman who must always have a lover. Admiration and what she would call love were essential to her. She attracted men without even trying, and when she did try the effect was great. I had intercepted glances between her and a certain Major Pennington Brown. He was a man in his early forties with a mouse of a wife who, I imagined, at one time had thought him wonderful. Perhaps she no longer did. I thought him rather foppish and affected; but he certainly was handsome.

I tackled Lavinia about him. She said: 'Oh, spying already, are you?'

'No great effort was needed. I just assumed there was an intrigue in progress. I know the signs. They haven't changed much since your French comte put in his untimely appearance.'

'Garry is rather sweet and he absolutely dotes on me.'

So Major Pennington Brown was Garry!

'I am sure his wife agrees with you.'

'She's a poor little thing.'

'Evidently he didn't think so once. He must have found her attractive to have married her.'

'Her fortune was very attractive.'

'I see; and you find such conduct "rather sweet"?'

'Now please don't take up that tone. Remember . . .'

'I am the servant. Very well . . .'

'Hush! Hush! I shall certainly not allow you to go home in high dudgeon . . . whatever that is. I like Garry if you don't, and why shouldn't he find *me* attractive?'

'As he is looking for just a light love-affair I suppose he would.'

'Just a light love-affair! Don't speak so slightingly of such a delightful occupation. What do you know of light love-affairs?'

671

'Nothing, and never want to.'

'Oh, we are so virtuous, are we?'

'We are not stupid, if that's what you mean.'

'Well, I think you are if you refuse to indulge in what is really a great pleasure.' Her eyes narrowed. 'I'll make you change your mind one day . . . you'll see.'

Now I knew what she was planning for me. She wanted me to find someone among that social circle of hers, someone with whom I should have a light love-affair. She wanted someone to giggle with, to share chat of our experiences. I could not really think why Lavinia should be so eager to have me here when she could find so many Army or Company wives who would much more suitably fill her need for companionship.

I did not like her circle of friends; they seemed to me superficial and not very interesting. But I enjoyed my sessions with Louise, who was a delightful child interested in the picture-books I had brought with me; she liked me to tell her simple stories and when I came into the nursery she would hurry to me and bury her head in my skirts in enthusiastic welcome. Already I loved the child.

The ayah would sometimes sit watching us, nodding her head and smiling. Our love for Louise had made a bond between us.

It was in the gardens that I came upon her on one occasion. I had a feeling that she had followed me from the house and had chosen a suitable moment to speak to me.

There was a gazebo in the gardens – a favourite spot of mine. It looked over a beautiful lawn in the centre of which was a spreading banyan tree.

She approached me and said: 'Please . . . may I talk?'

'Of course,' I replied. 'Do sit down. Isn't it beautiful here? How lovely that tree is . . . and the grass is so green.'

'Much rain make it so.'

'Do you want to talk about Louise?'

She nodded.

'She loves to learn,' I said. 'It is a joy to teach her. I think she is an enchanting little girl.'

'She is to me . . . my own baby.'

'Yes,' I said. 'I know.'

'And now . . .'

'Are you afraid that now the nanny is here you will be sent away?'

She looked at me with wide, piteous eyes. 'Louise . . .' she said, 'is like my baby . . . I do not want to lose.'

I took her hand and pressed it. 'I understand,' I told her.

'Missie Alice . . . she new nanny. Poor ayah . . . no more.'

'The children love you,' I said.

A smile spread across her face and the sorrow returned.

'I will be told,' she said. 'I will be told . . . go.'

'And that would make you very sad.'

'Very sad,' she repeated.

'Why do you tell me? Do you think I could change this?'

She nodded.

'Memsahib Countess like you very much. She listen. She is very happy you come. All the time say: "Where is Missie Drusilla?"' She pointed at me. 'You listen . . . but she not listen. I think she will say Go.'

'I tell you what I'll do. I will speak to her. I will tell her how the children love you. I will say it is best that you stay.'

Her smile was dazzling. She stood up, put her hands together and bowed her head as though in prayer. Then she moved gracefully away, leaving me staring at the banyan tree but seeing nothing but the ayah coming to the house, taking over the care of Louise, growing to love the child, being excited at the prospect of another child and in due course giving the same devotion to Alan. And then all this love and care was to be terminated because of Lady Harriet's whim. Lady Harriet knew nothing of the true circumstances here and would not understand the love that could exist between an Indian nurse and her English charges.

I took the first opportunity to speak to Lavinia. She was

673

taking a rest before preparing for the evening, which would be a gathering of friends before dinner. I had been present on several of these occasions where she graciously introduced me as her friend from England. I had been quizzed by the men who might have thought I would be an easy conquest but the effort of attempting my seduction must have seemed hardly worthwhile to them; and when it was discovered that I was the governess and brought into contact with them through the generosity of Lavinia I was more or less politely ignored. These sessions had become ones which I wanted to avoid whenever possible.

She was lying on her bed, pads of cotton wool over her eyes.

'Lavinia,' I said, 'I want to have a word with you.'

'Didn't they tell you I was resting?'

'Yes, but I came all the same.'

'Something important?' She lifted the cotton wool from her right eye and looked at me.

'Very important.'

'Do tell me. You've changed your mind and want to come to the party? All right. Wear the mauve Bokhara. It's the best thing you have.'

'It is not that. How many servants do you employ here?'

'What a question to ask me! Ask the Khansamah. He's the one who would know.'

'So many that one makes little or no difference.'

'I suppose you are right.'

'I wanted to speak to you about the ayah.'

'What about her? She'll be going soon.'

'I don't think she should go.'

'Well, Nanny Philwright will want to be rid of her, I'm sure.'

'She doesn't want to.'

'She has told you so?'

'Yes. You see Louise loves her.'

'Oh, children love everybody.'

'That's not true. Listen, Lavinia. That ayah has been

with those children since Louise was born. She represents something to the child. Security, stability. Can't you see that?'

Lavinia was beginning to look bored. She wanted to talk to me about a certain Captain Ferryman who was making Major Pennington Brown decidedly jealous.

But I was determined. 'Lavinia, it won't make any difference to you whether the ayah is here or not.'

'Then why bother me with it?'

'Because you can change everything for her. She is a most unhappy woman.'

'Is she?'

'Listen, Lavinia, I want you to do something for *me*.'

'Unto half of my kingdom, as they say in the fairy stories.'

'Oh, not as much as that.'

'Then it is yours.'

'Be serious. I want you to let the ayah stay.'

'Is that all?'

'It's a great deal to her.'

'And what is it to you?'

'I care, Lavinia. I want her to be happy. I want Louise to be happy. If she goes away they will both be miserable.'

'Look here, Drusilla. Why are you so intense about it? Why should I care whether the woman goes or stays?'

'I know you don't care about these things, but I do.'

She laughed at me. 'You're such an odd creature, Drusilla. You have the most queer obsessions. I don't care what you do. Keep the ayah if you want to, as long as Nanny Philwright doesn't mind. I don't want trouble there. She mustn't be upset. Mama would be cross because she is her choice.'

'I can assure you that Alice Philwright will agree with me. She has the welfare of Louise at heart. Alan already loves her, too.'

'Pass me the mirror. Do you think I am getting too plump?'

'As far as your looks go you are beautiful.'

675

'So it is only my soul that is black?'

'Not exactly black.'

'Not shining white either.'

'No. But I think you are not entirely beyond redemption.'

'And if I grant your wish will you plead for me when you reap the rewards of your virtue and I am consigned to the flames?'

'I promise.'

'All right then. Request granted.'

'I may tell ayah that you wish her to stay on?'

'Tell her what you want to.'

I went to the bed and kissed the top of her head. 'Thank you, Lavinia. You don't know how happy you've made me.'

'Then stop and talk to me till it is time for them to come and dress me. I want to tell you about Captain Ferryman who is really very good-looking. He's quite clever, too. They say he has wit.'

So I listened and made the comments she expected until the maid came in to help prepare her.

It was a small price to pay for victory.

When I told the ayah that there was no question of her being sent away, she took my hand and kissed it reverently.

I drew it away murmuring: 'It was nothing . . . it is right that you should stay.'

But she continued to regard me with her soulful eyes.

Alice said to me afterwards: 'The ayah looks upon you as a kind of all-powerful goddess.'

I told her what had happened.

'I think you have earned her eternal gratitude,' she said.

Louise was changing. She was now a very happy child. She was ready to love anyone who showed her affection. She had her ayah and along we had come: Nanny and myself. Alice was strict but loving; she was completely fitted for the job and she filled it with efficiency. Alan loved her, too. Young as he was, I was teaching him. He liked the pictures in the books I had brought and could already pick out certain animals which I had pointed out to him.

Louise liked to sing. She loved the nursery rhymes I taught her and the strains of *Ba, Ba, Black Sheep* and *Ring a Ring of Roses* could often be heard.

It was a happy nursery. I was delighted with my task and so was Alice. But I had, though, a strong feeling of transience. This was ephemeral.

There was talk of our going to Delhi, which we must do sooner or later.

'We shall leave the Army personnel here, I expect,' said Lavinia ruefully. She was enjoying the rivalry between her captain and major. She had repeatedly tried to bring me into her circle of friends; but my reception of them was as lukewarm as theirs of me.

Lavinia was irritated. 'You make me angry,' she said. 'You take no pains. You make no effort.'

'Do you want me to roll my eyes and flutter my fan as you do?'

'You'll never get anyone with that Keep Off air of yours. You might just as well write it on a board and carry it round your neck.'

'It's in contrast to your Come Hither approach.'

That made her laugh. 'Drusilla, you'll be the death of me. I shall die of laughing at you.'

'What I say is true.'

'Come Hither anyway is more friendly than Keep Off.'

'It helps to maintain that devastating attraction of yours. Your way of going on is tantamount to an invitation to all and sundry. Lover wanted. No lengthy courtship necessary.'

'I wonder why I put up with you.'

'There is an alternative.'

'Oh, are we back at the dreary subject? I give in. You amuse me too much for me to let you go. I shall just ignore you and put on my Come Hither look whenever I wish.'

'I didn't expect anything else.'

And so we continued to banter and there was no doubt

677

that Lavinia was happy to have me here. One of the things she enjoyed most was shocking me.

One day when I went to the schoolroom the ayah was there with a young girl who must have been about eleven or twelve years old. She was a strikingly lovely child. Her long black hair was tied back with a silver ribbon and she wore a pale pink sari which set off the smoothness of dark skin. Her eyes were large and luminous.

'This, Missie, my niece.'

I said I was very pleased to make her acquaintance.

'She . . . Roshanara.'

'Roshanara,' I repeated. 'What a lovely name.'

The ayah smiled and nodded.

'Is she visiting you?'

The ayah nodded. 'Missie let her stay . . . listen to Missie Louise,'

'But, of course,' I said.

And as I sat with Louise over the books, Roshanara watched and listened intently.

Roshanara was exceptionally beautiful even for an Indian girl. Her natural grace was delightful to watch. She already spoke English tolerably well. She loved learning and it was delightful to see her rather solemn little face break into a smile when she mastered some unfamiliar word. Louise loved having her with us and those two hours teaching were some of the most enjoyable of my days.

I learned a little about Roshanara. She was the ayah's niece, her father being a prosperous tradesman, and she was heiress to a little money which meant that her marriage prospects were good. She was already betrothed to a young man a year older than herself. He was the son of the Great Khansamah who presided over the house in Delhi.

'The house,' Ayah told me, 'where live the great sahibs . . . Memsahib Countess's Sahib and her Sahib brother.'

I found out more about this house from Lavinia. It was a Company house, as most of the houses were, and they were kept up for the convenience of important directors of the Company. The house in Delhi was grander than this one in Bombay, but Lavinia found this more cosy. I think she meant that here she was free of her husband and the censorious eye of her brother.

According to Roshanara, the house in Delhi was under the command of the Great Khansamah who was a very important gentleman indeed. He was employed by the Company, as the Khansamah in Bombay was, and it was their duty to look after the comforts of important gentlemen sent out from England – I presumed such as Fabian and Dougal.

The man in Delhi was known as the Great Khansamah Nana. Later I wondered whether this was his real name or one given to him for his authoritative attitude to all those who came under his sway. I had not heard then of Nana Sahib, the revolutionary leader who was obsessed by his hatred of the British. It seems strange, looking back, that we should have been completely unaware of the gathering storm.

The Great Khansamah Nana had a son and it was to this son that Roshanara was betrothed. When the household moved to Delhi, which would be before long, the marriage would be celebrated.

'You are looking forward to it?' I asked Roshanara.

I looked into those limpid eyes and saw a hint of fear over-shadowed by resignation.

'It is what must be,' she said.

'You are too young to be married.'

'It is the age to be married.'

'And you have never seen your bridegroom!'

'No. I shall not until we are married.'

Poor child! I thought; and I felt very tender towards her. We were becoming good friends. I talked to her often and I fancied she found confidence which grew out of our friendship.

As for the ayah, she looked on with contentment. She

was happy. She was to remain with her beloved children and her beloved niece was with her, learning, as she said, from a very clever lady.

I had been apprehensive as to my skill as a governess, but I really was beginning to congratulate myself that I was rather good at it.

In two years' time we were to return to England. Then, of course, Louise, probably under the guidance of Lady Harriet, would have a professional governess and be taught all the things an English young lady should know. In the meantime I would suffice.

Lavinia sent for me. It was afternoon when a silence lay over the house. There was no sound but that of the creaking *punkahs* as the sleepy boys worked the pulleys.

Lavinia was lying on her bed, looking languid in a green peignoir which contrasted charmingly with the tawny shades of her hair.

I sat on the edge of the bed.

'We're going to Delhi,' she said. 'Orders from above.'

'Oh?' I said. 'Are you pleased?'

She grimaced. 'Not really. It was getting quite interesting here.'

'You mean the rivalry between the handsome major and the ambitious captain?'

'Oh, is he ambitious?'

'To enjoy your obvious charms.'

'Oh, thank you. A compliment from you means a good deal because you don't give them often. You're one of the dreadful honest people who have to tell the truth at all costs. You're the sort who'd go through fire and torment rather than tell one little white lie.'

'And you would tell them without compunction.'

'I knew you couldn't continue to praise me. Seriously, Drusilla. We have to depart next week.'

'That's short notice, surely.'

"They think it rather long and I'm only getting it because of the children. Otherwise it would be up and away with

680

twenty-four hours notice. Someone is coming out to Bombay ... Papa, Mama and three children. They want the house, so we have to go to Delhi ... where we should be in any case.'

'So we set out next week?'

She nodded.

'It will be interesting to see Delhi.'

'Dougal will be there and I expect ... Fabian.'

'You will be delighted to see your husband and your brother again.'

She pursed her voluptuous lips with faint distaste.

'Oh,' I said, 'I suppose it will mean you have to behave with a little more decorum than you usually display.'

'Can you see me acting with decorum? I shall be myself. No one is going to change me. It's quite a business moving the nursery. It's a good thing ayah is here. We have to ride in those wretched *dâk-gharis*, as they call the awful things. I can tell you it will be most uncomfortable.'

'Well, I did survive that journey across the desert, which is not exactly the most comfortable I have undertaken.'

'You wait till you see our *dâk*. It's a long journey and there are the children.'

'I don't suppose you will worry much about them.'

'They will have Nanny Philwright and the ayah ... not to mention their resourceful governess.'

'What about Roshanara?' I asked.

'Oh, that young girl who is going to marry the Great Khansamah's son. She'll go with us. We can't afford to offend G. K.'

'G. K.?'

'Oh, come. Where are your wits? Great Khansamah, of course. He rules the household, I gather, with a rod of iron. You need someone of Mama's calibre to stand up to him. Dougal could never do it. Fabian could, of course. But he would consider it a waste of time.'

'So,' I said, 'we in the nursery shall be making tracks for Delhi?'

'Exactly so . . . with the rest of us.'

'I shall look forward to seeing more of India,' I said. And I was thinking; Fabian will be there. I wonder what he will be like now?

Preparation went on apace. Ayah was delighted that she was accompanying us. She told me she owed her happiness to me. She knew that it was my word with Memsahib Countess which had made it possible for her to stay.

'This I never forget,' she told me earnestly.

'It was nothing,' I assured her; but she would not have it so. She told me she was happy because she would see her niece married. She loved Roshanara dearly and she was delighted that she would make a grand marriage.

Roshanara was less content and as the days passed she grew more and more apprehensive.

'You see . . . I do not know him,' she confided to me.

'It seems wrong to marry you to someone whom you have never seen.'

She turned her sad, fatalistic eyes on me. 'It happens to all girls,' she said. 'Sometimes happy . . . sometimes not.'

'I heard he is an important young man.'

'Son of Great Khansamah in Delhi,' she told me, not without pride. 'He is very great gentleman. It is an honour, they say, for me to marry his son.'

'He is about your age. You'll grow up together. That might be good.'

She shivered a little. I could see she was trying to comfort herself by painting a rosy picture but it was one in which she could not believe.

In due course we were ready to leave. Baggage had already gone off in horsedrawn carriages, all cleverly packed by the servants on the instructions of the Khansamah – not the great one, of course, but a very impressive gentleman for all that. Now it was our turn.

It was a long journey and having travelled before I was prepared for acute discomfort.

I was, perhaps on the whole, a little too pessimistic.

Our *dâk-ghari* was a badly constructed carriage drawn by a wild-looking horse. There were several of these vehicles for our party. I was with Lavinia and a certain Captain Cranly who, I suppose, was there to protect us. The children travelled in a *dâk* which they shared with Alice, the ayah and Roshanara with the small amount of luggage which we should need for the journey. In another *dâk* we had our brass pots which we should use for washing and mattresses on which we could sleep if there were no beds in the rest-houses where we should stay during the journey.

And so we set off.

It was, as India always would be, interesting, stimulating and intensely exciting, but so intent were we on keeping our balance as the *dâk* lurched along that we could not give our full attention to the scenery.

Lavinia was sighing for a *palanquin* which would have made the journey so much more comfortable. A *palanquin*, she told me, was a kind of litter, with bedding inside on which the occupant could recline in comfort. They were suspended on poles which four men carried.

'Rather hard on the men,' I commented.

'They are used to it. I think I shall refuse to travel any more without a *palanquin*.'

The journey seemed long. We stopped at several of the *dâk*-bungalows which bore a striking resemblance to the caravanserai which we had discovered in the desert on the way from Cairo to Suez. We were usually given chicken and oatmeal bread there and we had tea, too, with goat's milk, which I did not like very much. Still, hunger seasons all dishes, they say; and it certainly did on that journey to Delhi.

Every time we stopped the children greeted us as though they had not seen us for months, which amused us very much.

And in due course we saw in the distance the red stone walls of beautiful Delhi.

To ride through that city was an exhilarating experience. My first impressions filled me with excited anticipation. I wished that I had a guide with me to answer my eager questions and explain what these impressive buildings were.

The walled city stood on high ground with a commanding view over verdant woods. Domes, minarets and gardens gave it a touch of mystery which enthralled me. I saw the red walls of the Fort, the old palace of Shah Jehan. I yearned to know more of its history. I thought suddenly: How Dougal must enjoy this.

We went through the city past Jama Masjid, the great mosque, which was surely one of the finest structures in India. I caught a glimpse of the imperial tombs. I did not know what the future held but I did know I should always be glad that I had seen India.

And so we came to Delhi.

The house was much grander than the one in Bombay.

We were met by the Great Khansamah, a middle-aged man with more dignity that I have ever seen in any other person. The house might have been his and we distinguished guests but not quite of his high caste.

He clapped his hands and servants came running. He cast an eye on Roshanara and his expression was censorious. I remembered that this was her future father-in-law; and I hoped for her sake he would not live too close to the married couple.

'Welcome to Delhi,' he said, as though he owned the city.

We found ourselves talking to him deferentially. Watching him, I saw his eyes linger on Lavinia with a certain gleam in them which I had noticed in the eyes of others when they looked at her. She was aware of it and did not resent it.

We were taken to the rooms which had been assigned to us. There were *punkahs* everywhere and I noticed there was no surreptitious idling here.

I kept thinking of one thing: I shall soon meet Dougal
... and Fabian.

Alice, with the ayah, took the children to their quarters.
I was shown to my room which looked down across the
veranda to the stately pipal tree with its abundant green
foliage. The garden on to which I gazed was beautiful. In
the pond water-lilies and lotus flowers floated under a tall
feathery tamarind tree.

There was a feeling of serenity and peaceful beauty. Later
I tried to tell myself that it was a brooding calm before
the storm but I believe that did not occur to me at the
time.

After a while I went along to see how Alice was settling
the children in. Their quarters were more spacious than
those in Bombay. Roshanara was there. I noticed she
shivered intermittently.

I said: 'All will be well.'

She looked at me pleadingly as though I had the power
to help her.

'I feel it in my bones,' I added with a smile.

'My bones tell different.'

I believed it was the overbearing Great Khansamah who
had struck fear into her heart.

I said: 'Stern fathers often have gentle sons. You see, they
have been brought up strictly and perhaps suffered. It makes
them kind and understanding.'

She listened attentively. I thought: Poor child! What a
sad fate to be given in marriage to a stranger. I, who had
successfully evaded the efforts of Lady Harriet to marry me
off to Colin Brady, could feel especially sorry for frail
Roshanara.

Alice was delighted with the new nursery; she too was
finding life strange and exhilarating; but sometimes I detected a wistfulness in her eyes and I guessed then that she
was thinking of Tom Keeping. A thought struck me: He
had come to Delhi; he worked for the Company. Perhaps
we should see him again soon. That thought delighted me.

Alice was such a good sort. She should have children of her own rather than lavish affection on those of other people who, as the ayah had stressed, could so easily be snatched from her.

After leaving the children I went back to my room. Lavinia was there sprawling in one of the armchairs.

'Where have you been?' she demanded.

'Just giving them a hand in the nursery.'

'I've been waiting for you.'

I did not apologize. I was a little irritated by her lack of interest in the children's welfare.

'You will dine with us tonight?'

'Oh, should I?'

'Dougal will be there. So will Fabian, I expect . . . unless they are dining somewhere else, which they often have to do. Company business crops up.'

'I see. But I am here as the governess.'

'Don't talk nonsense. They know you. Dougal rather well, I fancy. There would be an outcry if you were put in the category of servant . . . even higher servant.'

'I don't suppose they would notice.'

'Don't you fish for compliments from me. That's my province. I want you there. There'll be lots of boring conversation about the Company, of course. You and I can chatter on the side.'

'Well, if I shall serve a useful purpose . . .'

She laughed at me. 'I wish we'd stayed in Bombay. Those awful *dâk* things. They were horrible. I shall reprimand Dougal for not sending *palanquins* for us to ride in. I shall say it is an insult to the Company to have Company people's memsahibs riding around in those awful things. They might take some notice if I put it that way. Why couldn't we have stayed?'

'I know you hate to leave the romantic major and the aspiring captain behind.'

She snapped her fingers. 'Oh, they'll have a regiment here. They'll have to. This is, after all, the important place,

where most of the business is done. Here and Calcutta . . .
I'd rather Delhi than there . . . I must say.'

'So there will be replacements for the gallant pair.'

'There is no need for you to worry on that account.
What shall I wear tonight? That's what I wanted to ask
you.'

She chattered on about her clothes and I listened halfheartedly, my mind on what it would be like to see Dougal
and Fabian again.

I was soon to find out.

I saw Dougal first. I had found my way to that room which
was a kind of ante-room to the dining-room. Dougal was
already there. I had a notion that he would have heard that
we had arrived and was waiting for me.

He came forward and took both my hands.

'Drusilla! What a great pleasure?'

He had aged quite a bit. He had lost that air of looking
out on the world and finding it full of interest. There was
a faint furrow between his eyes.

'How are you, Dougal?' I asked.

He hesitated just for a second. 'Oh, well, thank you. And
you?'

'The same,' I said.

'I was delighted when I heard you were coming . . . and
so sorry to hear about your father.'

'Yes. It was a great sadness.'

'I shall always remember those days when we talked
together.' A wistful look came into his eyes. It had always
been easy to read Dougal's thoughts . . . though perhaps
not always, for had I not believed at one time that he was
growing fond of me? Fond of me he was. But not in the
way I had thought.

And then Fabian came into the room and my attention
was all for him.

He stood still, legs apart, studying me. But I was not able
to read him as I did Dougal. I did see his mouth turn up a

little at the corners as though he found something amusing in the fact that I was here.

'Well,' he said. 'Miss Drusilla Delany. Welcome to India.'

'Thank you,' I said.

He had advanced, and he took my hands, looking intently into my face as he did so.

'Ah . . . still the same Miss Delany.'

'Did you expect someone different?'

'I was hoping I should find no change. And now I am content.' He spoke lightly. 'What did you think of the journey?'

'Tremendously interesting. A trifle uncomfortable but a stimulating experience.'

'You take a philosophical view, I see. I knew you would, of course. And I do hope the interest and stimulation outweighed the discomfort.'

Lavinia had come into the room. Both men turned to her. She looked beautiful with her hair dressed high on her head and her somewhat diaphanous gown clinging to her superb figure.

I immediately felt like an insignificant wren in the presence of a peacock.

Dougal went to her and they kissed perfunctorily. It was not what one would have expected from a husband and wife deprived of each other's company for some months. I noticed the change in Dougal. He seemed apprehensive.

She turned to Fabian.

'Well, sister,' he was saying. 'You seem to look better than ever. I guess you are delighted that Miss Drusilla has joined you.'

Lavinia pouted. 'Oh, she disapproves of me, don't you, Drusilla?'

'I expect with reason,' said Fabian.

'Drusilla would always be reasonable,' added Dougal with an air of resignation.

'Of course Drusilla is a paragon of virtue,' said Lavinia mockingly.

'Well, let us hope that you profit from her example,' added Fabian.

'We had better go in to dinner,' said Dougal. 'The Great Khansamah will be annoyed if we do not.'

'Then let us delay,' said Fabian. 'I believe that we should make the rules.'

'He can be very difficult in many ways,' Dougal reminded him. He turned to me: 'He has complete control over the servants.'

'All the same,' protested Fabian, 'I don't intend to let him govern my life. But I suppose the food will be spoiled if we don't go in. So perhaps the Great Khansamah has reason on his side. We don't want to give Miss Drusilla a bad impression, do we?'

It was cool in the dining-room – a large salon-like place with French windows looking out on to a beautiful lawn with a pond on which floated the familiar water-lilies and lotus flowers. There was a faint hum in the air from the countless insects and I already knew that when the lamps were lighted the curtains would have to be drawn to prevent certain obnoxious creatures invading the room.

'You must tell us all about your journey,' said Fabian.

I told them and mentioned our hazardous progress across the desert.

'Did you become friendly with any of your fellow passengers?' asked Fabian. 'One does on ships.'

'Well, there was a Frenchman. He was very helpful to us but he was taken ill on the journey through the desert and we didn't see him again. We met someone from the Company. You will know him, I expect. A Mr Tom Keeping.'

Fabian nodded. 'I trust he was helpful.'

'Oh, very.'

'And what do you think of India?' asked Dougal.

'I feel I have seen very little of it so far.'

'Everything is different here from in England,' he said a little ruefully.

'That is what I expected.'

The Great Khansamah had come into the room. He was dressed in a pale blue shirt over baggy white trousers; his puggaree was white and he wore a pair of dark red shoes of which I discovered he was very proud. He wore them with an air which was meant to imply that they were a sign of his great position.

'Everything is to the satisfaction,' he said in a voice daring us to say that it was not.

Lavinia smiled at him warmly. 'It is very good,' she told him. 'Thank you.'

'And the Sahibs . . .?' he said.

Fabian and Dougal told him that it was very satisfactory. Then he bowed and retired.

'He really has a great opinion of himself,' murmured Dougal.

'The trouble is,' replied Fabian, 'so has the rest of the household.'

'Why is he so important?' I asked.

'He is employed by the Company. This is for him a permanent post. He regards the house as his and those of us who use it are merely his passing guests. That is how he sees it. Of course he is very efficient. I suppose that is why he is tolerated.'

'I think he will be easy to get along with,' said Lavinia.

'He will if he gets complete subservience,' Fabian told her.

'Which you resent,' I said.

'I won't have my life ruled by servants.'

'I don't think he sees himself as that,' said Dougal. 'To himself he is the great Nabob, the ruler of us all.'

'There is something about him that makes me wary,' said Fabian. 'If he becomes too arrogant I shall do my best to get him replaced. Now, what news from home?'

'You know the war is over,' I asked.

'It is about time, too.'

'They have brought the men home from the Crimea and

690

the nurses are looking after them. They did a wonderful job.'

'Thanks to the redoubtable Miss Nightingale.'

'Yes,' I said. 'It took a great deal of hard work to make people listen to her.'

'Well, the war is over,' said Fabian. 'And it ended in victory for us – a Pyrrhic victory, I fear. The losses were tremendous and the French and Russians suffered more than we did, I believe. But our losses were great.'

'Thank Heaven it is all over,' said Dougal.

'It took us a long time,' commented Fabian. 'And . . . I don't think it has done us much good here.'

'You mean in India?' I asked.

'They watch closely what the British are doing and I have come to the conclusion that attitudes have changed a little since it started.'

He was frowning as he looked into his glass.

Lavinia yawned. She said: 'I believe the shops here are very much like those in Bombay.'

Fabian laughed. 'And that is a matter of the utmost importance which you will no doubt quickly investigate.'

'Why should the attitude change because of a war far away?' I asked.

Fabian leaned his arms on the table and looked intently at me. 'The Company has brought great good to India . . . so we think. But it is never easy for one country to impose its customs on another. Even though the changes in some cases may be for the better, there is necessarily a certain resentment.'

'There is undoubtedly resentment here,' agreed Dougal.

'And it alarms you?' I asked.

'Not exactly,' replied Fabian. 'But I think we have to be watchful.'

'Is that one of the reasons why the despotic rule of the Great Khansamah is tolerated?'

'I see you have grasped the situation very quickly.'

'Oh, Drusilla is so clever,' said Lavinia. 'Far cleverer than I could ever be.'

'You do show a certain perception since you are able to see it,' said her brother. 'Although I must say it is rather obvious.'

'Fabian is always beastly to me,' said Lavinia, pouting.

'I am truthful, dear sister.' He turned to me. 'Things have changed a little in the last year or so. And I think it may have something to do with the war. There were accounts in the papers of the suffering endured by our men and of the long siege of Sebastopol. I sensed that some were regarding that with a certain satisfaction.'

'But surely our prosperity helps *them*.'

'It does, but all people are not so logical as you and I. There is something such as cutting off one's nose to spite one's face. I fancy there are many here who would be ready to do just that . . . to let their own prosperity suffer for the sake of seeing us humiliated.'

'It sounds rather a senseless attitude to take up.'

'There is a strong sense of national pride in us all,' put in Dougal. 'Independence is dear to most of us and some fear to lose it even if retaining it means dispensing with certain comforts.'

'What would be the result of this feeling?' I asked.

'Nothing we shouldn't be able to handle,' said Fabian. 'But it shows itself now and then. The Khansamah of this house is a man of overweening pride, as you have seen.'

'I think he is rather fun,' said Lavinia.

'If you recognize that he is the head of the household, all will be well,' said Fabian. 'I believe he is not a man whom it would be wise to cross.'

'What could he do?'

'Make things uncomfortable in a hundred ways. The servants would obey him. They daren't do anything else. If there is a growing restlessness in the country it is probably due to the way we have brought in new laws. They are afraid we are going to impose our ways on them to such an extent that their native institutions will be stifled out of existence.'

'Is it right to do that?' I asked.

Fabian looked at me and nodded. 'Thuggery. Suttee . . . they are evils which have been suppressed by the British. You looked surprised. I see you are unaware of these matters. Both are pernicious, wicked, cruel customs long overdue for suppression. We have made the performance of them against the law. There were many Indians who lived in fear of these practices, but at the same time they resent our coming here and making them criminal acts. Dougal, of course, has made a study of all this.'

'He would,' said Lavinia.

Dougal did not glance at her. He turned to me. 'It is the Hindustani Thaga. We have called it Thuggery. It is a worship of the goddess Kali, who must be the most blood-thirsty of all gods and goddesses ever thought of. She demands perpetual blood. Those who take the oath to her are by profession murderers. It is considered an honourable profession . . . to murder.'

'Surely everyone agrees that it is good to stop that,' I said.

'Everyone . . . except the Thugs themselves. But it is interference by foreigners with the customs of the country.'

'People must have been terrified.'

'It was a religious community. These people who took the oath lived by murder. It was not important whom they murdered as long as they killed. They lived on the plunder they took from their victims, but the motive was not robbery but to placate their goddess. They banded together in groups, falling in with travellers, seeking their confidences and choosing the appropriate moment to murder them.'

'How . . . diabolical!'

'They usually killed by strangulation.'

'Quite a number of them made use of the Thorn Apple,' said Fabian.

'Oh, that's a special sort of drug,' said Dougal. 'It grows

693

profusely here. The leaves and seeds are used in medicine. When the leaves are dry they have a narcotic smell. You'd recognize the plant when you see it. The name is actually Datura but they call it Thorn Apple. You can see the tubular five-cleft calyx with a large corolla, shaped rather like a funnel. It has a prickly sort of capsule.'

'Trust Dougal to get the scientific description,' said Lavinia mockingly.

'There's nothing scientific about that,' said Dougal. 'It is just easy for anyone to see.'

'I bet I shouldn't recognize it if I saw it,' said Lavinia. 'Would you, Drusilla?'

'I don't think so for a moment.'

'There you are, Dougal. You're boring us with your description. I want to hear more about the poison.'

'It's deadly,' said Dougal. 'A peculiar alkaloid called Daturina can be distilled from it. Some of the natives use it as a drug. When they do, they become wildly excited. The world seems a beautiful place and they are almost delirious.'

'And they like that?' I asked.

'Oh yes, indeed,' said Dougal. 'It makes them feel wonderful . . . while it lasts. But I believe it is followed by acute depression, which is usual in the case of these substances. Moreover, it can be very dangerous and in the end fatal.'

'You were saying that these Thugs used it to kill their victims.'

'It was one of their methods,' replied Fabian, 'but I believe the more usual was strangulation.'

'I should have thought most people would have been greatly relieved that these Thugs had been put out of action by the law.'

Fabian lifted his shoulders and looked at the ceiling.

'It is a matter of what we were saying . . . Independence or better rule. There are those who will always want the former. It is the same with Suttee.'

'That was abolished about the same time as Thuggery,'

Dougal told me. 'They really have a great deal to be thankful for to Lord William Bentinck. He was the governor of Madras for twenty years and then he became Governor General from 1828 to '35. You know what happens in Suttee. A husband dies and his wife leaps into his funeral pyre and is burned to death with his body.'

'How terrible!'

'So thought we all and Lord William brought in the laws condemning Suttee and Thuggery,' added Fabian.

'It was a great step forward,' commented Dougal.

'Do you know,' put in Fabian, 'I believe both are still practised in some remote places. It is a defiance of British rule.'

Lavinia yawned again and said: 'Really this is getting like a history lesson!'

'A fascinating one,' I said.

'Drusilla, don't be such a prig! You infuriate me. You just encourage them. I know what she's going to say. "If you don't like it, I'll go back home." She's always threatening me with going back home.'

'That,' said Fabian gravely, 'is something we must persuade her not to do.'

I was happy suddenly. It was the experience I had known before. It was like coming alive.

For the rest of the evening we talked of India, of the various castes and religions. Looking out on the lawn, I thought it was one of the most peaceful scenes I had ever encountered.

When I retired that night it was long before I slept. I kept thinking about the evening, the old cruel customs of the country and the fact that I was living under the same roof as the two men – I had to admit it – who had been most important in my life: Dougal and Fabian! How different they were! I was a little alarmed by the wistfulness I saw in Dougal's eyes; he was sad and regretful. It was not difficult to see that his marriage had brought disillusionment to him; and he seemed, even in the brief time we had been together, to be turning to me for solace. I thought I should have to be careful. As for Fabian, he had changed little. I must not allow myself to become too impressed by him. I must remember that he was a Framling and they did not change. They would always believe that the world was made for them and all the people in it to suit their purpose. Moreover, I must not forget that Lady Geraldine might soon be coming out to marry him.

Almost immediately Roshanara was married. We did not attend the ceremony, which was carried out in accordance with the ancient Indian custom. Asraf, the young bridegroom, I heard from the ayah, was about two years older than Roshanara.

'Poor children,' said Alice. 'I pray that life will not be too difficult for little Roshanara and her husband.'

We saw the decorated carriages, for it was a grand occasion presided over by the Great Khansamah, who looked very magnificent: I saw the glitter of jewels in his puggaree.

I did not see Roshanara after her wedding. She was leaving with her husband for the tea plantation where he worked for his uncle and it was some distance away. I wondered whether the uncle was as grand as Asraf's father; but it was difficult to imagine that anyone could be that.

We had settled into a routine. We had made a schoolroom in the nursery and there I taught the children. We all missed Roshanara. Alan was becoming quite a little person now.

They were happy. The change of scene had affected them very little while they had those they loved and relied on about them. It was rumoured, Alice said, that their mother was not very interested in them, but I replied that she never had been, so they would not notice. True, she was their mother, but titles were not important and they were content with Alice, the ayah and me. We represented their close little world and they asked for nothing more.

Lavinia was somewhat pleased with the move now that

she was settling in. Delhi was more fashionable than Bombay; there was more going on and naturally there was a greater military presence here, which pleased her.

'More handsome officers to choose from,' I told her sardonically.

She put her tongue out at me.

'Jealous?' she asked.

'Not in the least.'

'Liar.'

I shrugged my shoulders. 'Have it your way.'

'Poor Drusilla, if you'd only *pretend* to think they're marvellous they would like you.'

'I leave all that to you.'

She laughed secretly.

As usual, she was very preoccupied with her appearance and what clothes she should wear to enhance it. She had found some exotic perfume which pleased her. I was amazed how little her experiences had changed her. The sordid affair with the mock comte had passed her, leaving her unrepentant and able to forget Fleur as though she did not exist. Others had taken care of that misdemeanour. I think she must have imagined that there would always be those around her to do that. But in her way she was fond of me. She enjoyed shocking me; she liked my veiled criticism. If ever I suggested going she was alarmed. That gave me the weapon I needed against her now and then. She realized this and accepted it. And in spite of everything I had a fondness for her too, though often I thought her behaviour outrageous.

She had followed the custom of the ladies of the household by interviewing the Khansamah each morning to discuss the day's menu. This surprised me, for in Bombay where it had also been her duty, she had shirked it. But now she did it regularly. I was to discover why.

The Great Khansamah would come with his usual pomp to the upper part of the house and Lavinia would receive him in the little boudoir-type room close to her bedroom.

697

She would be wearing a be-ribboned peignoir or some equally feminine garment, which I thought unwise.

She did not seem to be aware that this was a ceremony – a ritual almost. The lady of the house should sit at a table, dignified and precise, and listen attentively to the suggestions made by the Khansamah, sometimes query them, and then make a suggestion herself; and then perhaps give way or insist, whichever etiquette demanded.

The procedure was quite different with Lavinia. I knew why she bothered. It was because the dignified Khansamah emerged sufficiently from his regal aura to imply that he considered her beautiful.

Dougal and Fabian were away for most of the day; sometimes they dined at the house; at others they did so elsewhere. Dougal came more often than Fabian, who seemed to be more closely involved with the Company.

I took my meals with them. I had wondered how Alice felt about this because she had hers in the nursery or her own room. I tried to explain to her. 'I think it's because I'm supposed to be here as a sort of companion to the Countess. I knew her from my childhood . . . you see . . . living close. She seems to want me there at the moment. Of course she could change. She is very unpredictable.'

'I'm happier this way,' said Alice. 'It suits me.'

'I hope you don't mind . . . really.'

'My dear Drusilla, why should I? I'm sorry for you sometimes . . . having to spend so much time with the Countess.'

'I know her well. I don't let her bully me.'

'She seems to be a very reckless woman.'

'She has always been that.'

'I guessed that, but I thought it would be different here from how it was in England.'

I agreed; and I often had uneasy twinges about Lavinia. Well, if there were scrapes here she had a husband and a brother to look after her.

We had dined. Fabian was not with us; there was just

Dougal, Lavinia and myself. We had talked generally about things and as soon as the meal was over, Lavinia said that she was going to bed.

Thus Dougal and I were left alone together.

We were in the drawing-room. The heat of the day was gone and the cool of the evening was delightful.

'The gardens are so beautiful in the moonlight,' said Dougal. 'If we put out the lamps we could draw the curtains and enjoy the scene.'

This he did, drawing back the curtains. He was right. The scene was breathtakingly beautiful. I could see the pond with the blooms floating on its surface; and the banyan tree looked mysterious in the pale light.

Dougal said: 'It isn't often that we get an opportunity to talk alone. It's a rare luxury, Drusilla.'

'I know you are a little homesick, Dougal.'

'Each day brings Home a little nearer.'

'Are you determined to break away when your two years are up?'

He nodded. 'I think so. People must live their own lives as they want to, don't you agree?'

'Yes, I think you are right . . . providing they don't hurt anyone in doing so.'

'I was never meant for this.'

'No. You were meant to live quietly surrounded by your books in the shades of academe.'

'I think you know me well, Drusilla.'

'One wouldn't have to, to realize what you want from life.'

'I should like to be reading . . . learning all the time. There is nothing so exciting as discovering facts about the world we live in. I wonder more people don't realize it. It seems to me that most of them are chasing shadows.'

'Perhaps they think you are doing the same. All people view life differently. What is excitement to one is boredom to another.'

'How right you are.'

'It is something we have to remember.'

'I want very much to go home. I don't feel happy here. There is a brooding sense of evil in the air, I fancy.'

'Do you really feel that?'

'It seems to me that these people watch us . . . purposefully. It seems they are saying, "You don't belong here. Get out."'

'Have you told Fabian?'

'My brother-in-law is a practical man. As they say, his feet are firmly on the ground. To be in authority here suits him as it would never suit me. So you see why I plan definitely to go home when the two years are up and stay there.'

'If you feel that, why do you not go before?'

'I have to give a good warning. So far I have hinted. I have certain commitments at home, I tell them. The trouble is, the family has been connected with the Company for years. If one comes from such a family one is expected to uphold tradition.'

'Poor Dougal!'

'Oh, I deserve my fate. I have made one mistake after another.'

'I think that is not uncommon with most of us.'

'You have made none.'

I raised my eyebrows and laughed. 'I am sure I have.'

'No major ones. Drusilla, there is no sense in trying to cover up what is obvious. I have made just about the most ghastly mistake a man can make.'

'Are you sure you want to talk to me about this, Dougal?'

'To whom else should I talk?'

'Fabian, perhaps.'

'Fabian? These Framlings are too self-centred to concern themselves very much with other people's problems.'

'I'm sure Fabian would be sympathetic.' He did not answer and I went on: 'Is it your marriage?'

'Lavinia and I have absolutely nothing in common.'

A sudden wave of anger swept over me. I thought: Why

do you realize this only now? It must have been obvious from the first and why tell *me*?

'I used to enjoy our times at the rectory,' he went on wistfully.

'My father did, too.'

'I got the impression that we all did.'

'Oh yes. We talked of interesting things.'

'You always took up any subject with enthusiasm. If only . . .'

'That must be one of the most used phrases in the language.'

'Do you never use it?'

'I suppose so. But it is always ineffectual. Nothing that has ever gone before can be changed.'

'That doesn't prevent my saying . . . if only . . .'

'You will not be here always and if you have made up your mind to go back and study when you get home . . . well, that is something to look forward to.'

'Lavinia would never agree to live the kind of life I would want.'

'That seems very likely, but why did you not think of that before?'

'I was bemused.'

'Ah yes, I know.'

Silence fell on us. It was broken only by the sound of an enormous flying insect passing the open door.

'He would have been in the room if we had had the lamp burning,' said Dougal.

'He looked very beautiful.'

'There is so much beauty here,' said Dougal. 'Look at the garden. Is it not exquisite . . . the trees, the pond, the flowers. There is a feeling of deep peace . . . but it is quite false in fact. Everything in this country is mysterious. It seems to me that nothing is what it appears to be.'

'Does that apply here particularly.'

'I think so. These servants who come to do our bidding

701

. . . I often wonder what is going on in their minds. They seem almost accusing sometimes, as though they harbour resentment and blame us for it. Look at that garden. Where could you see a more peaceful-looking spot, and yet out there among the grass lurk Russelian snakes. You could even come face to face with a cobra lurking in the undergrowth.'

'You make it sound like the Garden of Eden with the serpent lurking,' I said with a laugh.

'It is not dissimilar. You must be careful in the garden, Drusilla. These snakes are everywhere.'

'I have seen one or two. Are they the pale yellowish kind?'

'Yes . . . the variegated ones. They have big oval spots, brown with a white edge to them. Avoid them. Their bite could be fatal.'

'I have seen them in the bazaar emerging from the snake charmers' baskets.'

'Ah yes, but those have had their poisonous fangs removed. The kind you find in the garden have not.'

'It makes me shiver to think of the peaceful aspect of this place and all that danger lurking beneath it.'

'It is like a mirror to life. Often great beauty will disguise emptiness . . . and sometimes evil.'

In the half-light I saw his sad smile. I knew he was thinking of Lavinia and I wanted to comfort him.

We sat in silence for a few moments and it was thus that Fabian found us.

He came into the room suddenly.

'Ah,' he said. 'Forgive me. I did not know that anyone was here. So you are sitting in the dark.'

'We wanted the air but not the insects,' I said.

'Well, I dare say a few of them have found their way in.'

He sat down near me.

'You have had a tiring day?' I asked.

He shrugged his shoulders. 'No more than usual.' He

702

stretched his long legs. 'You are right,' he went on. 'It seems very peaceful here sitting in the dark. Tell me, have I interrupted some interesting conversation?'

'We were talking of the contrasts here. The beauty and the ugliness beneath the surface. The beautiful flowers, the green grass, and the Russelian snakes out of sight and ready to strike the fatal blow.'

'Danger lurking everywhere,' said Fabian lightly. 'But isn't that what makes it exciting?'

'I suppose most people would say yes,' said Dougal.

'And what of you?' asked Fabian of me.

'I am not sure. I suppose it would depend on the lurking danger.'

'And whether, having met it, you could escape it?' suggested Fabian.

'I suppose so.' I stood up. 'I dare say you have business to talk of. I will say good night.'

'Oh, you mustn't let my coming break up this pleasant tête-à-tête.'

'We were just talking idly,' I said. 'And I will go now.'

Fabian accompanied me to the door.

'Good night,' he said, and there was a quizzical expression in his eyes.

I was reminded of that conversation a few days later. I was in the garden with Alice and the children. The ayah was with us. I was talking to her about Roshanara and asking if she had heard anything of her.

She shook her head. 'No . . . no. She go far away. Perhaps I never see her again.'

'Oh, but she will come and see you!' I protested. 'She can't be so very far.'

The ayah lifted her hands and gently rocked from side to side. There was something fatalistic in her attitude.

Louise came running up to us. She was holding something in her hand.

'What is it?' I asked.

'I picked it for you,' she said and handed a plant to me. I stared at it. I had never seen anything like it before.

The ayah had taken it. Her face had turned pale. She said in a frightened voice: 'Thorn Apple.'

Memory stirred in me. What had I heard about the Thorn Apple? Snatches of conversation came back. It was the Thorn Apple from which drugs were distilled. The Thugs had used it in the past to poison their victims when they did not dispatch them by strangulation.

And here was Louise . . . picking it in the garden.

I could see that the ayah knew about it.

I said: 'I . . . I have heard something of this plant.'

She nodded.

'Where did Louise find it?'

She shook her head. 'Not here. It could not be. It would not be permitted . . .'

Louise was watching us with some dismay. She was a bright child and would understand immediately that something was wrong.

'Thank you, Louise,' I said. 'It was kind of you to bring me the flower.' I kissed her. 'Tell me. Where did you find it?'

She spread her arms and waved them as though to embrace the whole of the garden.

'Here?' I said. 'In the garden?'

She nodded.

I looked at the ayah. 'Show us,' I said.

I was holding the thing gingerly. I could smell a faint narcotic odour.

Louise was leading the way to a small gate. It was locked but possible for one of Louise's size to crawl under it, which she proceeded to do.

'This Great Khansamah's garden,' said Ayah, shaking her head.

'Come back, Louise,' I called.

She stood on the other side of the gate looking at us wonderingly.

'It was in here I found your flower,' she said, pointing. 'Over there.'

'This Great Khansamah's garden,' repeated Ayah. 'You must not go there. Great Khansamah . . . he be very angry.'

Louise scrambled back looking alarmed.

'Never go there again,' said Ayah. 'It is not good.'

Louise gripped her sari as though for protection. Everyone had heard of the power of the Great Khansamah.

I took the sprig into the house and burned it. Then I realized that I should have kept it and shown it to Dougal or Fabian.

I saw Dougal soon after that and told him what had happened.

'Are you sure?' he said.

'The ayah called it Thorn Apple and I remembered what you have said.'

'Could you recognize it from my description?'

'Well, no . . . not exactly but it could have been. But the ayah knew it. She would surely know and she recognized it at once.'

He was silent. Then he said: 'The Great Khansamah's garden is his own property and we cannot tell him what he can and cannot grow there.'

'But if he is growing this drug . . .'

'He is a law unto himself.'

'But he is employed by the Company and if he breaks the law . . .'

'I think it wiser to say nothing about this just yet. After all, we have to have proof and it could cause a great deal of trouble if we tried to prevent his growing what he wants to in that patch of land which the Company has decided shall be for his sole use.'

I wished that I had spoken to Fabian about it. I was sure his reaction would have been different.

But on the other hand I had only the ayah's word for it that it was the dreaded Datura; she could so easily have been wrong; and I could imagine the outcry there would

705

have been if we had tried to interfere with the Great Khansa-mah's right to grow what he wanted to in his own garden.

That very day we had a great surprise and perhaps that is why I was not more concerned at the time with the discovery of the deadly plant in the garden.

Tom Keeping came to the house.

He came face to face with us as Alice and I were preparing to take the children into the gardens.

'Miss Philwright, Miss Delany,' he cried, his face breaking into a delighted smile.

I was aware of Alice, a little tense beside me.

'I knew you were here,' he went on. 'It is a great pleasure to see you again. Are you well? Are you enjoying being here?'

I said we were and Alice agreed with me.

'I knew we should meet again sometime and urgent business has brought me here.'

'Shall you be staying?'

'That depends on many things. However, we shall be able to meet at times.' He was looking at Alice. 'You find it congenial?'

'Yes,' she said. 'I get on well with the children. Don't we?' she said, looking at Louise.

Louise nodded vigorously, staring up at Tom Keeping with interest.

'Me too,' said Alan.

'Yes,' said Alice, ruffling his hair. 'You too, darling.'

'I want to see Sir Fabian urgently,' said Tom. 'I am told he will be here this afternoon.'

'We never know when he will be here,' I told him.

'We should be getting along into the garden,' said Alice.

Tom Keeping smiled. 'We shall meet again soon. *Au revoir*,' he said.

Dougal had appeared. He said: 'Sir Fabian will be here very soon. In the meantime, come into the study and we can talk things over.'

They left us and we went into the garden.

'What a surprise!' I said.

'Yes, but I suppose as he is employed by the Company . . .' Alice's voice trailed off.

'He is such a nice man.'

Alice was silent. She looked pink and flushed and younger; I noticed, too, that she was rather absentminded. I thought: It would be wonderful if he cared for her, but if he does not it would have been better if he had not come back.

Fabian returned later that day. He was closeted in his study with Dougal and Tom Keeping. They did not appear at dinner but had something sent to the study.

Lavinia and I were alone.

'Thank goodness,' she said. 'I can't bear all this Company talk. You'd think there was nothing else in the world.'

She chattered on about a certain young captain whom she had met the previous evening.

'So handsome and married to the plainest girl . . . I expect it was for her money. She doesn't even know how to make the best of herself. Fancy anyone with her dark skin wearing brown.'

I could not give much attention to such matters. I was thinking about Alice and Tom Keeping.

The next day we took the children into the gardens. Tom Keeping joined us. I made an excuse and left him and Alice together. Alice looked a little alarmed, but I was firm. There was something I had to do for the Countess, I lied.

I could not help feeling that Tom Keeping was rather pleased.

On the way into the house I came face to face with Fabian.

He said: 'Hello. Are you busy?'

'Not particularly.'

'I'd like to have a talk.'

'What about?' I asked.

'Things,' he said.

'Where?'

'I think in my study.'

I must have shown some apprehension. I had never forgotten that occasion when he had made some sort of advance when he had been under the impression that I was Fleur's mother. I could never be alone with him without wondering whether he was going to do the same again. He knew now that I was not a woman of easy virtue, but I fancied that would not prevent his belief that as a Framling and so much above me in the social scale, it would be in order to amuse himself with me for a while. Perhaps that was why I always seemed to be on the defensive. He was aware of this, I was sure. That was what was so disconcerting. He seemed to read my thoughts with ease. I had always felt that he was faintly attracted by me – not for my good looks which were non-existent, not for my feminine appeal, but because I was, as Lavinia had pointed out many times, prim and a man such as he was would find it diverting to break through my armour and to see me submit to him.

I was determined not to show him that I felt excited as well as apprehensive.

He shut the door, his lips turning up at the corners. He held the chair for me and as I sat down his hand touched my shoulder. He took a chair by the table which was between us.

'You know Tom Keeping is here,' he said.

'Yes, he is in the garden with Miss Philwright and the children.'

'I noticed the little charade. You discreetly left them together. Is there some relationship between Keeping and the nanny?'

'That is something you should ask them.'

I saw the amused look in his eyes. It faded suddenly. 'Drusilla,' he said seriously, 'you are a sensible girl. I wish I could say the same for my sister.' He hesitated. 'We are a little alarmed.'

'About what?'

He waved his hands. 'Everything,' he said.

'I don't understand.'

'I wish we did . . . more fully. Tom Keeping has a special position in the Company. He travels around a great deal. He keeps an eye . . . on things.'

'You mean he is a sort of Company spy?'

'That is hardly the description I would use. You see the position we are in here. It is after all an alien country. Their customs are so different from ours. There are bound to be clashes. We think we could help improve conditions here. They are thinking we are an Imperialistic conqueror. That is not so. We want the best for them . . . providing it is also the best for ourselves. We have made good laws for them . . . but they are our laws, not theirs, and they often resent them.'

'I know. You have told us.'

'They act in defiance of us. That is the trouble. That is what Tom is here to talk about. There has been a rather bad outbreak of Thuggery some thirty miles from here. A group of four travellers have been murdered. We recognize the methods. They had no enemies . . . four innocuous men, travelling together for company. They have all been found dead in the forest near a certain inn. The innkeeper admits they stayed there. There were two men at the inn who dined with them. A few hours later the four travellers were found dead in the forest. They had died of poison, which must have been administered in some drink just before they left the inn. There was no reason for the deaths . . . except to placate the bloodthirsty Kali. It seems to me that in defiance of our law there is a return to this old barbaric custom.'

'How dreadful! Innocent travellers . . . murdered by strangers!'

'That is the way of the Thagi. It makes me very uneasy. There have not been many cases lately and we were beginning to think we had wiped the whole thing out. It's a return to it . . . a defiance . . . That is what is so upsetting.

Tom is investigating. If we could find the source of the trouble . . . if we could find the murderers and where they come from we might be able to stamp it out, and we must stamp it out quickly. To allow it to go on would not only bring terror to countless Indians, but worse still, it is an open defiance of British law.'

'What are you going to do about it?'

'No doubt there is some sort of central control. These people have their meetings, you know. Wild ceremonies with blood offerings to Kali – strange oaths and so on. If we could find the leaders and root them out, we'd stop the whole thing. No sensible Indian would want to continue with that.'

'But Dougal was saying that people value their independence more than anything. They don't want improvements if they are going to interfere with that.'

'Oh, Dougal. He's a dreamer. We've got to find out what this means and root it out.'

'Perhaps it could be explained to the people.'

He looked at me in exasperation. 'Drusilla, you are a child in these matters. The sentimental view will only make matters worse. We have to stamp out these evils if we are going to have a reasonable country here where we can live and work and bring benefits to them as well as to ourselves. If they won't accept that we have to make them.'

'Do you think you will ever do that?'

'We have to try.'

'What would you do if you found the murderers?'

'Hang them.'

'Would that be wise? They are following what seems to be a religion with them. It is the worship of the goddess Kali which makes them do such things.'

'You are a clever young lady, my dear Drusilla, but in these matters you are . . . infantile.'

'Then why do you bother to tell me of them?'

'Because I think we should all be warned. Keeping doesn't like the way things are going. He says he is aware of an undercurrent. He has detected insolence in certain people. He is trained to recognize these moods. He is a very experienced man, and he is disturbed.'

'What should one do about it?'

'Take great care. Watch the way the wind blows. It is no use talking to Lavinia.'

'No use at all. But why do you talk to me?'

'Because I expect you to be . . . sensible.'

'In what way?'

'Be watchful. Tell one of us if you see anything that may seem strange. We are going through an uneasy patch. We have them from time to time. We must be careful not to offend . . . not to show arrogance . . . to respect their customs.'

'Except. Thuggery.'

'That is true. But we are hoping that this is an isolated outbreak. If we could track it down and put an end to it there might be no more. If it goes undetected it might grow.'

'I understand your anxiety. Thank you for telling me.'

'I dare say Tom Keeping will tell Miss Philwright. In fact I am sure he will. He has a great respect for her intelligence. He seems to be very interested in her.'

'It was obvious when we travelled with him.'

'And she . . . what are her feelings?'

'I am not sure. She is not one to betray them.'

'There are some like that,' he said, smiling at me.

'It is often wise.'

'I am sure anything Miss Philwright – and you also – would do would be wise. Tom Keeping is a good fellow . . . a very faithful member of the Company. I owe him a good deal.'

'Yes, he is clearly very efficient.'

'You owe him something, too.'

'You mean because he looked after us during the latter part of our voyage?'

'He looked after you very well. I don't think you are aware of how well.'

711

I waited.

He went on: 'Do you know he rescued you from a rather tricky situation?'

I looked at him in surprise. 'I know he was very kind and helpful.'

'How good a student of human nature are you, Miss Drusilla?'

'Do you mean can I judge people? Oh, tolerably well, I believe.'

'I imagine that might be so . . . among ordinary people with whom you come into contact. The lady helpers at the church and the garden bazaar and so on; who must arrange the flowers in the church for Easter; who must be given that best stall at the sale of work; who is a little jealous because someone had too friendly a smile from the delectable Reverend Brady . . . By the way, Brady is married. He married the doctor's daughter.'

He was watching me intently.

'A very suitable match,' I said. 'I trust it satisfies Lady Harriet?'

'There might not have been a marriage if it had not.'

'I suppose not. Colin Brady is a very docile subject.'

'You were less so.'

'I like to manage my own life, don't you?'

'Precisely. But we stray from the point, which was an assessment of your ability to judge human nature. I can tell you this, Miss Drusilla: you may be an expert in your narrow field, but when you stray outside that you are an utter ignoramus.'

'Indeed.'

'Indeed yes. You were completely taken in by the charming Lasseur.'

I was startled.

'He was attractive, was he not? The attentive Frenchman. Were you just a little impressed by him? Did you find him quite attractive?'

'Monsieur Lasseur . . .' I murmured.

'The very same. He was not really a Frenchman, you know.'

'But . . .'

He laughed at me. 'You were an innocent . . . a sheep among wolves. I think it would always be well to know when one is out of one's depth.'

'You are talking in riddles.'

'Always an amusing way to talk, don't you think?'

'No. I would like plain speaking.'

'Then I will speak plainly. Monsieur Lasseur, no Frenchman but a gentleman of obscure origins, was playing a part. The gallant gentleman was out to deceive unsuspecting ladies who believe they have such a good understanding of life and its little vicissitudes that they are ready to fall into his trap. Your Monsieur Lasseur . . .'

'Mine?'

'Monsieur Lasseur is what is known in certain quarters as a procurer for a very wealthy employer, an oriental gentleman who has his own country's traditional ideas about the uses of women . . . with which a young lady such as yourself would never agree. In other words, Monsieur Lasseur had selected you as an interesting addition to his master's harem.'

I felt myself blushing scarlet and I could see this amused him very much.

'I don't believe it,' I said.

'Nevertheless, he is known to some of us. English young ladies are very desirable in certain circumstances. First they belong to that proud country which sees itself as master of the world. They have had a different upbringing from the women of eastern countries. They have had more independence; they have not all been brought up to believe that their mission in life is to serve men in any way in which they are called on to do so. I am sorry if this conversation shocks you, but you see, if you are going adventuring through the world you must be made aware of the facts of life. Lasseur travelled with the ship from England. He was there on his master's

713

more legitimate business; but if he could find someone delectable enough to titillate his master's somewhat jaded palate and bring her back in triumph, he would win the great man's approval and gratitude. He would have done more than merely complete his master's business which he had been sent to England to do. Well, he saw you.'

'I really don't believe a word of this.'

'You can ask Keeping. He saw what was happening. It would not have been exactly the first time a young woman had disappeared in the desert with him and been heard of no more. By the way, you owe a little gratitude to me. I sent word to him to look out for you when you left the ship at Alexandria. He did. He made you his concern, for he knew that was what I would wish. You look stunned.'

I was. I was remembering it all. The meeting with Monsieur Lasseur . . . the conversations . . . the coming of Tom Keeping. And Monsieur Lasseur had intended to arrange that we travel without the rest of the party. Good heavens! I thought. It is feasible.

Fabian was smiling, reading my thoughts.

'I hope you are not disappointed to have been snatched from a Sultan's harem.'

'I am sure the Sultan would have been. I should have thought I was hardly worth the trouble.'

'You underestimate yourself,' he said. 'I believe that you are worth a great deal of trouble.'

He rose from his chair and came over to me. I rose too. He put his hands on my shoulders.

'I'm glad Keeping rescued you and brought you safely to us,' he said seriously.

'Thank you.'

'You still look bewildered.'

'I have been astonished by what you have told me. I really find it hard to believe.'

'That is because you have lived most of your life in a rectory where cunning eastern gentlemen are unheard of.'

714

'There are predatory creatures the whole world over, I suppose.'

'Yes,' he said with a smile, 'but their methods would be different.'

'I must tell Mr Keeping how grateful I am to him.'

'He will tell you he was doing it all as a matter of duty . . . obeying orders.'

'The Company's orders?'

'The Company is only those who work for it. Shall we say my orders. I am the one to whom you should show gratitude.'

'Then if that is so, I thank you.'

He inclined his head. 'I might ask your help one day.'

'I can't imagine my feeble efforts would be of any use to you.'

'You underestimate yourself again. You mustn't, you know. There is a belief that people take you at your own valuation. You see, for all his faults the discerning Monsieur Lasseur recognized your worth. Others might too . . . if you let them.'

'I think I should join the children. I am usually with them at this time.'

'And spoil the tête-à-tête between Miss Philwright and Tom Keeping?'

'Perhaps I should take the children off her hands. They should be able to talk more easily then.'

'Drusilla . . .'

'Yes?'

'Are you a little grateful to me?'

I hesitated. I still found the story incredible.

'I . . . I suppose so,' I said.

'You suppose! That is a very hesitant comment from a young lady who is usually so determined.'

'I am grateful to Mr Keeping, of course. What did he do to the man?'

'He will tell you. There was a stop at one of those places.'

'Yes. It was where he was taken ill.'

'Helped by Tom, of course.'

'It must have been something he put in the wine. I remember there was wine.'

'Of course. He did tell me. He slipped it into the fellow's glass knowing the effect would be quick. He went in with him to the men's rest-room so that he was handy when Lasseur began to feel strange. He looked after him, called the manager of the place and arranged for him to stay there until he was fit to travel. By the time he had recovered the ship would be sailing from Suez with you out of harm's way.'

'It was very cleverly done. What did he give him?'

'Something to get the desired effect. In the course of his business Tom has learned of such things.'

'Perhaps it was Datura,' I said. 'The Thorn Apple.'

'Oh, that . . . Dougal was talking about it, wasn't he?'

'Yes. He explained what it looked like. I could hardly recognize it from his description.'

'You have seen it, then?'

I said: 'It seems the Khansamah grows it in his garden.'

Fabian dropped his bantering manner. 'G. K.!' he said. 'In his garden! But . . . the cultivation is forbidden . . . except in certain cases.'

'Perhaps he is one of the certain cases.'

'I should not think so. How did you know of this?'

I told him how Louise had brought the sprig to me.

'Good God!' he said. 'He is growing it in his garden!'

'Shall you speak to him? Ayah was very upset. You see, Louise crawled under the fence and thought she was bringing me a nice flower.'

'The child took it . . .' he murmured. 'You have said nothing of this to the Khansamah?'

'No. You know how important he is.'

'I do indeed,' said Fabian grimly. 'Did you tell anyone about this?'

'I told Dougal, but foolishly I had burned the thing so I couldn't show him. I am sure he thought I had been mistaken and I think he felt it was not possible to question the Khansamah.'

'H'm,' said Fabian slowly. 'That would be difficult, I admit. Perhaps it is one of those pieces of information best hidden . . . for a while. I want to see Tom Keeping. Perhaps you could go out there and tell him I'm in my study. Would you do that?'

'Of course.'

I could see that the possibility of the Khansamah's growing the Thorn Apple in his garden had driven all frivolous thoughts from his mind.

I sat on in the garden talking to Alice. Tom Keeping had immediately gone in to Fabian when I had told him where he was.

Alice was different. There was a lilt in her voice. I thought to myself: This is Alice in love.

She said how strange it was that Tom Keeping had come to the house.

'It's not strange at all,' I said. 'He is the Company's servant, as they all are. Sir Fabian has just told me the strangest thing. I don't know whether to believe him or not.'

I explained.

She stared at me in amazement. 'It was all rather odd, wasn't it!' she said. 'The way in which he was so suddenly taken ill.'

'It fits,' I agreed. 'But it does seem a rather wild story to me.'

'Well, we were in a wild country. Things are different there . . . and here . . . from what they are at home. It just seems improbable because you are putting it into an English setting. I think Tom acted splendidly, so quickly . . . so efficiently.'

'Yes, I shall have to thank him.'

'What would have happened if he hadn't been there!' She shivered. 'It is too awful to contemplate.'

'Sir Fabian says that Tom was acting on his orders.'

'He would, wouldn't he?'

'It sounds . . . possible.'

Alice lifted her shoulders. 'I think Tom was wonderful,' she said.

I could see that she was obsessed by Tom and I wondered what the outcome would be.

We chatted in the nursery together when the children had gone to bed. Alice was more talkative than usual.

'Tom is apparently a wonderful man,' I said. 'They all seem to think highly of him.'

'His life is very adventurous. I don't suppose he'll stay here long. He is always on the move. He was delighted to see us.'

'He was delighted to see *you*.'

'He did say that he was. Then . . . he said a strange thing . . . how glad he was to have met us but he did not think it was a good time for us to be here. I asked him what he meant by that but he was rather noncommital.'

'I told Sir Fabian about the discovery of that plant in the Khansamah's garden. He was rather disturbed.'

'There is a strange feeling in the air. This matter of the Thugs . . . I think it is causing them a great deal of concern.'

'Naturally it would. It's rebelling against the law.'

'Tom says he expects to be here only a few days and he never knows where he will go next.' She was silent for a while; then she went on: 'It was really wonderful what he did in the desert.'

She smiled proudly. I hoped everything would turn out well for her. She deserved some good fortune.

As soon as I saw Tom Keeping I told him I now knew what he had done and I thanked him.

'It was a pleasure,' he said. 'I only wish I could have had that man arrested. But it is not easy in such places. I recognized him at once, for he had tried the same tactics before. There was a young girl who was going out to be

718

married. Lasseur was one of the party and they disappeared together on the journey across the desert. He had procured a small carriage at the stables, persuaded the girl that they would take the last stage of the journey in greater comfort and . . . she was never seen again.'

'I don't know what to say to you. It is so bewildering. When I try to think of what might have been . . .'

He laid a hand on my arm. 'Well, it didn't happen. Sir Fabian did not like the idea of you two ladies travelling unaccompanied and he told me to look out for you as I was in the neighbourhood and would be making the last part of the journey back to India with you. I saw at once that he was trying the same trick again. I thoroughly enjoyed foiling the loathesome creature.'

'He will probably do it again.'

'Doubtless he will. I should have liked to expose him, but it is a tricky thing to do. His employer is, I believe, a man of great wealth and power. Heaven knows what the consequences would be if anyone interfered with one of his men. It could be an international incident! Discretion had to be the better part of valour on that occasion and I had to content myself with bringing you safely to your destination.'

'Well, thank you.'

'You should thank Sir Fabian. Your safe arrival was a matter of the utmost importance to him.'

I felt a glow of pleasure which, ridiculously, seemed to make the dangers through which I had passed worthwhile.

Then something disturbing did occur. It was afternoon, that time when the day was at its hottest and the household was quiet.

Lavinia had asked me to go to her. She wanted to chat and ask my opinion about a new dress she was having made up. Not that she would take my advice on such a matter; but she wanted to talk.

I thought this would be a good time. She usually rested

at this hour, though she did not sleep, so I guessed I would find her alone.

As I approached her door I heard the sound of voices. Lavinia's was high-pitched. She sounded alarmed.

I ran to the door and opened it. For a few seconds I stared in blank amazement. She was standing by the bed; her peignoir had fallen from her shoulders. She looked startled and afraid – and with her was the Great Khansamah. He was there beside her, his puggaree awry . . . his face distorted. It seemed to me that he was attacking Lavinia. His eyes were glazed and there was something odd about him.

As for Lavinia, her hair was loose about her bare shoulders. She was very flushed. When she looked at me I saw the fear fade from her face and an almost smug expression cross her features.

'I think,' she said to the Khansamah, 'that it would be better if you left now.'

I could see that he was desperately trying to recover his dignity. His hand went to his half-opened shirt. He looked at me and said haltingly: 'Missie come to see Memsahib Countess. I will go.'

'Yes, Khansamah,' said Lavinia, a trifle imperiously. 'You should go now.'

He bowed and, throwing a look of dislike in my direction, he departed.

I said: 'What was that all about?'

'My dear Drusilla, I was most surprised. The fellow thought I might allow him to make love to me.'

'Lavinia!'

'Don't look so surprised. He thinks he is better than any of us.'

'How could you allow it?'

'I didn't allow it. I protested vigorously.'

'Why should he have thought it would be possible?'

'I tell you, he has a high opinion of himself.'

'You must have given him some encouragement.'

She pouted. 'That's right. Blame me . . . as you always do.'

'Don't you see how dangerous this is?'

'Dangerous? I could have handled him.'

'You looked rather alarmed when I came in.'

'In the nick of time!' she said dramatically.

'You should never have received him the way you have. You should have seen him downstairs for your daily consultations.'

'What nonsense! I was only doing what all the women do. They see their khansamahs every morning.'

'This one is different. You have behaved foolishly. You have flirted with him. You must have made him think that he might be successful with you. It would never have entered his mind if you had behaved with decorum as the others do. Who else would dream of encouraging the servants to have such ideas?'

'I did nothing of the sort.'

'You did. I have seen you. Receiving him in your negligée . . . smiling at him, accepting his compliments. Naturally he thought he was making headway with you.'

'But he is a servant here. He should remember that.'

'Not when you behave like a slut.'

'Be careful, Drusilla.'

'It is you who have to be careful. If you do not want plain speaking there is no point in our going on talking.'

'I thought you would be sympathetic.'

'Lavinia, don't you realize the situation here? Tom Keeping is here because of it. There is unease . . . unrest . . . and you create this situation with that man!'

'I didn't make it. He did. I didn't ask him to come to my room.'

'No. But you have implied your interest in him.'

'I have never said a word.'

'Looks speak as loud as words. You are just as bad as you were at school.'

'Oh, you are going to bring all that up, are you?'

721

'Yes, I am . . . as an example of one piece of folly. This is almost as bad.'

She raised her eyebrows. 'Really, Drusilla, you do give yourself airs . . . just because I have been friendly towards you.'

'If you don't like my manner . . .'

'I know. You'll go home. You would go back to that boring old rectory . . . so you think. But you can't. You can't marry Colin Brady because he's already married.'

'I never intended to marry him. And I don't want to be where I am not wanted.'

'Fabian would never let you go.'

I flushed slightly. She saw it and laughed. 'He's quite interested in you . . . but don't deceive yourself. He'd never marry *you*. Fabian is no better than I am really. But . . . you shouldn't be so stand-offish with him, you know.'

I prepared to go but she cried piteously: 'Drusilla, wait a minute. I'm so glad you came in when you did. I think the Khansamah would be very determined. I was really getting just a little scared that he might rape me.'

'I don't want to hear any more, Lavinia. What happened was largely your fault. I think you ought to be a little more responsible. I believe he was drugged. I know he grows Datura in his garden. This would account for his indiscretion, for I cannot believe that even he would dare presume so much in the normal way.'

'So what are you going to do now? Tell Dougal what a terrible wife he has? Don't bother. He knows already. Tell him he's such a bore and that is why I have to find a little divertissement.'

'Of course I shall not tell Dougal.'

'I know. You'll tell Fabian. Drusilla, for Heaven's sake don't do that.'

'I think perhaps it ought to be mentioned. It's intolerable . . . his coming to your bedroom like that.'

'Well, I am rather irresistible.'

'And full of implied promises.'

'Drusilla, please don't tell Fabian.'

I paused. Then I said: 'I think it might be important in view of . . .'

'Oh, don't be so profound! He's a man like any other. They are all the same if you give them half an inch.'

'Then stop giving away inches . . . though in your case it must go into yards.'

'I promise . . . Drusilla, I promise. I'll behave . . . only don't tell Fabian.'

At length I agreed but somewhat uneasily, for I felt that the fact that a member of the Indian household should contemplate such a relationship with the lady of the house was significant.

It was about two days later when the news was brought to the house.

I had seen the Khansamah once during that time. He was his old dignified self. He bowed his head in the customary greeting and made no sign that he remembered that scene in Lavinia's bedroom and the part I played in it.

Lavinia said that when he came to pay his daily call she received him in her sitting-room and she was dressed for the day. It had gone off in a calm manner – much as many such meetings must be going on in houses in the British quarter, where matrons were discussing the day's menus with their khansamahs. There had been no reference to what had happened.

'You should have seen me,' said Lavinia. 'You would have been proud of me. Yes, even you, Drusilla. I just discussed the food and he made suggestions as to what would be suitable. I said, "Yes, Khansamah, I will leave that to you," just as I am sure the most dignified ladies do it. Then . . . it was over.'

'He will understand that he behaved in a way which will not be tolerated,' I said. 'He wouldn't apologize, of course. That would be asking too much. Besides, the fault was largely yours. He has decided to ignore the whole thing, which after all is the best way of dealing with it.'

A young man came to the house. He had ridden from afar. He was quite exhausted and wanted to be taken to the Great Khansamah without delay.

In due course we learned that the message which had been brought was from the Khansamah's brother, and that the Khansamah's son, Asraf, who had recently been married to Roshanara, was dead. He had been murdered.

The Khansamah shut himself into his room in mourning. A pall of gloom fell over the house. Fabian was deeply disturbed. Tom Keeping and Dougal were in the study with Fabian for a long time. They did not emerge for dinner and as on other occasions, trays were sent to the study.

Lavinia and I met over dinner alone. We talked, as the whole household was talking, about Asraf's death.

'He was so young,' I said. 'He and Roshanara have only just been married. Who could have wanted to kill him?'

Even Lavinia was shocked.

'Poor Khansamah. It is such a blow to him. His only son!'

'It is terrible,' I said, and felt sorry for the man in spite of the fact that he was fast becoming a sinister figure in my imagination.

Lavinia said she would retire early and she went to her room. I was in no mood for sleep. I felt very disturbed. I wondered what would happen to Roshanara. Poor child, she was so young.

I sat in the drawing-room in the dark, with the curtains drawn back so that I could look out on the beauty of the moonlit garden.

Just as I was thinking I would retire the door opened and Fabian came in.

'Hello,' he said. 'Still up? Where is Lavinia?'

'She has gone to bed.'

'And you are sitting here alone?'

'Yes. All this is so disturbing.'

He shut the door and advanced into the room. 'I agree,' he said. 'Very disturbing.'

'What does it mean?' I asked.

'It means that for some reason Asraf has been murdered.'

'Perhaps it is one of those Thugs. They murder without reason.'

He was silent for a while. Then he said: 'No . . . I do not think it was the Thugs this time . . . although it might be connected with them.'

'You think that someone murdered . . . not just for the sake of killing . . . but for a definite reason?'

He sat down opposite me. 'It is imperative that we find out what is going on.'

'I understand that.'

'It could be of the most importance to us. I don't like the way things look. I have been discussing with Dougal and Tom the possibility of getting Lavinia and you away with the children.'

'Away! You mean . . .'

'I should feel happier.' He smiled at me a little sardonically. 'I don't mean happier . . . exactly . . . I mean relieved.'

'I don't think Lavinia would go.'

'Lavinia? She will go where and when she is told to go.'

'She has a will of her own.'

'It's a pity she hasn't some sense to go with it.'

'I don't think I should like to be sent here and there . . . like a parcel.'

'Please don't be difficult. Things are hard enough to decide, so don't make them worse.'

'It is just that one wants to have a little say in what happens to one.'

'You have no idea what is going on and yet you want to make decisions. Women and children should not be here.'

'You raised no objections to Lavinia's coming out here. The children were born out here.'

'She came with her husband. I could not arrange where the children were born. I am just stating that it is unfortu-

725

nate that she and they and you are here. But all that came
about naturally enough. I blame myself for bringing you
and Miss Philwright out.'

'*You* did not bring us out.'

'It was my suggestion that you come.'

'Why?'

'I thought perhaps you would have some influence on
Lavinia. You did in the past, and I believe I told you . . .
or implied at least . . . that I also considered the benefits
your presence here would give me.'

'Because you think with your mother that it is necessary
for the children to have an English governess and an English
nanny.'

'But of course . . .'

'And now you regret it.'

'For one reason only. I don't like the situation here and
I think it would be better not to have too many women and
children around.'

'I think your concern does you credit.'

He said with a touch of sarcasm: 'You know the real
reason why I manœuvred your visit. It was because I wanted
a little pleasure for myself.'

'I am surprised that you should think I could provide
it.'

'You can't be. You know for one thing how I enjoy these
spirited conversations . . . Also, I wanted to get you away
from the odious Colin Brady.'

'I thought he was regarded as a devoted Framling subject.'

'All the more reason why I should dislike him. I wanted
to see you . . . so I arranged it. Besides, what would you
have done at home? You couldn't stay at the rectory without
marrying Brady. Where would you have gone?'

'Where I did go. To my old nurse.'

'Ah yes, that good woman. I wanted you here, that was
all. In spite of your indifference to me, I am fond of you,
Drusilla.'

I hoped I did not show the pleasure I felt. He was

irrepressible. He must know that I would never indulge in a light love-affair with him; but he never gave up.

I changed the subject. 'Why are you so disturbed now?'

'This Asraf business.'

'The murder?'

'Exactly. Why was he killed? He was little more than a boy. Why? It is something we have to find out . . . quickly. If it were the Thugs I think I should feel easier. But this was an isolated killing. Thugs deal in numbers. The blood of one innocent boy would not placate Kali for long. As much as I would deplore further outbreaks, I feel that would be more understandable than this mystery. You see, this comes back to our own household. I have a feeling that that is significant.'

'Can you question the Khansamah?'

He shook his head. 'It might be dangerous. We have to find out what is going on. Why was Asraf murdered? We must know whether it was a ritual killing or for some other reason. Tom has left at once to investigate. We may have some news when he gets back.'

'It is all very mysterious.'

'There are many mysteries in this country. Drusilla, I think I should warn you. I may decide that you would have to go at a moment's notice. I should have sent you off before now but travelling is so difficult and the journey might prove more dangerous than staying here. It might be necessary to move you to another town here in India. But we have to understand what this murder means first. So much depends on what is behind it.'

There was silence for a few moments. Then he said: 'How peaceful it seems out there . . .' He did not go on. I stood up suddenly. I wondered what Lavinia would think if she came down and found me in this darkened room with her brother.

I said: 'I will say good night.'

I heard him laugh. 'You think being here alone with me . . . is a little improper?'

727

Again he was reading my thoughts, which surprised and disconcerted me every time I discovered it.

'Oh . . . certainly not.'

'No? Perhaps you are not quite so conventional as I sometimes think. Well, you came on a very hazardous journey. You came with great risk across the desert . . . so it is hardly likely that you can be afraid of me just because we are alone and in a darkened room.'

'What an idea!' I said lightly.

'Yes, it is, isn't it? Stay a while, Drusilla.'

'Oh, I am very tired. I think I should go to bed.'

'Don't worry too much about what I have told you. I may be wrong. There could be a logical answer to all these things . . . chains of coincidence and that sort of thing. But one must find out and be prepared.'

'Of course.'

'I should be most unhappy if you had to go.'

'It is kind of you to say so.'

'It is merely truthful. I wish you were not so afraid.'

'I am not afraid of you, you know.'

'Afraid of yourself, perhaps?'

'I assure you I am by no means overawed or in terror of myself.'

'I didn't mean in that way.'

'I must go.'

He took my hand and kissed it.

'Drusilla, you know I am very fond of you.'

'Thank you.'

'Don't thank me for what I can't help. Stay awhile. Let's talk. Let's stop hedging, shall we?'

'I was not aware of hedging.'

'It's built up between us. You planted the seeds and they grow like weeds . . . of the most prolific kind. I know what started it. It was that business in France. It had more effect on you than it had on Lavinia. You decided that all men are liars and deceivers and you have made up your mind never to be lied to or deceived.'

728

'I think you are talking about something of which you are quite ignorant.'

'Well, give me a chance to learn. I shall be your humble pupil.'

'I am sure you would never be humble ... nor take instruction from me. So I'll say good night. I will remember what you told me and hold myself in readiness for departure at any moment.'

'I hope it doesn't come to that.'

'Nevertheless I shall be prepared.'

'Do you insist on going?'

'I must,' I said. 'Good night.'

I went upstairs in a mood of exhilaration. I wished that I could believe it when I told myself I was indifferent to him.

Alice showed me a letter Tom Keeping had left for her to read after he had gone. He was expecting to return before long and then perhaps she would have an answer for him. He was asking her to marry him. He knew that she would not want to give a hasty reply and would need time to think. They had known each other such a short time but he himself was certain that he wanted to marry her.

'The times are somewhat uneasy,' he wrote. 'I shall be here for some years, I imagine. You would be travelling with me. It could be dangerous at times and there would be occasions when we should be apart. I do want you to consider all this. I thought it better to write, for I did not want my feelings to carry me away to such an extent that I glossed over the difficulties. Everything will be different from what you have known. But I love you, Alice, and if you care for me I should be the happiest man on Earth.'

I was deeply moved when I read it. It might not have been an effusive love-letter but it conveyed a deep sincerity.

I looked at Alice and I did not have to ask what her answer would be.

'I would not have believed such a thing could happen to

me,' she said. 'I never thought for one moment that any man would want to marry me . . . and a man like Tom. I feel I must be dreaming.'

Dear Alice! She did look bemused, but incredibly happy.

'Oh, Alice,' I said. 'It's wonderful. It's a beautiful romance.'

'That it should happen to me! I can't believe it. Do you think he really means it?'

'Of course he means it. I'm so happy for you.'

'I couldn't marry him yet.'

'Why not?'

'What about my job here? The Countess . . .'

'The Countess wouldn't care about you if it suited her. Of course you must marry him. You must begin this wonderful life as soon as you can.'

'What about the children?'

'They have a good nurse in Ayah and an excellent governess in me.'

'Oh, Drusilla, we have been such friends!'

'Why the past tense? We *are* good friends. We always shall be.'

It was wonderful to see the change in Alice. She was like a different person. She had never thought to meet someone like Tom Keeping who would love her and whom she loved. She was very fond of children and wanted to have her own; but she had long thought that it would be her mission in life to look after other people's.

A wonderful vista was opening out before her. An adventurous life . . . travelling through India with a man who had a most unusual and exciting job – and she would be with him for ever more.

She looked at me rather wistfully, and I guessed that like many people in love – unselfish ones like Alice, that is – she wanted to see others in the same state, and especially me.

'I wish . . .' she said rather sadly.

I knew what she was going to say and added quickly:

730

'You wish that Tom would come back quickly and you are wondering when you can be married. It will be quite simple, I imagine. Think of all the girls who come out to be married. They must be quite used to it by now.'

'I was wishing that you could find someone . . .'

'Oh,' I said lightly, 'there aren't enough of Tom Keeping's kind to go round. Only the fortunate ones get them.'

She was frowning. 'I shan't like leaving you.'

'My dear Alice, I shall be perfectly all right.'

'I shall worry about you.'

'Oh come, Alice. You know I'm not a wilting blossom. I shall manage the children perfectly with Ayah's help.'

'I wasn't thinking of that, Drusilla. We have been very close. Oh, I feel I can talk to you. How do you feel about Fabian Framling?'

'Oh . . . an interesting man. Very much aware of his own importance.'

'How important is he to you?'

'I suppose the same as he is to everyone else. He seems to be quite a power around here.'

'That isn't quite what I meant.'

'Then what did you mean?'

'I think he is not indifferent to you.'

'He is not indifferent to anything that goes on around here.'

'You know what I mean. He's interested . . .'

'In seduction?'

'Well . . . I did think of something like that.'

'And I think it might enter his mind . . . as it would where any youngish woman was concerned.'

'That is what I'm afraid of. It wouldn't be wise to feel too strongly.'

'Don't worry. I know him very well.'

'Isn't that Lady Somebody coming out to marry him?'

'I should imagine all that is shelved because of the uneasiness here.'

'But eventually the marriage will take place.'

'I think it is Lady Harriet's will . . . and that is usually obeyed by all.'

'I see. I wish you could come away with me when I go.'

'I don't think Tom would want a third person to share his honeymoon.'

'I do hope you will be all right. Of course you are very sensible. I don't like your being here . . . with the Countess, who is very reckless and selfish . . . and as for her husband . . . I think he is half in love with you.'

'Don't worry, I tell you. Dougal would always be half in love . . . never wholly so.'

'I don't like the situation at all. You must never let anyone take you off your guard.'

'Thank you. I suppose you feel that as an about-to-be-married woman you should look after your less experienced and fragile sisters. Oh, Alice, just concentrate on being happy. For I am happy for you.'

Lavinia was amused when she heard that Tom and Alice were to be married.

'Who would have thought it of her! She seems a born old maid. Frankly I can't understand what he sees in her. She's very *plain*.'

'There is more to people than waving tendrils and tigerish looks, you know. She's highly intelligent.'

'Which you imply I'm not.'

'Nobody could call you plain.'

'Nor intelligent either?'

'Well, the way in which you behave does rather suggest a sparsity of that valuable asset.'

'Oh, shut up. Anyway, I think it's funny. Nanny Alice and Tom Keeping. And what about the children? Mama will be furious. She sent Alice Philwright out to look after the children, not to get married.'

'The matter will have passed out of your mother's jurisdiction. She may rule Framling but not all India.'

'She'll be extremely put out. I wonder if she will send out another English nanny.'

'I shouldn't think so. After all, your time out here is not very long, is it?'

'Thank you for reminding me of that blessed fact.'

'You might not enjoy such male adoration on the Carruthers' country estate as you do here.'

'No. That is a point. And Mama will not be so far off. I shall have to reconsider. Perhaps I shall persuade Dougal to stay after all.'

'I think he longs to get home.'

'To those dry old books which he can't get here. Serve him right.'

'Such a dutiful spouse,' I murmured; and she was laughing.

Fabian's reaction to the news was one of surprise.

We were at dinner when the matter was brought up.

'I thought Keeping was a confirmed bachelor,' he said.

'Some men are until they meet someone they really care about,' I replied.

He threw me an amused glance.

'Nobody could be more surprised than I,' said Lavinia. 'I thought people like Nanny Philwright never got married. They're supposed to be devoted to their charges all their lives and in the end live in a little house bought for them by some grateful one who visits Nanny every Christmas and on her birthday and makes sure she is comfortable for the rest of her days.'

'I am not surprised at all,' I said. 'They are a delightful couple. I could see there was a rapport between them from the moment they met.'

'On the road across the desert,' said Fabian, smiling at me significantly and reminding me how Tom Keeping at his command had saved me from a fate too horrible to contemplate.

'It means we are losing our nanny,' said Lavinia. 'That is a bore.'

733

'The ayah is very good,' I reminded her. 'I shall help to look after them, as I always have done. But we shall all be very sad to see her go.'

'She will visit the house with Tom from time to time, I dare say,' said Dougal.

'Then there can be a joyous reunion,' added Fabian.

'I am very happy for Alice,' I said. 'She is one of the best people I have ever known.'

'Then,' said Fabian, 'let us drink to them.' He lifted his glass. 'To lovers . . . wherever they may be.'

Mutiny

Asraf's body was brought to his father. It was kept in state in the little house in the grounds which was the Great Khansamah's home. There was to be a traditional burial, which meant that Asraf's body would be placed in a wooden cart and taken to a certain spot where it would be burned.

Roshanara had come back. She was staying under the protection of her father-in-law, the Great Khansamah. I wished that we could see her again. I should have liked to talk to her. I wanted to know what her future would be.

I was soon to learn.

Ayah came to me; she plucked my sleeve implying that she wished to see me alone.

I said: 'Is anything wrong?'

She did not answer that. Instead she said: 'Missie . . . come . . .'

She took me out to the garden and to the gazebo there among the tall grasses and shrubs. Few people went there. We were told that snakes abounded in the long grass. The Russelian snake had been seen there and on one or two occasions the dreaded cobra.

I drew back a little as we approached the gazebo. The ayah noticed. She said: 'We take care . . . great care. Follow where I go, please.'

I followed her and in the gazebo I came face to face with Roshanara. We looked at each other for a few seconds and then she was in my arms.

'Oh, Missie . . . Missie . . .' she said. 'So good . . . so kind.'

I held her at arms' length. I was a little shocked by her

appearance. She was no longer the child who had sat down with Louise and listened to my lessons.

She looked older, thinner and what alarmed me was her expression of apprehension which was immediately noticeable. I realized that here was a very frightened girl.

'So you are a widow now, Roshanara,' I said.

She gave me a sorrowful look.

'I am so sorry,' I said. 'It was terrible. You have been so briefly married. How sad to lose your husband.'

She shook her head and said nothing but her big frightened eyes never left my face.

'He was murdered,' I went on. 'It was so senseless. Was it some enemy?'

'He did nothing, Missie. He just frightened little boy. He die because of what was done . . . by another.'

'Do you want to talk about it?'

She shook her head. Then suddenly she was kneeling at my feet, clutching at my skirt.

'Help me, Missie,' she said. 'Do not let me burn.'

I looked at the ayah, who nodded. She said: 'Tell. Tell, Roshanara. Tell Missie.'

Roshanara looked up at me. 'There will be the funeral . . . the funeral pyre. I must throw myself into the flames.'

'No!' I said.

'Great Khansamah say Yes. He say it is the widow's duty.'

'No, no,' I said. 'That is Suttee. It is no longer permitted under British rule.'

'Great Khansamah he say this our way. He will not have the foreigners' way.'

'It is simply forbidden,' I told her. 'You just have to refuse. No one can make you. You have the law on your side.'

'Great Khansamah he say . . .'

'This is nothing to do with Great Khansamah.'

'Asraf is his son.'

'That is of no account. It is against the law.'

'Missie will know,' said Ayah.

Roshanara nodded.

'It is not going to happen,' I said. 'We shall see to that. Leave it with me. I shall see that it does not happen.'

Roshanara's terrified look was replaced by one of confidence. I was a little shaken that she put so much reliance on my powers.

I wanted to act quickly and I was not sure how to go about it. This was too big a matter for me to deal with alone. I must consult Fabian and Dougal. It would have to be Fabian. Dougal would be all sympathy but he was a little ineffectual. Fabian would know what was the best thing to do.

I must find him quickly and talk to him.

I said: 'Leave this to me. Now I must go. What will you do, Roshanara?'

'She will go back to Great Khansamah's house,' said Ayah. 'He must not know she come and tell you this. I take her back.'

I said: 'I am sure I shall soon be ready to tell you what you must do.'

I went at once to Fabian's study. By good fortune he was there.

He rose and showed his pleasure at the sight of me. I was annoyed with myself for feeling so elated when I had this terrible situation to face.

I said: 'I have to talk to you.'

'I'm glad of that. What is it?'

'It's Roshanara. She's here. I've just seen her. The poor child is terrified. The Great Khansamah is going to force her to leap into Asraf's funeral pyre.'

'What?'

'It is what she has been told she must do.'

'It's impossible.'

'It's the Great Khansamah's orders. What do we do about it?'

737

'I'd say we'd stop the proceedings.'

'That would not be difficult in view of the law, would it?'

'It wouldn't be difficult but it might be dangerously provocative. We have made a few alarming discoveries and it is my opinion that the situation is becoming explosive. I believe we have to act with the utmost caution.'

'But in a case of lawbreaking . . .'

'Drusilla,' he said seriously, 'I can trust your discretion?'

'Of course.'

'Don't speak of this to my sister, or anyone. When Tom Keeping returns I dare say he will put Miss Philwright in the picture . . . but she is a sensible girl. Tom wouldn't have fallen in love with her otherwise.'

'I have promised Roshanara that something will be done.'

'Something shall be done. This atrocious thing will not be allowed to take place. Rest assured of that. But we have discovered certain things. There is rebellion in the air. It would take very little to set a spark to the smouldering fires and when it comes — if it comes — the conflagration will be great. We've gone wrong somewhere . . . or perhaps it has all come about naturally. The Company has never wanted to make a subject race of the Indians. We have improved their lot in so many ways but there are bound to be mistakes. Perhaps we have made a few. I think our influence has been too rapidly felt. These people may believe that their civilization is threatened and that their native institutions are being squeezed out to make way for others.'

'But surely they must realize that they are better off without such evil practices as Suttee and Thuggery.'

'Perhaps. But still there will be some who object. You see, under Lord Dalhousie we have annexed the Punjab and Oude. But the real trouble at the moment is that a certain unrest is growing up here in Delhi round the deposed King Bahadur Shah and Dalhousie is now threatening to send the old Mogul family from their seat in Delhi.'

'Why?'

Fabian lifted his shoulders. 'We are watchful of the leader, Nana Sahib, who will seize the first opportunity to rouse the people to revolt against us. We are in a difficult position. I am telling you this so that you will see that we have to act with the utmost care.'

'What about Roshanara?'

'This must be stopped. There is no doubt of that. But we shall have to be careful how we act. We have made discoveries about the Great Khansamah and it seems we have trouble in our own household.'

'That does not surprise me. Can you not denounce him?'

'Certainly not. That would start the rebellion at once and Heaven knows where it would end. He is not only a khansamah. He has taken this position because this is a house frequented by officials of the Company.'

'You mean . . . in a way . . . he is a spy?'

'Oh, more than that. G. K. is a leader. He hates the intruders. I am sure of that. He is a follower of Nana Sahib who wants us out of the country.'

'He is Nana, too. Great Nana. I have heard him called that.'

'Whether he took the name after the leader or whether it is his by right, I do not know. All I do know is that we have made discoveries about him and because of what he is we must act with the greatest caution.'

'What discoveries?'

'He is growing Datura in the garden. Because Thuggery has been abolished by our law he wants to defy that law. Keeping suspected . . . and he has now found evidence to prove that he was right and that G. K. was helping his friends to go back to Thuggery. The travellers who had been found in the forest had been poisoned and we believe that the poison came through G. K. This seems likely, for a relative of one of the travellers who died took his revenge by murdering Asraf.'

'Oh, poor Asraf to be the victim of someone's revenge on someone else!'

'His own father, of course. Asraf is G. K.'s only son. It would have been harder to inflict a greater injury. So you see we have the seeds of deception in our own household.'

'But what can we do about Roshanara?'

'We shall stop it . . . but subtly and in secret. To make a scene at the funeral pyre would be the utmost folly and could start an instant revolt. I feel certain that if we did there would be an immediate uprising in this very house. We must avoid that. When Keeping comes back I shall discuss with him the urgency of getting you with Lavinia and the children out of Delhi.'

'You expect trouble in Delhi?'

'Delhi is an important city. When there is trouble it is likely to be at the heart of it.'

'Tell me what you propose to do about Roshanara.'

'I shall have to give the matter some thought, but at the moment it seems to me that what we must do is smuggle her out of the city.'

'The Great Khansamah would never allow that.'

'I will do it without his knowledge, of course.'

'Is it possible?'

'We must make it possible. The Company owns several houses in various places. There it is possible for people to live in secret for a little while. I do believe this is the best way to act. We must be very, very careful, though. Tom should return tonight. He comes and goes with frequency so it will not arouse much comment if he leaves again. When is the funeral to be?'

'Very soon, I believe. I think in two days' time.'

'Then prompt action is necessary. Be ready. I may need your help. And remember, not a word to anyone.'

'I'll remember,' I said.

He smiled at me and leaned towards me. I thought he was going to kiss me but he did not. I think he must have seen the alarm leap into my eyes. I must disguise my feelings.

Alice had noticed something. I must be sure no one else did
. . . especially Fabian.

The events of that day stay clearly in my mind.

As soon as I could I saw the ayah, which happened almost
immediately because she was as eager to see me as I was
her.

I said to her: 'It is all right. It is going to be stopped but
we have to be careful. There must be no betrayal of what
we are going to do.'

She nodded gravely.

'Sir Fabian is going to see that it is all right. You must
do exactly what you are told and not whisper a word to
anyone.'

She nodded again. 'Now?' she asked.

'When we are ready I will tell you. In the meantime you
must behave as though nothing has happened.'

I knew she would. She was terrified of what would
happen to her if the Great Khansamah ever discovered she
had been involved in a plot to undermine his authority.

Later that day Tom Keeping arrived.

Fabian summoned Dougal and me to the study and said
that Miss Philwright must come too, for her help might be
needed and now she was engaged to Tom she would work
with us.

It was obvious that Tom already knew that Alice had
accepted him. His look of contentment mingled with that
of apprehension for which the situation was responsible.

'Sit down,' said Fabian. 'You too, Miss Philwright. You
have heard what is happening?' He looked questioningly
at Alice.

Alice said she did know.

'Well, we have to get this girl out of the house. Tom is
seeing to that. There are several small houses owned by the
Company to which many of its members can go if ever
there is the need to hide. They are run as little inns in the
country. There anyone who has to hide for a while can pass

as a traveller and little notice is taken of them. Tom, tell your plan.'

'We are going to get the Indian girl out of danger,' said Tom. 'We could, of course, forbid the ceremony and call in the law. That is what I would suggest normally. But we think that would not be wise in view of the explosive state of affairs at present.'

Fabian said: 'I believe that both Miss Delany and Miss Philwright are aware of the growing tension among the people here. Our enemies are spreading rumours among the Sepoys that the bullets they use have been greased with the fat of beef and pork which they consider unclean. They think that we are trying to suppress their old customs by treating them with contempt. Several fires have been started in Barrackpur. I'm sorry, Tom. I digress, but I do think it is important for the young ladies to understand the gravity of the situation and why we have to act in this devious manner. There have been outbursts of rebellion which we have suppressed, but rumours are running through Oude and Bundelkhund which are undermining our prestige. Now carry on, Tom.'

'We're highly suspicious of the Khansamah. He is a man who seems able to lead people. It is because of his presence in this household that we have to proceed with the greatest caution, and Sir Fabian and I have come to the conclusion that until we are more sure of his intentions, we must concentrate – for the moment – more on saving the life of this girl than on seeing justice done. Our plan, therefore, is to get Roshanara out of harm's way.'

'How?' asked Dougal.

'By taking her away from here.'

'You will be seen leaving,' said Dougal.

'Not if we do it this way. She will not leave until after dark.'

'She will be missed from the Khansamah's house,' I said.

'We hope that she is supposed to remain alone in her room, prostrate with grief for the loss of her husband.

742

According to tradition, she should be spending what they believe will be her last night on Earth in meditation and prayer. They will leave her in solitude to do this. What she must do is slip out of his house but not come into this one. She will go to the gazebo.'

'The grass around it is infested with snakes,' said Dougal. 'I can tell you that some of them are . . . lethal.'

'I know how interested you are in the various species, Dougal,' said Fabian impatiently, 'but there is no time to discuss them now.'

'I merely thought the approach to the place is dangerous.'

'The danger is minor compared with what we should have to face if we did not take this action. Go on, Tom.'

'Well,' said Tom, 'we must disguise Roshanara. This is where you ladies will help. I have a wig here which will transform her appearance.' He opened a small bag and brought out the wig. It was made of human hair and looked quite realistic. It was light brown in colour.

'It will make a good deal of difference to her appearance,' I commented.

'A little face powder might lighten her skin,' said Alice.

'I am sure it would,' I said. 'Lavinia has lots of pots and bottles on her dressing-table. I'll ask her.'

'No,' said Fabian. 'Don't ask her. Take what you want.'

'She may miss them.'

'You must make sure that she does not. You will only need them briefly and they can be replaced before she notices they have been taken away. So you really think you could alter her appearance . . . make her look . . . European?'

'I think we might,' I said. 'We can try.'

'But you must not tell Lavinia a word.'

'It will mean purloining these things.'

'Then purloin.'

'The plan is,' went on Tom, 'to get Roshanara here at midnight. She must in no circumstances come into this house. Servants have sharp ears and eyes and are always

743

on the alert, but particularly so now. She should make her way to the gazebo.'

'In spite of possible snakes,' added Fabian, throwing a glance at Dougal.

'There,' went on Tom, 'she will be dressed in some garments which you will find for her . . . European style. Her appearance should be entirely changed. She and I will leave at once. I shall get her to a house on the fringe of the city. Mr and Mrs Sheldrake will arrive. Sheldrake is one of the Company's men. His wife will be a help. Roshanara will pose as their daughter. Mrs Sheldrake and the girl can travel in a *palanquin* . . . the girl being ill, we shall say. That will insure against too many questions being asked, for no one will want to go too near her for fear of catching some infectious disease. Thus we will get her to a house of safety where she will remain until we can review the situation.'

Fabian looked at me. 'You are thinking this a little melodramatic. Why do we not simply stop the proceedings? Believe me, it is what I should prefer to do.'

'I do understand,' I assured him. 'It must be done as you have arranged. Alice and I will do our best to disguise her.'

'The thing is to find something to fit her,' said Alice. 'She is so young and slight.'

'Any garment will do,' said Fabian. 'She will be in the *palanquin* most of the time . . . except at first of course.'

'And that I should imagine is the most dangerous part,' I said. I turned to Alice. 'Where shall we find the clothes?'

Alice studied me for a few seconds. 'You are very slim, though much taller than the girl. We could cut off the bottom of one of your dresses.'

'That's the answer,' said Tom looking proudly at Alice who had produced it.

'And don't forget,' said Fabian, 'my sister must not be in the secret. She would be unable to stop herself blurting out something about it.'

'We must first get the message to Roshanara,' said Tom.

'I will speak to the ayah at once,' I told him.

'I don't like a native being involved,' said Fabian.

I looked at him with exasperation. 'Don't you see, Ayah wants this to succeed as much as any of us. She is her aunt. She brought her up. She will do everything she can to save her. I know.'

'It doesn't do to get emotionally involved,' said Fabian. 'It leads to misjudgement. Impress on the ayah . . .'

'Of course I will, but she will understand that without telling. We can trust her discretion absolutely.'

'It is a mistake to trust absolutely.'

Why was it, I asked myself, that I could never be with him without this argumentative mood overtaking me? This was no time for it. We had to concentrate all our efforts on making the plan work.

As soon as I left the house I saw the ayah. I suggested she go to the gazebo where we could talk. Fabian was right. One should not be too trusting and although I was sure there must be many of the servants who would be sad to see Roshanara burned to death, they would never know where the wrath of the Khansamah would end and some might feel a patriotic desire to drive the British out of India and defy their laws.

I told Ayah what we planned. Roshanara would hear what she had to do when she arrived at the gazebo. We would tell her while we dressed her. It was pathetic to see the hope in her eyes. She believed Roshanara's chances of survival had come through my goddess-like power. I wanted to tell her that it was Fabian and Tom Keeping who had formulated the plan between them.

She listened carefully to what I said. Roshanara would come to the gazebo at midnight when the house of the Great Khansamah was quiet and all in it sleeping. It could be done, she knew, because the whole family would be in their rooms praying before the night of the funeral.

Alice and I would go to the gazebo during the day,

taking certain of the things we should need to change the appearance of Roshanara. Our great fear was that we might betray in some way that we were acting in an unusual manner.

Apparently we did not, for all went smoothly.

Alice and I dressed Roshanara. The poor child was trembling with fright. She could not believe that anyone could challenge the orders of the Great Khansamah; but at the same time she had great confidence in me.

There was no need to warn either Indian of the consequences to themselves if the plan went wrong. They were as aware of that as we were.

So in due course Roshanara was ready. She did not look in the least like her old self. The cut down dress hung on her a little but it was not entirely ill-fitting, and the wig of light brown hair completely transformed her. She looked like a Eurasian. Her graceful movements and her striking dark eyes could not be disguised.

I knew how successful our plan had been when a few days later a note was delivered from Tom Keeping.

'All is well,' he wrote. 'Cargo will be safely delivered from the city tonight.'

That seemed satisfactory. We had saved Roshanara.

There was a great outcry the next day when the news of Roshanara's absence became known.

The Khansamah said nothing but I knew he was in a murderous rage. He had wanted the old custom of Suttee to be carried out to the letter. He wished to defy the British, which was apparently a sentiment gaining ground throughout the country.

The ayah told me that many questions had been asked. He had interrogated her particularly. What did she know? She must have an idea. Had the girl gone off on her own? They would find her, never fear. She should die in the fire if she were found, and she would not have the honour of making a sacrifice for her husband and her country.

But die she should, for defying the orders of the Great Khansamah and for being a traitor to her country.

Poor Roshanara! I hoped she had escaped from her formidable father-in-law for ever.

Lavinia had been kept in ignorance of all this on Fabian's orders, but now she was aware of Roshanara's escape. The reason for it had seeped out and everyone was talking of it.

'Poor girl,' she said. 'Did you know they wanted her to jump into the funeral pyre?'

'Well, it was an old custom at one time.'

'But it isn't now.'

'No. Thank goodness it has stopped.'

'But they still do it. The Great Khansamah wanted it done this time. It was out of respect for his son. He seems a little annoyed that his wishes were disobeyed.'

'Serve him right.'

'He's only following the old custom.'

'I wonder if he would be prepared to jump into a fire for the sake of an old custom.'

'Of course he wouldn't. Roshanara's well out of it. I wonder how she managed it? I shouldn't have thought she would have had the spirit.'

'When one is faced with death one finds the power to do all sorts of things.'

'How do you know? You've never faced death.'

'You're right. We none of us know how we should behave in certain circumstances if we have never faced them.'

'Philosophizing again! Trust old Drusilla. G. K. has been questioning them all. He is trying to find out who disobeyed his orders.'

'Has he been telling you?'

'Not he! He's very dignified now . . . since that time I sent him off with a flea in his ear.'

'As I remember; you did nothing of the sort. The encounter was brought to an end when I came in and rescued you.'

'Drusilla to the rescue! Because you did it once over that boring old comte, you think you do it all the time.'

'I am glad he has become that boring old comte. He was so wonderful at one time.'

'Well, the Khansamah has been behaving very well lately.'

'Very well! Trying to force his daughter-in-law to burn herself to death!'

'I was referring to his way with me.'

'Of course. You never give a thought to anything that does not concern you.'

Lavinia laughed. 'Stay with me. I love the way you treat me. I don't know why. Mama would have dismissed you long ago for insolence.'

'But you are not Mama and if I am dismissed I will take myself off without delay.'

'Huffy again! Of course I want you to stay. You're my best friend, Drusilla. What a name! It suits you. You look like a Drusilla.'

'Prim? Disapproving of all the fun?'

'That's right.'

'It's not true. I only disapprove of the so-called fun you like to have with the opposite sex which has once had dire consequences which you should remember.'

'Are we back to that!'

'Yes . . . and be careful of the Khansamah. He may not be what you think.'

'Oh, he's polite to me always. He's quite humble now.'

'I wouldn't trust him.'

'You wouldn't trust your maiden aunt who goes to church four times a day and prays for an hour kneeling by her bedside every night.'

'I have no such maiden aunt.'

'You ought to be one yourself – only you haven't any family to be aunt to. That's why you impress your prim propriety on me.'

'I tell you . . .'

'I'm going home!' she mimicked. 'Oh no you won't. What

was I telling you? Oh, I know. How G. K. is with me. He is rather sweet, really. Do you know he brought me a present the other day. I know what it is for. He's asking for forgiveness for that outburst. Of course I forgive him. He just admired me so much.'

'I believe you would have surrendered if I hadn't come in.'

'Give up my virtue! What an experience it would have been!'

'You have so little virtue that you would hardly be aware of its loss. As to experience . . . so is jumping into the sea and drowning yourself, but I don't suggest you try that for the sake of sweet experience.'

'Oh, shut up and look at the present G. K. brought to me.'

She went to a drawer and took out a case.

'You mean you accepted a gift . . . from him!'

'Of course I accepted it. One has to accept gifts in the spirit in which they are given. It's extremely impolite not to do so.'

She opened the box and drew out its contents. She held it to her face, peering over the top coquettishly.

I was staring in horror at a peacock feather fan.

The weeks that followed were marked by increasing tension. In certain parts of the country open rebellion had broken out, but so far it had been kept under control.

At the beginning of March of that year 1857 Alice and Tom Keeping were married. It was a simple ceremony which I attended with Dougal, Lavinia and Fabian, who had made a flying visit to Delhi for the occasion and left immediately afterwards. He did say that he had urgent Company business and must keep in touch with the Army. He was going to the Punjab where, so far, everything was quiet.

Dougal remained in Delhi and I had several opportunities of talking to him.

He said he would very much like to get out of the country and Fabian had agreed with him on this. Undercurrents of rebellion were springing up everywhere and the journey to the coast might prove very hazardous. But for the children he thought it would be advisable to attempt to leave. Both he and Fabian agreed that Delhi might perhaps be the safest place for us to be after all, for the biggest concentration of Army personnel was stationed there.

I had thought a great deal about the Khansamah's gift of the peacock feather fan to Lavinia. I could not help feeling that there was some sinister implication in this. I chided myself. It was a small matter compared with the cloud of uncertainty which hung over us. Fans made of peacock feathers were common enough in the bazaars and market-places. True, they were mostly bought by foreigners who would not know of their reputation . . . whatever that was. But what was the significance of the Khansamah's gift of one to Lavinia?'

She believed it was a form of apology for his behaviour; but then Lavinia would always believe what she wanted to.

I did ask Dougal about peacock feathers. He was very interested in old customs and he had probably heard that they were considered to be unlucky. He had not, but being Dougal, he set himself the task of finding out.

As he had known that one day he would have to visit India he had made it his duty to find out all he could about that country; and in his possession were several books which he had brought out with him from England.

There was not much that he could tell me, however, but he did discover that there were suspicions regarding peacocks' feathers and one or two sources stated that in some quarters they were considered to be bringers of ill luck.

I told him that I had one in my possession which had been given to me by Miss Lucille Framling who had certainly believed in its evil influence.

'Odd that she should wish to pass it on to you,' he said.

I told him of the incident when I had taken the fan. He smiled and said: 'I believe she was a little unbalanced.'

'Yes, she had a great tragedy. Her lover was murdered and it seemed to her that it was all due to the fan.'

'Well, that's a lot of nonsense.'

I did not tell him that the Khansamah had presented Lavinia with one. I wondered what he would say if he knew that she had carried on a mild flirtation with the man. Sometimes I thought he did not care what Lavinia did.

'It goes back to the legend of Argus whose eyes went to the peacock's tail. Some believe that Argus wants revenge and that the spots are eyes which see everything that is going on . . . not only what is visible but what is in the mind. There are quite a number of people in this country who never have peacock feathers in their houses.'

'They don't all feel like that I suppose. Some might think the fans made pleasant gifts. They are really very beautiful.'

'It might be that the fact that they are would make them more evil in the eyes of the superstitious.'

I tried to forget that the Khansamah had given Lavinia the fan. Heaven knew, there were far more important matters to concern me.

I received a letter from Alice. She was very happy. She wrote: 'Tom is wonderful and we often marvel at the fortuitous way in which we met. Tom is wondering what is going to happen next. I think he realizes the danger of the situation more than most, for his work takes him all over the country. His work is so exciting and it is marvellous to be able to help him. You will be happy to know that the cargo is settled and being taken care of. I look forward to meeting you some time. Perhaps we shall come back to Delhi. Tom is never sure where his work will take him and things are a little uncertain now. It would be wonderful to have a real talk about everything.'

I was so pleased to read her letter. How wonderfully life had turned out for Alice!

Meanwhile as the uneasy weeks passed, rumour intensified. April had passed and May was with us. Lord Canning made a proclamation assuring the Sepoy troops that the cartridges they used were not greased with pork or beef, but it was, I believed, received with scepticism.

Dougal was called away. He went reluctantly.

'I don't like leaving you here alone,' he said. 'Major Cummings will keep an eye on the house. You must do whatever he tells you.'

Lavinia was rather pleased. She was developing a fondness for Major Cummings.

The day Dougal left Fabian returned.

He asked me to go to his study and when I arrived, I saw how serious he was.

He said: 'I can't talk to Lavinia. She has no sense of responsibility. I can't tell you how worrying this is, Drusilla. It seems to me you are the only sensible one here now that Alice Philwright has gone. A pity. She is a practical young woman.'

'What has happened?'

'God knows. There is a terrible feeling of uneasiness throughout the Company and the Army. It was a mistake to depose the King of Delhi – old Bahadur Shah was quite harmless – and an even greater one to try to turn them out of the family mansion. You see, Drusilla, we have won many a battle with the Sepoy troops. Now they say to themselves: Who won these battles? It is the soldier who wins the battles . . . not those in command. What we could do for the British we could do for ourselves. They are against us, Drusilla . . . and they are part of the Army.'

'Do you really think they would revolt?'

'Some would. The Sikhs are loyal . . . so far. I think they can see what benefits have come through us and they care enough for the country to want us to continue. But this headlong nationalism . . . we can't stop it. What worries me is you and Lavinia and the children. I do wish I could get you home.'

'I don't think that would be easy, would it?'

'Far from easy . . . but just possible. You see, if we got you out of Delhi, where would you go? One doesn't know from one hour to the next where revolt will break out. We might be sending you into disaster . . . whereas here in Delhi . . . at least we are well represented and we know where we are.'

'There must be more important things to worry about than us.'

'That is not the case,' he said. 'I wish to God you had never come. I wish I could stay here. I want to keep my eyes on things . . . here. But I can't. Drusilla, you will have to think for yourself and Lavinia.'

'Have you talked to Lavinia?'

'I have tried to. It doesn't make much impression. She doesn't really see danger. I don't like leaving you here with the Khansamah. I wish I could get rid of him. I am certain that he was responsible for that outbreak of Thuggery. He would regard it as a gesture of defiance . . . against us, you see. He is at variance with the laws because *we* have imposed them. But someone took revenge on *him*, for the murder of young Asraf was revenge by the family of one of the victims. Now he may suspect that we were involved in the plot to spirit Roshanara away. I want you to be ready to leave at a moment's notice.'

'I will be.'

'There may not be much warning. I wish I could stay in Delhi but I have to leave tonight.'

'Don't worry about us. I will be prepared.'

'The children . . .'

'I shall manage that. I shall tell them it is a new game. It will be easy to handle them.'

'I'm sure you'll manage. Sometimes I thank God you are here and at others I curse myself for having brought you.'

I smiled at him. 'Please don't do that,' I said. 'It has been . . . illuminating.'

He looked at me steadily for a moment and then suddenly

753

he put his arms round me and held me tightly against him.

Then I felt that everything was worthwhile.

When he had gone I felt a frightening loneliness. There seemed to be a special stillness in the air ... a tension as though something terrible was lurking, ready to spring out on us and destroy us.

It was early evening. The children were in bed. The ayah's cousin had joined her to help her look after the children. She was a quiet, gentle girl and both Louise and Alan were already fond of her.

I heard a gentle knock at the door. I went to it and there was the ayah.

'Is anything wrong?' I cried in alarm.

She put her fingers to her lips and came into the room.

'I want you to come ... see my brother. He must see you.'

'Why does he want to see me?'

'He want to say thank-you.' She lowered her voice. 'For saving Roshanara.'

'There is no need for that.'

'Yes ... great need.'

I knew how easily susceptibilities could be wounded so I said: 'I shall be home tomorrow. Perhaps he would call then.'

'He not come. He say you go to him.'

'When?'

'Now.'

'The children ...'

'They are in good care.'

I knew that she had set her little cousin to watch over them.

'Very important,' she said, and added mysteriously: 'For plan.'

I was very puzzled and she went on: 'Come on. Go to gazebo. Wait there.'

I was very curious but I did sense an urgency in her

manner and because I knew that I must be prepared for any extraordinary occurrence I fell in at once with her suggestion.

I looked in at the children. They were sleeping peacefully and the ayah's cousin was seated by Alan's bed.

'I watch,' she said.

I went with all speed to the gazebo. The ayah was already there. She opened a box and took out a blue sari which she asked me to put on. It seemed to become more and more mysterious but remembering Fabian's warnings and the dangers in which we were living, I complied. She gave me a piece of material rather like a shawl to put round my head.

'We go,' she said.

We left the garden, avoiding coming in view of the house and we were soon hurrying along the streets.

I knew the way well. It was near the bazaar.

We came to a house. I had noticed it before because it had a magnificent mango tree in front of it. Now it was full of blossom.

'This is my brother's house,' said the ayah.

The brother came out to greet us. He bowed twice and took us into the house. He drew aside a beaded curtain and invited us into a room which seemed full of carved wooden furniture.

'Salar very happy,' he said. 'He want thank for Roshanara . . .' He shook his head and there were tears in his eyes. 'She safe now . . . she well. She happy. Missie Drusilla, she say, she very great lady.'

'Oh, it was nothing,' I told him. 'Naturally we wouldn't have allowed it to happen. It is against the law.'

'Salar . . . he wish to do service. He wish to say not good in big house. Not good stay.'

'Yes,' I said, 'there is trouble everywhere.'

'Not good,' he went on, nodding. 'Salar want to say big thank.'

'Well, you must not think any more of it. We were fond

755

of Roshanara. We could not allow her to do as they wanted her to. Naturally we did what we could.'

The ayah said: 'My brother does not understand. He say you must leave big house. It not good.'

'I know,' I said. 'We shall go when we can.'

'My brother say best go back across sea.'

'Tell him we shall when the opportunity comes.'

They talked together, Salar shaking his head and the ayah nodding with him.

'He say will help,' she told me.

'Will you thank him very, very much and say that I shall not forget his kindness.'

'He owe debt. He like not to owe. He like to pay.'

'I am sure he does and I do appreciate it. Tell him that if I need his help I will ask.'

In due course we were ushered out of the house.

Salar evidently felt relieved, for he had made his gratitude known to me.

It was a few days later when I heard that incendiary fires were springing up all over Meerut and that mutiny had broken out there.

The tension in the household increased. The Great Khansamah had grown in importance over the past weeks. He strutted about the house as though he were indeed master of us all. I was very much afraid of what he might do.

I talked to Lavinia about it.

I said: 'Lavinia, aren't you afraid?'

'What of?'

'Are you completely oblivious of what is going on around you?'

'Oh, all this talk, you mean? There's always talk.'

'You know that Fabian and Dougal are worried about us?'

'There is no need to be. Major Cummings is here to protect us. He says he will make sure that I am all right.'

'What about the children?'

'They are all right. They are only children. They know nothing of all this whispering. Besides, you'll look after them . . . and Ayah, of course.'

'Lavinia, you don't seem to have an inkling of what is going on. This is an explosive situation.'

'I tell you we shall be all right. The Khansamah will make sure of that.'

'He is against us.'

'He's not against me. We understand each other . . . Besides, he's one of my great admirers.'

'I marvel at you, Lavinia.'

'All right. Marvel away. It is what I expect.'

I knew it was no use trying to impress on her the gravity of the situation.

It was only a day or so later when, in the evening, the ayah came to my room.

She said: 'We must go . . . go now. I will take the children to the gazebo. Come there . . . as quick as you can. I take children . . . now.'

I could see that she was aware of some impending danger and that it was very close. The urgency of her voice convinced me that I must obey at once without question.

'I will go and bring the Countess.'

'Quick. No time to lose.'

'The children are in bed.'

'No matter. I tell them new game. I keep them quiet. We will bring them. Must be quick. No time.'

'Why . . .?'

'Not now. Just come. I tell . . .'

I ran to Lavinia's room. Fortunately she was alone. She was seated by the mirror, combing her hair.

I said: 'Lavinia, we have to go at once.'

'Where?'

'Down to the gazebo.'

'What for?'

'Look. There is no time to explain. I don't know myself

757

yet. Just come. I know it is important. The children will be there.'

'But whatever for?'

'Don't argue. Come.'

'I'm not dressed.'

'Never mind.'

'I won't be ordered like this.'

'Lavinia, Ayah will be frantic. Promise me you'll come at once. And come quickly. Don't let anyone know where you are going.'

'Really, Drusilla.'

'Look, you must have some idea of the danger we're in.' She did look slightly alarmed. Even she must have been aware of the changing atmosphere.

She said: 'All right . . . I'll come.'

'I'll go on ahead. I must tell Ayah. She'll be wondering why I'm so long. Don't forget. Don't tell anyone *not anyone* where you are going and try not to let anyone see you. It's very important.'

I went down by means of a back staircase. I reached the garden without seeing anyone, and sped across the grass to the gazebo.

Ayah was there with the children. I could see the panic in her eyes.

'We must go . . . quick . . .' she whispered. 'It is dangerous to wait.'

Louise said: 'It's a new game, Drusilla. It is hide-and-seek, isn't it, Ayah?'

'Yes, yes . . . we now hide and seek. Come.'

'I must wait for the Countess,' I said.

'No wait.'

'She will come down here and not know what to do.'

'We must take the children now. You come, too.'

I said: 'I have to wait.'

'We cannot. No wait.'

'Where are you going?'

'To my brother's house.'

'To Salar!'

She nodded. 'This what he say. When time come you must be here . . . with Missie . . . with children . . . Time come. We must go.'

'Take the children. I will bring the Countess there. I have told her I will wait for her here. I must stay for her.'

The ayah shook her head. 'No. Bad. Bad . . . not good.'

She had wrapped the children in cloaks so that I could hardly see them. She put the box she had brought to the gazebo into my hands. 'You wear,' she said. 'Cover head. You look Indian woman . . . a little then. Come. Do not wait.'

I put on the sari and the shawl over my head.

'Drusilla, you do look funny,' said Louise.

'Now we go. I take children. You come to brother. We want do this for you.'

'As soon as the Countess arrives I will bring her. She can't be long. I think she is realizing the danger at last.'

'Tell her cover head. Wear shawl . . .'

I was dismayed but I knew I must deal with such problems when they came.

Taking Alan's hand and commanding Louise to keep close, Ayah hurried out of the gazebo.

The stillness was broken only by the sound of insects with which I had now become familiar. I could hear the beating of my own heart. I was aware the ayah was better informed of danger than I could be and I could see that it had become more acute.

I felt alone and helpless. As soon as I had let the children go I believed I should have gone with them. They were in my charge, but how could I have left Lavinia? The folly of Lavinia had once before had a great effect on my life. I now believed that it was about to do so again.

If only she had come with me at once. It might well be that there was no need for the flight from the house, but Ayah believed so. I went to the door of the arbour and looked towards the house. And then . . . suddenly I heard shouting. I saw dark figures at the window. It seemed that the entire household was invading the upper rooms.

My heart was thundering, my throat parched. I kept whispering: 'Lavinia . . . Lavinia, where are you? Why don't you come?'

There was nothing I wanted so much as to see her stealthily creeping across the grass to the gazebo.

But she did not come.

Instinctively I knew that I should go, that I should find my way to the house with the mango tree. I knew my way there. I had passed it many times.

Go! Go! said my common sense. But I could not go without Lavinia.

What if she came to the gazebo and found me gone? Where would she go? What would she do? She did not know that there would be sanctuary in that house.

I must wait for Lavinia.

I did not know how long I waited. I could see Lavinia's window from where I was. Some of the lamps had been lighted. And as I watched I saw the Khansamah at her window. So he was in her room! He was gone in a second and I wondered if I had been mistaken.

I stood there shivering. I did not know what to do. I prayed for guidance.

Go . . . go now, said the voice within me. But I could not go while Lavinia was in the house.

It must have been an hour later. The night was hot but I was shivering. I heard the far-off sound of singing . . . drunken singing. It was coming from the lower part of the house.

I hestitated. Then I ventured across the grass. I knew it was folly. Something dreadful had happened in the house. I should run from it as quickly as I could. I should find my way to Salar's house where Ayah and the children would be waiting for me.

But still I could not do it.

'Lavinia,' I heard myself whispering. 'Where are you? Why don't you come?'

The waiting was unbearable. I could not endure it. I knew I had to go into the house and find her.

It was folly, of course. The ayah had known that it was imperative for us to get away. She had saved us just in time. But how could I leave Lavinia there?

I told myself that my duty lay with the children. They would need me now. But they were safe with the ayah. If she had reached her brother's house they would be there waiting for me now.

I knew what I had to do. I had to find Lavinia. I could not leave without her. She should have come with me, of course; she was foolish. She always had been foolish. But still I was fond of her. It seemed to me that my life was somehow bound up in hers and I could not desert her now.

I was outside the house. I stood leaning against the wall, listening. The sounds of revelry were coming from the servants' quarters. I pictured the Khansamah there. But where was Lavinia?

She had said she would come. What was she waiting for?

The door was open. I stepped into the hall. I could hear the shouts and laughter more distinctly now. They were very merry . . . the merriment of intoxication, I was sure.

Silently, fearing the Khansamah would appear at any moment, I crept up the stairs. Fortunately that part of the house seemed to be deserted.

The door of Lavinia's room was wide open. I crept along the corridor and paused there.

The sight which met my eyes was one which will be forever imprinted on my mind. Disorder . . . and horror. The walls of the room were splashed with blood. And there, spreadeagled across the bed, was Lavinia's nude body. Something about its posture was obscene and I knew it had been placed deliberately so. Her eyes were wide and staring with horror. Her glorious hair was matted with blood, and spread out at her feet was the blood-spattered peacock

761

feather fan. I knew then that the Khansamah had done this.

I felt sick and faint, for I saw that her throat had been cut.

Lavinia was dead. That beauty which had been her pride, which had obsessed her and made her what she was, had in the end destroyed her.

Instinctively I knew that the Khansamah had taken his revenge in his own way, because she had encouraged him and then rejected him. She had committed the great crime in his eyes of insulting his dignity. He had been waiting to avenge his lost prestige; the gift of the peacock feather fan had been a warning.

For some moments I could see nothing but the horror of this.

'Lavinia . . . Lavinia . . . why did you not come? Why did you hesitate? You have destroyed yourself.'

How can I tell the children? I asked myself, as though that was the most important thing in the world.

The children! I must get back to them. I should be looking after them. I should have to plan for them as I had planned for Fleur.

I must get out of this house of death immediately. If I were discovered my fate would be that of Lavinia. I was needed. I must look after the children.

I turned away from that scene of horror. I crept down the stairs. Luck was with me, for no one appeared. I was out through the open door speeding across the grass.

The night air sobered me. I went inside the gazebo and allowed myself a few seconds to regain my breath. I must get to the children. To do so I had to pass through the streets. I could guess what was happening in every house where Europeans were living. The Mutiny had started in earnest. What we had feared for all these weeks had erupted and it was far worse than anything I had imagined.

There were few people in the streets. I was glad of the

shawl and the sari. Ayah had been wise to provide them. I stooped a little for I was tall and my height might betray me.

That journey through the streets seemed to take a long time. I saw several bloodied bodies lying in the roads. They were all Europeans. I guessed what was happening and as I turned each corner I expected to come face to face with someone who would recognize me as belonging to the race they hated.

My good fortune was great that night. I realized how great later.

I reached the house.

Ayah embraced me when she saw me.

'I have been worried.'

'Ayah,' I stammered. 'They've killed her. She's dead.'

She nodded. 'She should have come.'

'Oh yes . . . yes . . . She wouldn't believe it. It was awful. Blood . . . blood all over the room.'

'Remember the children,' she said.

'Where are they?'

'Asleep now. You have been long.'

'Ayah . . . what are we going to do?'

She said resignedly: 'We wait. We see. You rest now. Safe for a while. My brother, he happy. He pay debt.'

She took me into the workshop. Carved wooden objects were scattered about the place. There was a smell of wood in the air. I noticed a window which looked out on to a courtyard.

'All right,' she said. 'Out there courtyard. Salar's courtyard. No one see.'

She took me into a small room which led from the workroom. There was no window in this room. The children lay on a pallet on the floor, fast asleep. There was another pallet beside them.

'You here,' said the ayah, pointing to it. 'You rest now. You feel very bad.'

Feel bad? Indeed I did. I was desperately trying to shut

763

out of my mind that scene which I knew I should never be able to forget.

I lay on the pallet. I was seeing it all again. That once pleasant room transformed into a scene from some hellish horror . . . something I could never have imagined. Blood . . . blood everywhere . . . and Lavinia's body placed across the bed, her once flaunted beauty degraded and gone for ever.

I lay there thinking of the first time we had met, going away to school . . . Lavinia, who had been so much a part of my life almost always . . .

And now . . . no more.

What could I have done to save her? I should have impressed on her the need to go more urgently. I should have made her understand the danger. But who could make Lavinia do what she did not want to?

My face was wet. I was weeping. It helped a little. It soothed me somehow.

Oh Lavinia . . . Lavinia . . . dead.

One of the children stirred in sleep as though to remind me that it was my duty to calm myself, not to give way to grief, to cherish them, to make them as my own.

I often wondered how the woodcarver Salar managed to keep us hidden in his house for all those weeks. It was an amazing feat.

The house was not big. He lived alone, for he was unmarried. He carved his wooden objects and took them along to the shops who bought them from him. He had always lived a lonely life, so this was a help.

I learned a little about him from Ayah, who told me that his niece Roshanara had meant a great deal to him. He loved the girl more than he had ever loved anyone else and he would never forget that we had saved her life. One day he would visit her; perhaps he would live close to her; and he owed that to us. He was happy now, for he was paying his debt . . . more than paying it. Three lives for one. He was pleased about that. But he had not yet saved us. Only the first part of the operation had been carried out. The debt would not be wiped out until we could walk freely in the streets again.

On the very night of our escape Ayah went back to the house. She did not want suspicion to fall on her, for that could lead the Khansamah to Salar's house and if he came that would be the end of us all. Salar would not be able to protect us then; and whatever happened Salar must pay his debt.

This was a blessing, for she could keep me informed of what was happening there; also she could walk the streets and get an idea of the general situation.

It was very difficult to keep the children amused and to answer their questions. The little courtyard which I had seen from the window was shut in by very high walls; but at least it was open to the sky and this was the only fresh air that the children could have. We dared not let them be seen. Ayah brought some little trousers and tunics so that they were dressed like the natives; but their fair hair betrayed them and we toyed with the idea of dying it black, but we doubted whether we could do this satisfactorily. In any case we should be afraid to let them venture out. We could not keep up the pretence that this was merely a game of hide-and-seek. Louise was too intelligent for that.

I said to her: 'We have to hide here for a little while because there are some bad men who are trying to find us.'

Her eyes widened. 'What bad men?' she asked.

'Just . . . bad men.'

'Great Khansamah?' she asked.

How much does she know? I wondered. I had often been startled by the mingling of innocence and shrewdness displayed by children.

I decided to tell her the truth. 'Yes,' I said.

She regarded me seriously. 'He does not like us,' she said. 'I know.'

'How did you know?' I asked.

She merely nodded. 'I know,' she said.

'So we have to stay here for a little while until . . .'

'Until he has gone away?'

'Yes,' I said.

'Where is my Mama?' asked Alan.

Louise was regarding me intently and I knew I had to tell them. I made up my mind quickly. 'Your Mama has gone away.'

'When is she coming back?' asked Louise.

'Well . . . she has gone a long way.'

'Home to England?' asked Louise.

'Well . . . not exactly. She has gone farther than that.'

'There isn't farther than that,' said Louise gravely.

'Yes, there is. There's Heaven.'

'Is that where she's gone?'

'Yes.'

'How long will she stay?' asked Alan.

'Well, when people go to Heaven it is usually for a long time.'

'Will she be with the angels?' asked Louise.

'I'm an angel,' said Alan.

'You're not an angel,' said Louise. 'You haven't got any wings. You're only a little boy.'

'I'm Drusilla's angel,' he said. 'Aren't I, Drusilla?'

I hugged him and said he was.

I was near to tears and Louise was watching me intently. She was a very serious little girl and I think she did not entirely accept stories of what was happening.

'*You* won't go away, will you?' she said.

I shook my head and said if I had my way I should never go.

Days passed. Each morning I awoke and wondered whether this would be my last day on Earth, and each night when I lay on my pallet I wondered whether I should live through to the next day.

I tried to carry on with lessons. I invented games which we could play. We had guessing games and I was continually trying to devise versions of old ones. Alan was often fretful. He wanted to go out into the garden. It was difficult to explain to him. Louise understood, I think, that we were in real danger; she was a sensible and clever little girl.

Ayah visited us often. It was quite natural that she should call on her brother. She brought news of what was happening.

The Sepoys who had murdered their officers were now the Army and they were in Delhi. Moreover, Bahadur Shah had been restored. Everyone must do homage to the King. The British had been driven out of Delhi. Any found on the streets would be instantly dispatched. India was now for the Indians. The great Nana Sahib, who bore the same name as our Great Khansamah, was marching through Oude to the North West Provinces preaching rebellion and the need to throw off the foreigners' yoke. Risings had taken place in Lahore and Peshawar. Soon the British would be driven out of India, said Salar.

I did not believe my countrymen would allow themselves to be so easily dismissed and it seemed that I might be right in this, for soon after we heard that Sir John Lawrence had armed the Sikhs and with their help had curbed the power of the Sepoys. The Punjab remained faithful to the British and rumour had it that Sir John Lawrence was sending an army to the relief of Delhi.

I guessed that we were in acute danger and if any man, woman or child of European origin was found in the streets they would be instantly killed.

I gave myself entirely up to the care of the children. I had to keep them happy and myself occupied. I gave my entire attention to them; it was one way of shutting out that fearful memory.

I wished that I had never seen it. To have heard vaguely that Lavinia had been killed, as had thousands of others, would have shocked me deeply, but that I should have seen the manner in which she died, seemed more than I could bear to think of.

The children were a blessing. They were very good in the circumstances. At least we were not so much in the dark as we had been. Louise had a strong sense of danger. Sometimes she would come and stand beside me for no apparent reason. I understood. She was old enough to realize that we were living through dangerous times. She clung to both me and the ayah. I knew she was very disturbed when the ayah was not with us.

They were wonderful, those two ... the ayah and her brother. I had complete trust in them; the fidelity of Ayah, the integrity of Salar, were an example to us all.

All the time I was wondering about Fabian and Dougal. Where were they? How had they fared in this holocaust? I guessed that Fabian at least would be somewhere in the heart of the trouble. I longed for news of him. Lying on my pallet at night, I would think of him and because I felt life was so uncertain and death was hovering all the time behind any door, I faced my true feelings for him.

I longed to be with him. The times I had spent with him had been the highlights of my life. I liked to brood on the childish episode when he had seen me as a baby and taken me for his own. He might have kept me there always. What a difference that would have made to my life! I thought of him as he had been, stretched out on the settee ... with Lavinia kneeling before him with a chalice of wine while I fanned him with Miss Lucille's peacock feather fan.

Then my mind switched to that terrible scene ... the sight of the bloodstained feathers of the fan which the Khansamah had given to Lavinia. How strange that there should be yet another feather fan to haunt me. When he had given that fan to Lavinia she had believed it meant contrition on his part. How little she understood. It meant disaster was coming to her ... revenge because she had slighted him.

I must cling to something to blot out the memory. Fabian would save us, I told myself. I prayed that he might still be alive and that I should soon see him again.

I must face the truth. He was more important to me than I dared admit; but what was the point of deceiving myself now? Why did I not admit to my obsession with him? It had been there ever since we had been children. I supposed I was in love with him. I had always been what was called a sensible girl. Even Lady Harriet had admitted that. Had she not sent me to the finishing school in France – which my father could never have afforded – for the purpose of looking after Lavina?

And I *had* looked after her. I had brought her through a difficult situation which, had we not been successful, would have ruined her prospects for a grand marriage. That was something of which Lady Harriet was ignorant but I was sure she would have approved of my action had she known.

I was a sensible girl. I must go on being sensible. Just because I was overwrought . . . just because I had witnessed something more terrible than I could ever have imagined, I must not allow it to unnerve me.

The ayah came in to tell me the news. Something was happening. The British were advancing on Delhi and there was great consternation throughout the city.

'Take great care,' said Salah. 'They must not find you.'

We waited. Could this life be going to change? The weeks were passing. Surely something must happen soon?

It was a hot June day when an attempt was made to blow open the gates of the city. Perhaps Delhi would be taken. Then perhaps I might see Fabian.

However, this was not to be. The people rose in their determination to hold the city. The Sepoys were well trained and they were brave soldiers; and they did not fight the less boldly and skilfully because they were fighting for India.

It was a bitter disappointment when the attempt failed.

But of course that was not the end.

There followed more long weeks of waiting and speculation, wondering if each day would be our last.

We had come to Salar's house in May and it was not until September that the city of Delhi was taken by the Sikhs and the British.

It was still unsafe to venture out. Fighting was going on in the streets and anyone not of the Indian race would be shot on sight.

But hope had returned. Something must happen soon. Louise was aware of this.

'Will my mother come back now?' she asked.

'No, Louise. She can't come back.'

'Will my father?'

'Perhaps.'

'And my uncle?'

'I don't know. They will come if they can. They will want to make sure that we are all safe.'

'Shall we go away from here then?'

'Yes, we shall go away.'

'On a big ship? Home?'

It was pleasant to hear her speak of England as Home for she had never seen it. Yet it meant Home to her.

'Yes,' I told her. 'One day . . .'

'Soon?'

'Perhaps that may well be.'

She nodded, smiling. She knew that if she asked some questions she would get evasive answers and her instinct told her that they might not be true.

And so we waited.

One day the ayah came to me. It was in the late afternoon. I thought this was simply one of her periodic visits but it was quite different.

She said: 'We all leave house. Khansamah say it is not safe. He says enemy come. Soldiers in all houses, British soldiers now. He say they blame us . . . kill us.'

'They wouldn't kill you.'

'Khansamah he say . . .'

'Where is the Khansamah?'

770

'I do not know. He say all go. They all go different places.'

She stayed in her brother's house all that day and the next night. We waited eagerly for news.

The following day she went out. She still thought it might be unsafe for me to venture into the streets with the children. People were still being killed and even though the British Army had taken over the town there were still pockets of resistance.

When she came back she said: 'I see Sir Fabian. He is at house.'

I was speechless but I think she must have been aware of the joy which was surging through me.

'Did you see him? Did you speak to him?'

She nodded. 'I go to him. He say, "Where Missie Drusilla and children? Where Memsahib Countess?"'

'You . . . you told him?'

She shook her head. 'I fear Khansamah. He watch me. I think he know.' She began to tremble. 'I think he watch me.'

'But where is he?'

She hesitated. 'I didn't see . . . but I think he watch. I think he follow me. I did not see, but I know.'

'Well,' I said, 'he won't be able to do any harm now. He is no longer at the house. What did you tell Sir Fabian?'

'I tell him Countess dead, children safe with you.'

'So you did tell him that?'

She nodded. 'He say, "Where? Where?" But I did not tell. I fear Khansamah come here. I fear he watch. I say, "I bring Missie Drusilla to you." He say, "Yes, Yes." And then I run away.'

'I must go to him,' I said.

'Not in day. Wait for night.'

How did I live through that day? I felt light-headed. An exultation had taken hold of me. Then I experienced guilty feelings. There was death and destruction all around me. How could I feel this joy when I was still mourning Lavinia's

771

death and that of all the others who had died with her?

At last it was evening.

'Wear sari,' said Ayah. 'Cover up head best. Then come.'

I went through the streets with Ayah, hurrying along, being able to think of nothing but the possibility of seeing him, yet fearing that I never should. I imagined an assassin at every turn.

I had an uneasy feeling that we were being followed. A light footfall . . . a hasty glance over my shoulder. Nothing. Only imagination stretched beyond belief because of all the terrible things which had happened in the last months of my life.

I must live through the next moments. I must see Fabian again.

And there was the house.

'I wait for you in the gazebo,' said Ayah.

I went swiftly across the grass. There were lights in several of the windows. I wanted to call out: Fabian. I'm here, Fabian.

There was a clump of flowering shrubs near the house. As I passed this I heard a movement behind me. I turned sharply and as I did so, terror swept over me. I was looking into the murderous eyes of the Khansamah.

'Missie Drusilla,' he said softly.

'What . . . what are you doing here?'

'My home,' he said.

'No more. You have betrayed those who trusted you.'

'You very bold, Missie Drusilla,' he said. 'You go . . . you take children . . . you hide. I know now where. I kill Ayah . . . but you first.'

I screamed for help as he sprang towards me. I saw the knife in his upraised hand. I called out again and with all my strength pushed him from me.

It was a feeble effort but it did cause him to reel back a little. He regained his balance immediately and was coming nearer. Those seconds seemed to go on for a long time. It amazes me, thinking back, how much can pass through the mind at such a moment. My first thought was: Has Ayah betrayed me? Is it for this she brought me here? No. She would never do that. She loved the children. She was fond of me for what I had done for Roshanara. It was an unworthy thought. I believed in that fearful moment that this was the end. I shall never see Fabian again, I thought. And who will look after the children?

Then there was a shattering explosion. The Khansamah threw up his hands. I heard the knife fall to the ground; he reeled drunkenly before he collapsed in a heap at my feet.

Fabian was coming towards me, a pistol in his hand.

'Drusilla!' he said.

I felt faint with shock. I thought I must be dead and dreaming.

His arms were round me. He was holding me tightly against him. I was trembling.

I heard him mutter. 'Are you all right? Thank God you are safe . . .'

'Fabian,' I whispered. 'Fabian . . .' Repeating his name seemed to relieve me.

'Let's get inside . . . away from that.'

'He's dead,' I murmured.

'Yes, he's dead.'

'You . . . saved me.'

'Just in time. The old villain. It's his just deserts. Tell me . . . I've wondered so much . . . such nightmare thoughts. You're shivering. Come into the house. Don't be afraid. They've all gone . . . none of them stayed when we came in. The house is safe now. There's so much to say . . .'

He put his arm round me and led me into the house. It was quiet.

'I'll find some brandy or something,' he said.

A soldier in uniform came into the hall.

'Can you find some brandy, Jim?' said Fabian. 'There's been a nasty accident out there. Get rid of the body, will you? It's an old rascal who used to work here. He tried to kill Miss Delany.'

773

'Yes, sir,' said the man. He was clearly no more moved by one request than the other.

We went into the drawing-room which no longer looked familiar and after a few moments the man returned with the brandy and two glasses.

Fabian poured it out. 'Drink this,' he said. 'You'll feel better.'

I took the glass with trembling hands.

'That man . . .' I began.

'Stop thinking of him. It was you or him. So he had to go. Moreover, he has caused a lot of trouble. He's had that coming to him for a long time.'

'Lavinia . . .' I said. And I told him.

He was deeply shocked. 'My poor foolish sister . . . she never learned, did she?' He took a sip of brandy and stared ahead of him. He had cared for her, I knew, although he had deplored her conduct and had usually treated her with an affectionate contempt. He had done what he could for Fleur's future. It was a terrible blow to him that she was dead.

'It was that man . . .' I said, and I heard myself blurting out what I had seen. 'The peacock feather fan was at her feet. It was spattered with blood. He must have put it there.'

Fabian put an arm round me and held me close to him. I fancied we comforted each other.

'I have avenged her, then,' he said at length. 'I am glad I was the one. We have been looking for him for some time. He was one of the leaders. Fancied himself a Nana Sahib. Thank God we've got him now. It will be over in a little time, Drusilla. But there's a good deal to do yet. We'll get away from it all . . . we'll be able to put all this behind us . . . once we are out of this mess.'

I started to talk about the children . . . about Salar and his workshop and the way in which he had sheltered us all this time.

'Good man. He shall be rewarded.'

'He doesn't want rewards,' I said. 'He wants to pay his debt for what we did for Roshanara.'

'Yes,' he said. 'I understand that.'

'What was the Khansamah doing here?' I asked.

'Probably trying to get me. He was lurking in the grounds, I suspect. So that must have been his idea. We have some of the military here and I dare say there were attempts at sniping. We'll have to take the greatest care.'

'And Dougal?' I asked. 'Where is Dougal?'

'I haven't heard from him for some time. I think he may be in Lucknow. Alice and Tom will be there, too.'

I shivered. 'If only this were over.'

'It will be,' he assured me. 'But there is plenty of danger yet. You must go back to Salar's shop. You've been safe there so far. The children must stay there. How are they?'

'Restive . . . but otherwise all right. I can't tell you what I owe to the ayah and her brother. It's really all because of Roshanara.'

'Well, we foiled the old devil over that little matter. It is comforting to know he is beyond seeking revenge now. You have been constantly in my thoughts, Drusilla . . . all of you.'

'And you have been in mine . . . with Dougal . . . Alice and Tom.'

'I know the children will be as safe as it is possible to be with you. The thing is, where do we go from here? I wouldn't want you to come to the house . . . yet. I feel that would be unsafe. I am going to move Heaven and Earth to get you all home as soon as possible.'

'You said the trouble was dying down.'

'It will be a slow death, I fear. Although we are here in force there is going to be trouble yet. I'd be so much easier in my mind if I thought that you and the children were out of it. A pity we're not in Bombay. Then it might be possible to get you away. But here . . . you'd have to travel across country and Heaven knows what you might run into. Now what you have to do is get back to Salar's. Stay there as you were for a few days and then we'll see how things are. I shall know where you are . . . and I am going to concentrate on getting you out of the country and home.'

I could not think clearly. It was all-important that he was alive . . . that we had met again . . . that he was so moved and delighted to see me, that he was the one who had saved my life when I was on the brink of death. Perhaps in such circumstances one thinks more lightly of death than one does normally. This night I had seen a man shot dead before my eyes and I could only feel a numbed sense of shock which was overpowered by a tremendous happiness.

He took me back to the gazebo where the ayah was waiting. She had heard the shot and had crept out to see what had happened. She had thought at first that I might have been killed. I think she must have been relieved when she saw the dead man, for she herself had lived in fear of him for a very long time. There was no doubt that he had been arrogant, cruel and sadistic. I supposed I should not feel so disturbed because he had been treated as he had treated so many. But death is shocking and I could not throw off the effects of that shock.

Ayah was delighted to see me safe but she was a little worried to see Fabian and more so when he told us that he was going to see us safely to her brother's house where I was to stay for a while longer. She was very disturbed. He must not be seen with us. Who knew who would watch?

She was really frightened, and Fabian saw reason in her fear, so it was arranged that she and I should walk ahead of him, and Fabian, watchful of us but keeping his distance, his pistol ready, in case he should have to come to our assistance.

And so I went back to Salar's house.

I lay on my pallet in a bemused state for the rest of that night.

Life had changed. The streets of Delhi were safer now, though there were periodic outbreaks of violence. Nana

Sahib had been defeated, but the Mutiny was by no means quelled, though the British were gaining success after success, and it was becoming clear that although it might take time, order would eventually be restored. I could go out, but I never went far. Fabian was still at the house and I saw him now and then.

We talked a great deal about the position here. He never discussed the future. Later I thought that was because he did not believe then that there would be one for us.

Death had receded a little. It was no longer lurking beside us, but it was still not very far away.

Fabian's great concern was to get us out of the country. He was continually making enquiries as to how safe it would be for us to travel to the coast. There were big British successes at Rajputana, Malwa, Berar and some remote places.

It was safe for me to go to the house now but Fabian did not wish me to go there too often. He thought that some of the Khansamah's men might be around and take it into their heads to avenge his death and they would shoot anyone connected with the house for that purpose. I was to stay at Salar's house until something could be arranged to get us to the country.

Fabian did not leave Delhi.

He told me that this would probably be the end of the Company as such. It was being realized, he had heard, that a trading company was not fitted to govern a country and it could be said that the Company had done that with the aid of the Army. It was not very satisfactory and he believed that some other form of government would take its place when all this was settled.

'You mean we shall still keep our interests in India?'

'Most certainly, yes. There is no question of that. But there will be new legislation, I am convinced.'

I loved those sessions with him. We seemed to grow very close. I was greatly soothed, for the terrible things which I had witnessed had changed me forever. I should never forget the sight of Lavinia, spreadeagled across the bed. I should never be rid of the memory of the peacock feather fan. I should always remember the look of startled horror on her face. I thought so often of her . . . she who had lived in a world of dreams where she was always the beautiful siren, adored by gallant knights. What had she thought when she had found herself face to face with horrific reality? Perhaps the answer was in those wild staring eyes.

I often spoke her name aloud. 'Lavinia . . . Lavinia, why would you not come with me when I begged you to? Why did you delay? Could you really have believed that the Khansamah was your devoted slave, that no harm would come to you while he was there?' Oh, poor deluded Lavinia!

Fabian had been deeply shocked by what had occurred, but he was a realist. She was dead. Nothing could bring her back. Her death was in a way due to her folly. What we had to do now was think of the children.

The coming of the new year saw the end of rebellion in Bengal, and in most of Central India. Bahadur Shah, the last of the Moguls, had been tried and convicted of treason and sent to Burma. Order was slowly being restored. I still thought a good deal about Dougal, Alice and Tom. It seemed they must still be in Lucknow, for we had heard no news of them. I was desperately afraid of what might have happened.

Life was more tolerable. We were still living at Salar's house but we were freer now and there was no need for us to keep our identity secret. Our own people were back in command in Delhi. We had nothing to fear from the Sikhs who had always been loyal to British rule and had realized the benefits it brought to them.

I did not take the children to the house, for I feared it would bring back memories and start them asking questions about their mother; but Fabian came to Salar's house. They were pleased to see him and showed some rather restrained affection towards him, for they were still a little in awe of him.

He had changed somewhat. He was more serious now. What had happened to Lavinia had affected him more deeply than I realized. Moreover, he had lost several friends and colleagues in the débâcle. I supposed no one who had lived through all that could ever be the same carefree person again. One must take life seriously when one could never be sure when one could be plunged into horror.

Our conversation was very sober now and we talked a great deal about what was happening in this country. Those verbal battles between us were no more. I felt that our relationship – however deep it was now – must change when we returned to more normal circumstances. Perhaps we had been drawn together closely but superficially. I had a sense of transience.

I thought often: I shall never be the same person again. I told myself repeatedly that I must not attach too much importance to my new relationship with Fabian, for neither of us were living a normal life.

The year was advancing. At any moment I was prepared to hear that I must make ready to go.

Then it came. I was to prepare to set out for Bombay in two days' time, taking the children with me. The ayah would remain behind in her brother's household. I should travel in the company of a party of women and children. For a long time plans had been in progress to get them home.

'So,' I said blankly. 'I shall travel alone.'

'I shall accompany you as far as Bombay,' said Fabian. 'I cannot contemplate your making that journey, which may be highly dangerous . . . without me.'

I felt my heart leap with joy while I chided myself for my folly.

How sad it was to say goodbye to the ayah. Salar was triumphant. He had successfully paid his debt. Ayah was calm; the children were quiet. It was a great wrench for them – perhaps their first real sorrow.

I said: 'Dear Ayah, it may be that we shall meet again.'

She gave me that infinitely sad smile of hers, and told me of her deep unhappiness, but that she knew she must accept her fate.

That journey to Bombay seems unreal to me even now.

We set out in a *dâk-ghari* type of vehicle in which I had travelled before. I knew that in those rough carts drawn by one unkempt-looking horse we must prepare for a somewhat uncomfortable journey. The children, sad as they were to leave Ayah, were glad to escape from the confinement of Salar's house. They were going home, Louise told Alan, and the little boy so far forgot his sorrow at parting with his beloved ayah as to jump up and down and sing 'Home, Home'.

There was a magic in that word.

We had set out from the house very early in the morning, I riding in the cart with the children, and Fabian on horseback beside us with half a dozen armed men. We did not have to wait long before more joined the party, and by the time we left Delhi our numbers had increased considerably. There were women and children in *dâk-gharis* like ours. More soldiers joined us. And the long trek began.

We knew that the Mutiny was by no means over and that it was possible that we could be attacked by hostile natives. The fact that we were women and children and elderly people would not save us. This was a war against a race not against individual people. It was moving to see how everyone wanted to help one another. If anyone was sick or some minor accident occurred everyone without exception wanted to give whatever possible. It amazed me how the sense of impending danger could have that effect on people.

Most of us had seen death in some form over the last months; we knew that its shadow still hung over us and that any moment could be our last: but for some reason we had lost our fear and awe of death. It had become an everyday occurrence. We had learned that life was transient.

Perhaps we had become more spiritual, less materialistic. I did not know. But, looking back, I see that it was a strange and elevating experience to have lived through.

We stopped now and then at the *dâk-bungalows* for food and to rest or change horses. We did not sleep there. There was a sense of urgency among the company. Everyone knew that we must get on the ship before we were safe.

The stops were a relief. It meant that we escaped for a spell the violent jolting of the *dâk-gharis*. We snatched a few hours' sleep here and there. The children usually closed their eyes when the sun set and slept through the nights.

I was always aware of Fabian's presence and it comforted me. While he was there I felt assured that we should come safely through. In one way I did not want the journey to end because I knew it would mean saying goodbye to him, and in spite of the discomfort I found it exhilarating.

When we reached Bombay, he would return to Delhi and we should sail away. We might be safe, but he would be going back into danger. Often I wondered what was happening to Tom, Alice and Dougal.

During our little halts Fabian and I would talk together. We would wander a little distance from the others.

He said: 'Once you are on the ship all should be well. You will have the journey across land, of course, from Suez to Alexandria . . . but you know of the pitfalls now. You will be with a great number of people and you are not likely to get taken in by handsome strangers of the Lasseur breed.'

'No,' I answered. 'I know better now.'

'When you get home you will stay with the children?'

'Lady Harriet will want to have them with her.'

'Of course. But you will be there, too. You can't desert them. Think what that would mean to them. They have lost their mother and the ayah. They cling to you, I notice. You represent security to them. You must stay with them at Framling. I have written to my mother to tell her this.'

'You think a letter will reach her?'

'I have already given it to one of our people who left two

781

weeks ago. I have told her that you will be arriving with
the children and I shall want you to remain with them until
I come home.'

'When will that be?'

He lifted his shoulders. 'Who can say? But you must be
with them. My mother might be a little . . . formidable . . .
just at first. They will need you there to help them understand her. Poor children, they have suffered enough through
their experiences.'

'It does not seem to have affected them adversely. I believe
children soon come to accept everything as normal. They
are used now to this hole and corner existence. They had
all those weeks at Salar's.'

'And their mother?'

'They accept her death. They think she has gone to
Heaven.'

'They will still be wondering.'

'So much has happened and Lavinia did not see very
much of them. She was a rather remote person to
them.'

'Perhaps that is as well.'

'They miss the ayah, of course.'

'That has made them turn more to you. So you see,
Drusilla, you must not leave them. I've explained that to
my mother.'

'You want me to remain at Framling . . . as a sort of
governess.'

'You are a friend of the family. When I come home we
can make arrangements. Until then, I want you to make
sure they are all right. Promise me.'

I promised.

'There is something else,' he went on. 'I have told my
mother about . . . the other child.'

'You mean Fleur?'

'Yes. I thought she should know.'

'But Polly and her sister . . .'

'I know. They have looked after her . . . and very well,

782

too. But what if anything should happen to them? It is right that Fleur should be with her family.'

'So Lady Harriet knows at last.'

'Well, she had to know sometime. I could not break it to her gently. Who knows what is going to happen here?'

'What do you think she will do?'

'She will probably try to get the child.'

'Oh no!'

I could imagine the confrontation with Polly and Eff on one side and Lady Harriet on the other. It would be the meeting of two formidable contingents. I wondered who would be the stronger.

'I do hope . . .' I began.

'My mother will make up her mind what should be done about the child. And in any case, whatever happens, we know that Fleur will have a home.'

I heard myself say faintly: 'I suppose you are right.'

'I think so.'

'Polly and her sister will never let Fleur go.'

'I fancy there will be some sort of battle but I am not sure which side will be victorious. My mother is a very determined lady.'

'So are Eff and Polly.'

'It will be a battle of the Titans.'

He laughed and I found myself laughing with him.

I felt suddenly secure, unafraid.

I shall never forget that night . . . the line of vehicles, the grazing horses . . . the warm balmy air, the hum of insects . . . and Fabian there beside me.

I wanted it to go on. It was absurd, but I was in no hurry to reach Bombay.

There were other pauses. We talked and sometimes were silent but there was a great bond between us. More than ever I was sure that my life was bound up with the Framlings. Sometimes we talked of the past, and again of those days when he had captured me and made me his child, when he had pretended he was my father.

'You thought you could take what you wanted,' I told him, 'including other people's children.'

'I suppose I did.'

'Perhaps you still do.'

'Old habits persist.'

I thought of the peacock feather fan, but I did not speak of it. To brood on it brought back that memory which I knew I should never entirely forget — Lavinia on the bloodied bed, with the fan at her feet.

I must put all that behind me. I must live for the future. I had a great task to do. I had to get the children home, to give my life to them . . . until Fabian returned.

At last we were in Bombay. There were the familiar buildings, their walls brilliant white in the dazzling sun, the sea, the gateway to India, as they called it. Now we were to pass through those gates . . . on our way home.

We had to wait a few days for the ship; and at last it came. We were taken on board. Fabian came on board to see us settled. There was a small cabin which I was to share with the children.

There was no time to be wasted. Soon after we were on board we were ready to sail.

Fabian took his farewells of the children, admonishing them to obey me in all things. They listened solemnly.

Then he took my hands.

'Goodbye, Drusilla,' he said. 'I'll come home as soon as it is possible.' He smiled at me. 'We'll have lots to talk about and plenty of time to do it in then.'

'Yes,' I answered.

He kissed me twice, once on either cheek.

'Take great care,' he said.

'You, too,' I told him.

And that was all. I sailed out of Bombay with the children, leaving Fabian behind in that strife-torn land.

ENGLAND

Homecoming

❧

I remember little of the journey. I suppose it was eventful as all such journeys are, but everything that happened seemed trivial after what had gone before.

There were the children to look after. There seemed to be children everywhere and they needed constant attention. A sailing ship is not the easiest of nurseries. There was a certain tension among the older passengers. Many of them had left husbands and other relatives behind in India and were constantly wondering what had happened to them.

We had no news; we were a little band of refugees from a strange land.

The children, of course, were excited by everything they saw and the crew were happy to have them around. I saw Louise on deck, with others of her age, while seamen pointed out to them the dolphins and flying fish. I remember the great excitement when a whale was seen.

We had the inevitable storms which kept us to our cabins and the children shrieked with laughter when they could not stand up straight and small objects rolled about the cabin. Everything was new and exciting to them and at the end of it they were going to that wonderful place called Home.

What they were expecting I could not imagine. I hoped they would not be disappointed.

So we reached Suez.

I was not looking forward to the ride across the desert, but it was of immense excitement to the children. They did not appear to notice the discomfort of the wagons and the wildness of the horses which carried them along. They were thrilled when we stopped at the caravanserais. I could hear

787

Louise telling Alan all about it while he jumped up and down as he always did to express excitement.

How it all came back to me! The journey with Alice, our acquaintance with Monsieur Lasseur, and then the arrival of Tom Keeping and the mysterious end of the so-called Frenchman.

I shivered to contemplate where I might be now but for the intervention of Tom on Fabian's orders.

All my thoughts led back to Fabian.

At last we arrived at Southampton.

'Is this Home?' asked Louise.

'Yes,' I said with emotion. 'This is Home.'

How strange England seemed after that land of brilliant sunshine, often overpowering heat, lotus flowers, banyan trees and dark silent-footed people with their soft melodious voices.

It was April when we arrived. A lovely time of year to return to England with the trees in bud and the spring flowers just beginning to show themselves, the gentle rain, the sun which was warm without being hot, no longer fierce, merely benign and a little coy since it so often hid behind the clouds. I watched the children's eyes grow wide with excitement. I think they had long ago made up their minds that Home was a kind of Mecca, the promised land, and in it everything would be wonderful.

We were taken to an inn where we could make our arrangements to return to those who were waiting for us.

I had a message sent off at once to Framling to tell Lady Harriet that I had arrived with the children.

There we heard the news. Sir Colin Campbell had relieved Lucknow. There had been great rejoicing at home at this news. It was believed that the Mutiny was grinding to a halt.

Everyone in the inn wanted to make much of us. We had been through the terrible Mutiny and we had survived. They could not do enough for us.

I was thinking of those I had left behind. How was Fabian? Had the relief of Lucknow come in time for Alice, Tom and Dougal? I could not bear to think that the love Alice planned to share with Tom should be snatched from her.

Lady Harriet was never one for delays. As soon as she received my note, a carriage was sent to take us to Framling. And there we were, riding through English country lanes, past fields like neat green squares, past woodland, streams and rivers. The children were entranced. Louise sat silent while Alan could not curb his desire to jump up and down.

And there was the familiar village, the green, the rectory, the House, the scene of my childhood. How was Colin Brady? I wondered. Still the humble servant of Lady Harriet, I was sure.

I watched the children as we approached Framling. It looked splendid in the pale sunshine . . . arrogant, formidable and heartbreakingly beautiful.

'Is this Home?' asked Louise.

'Yes,' I said. 'You will soon see your grandmother.'

I had to restrain Alan who was almost jumping out of the carriage.

Up the drive we went . . . so many memories crowding in. Lavinia . . . oh no. I could not bear to think of the last time I had seen her. Fabian . . . I dared not think of him either. Perhaps I had had wild dreams. Now, face to face with that magnificent pile of bricks and soon to see Lady Harriet, I knew how absurd my dreams had been.

He would come back and everything would be as it always had been, except that I was the plain girl from the rectory who would have a good post as governess to Lady Harriet's grandchildren: a good sensible girl who would remember her place. That was what Lady Harriet would want and expect; and Lady Harriet always had what she wanted.

The carriage had pulled up. One of the servants appeared.

Jane? Dolly? Bet? I couldn't remember; but I knew her and she knew me.

'Oh, Miss Delany, Lady Harriet said you're to go to her with the children as soon as you come.'

The children could hardly wait to get out of the carriage.

Into the hall . . . the familiar hall with its high vaulted roof and the weapons on the walls, weapons used by long-dead Framlings to protect the House against any who came against it. Up the staircase to the drawing-room where Lady Harriet would be sitting waiting.

'They're here, Lady Harriet.'

She rose. She looked as ever stately and formidable. There was a faint colour in her cheeks and her eyes immediately alighted on the children.

I felt their grip on my hands tighten.

'This is your grandmother, children,' I said.

They stared at her and she at them. I believed she was deeply touched by the sight of them and she would be thinking of Lavinia, of course. I was glad she did not know the nature of her dying. Fabian would never tell her; nor should I. So many people had died in the Mutiny. It was accepted that it might have been the fate of any one of us.

She looked at me. 'Good day, Drusilla,' she said. 'Welcome home. Come along in. And this is Louise.'

Louise nodded.

'I'm Alan,' said the boy. 'This is Home, isn't it?'

Did I see the blink of the eyes as though she feared she might betray her tears? I believed that was so. I heard the faint catch in her voice when she said: 'Yes, my dear child, you have come Home.' Then she was immediately the familiar Lady Harriet. 'How are you, Drusilla? You look well. Sir Fabian has written to me about you. I know you have been very sensible. You were always a sensible girl. Your room is next to the children's. Temporarily perhaps . . . but just at first . . . they would no doubt like that best. Sometime you must tell me of your adventures. Now, Louise, come here, my dear.'

790

Louise released my hand reluctantly.

'My dear child,' said Lady Harriet. 'How tall you are! All the Framlings are tall. This will be your home now. I am your grandmama. I shall look after you now.'

Louise turned to look up at me anxiously.

'Miss Delany . . . Drusilla . . . will be here, too. We shall all be here together. And then you shall have a nanny . . . an English one . . . like Miss Philwright.' A faint look of criticism came into her eyes. How dared Nanny Philwright be so forgetful of her duties as to marry and leave the Framling children! She was still the old Lady Harriet. There was no change. I had thought there might be as I had seen a little emotion. But of course that was merely for the Framling family. It did not extend to outsiders.

Both children watched her with a kind of wonder. I think the sight of them moved her deeply. Perhaps she feared she would show how much and that made her brisk.

'I dare say the children would like something to eat,' she said. 'What about some broth . . . some milk, bread and butter? What do you think, Drusilla?'

I felt it was an indication of her emotion that she should ask my opinion.

'They will be having their luncheon soon,' she said.

'Then I think a little milk and perhaps a slice of bread and butter would be best.' I turned to the children. 'Would you like that?' I asked.

Louise said Yes please and Alan nodded gravely.

'Good,' said Lady Harriet. 'It will be sent to your rooms. I shall show them to you myself. I have had the old nursery made ready. And later, Drusilla, I will have a talk with you. You are in the room next to the night nursery for the time being. Later we shall have a nanny . . . but perhaps just at first . . .'

I said I thought that was an excellent arrangement.

We went up the stairs to the old nursery and on the way up Lady Harriet dispatched one of the servants for the refreshments.

The rooms were light and airy. I remembered seeing them in the old days when I had come to play with Lavinia. Then I was seeing her again, just as I had that last time and a terrible sense of doom descended on me. Here in these rooms Fabian had held autocratic sway over, so it was said, even his mother. He had been the pampered one whose slightest whim was to be indulged even when it meant taking a child from her family.

There would be so many memories here and in that moment I felt that I wanted to go right away, for I could never be anything but an outsider in this house . . . the rector's daughter, not quite good enough to mingle with Framling society except when she could be some use to it.

'I will leave you to settle in,' said Lady Harriet.

I had the feeling that she wanted to get away, that she could not bear to be in this room where her dead daughter had lived and played as a child, as these grandchildren of hers would now do. Could she really be overcome by emotion? I was sure it was something she would never admit.

At last she had gone and I was alone with the children.

'Is she the Queen?' asked Louise.

That was a strange day. I took the children round the house and the garden. They thought it was all wonderful. We met some of the servants, who could not hide their pleasure at the prospect of having children in the house.

I thought: They will be happy here in time. They clung to me with a little more intensity than before, which told me that they were a little uneasy about the change in their lives: and they were certainly in awe of their formidable grandmother.

My food was sent up on a tray.

Lady Harriet had intimated that she wished to talk to me that evening and I was invited to her sitting-room after she had had her dinner.

'Sit down, Drusilla,' she said. 'There is so much I wish

to say to you. I know you have endured a great deal. Sir Fabian has told me how you looked after the children and kept them safely during that dreadful time for which we are both extremely grateful to you. Sir Fabian says you are to stay with the children, at least until his return, which he hopes will not be very long. He believes there will be changes in India because of this awful mutiny. Louise and Alan are now out of danger, but there is that other child. I know about that and your part in it. It was very unfortunate but we will not dwell on that. I have had the whole story from my son and I have been to see those people who have the child. That dreadful place where they are living! I sent for them to come here but they rudely ignored my request ... and I went to them. What a pity they took the child.'

'I must tell you, Lady Harriet, that they were wonderful to us. I don't know what we should have done without them.'

'I am not blaming you, Drusilla. Your part in the affair was ... commendable. That nursemaid of yours ... she is a forthright woman.' I fancied she conceded a grudging admiration for one not unlike herself. 'I suppose what they did at the time was ... admirable. But we have now to think of the child. However unfortunate her birth, she is *my* granddaughter and she must be brought up here at Framling.'

'Lady Harriet, they have cared for her since she was a baby. They love her as they would their own. They will never let her go.'

'We shall have to see about that,' said Lady Harriet firmly. 'Sir Fabian thinks she should be here with her half-sister and -brother.'

'I know they will never give her up.'

'She is a Framling and I am her grandmother. I have my rights.'

'It would not be good for the child to take her away immediately.'

'We shall in time make them see sense.'

'But, Lady Harriet, sense to you might not be sense to them.'

She looked at me in surprise that I could make such a suggestion. I did not flinch. I had made up my mind, as I had with Lavinia, that she should not dominate me. If she objected to my behaviour, I should simply have to make her understand that I was here only because I did not want to leave the children. I was more useful to Lady Harriet at this time than she was to me and that gave me an advantage. My status was not that of an ordinary nursery governess.

'We shall see,' she said ominously. Then she added: 'I want you to go along and see these people.'

'I intend to. Polly is very dear to me and so are her sister and Fleur.'

'Then I should like you to go as soon as possible.'

'It is what I intend.'

She nodded. 'Explain to them the advantages the child would have here. In spite of her birth she is still my grandchild. I think they should be made to understand what that means.'

'I think they will want to do what is best for the child.'

'Ah. Then you can make them see good sense.'

'I am not sure what their reaction will be, Lady Harriet.'

'I have confidence in you, Drusilla.' She bestowed a smile on me – a reward in advance for bringing her ill-begotten grandchild back to the flock, I thought. But it was not going to be as easy as that. I knew Polly and I knew Eff. They would be as resolute as Lady Harriet herself. 'Well,' she went on. 'Now Louise and Alan are here, their future is assured.'

'What of their father?' I asked. 'When he returns he may have plans for them.'

'Oh no.' She laughed. 'He will do nothing. He will see that they are better with me.'

'Is there news . . .'

'We have had very little. He was in Lucknow with that

794

nanny and her husband.' She sniffed to show distaste. 'They were all safe. We did hear that. But, of course, those dreadful things are still going on. Those wicked people to murder those who have done so much for them. *English* men, women and little children . . . murdered by natives! They will get their just deserts, never fear.'

I said: 'I am glad to hear they are safe.'

Lady Harriet nodded. 'Well, Drusilla, it has been a long day for you . . . and for me. I will say goodnight now. The children are sleeping, I suppose.'

'Oh yes, they are very tired.'

'I have no doubt of that. I am sorry to impose the duties of nursery maid upon you. But they are used to you and it is best for the time being. I think too many changes would not be good for them at the moment. But I have a good nanny in mind.'

'I certainly think that for the time being they are best with me. I have looked after them throughout the journey . . . and before. They very much miss their Indian nurse.'

A look of disapproval crossed her face. 'Well, we shall have a good English nanny . . . and that will be an end to all that. Good night, Drusilla.'

'Good night, Lady Harriet.'

How strange it was to be in this house once more . . . to be actually living under its roof!

I went to my room. The sheets seemed very clean and cold, and the room airy and a little austere. There were too many memories . . . beyond the gardens . . . the green, the old church . . . and the rectory . . . the scenes of my childhood.

I thought of my father. I could see him, walking from the rectory to the church, his prayer book under his arm, his fine hair blowing untidily in the wind . . . his thoughts far away . . . in ancient Greece most likely.

So much had happened since I left.

I did not feel tired and yet as soon as I lay between those

cool clean sheets I fell into a deep sleep, so exhausted was I both physically and emotionally.

The next day I spent with the children. I took them for a walk through the old churchyard. I saw Colin Brady and his wife. There was a young baby now.

Ellen Brady, the doctor's daughter, now Colin's wife, insisted that I come into the rectory where she gave me a glass of her elderberry wine. Colin came and joined us. The children sat quietly by.

I thought *I* might be sitting there by the tray dispensing glasses of *my* elderberry wine to visitors. No. I should never have settled for that, although I had no doubt that Lady Harriet still considered it foolish of me not to have done so.

'We thought of you when we heard the news, didn't we, Ellen?' said Colin.

Ellen said they had.

'All those terrible things. How could they! It must have been really frightening.'

The children had been taken by the maid to look at the garden so they could speak freely by this time.

'And Miss Lavinia ... the Countess. What a terrible thing to die like that ... and so young ...'

I agreed, thinking: You have no idea how she died. You could never have imagined it.

When I went into the village people came to speak to me. Shopkeepers came out of their shops as I passed.

'Oh, I'm glad to see you back, Miss Drusilla. It must have been terrible. All those awful things ...'

They were interested in the children.

'It will be nice to have little ones at Framling. Lady Harriet will be pleased.'

There was no doubt that she was. She mourned Lavinia, I knew. It seemed outrageous to her that natives should attack the English but that they should *murder* her daughter was even more outrageous. Perhaps I had never really understood her. One thing she did care for was children – and now her grandchildren. I knew there was going to be a great battle for Fleur.

I thought about that a good deal and as soon as I was assured that the children were sufficiently settled to do without me for a few days, I decided to go to see Polly. So I wrote to her.

Lady Harriet visited the nursery. I encouraged the children to talk to her; but I noticed they kept close to me when she was around.

She did not force herself upon them. That would not be Lady Harriet's way. But I could see how pleased she was when Louise addressed her directly. Alan averted his eyes when she was near and refrained from jumping.

'The children seem to be very quiet,' she said to me once when they had gone to bed.

'They have to get used to their surroundings,' I told her. 'They have lived through so many changes. But they will settle in time.'

'They shall be taught to ride.'

I said I thought that an excellent idea.

'I shall delay getting the nanny . . . just for a little while yet.'

I told her I thought that was a good idea. 'Let them get accustomed to new faces for a while.'

She nodded with approval.

'The news is getting better,' she said. 'General Roberts is working wonders. He is showing those dreadful people who are the masters and Sir John Lawrence, they seem to think, deserves great praise for the part he has played. It seems that soon things will be more or less normal out there . . . as normal as they can be in such a place. It may well be that we shall have Sir Fabian and the children's father home sooner than I had hoped.'

'That will be a great relief for you, Lady Harriet.'

'Indeed yes. Then, of course, we shall have wedding bells. Lady Geraldine has waited long enough.'

I did not want to look at her. I thought I might betray something.

'There will be no delay,' she went on, 'not once Sir Fabian is home. It is the last thing he would want.' She smiled indulgently. 'He is rather impatient, I'm afraid. He always has been. When he wants something he wants it at once. So . . . I am sure there will be a wedding . . . soon.'

It seemed so reasonable now. Everything was different at home. When we were in India, travelling from Delhi to Bombay, I had perhaps dreamed impossible dreams.

Here, I could realize how foolish I had been.

I had had a rapturously loving reply from Polly.

'I'm just singing all over the place. Eff says I'm driving her mad. It's just that I'm so happy you're safe and sound and back home. We'll be waiting, so come just as soon as you can.'

The papers heralded the good news. The Mutiny was fast coming to an end and black headlines in the papers proclaimed victory. General Roberts and Sir John Lawrence were the heroes. There was a great deal written about the loyal Sikhs and the treacherous Sepoys. But all would be well. The wicked had been shown the evil of their ways and the just were triumphant.

Old men sat by the pond and discussed the relief of Lucknow. Names like Bundelkhund and Jhansi were tossed about with abandon. They had all defeated the villainous Nana Sahib; they had triumphed over his ally Tantia Topi. They had put the mutineers where they belonged.

There was peace in the air. The spring was with us; the faint hum of insects mingled with the sound of clipping shears as the garden hedges were cut.

This was home. And I set out to see Polly.

I told the children that I should be away only for a few days. They had taken a great fancy to Molly, one of the parlourmaids, and I knew they would be happy with her. She would take them down to the drawing-room in the afternoons to spend an hour with Grandmama; this had become a ritual which they accepted; and they were indeed becoming less in awe of her. I felt I could leave them safely and in any case I did feel it was necessary for me to hear what Polly had to tell me.

She was waiting for me at the station. Her eyes filled with tears when she saw me and for a few moments we clung together.

Then she became practical. 'Eff stayed at home. She'll have the kettle boiling by the time we get back. My goodness, am I glad to see you! Let's have a look at you. Not bad. I've been that worried . . . you out there in all that. Enough to make your hair curl. When we heard you was back . . . you should have seen us . . . Eff and Fleur . . . Oh, she remembers you all right. To tell the truth sometimes Eff's a bit jealous. She is like that. But it's good to see you. I've told you I've been singing all over the place ever since . . . nearly driven Eff off her rocker. Well, here you are.'

We said little in the cab going to the house. And there it was, so dear and familiar.

The door was flung open and there were Eff and Fleur. Eff the same as ever and Fleur grown far more than I had expected . . . a beautiful dark-haired girl, who threw her arms round my neck and kissed me.

'Well, are we going to stand here all night?' demanded Eff. 'I've got the kettle on the boil. And there's muffins for tea. Got to be toasted. Didn't dare start till you come. Didn't want them all dried up, did we?'

And there we were sitting in the kitchen, too emotional to say very much at first but so happy to be together.

I had to meet the governess. 'Mrs Childers, a real lady,' I was told. 'Come down in the world,' Polly added. 'She's ever so particular and glad to be here. No airs and graces . . . just fond of Fleur, and my goodness, is Fleur fond of her. Clever, she is. History, geography and French, would you believe? Fleur's a natural for that. You should hear 'em parleyvousing. Eff and me just curl up, don't we, Eff?'

799

'You do,' said Eff. 'I know French when I hear it and it's not all that to laugh about. And it's right and proper that Fleur should speak French because most ladies do and that's what she's got to be.'

Mrs Childers turned out to be a very pleasant woman; she was in her late thirties, I imagined; she was a widow and very fond of children; she had obviously, as Eff told me, come down in the world but – Eff again – there was 'no side to her'. She faced facts, and, as Polly said, they might not be Lady High-and-Mighty or Lady Muck but they treated her like one of themselves and she could take it or leave it.

Mrs Childers had obviously taken it and she told me that she was happy in the house and fond of Fleur. So it seemed they had all come to an excellent arrangement.

Each morning Mrs Childers took Fleur into the park. They looked at flowers and things, Eff told me. It was something called botany.

Eff went often to the market to shop and this gave me an opportunity to be alone with Polly.

She very soon began to talk about Lady Harriet's visit.

'Sent for me, she did. "Please come to Framling without delay." Who does she think she is? "You go and take a running jump at yourself," I said, not to her . . . but to Eff. Then down she comes. You should have seen her. I would have took her into the kitchen but Eff would have her in the parlour. She was going to take Fleur with her, she said. "If you think that," I said, "you've got another think coming. This is Fleur's home and this is where she stays." She started to tell us how much more she could do for her. So could we, I told her. Do you know we own this house now? Yes, we bought it and we're on the way to getting next door. Eff talks about retiring to a little place in the country.'

'The country! You, Polly! But you love London.'

'Well, when you're getting on a bit it's different. Eff always liked a bit of green. Anyway, it's not for now. It's for later. But what I'm saying is we can look after Fleur without her ladyship's help. Now what about you? You're living there . . . with that woman.'

'The children are there, Polly . . . Louise and Alan. You'd love them.'

'If they're half as nice as their sister, I reckon I would. I reckon they're glad to have you, but it can't be much fun in that house with her ladyship.'

'I manage. She is fond of the children and she realizes that they need me. I was with them all through that terrible time in India, remember.'

Polly nodded. 'You know, if you couldn't stand her you could always come here. I reckon we'd manage all right the way we're getting on. Rents are coming in regular and now that we've got our own house . . . it's good. Mind you, we had a struggle to get it and we were a bit short at one time. That reminds me. I ought to have told you before. Well, I had to do it. You'll understand, I know.'

'I expect so, Polly. What is it?'

'Fleur's been ill.'

'You didn't tell me.'

'There wasn't no sense in worrying you when you were so far away. There was nothing you could have done. There was one time when it was touch and go.'

'Oh Polly! Do you mean that!'

'H'm. If that old grandmother had been there then I reckon Fleur would have been with her by now. We'd have had to let her go. Something in her throat it was. It could have been the end of her if she hadn't had this operation.'

'This is terrible, Polly. And I didn't know it.'

'There was this man . . . a clever surgeon or something. Dr Clement told us about him. He thought he was about the only man who could save her. Mind you, he was one of the Harley Street men . . . and it was fancy prices to get him to work. We had to find the money. We'd just bought the house. If it had been earlier we could have used that money and let the house go. But there we were . . . not much we could lay our hands on. Well, we'd got the house now but that wouldn't have meant much to us if we'd lost Fleur.'

I looked at her in horror but she shook her head and smiled at me. 'It's all right now. He did the job . . . it was a complete cure. I'll tell you what we did. Remember that fan you'd got . . . the one the old lady gave you?'

I nodded.

'There was a bit of jewellery in it.'

'Yes, Polly, yes.'

'I took it to the jeweller and he said that piece of glitter was worth quite a lot of money.' She looked at me apologetically. 'I said to Eff, "This is what Drusilla would want if she was here." She agreed with me. We had to have that money quick. I had to make up my mind there and then. And there were the jewels and there was dear little Fleur . . . so I took the fan to the jeweller and he bought the jewels . . . took them out he did . . . ever so careful . . . It saved Fleur's life. There was even some over so we took her to the seaside with that . . . Eff and me. A rare old time we had. You should have seen the colour come back into that little one's cheeks. You see . . .'

'Of course I see, Polly. I'm glad . . . I'm so glad.'

'I knew you would be. What's a bit of stone compared with a child's life, eh? That's what I said to Eff. And I tell you this. He's made a good job of the fan, that jeweller. It looks just like it did before. I've kept it very special here. Just a minute.'

I sat still feeling shaken while she went away to get it. I could never think of peacock feathers without seeing that terrible bloodstained fan lying at Lavinia's feet.

Polly stood before me and proudly opened the fan. It looked scarcely different from when I had last seen it; the place where the jewels had been was neatly covered.

'There!' said Polly. 'A pretty thing it is. I'll never forget what it's done for Fleur.'

*

As soon as I returned Lady Harriet wanted to know what had happened.

'They are adamant,' I told her. 'They will never give Fleur up.'

'But didn't you point out the advantages I could give her?'

'They think she is better with them. They have a governess, you know.'

'I did know. What any *good* governess would be doing in a place like that, I cannot imagine.'

'She seems to be a very intelligent woman and she is very fond of Fleur.'

'Rubbish!' said Lady Harriet. 'They must be brought to their senses. I can assert my rights, you know.'

'The circumstances are rather extraordinary.'

'What do you mean? Fleur is my grandchild.'

'But you have only just learned of her existence.'

'What of that? I know she is my grandchild. I have a right.'

'You mean you would go to law?'

'I will do anything that is necessary to get possession of my grandchild.'

'It would mean bringing out the facts of the child's birth.'

'Well?'

'Would you care for that?'

'If it is necessary it will have to be done.'

'But if you took this matter to law there would be publicity. That would not be good for Fleur.'

She hesitated for a moment. Then she said: 'I am determined to get the child.'

I felt it was a little ironical that when Fleur had been born she was unwanted by her mother and we had been at great pains to find a home for her. Now there were two strong factions – one determined to get her, the other to keep her.

I wondered who would win.

*

Time was slipping by. Louise and Alan were growing up into Framling children. They were given riding lessons, which delighted them, and each morning they spent half an hour in the paddock with a Framling groom. Lady Harriet used to watch them from her window with great satisfaction.

The nanny arrived. She was in her mid-forties, I thought, and had been looking after children for more than twenty-five years. Lady Harriet was pleased with her. She had worked in a ducal family, Lady Harriet told me – only a younger son, but still ducal.

'She will relieve you of the more onerous duties,' she said. 'You can confine yourself to the schoolroom now.'

The children accepted Nanny Morton and as she was in full possession of that nanny-like gift of keeping a firm hand and at the same time conveying the impression that she was one of those omniscient beings who would protect them against the world, she soon became part of the daily routine and she helped them gain a strong hold on that state which is all-important to the young: security.

Now and then they referred to their mother and the ayah, but these occasions were becoming more rare. Framling was now their home. They loved the spaciousness of that mysterious and yet now familiar house; they loved their riding; and although they were in awe of their formidable grandmother they had a certain affection for her and were gratified on those rare occasions when she expressed approval of something they had done; then they had Nanny Morton and myself.

Those weeks which they had spent cooped up in Salar's house and the general feeling of unease which they must have experienced made them appreciate the peace of Framling, the glorious gardens, the exciting riding and the general feeling of well-being.

Lady Harriet often talked of Lady Geraldine.

'There is some restoration to be done in the west wing,'

she told me. 'But I am doing nothing. Lady Geraldine may want to change it all when she comes.'

And then: 'Lady Geraldine is a great horsewoman. I dare say she will want to improve the stables.'

Lady Geraldine had a habit of cropping up in the conversation and as time passed the more frequently she did so.

'Surely there is nothing now to keep Sir Fabian in India,' she said. 'I am sure he will be home soon. I shall invite Lady Geraldine over so that she is here when he comes. That will be a nice surprise for him. Louise and Alan had better make the most of the nursery. They may have to be sharing it before long.'

'You mean Fleur . . .'

'Yes, Fleur, and when Sir Fabian marries . . .' She gave a little giggle. 'Lady Geraldine's family are noted for their fertility. They all have large families.'

She was getting more and more excited because she could not believe he would be away much longer.

Then Dougal came home.

We were at lessons in the schoolroom when he arrived. There was no warning.

Lady Harriet came in with him. I heard her say before she appeared: 'They are having their lessons with Drusilla. You remember Drusilla . . . that nice sensible girl from the rectory.

As if he needed reminding! We had been good friends. I had seen him in India; and he knew I had looked after the children there. But Lady Harriet was never very clear about the relationships of menials.

He came in and stood still smiling, his eyes on me, before they went to the children.

I stood up.

Lady Harriet said: 'Children, your papa is here.'

Louise said: 'Hello, Papa.'

Alan was silent.

'How are you?' said Dougal. 'And you, Drusilla?'

'Very well,' I answered. 'And you?'

He nodded, still looking at me. 'It has been so long.'

'We heard about Lucknow. That must have been terrible.'

'Terrible for us all,' said Dougal.

'I think the children might finish with their lesson,' said Lady Harriet, 'and as it is rather a special occasion, we will all go to my sitting-room.'

They left their books and I paused to shut them and put them away.

'You will want to be with your papa, children,' said Lady Harriet.

'Yes, Grandmama,' said Louise meekly.

Dougal looked at me: 'We'll talk later,' he said.

I was alone in the schoolroom, reminding myself that, in spite of all that had gone before, I was only the governess.

The children did not seem to be particularly excited to see their father; but Lady Harriet was delighted and the reason was that he brought news that Fabian would soon be coming home.

'This is good news from India,' she told me. 'My son will soon be on his way home. The wedding will take place almost immediately. They would have been married now but for those wicked natives. I have started thinking about what dress I shall wear. As the bridegroom's mother I shall have my part to play, and Lizzie Carter, although a good worker, is rather slow. Louise will make a charming bridesmaid and Alan will be quite a stalwart little page. I always enjoy planning weddings. I remember Lavinia . . .' Her voice faded briefly. 'Poor Dougal,' she went on briskly. 'He is a lost soul without her.'

I had never noticed his reliance on her but I did not say so. The mention of Lavinia was as painful to me as it was to Lady Harriet.

Dougal was staying for a few days at Framling; then he was going to his estates. He took an early opportunity of talking to me.

'It is wonderful to see you, Drusilla,' he said. 'There were times when I thought I should never see anyone again. What experiences we passed through.'

'We did . . . among thousands of others.'

'Sometimes I feel I shall never be the same again.'

'I think we all feel like that.'

'I am leaving the Company. I intended to in any case. Indeed, I think there will be changes. The feeling is that this will be the end of the Company as such. It will be passed over to the State. I intend to hand over my interests to a cousin.'

'What shall you do?'

'What I always wanted to. Study.'

'And the children?'

He looked surprised. 'Oh, they will be with their grandmother.'

'That is what she wants, of course.'

'It seems the most sensible thing. She has the big house . . . the nurseries . . . everything the children need and . . . er . . . she is determined to keep them. I was telling Louise about some of the newest discoveries in archæology and she was quite interested.'

'Louise is very intelligent . . . the sort of child who is interested in everything she hears.'

'Yes. It's fascinating to study a child's mind . . . to watch the dawning of intelligence. They have perfect brains . . . uncluttered . . . and quick to learn.'

'They have to be, to grasp what is necessary in life. It has often occurred to me that they think logically and clearly. All they lack is experience and therefore they have to learn how to deal with triumph and disaster.'

'It is good to be with you, Drusilla. I have missed you. I often think of the old days at the rectory. Do you remember them?'

'Of course.'

'Your father was such an interesting man.'

We were watching the children on their ponies and at

807

that moment Alan passed. He was riding without holding the reins. The groom was beside him.

'Look at me, Drusilla,' he cried. 'Look. No reins.'

I clapped my hands and he laughed joyously.

'They are so fond of you,' said Dougal.

'We grew close while we were in hiding. Both of them were aware of the danger, I think.'

'How fortunate that you came through all that.'

'You were with Tom and Alice.'

'Yes, they were in Lucknow. That was a time of real terror. We never knew from one moment to the next, what was going to happen. I can't explain to you what it was like when Campbell's troops took the city. It was a hard struggle. They fought like demons.'

'Will Tom and Alice come home?'

'Not for some time, I imagine. Things are in upheaval over there. Everyone is anticipating great change. Tom will be needed and is sure to be there some time yet. But he has Alice with him. They get along very well together. Fabian will be home quite soon. I don't know how it is all going to work out. He will want to see people in London. Everything is in a state of flux. There will be great changes in the Company and I don't know how this will affect Fabian.'

'Nor Tom Keeping, I suppose.'

'Tom will be all right. He is a lucky man. Alice is a fine person.' He looked a little wistful. 'Just imagine. They had known each other such a short time . . . and there it was. They seem as though they were just made for each other.'

'I suppose it happens like that sometimes.'

'To the lucky ones. To the rest of us . . .' He lapsed into silence and then went on: 'There should be no pretence between us, should there? We know each other too well. Drusilla, I have made a mess of things.'

'I suppose we all feel that about ourselves at some time.'

'I hope you don't. Here am I . . . adrift. A man with two children to whom sometimes I fancy I am a stranger.'

'That could soon be remedied.'

'They are so fond of you, Drusilla.'

'I have been with them for a long time. They were my charges when I came to India and have been ever since. Then we went through that fearful time together. They weren't aware of the enormity of the dangers but even young children can't live through a time like that without being affected. I represent a sort of rock to them, security, I suppose.'

'I understand that. It is how they would see you. There is a strength about you, Drusilla. I often think of the old days. We were very good friends then. I can't tell you how much I used to look forward to those sessions with you and your father.'

'Yes, we all enjoyed them.'

'We talked of interesting things . . . important things . . . and because we shared our pleasure we enjoyed it the more. Do you ever wish you could go back in time . . . to act differently . . . to change things?'

'I think everyone does that now and then.'

'Mine was not a happy marriage. Well . . . it was disastrous, really. You see, she was so beautiful.'

'I don't think I ever saw anyone as beautiful as Lavinia.'

'It was a blinding sort of beauty. I thought she was like Venus rising from the sea.'

'You worship beauty, I know. I have seen your eyes when they rest on certain pieces of statuary or great paintings.'

'I thought she was quite the most beautiful creature I had ever seen. She seemed to be fond of me and Lady Harriet was determined . . .'

'Ah yes,' I said. 'You became very eligible overnight.'

'That should never have happened to me. Well, she is dead now, and there are the children.'

'They will be your chief concern.'

'They will be brought up here, I suppose. They are well and happy here. I am not sure about the influence of the Framlings. I worry about them a little. I feel they might take their values from Lady Harriet. I am glad that you are with them, Drusilla.'

'I love them very much.'

'I can see that. But when Fabian returns . . . I believe he will soon get married. I gather there is already some understanding with Lady Geraldine Fitzbrock. Not an official engagement yet . . . but that will come, and Lady Harriet wants a quick marriage, so . . .'

'Yes, I too had gathered that from her.'

'Well, it will be a little time before Fabian has children, I suppose. But the nursery will be theirs and if his children are anything like him they will soon be dominating mine.'

The subject of Fabian's marriage filled me with deep depression which I hoped I did not show.

He went on: 'I wish I could take them away . . . have a place of my own.'

'You have, haven't you?'

'A rambling old place . . . more like a fortress than a home. It came along with the inheritance. It would not be much of a home for children, Drusilla.'

'Perhaps it could be made so.'

'With a family . . . children perhaps . . .'

'Well, it is all before you.'

'Yes. It's not too late, is it?'

'Some say it is never too late.'

'Drusilla . . .' He was smiling at me.

I thought in panic: He is going to ask me to marry him as my father thought he might all those years ago. He is thinking it could be a solution. I have already been a surrogate mother to his children and he knows that I will be interested in whatever he takes up. I am not beautiful . . . hardly like Venus rising from the sea . . . but I have other qualities. As Lady Harriet would say, I am a sensible girl.

Just at that moment the children ran up. Their riding lesson was over. I was glad of the diversion.

Louise said, not looking at her father: 'Drusilla, I did the jump today. Did you see?'

'Yes,' I told her. 'You did it beautifully.'

'Did I? Jim said it's going to get higher and higher.'

'Right up to the sky,' said Alan. 'Did you see *me?*'

'Yes,' I assured him. 'We both watched . . . your father and I.'

'You were very good,' Dougal told him.

Alan smiled at him and jumped.

'Stop, Alan,' said Louise. She looked apologetically at Dougal. 'He's always jumping,' she added.

'It shows he's happy,' I said.

'You wait until *I* do the jumps with my horse,' Alan cried.

'We will,' I told him. I turned to Dougal. 'Won't we?'

'You too?' said Alan, looking doubtfully at his father. '*You* and Drusilla?'

'We shall be there,' I replied.

Alan jumped again and we all laughed.

Then we walked back, Alan running on ahead and turning to look back at us every few seconds while Louise walked rather soberly between us.

Fabian was coming home. He was on the high seas and in a week or so he would be with us.

Lady Harriet was more excited than I had ever seen her. She was quite talkative to me.

'I have decided that I won't ask Lady Geraldine just at first. He will pay too much attention to her and as I have not seen my son for a long time I want him to myself. Besides, it will be more romantic for him to go down to her. He should propose in her father's house. Everything will be different when he comes. There will be no nonsense about the child from those two women. Fleur will be brought to her rightful home.'

'I dare say she will want to have some say in her future herself.'

'A mere child! What are you thinking of, Drusilla?'

'I was thinking that perhaps I should consider my position.'

'Your position! What do you mean?'

'I thought Lady Geraldine might want to make changes.'

'In the nursery? I am mistress of this house as I was when I came here as a bride and I intend to remain so. Moreover, you teach the children very well and *I* am satisfied with their progress. Louise is getting on admirably. You have a gift for teaching. *My* governess was with me from my earliest days to the time when I had my season.'

That was an end of the matter . . . for her. But not for me. I could not stay. I certainly would not remain when Fabian was married to Lady Geraldine. I knew I had had ridiculous dreams. I suppose those days in India which now seemed part of an unreal nightmare had had their effect on me. Back in Framling, I realized how impossible those dreams had been.

The Framlings were Framlings. They would never change. They looked upon the rest of us as pawns in a game to be moved around as benefited them. We were of no importance except in our usefulness.

During that week when Lady Harriet went around in a state of happiness which I had never seen her in before, I was getting more and more depressed. I did not want to be here when he came home. I could not join the general rejoicing because of the suitable marriage he was making. Fabian *would* marry suitably, I was sure. He was as much aware of family obligations as his mother was. He had been brought up to regard them as all-important. I had not been mistaken when I had thought there was an attraction between us. There always had been . . . with him as well as with me. I knew that he wanted to make love to me; but the question of marriage would never arise. I had heard whispers of past Framlings . . . the vivid lives they had led, the romantic adventures which had nothing to do with

812

marriage. They married suitably and that was all that was expected of them.

But that was not the life for me. I was too serious-minded; as Lady Harriet would have said, 'too sensible'.

I saw Dougal often. He did not ask me to marry him but I knew it was in his mind. He was afraid to ask me outright for fear I should refuse. I realized that Dougal was not the man to take quick decisions. He would always waver; others would have to make up his mind for him.

If I gave him that little bit of encouragement for which he looked, he would have asked me. Why did he want me? I asked myself. It was because I represented a certain security to him as I did to his children. I would be the surrogate mother for which post I had already qualified.

It would be convenient, wise no doubt. I could look to a peaceful life ahead with Dougal, quiet, pleasant, with a husband who would be considerate and caring . . . and the children growing up with us. We would study together. I should learn a great deal. Our excitement would be in the antiquities of the world . . . books, art . . . they would give us our interest.

Perhaps I should grow like him.

He was seeing me as the antithesis of Lavinia. But he would never forget that outstanding beauty which I believed he had marvelled at when he saw her.

Everyone would say I should be glad of the opportunity. What is your life? they would say. Are you going to spend it serving the Framlings? And what about Lady Geraldine? Would she sense her husband's feelings towards me? It could develop into an explosive, impossible situation.

I should have to go. Where? I had a little money, just about enough to keep me in a rather dreary comfortless style. What a fool I was to turn away from all that Dougal was offering me.

And Fabian would be home in a day or so.

I could not bear to be there when he came.

I said to Lady Harriet: 'I should like to go to see Polly again.'

'Well,' replied Lady Harriet, 'that is not a bad idea. You can tell them that Sir Fabian will soon be home and he will put a stop to their nonsense. They might as well give up Fleur with a good grace. Tell them we shall not be forgetful and shall reward them for what they have done.'

I did not remark that that was the very way to stiffen their resolve, if it needed stiffening – which it did not. But how could one explain such things to Lady Harriet?

I was happy to be with Polly again. I was taken back to my childhood when she was there to soothe away my little problems.

It was not long before she sensed there was something on my mind. She managed in that skilful way of hers that we should be alone together.

'Let's sit in the parlour,' she said. 'Eff won't know. Besides, you're a visitor and parlours are for visitors.'

So we sat there on the stiff unused chairs with their prim antimacassars on the backs and the aspidistra on the wicker table in the window and the clock which Father had thought such a lot of, ticking away on the mantelshelf.

'Now what's on your mind?'

'Oh, I'm all right, Polly.'

'Don't give me that. I know when something's wrong with you, and that's now.'

'Sir Fabian is coming home,' I said.

'Well, it's about time, I should think.'

I was silent.

'Here,' she said. 'Tell me. You know you can tell your old Polly anything.'

'I feel rather foolish. I've been so stupid.'

'Ain't we all?'

'You see, Polly, if you can imagine what it was like in India ... From one minute to the next we never knew whether it was going to be our last. That does something to you.'

'You tell me what it does to you.'

'Well . . . he was there and all those other people were too, but it was like being with him alone. He'd saved my life, Polly. I had seen him shoot a man who was going to kill me.'

She nodded slowly.

'I know,' she said. 'He seemed like some sort of hero to you, didn't he? You had this fancy for him. You'd always had it, really. You can't fool me.'

'Perhaps,' I said. 'It was silly of me.'

'I never thought he'd be any good to you. There was that other one.' She looked at me. 'And he goes and marries that Lavinia. I reckon you're better off without the both. Men . . . they're chancy things . . . Better none at all than the wrong one . . . and my goodness, the good ones don't grow on trees, I can tell you.'

'There *was* your Tom.'

'Ah . . . my Tom. Not many like him in this world, I can tell you, and he goes and gets himself drowned. I said to him, "You ought to get a job ashore, that's what." But would he listen? Oh no. No sense, men, that's about it.'

'Polly,' I said. 'I had to get away. You see, he's coming home and he is going to be married.'

'What?'

'Lady Harriet is making preparations. She is Lady Geraldine Fitzbrock.'

'What a name to go to bed with!'

'She will be Lady Geraldine Framling. I couldn't stay there. She wouldn't want me.'

'Not when she sees he's got a fancy for you.'

'It was only a passing fancy, Polly. He'd forget all about me if I was not there.'

'You'd better get out of that place, I can see. There's always a home for you here.'

'That's another thing, Polly. Lady Harriet says he will do something about Fleur.'

'What about her?'

'She says they will stand by their rights. She's the grandmother, you see.'

'Grandmother me foot! Fleur's ours. We brought her up. We had her since she was a few weeks old. Nobody's going to take her away from us now. I tell you straight.'

'If she took it to court . . . all their money and the fact that Fleur is their flesh and blood . . .'

'I won't have it. Eff won't either. They wouldn't want all that dragged through the courts . . . all about Madam Lavinia's affairs in France. 'Course they wouldn't.'

'Nor would you, Polly. You wouldn't want Fleur to be faced with all that.'

Polly was silent for once.

'Oh . . . it won't get to that,' she said at length.

'They are very determined and accustomed to having their own way.'

'Here's someone who's not letting them. But we're talking about you. You know, you want to get that Fabian out of your mind. That other one . . . well, it mightn't be such a bad idea.'

'You mean Dougal?'

'Yes, him. He's a bit of a ninny, but there are the children and you know how fond you are of them.'

'We were great friends, really. I liked him very much. But then Lavinia appeared. She was so beautiful, Polly. I think it ruined her life in a way. She couldn't resist admiration. She had to have it from everyone and in the end . . . she died.'

I found myself telling the story. It all came back to me so vividly. Roshanara . . . the Khansamah . . . his meetings with Lavinia in her boudoir . . . to that last terrible scene.

'She was lying on the bed, Polly. I knew what had happened. She had insulted his dignity and she paid for it in a special way. He gave her a peacock feather fan. She thought it was because he was contrite and so enamoured of her beauty. But it was the sign of death. That's what it meant. And there she lay with the bloodstained fan at her feet.'

'Well, I never!'

'You see, Polly, there is a legend about peacocks' feathers. They are bringers of ill fortune. You remember Miss Lucille and her fan.'

'I do indeed. And reason to be thankful for it. I reckon it saved our Fleur's life.'

'But getting the jewel cost her lover his.'

'I reckon those men would have got him at any time.'

'But it was when he was taking the fan to have the jewels set in it that it happened. Lucille believed it was the ill luck of the fan.'

'Well, she was off her rocker.'

'I know she was unbalanced . . . but it was due to what happened to her.'

'You want to get rid of all them fancy ideas about fans.'

'But it means something to them, Polly. They are a strange people. They are not like us. What seems plain common sense here is different there. Dougal found there was a legend about peacocks' feathers. The Khansamah must have believed it, for he gave Lavinia the fan and when he killed her he laid it at her feet. It was a sort of ritual.'

'Well, let them think what they like. A bundle of feathers is a bundle of feathers to me and I can't see anything to frighten yourself about that.'

'Polly, I have the fan. At one time my father . . . and others . . . thought Dougal would ask me to marry him. They all thought it would be good for me.'

'He'd have shown a lot more sense if he had asked you and I'm not sure you wouldn't have shown some if you'd said yes. He might not be all that you'd want . . . not one of them dashing heroes . . . he might be just a timid little man . . . but he's not so bad and you can't have everything in life. Sometimes it's best to take what you can get . . . providing it's all right in the main.'

'He didn't want me when he saw Lavinia. It was as though he were bewitched. He didn't *see* me after that. I was interested in what interested him, as my father was. He enjoyed being with us . . . talking to us . . . and then he saw Lavinia. He had seen her before, of course, but she was grown up and he saw her afresh. He forgot any feeling he might have had for me. You see, it's a sort of pattern.'

'I shall begin to think you're going wrong in the head. What's all this got to do with fans?'

'I think, Polly, that I shall never be happy in love because I took the fan. It was in my possession for a while. That is what Miss Lucille believed . . . and it seems as if . . . you see.'

'No, I don't see,' said Polly. 'This isn't like you. I always thought you had some sense.'

'Strange things happen in India.'

'Well, you're not there now. You're in plain sensible England where fans are just fans and nothing else.'

'I know you're right.'

'Of course I'm right. So don't let's have any more of this nonsense about fans. I reckon that fan done us all a good turn. When you look at young Fleur now and think what she was like at that time . . . it makes me tremble all over now to think of it. So you're not going to marry this Dougal?'

'He hasn't asked me yet, Polly.'

'Looks like he's just waiting for a shove in the right direction.'

'I shall not do the shoving.'

'Well, you'd have a grand title, wouldn't you? I never thought much of them myself but there's plenty as do.'

'I wouldn't want to marry for that, Polly.'

''Course you wouldn't. But he seems a nice enough fellow. All he needs is a bit of pushing and you'd be rather good at that. And there's the children, too. They're fond of you and they'd have you as their mum. I reckon that's what *they*'d like.'

'They probably would, but one doesn't marry for that reason.'

'You're still thinking of that old fan. You're thinking it's going to be bad luck and nothing will go right while you have it. Here. Wait a minute. Come into the kitchen. I want to show you something. Just a minute. I'll go and get it.'

I went into the kitchen. It was warm, for the fire was burning. It always was, for it heated the oven and the kettle was always on the hob.

Within a few minutes Polly came in; she was carrying the case which contained the peacock feather fan.

She took it out and unfurled it.

'Pretty thing,' she said.

Then she went to the fire and put the fan into the heart of it. The feathers were immediately alight – their deep blues mingling with the red of the flames. I gasped as I watched it disintegrate.

Nothing was left of it but the blackened frame.

I turned to her in dismay. She was looking at me half fearfully, half triumphant. I knew she felt unsure of what my reaction would be.

'Polly!' I stammered.

She looked a little truculent. 'There,' she said. 'It's gone. There's no need to worry about that any more. You was getting worked up about that fan. I could see it was beginning to get a hold of you. You was expecting things to go wrong . . . and somehow that's often a way of making them. It's gone now . . . that's the end of it. We make our own lives, you know. It's got nothing to do with a bunch of feathers.'

I had been in the park with Mrs Childers and Fleur and as soon as we returned Polly came hurrying into the hall, Eff just behind her. Polly looked anxious, Eff excited.

Eff called: 'A visitor for you, Drusilla.' And then in a

high-pitched, overawed sort of manner, she added: 'In the parlour.'

'Who . . .?' I began.

'You go and see,' said Polly.

I went in. He was standing there, smiling, making the parlour look smaller and less prim than it usually did.

'Drusilla!' He came to me and took my hands. He looked at me for a second or so and then he held me to him tightly. After a moment he released me, holding me slightly away from him, looking at me intently.

'Why did you go?' he demanded. 'Just when I was coming home.'

'I . . . I thought you would want to be with your family.'

He laughed, a happy, derisive sort of laughter.

'You knew I wanted to be with you more than anyone.'

I thought then: It is wonderful. I don't care what happens afterwards . . . this is wonderful *now*.

I began: 'I was not sure . . .'

'I did not know you could be so foolish, Drusilla. You knew I was coming and you went away.'

I tried to calm myself. 'You've come here because of . . . Fleur. You've come to try to take her away.'

'What on Earth is the matter with you? Have you forgotten? Remember the last time we were together . . . all those people around, when we wanted to be alone. The first thing I said when I came home was, "Where is Drusilla? Why isn't she here with the children?" And my mother told me you had come here. I said, "But I said she was to be here." I expected to find you at Framling as soon as I got back.'

'I didn't know you would want to see *me*.'

He looked at me incredulously.

'Drusilla, what's happened to you?' he demanded.

I said slowly: 'I've come home. Everything is different here. It seems to me now that in India I was living in a different world, where anything could happen. Here it is . . . as it always was.'

'What difference does it make where we are? We are *us*,

aren't we? We know what we want. At least I do. And I want you.'

'Have you thought . . .'

'I don't have to think. Why are you being so aloof? It wasn't like this when we were last together.'

'I tell you it is different now. How was it in India?'

'Chaotic.'

'Alice and Tom?'

'In a state of bliss . . . a most wonderful example of the joys of married life.'

I smiled. 'Ah,' he said. 'Now you are more like yourself. What is the matter? We're talking like strangers. Here am I come home to marry you and you behave as though we have just been introduced.'

'To marry *me*! But . . .'

'You are not going to raise objections, are you? You know my nature. I just ignore them.'

'What of Lady Geraldine?'

'She is well, I believe.'

'But your mother was arranging . . .'

'Arranging what?'

'The wedding.'

'*Our* wedding.'

'Your marriage to Lady Geraldine. Your mother has been arranging it.'

'I arrange my own wedding.'

'But Lady Geraldine . . .'

'What has my mother said to you?'

'That you were coming home to marry her.'

He laughed. 'Oh, she has had that in mind for some time. She forgot to consult me, that's all.'

'But she will be . . . furious.'

'My mother will agree with me. She always does. Though I believe I am the only one whose opinion she considers. Stop thinking about my mother and think of me. You're not marrying her.'

'I can't believe all this.'

821

'You're not going to say, "This is so sudden, sir," as so many well-brought-up ladies are supposed to?'

'But, Fabian, it *is* sudden . . .'

'I should have thought it was obvious. The way we were in India . . . have you forgotten?'

'I forget nothing of what happened there.'

'We went through all that together, didn't we? I blamed myself for bringing you out there. But now we're here . . . together . . . I think those times taught us a great deal about each other. It taught us that there was a special bond between us and it grows stronger every day. It's never going to break, Drusilla. We're together . . . forever.'

'Fabian, I think you go too fast.'

'I think I have gone unforgivably slowly. You are not going to refuse me, are you? You should know by now that I never take refusals. I should immediately abduct you and drag you to the altar.'

'Do you really mean that you want to marry *me*?'

'Good Heavens! Haven't I made that clear?'

'You do realize it is most unsuitable.'

'If it suits me it has to suit everyone else.'

'Lady Harriet would never allow it.'

'Lady Harriet will accept what I want. She already knows. I was enraged when I came back and found you weren't there. I said "I am going to marry Drusilla and there will be no delay about it."'

'She must have been outraged.'

'Only mildly surprised.'

I shook my head.

He said: 'I am disappointed in you, Drusilla. Have you forgotten everything? That night you came to the house . . .' I shook my head and he went on: 'That dreadful moment when I feared I might miss . . . that I might be too late. You've no idea what I went through. I lived a lifetime in those few seconds. Have you forgotten that trek to Bombay? I was desolate when you sailed away and I promised myself that the moment I was free of all that, we would be together

822

. . . and never part again. Drusilla, have you forgotten? Didn't I choose you when you were a baby? "That's mine," I said, and it has been like that ever since.'

I felt numb with happiness which I could not accept as real. He was holding me tightly. I felt protected against the fury of Lady Harriet, the disappointment of Lady Geraldine and the terrible fear that I should wake up and find I had been dreaming. Don't think of what's to come, I admonished myself. Live in the moment. This is the greatest happiness you could ever know.

He felt no such qualms. I knew, of course, that he would never have any doubts that he could have what he wanted.

'So,' he said. 'We'll go back. No delays. It will be the quickest wedding in Framling history. No more protests . . . please.'

'If it is true. If you mean it . . . if you really mean it, then . . .'

'Then what?'

'Then life is wonderful.'

We called in Polly and Eff and told them the news.

'So you are getting married,' said Polly. She was a trifle bellicose, I must admit. I saw the glint in her eyes. She was still a little uncertain whether her little ewe lamb was going to be devoured by the big bad wolf.

He knew how she regarded him and I saw the glint of amusement in his eyes.

'Soon,' he told her, 'you shall dance at our wedding.'

'My dancing days are over,' said Polly tersely.

'But on such an occasion they might be revived perhaps,' he suggested.

Eff's eyes glistened. I could see her choosing her dress. 'It's for a wedding, a rather special one. *Sir* Fabian Framling. He's marrying a special friend of ours.' I could hear her explaining to the tenants. 'Well, I suppose you'd call it one of them grand weddings. Polly and me, we've had our invitations. Such an old friend.'

Polly was less euphoric. She didn't trust any man except her Tom and her suspicion of Fabian was too deeply rooted to be dispersed by an offer of marriage.

I could smile at her fears and be happy.

Fabian wanted to stay on in London for a few days and then we should go back together. He had booked a room in a hotel. Eff was relieved. She had had an idea that she might have to 'put him up' but she did not really think there was a vacant room in any of the houses which would be worthy of a titled gentleman, although the prestige which would come from being able to say 'When *Sir* Fabian was in one of my rooms . . .' would be great.

Later that day Fabian and I went to a jeweller's to buy a ring. It was beautiful – an emerald set in diamonds. When it was on my finger I felt happier than I ever had been in my life . . . for the ring seemed to seal the bond and to proclaim to the world that I was to marry Fabian.

I believed I should be happy. I believed I could forget the horrible sights I had witnessed during the Mutiny. I was loved by Fabian, more deeply, more tenderly than I had ever believed possible; and somehow at the back of my mind I linked my happiness with the destruction of the peacock feather fan.

It was ridiculous, I knew – a flight of fancy. Perhaps I had been too long in India where mysticism seemed to flourish more than it could in the prosaic air of England. No blame could attach to me. I had not destroyed it; Polly had done that for me, and she had never owned it so it could not involve her. I closed my eyes and could see those beautiful blue feathers curling up in the flames. It was ridiculously fanciful. I had allowed the fan to take hold of my imagination: subconsciously I had endowed it with magical qualities and so it had seemed to influence my life.

But no more. I felt free. I wanted to live every moment ahead of me to the full. There would be difficulties to face. I could leave those for the future and live in this moment

. . . this wonderful moment . . . with the joy of loving and being loved.

Fabian and I sat in the gardens opposite the house and talked.

He said suddenly: 'There is the question of the child.'

'They will never give her up,' I told him.

'She can't stay in this place.'

'Fabian, you can't use people when they are useful and when you think they have served their purpose cast them aside.'

'I have an idea. They should bring her down to Framling.'

'Polly and Eff!'

'This is what I think. There are a couple of vacant houses on the estate. They could have one of these and the child would be there . . . near Framling. She could live between the two houses for a while. Then the time will come when she will go away to school. And she can think of both the house with those two in it *and* Framling as her home.'

'They have their houses. They wouldn't want to go to the country.'

'They'd want what was best for Fleur, and they'd be near you. I think they could be persuaded and you are the one to persuade.'

'I am not sure they will accept it . . . or even consider it.'

'You'll do it. You'll persuade them.'

'They are independent.'

'They own that house, don't they? They could sell it and buy this place.'

'What about the price?'

'It could be anything that fitted. They could have the place for nothing.'

'They would never accept that. They'd call it being beholden.'

'Then let them buy it . . . and whatever price will fit. It's quite simple.'

'You don't know Polly and Eff.'

825

'No, but I know you and I am sure you can make it work out.'

I talked to Polly first.

'Well I never!' she said. 'Give up this house. Take the one they've got empty. We want no charity from them.'

'It wouldn't be charity. You'd be absolutely independent of them. You could sell this house and with the proceeds buy the other.'

'Not on your life.'

'You'd be near me, Polly. That would be lovely.'

She nodded.

'And Fleur would have all that the Framlings could give her.'

'I know that. It's worried me at times. I've talked to Eff.'

'You gave her a home when she needed it. You gave her love. That was wonderful, Polly. But she will have to go to school. Framling will be a good background.'

'You don't think Eff and me haven't thought of that.'

'Why not speak to Eff?'

Polly was weighing the advantages. Most certainly she and Eff wanted the best for Fleur. It was more important to them than anything; and I could see Polly was liking the idea of being near me. She was thinking I might need a bit of advice, married to that one.

She was wavering. Eff had said she was getting tired of some of the tenants. She had had a lot of trouble with Second Floor No. 28.

I said: 'Polly, it would be wonderful for me.'

'I'll speak to Eff,' said Polly. 'She won't, though.'

'You might persuade her.'

'Oh, I know she wants the best for Fleur and I can see it would be a bit different there than here . . .'

'Think about it, Polly . . . seriously.'

Later I said to Fabian: 'I think it might work.'

*

Fabian and I travelled back to Framling together. I was bracing myself for facing Lady Harriet.

I was amazed at how graciously·she received me. There was a difference in her attitude. I had left the house as the governess to her grandchildren; I returned as the fiancée of her beloved son.

I wondered if she were asking herself what Fabian was doing, throwing himself away on the plain girl from the rectory – particularly when *her* choice had fallen on someone else.

I remembered that long-ago incident when he had brought me as a baby to his house and proclaimed that I was his child. Lady Harriet had insisted that her son's whim should be gratified. Now perhaps it was a similiar situation.

Smiling, she discussed the wedding.

'There is no point in delay,' she said. 'I have thought for long, Fabian, that it was time you were married. You can't be married from here, Drusilla, that would be quite irregular. Brides should not be living under the same roofs as their bridegrooms the day before their marriages. So you can go to the rectory. That will be the most appropriate because it was your old home. It's a pity Colin Brady can't give you away. He would have been the best person for that. But he will have to officiate in the church . . . so it will have to be the doctor. That will be an excellent alternative as his daughter is at the rectory now. The next best thing to Colin Brady himself.'

Lady Geraldine was mentioned only once. 'A nice girl . . . a little too fond of riding. She spent most of the day in the saddle. I believe that broadens the figure and can mean a lack of other interests.'

She gave no hint that she was disappointed. Here was a new side to Lady Harriet. Her love for her son went as deep as did that she had had for Lavinia . . . and perhaps deeper, for Fabian was perfect in her eyes. The fact that she rarely mentioned her daughter did not mean that she had forgotten her. She often went to Lavinia's old room and stayed there for a long time and she would be noticeably subdued when she emerged. As for Fabian, he could do no wrong. He was *her* son and therefore the perfect man. Fabian had chosen me, and because I was his choice, miraculously I had become hers.

I could not believe in such a *volte-face* until I began to understand Lady Harriet. She must of course always be right, so – wisely – she promptly adjusted her views to the inevitable and made herself believe that it was what she had wanted all the time. I felt warmer towards her because we both loved the same person and he was more important than any other to us. She recognized this and it made an instant bond between us.

History did seem to be repeating itself. I overheard a conversation and shamelessly I listened as I had on another occasion.

It was in this very garden that I had overheard her remark that I was the plain child from the rectory. It had affected me more deeply than I had realized at the time.

Lady Harriet was in the drawing-room with the doctor and his wife. The doctor was receiving his instructions as he had been chosen by her to play his part at the ceremony.

Her voice, resonant and authoritative, floated out to me.

'I had always meant Drusilla for Fabian and I am so happy that it has all turned out as I planned. She is so good with the children . . . and such a *sensible* girl.'

The sun was shining on the pool; the water-lilies were enchanting. A white butterfly paused and alighted on one of them. It rested a moment and was gone.

I was happier than I had believed possible.

Fabian loved me. Polly and Eff, I was sure, would soon be close at hand and Fleur with them. The qualms which my formidable mother-in-law might have aroused in me were stilled. Moreover, I felt an understanding of her which could develop into fondness.

Fabian would be beside me and life would be good.